COMBO

Great way to get the books you want for a lower overall price! Excellent reading.

EDWARD BELLAMY COMBO #1: THE JULIAN WEST NOVELS

LOOKING BACKWARD: 2000-1887
EQUALITY

EDWARD BELLAMY

2013

Edward Bellamy Combo #1: The Julian West Novels

Looking Backward: 2000-1887 (1888)
Equality (1897)

This edition prepared in 2013

ISBN-13: 978-1492765059
ISBN-10: 1492765058

LOOKING BACKWARD: 2000-1887

AUTHOR'S PREFACE

Historical Section Shawmut College, Boston,
December 26, 2000

Living as we do in the closing year of the twentieth century, enjoying the blessings of a social order at once so simple and logical that it seems but the triumph of common sense, it is no doubt difficult for those whose studies have not been largely historical to realize that the present organization of society is, in its completeness, less than a century old. No historical fact is, however, better established than that till nearly the end of the nineteenth century it was the general belief that the ancient industrial system, with all its shocking social consequences, was destined to last, with possibly a little patching, to the end of time. How strange and wellnigh incredible does it seem that so prodigious a moral and material transformation as has taken place since then could have been accomplished in so brief an interval! The readiness with which men accustom themselves, as matters of course, to improvements in their condition, which, when anticipated, seemed to leave nothing more to be desired, could not be more strikingly illustrated. What reflection could be better calculated to moderate the enthusiasm of reformers who count for their reward on the lively gratitude of future ages!

The object of this volume is to assist persons who, while desiring to gain a more definite idea of the social contrasts between the nineteenth and twentieth centuries, are daunted by the formal aspect of the histories which treat the subject. Warned by a teacher's experience that learning is accounted a weariness to the flesh, the author has sought to alleviate the instructive quality of the book by casting it in the form of a romantic narrative, which he would be glad to fancy not wholly devoid of interest on its own account.

The reader, to whom modern social institutions and their underlying principles are matters of course, may at times find Dr. Leete's explanations of them rather trite—but it must be remembered that to Dr. Leete's guest they were not matters of course, and that this book is written for the express purpose of inducing the reader to forget for the nonce that they are so to him. One word more. The almost universal theme of the writers and orators who have celebrated this bimillennial epoch has been the future rather than the past, not the advance that has been made, but the progress that shall be made, ever onward and upward, till the race shall achieve its ineffable destiny. This is well, wholly well, but it seems to me that nowhere can we find more solid ground for daring anticipations of human development during the next one thousand years, than by "Looking Backward" upon the progress of the last one hundred.

That this volume may be so fortunate as to find readers whose interest in the subject shall incline them to overlook the deficiencies of the treatment is the hope in which the author steps aside and leaves Mr. Julian West to speak for himself.

Chapter 1

I first saw the light in the city of Boston in the year 1857. "What!" you say, "eighteen fifty-seven? That is an odd slip. He means nineteen fifty-seven, of course." I beg pardon, but there is no mistake. It was about four in the afternoon of December the 26th, one day after Christmas, in the year 1857, not 1957, that I first breathed the east wind of Boston, which, I assure the reader, was at that remote period marked by the same penetrating quality characterizing it in the present year of grace, 2000.

These statements seem so absurd on their face, especially when I add that I am a young man apparently of about thirty years of age, that no person can be blamed for refusing to read another word of what promises to be a mere imposition upon his credulity. Nevertheless I earnestly assure the reader that no imposition is intended, and will undertake, if he shall follow me a few pages, to entirely convince him of this. If I may, then, provisionally assume, with the pledge of justifying the assumption, that I know better than the reader when I was born, I will go on with my narrative. As every schoolboy knows, in the latter part of the nineteenth century the civilization of to-day, or anything like it, did not exist, although the elements which were to develop it were already in ferment. Nothing had, however, occurred to modify the immemorial division of society into the four classes, or nations, as they may be more fitly called, since the differences between them were far greater than those between any nations nowadays, of the rich and the poor, the educated and the ignorant. I myself was rich and also educated, and possessed, therefore, all the elements of happiness enjoyed by the most fortunate in that age. Living in luxury, and occupied only with the pursuit of the pleasures and refinements of life, I derived the means of my support from the labor of others, rendering no sort of service in return. My parents and grand-parents had lived in the same way, and I expected that my descendants, if I had any, would enjoy a like easy existence.

But how could I live without service to the world? you ask. Why should the world have supported in utter idleness one who was able to render service? The answer is that my great-grandfather had accumulated a sum of money on which his descendants had ever since lived. The sum, you will naturally infer, must have been very large not to have been exhausted in supporting three generations in idleness. This, however, was not the fact. The sum had been originally by no means large. It was, in fact, much larger now that three generations had been supported upon it in idleness, than it was at first. This mystery of use without consumption, of warmth without combustion, seems like magic, but was merely an ingenious application of the art now happily lost but carried to great perfection by your ancestors, of shifting the burden of one's support on the shoulders of others. The man who had accomplished this, and it was the end all sought, was said to live on the income of his investments. To explain at this point how the ancient methods of industry made this possible would delay us too much. I shall only stop now to say that interest on investments was a species of tax in perpetuity upon the product of those engaged in industry which a person possessing or inheriting money was able to levy. It must not be supposed that an arrangement which seems so unnatural and preposterous according to modern notions was never criticized by your ancestors. It had been the effort of lawgivers and prophets from the earliest ages to abolish interest, or at least to limit it to the smallest possible rate. All these efforts had, however, failed, as they necessarily must so long as the ancient social organizations prevailed. At the time of which I write, the latter part of the nineteenth century, governments had generally given up trying to regulate the subject at all.

By way of attempting to give the reader some general impression of the way people lived together in those days, and especially of the relations of the rich and poor to one another, perhaps I cannot do better than to compare society as it then was to a prodigious coach which the masses of humanity were harnessed to and dragged toilsomely along a very hilly and sandy road. The driver was hunger, and permitted no lagging, though the pace was necessarily very slow. Despite the difficulty of drawing the coach at all along so hard a road, the top was covered with passengers who never got down, even at the steepest ascents. These seats on top were very breezy and comfortable. Well up out of the dust, their occupants could enjoy the scenery at their leisure, or critically discuss the merits of the straining team. Naturally such places were in great demand and the competition for them was keen, every one seeking as the first end in life to secure a seat on the coach for himself and to leave it to his child after him. By the rule of the coach a man could leave his seat to whom he wished, but on the other hand there were many accidents by which it might at any time be wholly lost. For all that they were so easy, the seats were very insecure, and at every sudden jolt of the coach persons were slipping out of them and falling to the ground, where they were instantly compelled to take hold of the rope and help to drag the coach on which they had before ridden so pleasantly. It was naturally regarded as a terrible misfortune to lose one's seat, and the apprehension that this might happen to them or their friends was a constant cloud upon the happiness of those who rode.

But did they think only of themselves? you ask. Was not their very luxury rendered intolerable to them by comparison with the lot of their brothers and sisters in the harness, and the knowledge that their own weight added to their toil? Had they no compassion for fellow beings from whom fortune only distinguished them? Oh, yes; commiseration was frequently expressed by those who rode for those who had to pull the coach, especially when the vehicle came to a bad place in the road, as it was constantly doing, or to a particularly steep hill. At such times, the desperate straining of the team, their agonized leaping and plunging under the pitiless lashing of hunger, the many who fainted at the rope and were trampled in the mire, made a very distressing spectacle, which often called forth highly creditable displays of feeling on the top of the coach. At such times the passengers would call down encouragingly to the toilers of the rope, exhorting them to patience, and holding out hopes of possible compensation in another world for the hardness of their lot, while others contributed to buy salves and liniments for the crippled and injured. It was agreed that it was a great pity that the coach should be so hard to pull, and there was a sense of general relief when the specially bad piece of road was gotten over. This relief was not, indeed, wholly on account of the team, for there was always some danger at these bad places of a general overturn in which all would lose their seats.

It must in truth be admitted that the main effect of the spectacle of the misery of the toilers at the rope was to enhance the passengers' sense of the value of their seats upon the coach, and to cause them to hold on to them more desperately than before. If the passengers could only have felt assured that neither they nor their friends would ever fall from the top, it is probable that, beyond contributing to the funds for liniments and bandages, they would have troubled themselves extremely little about those who dragged the coach.

I am well aware that this will appear to the men and women of the twentieth century an incredible inhumanity, but there are two facts, both very curious, which partly explain it. In the first place, it was firmly and sincerely believed that there was no other way in which Society could get along, except the many pulled at the rope and the few rode, and not only this, but that no very radical improvement even was possible, either in the harness, the coach, the roadway, or the distribution of the toil. It had always been as it was, and it always would be so. It was a pity, but it could not be helped, and philosophy forbade wasting compassion on what was beyond remedy.

The other fact is yet more curious, consisting in a singular hallucination which those on the top of the coach generally shared, that they were not exactly like their brothers and sisters who pulled at the rope, but of finer clay, in some way belonging to a higher order of beings who might justly expect to be drawn. This seems unaccountable, but, as I once rode on this very coach and shared that very hallucination, I ought to be believed. The strangest thing about the hallucination was that those who had but just climbed up from the ground, before they had outgrown the marks of the rope upon their hands, began to fall under its influence. As for those whose parents and grand-parents before them had been so fortunate as to keep their seats on the top, the conviction they cherished of the essential difference between their sort of humanity and the common article was absolute. The effect of such a delusion in moderating fellow feeling for the sufferings of the mass of men into a distant and philosophical compassion is obvious. To it I refer as the only extenuation I can offer for the indifference which, at the period I write of, marked my own attitude toward the misery of my brothers.

In 1887 I came to my thirtieth year. Although still unmarried, I was engaged to wed Edith Bartlett. She, like myself, rode on the top of the coach. That is to say, not to encumber ourselves further with an illustration which has, I hope, served its purpose of giving the reader some general impression of how we lived then, her family was wealthy. In that age, when money alone commanded all that was agreeable and refined in life, it was enough for a woman to be rich to have suitors; but Edith Bartlett was beautiful and graceful also.

My lady readers, I am aware, will protest at this. "Handsome she might have been," I hear them saying, "but graceful never, in the costumes which were the fashion at that period, when the head covering was a dizzy structure a foot tall, and the almost incredible extension of the skirt behind by means of artificial contrivances more thoroughly dehumanized the form than any former device of dressmakers. Fancy any one graceful in such a costume!" The point is certainly well taken, and I can only reply that while the ladies of the twentieth century are lovely demonstrations of the effect of appropriate drapery in accenting feminine graces, my recollection of their great-grandmothers enables me to maintain that no deformity of costume can wholly disguise them.

Our marriage only waited on the completion of the house which I was building for our occupancy in one of the most desirable parts of the city, that is to say, a part chiefly inhabited by the rich. For it must be understood that the comparative desirability of different parts of Boston for residence depended then, not on natural features, but on the character of the neighboring population. Each class or nation lived by itself, in quarters of its own. A rich man living among the poor, an educated man among the uneducated, was like one living in isolation among a jealous and alien race. When the house had been begun, its completion by the winter of 1886 had been expected. The spring of the following year found it, however, yet incomplete, and my marriage still a thing of the future. The cause of a delay calculated to be particularly exasperating to an ardent lover was a series of strikes, that is to say, concerted refusals to work on the part of the brick-layers, masons, carpenters, painters, plumbers, and other trades concerned in house building. What the specific causes of these strikes were I do not remember. Strikes had become so common at that period that people had ceased to inquire into their particular grounds. In one department of industry or another, they had been nearly incessant ever since the great business crisis of 1873. In fact it had come to be the exceptional thing to see any class of laborers pursue their avocation steadily for more than a few months at a time.

The reader who observes the dates alluded to will of course recognize in these disturbances of industry the first and incoherent phase of the great movement which ended in the establishment of the modern industrial system with all its social consequences. This is all so plain in the retrospect that a child can understand it, but not being prophets, we of that day had no clear idea what was happening to us. What we did see was that industrially the country was in a very queer way. The relation between the workingman and the employer, between labor and capital, appeared in some unaccountable manner to have become dislocated. The working classes had quite suddenly and very generally become infected with a profound discontent with their condition, and an idea that it could be greatly bettered if they only knew how to go about it. On every side, with one accord, they preferred demands for higher pay, shorter hours, better dwellings, better educational advantages, and a share in the refinements and luxuries of life, demands which it was impossible to see the way to granting unless the world were to become a great deal richer than it then was. Though they knew something of what they wanted, they knew nothing of how to accomplish it, and the eager enthusiasm with which they thronged about any one who seemed likely to give them any light on the subject lent sudden reputation to many would-be leaders, some of whom had little enough light to give. However chimerical the aspirations of the laboring classes might be deemed, the devotion with which they supported one another in the strikes, which were their chief weapon, and the sacrifices which they underwent to carry them out left no doubt of their dead earnestness.

As to the final outcome of the labor troubles, which was the phrase by which the movement I have described was most commonly referred to, the opinions of the people of my class differed according to individual temperament. The sanguine argued very forcibly that it was in the very nature of things impossible that the new hopes of the workingmen could be satisfied, simply because the world had not the wherewithal to satisfy them. It was only because the masses worked very hard and lived on short commons that the race did not starve outright, and no considerable improvement in their condition was possible while the world, as a whole, remained so poor. It was not the capitalists whom the laboring men were contending with, these maintained, but the iron-bound environment of humanity, and it was merely a question of the thickness of their skulls when they would discover the fact and make up their minds to endure what they could not cure.

The less sanguine admitted all this. Of course the workingmen's aspirations were impossible of fulfillment for natural reasons, but there were grounds to fear that they would not discover this fact until they had made a sad mess of society. They had the votes and the power to do so if they pleased, and their leaders meant they should. Some of these desponding observers went so far as to predict an impending social cataclysm. Humanity, they argued, having climbed to the top round of the ladder of civilization, was about to take a header into chaos, after which it would doubtless pick itself up, turn round, and begin to climb again. Repeated experiences of this sort in historic and prehistoric times possibly accounted for the puzzling bumps on the human cranium. Human history, like all great movements, was cyclical, and returned to the point of beginning. The idea of indefinite progress in a right line was a chimera of the imagination, with no analogue in nature. The parabola of a comet was perhaps a yet better illustration of the career of humanity. Tending upward and sunward from the aphelion of barbarism, the race attained the perihelion of civilization only to plunge downward once more to its nether goal in the regions of chaos.

This, of course, was an extreme opinion, but I remember serious men among my acquaintances who, in discussing the signs of the times, adopted a very similar tone. It was no doubt the common opinion of thoughtful men that society was approaching a critical period which might result in great changes. The labor troubles, their causes, course, and cure, took lead of all other topics in the public prints, and in serious conversation.

The nervous tension of the public mind could not have been more strikingly illustrated than it was by the alarm resulting from the talk of a small band of men who called themselves anarchists, and proposed to terrify the American people into adopting their ideas by threats of violence, as if a mighty nation which had but just put down a rebellion of half its own numbers, in order to maintain its political system, were likely to adopt a new social system out of fear.

As one of the wealthy, with a large stake in the existing order of things, I naturally shared the apprehensions of my class. The particular grievance I had against the working classes at the time of which I write, on account of the effect of their strikes in postponing my wedded bliss, no doubt lent a special animosity to my feeling toward them.

Chapter 2

The thirtieth day of May, 1887, fell on a Monday. It was one of the annual holidays of the nation in the latter third of the nineteenth century, being set apart under the name of Decoration Day, for doing honor to the memory of the soldiers of the North who took part in the war for the preservation of the union of the States. The survivors of the war, escorted by military and civic processions and bands of music, were wont on this occasion to visit the cemeteries and lay wreaths of flowers upon the graves of their dead comrades, the ceremony being a very solemn and touching one. The eldest brother of Edith Bartlett had fallen in the war, and on Decoration Day the family was in the habit of making a visit to Mount Auburn, where he lay.

I had asked permission to make one of the party, and, on our return to the city at nightfall, remained to dine with the family of my betrothed. In the drawing-room, after dinner, I picked up an evening paper and read of a fresh strike in the building trades, which would probably still further delay the completion of my unlucky house. I remember distinctly how exasperated I was at this, and the objurgations, as forcible as the presence of the ladies permitted, which I lavished upon workmen in general, and these strikers in particular. I had abundant sympathy from those about me, and the remarks made in the desultory conversation which followed, upon the unprincipled conduct of the labor agitators, were calculated to make those gentlemen's ears tingle. It was agreed that affairs were going from bad to worse very fast, and that there was no telling what we should come to soon. "The worst of it," I remember Mrs. Bartlett's saying, "is that the working classes all over the world seem to be going crazy at once. In Europe it is far worse even than here. I'm sure I should not dare to live there at all. I asked Mr. Bartlett the other day where we should emigrate to if all the terrible things took place which those socialists threaten. He said he did not know any place now where society could be called stable except Greenland, Patagonia, and the Chinese Empire." "Those Chinamen knew what they were about," somebody added, "when they refused to let in our western civilization. They knew what it would lead to better than we did. They saw it was nothing but dynamite in disguise."

After this, I remember drawing Edith apart and trying to persuade her that it would be better to be married at once without waiting for the completion of the house, spending the time in travel till our home was ready for us. She was remarkably handsome that evening, the mourning costume that she wore in recognition of the day setting off to great advantage the purity of her complexion. I can see her even now with my mind's eye just as she looked that night. When I took my leave she followed me into the hall and I kissed her good-by as usual. There was no circumstance out of the common to distinguish this parting from previous occasions when we had bade each other good-by for a night or a day. There was absolutely no premonition in my mind, or I am sure in hers, that this was more than an ordinary separation.

Ah, well!

The hour at which I had left my betrothed was a rather early one for a lover, but the fact was no reflection on my devotion. I was a confirmed sufferer from insomnia, and although otherwise perfectly well had been completely fagged out that day, from having slept scarcely at all the two previous nights. Edith knew this and had insisted on sending me home by nine o'clock, with strict orders to go to bed at once.

The house in which I lived had been occupied by three generations of the family of which I was the only living representative in the direct line. It was a large, ancient wooden mansion, very elegant in an old-fashioned way within, but situated in a quarter that had long since become undesirable for residence, from its invasion by tenement houses and manufactories. It was not a house to which I could think of bringing a bride, much less so dainty a one as Edith Bartlett. I had advertised it for sale, and meanwhile merely used it for sleeping purposes, dining at my club. One servant, a faithful colored man by the name of Sawyer, lived with me and attended to my few wants. One feature of the house I expected to miss greatly when I should leave it, and this was the sleeping chamber which I had built under the foundations. I could not have slept in the city at all, with its never ceasing nightly noises, if I had been obliged to use an upstairs chamber. But to this subterranean room no murmur from the upper world ever penetrated. When I had entered it and closed the door, I was surrounded by the silence of the tomb. In order to prevent the dampness of the subsoil from penetrating the chamber, the walls had been laid in hydraulic cement and were very thick, and the floor was likewise protected. In order that the room might serve also as a vault equally proof against violence and flames, for the storage of valuables, I had roofed it with stone slabs hermetically sealed, and the outer door was of iron with a thick coating of asbestos. A small pipe, communicating with a wind-mill on the top of the house, insured the renewal of air.

It might seem that the tenant of such a chamber ought to be able to command slumber, but it was rare that I slept well, even there, two nights in succession. So accustomed was I to wakefulness that I minded little the loss of one night's rest. A second night, however, spent in my reading chair instead of my bed, tired me out, and I never allowed myself to go longer than that without slumber, from fear of nervous disorder. From this statement it will be inferred that I had at my command some artificial means for inducing sleep in the last resort, and so in fact I had. If after two sleepless nights I found myself on the approach of the third without sensations of drowsiness, I called in Dr. Pillsbury.

He was a doctor by courtesy only, what was called in those days an "irregular" or "quack" doctor. He called himself a "Professor of Animal Magnetism." I had come across him in the course of some amateur investigations into the phenomena of animal magnetism. I don't think he knew anything about medicine, but he was certainly a remarkable mesmerist. It was for the purpose of being put to sleep by his manipulations that I used to send for him when I found a third night of sleeplessness impending. Let my nervous excitement or mental preoccupation be however great, Dr. Pillsbury never failed, after a short time, to leave me in a deep slumber, which continued till I was aroused by a reversal of the mesmerizing process. The process for awaking the sleeper was much simpler than that for putting him to sleep, and for convenience I had made Dr Pillsbury teach Sawyer how to do it.

My faithful servant alone knew for what purpose Dr. Pillsbury visited me, or that he did so at all. Of course, when Edith became my wife I should have to tell her my secrets. I had not hitherto told her this, because there was unquestionably a slight risk in the mesmeric sleep, and I knew she would set her face against my practice. The risk, of course, was that it might become too profound and pass into a trance beyond the mesmerizer's power to break, ending in death. Repeated experiments had fully convinced me that the risk was next to nothing if reasonable precautions were exercised, and of this I hoped, though doubtingly, to convince Edith. I went directly home after leaving her, and at once sent Sawyer to fetch Dr. Pillsbury. Meanwhile I sought my subterranean sleeping chamber, and exchanging my costume for a comfortable dressing-gown, sat down to read the letters by the evening mail which Sawyer had laid on my reading table.

One of them was from the builder of my new house, and confirmed what I had inferred from the newspaper item. The new strikes, he said, had postponed indefinitely the completion of the contract, as neither masters nor workmen would concede the point at issue without a long struggle. Caligula wished that the Roman people had but one neck that he might cut it off, and as I read this letter I am afraid that for a moment I was capable of wishing the same thing concerning the laboring classes of America. The return of Sawyer with the doctor interrupted my gloomy meditations.

It appeared that he had with difficulty been able to secure his services, as he was preparing to leave the city that very night. The doctor explained that since he had seen me last he had learned of a fine professional opening in a distant city, and decided to take prompt advantage of it. On my asking, in some panic, what I was to do for some one to put me to sleep, he gave me the names of several mesmerizers in Boston who, he averred, had quite as great powers as he.

Somewhat relieved on this point, I instructed Sawyer to rouse me at nine o'clock next morning, and, lying down on the bed in my dressing-gown, assumed a comfortable attitude, and surrendered myself to the manipulations of the mesmerizer. Owing, perhaps, to my unusually nervous state, I was slower than common in losing consciousness, but at length a delicious drowsiness stole over me.

Chapter 3

"He is going to open his eyes. He had better see but one of us at first."

"Promise me, then, that you will not tell him."

The first voice was a man's, the second a woman's, and both spoke in whispers.

"I will see how he seems," replied the man.

"No, no, promise me," persisted the other.

"Let her have her way," whispered a third voice, also a woman.

"Well, well, I promise, then," answered the man. "Quick, go! He is coming out of it."

There was a rustle of garments and I opened my eyes. A fine looking man of perhaps sixty was bending over me, an expression of much benevolence mingled with great curiosity upon his features. He was an utter stranger. I raised myself on an elbow and looked around. The room was empty. I certainly had never been in it before, or one furnished like it. I looked back at my companion. He smiled.

"How do you feel?" he inquired.

"Where am I?" I demanded.

"You are in my house," was the reply.

"How came I here?"

"We will talk about that when you are stronger. Meanwhile, I beg you will feel no anxiety. You are among friends and in good hands. How do you feel?"

"A bit queerly," I replied, "but I am well, I suppose. Will you tell me how I came to be indebted to your hospitality? What has happened to me? How came I here? It was in my own house that I went to sleep."

"There will be time enough for explanations later," my unknown host replied, with a reassuring smile. "It will be better to avoid agitating talk until you are a little more yourself. Will you oblige me by taking a couple of swallows of this mixture? It will do you good. I am a physician."

I repelled the glass with my hand and sat up on the couch, although with an effort, for my head was strangely light.

"I insist upon knowing at once where I am and what you have been doing with me," I said.

"My dear sir," responded my companion, "let me beg that you will not agitate yourself. I would rather you did not insist upon explanations so soon, but if you do, I will try to satisfy you, provided you will first take this draught, which will strengthen you somewhat."

I thereupon drank what he offered me. Then he said, "It is not so simple a matter as you evidently suppose to tell you how you came here. You can tell me quite as much on that point as I can tell you. You have just been roused from a deep sleep, or, more properly, trance. So much I can tell you. You say you were in your own house when you fell into that sleep. May I ask you when that was?"

"When?" I replied, "when? Why, last evening, of course, at about ten o'clock. I left my man Sawyer orders to call me at nine o'clock. What has become of Sawyer?"

"I can't precisely tell you that," replied my companion, regarding me with a curious expression, "but I am sure that he is excusable for not being here. And now can you tell me a little more explicitly when it was that you fell into that sleep, the date, I mean?"

"Why, last night, of course; I said so, didn't I? that is, unless I have overslept an entire day. Great heavens! that cannot be possible; and yet I have an odd sensation of having slept a long time. It was Decoration Day that I went to sleep."

"Decoration Day?"

"Yes, Monday, the 30th."

"Pardon me, the 30th of what?"

"Why, of this month, of course, unless I have slept into June, but that can't be."

"This month is September."

"September! You don't mean that I've slept since May! God in heaven! Why, it is incredible."

"We shall see," replied my companion; "you say that it was May 30th when you went to sleep?"

"Yes."

"May I ask of what year?"

I stared blankly at him, incapable of speech, for some moments.

"Of what year?" I feebly echoed at last.

"Yes, of what year, if you please? After you have told me that I shall be able to tell you how long you have slept."

"It was the year 1887," I said.

My companion insisted that I should take another draught from the glass, and felt my pulse.

"My dear sir," he said, "your manner indicates that you are a man of culture, which I am aware was by no means the matter of course in your day it now is. No doubt, then, you have yourself made the observation that nothing in this world can be truly said to be more wonderful than anything else. The causes of all phenomena are equally adequate, and the results equally matters of course. That you should be startled by what I shall tell you is to be expected; but I am confident that you will not permit it to affect your equanimity unduly. Your appearance is that of a young man of barely thirty, and your bodily condition seems not greatly different from that of one just roused from a somewhat too long and profound sleep, and yet this is the tenth day of September in the year 2000, and you have slept exactly one hundred and thirteen years, three months, and eleven days."

Feeling partially dazed, I drank a cup of some sort of broth at my companion's suggestion, and, immediately afterward becoming very drowsy, went off into a deep sleep.

When I awoke it was broad daylight in the room, which had been lighted artificially when I was awake before. My mysterious host was sitting near. He was not looking at me when I opened my eyes, and I had a good opportunity to study him and meditate upon my extraordinary situation, before he observed that I was awake. My giddiness was all gone, and my mind perfectly clear. The story that I had been asleep one hundred and thirteen years, which, in my former weak and bewildered condition, I had accepted without question, recurred to me now only to be rejected as a preposterous attempt at an imposture, the motive of which it was impossible remotely to surmise.

Something extraordinary had certainly happened to account for my waking up in this strange house with this unknown companion, but my fancy was utterly impotent to suggest more than the wildest guess as to what that something might have been. Could it be that I was the victim of some sort of conspiracy? It looked so, certainly; and yet, if human lineaments ever gave true evidence, it was certain that this man by my side, with a face so refined and ingenuous, was no party to any scheme of crime or outrage. Then it occurred to me to question if I might not be the butt of some elaborate practical joke on the part of friends who had somehow learned the secret of my underground chamber and taken this means of impressing me with the peril of mesmeric experiments. There were great difficulties in the way of this theory; Sawyer would never have betrayed me, nor had I any friends at all likely to undertake such an enterprise; nevertheless the supposition that I was the victim of a practical joke seemed on the whole the only one tenable. Half expecting to catch a glimpse of some familiar face grinning from behind a chair or curtain, I looked carefully about the room. When my eyes next rested on my companion, he was looking at me.

"You have had a fine nap of twelve hours," he said briskly, "and I can see that it has done you good. You look much better. Your color is good and your eyes are bright. How do you feel?"

"I never felt better," I said, sitting up.

"You remember your first waking, no doubt," he pursued, "and your surprise when I told you how long you had been asleep?"

"You said, I believe, that I had slept one hundred and thirteen years."

"Exactly."

"You will admit," I said, with an ironical smile, "that the story was rather an improbable one."

"Extraordinary, I admit," he responded, "but given the proper conditions, not improbable nor inconsistent with what we know of the trance state. When complete, as in your case, the vital functions are absolutely suspended, and there is no waste of the tissues. No limit can be set to the possible duration of a trance when the external conditions protect the body from physical injury. This trance of yours is indeed the longest of which there is any positive record, but there is no known reason wherefore, had you not been discovered and had the chamber in which we found you continued intact, you might not have remained in a state of suspended animation till, at the end of indefinite ages, the gradual refrigeration of the earth had destroyed the bodily tissues and set the spirit free."

I had to admit that, if I were indeed the victim of a practical joke, its authors had chosen an admirable agent for carrying out their imposition. The impressive and even eloquent manner of this man would have lent dignity to an argument that the moon was made of cheese. The smile with which I had regarded him as he advanced his trance hypothesis did not appear to confuse him in the slightest degree.

"Perhaps," I said, "you will go on and favor me with some particulars as to the circumstances under which you discovered this chamber of which you speak, and its contents. I enjoy good fiction."

"In this case," was the grave reply, "no fiction could be so strange as the truth. You must know that these many years I have been cherishing the idea of building a laboratory in the large garden beside this house, for the purpose of chemical experiments for which I have a taste. Last Thursday the excavation for the cellar was at last begun. It was completed by that night, and Friday the masons were to have come. Thursday night we had a tremendous deluge of rain, and Friday morning I found my cellar a frog-pond and the walls quite washed down. My daughter, who had come out to view the disaster with me, called my attention to a corner of masonry laid bare by the crumbling away of one of the walls. I cleared a little earth from it, and, finding that it seemed part of a large mass, determined to investigate it. The workmen I sent for unearthed an oblong vault some eight feet below the surface, and set in the corner of what had evidently been the foundation walls of an ancient house. A layer of ashes and charcoal on the top of the vault showed that the house above had perished by fire. The vault itself was perfectly intact, the cement being as good as when first applied. It had a door, but this we could not force, and found entrance by removing one of the flagstones which formed the roof. The air which came up was stagnant but pure, dry and not cold. Descending with a lantern, I found myself in an apartment fitted up as a bedroom in the style of the nineteenth century. On the bed lay a young man. That he was dead and must have been dead a century was of course to be taken for granted; but the extraordinary state of preservation of the body struck me and the medical colleagues whom I had summoned with amazement. That the art of such embalming as this had ever been known we should not have believed, yet here seemed conclusive testimony that our immediate ancestors had possessed it. My medical colleagues, whose curiosity was highly excited, were at once for undertaking experiments to test the nature of the process employed, but I withheld them. My motive in so doing, at least the only motive I now need speak of, was the recollection of something I once had read about the extent to which your contemporaries had cultivated the subject of animal magnetism. It had occurred to me as just conceivable that you might be in a trance, and that the secret of your bodily integrity after so long a time was not the craft of an embalmer, but life. So extremely fanciful did this idea seem, even to me, that I did not risk the ridicule of my fellow physicians by mentioning it, but gave some other reason for postponing their experiments. No sooner, however, had they left me, than I set on foot a systematic attempt at resuscitation, of which you know the result."

Had its theme been yet more incredible, the circumstantiality of this narrative, as well as the impressive manner and personality of the narrator, might have staggered a listener, and I had begun to feel very strangely, when, as he closed, I chanced to catch a glimpse of my reflection in a mirror hanging on the wall of the room. I rose and went up to it. The face I saw was the face to a hair and a line and not a day older than the one I had looked at as I tied my cravat before going to Edith that Decoration Day, which, as this man would have me believe, was celebrated one hundred and thirteen years before. At this, the colossal character of the fraud which was being attempted on me, came over me afresh. Indignation mastered my mind as I realized the outrageous liberty that had been taken.

"You are probably surprised," said my companion, "to see that, although you are a century older than when you lay down to sleep in that underground chamber, your appearance is unchanged. That should not amaze you. It is by virtue of the total arrest of the vital functions that you have survived this great period of time. If your body could have undergone any change during your trance, it would long ago have suffered dissolution."

"Sir," I replied, turning to him, "what your motive can be in reciting to me with a serious face this remarkable farrago, I am utterly unable to guess; but you are surely yourself too intelligent to suppose that anybody but an imbecile could be deceived by it. Spare me any more of this elaborate nonsense and once for all tell me whether you refuse to give me an intelligible account of where I am and how I came here. If so, I shall proceed to ascertain my whereabouts for myself, whoever may hinder."

"You do not, then, believe that this is the year 2000?"

"Do you really think it necessary to ask me that?" I returned.

"Very well," replied my extraordinary host. "Since I cannot convince you, you shall convince yourself. Are you strong enough to follow me upstairs?"

"I am as strong as I ever was," I replied angrily, "as I may have to prove if this jest is carried much farther."

"I beg, sir," was my companion's response, "that you will not allow yourself to be too fully persuaded that you are the victim of a trick, lest the reaction, when you are convinced of the truth of my statements, should be too great."

The tone of concern, mingled with commiseration, with which he said this, and the entire absence of any sign of resentment at my hot words, strangely daunted me, and I followed him from the room with an extraordinary mixture of emotions. He led the way up two flights of stairs and then up a shorter one, which landed us upon a belvedere on the house-top. "Be pleased to look around you," he said, as we reached the platform, "and tell me if this is the Boston of the nineteenth century."

At my feet lay a great city. Miles of broad streets, shaded by trees and lined with fine buildings, for the most part not in continuous blocks but set in larger or smaller inclosures, stretched in every direction. Every quarter contained large open squares filled with trees, among which statues glistened and fountains flashed in the late afternoon sun. Public buildings of a colossal size and an architectural grandeur unparalleled in my day raised their stately piles on every side. Surely I had never seen this city nor one comparable to it before. Raising my eyes at last towards the horizon, I looked westward. That blue ribbon winding away to the sunset, was it not the sinuous Charles? I looked east; Boston harbor stretched before me within its headlands, not one of its green islets missing.

I knew then that I had been told the truth concerning the prodigious thing which had befallen me.

Chapter 4

I did not faint, but the effort to realize my position made me very giddy, and I remember that my companion had to give me a strong arm as he conducted me from the roof to a roomy apartment on the upper floor of the house, where he insisted on my drinking a glass or two of good wine and partaking of a light repast.

"I think you are going to be all right now," he said cheerily. "I should not have taken so abrupt a means to convince you of your position if your course, while perfectly excusable under the circumstances, had not rather obliged me to do so. I confess," he added laughing, "I was a little apprehensive at one time that I should undergo what I believe you used to call a knockdown in the nineteenth century, if I did not act rather promptly. I remembered that the Bostonians of your day were famous pugilists, and thought best to lose no time. I take it you are now ready to acquit me of the charge of hoaxing you."

"If you had told me," I replied, profoundly awed, "that a thousand years instead of a hundred had elapsed since I last looked on this city, I should now believe you."

"Only a century has passed," he answered, "but many a millennium in the world's history has seen changes less extraordinary."

"And now," he added, extending his hand with an air of irresistible cordiality, "let me give you a hearty welcome to the Boston of the twentieth century and to this house. My name is Leete, Dr. Leete they call me."

"My name," I said as I shook his hand, "is Julian West."

"I am most happy in making your acquaintance, Mr. West," he responded. "Seeing that this house is built on the site of your own, I hope you will find it easy to make yourself at home in it."

After my refreshment Dr. Leete offered me a bath and a change of clothing, of which I gladly availed myself.

It did not appear that any very startling revolution in men's attire had been among the great changes my host had spoken of, for, barring a few details, my new habiliments did not puzzle me at all.

Physically, I was now myself again. But mentally, how was it with me, the reader will doubtless wonder. What were my intellectual sensations, he may wish to know, on finding myself so suddenly dropped as it were into a new world. In reply let me ask him to suppose himself suddenly, in the twinkling of an eye, transported from earth, say, to Paradise or Hades. What does he fancy would be his own experience? Would his thoughts return at once to the earth he had just left, or would he, after the first shock, wellnigh forget his former life for a while, albeit to be remembered later, in the interest excited by his new surroundings? All I can say is, that if his experience were at all like mine in the transition I am describing, the latter hypothesis would prove the correct one. The impressions of amazement and curiosity which my new surroundings produced occupied my mind, after the first shock, to the exclusion of all other thoughts. For the time the memory of my former life was, as it were, in abeyance.

No sooner did I find myself physically rehabilitated through the kind offices of my host, than I became eager to return to the house-top; and presently we were comfortably established there in easy-chairs, with the city beneath and around us. After Dr. Leete had responded to numerous questions on my part, as to the ancient landmarks I missed and the new ones which had replaced them, he asked me what point of the contrast between the new and the old city struck me most forcibly.

"To speak of small things before great," I responded, "I really think that the complete absence of chimneys and their smoke is the detail that first impressed me."

"Ah!" ejaculated my companion with an air of much interest, "I had forgotten the chimneys, it is so long since they went out of use. It is nearly a century since the crude method of combustion on which you depended for heat became obsolete."

"In general," I said, "what impresses me most about the city is the material prosperity on the part of the people which its magnificence implies."

"I would give a great deal for just one glimpse of the Boston of your day," replied Dr. Leete. "No doubt, as you imply, the cities of that period were rather shabby affairs. If you had the taste to make them splendid, which I would not be so rude as to question, the general poverty resulting from your extraordinary industrial system would not have given you the means. Moreover, the excessive individualism which then prevailed was inconsistent with much public spirit. What little wealth you had seems almost wholly to have been lavished in private luxury. Nowadays, on the contrary, there is no destination of the surplus wealth so popular as the adornment of the city, which all enjoy in equal degree."

The sun had been setting as we returned to the house-top, and as we talked night descended upon the city.

"It is growing dark," said Dr. Leete. "Let us descend into the house; I want to introduce my wife and daughter to you."

His words recalled to me the feminine voices which I had heard whispering about me as I was coming back to conscious life; and, most curious to learn what the ladies of the year 2000 were like, I assented with alacrity to the proposition. The apartment in which we found the wife and daughter of my host, as well as the entire interior of the house, was filled with a mellow light, which I knew must be artificial, although I could not discover the source from which it was diffused. Mrs. Leete was an exceptionally fine looking and well preserved woman of about her husband's age, while the daughter, who was in the first blush of womanhood, was the most beautiful girl I had ever seen. Her face was as bewitching as deep blue eyes, delicately tinted complexion, and perfect features could make it, but even had her countenance lacked special charms, the faultless luxuriance of her figure would have given her place as a beauty among the women of the nineteenth century. Feminine softness and delicacy were in this lovely creature deliciously combined with an appearance of health and abounding physical vitality too often lacking in the maidens with whom alone I could compare her. It was a coincidence trifling in comparison with the general strangeness of the situation, but still striking, that her name should be Edith.

The evening that followed was certainly unique in the history of social intercourse, but to suppose that our conversation was peculiarly strained or difficult would be a great mistake. I believe indeed that it is under what may be called unnatural, in the sense of extraordinary, circumstances that people behave most naturally, for the reason, no doubt, that such circumstances banish artificiality. I know at any rate that my intercourse that evening with these representatives of another age and world was marked by an ingenuous sincerity and frankness such as but rarely crown long acquaintance. No doubt the exquisite tact of my entertainers had much to do with this. Of course there was nothing we could talk of but the strange experience by virtue of which I was there, but they talked of it with an interest so naive and direct in its expression as to relieve the subject to a great degree of the element of the weird and the uncanny which might so easily have been overpowering. One would have supposed that they were quite in the habit of entertaining waifs from another century, so perfect was their tact.

For my own part, never do I remember the operations of my mind to have been more alert and acute than that evening, or my intellectual sensibilities more keen. Of course I do not mean that the consciousness of my amazing situation was for a moment out of mind, but its chief effect thus far was to produce a feverish elation, a sort of mental intoxication.[1]

Edith Leete took little part in the conversation, but when several times the magnetism of her beauty drew my glance to her face, I found her eyes fixed on me with an absorbed intensity, almost like fascination. It was evident that I had excited her interest to an extraordinary degree, as was not astonishing, supposing her to be a girl of imagination. Though I supposed curiosity was the chief motive of her interest, it could but affect me as it would not have done had she been less beautiful.

Dr. Leete, as well as the ladies, seemed greatly interested in my account of the circumstances under which I had gone to sleep in the underground chamber. All had suggestions to offer to account for my having been forgotten there, and the theory which we finally agreed on offers at least a plausible explanation, although whether it be in its details the true one, nobody, of course, will ever know. The layer of ashes found above the chamber indicated that the house had been burned down. Let it be supposed that the conflagration had taken place the night I fell asleep. It only remains to assume that Sawyer lost his life in the fire or by some accident connected with it, and the rest follows naturally enough. No one but he and Dr. Pillsbury either knew of the existence of the chamber or that I was in it, and Dr. Pillsbury, who had gone that night to New Orleans, had probably never heard of the fire at all. The conclusion of my friends, and of the public, must have been that I had perished in the flames. An excavation of the ruins, unless thorough, would not have disclosed the recess in the foundation walls connecting with my chamber. To be sure, if the site had been again built upon, at least immediately, such an excavation would have been necessary, but the troublous times and the undesirable character of the locality might well have prevented rebuilding. The size of the trees in the garden now occupying the site indicated, Dr. Leete said, that for more than half a century at least it had been open ground.

[1] In accounting for this state of mind it must be remembered that, except for the topic of our conversations, there was in my surroundings next to nothing to suggest what had befallen me. Within a block of my home in the old Boston I could have found social circles vastly more foreign to me. The speech of the Bostonians of the twentieth century differs even less from that of their cultured ancestors of the nineteenth than did that of the latter from the language of Washington and Franklin, while the differences between the style of dress and furniture of the two epochs are not more marked than I have known fashion to make in the time of one generation.

Chapter 5

When, in the course of the evening the ladies retired, leaving Dr. Leete and myself alone, he sounded me as to my disposition for sleep, saying that if I felt like it my bed was ready for me; but if I was inclined to wakefulness nothing would please him better than to bear me company. "I am a late bird, myself," he said, "and, without suspicion of flattery, I may say that a companion more interesting than yourself could scarcely be imagined. It is decidedly not often that one has a chance to converse with a man of the nineteenth century."

Now I had been looking forward all the evening with some dread to the time when I should be alone, on retiring for the night. Surrounded by these most friendly strangers, stimulated and supported by their sympathetic interest, I had been able to keep my mental balance. Even then, however, in pauses of the conversation I had had glimpses, vivid as lightning flashes, of the horror of strangeness that was waiting to be faced when I could no longer command diversion. I knew I could not sleep that night, and as for lying awake and thinking, it argues no cowardice, I am sure, to confess that I was afraid of it. When, in reply to my host's question, I frankly told him this, he replied that it would be strange if I did not feel just so, but that I need have no anxiety about sleeping; whenever I wanted to go to bed, he would give me a dose which would insure me a sound night's sleep without fail. Next morning, no doubt, I would awake with the feeling of an old citizen.

"Before I acquired that," I replied, "I must know a little more about the sort of Boston I have come back to. You told me when we were upon the house-top that though a century only had elapsed since I fell asleep, it had been marked by greater changes in the conditions of humanity than many a previous millennium. With the city before me I could well believe that, but I am very curious to know what some of the changes have been. To make a beginning somewhere, for the subject is doubtless a large one, what solution, if any, have you found for the labor question? It was the Sphinx's riddle of the nineteenth century, and when I dropped out the Sphinx was threatening to devour society, because the answer was not forthcoming. It is well worth sleeping a hundred years to learn what the right answer was, if, indeed, you have found it yet."

"As no such thing as the labor question is known nowadays," replied Dr. Leete, "and there is no way in which it could arise, I suppose we may claim to have solved it. Society would indeed have fully deserved being devoured if it had failed to answer a riddle so entirely simple. In fact, to speak by the book, it was not necessary for society to solve the riddle at all. It may be said to have solved itself. The solution came as the result of a process of industrial evolution which could not have terminated otherwise. All that society had to do was to recognize and cooperate with that evolution, when its tendency had become unmistakable."

"I can only say," I answered, "that at the time I fell asleep no such evolution had been recognized."

"It was in 1887 that you fell into this sleep, I think you said."

"Yes, May 30th, 1887."

My companion regarded me musingly for some moments. Then he observed, "And you tell me that even then there was no general recognition of the nature of the crisis which society was nearing? Of course, I fully credit your statement. The singular blindness of your contemporaries to the signs of the times is a phenomenon commented on by many of our historians, but few facts of history are more difficult for us to realize, so obvious and unmistakable as we look back seem the indications, which must also have come under your eyes, of the transformation about to come to pass. I should be interested, Mr. West, if you would give me a little more definite idea of the view which you and men of your grade of intellect took of the state and prospects of society in 1887. You must, at least, have realized that the widespread industrial and social troubles, and the underlying dissatisfaction of all classes with the inequalities of society, and the general misery of mankind, were portents of great changes of some sort."

"We did, indeed, fully realize that," I replied. "We felt that society was dragging anchor and in danger of going adrift. Whither it would drift nobody could say, but all feared the rocks."

"Nevertheless," said Dr. Leete, "the set of the current was perfectly perceptible if you had but taken pains to observe it, and it was not toward the rocks, but toward a deeper channel."

"We had a popular proverb," I replied, "that 'hindsight is better than foresight,' the force of which I shall now, no doubt, appreciate more fully than ever. All I can say is, that the prospect was such when I went into that long sleep that I should not have been surprised had I looked down from your house-top to-day on a heap of charred and moss-grown ruins instead of this glorious city."

Dr. Leete had listened to me with close attention and nodded thoughtfully as I finished speaking. "What you have said," he observed, "will be regarded as a most valuable vindication of Storiot, whose account of your era has been generally thought exaggerated in its picture of the gloom and confusion of men's minds. That a period of transition like that should be full of excitement and agitation was indeed to be looked for; but seeing how plain was the tendency of the forces in operation, it was natural to believe that hope rather than fear would have been the prevailing temper of the popular mind."

"You have not yet told me what was the answer to the riddle which you found," I said. "I am impatient to know by what contradiction of natural sequence the peace and prosperity which you now seem to enjoy could have been the outcome of an era like my own."

"Excuse me," replied my host, "but do you smoke?" It was not till our cigars were lighted and drawing well that he resumed. "Since you are in the humor to talk rather than to sleep, as I certainly am, perhaps I cannot do better than to try to give you enough idea of our modern industrial system to dissipate at least the impression that there is any mystery about the process of its evolution. The Bostonians of your day had the reputation of being great askers of questions, and I am going to show my descent by asking you one to begin with. What should you name as the most prominent feature of the labor troubles of your day?"

"Why, the strikes, of course," I replied.

"Exactly; but what made the strikes so formidable?"

"The great labor organizations."

"And what was the motive of these great organizations?"

"The workmen claimed they had to organize to get their rights from the big corporations," I replied.

"That is just it," said Dr. Leete; "the organization of labor and the strikes were an effect, merely, of the concentration of capital in greater masses than had ever been known before. Before this concentration began, while as yet commerce and industry were conducted by innumerable petty concerns with small capital, instead of a small number of great concerns with vast capital, the individual workman was relatively important and independent in his relations to the employer. Moreover, when a little capital or a new idea was enough to start a man in business for himself, workingmen were constantly becoming employers and there was no hard and fast line between the two classes. Labor unions were needless then, and general strikes out of the question. But when the era of small concerns with small capital was succeeded by that of the great aggregations of capital, all this was changed. The individual laborer, who had been relatively important to the small employer, was reduced to insignificance and powerlessness over against the great corporation, while at the same time the way upward to the grade of employer was closed to him. Self-defense drove him to union with his fellows.

"The records of the period show that the outcry against the concentration of capital was furious. Men believed that it threatened society with a form of tyranny more abhorrent than it had ever endured. They believed that the great corporations were preparing for them the yoke of a baser servitude than had ever been imposed on the race, servitude not to men but to soulless machines incapable of any motive but insatiable greed. Looking back, we cannot wonder at their desperation, for certainly humanity was never confronted with a fate more sordid and hideous than would have been the era of corporate tyranny which they anticipated.

"Meanwhile, without being in the smallest degree checked by the clamor against it, the absorption of business by ever larger monopolies continued. In the United States there was not, after the beginning of the last quarter of the century, any opportunity whatever for individual enterprise in any important field of industry, unless backed by a great capital. During the last decade of the century, such small businesses as still remained were fast-failing survivals of a past epoch, or mere parasites on the great corporations, or else existed in fields too small to attract the great capitalists. Small businesses, as far as they still remained, were reduced to the condition of rats and mice, living in holes and corners, and counting on evading notice for the enjoyment of existence. The railroads had gone on combining till a few great syndicates controlled every rail in the land. In manufactories, every important staple was controlled by a syndicate. These syndicates, pools, trusts, or whatever their name, fixed prices and crushed all competition except when combinations as vast as themselves arose. Then a struggle, resulting in a still greater consolidation, ensued. The great city bazar crushed it country rivals with branch stores, and in the city itself absorbed its smaller rivals till the business of a whole quarter was concentrated under one roof, with a hundred former proprietors of shops serving as clerks. Having no business of his own to put his money in, the small capitalist, at the same time that he took service under the corporation, found no other investment for his money but its stocks and bonds, thus becoming doubly dependent upon it.

"The fact that the desperate popular opposition to the consolidation of business in a few powerful hands had no effect to check it proves that there must have been a strong economical reason for it. The small capitalists, with their innumerable petty concerns, had in fact yielded the field to the great aggregations of capital, because they belonged to a day of small things and were totally incompetent to the demands of an age of steam and telegraphs and the gigantic scale of its enterprises. To restore the former order of things, even if possible, would have involved returning to the day of stagecoaches. Oppressive and intolerable as was the regime of the great consolidations of capital, even its victims, while they cursed it, were forced to admit the prodigious increase of efficiency which had been imparted to the national industries, the vast economies effected by concentration of management and unity of organization, and to confess that since the new system had taken the place of the old the wealth of the world had increased at a rate before undreamed of. To be sure this vast increase had gone chiefly to make the rich richer, increasing the gap between them and the poor; but the fact remained that, as a means merely of producing wealth, capital had been proved efficient in proportion to its consolidation. The restoration of the old system with the subdivision of capital, if it were possible, might indeed bring back a greater equality of conditions, with more individual dignity and freedom, but it would be at the price of general poverty and the arrest of material progress.

"Was there, then, no way of commanding the services of the mighty wealth-producing principle of consolidated capital without bowing down to a plutocracy like that of Carthage? As soon as men began to ask themselves these questions, they found the answer ready for them. The movement toward the conduct of business by larger and larger aggregations of capital, the tendency toward monopolies, which had been so desperately and vainly resisted, was recognized at last, in its true significance, as a process which only needed to complete its logical evolution to open a golden future to humanity.

"Early in the last century the evolution was completed by the final consolidation of the entire capital of the nation. The industry and commerce of the country, ceasing to be conducted by a set of irresponsible corporations and syndicates of private persons at their caprice and for their profit, were intrusted to a single syndicate representing the people, to be conducted in the common interest for the common profit. The nation, that is to say, organized as the one great business corporation in which all other corporations were absorbed; it became the one capitalist in the place of all other capitalists, the sole employer, the final monopoly in which all previous and lesser monopolies were swallowed up, a monopoly in the profits and economies of which all citizens shared. The epoch of trusts had ended in The Great Trust. In a word, the people of the United States concluded to assume the conduct of their own business, just as one hundred odd years before they had assumed the conduct of their own government, organizing now for industrial purposes on precisely the same grounds that they had then organized for political purposes. At last, strangely late in the world's history, the obvious fact was perceived that no business is so essentially the public business as the industry and commerce on which the people's livelihood depends, and that to entrust it to private persons to be managed for private profit is a folly similar in kind, though vastly greater in magnitude, to that of surrendering the functions of political government to kings and nobles to be conducted for their personal glorification."

"Such a stupendous change as you describe," said I, "did not, of course, take place without great bloodshed and terrible convulsions."

"On the contrary," replied Dr. Leete, "there was absolutely no violence. The change had been long foreseen. Public opinion had become fully ripe for it, and the whole mass of the people was behind it. There was no more possibility of opposing it by force than by argument. On the other hand the popular sentiment toward the great corporations and those identified with them had ceased to be one of bitterness, as they came to realize their necessity as a link, a transition phase, in the evolution of the true industrial system. The most violent foes of the great private monopolies were now forced to recognize how invaluable and indispensable had been their office in educating the people up to the point of assuming control of their own business. Fifty years before, the consolidation of the industries of the country under national control would have seemed a very daring experiment to the most sanguine. But by a series of object lessons, seen and studied by all men, the great corporations had taught the people an entirely new set of ideas on this subject. They had seen for many years syndicates handling revenues greater than those of states, and directing the labors of hundreds of thousands of men with an efficiency and economy unattainable in smaller operations. It had come to be recognized as an axiom that the larger the business the simpler the principles that can be applied to it; that, as the machine is truer than the hand, so the system, which in a great concern does the work of the master's eye in a small business, turns out more accurate results. Thus it came about that, thanks to the corporations themselves, when it was proposed that the nation should assume their functions, the suggestion implied nothing which seemed impracticable even to the timid. To be sure it was a step beyond any yet taken, a broader generalization, but the very fact that the nation would be the sole corporation in the field would, it was seen, relieve the undertaking of many difficulties with which the partial monopolies had contended."

Chapter 6

Dr. Leete ceased speaking, and I remained silent, endeavoring to form some general conception of the changes in the arrangements of society implied in the tremendous revolution which he had described.

Finally I said, "The idea of such an extension of the functions of government is, to say the least, rather overwhelming."

"Extension!" he repeated, "where is the extension?"

"In my day," I replied, "it was considered that the proper functions of government, strictly speaking, were limited to keeping the peace and defending the people against the public enemy, that is, to the military and police powers."

"And, in heaven's name, who are the public enemies?" exclaimed Dr. Leete. "Are they France, England, Germany, or hunger, cold, and nakedness? In your day governments were accustomed, on the slightest international misunderstanding, to seize upon the bodies of citizens and deliver them over by hundreds of thousands to death and mutilation, wasting their treasures the while like water; and all this oftenest for no imaginable profit to the victims. We have no wars now, and our governments no war powers, but in order to protect every citizen against hunger, cold, and nakedness, and provide for all his physical and mental needs, the function is assumed of directing his industry for a term of years. No, Mr. West, I am sure on reflection you will perceive that it was in your age, not in ours, that the extension of the functions of governments was extraordinary. Not even for the best ends would men now allow their governments such powers as were then used for the most maleficent."

"Leaving comparisons aside," I said, "the demagoguery and corruption of our public men would have been considered, in my day, insuperable objections to any assumption by government of the charge of the national industries. We should have thought that no arrangement could be worse than to entrust the politicians with control of the wealth-producing machinery of the country. Its material interests were quite too much the football of parties as it was."

"No doubt you were right," rejoined Dr. Leete, "but all that is changed now. We have no parties or politicians, and as for demagoguery and corruption, they are words having only an historical significance."

"Human nature itself must have changed very much," I said.

"Not at all," was Dr. Leete's reply, "but the conditions of human life have changed, and with them the motives of human action. The organization of society with you was such that officials were under a constant temptation to misuse their power for the private profit of themselves or others. Under such circumstances it seems almost strange that you dared entrust them with any of your affairs. Nowadays, on the contrary, society is so constituted that there is absolutely no way in which an official, however ill-disposed, could possibly make any profit for himself or any one else by a misuse of his power. Let him be as bad an official as you please, he cannot be a corrupt one. There is no motive to be. The social system no longer offers a premium on dishonesty. But these are matters which you can only understand as you come, with time, to know us better."

"But you have not yet told me how you have settled the labor problem. It is the problem of capital which we have been discussing," I said. "After the nation had assumed conduct of the mills, machinery, railroads, farms, mines, and capital in general of the country, the labor question still remained. In assuming the responsibilities of capital the nation had assumed the difficulties of the capitalist's position."

"The moment the nation assumed the responsibilities of capital those difficulties vanished," replied Dr. Leete. "The national organization of labor under one direction was the complete solution of what was, in your day and under your system, justly regarded as the insoluble labor problem. When the nation became the sole employer, all the citizens, by virtue of their citizenship, became employees, to be distributed according to the needs of industry."

"That is," I suggested, "you have simply applied the principle of universal military service, as it was understood in our day, to the labor question."

"Yes," said Dr. Leete, "that was something which followed as a matter of course as soon as the nation had become the sole capitalist. The people were already accustomed to the idea that the obligation of every citizen, not physically disabled, to contribute his military services to the defense of the nation was equal and absolute. That it was equally the duty of every citizen to contribute his quota of industrial or intellectual services to the maintenance of the nation was equally evident, though it was not until the nation became the employer of labor that citizens were able to render this sort of service with any pretense either of universality or equity. No organization of labor was possible when the employing power was divided among hundreds or thousands of individuals and corporations, between which concert of any kind was neither desired, nor indeed feasible. It constantly happened then that vast numbers who desired to labor could find no opportunity, and on the other hand, those who desired to evade a part or all of their debt could easily do so."

"Service, now, I suppose, is compulsory upon all," I suggested.

"It is rather a matter of course than of compulsion," replied Dr. Leete. "It is regarded as so absolutely natural and reasonable that the idea of its being compulsory has ceased to be thought of. He would be thought to be an incredibly contemptible person who should need compulsion in such a case. Nevertheless, to speak of service being compulsory would be a weak way to state its absolute inevitableness. Our entire social order is so wholly based upon and deduced from it that if it were conceivable that a man could escape it, he would be left with no possible way to provide for his existence. He would have excluded himself from the world, cut himself off from his kind, in a word, committed suicide."

"Is the term of service in this industrial army for life?"

"Oh, no; it both begins later and ends earlier than the average working period in your day. Your workshops were filled with children and old men, but we hold the period of youth sacred to education, and the period of maturity, when the physical forces begin to flag, equally sacred to ease and agreeable relaxation. The period of industrial service is twenty-four years, beginning at the close of the course of education at twenty-one and terminating at forty-five. After forty-five, while discharged from labor, the citizen still remains liable to special calls, in case of emergencies causing a sudden great increase in the demand for labor, till he reaches the age of fifty-five, but such calls are rarely, in fact almost never, made. The fifteenth day of October of every year is what we call Muster Day, because those who have reached the age of twenty-one are then mustered into the industrial service, and at the same time those who, after twenty-four years' service, have reached the age of forty-five, are honorably mustered out. It is the great day of the year with us, whence we reckon all other events, our Olympiad, save that it is annual."

Chapter 7

"It is after you have mustered your industrial army into service," I said, "that I should expect the chief difficulty to arise, for there its analogy with a military army must cease. Soldiers have all the same thing, and a very simple thing, to do, namely, to practice the manual of arms, to march and stand guard. But the industrial army must learn and follow two or three hundred diverse trades and avocations. What administrative talent can be equal to determining wisely what trade or business every individual in a great nation shall pursue?"

"The administration has nothing to do with determining that point."

"Who does determine it, then?" I asked.

"Every man for himself in accordance with his natural aptitude, the utmost pains being taken to enable him to find out what his natural aptitude really is. The principle on which our industrial army is organized is that a man's natural endowments, mental and physical, determine what he can work at most profitably to the nation and most satisfactorily to himself. While the obligation of service in some form is not to be evaded, voluntary election, subject only to necessary regulation, is depended on to determine the particular sort of service every man is to render. As an individual's satisfaction during his term of service depends on his having an occupation to his taste, parents and teachers watch from early years for indications of special aptitudes in children. A thorough study of the National industrial system, with the history and rudiments of all the great trades, is an essential part of our educational system. While manual training is not allowed to encroach on the general intellectual culture to which our schools are devoted, it is carried far enough to give our youth, in addition to their theoretical knowledge of the national industries, mechanical and agricultural, a certain familiarity with their tools and methods. Our schools are constantly visiting our workshops, and often are taken on long excursions to inspect particular industrial enterprises. In your day a man was not ashamed to be grossly ignorant of all trades except his own, but such ignorance would not be consistent with our idea of placing every one in a position to select intelligently the occupation for which he has most taste. Usually long before he is mustered into service a young man has found out the pursuit he wants to follow, has acquired a great deal of knowledge about it, and is waiting impatiently the time when he can enlist in its ranks."

"Surely," I said, "it can hardly be that the number of volunteers for any trade is exactly the number needed in that trade. It must be generally either under or over the demand."

"The supply of volunteers is always expected to fully equal the demand," replied Dr. Leete. "It is the business of the administration to see that this is the case. The rate of volunteering for each trade is closely watched. If there be a noticeably greater excess of volunteers over men needed in any trade, it is inferred that the trade offers greater attractions than others. On the other hand, if the number of volunteers for a trade tends to drop below the demand, it is inferred that it is thought more arduous. It is the business of the administration to seek constantly to equalize the attractions of the trades, so far as the conditions of labor in them are concerned, so that all trades shall be equally attractive to persons having natural tastes for them. This is done by making the hours of labor in different trades to differ according to their arduousness. The lighter trades, prosecuted under the most agreeable circumstances, have in this way the longest hours, while an arduous trade, such as mining, has very short hours. There is no theory, no a priori rule, by which the respective attractiveness of industries is determined. The administration, in taking burdens off one class of workers and adding them to other classes, simply follows the fluctuations of opinion among the workers themselves as indicated by the rate of volunteering. The principle is that no man's work ought to be, on the whole, harder for him than any other man's for him, the workers themselves to be the judges. There are no limits to the application of this rule. If any particular occupation is in itself so arduous or so oppressive that, in order to induce volunteers, the day's work in it had to be reduced to ten minutes, it would be done. If, even then, no man was willing to do it, it would remain undone. But of course, in point of fact, a moderate reduction in the hours of labor, or addition of other privileges, suffices to secure all needed volunteers for any occupation necessary to men. If, indeed, the unavoidable difficulties and dangers of such a necessary pursuit were so great that no inducement of compensating advantages would overcome men's repugnance to it, the administration would only need to take it out of the common order of occupations by declaring it 'extra hazardous,' and those who pursued it especially worthy of the national gratitude, to be overrun with volunteers. Our young men are very greedy of honor, and do not let slip such opportunities. Of course you will see that dependence on the purely voluntary choice of avocations involves the abolition in all of anything like unhygienic conditions or special peril to life and limb. Health and safety are conditions common to all industries. The nation does not maim and slaughter its workmen by thousands, as did the private capitalists and corporations of your day."

"When there are more who want to enter a particular trade than there is room for, how do you decide between the applicants?" I inquired.

"Preference is given to those who have acquired the most knowledge of the trade they wish to follow. No man, however, who through successive years remains persistent in his desire to show what he can do at any particular trade, is in the end denied an opportunity. Meanwhile, if a man cannot at first win entrance into the business he prefers, he has usually one or more alternative preferences, pursuits for which he has some degree of aptitude, although not the highest. Every one, indeed, is expected to study his aptitudes so as to have not only a first choice as to occupation, but a second or third, so that if, either at the outset of his career or subsequently, owing to the progress of invention or changes in demand, he is unable to follow his first vocation, he can still find reasonably congenial employment. This principle of secondary choices as to occupation is quite important in our system. I should add, in reference to the counter-possibility of some sudden failure of volunteers in a particular trade, or some sudden necessity of an increased force, that the administration, while depending on the voluntary system for filling up the trades as a rule, holds always in reserve the power to call for special volunteers, or draft any force needed from any quarter. Generally, however, all needs of this sort can be met by details from the class of unskilled or common laborers."

"How is this class of common laborers recruited?" I asked. "Surely nobody voluntarily enters that."

"It is the grade to which all new recruits belong for the first three years of their service. It is not till after this period, during which he is assignable to any work at the discretion of his superiors, that the young man is allowed to elect a special avocation. These three years of stringent discipline none are exempt from, and very glad our young men are to pass from this severe school into the comparative liberty of the trades. If a man were so stupid as to have no choice as to occupation, he would simply remain a common laborer; but such cases, as you may suppose, are not common."

"Having once elected and entered on a trade or occupation," I remarked, "I suppose he has to stick to it the rest of his life."

"Not necessarily," replied Dr. Leete; "while frequent and merely capricious changes of occupation are not encouraged or even permitted, every worker is allowed, of course, under certain regulations and in accordance with the exigencies of the service, to volunteer for another industry which he thinks would suit him better than his first choice. In this case his application is received just as if he were volunteering for the first time, and on the same terms. Not only this, but a worker may likewise, under suitable regulations and not too frequently, obtain a transfer to an establishment of the same industry in another part of the country which for any reason he may prefer. Under your system a discontented man could indeed leave his work at will, but he left his means of support at the same time, and took his chances as to future livelihood. We find that the number of men who wish to abandon an accustomed occupation for a new one, and old friends and associations for strange ones, is small. It is only the poorer sort of workmen who desire to change even as frequently as our regulations permit. Of course transfers or discharges, when health demands them, are always given."

"As an industrial system, I should think this might be extremely efficient," I said, "but I don't see that it makes any provision for the professional classes, the men who serve the nation with brains instead of hands. Of course you can't get along without the brain-workers. How, then, are they selected from those who are to serve as farmers and mechanics? That must require a very delicate sort of sifting process, I should say."

"So it does," replied Dr. Leete; "the most delicate possible test is needed here, and so we leave the question whether a man shall be a brain or hand worker entirely to him to settle. At the end of the term of three years as a common laborer, which every man must serve, it is for him to choose, in accordance to his natural tastes, whether he will fit himself for an art or profession, or be a farmer or mechanic. If he feels that he can do better work with his brains than his muscles, he finds every facility provided for testing the reality of his supposed bent, of cultivating it, and if fit of pursuing it as his avocation. The schools of technology, of medicine, of art, of music, of histrionics, and of higher liberal learning are always open to aspirants without condition."

"Are not the schools flooded with young men whose only motive is to avoid work?"

Dr. Leete smiled a little grimly.

"No one is at all likely to enter the professional schools for the purpose of avoiding work, I assure you," he said. "They are intended for those with special aptitude for the branches they teach, and any one without it would find it easier to do double hours at his trade than try to keep up with the classes. Of course many honestly mistake their vocation, and, finding themselves unequal to the requirements of the schools, drop out and return to the industrial service; no discredit attaches to such persons, for the public policy is to encourage all to develop suspected talents which only actual tests can prove the reality of. The professional and scientific schools of your day depended on the patronage of their pupils for support, and the practice appears to have been common of giving diplomas to unfit persons, who afterwards found their way into the professions. Our schools are national institutions, and to have passed their tests is a proof of special abilities not to be questioned.

"This opportunity for a professional training," the doctor continued, "remains open to every man till the age of thirty is reached, after which students are not received, as there would remain too brief a period before the age of discharge in which to serve the nation in their professions. In your day young men had to choose their professions very young, and therefore, in a large proportion of instances, wholly mistook their vocations. It is recognized nowadays that the natural aptitudes of some are later than those of others in developing, and therefore, while the choice of profession may be made as early as twenty-four, it remains open for six years longer."

A question which had a dozen times before been on my lips now found utterance, a question which touched upon what, in my time, had been regarded the most vital difficulty in the way of any final settlement of the industrial problem. "It is an extraordinary thing," I said, "that you should not yet have said a word about the method of adjusting wages. Since the nation is the sole employer, the government must fix the rate of wages and determine just how much everybody shall earn, from the doctors to the diggers. All I can say is, that this plan would never have worked with us, and I don't see how it can now unless human nature has changed. In my day, nobody was satisfied with his wages or salary. Even if he felt he received enough, he was sure his neighbor had too much, which was as bad. If the universal discontent on this subject, instead of being dissipated in curses and strikes directed against innumerable employers, could have been concentrated upon one, and that the government, the strongest ever devised would not have seen two pay days."

Dr. Leete laughed heartily.

"Very true, very true," he said, "a general strike would most probably have followed the first pay day, and a strike directed against a government is a revolution."

"How, then, do you avoid a revolution every pay day?" if demanded. "Has some prodigious philosopher devised a new system of calculus satisfactory to all for determining the exact and comparative value of all sorts of service, whether by brawn or brain, by hand or voice, by ear or eye? Or has human nature itself changed, so that no man looks upon his own things but 'every man on the things of his neighbor'? One or the other of these events must be the explanation."

"Neither one nor the other, however, is," was my host's laughing response. "And now, Mr. West," he continued, "you must remember that you are my patient as well as my guest, and permit me to prescribe sleep for you before we have any more conversation. It is after three o'clock."

"The prescription is, no doubt, a wise one," I said; "I only hope it can be filled."

"I will see to that," the doctor replied, and he did, for he gave me a wineglass of something or other which sent me to sleep as soon as my head touched the pillow.

Chapter 8

When I awoke I felt greatly refreshed, and lay a considerable time in a dozing state, enjoying the sensation of bodily comfort. The experiences of the day previous, my waking to find myself in the year 2000, the sight of the new Boston, my host and his family, and the wonderful things I had heard, were a blank in my memory. I thought I was in my bed-chamber at home, and the half-dreaming, half-waking fancies which passed before my mind related to the incidents and experiences of my former life. Dreamily I reviewed the incidents of Decoration Day, my trip in company with Edith and her parents to Mount Auburn, and my dining with them on our return to the city. I recalled how extremely well Edith had looked, and from that fell to thinking of our marriage; but scarcely had my imagination begun to develop this delightful theme than my waking dream was cut short by the recollection of the letter I had received the night before from the builder announcing that the new strikes might postpone indefinitely the completion of the new house. The chagrin which this recollection brought with it effectually roused me. I remembered that I had an appointment with the builder at eleven o'clock, to discuss the strike, and opening my eyes, looked up at the clock at the foot of my bed to see what time it was. But no clock met my glance, and what was more, I instantly perceived that I was not in my room. Starting up on my couch, I stared wildly round the strange apartment.

I think it must have been many seconds that I sat up thus in bed staring about, without being able to regain the clew to my personal identity. I was no more able to distinguish myself from pure being during those moments than we may suppose a soul in the rough to be before it has received the ear-marks, the individualizing touches which make it a person. Strange that the sense of this inability should be such anguish! but so we are constituted. There are no words for the mental torture I endured during this helpless, eyeless groping for myself in a boundless void. No other experience of the mind gives probably anything like the sense of absolute intellectual arrest from the loss of a mental fulcrum, a starting point of thought, which comes during such a momentary obscuration of the sense of one's identity. I trust I may never know what it is again.

I do not know how long this condition had lasted—it seemed an interminable time—when, like a flash, the recollection of everything came back to me. I remembered who and where I was, and how I had come here, and that these scenes as of the life of yesterday which had been passing before my mind concerned a generation long, long ago mouldered to dust. Leaping from bed, I stood in the middle of the room clasping my temples with all my might between my hands to keep them from bursting. Then I fell prone on the couch, and, burying my face in the pillow, lay without motion. The reaction which was inevitable, from the mental elation, the fever of the intellect that had been the first effect of my tremendous experience, had arrived. The emotional crisis which had awaited the full realization of my actual position, and all that it implied, was upon me, and with set teeth and laboring chest, gripping the bedstead with frenzied strength, I lay there and fought for my sanity. In my mind, all had broken loose, habits of feeling, associations of thought, ideas of persons and things, all had dissolved and lost coherence and were seething together in apparently irretrievable chaos. There were no rallying points, nothing was left stable. There only remained the will, and was any human will strong enough to say to such a weltering sea, "Peace, be still"? I dared not think. Every effort to reason upon what had befallen me, and realize what it implied, set up an intolerable swimming of the brain. The idea that I was two persons, that my identity was double, began to fascinate me with its simple solution of my experience.

I knew that I was on the verge of losing my mental balance. If I lay there thinking, I was doomed. Diversion of some sort I must have, at least the diversion of physical exertion. I sprang up, and, hastily dressing, opened the door of my room and went down-stairs. The hour was very early, it being not yet fairly light, and I found no one in the lower part of the house. There was a hat in the hall, and, opening the front door, which was fastened with a slightness indicating that burglary was not among the perils of the modern Boston, I found myself on the street. For two hours I walked or ran through the streets of the city, visiting most quarters of the peninsular part of the town. None but an antiquarian who knows something of the contrast which the Boston of today offers to the Boston of the nineteenth century can begin to appreciate what a series of bewildering surprises I underwent during that time. Viewed from the house-top the day before, the city had indeed appeared strange to me, but that was only in its general aspect. How complete the change had been I first realized now that I walked the streets. The few old landmarks which still remained only intensified this effect, for without them I might have imagined myself in a foreign town. A man may leave his native city in childhood, and return fifty years later, perhaps, to find it transformed in many features. He is astonished, but he is not bewildered. He is aware of a great lapse of time, and of changes likewise occurring in himself meanwhile. He but dimly recalls the city as he knew it when a child. But remember that there was no sense of any lapse of time with me. So far as my consciousness was concerned, it was but yesterday, but a few hours, since I had walked these streets in which scarcely a feature had escaped a complete metamorphosis. The mental image of the old city was so fresh and strong that it did not yield to the impression of the actual city, but contended with it, so that it was first one and then the other which seemed the more unreal. There was nothing I saw which was not blurred in this way, like the faces of a composite photograph.

Finally, I stood again at the door of the house from which I had come out. My feet must have instinctively brought me back to the site of my old home, for I had no clear idea of returning thither. It was no more homelike to me than any other spot in this city of a strange generation, nor were its inmates less utterly and necessarily strangers than all the other men and women now on the earth. Had the door of the house been locked, I should have been reminded by its resistance that I had no object in entering, and turned away, but it yielded to my hand, and advancing with uncertain steps through the hall, I entered one of the apartments opening from it. Throwing myself into a chair, I covered my burning eyeballs with my hands to shut out the horror of strangeness. My mental confusion was so intense as to produce actual nausea. The anguish of those moments, during which my brain seemed melting, or the abjectness of my sense of helplessness, how can I describe? In my despair I groaned aloud. I began to feel that unless some help should come I was about to lose my mind. And just then it did come. I heard the rustle of drapery, and looked up. Edith Leete was standing before me. Her beautiful face was full of the most poignant sympathy.

"Oh, what is the matter, Mr. West?" she said. "I was here when you came in. I saw how dreadfully distressed you looked, and when I heard you groan, I could not keep silent. What has happened to you? Where have you been? Can't I do something for you?"

Perhaps she involuntarily held out her hands in a gesture of compassion as she spoke. At any rate I had caught them in my own and was clinging to them with an impulse as instinctive as that which prompts the drowning man to seize upon and cling to the rope which is thrown him as he sinks for the last time. As I looked up into her compassionate face and her eyes moist with pity, my brain ceased to whirl. The tender human sympathy which thrilled in the soft pressure of her fingers had brought me the support I needed. Its effect to calm and soothe was like that of some wonder-working elixir.

"God bless you," I said, after a few moments. "He must have sent you to me just now. I think I was in danger of going crazy if you had not come." At this the tears came into her eyes.

"Oh, Mr. West!" she cried. "How heartless you must have thought us! How could we leave you to yourself so long! But it is over now, is it not? You are better, surely."

"Yes," I said, "thanks to you. If you will not go away quite yet, I shall be myself soon."

"Indeed I will not go away," she said, with a little quiver of her face, more expressive of her sympathy than a volume of words. "You must not think us so heartless as we seemed in leaving you so by yourself. I scarcely slept last night, for thinking how strange your waking would be this morning; but father said you would sleep till late. He said that it would be better not to show too much sympathy with you at first, but to try to divert your thoughts and make you feel that you were among friends."

"You have indeed made me feel that," I answered. "But you see it is a good deal of a jolt to drop a hundred years, and although I did not seem to feel it so much last night, I have had very odd sensations this morning." While I held her hands and kept my eyes on her face, I could already even jest a little at my plight.

"No one thought of such a thing as your going out in the city alone so early in the morning," she went on. "Oh, Mr. West, where have you been?"

Then I told her of my morning's experience, from my first waking till the moment I had looked up to see her before me, just as I have told it here. She was overcome by distressful pity during the recital, and, though I had released one of her hands, did not try to take from me the other, seeing, no doubt, how much good it did me to hold it. "I can think a little what this feeling must have been like," she said. "It must have been terrible. And to think you were left alone to struggle with it! Can you ever forgive us?"

"But it is gone now. You have driven it quite away for the present," I said.

"You will not let it return again," she queried anxiously.

"I can't quite say that," I replied. "It might be too early to say that, considering how strange everything will still be to me."

"But you will not try to contend with it alone again, at least," she persisted. "Promise that you will come to us, and let us sympathize with you, and try to help you. Perhaps we can't do much, but it will surely be better than to try to bear such feelings alone."

"I will come to you if you will let me," I said.

"Oh yes, yes, I beg you will," she said eagerly. "I would do anything to help you that I could."

"All you need do is to be sorry for me, as you seem to be now," I replied.

"It is understood, then," she said, smiling with wet eyes, "that you are to come and tell me next time, and not run all over Boston among strangers."

This assumption that we were not strangers seemed scarcely strange, so near within these few minutes had my trouble and her sympathetic tears brought us.

"I will promise, when you come to me," she added, with an expression of charming archness, passing, as she continued, into one of enthusiasm, "to seem as sorry for you as you wish, but you must not for a moment suppose that I am really sorry for you at all, or that I think you will long be sorry for yourself. I know, as well as I know that the world now is heaven compared with what it was in your day, that the only feeling you will have after a little while will be one of thankfulness to God that your life in that age was so strangely cut off, to be returned to you in this."

Chapter 9

Dr. and Mrs. Leete were evidently not a little startled to learn, when they presently appeared, that I had been all over the city alone that morning, and it was apparent that they were agreeably surprised to see that I seemed so little agitated after the experience.

"Your stroll could scarcely have failed to be a very interesting one," said Mrs. Leete, as we sat down to table soon after. "You must have seen a good many new things."

"I saw very little that was not new," I replied. "But I think what surprised me as much as anything was not to find any stores on Washington Street, or any banks on State. What have you done with the merchants and bankers? Hung them all, perhaps, as the anarchists wanted to do in my day?"

"Not so bad as that," replied Dr. Leete. "We have simply dispensed with them. Their functions are obsolete in the modern world."

"Who sells you things when you want to buy them?" I inquired.

"There is neither selling nor buying nowadays; the distribution of goods is effected in another way. As to the bankers, having no money we have no use for those gentry."

"Miss Leete," said I, turning to Edith, "I am afraid that your father is making sport of me. I don't blame him, for the temptation my innocence offers must be extraordinary. But, really, there are limits to my credulity as to possible alterations in the social system."

"Father has no idea of jesting, I am sure," she replied, with a reassuring smile.

The conversation took another turn then, the point of ladies' fashions in the nineteenth century being raised, if I remember rightly, by Mrs. Leete, and it was not till after breakfast, when the doctor had invited me up to the house-top, which appeared to be a favorite resort of his, that he recurred to the subject.

"You were surprised," he said, "at my saying that we got along without money or trade, but a moment's reflection will show that trade existed and money was needed in your day simply because the business of production was left in private hands, and that, consequently, they are superfluous now."

"I do not at once see how that follows," I replied.

"It is very simple," said Dr. Leete. "When innumerable different and independent persons produced the various things needful to life and comfort, endless exchanges between individuals were requisite in order that they might supply themselves with what they desired. These exchanges constituted trade, and money was essential as their medium. But as soon as the nation became the sole producer of all sorts of commodities, there was no need of exchanges between individuals that they might get what they required. Everything was procurable from one source, and nothing could be procured anywhere else. A system of direct distribution from the national storehouses took the place of trade, and for this money was unnecessary."

"How is this distribution managed?" I asked.

"On the simplest possible plan," replied Dr. Leete. "A credit corresponding to his share of the annual product of the nation is given to every citizen on the public books at the beginning of each year, and a credit card issued him with which he procures at the public storehouses, found in every community, whatever he desires whenever he desires it. This arrangement, you will see, totally obviates the necessity for business transactions of any sort between individuals and consumers. Perhaps you would like to see what our credit cards are like.

"You observe," he pursued as I was curiously examining the piece of pasteboard he gave me, "that this card is issued for a certain number of dollars. We have kept the old word, but not the substance. The term, as we use it, answers to no real thing, but merely serves as an algebraical symbol for comparing the values of products with one another. For this purpose they are all priced in dollars and cents, just as in your day. The value of what I procure on this card is checked off by the clerk, who pricks out of these tiers of squares the price of what I order."

"If you wanted to buy something of your neighbor, could you transfer part of your credit to him as consideration?" I inquired.

"In the first place," replied Dr. Leete, "our neighbors have nothing to sell us, but in any event our credit would not be transferable, being strictly personal. Before the nation could even think of honoring any such transfer as you speak of, it would be bound to inquire into all the circumstances of the transaction, so as to be able to guarantee its absolute equity. It would have been reason enough, had there been no other, for abolishing money, that its possession was no indication of rightful title to it. In the hands of the man who had stolen it or murdered for it, it was as good as in those which had earned it by industry. People nowadays interchange gifts and favors out of friendship, but buying and selling is considered absolutely inconsistent with the mutual benevolence and disinterestedness which should prevail between citizens and the sense of community of interest which supports our social system. According to our ideas, buying and selling is essentially anti-social in all its tendencies. It is an education in self-seeking at the expense of others, and no society whose citizens are trained in such a school can possibly rise above a very low grade of civilization."

"What if you have to spend more than your card in any one year?" I asked.

"The provision is so ample that we are more likely not to spend it all," replied Dr. Leete. "But if extraordinary expenses should exhaust it, we can obtain a limited advance on the next year's credit, though this practice is not encouraged, and a heavy discount is charged to check it. Of course if a man showed himself a reckless spendthrift he would receive his allowance monthly or weekly instead of yearly, or if necessary not be permitted to handle it all."

"If you don't spend your allowance, I suppose it accumulates?"

"That is also permitted to a certain extent when a special outlay is anticipated. But unless notice to the contrary is given, it is presumed that the citizen who does not fully expend his credit did not have occasion to do so, and the balance is turned into the general surplus."

"Such a system does not encourage saving habits on the part of citizens," I said.

"It is not intended to," was the reply. "The nation is rich, and does not wish the people to deprive themselves of any good thing. In your day, men were bound to lay up goods and money against coming failure of the means of support and for their children. This necessity made parsimony a virtue. But now it would have no such laudable object, and, having lost its utility, it has ceased to be regarded as a virtue. No man any more has any care for the morrow, either for himself or his children, for the nation guarantees the nurture, education, and comfortable maintenance of every citizen from the cradle to the grave."

"That is a sweeping guarantee!" I said. "What certainty can there be that the value of a man's labor will recompense the nation for its outlay on him? On the whole, society may be able to support all its members, but some must earn less than enough for their support, and others more;

and that brings us back once more to the wages question, on which you have hitherto said nothing. It was at just this point, if you remember, that our talk ended last evening; and I say again, as I did then, that here I should suppose a national industrial system like yours would find its main difficulty. How, I ask once more, can you adjust satisfactorily the comparative wages or remuneration of the multitude of avocations, so unlike and so incommensurable, which are necessary for the service of society? In our day the market rate determined the price of labor of all sorts, as well as of goods. The employer paid as little as he could, and the worker got as much. It was not a pretty system ethically, I admit; but it did, at least, furnish us a rough and ready formula for settling a question which must be settled ten thousand times a day if the world was ever going to get forward. There seemed to us no other practicable way of doing it."

"Yes," replied Dr. Leete, "it was the only practicable way under a system which made the interests of every individual antagonistic to those of every other; but it would have been a pity if humanity could never have devised a better plan, for yours was simply the application to the mutual relations of men of the devil's maxim, 'Your necessity is my opportunity.' The reward of any service depended not upon its difficulty, danger, or hardship, for throughout the world it seems that the most perilous, severe, and repulsive labor was done by the worst paid classes; but solely upon the strait of those who needed the service."

"All that is conceded," I said. "But, with all its defects, the plan of settling prices by the market rate was a practical plan; and I cannot conceive what satisfactory substitute you can have devised for it. The government being the only possible employer, there is of course no labor market or market rate. Wages of all sorts must be arbitrarily fixed by the government. I cannot imagine a more complex and delicate function than that must be, or one, however performed, more certain to breed universal dissatisfaction."

"I beg your pardon," replied Dr. Leete, "but I think you exaggerate the difficulty. Suppose a board of fairly sensible men were charged with settling the wages for all sorts of trades under a system which, like ours, guaranteed employment to all, while permitting the choice of avocations. Don't you see that, however unsatisfactory the first adjustment might be, the mistakes would soon correct themselves? The favored trades would have too many volunteers, and those discriminated against would lack them till the errors were set right. But this is aside from the purpose, for, though this plan would, I fancy, be practicable enough, it is no part of our system."

"How, then, do you regulate wages?" I once more asked.

Dr. Leete did not reply till after several moments of meditative silence. "I know, of course," he finally said, "enough of the old order of things to understand just what you mean by that question; and yet the present order is so utterly different at this point that I am a little at loss how to answer you best. You ask me how we regulate wages; I can only reply that there is no idea in the modern social economy which at all corresponds with what was meant by wages in your day."

"I suppose you mean that you have no money to pay wages in," said I. "But the credit given the worker at the government storehouse answers to his wages with us. How is the amount of the credit given respectively to the workers in different lines determined? By what title does the individual claim his particular share? What is the basis of allotment?"

"His title," replied Dr. Leete, "is his humanity. The basis of his claim is the fact that he is a man."

"The fact that he is a man!" I repeated, incredulously. "Do you possibly mean that all have the same share?"

"Most assuredly."

The readers of this book never having practically known any other arrangement, or perhaps very carefully considered the historical accounts of former epochs in which a very different system prevailed, cannot be expected to appreciate the stupor of amazement into which Dr. Leete's simple statement plunged me.

"You see," he said, smiling, "that it is not merely that we have no money to pay wages in, but, as I said, we have nothing at all answering to your idea of wages."

By this time I had pulled myself together sufficiently to voice some of the criticisms which, man of the nineteenth century as I was, came uppermost in my mind, upon this to me astounding arrangement. "Some men do twice the work of others!" I exclaimed. "Are the clever workmen content with a plan that ranks them with the indifferent?"

"We leave no possible ground for any complaint of injustice," replied Dr. Leete, "by requiring precisely the same measure of service from all."

"How can you do that, I should like to know, when no two men's powers are the same?"

"Nothing could be simpler," was Dr. Leete's reply. "We require of each that he shall make the same effort; that is, we demand of him the best service it is in his power to give."

"And supposing all do the best they can," I answered, "the amount of the product resulting is twice greater from one man than from another."

"Very true," replied Dr. Leete; "but the amount of the resulting product has nothing whatever to do with the question, which is one of desert. Desert is a moral question, and the amount of the product a material quantity. It would be an extraordinary sort of logic which should try to determine a moral question by a material standard. The amount of the effort alone is pertinent to the question of desert. All men who do their best, do the same. A man's endowments, however godlike, merely fix the measure of his duty. The man of great endowments who does not do all he might, though he may do more than a man of small endowments who does his best, is deemed a less deserving worker than the latter, and dies a debtor to his fellows. The Creator sets men's tasks for them by the faculties he gives them; we simply exact their fulfillment."

"No doubt that is very fine philosophy," I said; "nevertheless it seems hard that the man who produces twice as much as another, even if both do their best, should have only the same share."

"Does it, indeed, seem so to you?" responded Dr. Leete. "Now, do you know, that seems very curious to me? The way it strikes people nowadays is, that a man who can produce twice as much as another with the same effort, instead of being rewarded for doing so, ought to be punished if he does not do so. In the nineteenth century, when a horse pulled a heavier load than a goat, I suppose you rewarded him. Now, we should have whipped him soundly if he had not, on the ground that, being much stronger, he ought to. It is singular how ethical standards change." The doctor said this with such a twinkle in his eye that I was obliged to laugh.

"I suppose," I said, "that the real reason that we rewarded men for their endowments, while we considered those of horses and goats merely as fixing the service to be severally required of them, was that the animals, not being reasoning beings, naturally did the best they could, whereas men could only be induced to do so by rewarding them according to the amount of their product. That brings me to ask why, unless human nature has mightily changed in a hundred years, you are not under the same necessity."

"We are," replied Dr. Leete. "I don't think there has been any change in human nature in that respect since your day. It is still so constituted that special incentives in the form of prizes, and advantages to be gained, are requisite to call out the best endeavors of the average man in any direction."

"But what inducement," I asked, "can a man have to put forth his best endeavors when, however much or little he accomplishes, his income remains the same? High characters may be moved by devotion to the common welfare under such a system, but does not the average man tend to rest back on his oar, reasoning that it is of no use to make a special effort, since the effort will not increase his income, nor its withholding diminish it?"

"Does it then really seem to you," answered my companion, "that human nature is insensible to any motives save fear of want and love of luxury, that you should expect security and equality of livelihood to leave them without possible incentives to effort? Your contemporaries did not really think so, though they might fancy they did. When it was a question of the grandest class of efforts, the most absolute self-devotion, they depended on quite other incentives. Not higher wages, but honor and the hope of men's gratitude, patriotism and the inspiration of duty, were the motives which they set before their soldiers when it was a question of dying for the nation, and never was there an age of the world when those motives did not call out what is best and noblest in men. And not only this, but when you come to analyze the love of money which was the general impulse to effort in your day, you find that the dread of want and desire of luxury was but one of several motives which the pursuit of money represented; the others, and with many the more influential, being desire of power, of social position, and reputation for ability and success. So you see that though we have abolished poverty and the fear of it, and inordinate luxury with the hope of it, we have not touched the greater part of the motives which underlay the love of money in former times, or any of those which prompted the supremer sorts of effort. The coarser motives, which no longer move us, have been replaced by higher motives wholly unknown to the mere wage earners of your age. Now that industry of whatever sort is no longer self-service, but service of the nation, patriotism, passion for humanity, impel the worker as in your day they did the soldier. The army of industry is an army, not alone by virtue of its perfect organization, but by reason also of the ardor of self-devotion which animates its members.

"But as you used to supplement the motives of patriotism with the love of glory, in order to stimulate the valor of your soldiers, so do we. Based as our industrial system is on the principle of requiring the same unit of effort from every man, that is, the best he can do, you will see that the means by which we spur the workers to do their best must be a very essential part of our scheme. With us, diligence in the national service is the sole and certain way to public repute, social distinction, and official power. The value of a man's services to society fixes his rank in it. Compared with the effect of our social arrangements in impelling men to be zealous in business, we deem the object-lessons of biting poverty and wanton luxury on which you depended a device as weak and uncertain as it was barbaric. The lust of honor even in your sordid day notoriously impelled men to more desperate effort than the love of money could."

"I should be extremely interested," I said, "to learn something of what these social arrangements are."

"The scheme in its details," replied the doctor, "is of course very elaborate, for it underlies the entire organization of our industrial army; but a few words will give you a general idea of it."

At this moment our talk was charmingly interrupted by the emergence upon the aerial platform where we sat of Edith Leete. She was dressed for the street, and had come to speak to her father about some commission she was to do for him.

"By the way, Edith," he exclaimed, as she was about to leave us to ourselves, "I wonder if Mr. West would not be interested in visiting the store with you? I have been telling him something about our system of distribution, and perhaps he might like to see it in practical operation."

"My daughter," he added, turning to me, "is an indefatigable shopper, and can tell you more about the stores than I can."

The proposition was naturally very agreeable to me, and Edith being good enough to say that she should be glad to have my company, we left the house together.

Chapter 10

"If I am going to explain our way of shopping to you," said my companion, as we walked along the street, "you must explain your way to me. I have never been able to understand it from all I have read on the subject. For example, when you had such a vast number of shops, each with its different assortment, how could a lady ever settle upon any purchase till she had visited all the shops? for, until she had, she could not know what there was to choose from."

"It was as you suppose; that was the only way she could know," I replied.

"Father calls me an indefatigable shopper, but I should soon be a very fatigued one if I had to do as they did," was Edith's laughing comment.

"The loss of time in going from shop to shop was indeed a waste which the busy bitterly complained of," I said; "but as for the ladies of the idle class, though they complained also, I think the system was really a godsend by furnishing a device to kill time."

"But say there were a thousand shops in a city, hundreds, perhaps, of the same sort, how could even the idlest find time to make their rounds?"

"They really could not visit all, of course," I replied. "Those who did a great deal of buying, learned in time where they might expect to find what they wanted. This class had made a science of the specialties of the shops, and bought at advantage, always getting the most and best for the least money. It required, however, long experience to acquire this knowledge. Those who were too busy, or bought too little to gain it, took their chances and were generally unfortunate, getting the least and worst for the most money. It was the merest chance if persons not experienced in shopping received the value of their money."

"But why did you put up with such a shockingly inconvenient arrangement when you saw its faults so plainly?" Edith asked me.

"It was like all our social arrangements," I replied. "You can see their faults scarcely more plainly than we did, but we saw no remedy for them."

"Here we are at the store of our ward," said Edith, as we turned in at the great portal of one of the magnificent public buildings I had observed in my morning walk. There was nothing in the exterior aspect of the edifice to suggest a store to a representative of the nineteenth century. There was no display of goods in the great windows, or any device to advertise wares, or attract custom. Nor was there any sort of sign or legend on the front of the building to indicate the character of the business carried on there; but instead, above the portal, standing out from the front of the building, a majestic life-size group of statuary, the central figure of which was a female ideal of Plenty, with her cornucopia. Judging from the composition of the throng passing in and out, about the same proportion of the sexes among shoppers obtained as in the nineteenth century. As we entered, Edith said that there was one of these great distributing establishments in each ward of the city, so that no residence was more than five or ten minutes' walk from one of them. It was the first interior of a twentieth-century public building that I had ever beheld, and the spectacle naturally impressed me deeply. I was in a vast hall full of light, received not alone from the windows on all sides, but from the dome, the point of which was a hundred feet above. Beneath it, in the centre of the hall, a magnificent fountain played, cooling the atmosphere to a delicious freshness with its spray. The walls and ceiling were frescoed in mellow tints, calculated to soften without absorbing the light which flooded the interior. Around the fountain was a space occupied with chairs and sofas, on which many persons were seated conversing. Legends on the walls all about the hall indicated to what classes of commodities the counters below were devoted. Edith directed her steps towards one of these, where samples of muslin of a bewildering variety were displayed, and proceeded to inspect them.

"Where is the clerk?" I asked, for there was no one behind the counter, and no one seemed coming to attend to the customer.

"I have no need of the clerk yet," said Edith; "I have not made my selection."

"It was the principal business of clerks to help people to make their selections in my day," I replied.

"What! To tell people what they wanted?"

"Yes; and oftener to induce them to buy what they didn't want."

"But did not ladies find that very impertinent?" Edith asked, wonderingly. "What concern could it possibly be to the clerks whether people bought or not?"

"It was their sole concern," I answered. "They were hired for the purpose of getting rid of the goods, and were expected to do their utmost, short of the use of force, to compass that end."

"Ah, yes! How stupid I am to forget!" said Edith. "The storekeeper and his clerks depended for their livelihood on selling the goods in your day. Of course that is all different now. The goods are the nation's. They are here for those who want them, and it is the business of the clerks to wait on people and take their orders; but it is not the interest of the clerk or the nation to dispose of a yard or a pound of anything to anybody who does not want it." She smiled as she added, "How exceedingly odd it must have seemed to have clerks trying to induce one to take what one did not want, or was doubtful about!"

"But even a twentieth century clerk might make himself useful in giving you information about the goods, though he did not tease you to buy them," I suggested.

"No," said Edith, "that is not the business of the clerk. These printed cards, for which the government authorities are responsible, give us all the information we can possibly need."

I saw then that there was fastened to each sample a card containing in succinct form a complete statement of the make and materials of the goods and all its qualities, as well as price, leaving absolutely no point to hang a question on.

"The clerk has, then, nothing to say about the goods he sells?" I said.

"Nothing at all. It is not necessary that he should know or profess to know anything about them. Courtesy and accuracy in taking orders are all that are required of him."

"What a prodigious amount of lying that simple arrangement saves!" I ejaculated.

"Do you mean that all the clerks misrepresented their goods in your day?" Edith asked.

"God forbid that I should say so!" I replied, "for there were many who did not, and they were entitled to especial credit, for when one's livelihood and that of his wife and babies depended on the amount of goods he could dispose of, the temptation to deceive the customer—or let him deceive himself—was wellnigh overwhelming. But, Miss Leete, I am distracting you from your task with my talk."

"Not at all. I have made my selections." With that she touched a button, and in a moment a clerk appeared. He took down her order on a tablet with a pencil which made two copies, of which he gave one to her, and enclosing the counterpart in a small receptacle, dropped it into a transmitting tube.

"The duplicate of the order," said Edith as she turned away from the counter, after the clerk had punched the value of her purchase out of the credit card she gave him, "is given to the purchaser, so that any mistakes in filling it can be easily traced and rectified."

"You were very quick about your selections," I said. "May I ask how you knew that you might not have found something to suit you better in some of the other stores? But probably you are required to buy in your own district."

"Oh, no," she replied. "We buy where we please, though naturally most often near home. But I should have gained nothing by visiting other stores. The assortment in all is exactly the same, representing as it does in each case samples of all the varieties produced or imported by the United States. That is why one can decide quickly, and never need visit two stores."

"And is this merely a sample store? I see no clerks cutting off goods or marking bundles."

"All our stores are sample stores, except as to a few classes of articles. The goods, with these exceptions, are all at the great central warehouse of the city, to which they are shipped directly from the producers. We order from the sample and the printed statement of texture, make, and qualities. The orders are sent to the warehouse, and the goods distributed from there."

"That must be a tremendous saving of handling," I said. "By our system, the manufacturer sold to the wholesaler, the wholesaler to the retailer, and the retailer to the consumer, and the goods had to be handled each time. You avoid one handling of the goods, and eliminate the retailer altogether, with his big profit and the army of clerks it goes to support. Why, Miss Leete, this store is merely the order department of a wholesale house, with no more than a wholesaler's complement of clerks. Under our system of handling the goods, persuading the customer to buy them, cutting them off, and packing them, ten clerks would not do what one does here. The saving must be enormous."

"I suppose so," said Edith, "but of course we have never known any other way. But, Mr. West, you must not fail to ask father to take you to the central warehouse some day, where they receive the orders from the different sample houses all over the city and parcel out and send the goods to their destinations. He took me there not long ago, and it was a wonderful sight. The system is certainly perfect; for example, over yonder in that sort of cage is the dispatching clerk. The orders, as they are taken by the different departments in the store, are sent by transmitters to him. His assistants sort them and enclose each class in a carrier-box by itself. The dispatching clerk has a dozen pneumatic transmitters before him answering to the general classes of goods, each communicating with the corresponding department at the warehouse. He drops the box of orders into the tube it calls for, and in a few moments later it drops on the proper desk in the warehouse, together with all the orders of the same sort from the other sample stores. The orders are read off, recorded, and sent to be filled, like lightning. The filling I thought the most interesting part. Bales of cloth are placed on spindles and turned by machinery, and the cutter, who also has a machine, works right through one bale after another till exhausted, when another man takes his place; and it is the same with those who fill the orders in any other staple. The packages are then delivered by larger tubes to the city districts, and thence distributed to the houses. You may understand how quickly it is all done when I tell you that my order will probably be at home sooner than I could have carried it from here."

"How do you manage in the thinly settled rural districts?" I asked.

"The system is the same," Edith explained; "the village sample shops are connected by transmitters with the central county warehouse, which may be twenty miles away. The transmission is so swift, though, that the time lost on the way is trifling. But, to save expense, in many counties one set of tubes connect several villages with the warehouse, and then there is time lost waiting for one another. Sometimes it is two or three hours before goods ordered are received. It was so where I was staying last summer, and I found it quite inconvenient."[1]

"There must be many other respects also, no doubt, in which the country stores are inferior to the city stores," I suggested.

"No," Edith answered, "they are otherwise precisely as good. The sample shop of the smallest village, just like this one, gives you your choice of all the varieties of goods the nation has, for the county warehouse draws on the same source as the city warehouse."

As we walked home I commented on the great variety in the size and cost of the houses. "How is it," I asked, "that this difference is consistent with the fact that all citizens have the same income?"

"Because," Edith explained, "although the income is the same, personal taste determines how the individual shall spend it. Some like fine horses; others, like myself, prefer pretty clothes; and still others want an elaborate table. The rents which the nation receives for these houses vary, according to size, elegance, and location, so that everybody can find something to suit. The larger houses are usually occupied by large families, in which there are several to contribute to the rent; while small families, like ours, find smaller houses more convenient and economical. It is a matter of taste and convenience wholly. I have read that in old times people often kept up establishments and did other things which they could not afford for ostentation, to make people think them richer than they were. Was it really so, Mr. West?"

"I shall have to admit that it was," I replied.

"Well, you see, it could not be so nowadays; for everybody's income is known, and it is known that what is spent one way must be saved another."

[1] I am informed since the above is in type that this lack of perfection in the distributing service of some of the country districts is to be remedied, and that soon every village will have its own set of tubes.

Chapter 11

When we arrived home, Dr. Leete had not yet returned, and Mrs. Leete was not visible. "Are you fond of music, Mr. West?" Edith asked.

I assured her that it was half of life, according to my notion.

"I ought to apologize for inquiring," she said. "It is not a question that we ask one another nowadays; but I have read that in your day, even among the cultured class, there were some who did not care for music."

"You must remember, in excuse," I said, "that we had some rather absurd kinds of music."

"Yes," she said, "I know that; I am afraid I should not have fancied it all myself. Would you like to hear some of ours now, Mr. West?"

"Nothing would delight me so much as to listen to you," I said.

"To me!" she exclaimed, laughing. "Did you think I was going to play or sing to you?"

"I hoped so, certainly," I replied.

Seeing that I was a little abashed, she subdued her merriment and explained. "Of course, we all sing nowadays as a matter of course in the training of the voice, and some learn to play instruments for their private amusement; but the professional music is so much grander and more perfect than any performance of ours, and so easily commanded when we wish to hear it, that we don't think of calling our singing or playing music at all. All the really fine singers and players are in the musical service, and the rest of us hold our peace for the main part. But would you really like to hear some music?"

I assured her once more that I would.

"Come, then, into the music room," she said, and I followed her into an apartment finished, without hangings, in wood, with a floor of polished wood. I was prepared for new devices in musical instruments, but I saw nothing in the room which by any stretch of imagination could be conceived as such. It was evident that my puzzled appearance was affording intense amusement to Edith.

"Please look at to-day's music," she said, handing me a card, "and tell me what you would prefer. It is now five o'clock, you will remember."

The card bore the date "September 12, 2000," and contained the longest programme of music I had ever seen. It was as various as it was long, including a most extraordinary range of vocal and instrumental solos, duets, quartettes, and various orchestral combinations. I remained bewildered by the prodigious list until Edith's pink finger tip indicated a particular section of it, where several selections were bracketed, with the words "5 P.M." against them; then I observed that this prodigious programme was an all-day one, divided into twenty-four sections answering to the hours. There were but a few pieces of music in the "5 P.M." section, and I indicated an organ piece as my preference.

"I am so glad you like the organ," said she. "I think there is scarcely any music that suits my mood oftener."

She made me sit down comfortably, and, crossing the room, so far as I could see, merely touched one or two screws, and at once the room was filled with the music of a grand organ anthem; filled, not flooded, for, by some means, the volume of melody had been perfectly graduated to the size of the apartment. I listened, scarcely breathing, to the close. Such music, so perfectly rendered, I had never expected to hear.

"Grand!" I cried, as the last great wave of sound broke and ebbed away into silence. "Bach must be at the keys of that organ; but where is the organ?"

"Wait a moment, please," said Edith; "I want to have you listen to this waltz before you ask any questions. I think it is perfectly charming"; and as she spoke the sound of violins filled the room with the witchery of a summer night. When this had also ceased, she said: "There is nothing in the least mysterious about the music, as you seem to imagine. It is not made by fairies or genii, but by good, honest, and exceedingly clever human hands. We have simply carried the idea of labor saving by cooperation into our musical service as into everything else. There are a number of music rooms in the city, perfectly adapted acoustically to the different sorts of music. These halls are connected by telephone with all the houses of the city whose people care to pay the small fee, and there are none, you may be sure, who do not. The corps of musicians attached to each hall is so large that, although no individual performer, or group of performers, has more than a brief part, each day's programme lasts through the twenty-four hours. There are on that card for to-day, as you will see if you observe closely, distinct programmes of four of these concerts, each of a different order of music from the others, being now simultaneously performed, and any one of the four pieces now going on that you prefer, you can hear by merely pressing the button which will connect your house-wire with the hall where it is being rendered. The programmes are so coordinated that the pieces at any one time simultaneously proceeding in the different halls usually offer a choice, not only between instrumental and vocal, and between different sorts of instruments; but also between different motives from grave to gay, so that all tastes and moods can be suited."

"It appears to me, Miss Leete," I said, "that if we could have devised an arrangement for providing everybody with music in their homes, perfect in quality, unlimited in quantity, suited to every mood, and beginning and ceasing at will, we should have considered the limit of human felicity already attained, and ceased to strive for further improvements."

"I am sure I never could imagine how those among you who depended at all on music managed to endure the old-fashioned system for providing it," replied Edith. "Music really worth hearing must have been, I suppose, wholly out of the reach of the masses, and attainable by the most favored only occasionally, at great trouble, prodigious expense, and then for brief periods, arbitrarily fixed by somebody else, and in connection with all sorts of undesirable circumstances. Your concerts, for instance, and operas! How perfectly exasperating it must have been, for the sake of a piece or two of music that suited you, to have to sit for hours listening to what you did not care for! Now, at a dinner one can skip the courses one does not care for. Who would ever dine, however hungry, if required to eat everything brought on the table? and I am sure one's hearing is quite as sensitive as one's taste. I suppose it was these difficulties in the way of commanding really good music which made you endure so much playing and singing in your homes by people who had only the rudiments of the art."

"Yes," I replied, "it was that sort of music or none for most of us."

"Ah, well," Edith sighed, "when one really considers, it is not so strange that people in those days so often did not care for music. I dare say I should have detested it, too."

"Did I understand you rightly," I inquired, "that this musical programme covers the entire twenty-four hours? It seems to on this card, certainly; but who is there to listen to music between say midnight and morning?"

"Oh, many," Edith replied. "Our people keep all hours; but if the music were provided from midnight to morning for no others, it still would be for the sleepless, the sick, and the dying. All our bedchambers have a telephone attachment at the head of the bed by which any person who may be sleepless can command music at pleasure, of the sort suited to the mood."

"Is there such an arrangement in the room assigned to me?"

"Why, certainly; and how stupid, how very stupid, of me not to think to tell you of that last night! Father will show you about the adjustment before you go to bed to-night, however; and with the receiver at your ear, I am quite sure you will be able to snap your fingers at all sorts of uncanny feelings if they trouble you again."

That evening Dr. Leete asked us about our visit to the store, and in the course of the desultory comparison of the ways of the nineteenth century and the twentieth, which followed, something raised the question of inheritance. "I suppose," I said, "the inheritance of property is not now allowed."

"On the contrary," replied Dr. Leete, "there is no interference with it. In fact, you will find, Mr. West, as you come to know us, that there is far less interference of any sort with personal liberty nowadays than you were accustomed to. We require, indeed, by law that every man shall serve the nation for a fixed period, instead of leaving him his choice, as you did, between working, stealing, or starving. With the exception of this fundamental law, which is, indeed, merely a codification of the law of nature—the edict of Eden—by which it is made equal in its pressure on men, our system depends in no particular upon legislation, but is entirely voluntary, the logical outcome of the operation of human nature under rational conditions. This question of inheritance illustrates just that point. The fact that the nation is the sole capitalist and land-owner of course restricts the individual's possessions to his annual credit, and what personal and household belongings he may have procured with it. His credit, like an annuity in your day, ceases on his death, with the allowance of a fixed sum for funeral expenses. His other possessions he leaves as he pleases."

"What is to prevent, in course of time, such accumulations of valuable goods and chattels in the hands of individuals as might seriously interfere with equality in the circumstances of citizens?" I asked.

"That matter arranges itself very simply," was the reply. "Under the present organization of society, accumulations of personal property are merely burdensome the moment they exceed what adds to the real comfort. In your day, if a man had a house crammed full with gold and silver plate, rare china, expensive furniture, and such things, he was considered rich, for these things represented money, and could at any time be turned into it. Nowadays a man whom the legacies of a hundred relatives, simultaneously dying, should place in a similar position, would be considered very unlucky. The articles, not being salable, would be of no value to him except for their actual use or the enjoyment of their beauty. On the other hand, his income remaining the same, he would have to deplete his credit to hire houses to store the goods in, and still further to pay for the service of those who took care of them. You may be very sure that such a man would lose no time in scattering among his friends possessions which only made him the poorer, and that none of those friends would accept more of them than they could easily spare room for and time to attend to. You see, then, that to prohibit the inheritance of personal property with a view to prevent great accumulations would be a superfluous precaution for the nation. The individual citizen can be trusted to see that he is not overburdened. So careful is he in this respect, that the relatives usually waive claim to most of the effects of deceased friends, reserving only particular objects. The nation takes charge of the resigned chattels, and turns such as are of value into the common stock once more."

"You spoke of paying for service to take care of your houses," said I; "that suggests a question I have several times been on the point of asking. How have you disposed of the problem of domestic service? Who are willing to be domestic servants in a community where all are social equals? Our ladies found it hard enough to find such even when there was little pretense of social equality."

"It is precisely because we are all social equals whose equality nothing can compromise, and because service is honorable, in a society whose fundamental principle is that all in turn shall serve the rest, that we could easily provide a corps of domestic servants such as you never dreamed of, if we needed them," replied Dr. Leete. "But we do not need them."

"Who does your house-work, then?" I asked.

"There is none to do," said Mrs. Leete, to whom I had addressed this question. "Our washing is all done at public laundries at excessively cheap rates, and our cooking at public kitchens. The making and repairing of all we wear are done outside in public shops. Electricity, of course, takes the place of all fires and lighting. We choose houses no larger than we need, and furnish them so as to involve the minimum of trouble to keep them in order. We have no use for domestic servants."

"The fact," said Dr. Leete, "that you had in the poorer classes a boundless supply of serfs on whom you could impose all sorts of painful and disagreeable tasks, made you indifferent to devices to avoid the necessity for them. But now that we all have to do in turn whatever work is done for society, every individual in the nation has the same interest, and a personal one, in devices for lightening the burden. This fact has given a prodigious impulse to labor-saving inventions in all sorts of industry, of which the combination of the maximum of comfort and minimum of trouble in household arrangements was one of the earliest results.

"In case of special emergencies in the household," pursued Dr. Leete, "such as extensive cleaning or renovation, or sickness in the family, we can always secure assistance from the industrial force."

"But how do you recompense these assistants, since you have no money?"

"We do not pay them, of course, but the nation for them. Their services can be obtained by application at the proper bureau, and their value is pricked off the credit card of the applicant."

"What a paradise for womankind the world must be now!" I exclaimed. "In my day, even wealth and unlimited servants did not enfranchise their possessors from household cares, while the women of the merely well-to-do and poorer classes lived and died martyrs to them."

"Yes," said Mrs. Leete, "I have read something of that; enough to convince me that, badly off as the men, too, were in your day, they were more fortunate than their mothers and wives."

"The broad shoulders of the nation," said Dr. Leete, "bear now like a feather the burden that broke the backs of the women of your day. Their misery came, with all your other miseries, from that incapacity for cooperation which followed from the individualism on which your social system was founded, from your inability to perceive that you could make ten times more profit out of your fellow men by uniting with them than by contending with them. The wonder is, not that you did not live more comfortably, but that you were able to live together at all, who were all confessedly bent on making one another your servants, and securing possession of one another's goods.

"There, there, father, if you are so vehement, Mr. West will think you are scolding him," laughingly interposed Edith.

"When you want a doctor," I asked, "do you simply apply to the proper bureau and take any one that may be sent?"

"That rule would not work well in the case of physicians," replied Dr. Leete. "The good a physician can do a patient depends largely on his acquaintance with his constitutional tendencies and condition. The patient must be able, therefore, to call in a particular doctor, and he does so just as patients did in your day. The only difference is that, instead of collecting his fee for himself, the doctor collects it for the nation by pricking off the amount, according to a regular scale for medical attendance, from the patient's credit card."

"I can imagine," I said, "that if the fee is always the same, and a doctor may not turn away patients, as I suppose he may not, the good doctors are called constantly and the poor doctors left in idleness."

"In the first place, if you will overlook the apparent conceit of the remark from a retired physician," replied Dr. Leete, with a smile, "we have no poor doctors. Anybody who pleases to get a little smattering of medical terms is not now at liberty to practice on the bodies of citizens, as in your day. None but students who have passed the severe tests of the schools, and clearly proved their vocation, are permitted to practice. Then, too, you will observe that there is nowadays no attempt of doctors to build up their practice at the expense of other doctors. There would be no motive for that. For the rest, the doctor has to render regular reports of his work to the medical bureau, and if he is not reasonably well employed, work is found for him."

Chapter 12

The questions which I needed to ask before I could acquire even an outline acquaintance with the institutions of the twentieth century being endless, and Dr. Leete's good-nature appearing equally so, we sat up talking for several hours after the ladies left us. Reminding my host of the point at which our talk had broken off that morning, I expressed my curiosity to learn how the organization of the industrial army was made to afford a sufficient stimulus to diligence in the lack of any anxiety on the worker's part as to his livelihood.

"You must understand in the first place," replied the doctor, "that the supply of incentives to effort is but one of the objects sought in the organization we have adopted for the army. The other, and equally important, is to secure for the file-leaders and captains of the force, and the great officers of the nation, men of proven abilities, who are pledged by their own careers to hold their followers up to their highest standard of performance and permit no lagging. With a view to these two ends the industrial army is organized. First comes the unclassified grade of common laborers, men of all work, to which all recruits during their first three years belong. This grade is a sort of school, and a very strict one, in which the young men are taught habits of obedience, subordination, and devotion to duty. While the miscellaneous nature of the work done by this force prevents the systematic grading of the workers which is afterwards possible, yet individual records are kept, and excellence receives distinction corresponding with the penalties that negligence incurs. It is not, however, policy with us to permit youthful recklessness or indiscretion, when not deeply culpable, to handicap the future careers of young men, and all who have passed through the unclassified grade without serious disgrace have an equal opportunity to choose the life employment they have most liking for. Having selected this, they enter upon it as apprentices. The length of the apprenticeship naturally differs in different occupations. At the end of it the apprentice becomes a full workman, and a member of his trade or guild. Now not only are the individual records of the apprentices for ability and industry strictly kept, and excellence distinguished by suitable distinctions, but upon the average of his record during apprenticeship the standing given the apprentice among the full workmen depends.

"While the internal organizations of different industries, mechanical and agricultural, differ according to their peculiar conditions, they agree in a general division of their workers into first, second, and third grades, according to ability, and these grades are in many cases subdivided into first and second classes. According to his standing as an apprentice a young man is assigned his place as a first, second, or third grade worker. Of course only men of unusual ability pass directly from apprenticeship into the first grade of the workers. The most fall into the lower grades, working up as they grow more experienced, at the periodical regradings. These regradings take place in each industry at intervals corresponding with the length of the apprenticeship to that industry, so that merit never need wait long to rise, nor can any rest on past achievements unless they would drop into a lower rank. One of the notable advantages of a high grading is the privilege it gives the worker in electing which of the various branches or processes of his industry he will follow as his specialty. Of course it is not intended that any of these processes shall be disproportionately arduous, but there is often much difference between them, and the privilege of election is accordingly highly prized. So far as possible, indeed, the preferences even of the poorest workmen are considered in assigning them their line of work, because not only their happiness but their usefulness is thus enhanced. While, however, the wish of the lower grade man is consulted so far as the exigencies of the service permit, he is considered only after the upper grade men have been provided for, and often he has to put up with second or third choice, or even with an arbitrary assignment when help is needed. This privilege of election attends every regrading, and when a man loses his grade he also risks having to exchange the sort of work he likes for some other less to his taste. The results of each regrading, giving the standing of every man in his industry, are gazetted in the public prints, and those who have won promotion since the last regrading receive the nation's thanks and are publicly invested with the badge of their new rank."

"What may this badge be?" I asked.

"Every industry has its emblematic device," replied Dr. Leete, "and this, in the shape of a metallic badge so small that you might not see it unless you knew where to look, is all the insignia which the men of the army wear, except where public convenience demands a distinctive uniform. This badge is the same in form for all grades of industry, but while the badge of the third grade is iron, that of the second grade is silver, and that of the first is gilt.

"Apart from the grand incentive to endeavor afforded by the fact that the high places in the nation are open only to the highest class men, and that rank in the army constitutes the only mode of social distinction for the vast majority who are not aspirants in art, literature, and the professions, various incitements of a minor, but perhaps equally effective, sort are provided in the form of special privileges and immunities in the way of discipline, which the superior class men enjoy. These, while intended to be as little as possible invidious to the less successful, have the effect of keeping constantly before every man's mind the great desirability of attaining the grade next above his own.

"It is obviously important that not only the good but also the indifferent and poor workmen should be able to cherish the ambition of rising. Indeed, the number of the latter being so much greater, it is even more essential that the ranking system should not operate to discourage them than that it should stimulate the others. It is to this end that the grades are divided into classes. The grades as well as the classes being made numerically equal at each regrading, there is not at any time, counting out the officers and the unclassified and apprentice grades, over one-ninth of the industrial army in the lowest class, and most of this number are recent apprentices, all of whom expect to rise. Those who remain during the entire term of service in the lowest class are but a trifling fraction of the industrial army, and likely to be as deficient in sensibility to their position as in ability to better it.

"It is not even necessary that a worker should win promotion to a higher grade to have at least a taste of glory. While promotion requires a general excellence of record as a worker, honorable mention and various sorts of prizes are awarded for excellence less than sufficient for promotion, and also for special feats and single performances in the various industries. There are many minor distinctions of standing, not only within the grades but within the classes, each of which acts as a spur to the efforts of a group. It is intended that no form of merit shall wholly fail of recognition.

"As for actual neglect of work positively bad work, or other overt remissness on the part of men incapable of generous motives, the discipline of the industrial army is far too strict to allow anything whatever of the sort. A man able to do duty, and persistently refusing, is sentenced to solitary imprisonment on bread and water till he consents.

"The lowest grade of the officers of the industrial army, that of assistant foremen or lieutenants, is appointed out of men who have held their place for two years in the first class of the first grade. Where this leaves too large a range of choice, only the first group of this class are eligible. No one thus comes to the point of commanding men until he is about thirty years old. After a man becomes an officer, his rating of course no longer depends on the efficiency of his own work, but on that of his men. The foremen are appointed from among the assistant foremen, by the same exercise of discretion limited to a small eligible class. In the appointments to the still higher grades another principle is introduced, which it would take too much time to explain now.

"Of course such a system of grading as I have described would have been impracticable applied to the small industrial concerns of your day, in some of which there were hardly enough employees to have left one apiece for the classes. You must remember that, under the national organization of labor, all industries are carried on by great bodies of men, many of your farms or shops being combined as one. It is also owing solely to the vast scale on which each industry is organized, with co-ordinate establishments in every part of the country, that we are able by exchanges and transfers to fit every man so nearly with the sort of work he can do best.

"And now, Mr. West, I will leave it to you, on the bare outline of its features which I have given, if those who need special incentives to do their best are likely to lack them under our system. Does it not seem to you that men who found themselves obliged, whether they wished or not, to work, would under such a system be strongly impelled to do their best?"

I replied that it seemed to me the incentives offered were, if any objection were to be made, too strong; that the pace set for the young men was too hot; and such, indeed, I would add with deference, still remains my opinion, now that by longer residence among you I become better acquainted with the whole subject.

Dr. Leete, however, desired me to reflect, and I am ready to say that it is perhaps a sufficient reply to my objection, that the worker's livelihood is in no way dependent on his ranking, and anxiety for that never embitters his disappointments; that the working hours are short, the vacations regular, and that all emulation ceases at forty-five, with the attainment of middle life.

"There are two or three other points I ought to refer to," he added, "to prevent your getting mistaken impressions. In the first place, you must understand that this system of preferment given the more efficient workers over the less so, in no way contravenes the fundamental idea of our social system, that all who do their best are equally deserving, whether that best be great or small. I have shown that the system is arranged to encourage the weaker as well as the stronger with the hope of rising, while the fact that the stronger are selected for the leaders is in no way a reflection upon the weaker, but in the interest of the common weal.

"Do not imagine, either, because emulation is given free play as an incentive under our system, that we deem it a motive likely to appeal to the nobler sort of men, or worthy of them. Such as these find their motives within, not without, and measure their duty by their own endowments, not by those of others. So long as their achievement is proportioned to their powers, they would consider it preposterous to expect praise or blame because it chanced to be great or small. To such natures emulation appears philosophically absurd, and despicable in a moral aspect by its substitution of envy for admiration, and exultation for regret, in one's attitude toward the successes and the failures of others.

"But all men, even in the last year of the twentieth century, are not of this high order, and the incentives to endeavor requisite for those who are not must be of a sort adapted to their inferior natures. For these, then, emulation of the keenest edge is provided as a constant spur. Those who need this motive will feel it. Those who are above its influence do not need it.

"I should not fail to mention," resumed the doctor, "that for those too deficient in mental or bodily strength to be fairly graded with the main body of workers, we have a separate grade, unconnected with the others,—a sort of invalid corps, the members of which are provided with a light class of tasks fitted to their strength. All our sick in mind and body, all our deaf and dumb, and lame and blind and crippled, and even our insane, belong to this invalid corps, and bear its insignia. The strongest often do nearly a man's work, the feeblest, of course, nothing; but none who can do anything are willing quite to give up. In their lucid intervals, even our insane are eager to do what they can."

"That is a pretty idea of the invalid corps," I said. "Even a barbarian from the nineteenth century can appreciate that. It is a very graceful way of disguising charity, and must be grateful to the feelings of its recipients."

"Charity!" repeated Dr. Leete. "Did you suppose that we consider the incapable class we are talking of objects of charity?"

"Why, naturally," I said, "inasmuch as they are incapable of self-support."

But here the doctor took me up quickly.

"Who is capable of self-support?" he demanded. "There is no such thing in a civilized society as self-support. In a state of society so barbarous as not even to know family cooperation, each individual may possibly support himself, though even then for a part of his life only; but from the moment that men begin to live together, and constitute even the rudest sort of society, self-support becomes impossible. As men grow more civilized, and the subdivision of occupations and services is carried out, a complex mutual dependence becomes the universal rule. Every man, however solitary may seem his occupation, is a member of a vast industrial partnership, as large as the nation, as large as humanity. The necessity of mutual dependence should imply the duty and guarantee of mutual support; and that it did not in your day constituted the essential cruelty and unreason of your system."

"That may all be so," I replied, "but it does not touch the case of those who are unable to contribute anything to the product of industry."

"Surely I told you this morning, at least I thought I did," replied Dr. Leete, "that the right of a man to maintenance at the nation's table depends on the fact that he is a man, and not on the amount of health and strength he may have, so long as he does his best."

"You said so," I answered, "but I supposed the rule applied only to the workers of different ability. Does it also hold of those who can do nothing at all?"

"Are they not also men?"

"I am to understand, then, that the lame, the blind, the sick, and the impotent, are as well off as the most efficient and have the same income?"

"Certainly," was the reply.

"The idea of charity on such a scale," I answered, "would have made our most enthusiastic philanthropists gasp."

"If you had a sick brother at home," replied Dr. Leete, "unable to work, would you feed him on less dainty food, and lodge and clothe him more poorly, than yourself? More likely far, you would give him the preference; nor would you think of calling it charity. Would not the word, in that connection, fill you with indignation?"

"Of course," I replied; "but the cases are not parallel. There is a sense, no doubt, in which all men are brothers; but this general sort of brotherhood is not to be compared, except for rhetorical purposes, to the brotherhood of blood, either as to its sentiment or its obligations."

"There speaks the nineteenth century!" exclaimed Dr. Leete. "Ah, Mr. West, there is no doubt as to the length of time that you slept. If I were to give you, in one sentence, a key to what may seem the mysteries of our civilization as compared with that of your age, I should say that it is the fact that the solidarity of the race and the brotherhood of man, which to you were but fine phrases, are, to our thinking and feeling, ties as real and as vital as physical fraternity.

"But even setting that consideration aside, I do not see why it so surprises you that those who cannot work are conceded the full right to live on the produce of those who can. Even in your day, the duty of military service for the protection of the nation, to which our industrial service corresponds, while obligatory on those able to discharge it, did not operate to deprive of the privileges of citizenship those who were unable. They stayed at home, and were protected by those who fought, and nobody questioned their right to be, or thought less of them. So, now, the requirement of industrial service from those able to render it does not operate to deprive of the privileges of citizenship, which now implies the citizen's maintenance, him who cannot work. The worker is not a citizen because he works, but works because he is a citizen. As you recognize the duty of the strong to fight for the weak, we, now that fighting is gone by, recognize his duty to work for him.

"A solution which leaves an unaccounted-for residuum is no solution at all; and our solution of the problem of human society would have been none at all had it left the lame, the sick, and the blind outside with the beasts, to fare as they might. Better far have left the strong and well unprovided for than these burdened ones, toward whom every heart must yearn, and for whom ease of mind and body should be provided, if for no others. Therefore it is, as I told you this morning, that the title of every man, woman, and child to the means of existence rests on no basis less plain, broad, and simple than the fact that they are fellows of one race-members of one human family. The only coin current is the image of God, and that is good for all we have.

"I think there is no feature of the civilization of your epoch so repugnant to modern ideas as the neglect with which you treated your dependent classes. Even if you had no pity, no feeling of brotherhood, how was it that you did not see that you were robbing the incapable class of their plain right in leaving them unprovided for?"

"I don't quite follow you there," I said. "I admit the claim of this class to our pity, but how could they who produced nothing claim a share of the product as a right?"

"How happened it," was Dr. Leete's reply, "that your workers were able to produce more than so many savages would have done? Was it not wholly on account of the heritage of the past knowledge and achievements of the race, the machinery of society, thousands of years in contriving, found by you ready-made to your hand? How did you come to be possessors of this knowledge and this machinery, which represent nine parts to one contributed by yourself in the value of your product? You inherited it, did you not? And were not these others, these unfortunate and crippled brothers whom you cast out, joint inheritors, co-heirs with you? What did you do with their share? Did you not rob them when you put them off with crusts, who were entitled to sit with the heirs, and did you not add insult to robbery when you called the crusts charity?

"Ah, Mr. West," Dr. Leete continued, as I did not respond, "what I do not understand is, setting aside all considerations either of justice or brotherly feeling toward the crippled and defective, how the workers of your day could have had any heart for their work, knowing that their children, or grand-children, if unfortunate, would be deprived of the comforts and even necessities of life. It is a mystery how men with children could favor a system under which they were rewarded beyond those less endowed with bodily strength or mental power. For, by the same discrimination by which the father profited, the son, for whom he would give his life, being perchance weaker than others, might be reduced to crusts and beggary. How men dared leave children behind them, I have never been able to understand."

Note.—Although in his talk on the previous evening Dr. Leete had emphasized the pains taken to enable every man to ascertain and follow his natural bent in choosing an occupation, it was not till I learned that the worker's income is the same in all occupations that I realized how absolutely he may be counted on to do so, and thus, by selecting the harness which sets most lightly on himself, find that in which he can pull best. The failure of my age in any systematic or effective way to develop and utilize the natural aptitudes of men for the industries and intellectual avocations was one of the great wastes, as well as one of the most common causes of unhappiness in that time. The vast majority of my contemporaries, though nominally free to do so, never really chose their occupations at all, but were forced by circumstances into work for which they were relatively inefficient, because not naturally fitted for it. The rich, in this respect, had little advantage over the poor. The latter, indeed, being generally deprived of education, had no opportunity even to ascertain the natural aptitudes they might have, and on account of their poverty were unable to develop them by cultivation even when ascertained. The liberal and technical professions, except by favorable accident, were shut to them, to their own great loss and that of the nation. On the other hand, the well-to-do, although they could command education and opportunity, were scarcely less hampered by social prejudice, which forbade them to pursue manual avocations, even when adapted to them, and destined them, whether fit or unfit, to the professions, thus wasting many an excellent handicraftsman. Mercenary considerations, tempting men to pursue money-making occupations for which they were unfit, instead of less remunerative employments for which they were fit, were responsible for another vast perversion of talent. All these things now are changed. Equal education and opportunity must needs bring to light whatever aptitudes a man has, and neither social prejudices nor mercenary considerations hamper him in the choice of his life work.

Chapter 13

As Edith had promised he should do, Dr. Leete accompanied me to my bedroom when I retired, to instruct me as to the adjustment of the musical telephone. He showed how, by turning a screw, the volume of the music could be made to fill the room, or die away to an echo so faint and far that one could scarcely be sure whether he heard or imagined it. If, of two persons side by side, one desired to listen to music and the other to sleep, it could be made audible to one and inaudible to another.

"I should strongly advise you to sleep if you can to-night, Mr. West, in preference to listening to the finest tunes in the world," the doctor said, after explaining these points. "In the trying experience you are just now passing through, sleep is a nerve tonic for which there is no substitute."

Mindful of what had happened to me that very morning, I promised to heed his counsel.

"Very well," he said, "then I will set the telephone at eight o'clock."

"What do you mean?" I asked.

He explained that, by a clock-work combination, a person could arrange to be awakened at any hour by the music.

It began to appear, as has since fully proved to be the case, that I had left my tendency to insomnia behind me with the other discomforts of existence in the nineteenth century; for though I took no sleeping draught this time, yet, as the night before, I had no sooner touched the pillow than I was asleep.

I dreamed that I sat on the throne of the Abencerrages in the banqueting hall of the Alhambra, feasting my lords and generals, who next day were to follow the crescent against the Christian dogs of Spain. The air, cooled by the spray of fountains, was heavy with the scent of flowers. A band of Nautch girls, round-limbed and luscious-lipped, danced with voluptuous grace to the music of brazen and stringed instruments. Looking up to the latticed galleries, one caught a gleam now and then from the eye of some beauty of the royal harem, looking down upon the assembled flower of Moorish chivalry. Louder and louder clashed the cymbals, wilder and wilder grew the strain, till the blood of the desert race could no longer resist the martial delirium, and the swart nobles leaped to their feet; a thousand scimetars were bared, and the cry, "Allah il Allah!" shook the hall and awoke me, to find it broad daylight, and the room tingling with the electric music of the "Turkish Reveille."

At the breakfast-table, when I told my host of my morning's experience, I learned that it was not a mere chance that the piece of music which awakened me was a reveille. The airs played at one of the halls during the waking hours of the morning were always of an inspiring type.

"By the way," I said, "I have not thought to ask you anything about the state of Europe. Have the societies of the Old World also been remodeled?"

"Yes," replied Dr. Leete, "the great nations of Europe as well as Australia, Mexico, and parts of South America, are now organized industrially like the United States, which was the pioneer of the evolution. The peaceful relations of these nations are assured by a loose form of federal union of world-wide extent. An international council regulates the mutual intercourse and commerce of the members of the union and their joint policy toward the more backward races, which are gradually being educated up to civilized institutions. Complete autonomy within its own limits is enjoyed by every nation."

"How do you carry on commerce without money?" I said. "In trading with other nations, you must use some sort of money, although you dispense with it in the internal affairs of the nation."

"Oh, no; money is as superfluous in our foreign as in our internal relations. When foreign commerce was conducted by private enterprise, money was necessary to adjust it on account of the multifarious complexity of the transactions; but nowadays it is a function of the nations as units. There are thus only a dozen or so merchants in the world, and their business being supervised by the international council, a simple system of book accounts serves perfectly to regulate their dealings. Customs duties of every sort are of course superfluous. A nation simply does not import what its government does not think requisite for the general interest. Each nation has a bureau of foreign exchange, which manages its trading. For example, the American bureau, estimating such and such quantities of French goods necessary to America for a given year, sends the order to the French bureau, which in turn sends its order to our bureau. The same is done mutually by all the nations."

"But how are the prices of foreign goods settled, since there is no competition?"

"The price at which one nation supplies another with goods," replied Dr. Leete, "must be that at which it supplies its own citizens. So you see there is no danger of misunderstanding. Of course no nation is theoretically bound to supply another with the product of its own labor, but it is for the interest of all to exchange some commodities. If a nation is regularly supplying another with certain goods, notice is required from either side of any important change in the relation."

"But what if a nation, having a monopoly of some natural product, should refuse to supply it to the others, or to one of them?"

"Such a case has never occurred, and could not without doing the refusing party vastly more harm than the others," replied Dr. Leete. "In the fist place, no favoritism could be legally shown. The law requires that each nation shall deal with the others, in all respects, on exactly the same footing. Such a course as you suggest would cut off the nation adopting it from the remainder of the earth for all purposes whatever. The contingency is one that need not give us much anxiety."

"But," said I, "supposing a nation, having a natural monopoly in some product of which it exports more than it consumes, should put the price away up, and thus, without cutting off the supply, make a profit out of its neighbors' necessities? Its own citizens would of course have to pay the higher price on that commodity, but as a body would make more out of foreigners than they would be out of pocket themselves."

"When you come to know how prices of all commodities are determined nowadays, you will perceive how impossible it is that they could be altered, except with reference to the amount or arduousness of the work required respectively to produce them," was Dr. Leete's reply. "This principle is an international as well as a national guarantee; but even without it the sense of community of interest, international as well as national, and the conviction of the folly of selfishness, are too deep nowadays to render possible such a piece of sharp practice as you apprehend. You must understand that we all look forward to an eventual unification of the world as one nation. That, no doubt, will be the ultimate form of society, and will realize certain economic advantages over the present federal system of autonomous nations. Meanwhile, however, the present system works so nearly perfectly that we are quite content to leave to posterity the completion of the scheme. There are, indeed, some who hold that it never will be completed, on the ground that the federal plan is not merely a provisional solution of the problem of human society, but the best ultimate solution."

"How do you manage," I asked, "when the books of any two nations do not balance? Supposing we import more from France than we export to her."

"At the end of each year," replied the doctor, "the books of every nation are examined. If France is found in our debt, probably we are in the debt of some nation which owes France, and so on with all the nations. The balances that remain after the accounts have been cleared by the international council should not be large under our system. Whatever they may be, the council requires them to be settled every few years, and may require their settlement at any time if they are getting too large; for it is not intended that any nation shall run largely in debt to another, lest feelings unfavorable to amity should be engendered. To guard further against this, the international council inspects the commodities interchanged by the nations, to see that they are of perfect quality."

"But what are the balances finally settled with, seeing that you have no money?"

"In national staples; a basis of agreement as to what staples shall be accepted, and in what proportions, for settlement of accounts, being a preliminary to trade relations."

"Emigration is another point I want to ask you about," said I. "With every nation organized as a close industrial partnership, monopolizing all means of production in the country, the emigrant, even if he were permitted to land, would starve. I suppose there is no emigration nowadays."

"On the contrary, there is constant emigration, by which I suppose you mean removal to foreign countries for permanent residence," replied Dr. Leete. "It is arranged on a simple international arrangement of indemnities. For example, if a man at twenty-one emigrates from England to America, England loses all the expense of his maintenance and education, and America gets a workman for nothing. America accordingly makes England an allowance. The same principle, varied to suit the case, applies generally. If the man is near the term of his labor when he emigrates, the country receiving him has the allowance. As to imbecile persons, it is deemed best that each nation should be responsible for its own, and the emigration of such must be under full guarantees of support by his own nation. Subject to these regulations, the right of any man to emigrate at any time is unrestricted."

"But how about mere pleasure trips; tours of observation? How can a stranger travel in a country whose people do not receive money, and are themselves supplied with the means of life on a basis not extended to him? His own credit card cannot, of course, be good in other lands. How does he pay his way?"

"An American credit card," replied Dr. Leete, "is just as good in Europe as American gold used to be, and on precisely the same condition, namely, that it be exchanged into the currency of the country you are traveling in. An American in Berlin takes his credit card to the local office of the international council, and receives in exchange for the whole or part of it a German credit card, the amount being charged against the United States in favor of Germany on the international account."

"Perhaps Mr. West would like to dine at the Elephant to-day," said Edith, as we left the table.

"That is the name we give to the general dining-house in our ward," explained her father. "Not only is our cooking done at the public kitchens, as I told you last night, but the service and quality of the meals are much more satisfactory if taken at the dining-house. The two minor meals of the day are usually taken at home, as not worth the trouble of going out; but it is general to go out to dine. We have not done so since you have been with us, from a notion that it would be better to wait till you had become a little more familiar with our ways. What do you think? Shall we take dinner at the dining-house to-day?"

I said that I should be very much pleased to do so.

Not long after, Edith came to me, smiling, and said:

"Last night, as I was thinking what I could do to make you feel at home until you came to be a little more used to us and our ways, an idea occurred to me. What would you say if I were to introduce you to some very nice people of your own times, whom I am sure you used to be well acquainted with?"

I replied, rather vaguely, that it would certainly be very agreeable, but I did not see how she was going to manage it.

"Come with me," was her smiling reply, "and see if I am not as good as my word."

My susceptibility to surprise had been pretty well exhausted by the numerous shocks it had received, but it was with some wonderment that I followed her into a room which I had not before entered. It was a small, cosy apartment, walled with cases filled with books.

"Here are your friends," said Edith, indicating one of the cases, and as my eye glanced over the names on the backs of the volumes, Shakespeare, Milton, Wordsworth, Shelley, Tennyson, Defoe, Dickens, Thackeray, Hugo, Hawthorne, Irving, and a score of other great writers of my time and all time, I understood her meaning. She had indeed made good her promise in a sense compared with which its literal fulfillment would have been a disappointment. She had introduced me to a circle of friends whom the century that had elapsed since last I communed with them had aged as little as it had myself. Their spirit was as high, their wit as keen, their laughter and their tears as contagious, as when their speech had whiled away the hours of a former century. Lonely I was not and could not be more, with this goodly companionship, however wide the gulf of years that gaped between me and my old life.

"You are glad I brought you here," exclaimed Edith, radiant, as she read in my face the success of her experiment. "It was a good idea, was it not, Mr. West? How stupid in me not to think of it before! I will leave you now with your old friends, for I know there will be no company for you like them just now; but remember you must not let old friends make you quite forget new ones!" and with that smiling caution she left me.

Attracted by the most familiar of the names before me, I laid my hand on a volume of Dickens, and sat down to read. He had been my prime favorite among the bookwriters of the century,—I mean the nineteenth century,—and a week had rarely passed in my old life during which I had not taken up some volume of his works to while away an idle hour. Any volume with which I had been familiar would have produced an extraordinary impression, read under my present circumstances, but my exceptional familiarity with Dickens, and his consequent power to call up the associations of my former life, gave to his writings an effect no others could have had, to intensify, by force of contrast, my appreciation of the strangeness of my present environment. However new and astonishing one's surroundings, the tendency is to become a part of them so soon that almost from the first the power to see them objectively and fully measure their strangeness, is lost. That power, already dulled in my case, the pages of Dickens restored by carrying me back through their associations to the standpoint of my former life.

With a clearness which I had not been able before to attain, I saw now the past and present, like contrasting pictures, side by side.

The genius of the great novelist of the nineteenth century, like that of Homer, might indeed defy time; but the setting of his pathetic tales, the misery of the poor, the wrongs of power, the pitiless cruelty of the system of society, had passed away as utterly as Circe and the sirens, Charybdis and Cyclops.

During the hour or two that I sat there with Dickens open before me, I did not actually read more than a couple of pages. Every paragraph, every phrase, brought up some new aspect of the world-transformation which had taken place, and led my thoughts on long and widely ramifying excursions. As meditating thus in Dr. Leete's library I gradually attained a more clear and coherent idea of the prodigious spectacle which I had been so strangely enabled to view, I was filled with a deepening wonder at the seeming capriciousness of the fate that had given to one who so little deserved it, or seemed in any way set apart for it, the power alone among his contemporaries to stand upon the earth in this latter day. I had neither foreseen the new world nor toiled for it, as many about me had done regardless of the scorn of fools or the misconstruction of the good. Surely it would have been more in accordance with the fitness of things had one of those prophetic and strenuous souls been enabled to see the travail of his soul and be satisfied; he, for example, a thousand times rather than I, who, having beheld in a vision the world I looked on, sang of it in words that again and again, during these last wondrous days, had rung in my mind:

For I dipt into the future, far as human eye could see,
Saw the vision of the world, and all the wonder that would be
Till the war-drum throbbed no longer, and the battle-flags were furled.
In the Parliament of man, the federation of the world.
Then the common sense of most shall hold a fretful realm in awe,
And the kindly earth shall slumber, lapt in universal law.
For I doubt not through the ages one increasing purpose runs,
And the thoughts of men are widened with the process of the suns.

What though, in his old age, he momentarily lost faith in his own prediction, as prophets in their hours of depression and doubt generally do; the words had remained eternal testimony to the seership of a poet's heart, the insight that is given to faith.

I was still in the library when some hours later Dr. Leete sought me there. "Edith told me of her idea," he said, "and I thought it an excellent one. I had a little curiosity what writer you would first turn to. Ah, Dickens! You admired him, then! That is where we moderns agree with you. Judged by our standards, he overtops all the writers of his age, not because his literary genius was highest, but because his great heart beat for the poor, because he made the cause of the victims of society his own, and devoted his pen to exposing its cruelties and shams. No man of his time did so much as he to turn men's minds to the wrong and wretchedness of the old order of things, and open their eyes to the necessity of the great change that was coming, although he himself did not clearly foresee it."

Chapter 14

A heavy rainstorm came up during the day, and I had concluded that the condition of the streets would be such that my hosts would have to give up the idea of going out to dinner, although the dining-hall I had understood to be quite near. I was much surprised when at the dinner hour the ladies appeared prepared to go out, but without either rubbers or umbrellas.

The mystery was explained when we found ourselves on the street, for a continuous waterproof covering had been let down so as to inclose the sidewalk and turn it into a well lighted and perfectly dry corridor, which was filled with a stream of ladies and gentlemen dressed for dinner. At the corners the entire open space was similarly roofed in. Edith Leete, with whom I walked, seemed much interested in learning what appeared to be entirely new to her, that in the stormy weather the streets of the Boston of my day had been impassable, except to persons protected by umbrellas, boots, and heavy clothing. "Were sidewalk coverings not used at all?" she asked. They were used, I explained, but in a scattered and utterly unsystematic way, being private enterprises. She said to me that at the present time all the streets were provided against inclement weather in the manner I saw, the apparatus being rolled out of the way when it was unnecessary. She intimated that it would be considered an extraordinary imbecility to permit the weather to have any effect on the social movements of the people.

Dr. Leete, who was walking ahead, overhearing something of our talk, turned to say that the difference between the age of individualism and that of concert was well characterized by the fact that, in the nineteenth century, when it rained, the people of Boston put up three hundred thousand umbrellas over as many heads, and in the twentieth century they put up one umbrella over all the heads.

As we walked on, Edith said, "The private umbrella is father's favorite figure to illustrate the old way when everybody lived for himself and his family. There is a nineteenth century painting at the Art Gallery representing a crowd of people in the rain, each one holding his umbrella over himself and his wife, and giving his neighbors the drippings, which he claims must have been meant by the artist as a satire on his times."

We now entered a large building into which a stream of people was pouring. I could not see the front, owing to the awning, but, if in correspondence with the interior, which was even finer than the store I visited the day before, it would have been magnificent. My companion said that the sculptured group over the entrance was especially admired. Going up a grand staircase we walked some distance along a broad corridor with many doors opening upon it. At one of these, which bore my host's name, we turned in, and I found myself in an elegant dining-room containing a table for four. Windows opened on a courtyard where a fountain played to a great height and music made the air electric.

"You seem at home here," I said, as we seated ourselves at table, and Dr. Leete touched an annunciator.

"This is, in fact, a part of our house, slightly detached from the rest," he replied. "Every family in the ward has a room set apart in this great building for its permanent and exclusive use for a small annual rental. For transient guests and individuals there is accommodation on another floor. If we expect to dine here, we put in our orders the night before, selecting anything in market, according to the daily reports in the papers. The meal is as expensive or as simple as we please, though of course everything is vastly cheaper as well as better than it would be prepared at home. There is actually nothing which our people take more interest in than the perfection of the catering and cooking done for them, and I admit that we are a little vain of the success that has been attained by this branch of the service. Ah, my dear Mr. West, though other aspects of your civilization were more tragical, I can imagine that none could have been more depressing than the poor dinners you had to eat, that is, all of you who had not great wealth."

"You would have found none of us disposed to disagree with you on that point," I said.

The waiter, a fine-looking young fellow, wearing a slightly distinctive uniform, now made his appearance. I observed him closely, as it was the first time I had been able to study particularly the bearing of one of the enlisted members of the industrial army. This young man, I knew from what I had been told, must be highly educated, and the equal, socially and in all respects, of those he served. But it was perfectly evident that to neither side was the situation in the slightest degree embarrassing. Dr. Leete addressed the young man in a tone devoid, of course, as any gentleman's would be, of superciliousness, but at the same time not in any way deprecatory, while the manner of the young man was simply that of a person intent on discharging correctly the task he was engaged in, equally without familiarity or obsequiousness. It was, in fact, the manner of a soldier on duty, but without the military stiffness. As the youth left the room, I said, "I cannot get over my wonder at seeing a young man like that serving so contentedly in a menial position."

"What is that word 'menial'? I never heard it," said Edith.

"It is obsolete now," remarked her father. "If I understand it rightly, it applied to persons who performed particularly disagreeable and unpleasant tasks for others, and carried with it an implication of contempt. Was it not so, Mr. West?"

"That is about it," I said. "Personal service, such as waiting on tables, was considered menial, and held in such contempt, in my day, that persons of culture and refinement would suffer hardship before condescending to it."

"What a strangely artificial idea," exclaimed Mrs. Leete wonderingly.

"And yet these services had to be rendered," said Edith.

"Of course," I replied. "But we imposed them on the poor, and those who had no alternative but starvation."

"And increased the burden you imposed on them by adding your contempt," remarked Dr. Leete.

"I don't think I clearly understand," said Edith. "Do you mean that you permitted people to do things for you which you despised them for doing, or that you accepted services from them which you would have been unwilling to render them? You can't surely mean that, Mr. West?"

I was obliged to tell her that the fact was just as she had stated. Dr. Leete, however, came to my relief.

"To understand why Edith is surprised," he said, "you must know that nowadays it is an axiom of ethics that to accept a service from another which we would be unwilling to return in kind, if need were, is like borrowing with the intention of not repaying, while to enforce such a service by taking advantage of the poverty or necessity of a person would be an outrage like forcible robbery. It is the worst thing about any system which divides men, or allows them to be divided, into classes and castes, that it weakens the sense of a common humanity. Unequal distribution of wealth, and, still more effectually, unequal opportunities of education and culture, divided society in your day into classes which in many respects regarded each other as distinct races. There is not, after all, such a difference as might appear between our ways of looking at this question of service. Ladies and gentlemen of the cultured class in your day would no more have permitted persons of their own class to render them services they would scorn to return than we would permit anybody to do so. The poor and the uncultured, however, they looked upon as of another kind from themselves. The equal wealth and equal opportunities of culture which all persons now enjoy have simply made us all members of one class, which corresponds to the most fortunate class with you. Until this equality of condition had come to pass, the idea of the solidarity of humanity, the brotherhood of all men, could never have become the real conviction and practical principle of action it is nowadays. In your day the same phrases were indeed used, but they were phrases merely."

"Do the waiters, also, volunteer?"

"No," replied Dr. Leete. "The waiters are young men in the unclassified grade of the industrial army who are assignable to all sorts of miscellaneous occupations not requiring special skill. Waiting on table is one of these, and every young recruit is given a taste of it. I myself served as a waiter for several months in this very dining-house some forty years ago. Once more you must remember that there is recognized no sort of difference between the dignity of the different sorts of work required by the nation. The individual is never regarded, nor regards himself, as the servant of those he serves, nor is he in any way dependent upon them. It is always the nation which he is serving. No difference is recognized between a waiter's functions and those of any other worker. The fact that his is a personal service is indifferent from our point of view. So is a doctor's. I should as soon expect our waiter today to look down on me because I served him as a doctor, as think of looking down on him because he serves me as a waiter."

After dinner my entertainers conducted me about the building, of which the extent, the magnificent architecture and richness of embellishment, astonished me. It seemed that it was not merely a dining-hall, but likewise a great pleasure-house and social rendezvous of the quarter, and no appliance of entertainment or recreation seemed lacking.

"You find illustrated here," said Dr. Leete, when I had expressed my admiration, "what I said to you in our first conversation, when you were looking out over the city, as to the splendor of our public and common life as compared with the simplicity of our private and home life, and the contrast which, in this respect, the twentieth bears to the nineteenth century. To save ourselves useless burdens, we have as little gear about us at home as is consistent with comfort, but the social side of our life is ornate and luxurious beyond anything the world ever knew before. All the industrial and professional guilds have clubhouses as extensive as this, as well as country, mountain, and seaside houses for sport and rest in vacations."

NOTE. In the latter part of the nineteenth century it became a practice of needy young men at some of the colleges of the country to earn a little money for their term bills by serving as waiters on tables at hotels during the long summer vacation. It was claimed, in reply to critics who expressed the prejudices of the time in asserting that persons voluntarily following such an occupation could not be gentlemen, that they were entitled to praise for vindicating, by their example, the dignity of all honest and necessary labor. The use of this argument illustrates a common confusion in thought on the part of my former contemporaries. The business of waiting on tables was in no more need of defense than most of the other ways of getting a living in that day, but to talk of dignity attaching to labor of any sort under the system then prevailing was absurd.

There is no way in which selling labor for the highest price it will fetch is more dignified than selling goods for what can be got. Both were commercial transactions to be judged by the commercial standard. By setting a price in money on his service, the worker accepted the money measure for it, and renounced all clear claim to be judged by any other. The sordid taint which this necessity imparted to the noblest and the highest sorts of service was bitterly resented by generous souls, but there was no evading it. There was no exemption, however transcendent the quality of one's service, from the necessity of haggling for its price in the market-place. The physician must sell his healing and the apostle his preaching like the rest. The prophet, who had guessed the meaning of God, must dicker for the price of the revelation, and the poet hawk his visions in printers' row. If I were asked to name the most distinguishing felicity of this age, as compared to that in which I first saw the light, I should say that to me it seems to consist in the dignity you have given to labor by refusing to set a price upon it and abolishing the market-place forever. By requiring of every man his best you have made God his task-master, and by making honor the sole reward of achievement you have imparted to all service the distinction peculiar in my day to the soldier's.

Chapter 15

When, in the course of our tour of inspection, we came to the library, we succumbed to the temptation of the luxurious leather chairs with which it was furnished, and sat down in one of the book-lined alcoves to rest and chat awhile.[1]

"Edith tells me that you have been in the library all the morning," said Mrs. Leete. "Do you know, it seems to me, Mr. West, that you are the most enviable of mortals."

"I should like to know just why," I replied.

"Because the books of the last hundred years will be new to you," she answered. "You will have so much of the most absorbing literature to read as to leave you scarcely time for meals these five years to come. Ah, what would I give if I had not already read Berrian's novels."

"Or Nesmyth's, mamma," added Edith.

"Yes, or Oates' poems, or 'Past and Present,' or, 'In the Beginning,' or—oh, I could name a dozen books, each worth a year of one's life," declared Mrs. Leete, enthusiastically.

"I judge, then, that there has been some notable literature produced in this century."

"Yes," said Dr. Leete. "It has been an era of unexampled intellectual splendor. Probably humanity never before passed through a moral and material evolution, at once so vast in its scope and brief in its time of accomplishment, as that from the old order to the new in the early part of this century. When men came to realize the greatness of the felicity which had befallen them, and that the change through which they had passed was not merely an improvement in details of their condition, but the rise of the race to a new plane of existence with an illimitable vista of progress, their minds were affected in all their faculties with a stimulus, of which the outburst of the mediaeval renaissance offers a suggestion but faint indeed. There ensued an era of mechanical invention, scientific discovery, art, musical and literary productiveness to which no previous age of the world offers anything comparable."

"By the way," said I, "talking of literature, how are books published now? Is that also done by the nation?"

"Certainly."

"But how do you manage it? Does the government publish everything that is brought it as a matter of course, at the public expense, or does it exercise a censorship and print only what it approves?"

"Neither way. The printing department has no censorial powers. It is bound to print all that is offered it, but prints it only on condition that the author defray the first cost out of his credit. He must pay for the privilege of the public ear, and if he has any message worth hearing we consider that he will be glad to do it. Of course, if incomes were unequal, as in the old times, this rule would enable only the rich to be authors, but the resources of citizens being equal, it merely measures the strength of the author's motive. The cost of an edition of an average book can be saved out of a year's credit by the practice of economy and some sacrifices. The book, on being published, is placed on sale by the nation."

"The author receiving a royalty on the sales as with us, I suppose," I suggested.

"Not as with you, certainly," replied Dr. Leete, "but nevertheless in one way. The price of every book is made up of the cost of its publication with a royalty for the author. The author fixes this royalty at any figure he pleases. Of course if he puts it unreasonably high it is his own loss, for the book will not sell. The amount of this royalty is set to his credit and he is discharged from other service to the nation for so long a period as this credit at the rate of allowance for the support of citizens shall suffice to support him. If his book be moderately successful, he has thus a furlough for several months, a year, two or three years, and if he in the mean time produces other successful work, the remission of service is extended so far as the sale of that may justify. An author of much acceptance succeeds in supporting himself by his pen during the entire period of service, and the degree of any writer's literary ability, as determined by the popular voice, is thus the measure of the opportunity given him to devote his time to literature. In this respect the outcome of our system is not very dissimilar to that of yours, but there are two notable differences. In the first place, the universally high level of education nowadays gives the popular verdict a conclusiveness on the real merit of literary work which in your day it was as far as possible from having. In the second place, there is no such thing now as favoritism of any sort to interfere with the recognition of true merit. Every author has precisely the same facilities for bringing his work before the popular tribunal. To judge from the complaints of the writers of your day, this absolute equality of opportunity would have been greatly prized."

"In the recognition of merit in other fields of original genius, such as music, art, invention, design," I said, "I suppose you follow a similar principle."

"Yes," he replied, "although the details differ. In art, for example, as in literature, the people are the sole judges. They vote upon the acceptance of statues and paintings for the public buildings, and their favorable verdict carries with it the artist's remission from other tasks to devote himself to his vocation. On copies of his work disposed of, he also derives the same advantage as the author on sales of his books. In all these lines of original genius the plan pursued is the same to offer a free field to aspirants, and as soon as exceptional talent is recognized to release it from all trammels and let it have free course. The remission of other service in these cases is not intended as a gift or reward, but as the means of obtaining more and higher service. Of course there are various literary, art, and scientific institutes to which membership comes to the famous and is greatly prized. The highest of all honors in the nation, higher than the presidency, which calls merely for good sense and devotion to duty, is the red ribbon awarded by the vote of the people to the great authors, artists, engineers, physicians, and inventors of the generation. Not over a certain number wear it at any one time, though every bright young fellow in the country loses innumerable nights' sleep dreaming of it. I even did myself."

"Just as if mamma and I would have thought any more of you with it," exclaimed Edith; "not that it isn't, of course, a very fine thing to have."

"You had no choice, my dear, but to take your father as you found him and make the best of him," Dr. Leete replied; "but as for your mother, there, she would never have had me if I had not assured her that I was bound to get the red ribbon or at least the blue."

On this extravagance Mrs. Leete's only comment was a smile.

"How about periodicals and newspapers?" I said. "I won't deny that your book publishing system is a considerable improvement on ours, both as to its tendency to encourage a real literary vocation, and, quite as important, to discourage mere scribblers; but I don't see how it can be made to apply to magazines and newspapers. It is very well to make a man pay for publishing a book, because the expense will be only occasional; but no man could afford the expense of publishing a newspaper every day in the year. It took the deep pockets of our private capitalists to do that, and often exhausted even them before the returns came in. If you have newspapers at all, they must, I fancy, be published by the government at the public expense, with government editors, reflecting government opinions. Now, if your system is so perfect that there is never anything to criticize in the conduct of affairs, this arrangement may answer. Otherwise I should think the lack of an independent unofficial medium for the expression of public opinion would have most unfortunate results. Confess, Dr. Leete, that a free newspaper press, with all that it implies, was a redeeming incident of the old system when capital was in private hands, and that you have to set off the loss of that against your gains in other respects."

"I am afraid I can't give you even that consolation," replied Dr. Leete, laughing. "In the first place, Mr. West, the newspaper press is by no means the only or, as we look at it, the best vehicle for serious criticism of public affairs. To us, the judgments of your newspapers on such themes seem generally to have been crude and flippant, as well as deeply tinctured with prejudice and bitterness. In so far as they may be taken as expressing public opinion, they give an unfavorable impression of the popular intelligence, while so far as they may have formed public opinion, the nation was not to be felicitated. Nowadays, when a citizen desires to make a serious impression upon the public mind as to any aspect of public affairs, he comes out with a book or pamphlet, published as other books are. But this is not because we lack newspapers and magazines, or that they lack the most absolute freedom. The newspaper press is organized so as to be a more perfect expression of public opinion than it possibly could be in your day, when private capital controlled and managed it primarily as a money-making business, and secondarily only as a mouthpiece for the people."

"But," said I, "if the government prints the papers at the public expense, how can it fail to control their policy? Who appoints the editors, if not the government?"

"The government does not pay the expense of the papers, nor appoint their editors, nor in any way exert the slightest influence on their policy," replied Dr. Leete. "The people who take the paper pay the expense of its publication, choose its editor, and remove him when unsatisfactory. You will scarcely say, I think, that such a newspaper press is not a free organ of popular opinion."

"Decidedly I shall not," I replied, "but how is it practicable?"

"Nothing could be simpler. Supposing some of my neighbors or myself think we ought to have a newspaper reflecting our opinions, and devoted especially to our locality, trade, or profession. We go about among the people till we get the names of such a number that their annual subscriptions will meet the cost of the paper, which is little or big according to the largeness of its constituency. The amount of the subscriptions marked off the credits of the citizens guarantees the nation against loss in publishing the paper, its business, you understand, being that of a publisher purely, with no option to refuse the duty required. The subscribers to the paper now elect somebody as editor, who, if he accepts the office, is discharged from other service during his incumbency. Instead of paying a salary to him, as in your day, the subscribers pay the nation an indemnity equal to the cost of his support for taking him away from the general service. He manages the paper just as one of your editors did, except that he has no counting-room to obey, or interests of private capital as against the public good to defend. At the end of the first year, the subscribers for the next either re-elect the former editor or choose any one else to his place. An able editor, of course, keeps his place indefinitely. As the subscription list enlarges, the funds of the paper increase, and it is improved by the securing of more and better contributors, just as your papers were."

"How is the staff of contributors recompensed, since they cannot be paid in money?"

"The editor settles with them the price of their wares. The amount is transferred to their individual credit from the guarantee credit of the paper, and a remission of service is granted the contributor for a length of time corresponding to the amount credited him, just as to other authors. As to magazines, the system is the same. Those interested in the prospectus of a new periodical pledge enough subscriptions to run it for a year; select their editor, who recompenses his contributors just as in the other case, the printing bureau furnishing the necessary force and material for publication, as a matter of course. When an editor's services are no longer desired, if he cannot earn the right to his time by other literary work, he simply resumes his place in the industrial army. I should add that, though ordinarily the editor is elected only at the end of the year, and as a rule is continued in office for a term of years, in case of any sudden change he should give to the tone of the paper, provision is made for taking the sense of the subscribers as to his removal at any time."

"However earnestly a man may long for leisure for purposes of study or meditation," I remarked, "he cannot get out of the harness, if I understand you rightly, except in these two ways you have mentioned. He must either by literary, artistic, or inventive productiveness indemnify the nation for the loss of his services, or must get a sufficient number of other people to contribute to such an indemnity."

"It is most certain," replied Dr. Leete, "that no able-bodied man nowadays can evade his share of work and live on the toil of others, whether he calls himself by the fine name of student or confesses to being simply lazy. At the same time our system is elastic enough to give free play to every instinct of human nature which does not aim at dominating others or living on the fruit of others' labor. There is not only the remission by indemnification but the remission by abnegation. Any man in his thirty-third year, his term of service being then half done, can obtain an honorable discharge from the army, provided he accepts for the rest of his life one half the rate of maintenance other citizens receive. It is quite possible to live on this amount, though one must forego the luxuries and elegancies of life, with some, perhaps, of its comforts."

When the ladies retired that evening, Edith brought me a book and said:

"If you should be wakeful to-night, Mr. West, you might be interested in looking over this story by Berrian. It is considered his masterpiece, and will at least give you an idea what the stories nowadays are like."

I sat up in my room that night reading "Penthesilia" till it grew gray in the east, and did not lay it down till I had finished it. And yet let no admirer of the great romancer of the twentieth century resent my saying that at the first reading what most impressed me was not so much what was in the book as what was left out of it. The story-writers of my day would have deemed the making of bricks without straw a light task compared with the construction of a romance from which should be excluded all effects drawn from the contrasts of wealth and poverty, education and ignorance, coarseness and refinement, high and low, all motives drawn from social pride and ambition, the desire of being richer or the fear of being poorer, together with sordid anxieties of any sort for one's self or others; a romance in which there should, indeed, be love galore, but love unfretted by artificial barriers created by differences of station or possessions, owning no other law but that of the heart. The reading of "Penthesilia" was of more value than almost any amount of explanation would have been in giving me something like a general impression of the social aspect of the twentieth century. The information Dr. Leete had imparted was indeed extensive as to facts, but they had affected my mind as so many separate impressions, which I had as yet succeeded but imperfectly in making cohere. Berrian put them together for me in a picture.

[1] I cannot sufficiently celebrate the glorious liberty that reigns in the public libraries of the twentieth century as compared with the intolerable management of those of the nineteenth century, in which the books were jealously railed away from the people, and obtainable only at an expenditure of time and red tape calculated to discourage any ordinary taste for literature.

Chapter 16

Next morning I rose somewhat before the breakfast hour. As I descended the stairs, Edith stepped into the hall from the room which had been the scene of the morning interview between us described some chapters back.

"Ah!" she exclaimed, with a charmingly arch expression, "you thought to slip out unbeknown for another of those solitary morning rambles which have such nice effects on you. But you see I am up too early for you this time. You are fairly caught."

"You discredit the efficacy of your own cure," I said, "by supposing that such a ramble would now be attended with bad consequences."

"I am very glad to hear that," she said. "I was in here arranging some flowers for the breakfast table when I heard you come down, and fancied I detected something surreptitious in your step on the stairs."

"You did me injustice," I replied. "I had no idea of going out at all."

Despite her effort to convey an impression that my interception was purely accidental, I had at the time a dim suspicion of what I afterwards learned to be the fact, namely, that this sweet creature, in pursuance of her self-assumed guardianship over me, had risen for the last two or three mornings at an unheard-of hour, to insure against the possibility of my wandering off alone in case I should be affected as on the former occasion. Receiving permission to assist her in making up the breakfast bouquet, I followed her into the room from which she had emerged.

"Are you sure," she asked, "that you are quite done with those terrible sensations you had that morning?"

"I can't say that I do not have times of feeling decidedly queer," I replied, "moments when my personal identity seems an open question. It would be too much to expect after my experience that I should not have such sensations occasionally, but as for being carried entirely off my feet, as I was on the point of being that morning, I think the danger is past."

"I shall never forget how you looked that morning," she said.

"If you had merely saved my life," I continued, "I might, perhaps, find words to express my gratitude, but it was my reason you saved, and there are no words that would not belittle my debt to you." I spoke with emotion, and her eyes grew suddenly moist.

"It is too much to believe all this," she said, "but it is very delightful to hear you say it. What I did was very little. I was very much distressed for you, I know. Father never thinks anything ought to astonish us when it can be explained scientifically, as I suppose this long sleep of yours can be, but even to fancy myself in your place makes my head swim. I know that I could not have borne it at all."

"That would depend," I replied, "on whether an angel came to support you with her sympathy in the crisis of your condition, as one came to me." If my face at all expressed the feelings I had a right to have toward this sweet and lovely young girl, who had played so angelic a role toward me, its expression must have been very worshipful just then. The expression or the words, or both together, caused her now to drop her eyes with a charming blush.

"For the matter of that," I said, "if your experience has not been as startling as mine, it must have been rather overwhelming to see a man belonging to a strange century, and apparently a hundred years dead, raised to life."

"It seemed indeed strange beyond any describing at first," she said, "but when we began to put ourselves in your place, and realize how much stranger it must seem to you, I fancy we forgot our own feelings a good deal, at least I know I did. It seemed then not so much astounding as interesting and touching beyond anything ever heard of before."

"But does it not come over you as astounding to sit at table with me, seeing who I am?"

"You must remember that you do not seem so strange to us as we must to you," she answered. "We belong to a future of which you could not form an idea, a generation of which you knew nothing until you saw us. But you belong to a generation of which our forefathers were a part. We know all about it; the names of many of its members are household words with us. We have made a study of your ways of living and thinking; nothing you say or do surprises us, while we say and do nothing which does not seem strange to you. So you see, Mr. West, that if you feel that you can, in time, get accustomed to us, you must not be surprised that from the first we have scarcely found you strange at all."

"I had not thought of it in that way," I replied. "There is indeed much in what you say. One can look back a thousand years easier than forward fifty. A century is not so very long a retrospect. I might have known your great-grand-parents. Possibly I did. Did they live in Boston?"

"I believe so."

"You are not sure, then?"

"Yes," she replied. "Now I think, they did."

"I had a very large circle of acquaintances in the city," I said. "It is not unlikely that I knew or knew of some of them. Perhaps I may have known them well. Wouldn't it be interesting if I should chance to be able to tell you all about your great-grandfather, for instance?"

"Very interesting."

"Do you know your genealogy well enough to tell me who your forbears were in the Boston of my day?"

"Oh, yes."

"Perhaps, then, you will some time tell me what some of their names were."

She was engrossed in arranging a troublesome spray of green, and did not reply at once. Steps upon the stairway indicated that the other members of the family were descending.

"Perhaps, some time," she said.

After breakfast, Dr. Leete suggested taking me to inspect the central warehouse and observe actually in operation the machinery of distribution, which Edith had described to me. As we walked away from the house I said, "It is now several days that I have been living in your household on a most extraordinary footing, or rather on none at all. I have not spoken of this aspect of my position before because there were so many other aspects yet more extraordinary. But now that I am beginning a little to feel my feet under me, and to realize that, however I came here, I am here, and must make the best of it, I must speak to you on this point."

"As for your being a guest in my house," replied Dr. Leete, "I pray you not to begin to be uneasy on that point, for I mean to keep you a long time yet. With all your modesty, you can but realize that such a guest as yourself is an acquisition not willingly to be parted with."

"Thanks, doctor," I said. "It would be absurd, certainly, for me to affect any oversensitiveness about accepting the temporary hospitality of one to whom I owe it that I am not still awaiting the end of the world in a living tomb. But if I am to be a permanent citizen of this century I must have some standing in it. Now, in my time a person more or less entering the world, however he got in, would not be noticed in the unorganized throng of men, and might make a place for himself anywhere he chose if he were strong enough. But nowadays everybody is a part of a system with a distinct place and function. I am outside the system, and don't see how I can get in; there seems no way to get in, except to be born in or to come in as an emigrant from some other system."

Dr. Leete laughed heartily.

"I admit," he said, "that our system is defective in lacking provision for cases like yours, but you see nobody anticipated additions to the world except by the usual process. You need, however, have no fear that we shall be unable to provide both a place and occupation for you in due time. You have as yet been brought in contact only with the members of my family, but you must not suppose that I have kept your secret. On the contrary, your case, even before your resuscitation, and vastly more since has excited the profoundest interest in the nation. In view of your precarious nervous condition, it was thought best that I should take exclusive charge of you at first, and that you should, through me and my family, receive some general idea of the sort of world you had come back to before you began to make the acquaintance generally of its inhabitants. As to finding a function for you in society, there was no hesitation as to what that would be. Few of us have it in our power to confer so great a service on the nation as you will be able to when you leave my roof, which, however, you must not think of doing for a good time yet."

"What can I possibly do?" I asked. "Perhaps you imagine I have some trade, or art, or special skill. I assure you I have none whatever. I never earned a dollar in my life, or did an hour's work. I am strong, and might be a common laborer, but nothing more."

"If that were the most efficient service you were able to render the nation, you would find that avocation considered quite as respectable as any other," replied Dr. Leete; "but you can do something else better. You are easily the master of all our historians on questions relating to the social condition of the latter part of the nineteenth century, to us one of the most absorbingly interesting periods of history: and whenever in due time you have sufficiently familiarized yourself with our institutions, and are willing to teach us something concerning those of your day, you will find an historical lectureship in one of our colleges awaiting you."

"Very good! very good indeed," I said, much relieved by so practical a suggestion on a point which had begun to trouble me. "If your people are really so much interested in the nineteenth century, there will indeed be an occupation ready-made for me. I don't think there is anything else that I could possibly earn my salt at, but I certainly may claim without conceit to have some special qualifications for such a post as you describe."

Chapter 17

I found the processes at the warehouse quite as interesting as Edith had described them, and became even enthusiastic over the truly remarkable illustration which is seen there of the prodigiously multiplied efficiency which perfect organization can give to labor. It is like a gigantic mill, into the hopper of which goods are being constantly poured by the train-load and shipload, to issue at the other end in packages of pounds and ounces, yards and inches, pints and gallons, corresponding to the infinitely complex personal needs of half a million people. Dr. Leete, with the assistance of data furnished by me as to the way goods were sold in my day, figured out some astounding results in the way of the economies effected by the modern system.

As we set out homeward, I said: "After what I have seen to-day, together with what you have told me, and what I learned under Miss Leete's tutelage at the sample store, I have a tolerably clear idea of your system of distribution, and how it enables you to dispense with a circulating medium. But I should like very much to know something more about your system of production. You have told me in general how your industrial army is levied and organized, but who directs its efforts? What supreme authority determines what shall be done in every department, so that enough of everything is produced and yet no labor wasted? It seems to me that this must be a wonderfully complex and difficult function, requiring very unusual endowments."

"Does it indeed seem so to you?" responded Dr. Leete. "I assure you that it is nothing of the kind, but on the other hand so simple, and depending on principles so obvious and easily applied, that the functionaries at Washington to whom it is trusted require to be nothing more than men of fair abilities to discharge it to the entire satisfaction of the nation. The machine which they direct is indeed a vast one, but so logical in its principles and direct and simple in its workings, that it all but runs itself; and nobody but a fool could derange it, as I think you will agree after a few words of explanation. Since you already have a pretty good idea of the working of the distributive system, let us begin at that end. Even in your day statisticians were able to tell you the number of yards of cotton, velvet, woolen, the number of barrels of flour, potatoes, butter, number of pairs of shoes, hats, and umbrellas annually consumed by the nation. Owing to the fact that production was in private hands, and that there was no way of getting statistics of actual distribution, these figures were not exact, but they were nearly so. Now that every pin which is given out from a national warehouse is recorded, of course the figures of consumption for any week, month, or year, in the possession of the department of distribution at the end of that period, are precise. On these figures, allowing for tendencies to increase or decrease and for any special causes likely to affect demand, the estimates, say for a year ahead, are based. These estimates, with a proper margin for security, having been accepted by the general administration, the responsibility of the distributive department ceases until the goods are delivered to it. I speak of the estimates being furnished for an entire year ahead, but in reality they cover that much time only in case of the great staples for which the demand can be calculated on as steady. In the great majority of smaller industries for the product of which popular taste fluctuates, and novelty is frequently required, production is kept barely ahead of consumption, the distributive department furnishing frequent estimates based on the weekly state of demand.

"Now the entire field of productive and constructive industry is divided into ten great departments, each representing a group of allied industries, each particular industry being in turn represented by a subordinate bureau, which has a complete record of the plant and force under its control, of the present product, and means of increasing it. The estimates of the distributive department, after adoption by the administration, are sent as mandates to the ten great departments, which allot them to the subordinate bureaus representing the particular industries, and these set the men at work. Each bureau is responsible for the task given it, and this responsibility is enforced by departmental oversight and that of the administration; nor does the distributive department accept the product without its own inspection; while even if in the hands of the consumer an article turns out unfit, the system enables the fault to be traced back to the original workman. The production of the commodities for actual public consumption does not, of course, require by any means all the national force of workers. After the necessary contingents have been detailed for the various industries, the amount of labor left for other employment is expended in creating fixed capital, such as buildings, machinery, engineering works, and so forth."

"One point occurs to me," I said, "on which I should think there might be dissatisfaction. Where there is no opportunity for private enterprise, how is there any assurance that the claims of small minorities of the people to have articles produced, for which there is no wide demand, will be respected? An official decree at any moment may deprive them of the means of gratifying some special taste, merely because the majority does not share it."

"That would be tyranny indeed," replied Dr. Leete, "and you may be very sure that it does not happen with us, to whom liberty is as dear as equality or fraternity. As you come to know our system better, you will see that our officials are in fact, and not merely in name, the agents and servants of the people. The administration has no power to stop the production of any commodity for which there continues to be a demand. Suppose the demand for any article declines to such a point that its production becomes very costly. The price has to be raised in proportion, of course, but as long as the consumer cares to pay it, the production goes on. Again, suppose an article not before produced is demanded. If the administration doubts the reality of the demand, a popular petition guaranteeing a certain basis of consumption compels it to produce the desired article. A government, or a majority, which should undertake to tell the people, or a minority, what they were to eat, drink, or wear, as I believe governments in America did in your day, would be regarded as a curious anachronism indeed. Possibly you had reasons for tolerating these infringements of personal independence, but we should not think them endurable. I am glad you raised this point, for it has given me a chance to show you how much more direct and efficient is the control over production exercised by the individual citizen now than it was in your day, when what you called private initiative prevailed, though it should have been called capitalist initiative, for the average private citizen had little enough share in it."

"You speak of raising the price of costly articles," I said. "How can prices be regulated in a country where there is no competition between buyers or sellers?"

"Just as they were with you," replied Dr. Leete. "You think that needs explaining," he added, as I looked incredulous, "but the explanation need not be long; the cost of the labor which produced it was recognized as the legitimate basis of the price of an article in your day, and so it is in ours. In your day, it was the difference in wages that made the difference in the cost of labor; now it is the relative number of hours constituting a day's work in different trades, the maintenance of the worker being equal in all cases. The cost of a man's work in a trade so difficult that in order to attract volunteers the hours have to be fixed at four a day is twice as great as that in a trade where the men work eight hours. The result as to the cost of labor, you see, is just the same as if the man working four hours were paid, under your system, twice the wages the others get. This calculation applied to the labor employed in the various processes of a manufactured article gives its price relatively to other articles. Besides the cost of production and transportation, the factor of scarcity affects the prices of some commodities. As regards the great staples of life, of which an abundance can always be secured, scarcity is eliminated as a factor. There is always a large surplus kept on hand from which any fluctuations of demand or supply can be corrected, even in most cases of bad crops. The prices of the staples grow less year by year, but rarely, if ever, rise. There are, however, certain classes of articles permanently, and others temporarily, unequal to the demand, as, for example, fresh fish or dairy products in the latter category, and the products of high skill and rare materials in the other. All that can be done here is to equalize the inconvenience of the scarcity. This is done by temporarily raising the price if the scarcity be temporary, or fixing it high if it be permanent. High prices in your day meant restriction of the articles affected to the rich, but nowadays, when the means of all are the same, the effect is only that those to whom the articles seem most desirable are the ones who purchase them. Of course the nation, as any other caterer for the public needs must be, is frequently left with small lots of goods on its hands by changes in taste, unseasonable weather and various other causes. These it has to dispose of at a sacrifice just as merchants often did in your day, charging up the loss to the expenses of the business. Owing, however, to the vast body of consumers to which such lots can be simultaneously offered, there is rarely any difficulty in getting rid of them at trifling loss. I have given you now some general notion of our system of production; as well as distribution. Do you find it as complex as you expected?"

I admitted that nothing could be much simpler.

"I am sure," said Dr. Leete, "that it is within the truth to say that the head of one of the myriad private businesses of your day, who had to maintain sleepless vigilance against the fluctuations of the market, the machinations of his rivals, and the failure of his debtors, had a far more trying task than the group of men at Washington who nowadays direct the industries of the entire nation. All this merely shows, my dear fellow, how much easier it is to do things the right way than the wrong. It is easier for a general up in a balloon, with perfect survey of the field, to manoeuvre a million men to victory than for a sergeant to manage a platoon in a thicket."

"The general of this army, including the flower of the manhood of the nation, must be the foremost man in the country, really greater even than the President of the United States," I said.

"He is the President of the United States," replied Dr. Leete, "or rather the most important function of the presidency is the headship of the industrial army."

"How is he chosen?" I asked.

"I explained to you before," replied Dr. Leete, "when I was describing the force of the motive of emulation among all grades of the industrial army, that the line of promotion for the meritorious lies through three grades to the officer's grade, and thence up through the lieutenancies to the captaincy or foremanship, and superintendency or colonel's rank. Next, with an intervening grade in some of the larger trades, comes the general of the guild, under whose immediate control all the operations of the trade are conducted. This officer is at the head of the national bureau representing his trade, and is responsible for its work to the administration. The general of his guild holds a splendid position, and one which amply satisfies the ambition of most men, but above his rank, which may be compared—to follow the military analogies familiar to you—to that of a general of division or major-general, is that of the chiefs of the ten great departments, or groups of allied trades. The chiefs of these ten grand divisions of the industrial army may be compared to your commanders of army corps, or lieutenant-generals, each having from a dozen to a score of generals of separate guilds reporting to him. Above these ten great officers, who form his council, is the general-in-chief, who is the President of the United States.

"The general-in-chief of the industrial army must have passed through all the grades below him, from the common laborers up. Let us see how he rises. As I have told you, it is simply by the excellence of his record as a worker that one rises through the grades of the privates and becomes a candidate for a lieutenancy. Through the lieutenancies he rises to the colonelcy, or superintendent's position, by appointment from above, strictly limited to the candidates of the best records. The general of the guild appoints to the ranks under him, but he himself is not appointed, but chosen by suffrage."

"By suffrage!" I exclaimed. "Is not that ruinous to the discipline of the guild, by tempting the candidates to intrigue for the support of the workers under them?"

"So it would be, no doubt," replied Dr. Leete, "if the workers had any suffrage to exercise, or anything to say about the choice. But they have nothing. Just here comes in a peculiarity of our system. The general of the guild is chosen from among the superintendents by vote of the honorary members of the guild, that is, of those who have served their time in the guild and received their discharge. As you know, at the age of forty-five we are mustered out of the army of industry, and have the residue of life for the pursuit of our own improvement or recreation. Of course, however, the associations of our active lifetime retain a powerful hold on us. The companionships we formed then remain our companionships till the end of life. We always continue honorary members of our former guilds, and retain the keenest and most jealous interest in their welfare and repute in the hands of the following generation. In the clubs maintained by the honorary members of the several guilds, in which we meet socially, there are no topics of conversation so common as those which relate to these matters, and the young aspirants for guild leadership who can pass the criticism of us old fellows are likely to be pretty well equipped. Recognizing this fact, the nation entrusts to the honorary members of each guild the election of its general, and I venture to claim that no previous form of society could have developed a body of electors so ideally adapted to their office, as regards absolute impartiality, knowledge of the special qualifications and record of candidates, solicitude for the best result, and complete absence of self-interest.

"Each of the ten lieutenant-generals or heads of departments is himself elected from among the generals of the guilds grouped as a department, by vote of the honorary members of the guilds thus grouped. Of course there is a tendency on the part of each guild to vote for its own general, but no guild of any group has nearly enough votes to elect a man not supported by most of the others. I assure you that these elections are exceedingly lively."

"The President, I suppose, is selected from among the ten heads of the great departments," I suggested.

"Precisely, but the heads of departments are not eligible to the presidency till they have been a certain number of years out of office. It is rarely that a man passes through all the grades to the headship of a department much before he is forty, and at the end of a five years' term he is usually forty-five. If more, he still serves through his term, and if less, he is nevertheless discharged from the industrial army at its termination. It would not do for him to return to the ranks. The interval before he is a candidate for the presidency is intended to give time for him to recognize fully that he has returned into the general mass of the nation, and is identified with it rather than with the industrial army. Moreover, it is expected that he will employ this period in studying the general condition of the army, instead of that of the special group of guilds of which he was the head. From among the former heads of departments who may be eligible at the time, the President is elected by vote of all the men of the nation who are not connected with the industrial army."

"The army is not allowed to vote for President?"

"Certainly not. That would be perilous to its discipline, which it is the business of the President to maintain as the representative of the nation at large. His right hand for this purpose is the inspectorate, a highly important department of our system; to the inspectorate come all complaints or information as to defects in goods, insolence or inefficiency of officials, or dereliction of any sort in the public service. The inspectorate, however, does not wait for complaints. Not only is it on the alert to catch and sift every rumor of a fault in the service, but it is its business, by systematic and constant oversight and inspection of every branch of the army, to find out what is going wrong before anybody else does. The President is usually not far from fifty when elected, and serves five years, forming an honorable exception to the rule of retirement at forty-five. At the end of his term of office, a national Congress is called to receive his report and approve or condemn it. If it is approved, Congress usually elects him to represent the nation for five years more in the international council. Congress, I should also say, passes on the reports of the outgoing heads of departments, and a disapproval renders any one of them ineligible for President. But it is rare, indeed, that the nation has occasion for other sentiments than those of gratitude toward its high officers. As to their ability, to have risen from the ranks, by tests so various and severe, to their positions, is proof in itself of extraordinary qualities, while as to faithfulness, our social system leaves them absolutely without any other motive than that of winning the esteem of their fellow citizens. Corruption is impossible in a society where there is neither poverty to be bribed nor wealth to bribe, while as to demagoguery or intrigue for office, the conditions of promotion render them out of the question."

"One point I do not quite understand," I said. "Are the members of the liberal professions eligible to the presidency? and if so, how are they ranked with those who pursue the industries proper?"

"They have no ranking with them," replied Dr. Leete. "The members of the technical professions, such as engineers and architects, have a ranking with the constructive guilds; but the members of the liberal professions, the doctors and teachers, as well as the artists and men of letters who obtain remissions of industrial service, do not belong to the industrial army. On this ground they vote for the President, but are not eligible to his office. One of its main duties being the control and discipline of the industrial army, it is essential that the President should have passed through all its grades to understand his business."

"That is reasonable," I said; "but if the doctors and teachers do not know enough of industry to be President, neither, I should think, can the President know enough of medicine and education to control those departments."

"No more does he," was the reply. "Except in the general way that he is responsible for the enforcement of the laws as to all classes, the President has nothing to do with the faculties of medicine and education, which are controlled by boards of regents of their own, in which the President is ex-officio chairman, and has the casting vote. These regents, who, of course, are responsible to Congress, are chosen by the honorary members of the guilds of education and medicine, the retired teachers and doctors of the country."

"Do you know," I said, "the method of electing officials by votes of the retired members of the guilds is nothing more than the application on a national scale of the plan of government by alumni, which we used to a slight extent occasionally in the management of our higher educational institutions."

"Did you, indeed?" exclaimed Dr. Leete, with animation. "That is quite new to me, and I fancy will be to most of us, and of much interest as well. There has been great discussion as to the germ of the idea, and we fancied that there was for once something new under the sun. Well! well! In your higher educational institutions! that is interesting indeed. You must tell me more of that."

"Truly, there is very little more to tell than I have told already," I replied. "If we had the germ of your idea, it was but as a germ."

Chapter 18

That evening I sat up for some time after the ladies had retired, talking with Dr. Leete about the effect of the plan of exempting men from further service to the nation after the age of forty-five, a point brought up by his account of the part taken by the retired citizens in the government.

"At forty-five," said I, "a man still has ten years of good manual labor in him, and twice ten years of good intellectual service. To be superannuated at that age and laid on the shelf must be regarded rather as a hardship than a favor by men of energetic dispositions."

"My dear Mr. West," exclaimed Dr. Leete, beaming upon me, "you cannot have any idea of the piquancy your nineteenth century ideas have for us of this day, the rare quaintness of their effect. Know, O child of another race and yet the same, that the labor we have to render as our part in securing for the nation the means of a comfortable physical existence is by no means regarded as the most important, the most interesting, or the most dignified employment of our powers. We look upon it as a necessary duty to be discharged before we can fully devote ourselves to the higher exercise of our faculties, the intellectual and spiritual enjoyments and pursuits which alone mean life. Everything possible is indeed done by the just distribution of burdens, and by all manner of special attractions and incentives to relieve our labor of irksomeness, and, except in a comparative sense, it is not usually irksome, and is often inspiring. But it is not our labor, but the higher and larger activities which the performance of our task will leave us free to enter upon, that are considered the main business of existence.

"Of course not all, nor the majority, have those scientific, artistic, literary, or scholarly interests which make leisure the one thing valuable to their possessors. Many look upon the last half of life chiefly as a period for enjoyment of other sorts; for travel, for social relaxation in the company of their life-time friends; a time for the cultivation of all manner of personal idiosyncrasies and special tastes, and the pursuit of every imaginable form of recreation; in a word, a time for the leisurely and unperturbed appreciation of the good things of the world which they have helped to create. But, whatever the differences between our individual tastes as to the use we shall put our leisure to, we all agree in looking forward to the date of our discharge as the time when we shall first enter upon the full enjoyment of our birthright, the period when we shall first really attain our majority and become enfranchised from discipline and control, with the fee of our lives vested in ourselves. As eager boys in your day anticipated twenty-one, so men nowadays look forward to forty-five. At twenty-one we become men, but at forty-five we renew youth. Middle age and what you would have called old age are considered, rather than youth, the enviable time of life. Thanks to the better conditions of existence nowadays, and above all the freedom of every one from care, old age approaches many years later and has an aspect far more benign than in past times. Persons of average constitution usually live to eighty-five or ninety, and at forty-five we are physically and mentally younger, I fancy, than you were at thirty-five. It is a strange reflection that at forty-five, when we are just entering upon the most enjoyable period of life, you already began to think of growing old and to look backward. With you it was the forenoon, with us it is the afternoon, which is the brighter half of life."

After this I remember that our talk branched into the subject of popular sports and recreations at the present time as compared with those of the nineteenth century.

"In one respect," said Dr. Leete, "there is a marked difference. The professional sportsmen, which were such a curious feature of your day, we have nothing answering to, nor are the prizes for which our athletes contend money prizes, as with you. Our contests are always for glory only. The generous rivalry existing between the various guilds, and the loyalty of each worker to his own, afford a constant stimulation to all sorts of games and matches by sea and land, in which the young men take scarcely more interest than the honorary guildsmen who have served their time. The guild yacht races off Marblehead take place next week, and you will be able to judge for yourself of the popular enthusiasm which such events nowadays call out as compared with your day. The demand for 'panem ef circenses' preferred by the Roman populace is recognized nowadays as a wholly reasonable one. If bread is the first necessity of life, recreation is a close second, and the nation caters for both. Americans of the nineteenth century were as unfortunate in lacking an adequate provision for the one sort of need as for the other. Even if the people of that period had enjoyed larger leisure, they would, I fancy, have often been at a loss how to pass it agreeably. We are never in that predicament."

Chapter 19

In the course of an early morning constitutional I visited Charlestown. Among the changes, too numerous to attempt to indicate, which mark the lapse of a century in that quarter, I particularly noted the total disappearance of the old state prison.

"That went before my day, but I remember hearing about it," said Dr. Leete, when I alluded to the fact at the breakfast table. "We have no jails nowadays. All cases of atavism are treated in the hospitals."

"Of atavism!" I exclaimed, staring.

"Why, yes," replied Dr. Leete. "The idea of dealing punitively with those unfortunates was given up at least fifty years ago, and I think more."

"I don't quite understand you," I said. "Atavism in my day was a word applied to the cases of persons in whom some trait of a remote ancestor recurred in a noticeable manner. Am I to understand that crime is nowadays looked upon as the recurrence of an ancestral trait?"

"I beg your pardon," said Dr. Leete with a smile half humorous, half deprecating, "but since you have so explicitly asked the question, I am forced to say that the fact is precisely that."

After what I had already learned of the moral contrasts between the nineteenth and the twentieth centuries, it was doubtless absurd in me to begin to develop sensitiveness on the subject, and probably if Dr. Leete had not spoken with that apologetic air and Mrs. Leete and Edith shown a corresponding embarrassment, I should not have flushed, as I was conscious I did.

"I was not in much danger of being vain of my generation before," I said; "but, really—"

"This is your generation, Mr. West," interposed Edith. "It is the one in which you are living, you know, and it is only because we are alive now that we call it ours."

"Thank you. I will try to think of it so," I said, and as my eyes met hers their expression quite cured my senseless sensitiveness. "After all," I said, with a laugh, "I was brought up a Calvinist, and ought not to be startled to hear crime spoken of as an ancestral trait."

"In point of fact," said Dr. Leete, "our use of the word is no reflection at all on your generation, if, begging Edith's pardon, we may call it yours, so far as seeming to imply that we think ourselves, apart from our circumstances, better than you were. In your day fully nineteen twentieths of the crime, using the word broadly to include all sorts of misdemeanors, resulted from the inequality in the possessions of individuals; want tempted the poor, lust of greater gains, or the desire to preserve former gains, tempted the well-to-do. Directly or indirectly, the desire for money, which then meant every good thing, was the motive of all this crime, the taproot of a vast poison growth, which the machinery of law, courts, and police could barely prevent from choking your civilization outright. When we made the nation the sole trustee of the wealth of the people, and guaranteed to all abundant maintenance, on the one hand abolishing want, and on the other checking the accumulation of riches, we cut this root, and the poison tree that overshadowed your society withered, like Jonah's gourd, in a day. As for the comparatively small class of violent crimes against persons, unconnected with any idea of gain, they were almost wholly confined, even in your day, to the ignorant and bestial; and in these days, when education and good manners are not the monopoly of a few, but universal, such atrocities are scarcely ever heard of. You now see why the word 'atavism' is used for crime. It is because nearly all forms of crime known to you are motiveless now, and when they appear can only be explained as the outcropping of ancestral traits. You used to call persons who stole, evidently without any rational motive, kleptomaniacs, and when the case was clear deemed it absurd to punish them as thieves. Your attitude toward the genuine kleptomaniac is precisely ours toward the victim of atavism, an attitude of compassion and firm but gentle restraint."

"Your courts must have an easy time of it," I observed. "With no private property to speak of, no disputes between citizens over business relations, no real estate to divide or debts to collect, there must be absolutely no civil business at all for them; and with no offenses against property, and mighty few of any sort to provide criminal cases, I should think you might almost do without judges and lawyers altogether."

"We do without the lawyers, certainly," was Dr. Leete's reply. "It would not seem reasonable to us, in a case where the only interest of the nation is to find out the truth, that persons should take part in the proceedings who had an acknowledged motive to color it."

"But who defends the accused?"

"If he is a criminal he needs no defense, for he pleads guilty in most instances," replied Dr. Leete. "The plea of the accused is not a mere formality with us, as with you. It is usually the end of the case."

"You don't mean that the man who pleads not guilty is thereupon discharged?"

"No, I do not mean that. He is not accused on light grounds, and if he denies his guilt, must still be tried. But trials are few, for in most cases the guilty man pleads guilty. When he makes a false plea and is clearly proved guilty, his penalty is doubled. Falsehood is, however, so despised among us that few offenders would lie to save themselves."

"That is the most astounding thing you have yet told me," I exclaimed. "If lying has gone out of fashion, this is indeed the 'new heavens and the new earth wherein dwelleth righteousness,' which the prophet foretold."

"Such is, in fact, the belief of some persons nowadays," was the doctor's answer. "They hold that we have entered upon the millennium, and the theory from their point of view does not lack plausibility. But as to your astonishment at finding that the world has outgrown lying, there is really no ground for it. Falsehood, even in your day, was not common between gentlemen and ladies, social equals. The lie of fear was the refuge of cowardice, and the lie of fraud the device of the cheat. The inequalities of men and the lust of acquisition offered a constant premium on lying at that time. Yet even then, the man who neither feared another nor desired to defraud him scorned falsehood. Because we are now all social equals, and no man either has anything to fear from another or can gain anything by deceiving him, the contempt of falsehood is so universal that it is rarely, as I told you, that even a criminal in other respects will be found willing to lie. When, however, a plea of not guilty is returned, the judge appoints two colleagues to state the oppposite sides of the case. How far these men are from being like your hired advocates and prosecutors, determined to acquit or convict, may appear from the fact that unless both agree that the verdict found is just, the case is tried over, while anything like bias in the tone of either of the judges stating the case would be a shocking scandal."

"Do I understand," I said, "that it is a judge who states each side of the case as well as a judge who hears it?"

"Certainly. The judges take turns in serving on the bench and at the bar, and are expected to maintain the judicial temper equally whether in stating or deciding a case. The system is indeed in effect that of trial by three judges occupying different points of view as to the case. When they agree upon a verdict, we believe it to be as near to absolute truth as men well can come."

"You have given up the jury system, then?"

"It was well enough as a corrective in the days of hired advocates, and a bench sometimes venal, and often with a tenure that made it dependent, but is needless now. No conceivable motive but justice could actuate our judges."

"How are these magistrates selected?"

"They are an honorable exception to the rule which discharges all men from service at the age of forty-five. The President of the nation appoints the necessary judges year by year from the class reaching that age. The number appointed is, of course, exceedingly few, and the honor so high that it is held an offset to the additional term of service which follows, and though a judge's appointment may be declined, it rarely is. The term is five years, without eligibility to reappointment. The members of the Supreme Court, which is the guardian of the constitution, are selected from among the lower judges. When a vacancy in that court occurs, those of the lower judges, whose terms expire that year, select, as their last official act, the one of their colleagues left on the bench whom they deem fittest to fill it."

"There being no legal profession to serve as a school for judges," I said, "they must, of course, come directly from the law school to the bench."

"We have no such things as law schools," replied the doctor smiling. "The law as a special science is obsolete. It was a system of casuistry which the elaborate artificiality of the old order of society absolutely required to interpret it, but only a few of the plainest and simplest legal maxims have any application to the existing state of the world. Everything touching the relations of men to one another is now simpler, beyond any comparison, than in your day. We should have no sort of use for the hair-splitting experts who presided and argued in your courts. You must not imagine, however, that we have any disrespect for those ancient worthies because we have no use for them. On the contrary, we entertain an unfeigned respect, amounting almost to awe, for the men who alone understood and were able to expound the interminable complexity of the rights of property, and the relations of commercial and personal dependence involved in your system. What, indeed, could possibly give a more powerful impression of the intricacy and artificiality of that system than the fact that it was necessary to set apart from other pursuits the cream of the intellect of every generation, in order to provide a body of pundits able to make it even vaguely intelligible to those whose fates it determined. The treatises of your great lawyers, the works of Blackstone and Chitty, of Story and Parsons, stand in our museums, side by side with the tomes of Duns Scotus and his fellow scholastics, as curious monuments of intellectual subtlety devoted to subjects equally remote from the interests of modern men. Our judges are simply widely informed, judicious, and discreet men of ripe years.

"I should not fail to speak of one important function of the minor judges," added Dr. Leete. "This is to adjudicate all cases where a private of the industrial army makes a complaint of unfairness against an officer. All such questions are heard and settled without appeal by a single judge, three judges being required only in graver cases. The efficiency of industry requires the strictest discipline in the army of labor, but the claim of the workman to just and considerate treatment is backed by the whole power of the nation. The officer commands and the private obeys, but no officer is so high that he would dare display an overbearing manner toward a workman of the lowest class. As for churlishness or rudeness by an official of any sort, in his relations to the public, not one among minor offenses is more sure of a prompt penalty than this. Not only justice but civility is enforced by our judges in all sorts of intercourse. No value of service is accepted as a set-off to boorish or offensive manners."

It occurred to me, as Dr. Leete was speaking, that in all his talk I had heard much of the nation and nothing of the state governments. Had the organization of the nation as an industrial unit done away with the states? I asked.

"Necessarily," he replied. "The state governments would have interfered with the control and discipline of the industrial army, which, of course, required to be central and uniform. Even if the state governments had not become inconvenient for other reasons, they were rendered superfluous by the prodigious simplification in the task of government since your day. Almost the sole function of the administration now is that of directing the industries of the country. Most of the purposes for which governments formerly existed no longer remain to be subserved. We have no army or navy, and no military organization. We have no departments of state or treasury, no excise or revenue services, no taxes or tax collectors. The only function proper of government, as known to you, which still remains, is the judiciary and police system. I have already explained to you how simple is our judicial system as compared with your huge and complex machine. Of course the same absence of crime and temptation to it, which make the duties of judges so light, reduces the number and duties of the police to a minimum."

"But with no state legislatures, and Congress meeting only once in five years, how do you get your legislation done?"

"We have no legislation," replied Dr. Leete, "that is, next to none. It is rarely that Congress, even when it meets, considers any new laws of consequence, and then it only has power to commend them to the following Congress, lest anything be done hastily. If you will consider a moment, Mr. West, you will see that we have nothing to make laws about. The fundamental principles on which our society is founded settle for all time the strifes and misunderstandings which in your day called for legislation.

"Fully ninety-nine hundredths of the laws of that time concerned the definition and protection of private property and the relations of buyers and sellers. There is neither private property, beyond personal belongings, now, nor buying and selling, and therefore the occasion of nearly all the legislation formerly necessary has passed away. Formerly, society was a pyramid poised on its apex. All the gravitations of human nature were constantly tending to topple it over, and it could be maintained upright, or rather upwrong (if you will pardon the feeble witticism), by an elaborate system of constantly renewed props and buttresses and guy-ropes in the form of laws. A central Congress and forty state legislatures, turning out some twenty thousand laws a year, could not make new props fast enough to take the place of those which were constantly breaking down or becoming ineffectual through some shifting of the strain. Now society rests on its base, and is in as little need of artificial supports as the everlasting hills."

"But you have at least municipal governments besides the one central authority?"

"Certainly, and they have important and extensive functions in looking out for the public comfort and recreation, and the improvement and embellishment of the villages and cities."

"But having no control over the labor of their people, or means of hiring it, how can they do anything?"

"Every town or city is conceded the right to retain, for its own public works, a certain proportion of the quota of labor its citizens contribute to the nation. This proportion, being assigned it as so much credit, can be applied in any way desired."

Chapter 20

That afternoon Edith casually inquired if I had yet revisited the underground chamber in the garden in which I had been found.

"Not yet," I replied. "To be frank, I have shrunk thus far from doing so, lest the visit might revive old associations rather too strongly for my mental equilibrium."

"Ah, yes!" she said, "I can imagine that you have done well to stay away. I ought to have thought of that."

"No," I said, "I am glad you spoke of it. The danger, if there was any, existed only during the first day or two. Thanks to you, chiefly and always, I feel my footing now so firm in this new world, that if you will go with me to keep the ghosts off, I should really like to visit the place this afternoon."

Edith demurred at first, but, finding that I was in earnest, consented to accompany me. The rampart of earth thrown up from the excavation was visible among the trees from the house, and a few steps brought us to the spot. All remained as it was at the point when work was interrupted by the discovery of the tenant of the chamber, save that the door had been opened and the slab from the roof replaced. Descending the sloping sides of the excavation, we went in at the door and stood within the dimly lighted room.

Everything was just as I had beheld it last on that evening one hundred and thirteen years previous, just before closing my eyes for that long sleep. I stood for some time silently looking about me. I saw that my companion was furtively regarding me with an expression of awed and sympathetic curiosity. I put out my hand to her and she placed hers in it, the soft fingers responding with a reassuring pressure to my clasp. Finally she whispered, "Had we not better go out now? You must not try yourself too far. Oh, how strange it must be to you!"

"On the contrary," I replied, "it does not seem strange; that is the strangest part of it."

"Not strange?" she echoed.

"Even so," I replied. "The emotions with which you evidently credit me, and which I anticipated would attend this visit, I simply do not feel. I realize all that these surroundings suggest, but without the agitation I expected. You can't be nearly as much surprised at this as I am myself. Ever since that terrible morning when you came to my help, I have tried to avoid thinking of my former life, just as I have avoided coming here, for fear of the agitating effects. I am for all the world like a man who has permitted an injured limb to lie motionless under the impression that it is exquisitely sensitive, and on trying to move it finds that it is paralyzed."

"Do you mean your memory is gone?"

"Not at all. I remember everything connected with my former life, but with a total lack of keen sensation. I remember it for clearness as if it had been but a day since then, but my feelings about what I remember are as faint as if to my consciousness, as well as in fact, a hundred years had intervened. Perhaps it is possible to explain this, too. The effect of change in surroundings is like that of lapse of time in making the past seem remote. When I first woke from that trance, my former life appeared as yesterday, but now, since I have learned to know my new surroundings, and to realize the prodigious changes that have transformed the world, I no longer find it hard, but very easy, to realize that I have slept a century. Can you conceive of such a thing as living a hundred years in four days? It really seems to me that I have done just that, and that it is this experience which has given so remote and unreal an appearance to my former life. Can you see how such a thing might be?"

"I can conceive it," replied Edith, meditatively, "and I think we ought all to be thankful that it is so, for it will save you much suffering, I am sure."

"Imagine," I said, in an effort to explain, as much to myself as to her, the strangeness of my mental condition, "that a man first heard of a bereavement many, many years, half a lifetime perhaps, after the event occurred. I fancy his feeling would be perhaps something as mine is. When I think of my friends in the world of that former day, and the sorrow they must have felt for me, it is with a pensive pity, rather than keen anguish, as of a sorrow long, long ago ended."

"You have told us nothing yet of your friends," said Edith. "Had you many to mourn you?"

"Thank God, I had very few relatives, none nearer than cousins," I replied. "But there was one, not a relative, but dearer to me than any kin of blood. She had your name. She was to have been my wife soon. Ah me!"

"Ah me!" sighed the Edith by my side. "Think of the heartache she must have had."

Something in the deep feeling of this gentle girl touched a chord in my benumbed heart. My eyes, before so dry, were flooded with the tears that had till now refused to come. When I had regained my composure, I saw that she too had been weeping freely.

"God bless your tender heart," I said. "Would you like to see her picture?"

A small locket with Edith Bartlett's picture, secured about my neck with a gold chain, had lain upon my breast all through that long sleep, and removing this I opened and gave it to my companion. She took it with eagerness, and after poring long over the sweet face, touched the picture with her lips.

"I know that she was good and lovely enough to well deserve your tears," she said; "but remember her heartache was over long ago, and she has been in heaven for nearly a century."

It was indeed so. Whatever her sorrow had once been, for nearly a century she had ceased to weep, and, my sudden passion spent, my own tears dried away. I had loved her very dearly in my other life, but it was a hundred years ago! I do not know but some may find in this confession evidence of lack of feeling, but I think, perhaps, that none can have had an experience sufficiently like mine to enable them to judge me. As we were about to leave the chamber, my eye rested upon the great iron safe which stood in one corner. Calling my companion's attention to it, I said:

"This was my strong room as well as my sleeping room. In the safe yonder are several thousand dollars in gold, and any amount of securities. If I had known when I went to sleep that night just how long my nap would be, I should still have thought that the gold was a safe provision for my needs in any country or any century, however distant. That a time would ever come when it would lose its purchasing power, I should have considered the wildest of fancies. Nevertheless, here I wake up to find myself among a people of whom a cartload of gold will not procure a loaf of bread."

As might be expected, I did not succeed in impressing Edith that there was anything remarkable in this fact. "Why in the world should it?" she merely asked.

Chapter 21

It had been suggested by Dr. Leete that we should devote the next morning to an inspection of the schools and colleges of the city, with some attempt on his own part at an explanation of the educational system of the twentieth century.

"You will see," said he, as we set out after breakfast, "many very important differences between our methods of education and yours, but the main difference is that nowadays all persons equally have those opportunities of higher education which in your day only an infinitesimal portion of the population enjoyed. We should think we had gained nothing worth speaking of, in equalizing the physical comfort of men, without this educational equality."

"The cost must be very great," I said.

"If it took half the revenue of the nation, nobody would grudge it," replied Dr. Leete, "nor even if it took it all save a bare pittance. But in truth the expense of educating ten thousand youth is not ten nor five times that of educating one thousand. The principle which makes all operations on a large scale proportionally cheaper than on a small scale holds as to education also."

"College education was terribly expensive in my day," said I.

"If I have not been misinformed by our historians," Dr. Leete answered, "it was not college education but college dissipation and extravagance which cost so highly. The actual expense of your colleges appears to have been very low, and would have been far lower if their patronage had been greater. The higher education nowadays is as cheap as the lower, as all grades of teachers, like all other workers, receive the same support. We have simply added to the common school system of compulsory education, in vogue in Massachusetts a hundred years ago, a half dozen higher grades, carrying the youth to the age of twenty-one and giving him what you used to call the education of a gentleman, instead of turning him loose at fourteen or fifteen with no mental equipment beyond reading, writing, and the multiplication table."

"Setting aside the actual cost of these additional years of education," I replied, "we should not have thought we could afford the loss of time from industrial pursuits. Boys of the poorer classes usually went to work at sixteen or younger, and knew their trade at twenty."

"We should not concede you any gain even in material product by that plan," Dr. Leete replied. "The greater efficiency which education gives to all sorts of labor, except the rudest, makes up in a short period for the time lost in acquiring it."

"We should also have been afraid," said I, "that a high education, while it adapted men to the professions, would set them against manual labor of all sorts."

"That was the effect of high education in your day, I have read," replied the doctor; "and it was no wonder, for manual labor meant association with a rude, coarse, and ignorant class of people. There is no such class now. It was inevitable that such a feeling should exist then, for the further reason that all men receiving a high education were understood to be destined for the professions or for wealthy leisure, and such an education in one neither rich nor professional was a proof of disappointed aspirations, an evidence of failure, a badge of inferiority rather than superiority. Nowadays, of course, when the highest education is deemed necessary to fit a man merely to live, without any reference to the sort of work he may do, its possession conveys no such implication."

"After all," I remarked, "no amount of education can cure natural dullness or make up for original mental deficiencies. Unless the average natural mental capacity of men is much above its level in my day, a high education must be pretty nearly thrown away on a large element of the population. We used to hold that a certain amount of susceptibility to educational influences is required to make a mind worth cultivating, just as a certain natural fertility in soil is required if it is to repay tilling."

"Ah," said Dr. Leete, "I am glad you used that illustration, for it is just the one I would have chosen to set forth the modern view of education. You say that land so poor that the product will not repay the labor of tilling is not cultivated. Nevertheless, much land that does not begin to repay tilling by its product was cultivated in your day and is in ours. I refer to gardens, parks, lawns, and, in general, to pieces of land so situated that, were they left to grow up to weeds and briers, they would be eyesores and inconveniencies to all about. They are therefore tilled, and though their product is little, there is yet no land that, in a wider sense, better repays cultivation. So it is with the men and women with whom we mingle in the relations of society, whose voices are always in our ears, whose behavior in innumerable ways affects our enjoyment—who are, in fact, as much conditions of our lives as the air we breathe, or any of the physical elements on which we depend. If, indeed, we could not afford to educate everybody, we should choose the coarsest and dullest by nature, rather than the brightest, to receive what education we could give. The naturally refined and intellectual can better dispense with aids to culture than those less fortunate in natural endowments.

"To borrow a phrase which was often used in your day, we should not consider life worth living if we had to be surrounded by a population of ignorant, boorish, coarse, wholly uncultivated men and women, as was the plight of the few educated in your day. Is a man satisfied, merely because he is perfumed himself, to mingle with a malodorous crowd? Could he take more than a very limited satisfaction, even in a palatial apartment, if the windows on all four sides opened into stable yards? And yet just that was the situation of those considered most fortunate as to culture and refinement in your day. I know that the poor and ignorant envied the rich and cultured then; but to us the latter, living as they did, surrounded by squalor and brutishness, seem little better off than the former. The cultured man in your age was like one up to the neck in a nauseous bog solacing himself with a smelling bottle. You see, perhaps, now, how we look at this question of universal high education. No single thing is so important to every man as to have for neighbors intelligent, companionable persons. There is nothing, therefore, which the nation can do for him that will enhance so much his own happiness as to educate his neighbors. When it fails to do so, the value of his own education to him is reduced by half, and many of the tastes he has cultivated are made positive sources of pain.

"To educate some to the highest degree, and leave the mass wholly uncultivated, as you did, made the gap between them almost like that between different natural species, which have no means of communication. What could be more inhuman than this consequence of a partial enjoyment of education! Its universal and equal enjoyment leaves, indeed, the differences between men as to natural endowments as marked as in a state of nature, but the level of the lowest is vastly raised. Brutishness is eliminated. All have some inkling of the humanities, some appreciation of the things of the mind, and an admiration for the still higher culture they have fallen short of. They have become capable of receiving and imparting, in various degrees, but all in some measure, the pleasures and inspirations of a refined social life. The cultured society of the nineteenth century—what did it consist of but here and there a few microscopic oases in a vast, unbroken wilderness?

The proportion of individuals capable of intellectual sympathies or refined intercourse, to the mass of their contemporaries, used to be so infinitesimal as to be in any broad view of humanity scarcely worth mentioning. One generation of the world to-day represents a greater volume of intellectual life than any five centuries ever did before.

"There is still another point I should mention in stating the grounds on which nothing less than the universality of the best education could now be tolerated," continued Dr. Leete, "and that is, the interest of the coming generation in having educated parents. To put the matter in a nutshell, there are three main grounds on which our educational system rests: first, the right of every man to the completest education the nation can give him on his own account, as necessary to his enjoyment of himself; second, the right of his fellow-citizens to have him educated, as necessary to their enjoyment of his society; third, the right of the unborn to be guaranteed an intelligent and refined parentage."

I shall not describe in detail what I saw in the schools that day. Having taken but slight interest in educational matters in my former life, I could offer few comparisons of interest. Next to the fact of the universality of the higher as well as the lower education, I was most struck with the prominence given to physical culture, and the fact that proficiency in athletic feats and games as well as in scholarship had a place in the rating of the youth.

"The faculty of education," Dr. Leete explained, "is held to the same responsibility for the bodies as for the minds of its charges. The highest possible physical, as well as mental, development of every one is the double object of a curriculum which lasts from the age of six to that of twenty-one."

The magnificent health of the young people in the schools impressed me strongly. My previous observations, not only of the notable personal endowments of the family of my host, but of the people I had seen in my walks abroad, had already suggested the idea that there must have been something like a general improvement in the physical standard of the race since my day, and now, as I compared these stalwart young men and fresh, vigorous maidens with the young people I had seen in the schools of the nineteenth century, I was moved to impart my thought to Dr. Leete. He listened with great interest to what I said.

"Your testimony on this point," he declared, "is invaluable. We believe that there has been such an improvement as you speak of, but of course it could only be a matter of theory with us. It is an incident of your unique position that you alone in the world of to-day can speak with authority on this point. Your opinion, when you state it publicly, will, I assure you, make a profound sensation. For the rest it would be strange, certainly, if the race did not show an improvement. In your day, riches debauched one class with idleness of mind and body, while poverty sapped the vitality of the masses by overwork, bad food, and pestilent homes. The labor required of children, and the burdens laid on women, enfeebled the very springs of life. Instead of these maleficent circumstances, all now enjoy the most favorable conditions of physical life; the young are carefully nurtured and studiously cared for; the labor which is required of all is limited to the period of greatest bodily vigor, and is never excessive; care for one's self and one's family, anxiety as to livelihood, the strain of a ceaseless battle for life—all these influences, which once did so much to wreck the minds and bodies of men and women, are known no more. Certainly, an improvement of the species ought to follow such a change. In certain specific respects we know, indeed, that the improvement has taken place. Insanity, for instance, which in the nineteenth century was so terribly common a product of your insane mode of life, has almost disappeared, with its alternative, suicide."

Chapter 22

We had made an appointment to meet the ladies at the dining-hall for dinner, after which, having some engagement, they left us sitting at table there, discussing our wine and cigars with a multitude of other matters.

"Doctor," said I, in the course of our talk, "morally speaking, your social system is one which I should be insensate not to admire in comparison with any previously in vogue in the world, and especially with that of my own most unhappy century. If I were to fall into a mesmeric sleep tonight as lasting as that other and meanwhile the course of time were to take a turn backward instead of forward, and I were to wake up again in the nineteenth century, when I had told my friends what I had seen, they would every one admit that your world was a paradise of order, equity, and felicity. But they were a very practical people, my contemporaries, and after expressing their admiration for the moral beauty and material splendor of the system, they would presently begin to cipher and ask how you got the money to make everybody so happy; for certainly, to support the whole nation at a rate of comfort, and even luxury, such as I see around me, must involve vastly greater wealth than the nation produced in my day. Now, while I could explain to them pretty nearly everything else of the main features of your system, I should quite fail to answer this question, and failing there, they would tell me, for they were very close cipherers, that I had been dreaming; nor would they ever believe anything else. In my day, I know that the total annual product of the nation, although it might have been divided with absolute equality, would not have come to more than three or four hundred dollars per head, not very much more than enough to supply the necessities of life with few or any of its comforts. How is it that you have so much more?"

"That is a very pertinent question, Mr. West," replied Dr. Leete, "and I should not blame your friends, in the case you supposed, if they declared your story all moonshine, failing a satisfactory reply to it. It is a question which I cannot answer exhaustively at any one sitting, and as for the exact statistics to bear out my general statements, I shall have to refer you for them to books in my library, but it would certainly be a pity to leave you to be put to confusion by your old acquaintances, in case of the contingency you speak of, for lack of a few suggestions.

"Let us begin with a number of small items wherein we economize wealth as compared with you. We have no national, state, county, or municipal debts, or payments on their account. We have no sort of military or naval expenditures for men or materials, no army, navy, or militia. We have no revenue service, no swarm of tax assessors and collectors. As regards our judiciary, police, sheriffs, and jailers, the force which Massachusetts alone kept on foot in your day far more than suffices for the nation now. We have no criminal class preying upon the wealth of society as you had. The number of persons, more or less absolutely lost to the working force through physical disability, of the lame, sick, and debilitated, which constituted such a burden on the able-bodied in your day, now that all live under conditions of health and comfort, has shrunk to scarcely perceptible proportions, and with every generation is becoming more completely eliminated.

"Another item wherein we save is the disuse of money and the thousand occupations connected with financial operations of all sorts, whereby an army of men was formerly taken away from useful employments. Also consider that the waste of the very rich in your day on inordinate personal luxury has ceased, though, indeed, this item might easily be over-estimated. Again, consider that there are no idlers now, rich or poor—no drones.

"A very important cause of former poverty was the vast waste of labor and materials which resulted from domestic washing and cooking, and the performing separately of innumerable other tasks to which we apply the cooperative plan.

"A larger economy than any of these—yes, of all together—is effected by the organization of our distributing system, by which the work done once by the merchants, traders, storekeepers, with their various grades of jobbers, wholesalers, retailers, agents, commercial travelers, and middlemen of all sorts, with an excessive waste of energy in needless transportation and interminable handlings, is performed by one tenth the number of hands and an unnecessary turn of not one wheel. Something of what our distributing system is like you know. Our statisticians calculate that one eightieth part of our workers suffices for all the processes of distribution which in your day required one eighth of the population, so much being withdrawn from the force engaged in productive labor."

"I begin to see," I said, "where you get your greater wealth."

"I beg your pardon," replied Dr. Leete, "but you scarcely do as yet. The economies I have mentioned thus far, in the aggregate, considering the labor they would save directly and indirectly through saving of material, might possibly be equivalent to the addition to your annual production of wealth of one half its former total. These items are, however, scarcely worth mentioning in comparison with other prodigious wastes, now saved, which resulted inevitably from leaving the industries of the nation to private enterprise. However great the economies your contemporaries might have devised in the consumption of products, and however marvelous the progress of mechanical invention, they could never have raised themselves out of the slough of poverty so long as they held to that system.

"No mode more wasteful for utilizing human energy could be devised, and for the credit of the human intellect it should be remembered that the system never was devised, but was merely a survival from the rude ages when the lack of social organization made any sort of cooperation impossible."

"I will readily admit," I said, "that our industrial system was ethically very bad, but as a mere wealth-making machine, apart from moral aspects, it seemed to us admirable."

"As I said," responded the doctor, "the subject is too large to discuss at length now, but if you are really interested to know the main criticisms which we moderns make on your industrial system as compared with our own, I can touch briefly on some of them.

"The wastes which resulted from leaving the conduct of industry to irresponsible individuals, wholly without mutual understanding or concert, were mainly four: first, the waste by mistaken undertakings; second, the waste from the competition and mutual hostility of those engaged in industry; third, the waste by periodical gluts and crises, with the consequent interruptions of industry; fourth, the waste from idle capital and labor, at all times. Any one of these four great leaks, were all the others stopped, would suffice to make the difference between wealth and poverty on the part of a nation.

"Take the waste by mistaken undertakings, to begin with. In your day the production and distribution of commodities being without concert or organization, there was no means of knowing just what demand there was for any class of products, or what was the rate of supply. Therefore, any enterprise by a private capitalist was always a doubtful experiment. The projector having no general view of the field of industry and consumption, such as our government has, could never be sure either what the people wanted, or what arrangements other capitalists were making to supply them. In view of this, we are not surprised to learn that the chances were considered several to one in favor of the failure of any given business enterprise, and that it was common for persons who at last succeeded in making a hit to have failed repeatedly. If a shoemaker, for every pair of shoes he succeeded in completing, spoiled the leather of four or five pair, besides losing the time spent on them, he would stand about the same chance of getting rich as your contemporaries did with their system of private enterprise, and its average of four or five failures to one success.

"The next of the great wastes was that from competition. The field of industry was a battlefield as wide as the world, in which the workers wasted, in assailing one another, energies which, if expended in concerted effort, as to-day, would have enriched all. As for mercy or quarter in this warfare, there was absolutely no suggestion of it. To deliberately enter a field of business and destroy the enterprises of those who had occupied it previously, in order to plant one's own enterprise on their ruins, was an achievement which never failed to command popular admiration. Nor is there any stretch of fancy in comparing this sort of struggle with actual warfare, so far as concerns the mental agony and physical suffering which attended the struggle, and the misery which overwhelmed the defeated and those dependent on them. Now nothing about your age is, at first sight, more astounding to a man of modern times than the fact that men engaged in the same industry, instead of fraternizing as comrades and co-laborers to a common end, should have regarded each other as rivals and enemies to be throttled and overthrown. This certainly seems like sheer madness, a scene from bedlam. But more closely regarded, it is seen to be no such thing. Your contemporaries, with their mutual throat-cutting, knew very well what they were at. The producers of the nineteenth century were not, like ours, working together for the maintenance of the community, but each solely for his own maintenance at the expense of the community. If, in working to this end, he at the same time increased the aggregate wealth, that was merely incidental. It was just as feasible and as common to increase one's private hoard by practices injurious to the general welfare. One's worst enemies were necessarily those of his own trade, for, under your plan of making private profit the motive of production, a scarcity of the article he produced was what each particular producer desired. It was for his interest that no more of it should be produced than he himself could produce. To secure this consummation as far as circumstances permitted, by killing off and discouraging those engaged in his line of industry, was his constant effort. When he had killed off all he could, his policy was to combine with those he could not kill, and convert their mutual warfare into a warfare upon the public at large by cornering the market, as I believe you used to call it, and putting up prices to the highest point people would stand before going without the goods. The day dream of the nineteenth century producer was to gain absolute control of the supply of some necessity of life, so that he might keep the public at the verge of starvation, and always command famine prices for what he supplied. This, Mr. West, is what was called in the nineteenth century a system of production. I will leave it to you if it does not seem, in some of its aspects, a great deal more like a system for preventing production. Some time when we have plenty of leisure I am going to ask you to sit down with me and try to make me comprehend, as I never yet could, though I have studied the matter a great deal how such shrewd fellows as your contemporaries appear to have been in many respects ever came to entrust the business of providing for the community to a class whose interest it was to starve it. I assure you that the wonder with us is, not that the world did not get rich under such a system, but that it did not perish outright from want. This wonder increases as we go on to consider some of the other prodigious wastes that characterized it.

"Apart from the waste of labor and capital by misdirected industry, and that from the constant bloodletting of your industrial warfare, your system was liable to periodical convulsions, overwhelming alike the wise and unwise, the successful cut-throat as well as his victim. I refer to the business crises at intervals of five to ten years, which wrecked the industries of the nation, prostrating all weak enterprises and crippling the strongest, and were followed by long periods, often of many years, of so-called dull times, during which the capitalists slowly regathered their dissipated strength while the laboring classes starved and rioted. Then would ensue another brief season of prosperity, followed in turn by another crisis and the ensuing years of exhaustion. As commerce developed, making the nations mutually dependent, these crises became world-wide, while the obstinacy of the ensuing state of collapse increased with the area affected by the convulsions, and the consequent lack of rallying centres. In proportion as the industries of the world multiplied and became complex, and the volume of capital involved was increased, these business cataclysms became more frequent, till, in the latter part of the nineteenth century, there were two years of bad times to one of good, and the system of industry, never before so extended or so imposing, seemed in danger of collapsing by its own weight. After endless discussions, your economists appear by that time to have settled down to the despairing conclusion that there was no more possibility of preventing or controlling these crises than if they had been drouths or hurricanes. It only remained to endure them as necessary evils, and when they had passed over to build up again the shattered structure of industry, as dwellers in an earthquake country keep on rebuilding their cities on the same site.

"So far as considering the causes of the trouble inherent in their industrial system, your contemporaries were certainly correct. They were in its very basis, and must needs become more and more maleficent as the business fabric grew in size and complexity. One of these causes was the lack of any common control of the different industries, and the consequent impossibility of their orderly and coordinate development. It inevitably resulted from this lack that they were continually getting out of step with one another and out of relation with the demand.

"Of the latter there was no criterion such as organized distribution gives us, and the first notice that it had been exceeded in any group of industries was a crash of prices, bankruptcy of producers, stoppage of production, reduction of wages, or discharge of workmen. This process was constantly going on in many industries, even in what were called good times, but a crisis took place only when the industries affected were extensive. The markets then were glutted with goods, of which nobody wanted beyond a sufficiency at any price. The wages and profits of those making the glutted classes of goods being reduced or wholly stopped, their purchasing power as consumers of other classes of goods, of which there were no natural glut, was taken away, and, as a consequence, goods of which there was no natural glut became artificially glutted, till their prices also were broken down, and their makers thrown out of work and deprived of income. The crisis was by this time fairly under way, and nothing could check it till a nation's ransom had been wasted.

"A cause, also inherent in your system, which often produced and always terribly aggravated crises, was the machinery of money and credit. Money was essential when production was in many private hands, and buying and selling was necessary to secure what one wanted. It was, however, open to the obvious objection of substituting for food, clothing, and other things a merely conventional representative of them. The confusion of mind which this favored, between goods and their representative, led the way to the credit system and its prodigious illusions. Already accustomed to accept money for commodities, the people next accepted promises for money, and ceased to look at all behind the representative for the thing represented. Money was a sign of real commodities, but credit was but the sign of a sign. There was a natural limit to gold and silver, that is, money proper, but none to credit, and the result was that the volume of credit, that is, the promises of money, ceased to bear any ascertainable proportion to the money, still less to the commodities, actually in existence. Under such a system, frequent and periodical crises were necessitated by a law as absolute as that which brings to the ground a structure overhanging its centre of gravity. It was one of your fictions that the government and the banks authorized by it alone issued money; but everybody who gave a dollar's credit issued money to that extent, which was as good as any to swell the circulation till the next crises. The great extension of the credit system was a characteristic of the latter part of the nineteenth century, and accounts largely for the almost incessant business crises which marked that period. Perilous as credit was, you could not dispense with its use, for, lacking any national or other public organization of the capital of the country, it was the only means you had for concentrating and directing it upon industrial enterprises. It was in this way a most potent means for exaggerating the chief peril of the private enterprise system of industry by enabling particular industries to absorb disproportionate amounts of the disposable capital of the country, and thus prepare disaster. Business enterprises were always vastly in debt for advances of credit, both to one another and to the banks and capitalists, and the prompt withdrawal of this credit at the first sign of a crisis was generally the precipitating cause of it.

"It was the misfortune of your contemporaries that they had to cement their business fabric with a material which an accident might at any moment turn into an explosive. They were in the plight of a man building a house with dynamite for mortar, for credit can be compared with nothing else.

"If you would see how needless were these convulsions of business which I have been speaking of, and how entirely they resulted from leaving industry to private and unorganized management, just consider the working of our system. Overproduction in special lines, which was the great hobgoblin of your day, is impossible now, for by the connection between distribution and production supply is geared to demand like an engine to the governor which regulates its speed. Even suppose by an error of judgment an excessive production of some commodity. The consequent slackening or cessation of production in that line throws nobody out of employment. The suspended workers are at once found occupation in some other department of the vast workshop and lose only the time spent in changing, while, as for the glut, the business of the nation is large enough to carry any amount of product manufactured in excess of demand till the latter overtakes it. In such a case of over-production, as I have supposed, there is not with us, as with you, any complex machinery to get out of order and magnify a thousand times the original mistake. Of course, having not even money, we still less have credit. All estimates deal directly with the real things, the flour, iron, wood, wool, and labor, of which money and credit were for you the very misleading representatives. In our calculation of cost there can be no mistakes. Out of the annual product the amount necessary for the support of the people is taken, and the requisite labor to produce the next year's consumption provided for. The residue of the material and labor represents what can be safely expended in improvements. If the crops are bad, the surplus for that year is less than usual, that is all. Except for slight occasional effects of such natural causes, there are no fluctuations of business; the material prosperity of the nation flows on uninterruptedly from generation to generation, like an ever broadening and deepening river.

"Your business crises, Mr. West," continued the doctor, "like either of the great wastes I mentioned before, were enough, alone, to have kept your noses to the grindstone forever; but I have still to speak of one other great cause of your poverty, and that was the idleness of a great part of your capital and labor. With us it is the business of the administration to keep in constant employment every ounce of available capital and labor in the country. In your day there was no general control of either capital or labor, and a large part of both failed to find employment. 'Capital,' you used to say, 'is naturally timid,' and it would certainly have been reckless if it had not been timid in an epoch when there was a large preponderance of probability that any particular business venture would end in failure. There was no time when, if security could have been guaranteed it, the amount of capital devoted to productive industry could not have been greatly increased. The proportion of it so employed underwent constant extraordinary fluctuations, according to the greater or less feeling of uncertainty as to the stability of the industrial situation, so that the output of the national industries greatly varied in different years. But for the same reason that the amount of capital employed at times of special insecurity was far less than at times of somewhat greater security, a very large proportion was never employed at all, because the hazard of business was always very great in the best of times.

"It should be also noted that the great amount of capital always seeking employment where tolerable safety could be insured terribly embittered the competition between capitalists when a promising opening presented itself. The idleness of capital, the result of its timidity, of course meant the idleness of labor in corresponding degree. Moreover, every change in the adjustments of business, every slightest alteration in the condition of commerce or manufactures, not to speak of the innumerable business failures that took place yearly, even in the best of times, were constantly throwing a multitude of men out of employment for periods of weeks or months, or even years. A great number of these seekers after employment were constantly traversing the country, becoming in time professional vagabonds, then criminals. 'Give us work!' was the cry of an army of the unemployed at nearly all seasons, and in seasons of dullness in business this army swelled to a host so vast and desperate as to threaten the stability of the government. Could there conceivably be a more conclusive demonstration of the imbecility of the system of private enterprise as a method for enriching a nation than the fact that, in an age of such general poverty and want of everything, capitalists had to throttle one another to find a safe chance to invest their capital and workmen rioted and burned because they could find no work to do?

"Now, Mr. West," continued Dr. Leete, "I want you to bear in mind that these points of which I have been speaking indicate only negatively the advantages of the national organization of industry by showing certain fatal defects and prodigious imbecilities of the systems of private enterprise which are not found in it. These alone, you must admit, would pretty well explain why the nation is so much richer than in your day. But the larger half of our advantage over you, the positive side of it, I have yet barely spoken of. Supposing the system of private enterprise in industry were without any of the great leaks I have mentioned; that there were no waste on account of misdirected effort growing out of mistakes as to the demand, and inability to command a general view of the industrial field. Suppose, also, there were no neutralizing and duplicating of effort from competition. Suppose, also, there were no waste from business panics and crises through bankruptcy and long interruptions of industry, and also none from the idleness of capital and labor.

Supposing these evils, which are essential to the conduct of industry by capital in private hands, could all be miraculously prevented, and the system yet retained; even then the superiority of the results attained by the modern industrial system of national control would remain overwhelming.

"You used to have some pretty large textile manufacturing establishments, even in your day, although not comparable with ours. No doubt you have visited these great mills in your time, covering acres of ground, employing thousands of hands, and combining under one roof, under one control, the hundred distinct processes between, say, the cotton bale and the bale of glossy calicoes. You have admired the vast economy of labor as of mechanical force resulting from the perfect interworking with the rest of every wheel and every hand. No doubt you have reflected how much less the same force of workers employed in that factory would accomplish if they were scattered, each man working independently. Would you think it an exaggeration to say that the utmost product of those workers, working thus apart, however amicable their relations might be, was increased not merely by a percentage, but many fold, when their efforts were organized under one control? Well now, Mr. West, the organization of the industry of the nation under a single control, so that all its processes interlock, has multiplied the total product over the utmost that could be done under the former system, even leaving out of account the four great wastes mentioned, in the same proportion that the product of those millworkers was increased by cooperation. The effectiveness of the working force of a nation, under the myriad-headed leadership of private capital, even if the leaders were not mutual enemies, as compared with that which it attains under a single head, may be likened to the military efficiency of a mob, or a horde of barbarians with a thousand petty chiefs, as compared with that of a disciplined army under one general—such a fighting machine, for example, as the German army in the time of Von Moltke."

"After what you have told me," I said, "I do not so much wonder that the nation is richer now than then, but that you are not all Croesuses."

"Well," replied Dr. Leete, "we are pretty well off. The rate at which we live is as luxurious as we could wish. The rivalry of ostentation, which in your day led to extravagance in no way conducive to comfort, finds no place, of course, in a society of people absolutely equal in resources, and our ambition stops at the surroundings which minister to the enjoyment of life. We might, indeed, have much larger incomes, individually, if we chose so to use the surplus of our product, but we prefer to expend it upon public works and pleasures in which all share, upon public halls and buildings, art galleries, bridges, statuary, means of transit, and the conveniences of our cities, great musical and theatrical exhibitions, and in providing on a vast scale for the recreations of the people. You have not begun to see how we live yet, Mr. West. At home we have comfort, but the splendor of our life is, on its social side, that which we share with our fellows. When you know more of it you will see where the money goes, as you used to say, and I think you will agree that we do well so to expend it."

"I suppose," observed Dr. Leete, as we strolled homeward from the dining hall, "that no reflection would have cut the men of your wealth-worshiping century more keenly than the suggestion that they did not know how to make money. Nevertheless that is just the verdict history has passed on them. Their system of unorganized and antagonistic industries was as absurd economically as it was morally abominable. Selfishness was their only science, and in industrial production selfishness is suicide. Competition, which is the instinct of selfishness, is another word for dissipation of energy, while combination is the secret of efficient production; and not till the idea of increasing the individual hoard gives place to the idea of increasing the common stock can industrial combination be realized, and the acquisition of wealth really begin. Even if the principle of share and share alike for all men were not the only humane and rational basis for a society, we should still enforce it as economically expedient, seeing that until the disintegrating influence of self-seeking is suppressed no true concert of industry is possible."

Chapter 23

That evening, as I sat with Edith in the music room, listening to some pieces in the programme of that day which had attracted my notice, I took advantage of an interval in the music to say, "I have a question to ask you which I fear is rather indiscreet."

"I am quite sure it is not that," she replied, encouragingly.

"I am in the position of an eavesdropper," I continued, "who, having overheard a little of a matter not intended for him, though seeming to concern him, has the impudence to come to the speaker for the rest."

"An eavesdropper!" she repeated, looking puzzled.

"Yes," I said, "but an excusable one, as I think you will admit."

"This is very mysterious," she replied.

"Yes," said I, "so mysterious that often I have doubted whether I really overheard at all what I am going to ask you about, or only dreamed it. I want you to tell me. The matter is this: When I was coming out of that sleep of a century, the first impression of which I was conscious was of voices talking around me, voices that afterwards I recognized as your father's, your mother's, and your own. First, I remember your father's voice saying, "He is going to open his eyes. He had better see but one person at first." Then you said, if I did not dream it all, "Promise me, then, that you will not tell him." Your father seemed to hesitate about promising, but you insisted, and your mother interposing, he finally promised, and when I opened my eyes I saw only him."

I had been quite serious when I said that I was not sure that I had not dreamed the conversation I fancied I had overheard, so incomprehensible was it that these people should know anything of me, a contemporary of their great-grandparents, which I did not know myself. But when I saw the effect of my words upon Edith, I knew that it was no dream, but another mystery, and a more puzzling one than any I had before encountered. For from the moment that the drift of my question became apparent, she showed indications of the most acute embarrassment. Her eyes, always so frank and direct in expression, had dropped in a panic before mine, while her face crimsoned from neck to forehead.

"Pardon me," I said, as soon as I had recovered from bewilderment at the extraordinary effect of my words. "It seems, then, that I was not dreaming. There is some secret, something about me, which you are withholding from me. Really, doesn't it seem a little hard that a person in my position should not be given all the information possible concerning himself?"

"It does not concern you—that is, not directly. It is not about you exactly," she replied, scarcely audibly.

"But it concerns me in some way," I persisted. "It must be something that would interest me."

"I don't know even that," she replied, venturing a momentary glance at my face, furiously blushing, and yet with a quaint smile flickering about her lips which betrayed a certain perception of humor in the situation despite its embarrassment,—"I am not sure that it would even interest you."

"Your father would have told me," I insisted, with an accent of reproach. "It was you who forbade him. He thought I ought to know."

She did not reply. She was so entirely charming in her confusion that I was now prompted, as much by the desire to prolong the situation as by my original curiosity, to importune her further.

"Am I never to know? Will you never tell me?" I said.

"It depends," she answered, after a long pause.

"On what?" I persisted.

"Ah, you ask too much," she replied. Then, raising to mine a face which inscrutable eyes, flushed cheeks, and smiling lips combined to render perfectly bewitching, she added, "What should you think if I said that it depended on—yourself?"

"On myself?" I echoed. "How can that possibly be?"

"Mr. West, we are losing some charming music," was her only reply to this, and turning to the telephone, at a touch of her finger she set the air to swaying to the rhythm of an adagio. After that she took good care that the music should leave no opportunity for conversation. She kept her face averted from me, and pretended to be absorbed in the airs, but that it was a mere pretense the crimson tide standing at flood in her cheeks sufficiently betrayed.

When at length she suggested that I might have heard all I cared to, for that time, and we rose to leave the room, she came straight up to me and said, without raising her eyes, "Mr. West, you say I have been good to you. I have not been particularly so, but if you think I have, I want you to promise me that you will not try again to make me tell you this thing you have asked to-night, and that you will not try to find it out from any one else,—my father or mother, for instance."

To such an appeal there was but one reply possible. "Forgive me for distressing you. Of course I will promise," I said. "I would never have asked you if I had fancied it could distress you. But do you blame me for being curious?"

"I do not blame you at all."

"And some time," I added, "if I do not tease you, you may tell me of your own accord. May I not hope so?"

"Perhaps," she murmured.

"Only perhaps?"

Looking up, she read my face with a quick, deep glance. "Yes," she said, "I think I may tell you—some time": and so our conversation ended, for she gave me no chance to say anything more.

That night I don't think even Dr. Pillsbury could have put me to sleep, till toward morning at least. Mysteries had been my accustomed food for days now, but none had before confronted me at once so mysterious and so fascinating as this, the solution of which Edith Leete had forbidden me even to seek. It was a double mystery. How, in the first place, was it conceivable that she should know any secret about me, a stranger from a strange age? In the second place, even if she should know such a secret, how account for the agitating effect which the knowledge of it seemed to have upon her? There are puzzles so difficult that one cannot even get so far as a conjecture as to the solution, and this seemed one of them. I am usually of too practical a turn to waste time on such conundrums; but the difficulty of a riddle embodied in a beautiful young girl does not detract from its fascination. In general, no doubt, maidens' blushes may be safely assumed to tell the same tale to young men in all ages and races, but to give that interpretation to Edith's crimson cheeks would, considering my position and the length of time I had known her, and still more the fact that this mystery dated from before I had known her at all, be a piece of utter fatuity. And yet she was an angel, and I should not have been a young man if reason and common sense had been able quite to banish a roseate tinge from my dreams that night.

Chapter 24

In the morning I went down stairs early in the hope of seeing Edith alone. In this, however, I was disappointed. Not finding her in the house, I sought her in the garden, but she was not there. In the course of my wanderings I visited the underground chamber, and sat down there to rest. Upon the reading table in the chamber several periodicals and newspapers lay, and thinking that Dr. Leete might be interested in glancing over a Boston daily of 1887, I brought one of the papers with me into the house when I came.

At breakfast I met Edith. She blushed as she greeted me, but was perfectly self-possessed. As we sat at table, Dr. Leete amused himself with looking over the paper I had brought in. There was in it, as in all the newspapers of that date, a great deal about the labor troubles, strikes, lockouts, boycotts, the programmes of labor parties, and the wild threats of the anarchists.

"By the way," said I, as the doctor read aloud to us some of these items, "what part did the followers of the red flag take in the establishment of the new order of things? They were making considerable noise the last thing that I knew."

"They had nothing to do with it except to hinder it, of course," replied Dr. Leete. "They did that very effectually while they lasted, for their talk so disgusted people as to deprive the best considered projects for social reform of a hearing. The subsidizing of those fellows was one of the shrewdest moves of the opponents of reform."

"Subsidizing them!" I exclaimed in astonishment.

"Certainly," replied Dr. Leete. "No historical authority nowadays doubts that they were paid by the great monopolies to wave the red flag and talk about burning, sacking, and blowing people up, in order, by alarming the timid, to head off any real reforms. What astonishes me most is that you should have fallen into the trap so unsuspectingly."

"What are your grounds for believing that the red flag party was subsidized?" I inquired.

"Why simply because they must have seen that their course made a thousand enemies of their professed cause to one friend. Not to suppose that they were hired for the work is to credit them with an inconceivable folly.[1] In the United States, of all countries, no party could intelligently expect to carry its point without first winning over to its ideas a majority of the nation, as the national party eventually did."

"The national party!" I exclaimed. "That must have arisen after my day. I suppose it was one of the labor parties."

"Oh no!" replied the doctor. "The labor parties, as such, never could have accomplished anything on a large or permanent scale. For purposes of national scope, their basis as merely class organizations was too narrow. It was not till a rearrangement of the industrial and social system on a higher ethical basis, and for the more efficient production of wealth, was recognized as the interest, not of one class, but equally of all classes, of rich and poor, cultured and ignorant, old and young, weak and strong, men and women, that there was any prospect that it would be achieved. Then the national party arose to carry it out by political methods. It probably took that name because its aim was to nationalize the functions of production and distribution. Indeed, it could not well have had any other name, for its purpose was to realize the idea of the nation with a grandeur and completeness never before conceived, not as an association of men for certain merely political functions affecting their happiness only remotely and superficially, but as a family, a vital union, a common life, a mighty heaven-touching tree whose leaves are its people, fed from its veins, and feeding it in turn. The most patriotic of all possible parties, it sought to justify patriotism and raise it from an instinct to a rational devotion, by making the native land truly a father land, a father who kept the people alive and was not merely an idol for which they were expected to die."

[1] I fully admit the difficulty of accounting for the course of the anarchists on any other theory than that they were subsidized by the capitalists, but at the same time, there is no doubt that the theory is wholly erroneous. It certainly was not held at the time by any one, though it may seem so obvious in the retrospect.

Chapter 25

The personality of Edith Leete had naturally impressed me strongly ever since I had come, in so strange a manner, to be an inmate of her father's house, and it was to be expected that after what had happened the night previous, I should be more than ever preoccupied with thoughts of her. From the first I had been struck with the air of serene frankness and ingenuous directness, more like that of a noble and innocent boy than any girl I had ever known, which characterized her. I was curious to know how far this charming quality might be peculiar to herself, and how far possibly a result of alterations in the social position of women which might have taken place since my time. Finding an opportunity that day, when alone with Dr. Leete, I turned the conversation in that direction.

"I suppose," I said, "that women nowadays, having been relieved of the burden of housework, have no employment but the cultivation of their charms and graces."

"So far as we men are concerned," replied Dr. Leete, "we should consider that they amply paid their way, to use one of your forms of expression, if they confined themselves to that occupation, but you may be very sure that they have quite too much spirit to consent to be mere beneficiaries of society, even as a return for ornamenting it. They did, indeed, welcome their riddance from housework, because that was not only exceptionally wearing in itself, but also wasteful, in the extreme, of energy, as compared with the cooperative plan; but they accepted relief from that sort of work only that they might contribute in other and more effectual, as well as more agreeable, ways to the common weal. Our women, as well as our men, are members of the industrial army, and leave it only when maternal duties claim them. The result is that most women, at one time or another of their lives, serve industrially some five or ten or fifteen years, while those who have no children fill out the full term."

"A woman does not, then, necessarily leave the industrial service on marriage?" I queried.

"No more than a man," replied the doctor. "Why on earth should she? Married women have no housekeeping responsibilities now, you know, and a husband is not a baby that he should be cared for."

"It was thought one of the most grievous features of our civilization that we required so much toil from women," I said; "but it seems to me you get more out of them than we did."

Dr. Leete laughed. "Indeed we do, just as we do out of our men. Yet the women of this age are very happy, and those of the nineteenth century, unless contemporary references greatly mislead us, were very miserable. The reason that women nowadays are so much more efficient colaborers with the men, and at the same time are so happy, is that, in regard to their work as well as men's, we follow the principle of providing every one the kind of occupation he or she is best adapted to. Women being inferior in strength to men, and further disqualified industrially in special ways, the kinds of occupation reserved for them, and the conditions under which they pursue them, have reference to these facts. The heavier sorts of work are everywhere reserved for men, the lighter occupations for women. Under no circumstances is a woman permitted to follow any employment not perfectly adapted, both as to kind and degree of labor, to her sex. Moreover, the hours of women's work are considerably shorter than those of men's, more frequent vacations are granted, and the most careful provision is made for rest when needed. The men of this day so well appreciate that they owe to the beauty and grace of women the chief zest of their lives and their main incentive to effort, that they permit them to work at all only because it is fully understood that a certain regular requirement of labor, of a sort adapted to their powers, is well for body and mind, during the period of maximum physical vigor. We believe that the magnificent health which distinguishes our women from those of your day, who seem to have been so generally sickly, is owing largely to the fact that all alike are furnished with healthful and inspiring occupation."

"I understood you," I said, "that the women-workers belong to the army of industry, but how can they be under the same system of ranking and discipline with the men, when the conditions of their labor are so different?"

"They are under an entirely different discipline," replied Dr. Leete, "and constitute rather an allied force than an integral part of the army of the men. They have a woman general-in-chief and are under exclusively feminine regime. This general, as also the higher officers, is chosen by the body of women who have passed the time of service, in correspondence with the manner in which the chiefs of the masculine army and the President of the nation are elected. The general of the women's army sits in the cabinet of the President and has a veto on measures respecting women's work, pending appeals to Congress. I should have said, in speaking of the judiciary, that we have women on the bench, appointed by the general of the women, as well as men. Causes in which both parties are women are determined by women judges, and where a man and a woman are parties to a case, a judge of either sex must consent to the verdict."

"Womanhood seems to be organized as a sort of imperium in imperio in your system," I said.

"To some extent," Dr. Leete replied; "but the inner imperium is one from which you will admit there is not likely to be much danger to the nation. The lack of some such recognition of the distinct individuality of the sexes was one of the innumerable defects of your society. The passional attraction between men and women has too often prevented a perception of the profound differences which make the members of each sex in many things strange to the other, and capable of sympathy only with their own. It is in giving full play to the differences of sex rather than in seeking to obliterate them, as was apparently the effort of some reformers in your day, that the enjoyment of each by itself and the piquancy which each has for the other, are alike enhanced. In your day there was no career for women except in an unnatural rivalry with men. We have given them a world of their own, with its emulations, ambitions, and careers, and I assure you they are very happy in it. It seems to us that women were more than any other class the victims of your civilization. There is something which, even at this distance of time, penetrates one with pathos in the spectacle of their ennuied, undeveloped lives, stunted at marriage, their narrow horizon, bounded so often, physically, by the four walls of home, and morally by a petty circle of personal interests. I speak now, not of the poorer classes, who were generally worked to death, but also of the well-to-do and rich. From the great sorrows, as well as the petty frets of life, they had no refuge in the breezy outdoor world of human affairs, nor any interests save those of the family. Such an existence would have softened men's brains or driven them mad. All that is changed to-day. No woman is heard nowadays wishing she were a man, nor parents desiring boy rather than girl children. Our girls are as full of ambition for their careers as our boys. Marriage, when it comes, does not mean incarceration for them, nor does it separate them in any way from the larger interests of society, the bustling life of the world. Only when maternity fills a woman's mind with new interests does she withdraw from the world for a time. Afterward, and at any time, she may return to her place among her comrades, nor need she ever lose touch with them. Women are a very happy race nowadays, as compared with what they ever were before in the world's history, and their power of giving happiness to men has been of course increased in proportion."

"I should imagine it possible," I said, "that the interest which girls take in their careers as members of the industrial army and candidates for its distinctions might have an effect to deter them from marriage."

Dr. Leete smiled. "Have no anxiety on that score, Mr. West," he replied. "The Creator took very good care that whatever other modifications the dispositions of men and women might with time take on, their attraction for each other should remain constant. The mere fact that in an age like yours, when the struggle for existence must have left people little time for other thoughts, and the future was so uncertain that to assume parental responsibilities must have often seemed like a criminal risk, there was even then marrying and giving in marriage, should be conclusive on this point. As for love nowadays, one of our authors says that the vacuum left in the minds of men and women by the absence of care for one's livelihood has been entirely taken up by the tender passion. That, however, I beg you to believe, is something of an exaggestion. For the rest, so far is marriage from being an interference with a woman's career, that the higher positions in the feminine army of industry are intrusted only to women who have been both wives and mothers, as they alone fully represent their sex."

"Are credit cards issued to the women just as to the men?"

"Certainly."

"The credits of the women, I suppose, are for smaller sums, owing to the frequent suspension of their labor on account of family responsibilities."

"Smaller!" exclaimed Dr. Leete, "oh, no! The maintenance of all our people is the same. There are no exceptions to that rule, but if any difference were made on account of the interruptions you speak of, it would be by making the woman's credit larger, not smaller. Can you think of any service constituting a stronger claim on the nation's gratitude than bearing and nursing the nation's children? According to our view, none deserve so well of the world as good parents. There is no task so unselfish, so necessarily without return, though the heart is well rewarded, as the nurture of the children who are to make the world for one another when we are gone."

"It would seem to follow, from what you have said, that wives are in no way dependent on their husbands for maintenance."

"Of course they are not," replied Dr. Leete, "nor children on their parents either, that is, for means of support, though of course they are for the offices of affection. The child's labor, when he grows up, will go to increase the common stock, not his parents', who will be dead, and therefore he is properly nurtured out of the common stock. The account of every person, man, woman, and child, you must understand, is always with the nation directly, and never through any intermediary, except, of course, that parents, to a certain extent, act for children as their guardians. You see that it is by virtue of the relation of individuals to the nation, of their membership in it, that they are entitled to support; and this title is in no way connected with or affected by their relations to other individuals who are fellow members of the nation with them. That any person should be dependent for the means of support upon another would be shocking to the moral sense as well as indefensible on any rational social theory. What would become of personal liberty and dignity under such an arrangement? I am aware that you called yourselves free in the nineteenth century. The meaning of the word could not then, however, have been at all what it is at present, or you certainly would not have applied it to a society of which nearly every member was in a position of galling personal dependence upon others as to the very means of life, the poor upon the rich, or employed upon employer, women upon men, children upon parents. Instead of distributing the product of the nation directly to its members, which would seem the most natural and obvious method, it would actually appear that you had given your minds to devising a plan of hand to hand distribution, involving the maximum of personal humiliation to all classes of recipients.

"As regards the dependence of women upon men for support, which then was usual, of course, natural attraction in case of marriages of love may often have made it endurable, though for spirited women I should fancy it must always have remained humiliating. What, then, must it have been in the innumerable cases where women, with or without the form of marriage, had to sell themselves to men to get their living? Even your contemporaries, callous as they were to most of the revolting aspects of their society, seem to have had an idea that this was not quite as it should be; but, it was still only for pity's sake that they deplored the lot of the women. It did not occur to them that it was robbery as well as cruelty when men seized for themselves the whole product of the world and left women to beg and wheedle for their share. Why—but bless me, Mr. West, I am really running on at a remarkable rate, just as if the robbery, the sorrow, and the shame which those poor women endured were not over a century since, or as if you were responsible for what you no doubt deplored as much as I do."

"I must bear my share of responsibility for the world as it then was," I replied. "All I can say in extenuation is that until the nation was ripe for the present system of organized production and distribution, no radical improvement in the position of woman was possible. The root of her disability, as you say, was her personal dependence upon man for her livelihood, and I can imagine no other mode of social organization than that you have adopted, which would have set woman free of man at the same time that it set men free of one another. I suppose, by the way, that so entire a change in the position of women cannot have taken place without affecting in marked ways the social relations of the sexes. That will be a very interesting study for me."

"The change you will observe," said Dr. Leete, "will chiefly be, I think, the entire frankness and unconstraint which now characterizes those relations, as compared with the artificiality which seems to have marked them in your time. The sexes now meet with the ease of perfect equals, suitors to each other for nothing but love. In your time the fact that women were dependent for support on men made the woman in reality the one chiefly benefited by marriage. This fact, so far as we can judge from contemporary records, appears to have been coarsely enough recognized among the lower classes, while among the more polished it was glossed over by a system of elaborate conventionalities which aimed to carry the precisely opposite meaning, namely, that the man was the party chiefly benefited. To keep up this convention it was essential that he should always seem the suitor. Nothing was therefore considered more shocking to the proprieties than that a woman should betray a fondness for a man before he had indicated a desire to marry her. Why, we actually have in our libraries books, by authors of your day, written for no other purpose than to discuss the question whether, under any conceivable circumstances, a woman might, without discredit to her sex, reveal an unsolicited love. All this seems exquisitely absurd to us, and yet we know that, given your circumstances, the problem might have a serious side. When for a woman to proffer her love to a man was in effect to invite him to assume the burden of her support, it is easy to see that pride and delicacy might well have checked the promptings of the heart. When you go out into our society, Mr. West, you must be prepared to be often cross-questioned on this point by our young people, who are naturally much interested in this aspect of old-fashioned manners."[1]

"And so the girls of the twentieth century tell their love."

"If they choose," replied Dr. Leete. "There is no more pretense of a concealment of feeling on their part than on the part of their lovers. Coquetry would be as much despised in a girl as in a man. Affected coldness, which in your day rarely deceived a lover, would deceive him wholly now, for no one thinks of practicing it."

"One result which must follow from the independence of women I can see for myself," I said. "There can be no marriages now except those of inclination."

"That is a matter of course," replied Dr. Leete.

"Think of a world in which there are nothing but matches of pure love! Ah me, Dr. Leete, how far you are from being able to understand what an astonishing phenomenon such a world seems to a man of the nineteenth century!"

"I can, however, to some extent, imagine it," replied the doctor. "But the fact you celebrate, that there are nothing but love matches, means even more, perhaps, than you probably at first realize. It means that for the first time in human history the principle of sexual selection, with its tendency to preserve and transmit the better types of the race, and let the inferior types drop out, has unhindered operation. The necessities of poverty, the need of having a home, no longer tempt women to accept as the fathers of their children men whom they neither can love nor respect. Wealth and rank no longer divert attention from personal qualities. Gold no longer 'gilds the straitened forehead of the fool.' The gifts of person, mind, and disposition; beauty, wit, eloquence, kindness, generosity, geniality, courage, are sure of transmission to posterity. Every generation is sifted through a little finer mesh than the last. The attributes that human nature admires are preserved, those that repel it are left behind. There are, of course, a great many women who with love must mingle admiration, and seek to wed greatly, but these not the less obey the same law, for to wed greatly now is not to marry men of fortune or title, but those who have risen above their fellows by the solidity or brilliance of their services to humanity. These form nowadays the only aristocracy with which alliance is distinction.

"You were speaking, a day or two ago, of the physical superiority of our people to your contemporaries. Perhaps more important than any of the causes I mentioned then as tending to race purification has been the effect of untrammeled sexual selection upon the quality of two or three successive generations. I believe that when you have made a fuller study of our people you will find in them not only a physical, but a mental and moral improvement. It would be strange if it were not so, for not only is one of the great laws of nature now freely working out the salvation of the race, but a profound moral sentiment has come to its support. Individualism, which in your day was the animating idea of society, not only was fatal to any vital sentiment of brotherhood and common interest among living men, but equally to any realization of the responsibility of the living for the generation to follow. To-day this sense of responsibility, practically unrecognized in all previous ages, has become one of the great ethical ideas of the race, reinforcing, with an intense conviction of duty, the natural impulse to seek in marriage the best and noblest of the other sex. The result is, that not all the encouragements and incentives of every sort which we have provided to develop industry, talent, genius, excellence of whatever kind, are comparable in their effect on our young men with the fact that our women sit aloft as judges of the race and reserve themselves to reward the winners. Of all the whips, and spurs, and baits, and prizes, there is none like the thought of the radiant faces which the laggards will find averted.

"Celibates nowadays are almost invariably men who have failed to acquit themselves creditably in the work of life. The woman must be a courageous one, with a very evil sort of courage, too, whom pity for one of these unfortunates should lead to defy the opinion of her generation—for otherwise she is free—so far as to accept him for a husband. I should add that, more exacting and difficult to resist than any other element in that opinion, she would find the sentiment of her own sex. Our women have risen to the full height of their responsibility as the wardens of the world to come, to whose keeping the keys of the future are confided. Their feeling of duty in this respect amounts to a sense of religious consecration. It is a cult in which they educate their daughters from childhood."

After going to my room that night, I sat up late to read a romance of Berrian, handed me by Dr. Leete, the plot of which turned on a situation suggested by his last words, concerning the modern view of parental responsibility. A similar situation would almost certainly have been treated by a nineteenth century romancist so as to excite the morbid sympathy of the reader with the sentimental selfishness of the lovers, and his resentment toward the unwritten law which they outraged. I need not describe—for who has not read "Ruth Elton"?—how different is the course which Berrian takes, and with what tremendous effect he enforces the principle which he states: "Over the unborn our power is that of God, and our responsibility like His toward us. As we acquit ourselves toward them, so let Him deal with us."

[1] I may say that Dr. Leete's warning has been fully justified by my experience. The amount and intensity of amusement which the young people of this day, and the young women especially, are able to extract from what they are pleased to call the oddities of courtship in the nineteenth century, appear unlimited.

Chapter 26

I think if a person were ever excusable for losing track of the days of the week, the circumstances excused me. Indeed, if I had been told that the method of reckoning time had been wholly changed and the days were now counted in lots of five, ten, or fifteen instead of seven, I should have been in no way surprised after what I had already heard and seen of the twentieth century. The first time that any inquiry as to the days of the week occurred to me was the morning following the conversation related in the last chapter. At the breakfast table Dr. Leete asked me if I would care to hear a sermon.

"Is it Sunday, then?" I exclaimed.

"Yes," he replied. "It was on Friday, you see, when we made the lucky discovery of the buried chamber to which we owe your society this morning. It was on Saturday morning, soon after midnight, that you first awoke, and Sunday afternoon when you awoke the second time with faculties fully regained."

"So you still have Sundays and sermons," I said. "We had prophets who foretold that long before this time the world would have dispensed with both. I am very curious to know how the ecclesiastical systems fit in with the rest of your social arrangements. I suppose you have a sort of national church with official clergymen."

Dr. Leete laughed, and Mrs. Leete and Edith seemed greatly amused.

"Why, Mr. West," Edith said, "what odd people you must think us. You were quite done with national religious establishments in the nineteenth century, and did you fancy we had gone back to them?"

"But how can voluntary churches and an unofficial clerical profession be reconciled with national ownership of all buildings, and the industrial service required of all men?" I answered.

"The religious practices of the people have naturally changed considerably in a century," replied Dr. Leete; "but supposing them to have remained unchanged, our social system would accommodate them perfectly. The nation supplies any person or number of persons with buildings on guarantee of the rent, and they remain tenants while they pay it. As for the clergymen, if a number of persons wish the services of an individual for any particular end of their own, apart from the general service of the nation, they can always secure it, with that individual's own consent, of course, just as we secure the service of our editors, by contributing from their credit cards an indemnity to the nation for the loss of his services in general industry. This indemnity paid the nation for the individual answers to the salary in your day paid to the individual himself; and the various applications of this principle leave private initiative full play in all details to which national control is not applicable. Now, as to hearing a sermon to-day, if you wish to do so, you can either go to a church to hear it or stay at home."

"How am I to hear it if I stay at home?"

"Simply by accompanying us to the music room at the proper hour and selecting an easy chair. There are some who still prefer to hear sermons in church, but most of our preaching, like our musical performances, is not in public, but delivered in acoustically prepared chambers, connected by wire with subscribers' houses. If you prefer to go to a church I shall be glad to accompany you, but I really don't believe you are likely to hear anywhere a better discourse than you will at home. I see by the paper that Mr. Barton is to preach this morning, and he preaches only by telephone, and to audiences often reaching 150,000."

"The novelty of the experience of hearing a sermon under such circumstances would incline me to be one of Mr. Barton's hearers, if for no other reason," I said.

An hour or two later, as I sat reading in the library, Edith came for me, and I followed her to the music room, where Dr. and Mrs. Leete were waiting. We had not more than seated ourselves comfortably when the tinkle of a bell was heard, and a few moments after the voice of a man, at the pitch of ordinary conversation, addressed us, with an effect of proceeding from an invisible person in the room. This was what the voice said:

MR. BARTON'S SERMON

"We have had among us, during the past week, a critic from the nineteenth century, a living representative of the epoch of our great-grandparents. It would be strange if a fact so extraordinary had not somewhat strongly affected our imaginations. Perhaps most of us have been stimulated to some effort to realize the society of a century ago, and figure to ourselves what it must have been like to live then. In inviting you now to consider certain reflections upon this subject which have occurred to me, I presume that I shall rather follow than divert the course of your own thoughts."

Edith whispered something to her father at this point, to which he nodded assent and turned to me.

"Mr. West," he said, "Edith suggests that you may find it slightly embarrassing to listen to a discourse on the lines Mr. Barton is laying down, and if so, you need not be cheated out of a sermon. She will connect us with Mr. Sweetser's speaking room if you say so, and I can still promise you a very good discourse."

"No, no," I said. "Believe me, I would much rather hear what Mr. Barton has to say."

"As you please," replied my host.

When her father spoke to me Edith had touched a screw, and the voice of Mr. Barton had ceased abruptly. Now at another touch the room was once more filled with the earnest sympathetic tones which had already impressed me most favorably.

"I venture to assume that one effect has been common with us as a result of this effort at retrospection, and that it has been to leave us more than ever amazed at the stupendous change which one brief century has made in the material and moral conditions of humanity.

"Still, as regards the contrast between the poverty of the nation and the world in the nineteenth century and their wealth now, it is not greater, possibly, than had been before seen in human history, perhaps not greater, for example, than that between the poverty of this country during the earliest colonial period of the seventeenth century and the relatively great wealth it had attained at the close of the nineteenth, or between the England of William the Conqueror and that of Victoria. Although the aggregate riches of a nation did not then, as now, afford any accurate criterion of the masses of its people, yet instances like these afford partial parallels for the merely material side of the contrast between the nineteenth and the twentieth centuries. It is when we contemplate the moral aspect of that contrast that we find ourselves in the presence of a phenomenon for which history offers no precedent, however far back we may cast our eye. One might almost be excused who should exclaim, 'Here, surely, is something like a miracle!' Nevertheless, when we give over idle wonder, and begin to examine the seeming prodigy critically, we find it no prodigy at all, much less a miracle. It is not necessary to suppose a moral new birth of humanity, or a wholesale destruction of the wicked and survival of the good, to account for the fact before us. It finds its simple and obvious explanation in the reaction of a changed environment upon human nature. It means merely that a form of society which was founded on the pseudo self-interest of selfishness, and appealed solely to the anti-social and brutal side of human nature, has been replaced by institutions based on the true self-interest of a rational unselfishness, and appealing to the social and generous instincts of men.

"My friends, if you would see men again the beasts of prey they seemed in the nineteenth century, all you have to do is to restore the old social and industrial system, which taught them to view their natural prey in their fellow-men, and find their gain in the loss of others. No doubt it seems to you that no necessity, however dire, would have tempted you to subsist on what superior skill or strength enabled you to wrest from others equally needy. But suppose it were not merely your own life that you were responsible for. I know well that there must have been many a man among our ancestors who, if it had been merely a question of his own life, would sooner have given it up than nourished it by bread snatched from others. But this he was not permitted to do. He had dear lives dependent on him. Men loved women in those days, as now. God knows how they dared be fathers, but they had babies as sweet, no doubt, to them as ours to us, whom they must feed, clothe, educate. The gentlest creatures are fierce when they have young to provide for, and in that wolfish society the struggle for bread borrowed a peculiar desperation from the tenderest sentiments. For the sake of those dependent on him, a man might not choose, but must plunge into the foul fight—cheat, overreach, supplant, defraud, buy below worth and sell above, break down the business by which his neighbor fed his young ones, tempt men to buy what they ought not and to sell what they should not, grind his laborers, sweat his debtors, cozen his creditors. Though a man sought it carefully with tears, it was hard to find a way in which he could earn a living and provide for his family except by pressing in before some weaker rival and taking the food from his mouth. Even the ministers of religion were not exempt from this cruel necessity. While they warned their flocks against the love of money, regard for their families compelled them to keep an outlook for the pecuniary prizes of their calling. Poor fellows, theirs was indeed a trying business, preaching to men a generosity and unselfishness which they and everybody knew would, in the existing state of the world, reduce to poverty those who should practice them, laying down laws of conduct which the law of self-preservation compelled men to break. Looking on the inhuman spectacle of society, these worthy men bitterly bemoaned the depravity of human nature; as if angelic nature would not have been debauched in such a devil's school! Ah, my friends, believe me, it is not now in this happy age that humanity is proving the divinity within it. It was rather in those evil days when not even the fight for life with one another, the struggle for mere existence, in which mercy was folly, could wholly banish generosity and kindness from the earth.

"It is not hard to understand the desperation with which men and women, who under other conditions would have been full of gentleness and truth, fought and tore each other in the scramble for gold, when we realize what it meant to miss it, what poverty was in that day. For the body it was hunger and thirst, torment by heat and frost, in sickness neglect, in health unremitting toil; for the moral nature it meant oppression, contempt, and the patient endurance of indignity, brutish associations from infancy, the loss of all the innocence of childhood, the grace of womanhood, the dignity of manhood; for the mind it meant the death of ignorance, the torpor of all those faculties which distinguish us from brutes, the reduction of life to a round of bodily functions.

"Ah, my friends, if such a fate as this were offered you and your children as the only alternative of success in the accumulation of wealth, how long do you fancy would you be in sinking to the moral level of your ancestors?

"Some two or three centuries ago an act of barbarity was committed in India, which, though the number of lives destroyed was but a few score, was attended by such peculiar horrors that its memory is likely to be perpetual. A number of English prisoners were shut up in a room containing not enough air to supply one-tenth their number. The unfortunates were gallant men, devoted comrades in service, but, as the agonies of suffocation began to take hold on them, they forgot all else, and became involved in a hideous struggle, each one for himself, and against all others, to force a way to one of the small apertures of the prison at which alone it was possible to get a breath of air. It was a struggle in which men became beasts, and the recital of its horrors by the few survivors so shocked our forefathers that for a century later we find it a stock reference in their literature as a typical illustration of the extreme possibilities of human misery, as shocking in its moral as its physical aspect. They could scarcely have anticipated that to us the Black Hole of Calcutta, with its press of maddened men tearing and trampling one another in the struggle to win a place at the breathing holes, would seem a striking type of the society of their age. It lacked something of being a complete type, however, for in the Calcutta Black Hole there were no tender women, no little children and old men and women, no cripples. They were at least all men, strong to bear, who suffered.

"When we reflect that the ancient order of which I have been speaking was prevalent up to the end of the nineteenth century, while to us the new order which succeeded it already seems antique, even our parents having known no other, we cannot fail to be astounded at the suddenness with which a transition so profound beyond all previous experience of the race must have been effected. Some observation of the state of men's minds during the last quarter of the nineteenth century will, however, in great measure, dissipate this astonishment. Though general intelligence in the modern sense could not be said to exist in any community at that time, yet, as compared with previous generations, the one then on the stage was intelligent. The inevitable consequence of even this comparative degree of intelligence had been a perception of the evils of society, such as had never before been general. It is quite true that these evils had been even worse, much worse, in previous ages. It was the increased intelligence of the masses which made the difference, as the dawn reveals the squalor of surroundings which in the darkness may have seemed tolerable. The key-note of the literature of the period was one of compassion for the poor and unfortunate, and indignant outcry against the failure of the social machinery to ameliorate the miseries of men. It is plain from these outbursts that the moral hideousness of the spectacle about them was, at least by flashes, fully realized by the best of the men of that time, and that the lives of some of the more sensitive and generous hearted of them were rendered well nigh unendurable by the intensity of their sympathies.

"Although the idea of the vital unity of the family of mankind, the reality of human brotherhood, was very far from being apprehended by them as the moral axiom it seems to us, yet it is a mistake to suppose that there was no feeling at all corresponding to it. I could read you passages of great beauty from some of their writers which show that the conception was clearly attained by a few, and no doubt vaguely by many more. Moreover, it must not be forgotten that the nineteenth century was in name Christian, and the fact that the entire commercial and industrial frame of society was the embodiment of the anti-Christian spirit must have had some weight, though I admit it was strangely little, with the nominal followers of Jesus Christ.

"When we inquire why it did not have more, why, in general, long after a vast majority of men had agreed as to the crying abuses of the existing social arrangement, they still tolerated it, or contented themselves with talking of petty reforms in it, we come upon an extraordinary fact. It was the sincere belief of even the best of men at that epoch that the only stable elements in human nature, on which a social system could be safely founded, were its worst propensities. They had been taught and believed that greed and self-seeking were all that held mankind together, and that all human associations would fall to pieces if anything were done to blunt the edge of these motives or curb their operation. In a word, they believed—even those who longed to believe otherwise—the exact reverse of what seems to us self-evident; they believed, that is, that the anti-social qualities of men, and not their social qualities, were what furnished the cohesive force of society. It seemed reasonable to them that men lived together solely for the purpose of overreaching and oppressing one another, and of being overreached and oppressed, and that while a society that gave full scope to these propensities could stand, there would be little chance for one based on the idea of cooperation for the benefit of all. It seems absurd to expect any one to believe that convictions like these were ever seriously entertained by men; but that they were not only entertained by our great-grandfathers, but were responsible for the long delay in doing away with the ancient order, after a conviction of its intolerable abuses had become general, is as well established as any fact in history can be. Just here you will find the explanation of the profound pessimism of the literature of the last quarter of the nineteenth century, the note of melancholy in its poetry, and the cynicism of its humor.

"Feeling that the condition of the race was unendurable, they had no clear hope of anything better. They believed that the evolution of humanity had resulted in leading it into a cul de sac, and that there was no way of getting forward. The frame of men's minds at this time is strikingly illustrated by treatises which have come down to us, and may even now be consulted in our libraries by the curious, in which laborious arguments are pursued to prove that despite the evil plight of men, life was still, by some slight preponderance of considerations, probably better worth living than leaving. Despising themselves, they despised their Creator. There was a general decay of religious belief. Pale and watery gleams, from skies thickly veiled by doubt and dread, alone lighted up the chaos of earth. That men should doubt Him whose breath is in their nostrils, or dread the hands that moulded them, seems to us indeed a pitiable insanity; but we must remember that children who are brave by day have sometimes foolish fears at night. The dawn has come since then. It is very easy to believe in the fatherhood of God in the twentieth century.

"Briefly, as must needs be in a discourse of this character, I have adverted to some of the causes which had prepared men's minds for the change from the old to the new order, as well as some causes of the conservatism of despair which for a while held it back after the time was ripe. To wonder at the rapidity with which the change was completed after its possibility was first entertained is to forget the intoxicating effect of hope upon minds long accustomed to despair. The sunburst, after so long and dark a night, must needs have had a dazzling effect. From the moment men allowed themselves to believe that humanity after all had not been meant for a dwarf, that its squat stature was not the measure of its possible growth, but that it stood upon the verge of an avatar of limitless development, the reaction must needs have been overwhelming. It is evident that nothing was able to stand against the enthusiasm which the new faith inspired.

"Here, at last, men must have felt, was a cause compared with which the grandest of historic causes had been trivial. It was doubtless because it could have commanded millions of martyrs, that none were needed. The change of a dynasty in a petty kingdom of the old world often cost more lives than did the revolution which set the feet of the human race at last in the right way.

"Doubtless it ill beseems one to whom the boon of life in our resplendent age has been vouchsafed to wish his destiny other, and yet I have often thought that I would fain exchange my share in this serene and golden day for a place in that stormy epoch of transition, when heroes burst the barred gate of the future and revealed to the kindling gaze of a hopeless race, in place of the blank wall that had closed its path, a vista of progress whose end, for very excess of light, still dazzles us. Ah, my friends! who will say that to have lived then, when the weakest influence was a lever to whose touch the centuries trembled, was not worth a share even in this era of fruition?

"You know the story of that last, greatest, and most bloodless of revolutions. In the time of one generation men laid aside the social traditions and practices of barbarians, and assumed a social order worthy of rational and human beings. Ceasing to be predatory in their habits, they became co-workers, and found in fraternity, at once, the science of wealth and happiness. 'What shall I eat and drink, and wherewithal shall I be clothed?' stated as a problem beginning and ending in self, had been an anxious and an endless one. But when once it was conceived, not from the individual, but the fraternal standpoint, 'What shall we eat and drink, and wherewithal shall we be clothed?'—its difficulties vanished.

"Poverty with servitude had been the result, for the mass of humanity, of attempting to solve the problem of maintenance from the individual standpoint, but no sooner had the nation become the sole capitalist and employer than not alone did plenty replace poverty, but the last vestige of the serfdom of man to man disappeared from earth. Human slavery, so often vainly scotched, at last was killed. The means of subsistence no longer doled out by men to women, by employer to employed, by rich to poor, was distributed from a common stock as among children at the father's table. It was impossible for a man any longer to use his fellow-men as tools for his own profit. His esteem was the only sort of gain he could thenceforth make out of him. There was no more either arrogance or servility in the relations of human beings to one another. For the first time since the creation every man stood up straight before God. The fear of want and the lust of gain became extinct motives when abundance was assured to all and immoderate possessions made impossible of attainment. There were no more beggars nor almoners. Equity left charity without an occupation. The ten commandments became well nigh obsolete in a world where there was no temptation to theft, no occasion to lie either for fear or favor, no room for envy where all were equal, and little provocation to violence where men were disarmed of power to injure one another. Humanity's ancient dream of liberty, equality, fraternity, mocked by so many ages, at last was realized.

"As in the old society the generous, the just, the tender-hearted had been placed at a disadvantage by the possession of those qualities; so in the new society the cold-hearted, the greedy, and self-seeking found themselves out of joint with the world. Now that the conditions of life for the first time ceased to operate as a forcing process to develop the brutal qualities of human nature, and the premium which had heretofore encouraged selfishness was not only removed, but placed upon unselfishness, it was for the first time possible to see what unperverted human nature really was like. The depraved tendencies, which had previously overgrown and obscured the better to so large an extent, now withered like cellar fungi in the open air, and the nobler qualities showed a sudden luxuriance which turned cynics into panegyrists and for the first time in human history tempted mankind to fall in love with itself. Soon was fully revealed, what the divines and philosophers of the old world never would have believed, that human nature in its essential qualities is good, not bad, that men by their natural intention and structure are generous, not selfish, pitiful, not cruel, sympathetic, not arrogant, godlike in aspirations, instinct with divinest impulses of tenderness and self-sacrifice, images of God indeed, not the travesties upon Him they had seemed. The constant pressure, through numberless generations, of conditions of life which might have perverted angels, had not been able to essentially alter the natural nobility of the stock, and these conditions once removed, like a bent tree, it had sprung back to its normal uprightness.

"To put the whole matter in the nutshell of a parable, let me compare humanity in the olden time to a rosebush planted in a swamp, watered with black bog-water, breathing miasmatic fogs by day, and chilled with poison dews at night. Innumerable generations of gardeners had done their best to make it bloom, but beyond an occasional half-opened bud with a worm at the heart, their efforts had been unsuccessful. Many, indeed, claimed that the bush was no rosebush at all, but a noxious shrub, fit only to be uprooted and burned. The gardeners, for the most part, however, held that the bush belonged to the rose family, but had some ineradicable taint about it, which prevented the buds from coming out, and accounted for its generally sickly condition. There were a few, indeed, who maintained that the stock was good enough, that the trouble was in the bog, and that under more favorable conditions the plant might be expected to do better. But these persons were not regular gardeners, and being condemned by the latter as mere theorists and day dreamers, were, for the most part, so regarded by the people. Moreover, urged some eminent moral philosophers, even conceding for the sake of the argument that the bush might possibly do better elsewhere, it was a more valuable discipline for the buds to try to bloom in a bog than it would be under more favorable conditions. The buds that succeeded in opening might indeed be very rare, and the flowers pale and scentless, but they represented far more moral effort than if they had bloomed spontaneously in a garden.

"The regular gardeners and the moral philosophers had their way. The bush remained rooted in the bog, and the old course of treatment went on. Continually new varieties of forcing mixtures were applied to the roots, and more recipes than could be numbered, each declared by its advocates the best and only suitable preparation, were used to kill the vermin and remove the mildew. This went on a very long time. Occasionally some one claimed to observe a slight improvement in the appearance of the bush, but there were quite as many who declared that it did not look so well as it used to. On the whole there could not be said to be any marked change. Finally, during a period of general despondency as to the prospects of the bush where it was, the idea of transplanting it was again mooted, and this time found favor. 'Let us try it,' was the general voice. 'Perhaps it may thrive better elsewhere, and here it is certainly doubtful if it be worth cultivating longer.' So it came about that the rosebush of humanity was transplanted, and set in sweet, warm, dry earth, where the sun bathed it, the stars wooed it, and the south wind caressed it. Then it appeared that it was indeed a rosebush. The vermin and the mildew disappeared, and the bush was covered with most beautiful red roses, whose fragrance filled the world.

"It is a pledge of the destiny appointed for us that the Creator has set in our hearts an infinite standard of achievement, judged by which our past attainments seem always insignificant, and the goal never nearer. Had our forefathers conceived a state of society in which men should live together like brethren dwelling in unity, without strifes or envyings, violence or overreaching, and where, at the price of a degree of labor not greater than health demands, in their chosen occupations, they should be wholly freed from care for the morrow and left with no more concern for their livelihood than trees which are watered by unfailing streams,—had they conceived such a condition, I say, it would have seemed to them nothing less than paradise. They would have confounded it with their idea of heaven, nor dreamed that there could possibly lie further beyond anything to be desired or striven for.

"But how is it with us who stand on this height which they gazed up to? Already we have well nigh forgotten, except when it is especially called to our minds by some occasion like the present, that it was not always with men as it is now. It is a strain on our imaginations to conceive the social arrangements of our immediate ancestors. We find them grotesque. The solution of the problem of physical maintenance so as to banish care and crime, so far from seeming to us an ultimate attainment, appears but as a preliminary to anything like real human progress. We have but relieved ourselves of an impertinent and needless harassment which hindered our ancestor from undertaking the real ends of existence. We are merely stripped for the race; no more. We are like a child which has just learned to stand upright and to walk. It is a great event, from the child's point of view, when he first walks. Perhaps he fancies that there can be little beyond that achievement, but a year later he has forgotten that he could not always walk. His horizon did but widen when he rose, and enlarge as he moved. A great event indeed, in one sense, was his first step, but only as a beginning, not as the end. His true career was but then first entered on. The enfranchisement of humanity in the last century, from mental and physical absorption in working and scheming for the mere bodily necessities, may be regarded as a species of second birth of the race, without which its first birth to an existence that was but a burden would forever have remained unjustified, but whereby it is now abundantly vindicated. Since then, humanity has entered on a new phase of spiritual development, an evolution of higher faculties, the very existence of which in human nature our ancestors scarcely suspected. In place of the dreary hopelessness of the nineteenth century, its profound pessimism as to the future of humanity, the animating idea of the present age is an enthusiastic conception of the opportunities of our earthly existence, and the unbounded possibilities of human nature. The betterment of mankind from generation to generation, physically, mentally, morally, is recognized as the one great object supremely worthy of effort and of sacrifice. We believe the race for the first time to have entered on the realization of God's ideal of it, and each generation must now be a step upward.

"Do you ask what we look for when unnumbered generations shall have passed away? I answer, the way stretches far before us, but the end is lost in light. For twofold is the return of man to God 'who is our home,' the return of the individual by the way of death, and the return of the race by the fulfillment of the evolution, when the divine secret hidden in the germ shall be perfectly unfolded. With a tear for the dark past, turn we then to the dazzling future, and, veiling our eyes, press forward. The long and weary winter of the race is ended. Its summer has begun. Humanity has burst the chrysalis. The heavens are before it."

Chapter 27

I never could tell just why, but Sunday afternoon during my old life had been a time when I was peculiarly subject to melancholy, when the color unaccountably faded out of all the aspects of life, and everything appeared pathetically uninteresting. The hours, which in general were wont to bear me easily on their wings, lost the power of flight, and toward the close of the day, drooping quite to earth, had fairly to be dragged along by main strength. Perhaps it was partly owing to the established association of ideas that, despite the utter change in my circumstances, I fell into a state of profound depression on the afternoon of this my first Sunday in the twentieth century.

It was not, however, on the present occasion a depression without specific cause, the mere vague melancholy I have spoken of, but a sentiment suggested and certainly quite justified by my position. The sermon of Mr. Barton, with its constant implication of the vast moral gap between the century to which I belonged and that in which I found myself, had had an effect strongly to accentuate my sense of loneliness in it. Considerately and philosophically as he had spoken, his words could scarcely have failed to leave upon my mind a strong impression of the mingled pity, curiosity, and aversion which I, as a representative of an abhorred epoch, must excite in all around me.

The extraordinary kindness with which I had been treated by Dr. Leete and his family, and especially the goodness of Edith, had hitherto prevented my fully realizing that their real sentiment toward me must necessarily be that of the whole generation to which they belonged. The recognition of this, as regarded Dr. Leete and his amiable wife, however painful, I might have endured, but the conviction that Edith must share their feeling was more than I could bear.

The crushing effect with which this belated perception of a fact so obvious came to me opened my eyes fully to something which perhaps the reader has already suspected,—I loved Edith.

Was it strange that I did? The affecting occasion on which our intimacy had begun, when her hands had drawn me out of the whirlpool of madness; the fact that her sympathy was the vital breath which had set me up in this new life and enabled me to support it; my habit of looking to her as the mediator between me and the world around in a sense that even her father was not,—these were circumstances that had predetermined a result which her remarkable loveliness of person and disposition would alone have accounted for. It was quite inevitable that she should have come to seem to me, in a sense quite different from the usual experience of lovers, the only woman in this world. Now that I had become suddenly sensible of the fatuity of the hopes I had begun to cherish, I suffered not merely what another lover might, but in addition a desolate loneliness, an utter forlornness, such as no other lover, however unhappy, could have felt.

My hosts evidently saw that I was depressed in spirits, and did their best to divert me. Edith especially, I could see, was distressed for me, but according to the usual perversity of lovers, having once been so mad as to dream of receiving something more from her, there was no longer any virtue for me in a kindness that I knew was only sympathy.

Toward nightfall, after secluding myself in my room most of the afternoon, I went into the garden to walk about. The day was overcast, with an autumnal flavor in the warm, still air. Finding myself near the excavation, I entered the subterranean chamber and sat down there. "This," I muttered to myself, "is the only home I have. Let me stay here, and not go forth any more." Seeking aid from the familiar surroundings, I endeavored to find a sad sort of consolation in reviving the past and summoning up the forms and faces that were about me in my former life. It was in vain. There was no longer any life in them. For nearly one hundred years the stars had been looking down on Edith Bartlett's grave, and the graves of all my generation.

The past was dead, crushed beneath a century's weight, and from the present I was shut out. There was no place for me anywhere. I was neither dead nor properly alive.

"Forgive me for following you."

I looked up. Edith stood in the door of the subterranean room, regarding me smilingly, but with eyes full of sympathetic distress.

"Send me away if I am intruding on you," she said; "but we saw that you were out of spirits, and you know you promised to let me know if that were so. You have not kept your word."

I rose and came to the door, trying to smile, but making, I fancy, rather sorry work of it, for the sight of her loveliness brought home to me the more poignantly the cause of my wretchedness.

"I was feeling a little lonely, that is all," I said. "Has it never occurred to you that my position is so much more utterly alone than any human being's ever was before that a new word is really needed to describe it?"

"Oh, you must not talk that way—you must not let yourself feel that way—you must not!" she exclaimed, with moistened eyes. "Are we not your friends? It is your own fault if you will not let us be. You need not be lonely."

"You are good to me beyond my power of understanding," I said, "but don't you suppose that I know it is pity merely, sweet pity, but pity only. I should be a fool not to know that I cannot seem to you as other men of your own generation do, but as some strange uncanny being, a stranded creature of an unknown sea, whose forlornness touches your compassion despite its grotesqueness. I have been so foolish, you were so kind, as to almost forget that this must needs be so, and to fancy I might in time become naturalized, as we used to say, in this age, so as to feel like one of you and to seem to you like the other men about you. But Mr. Barton's sermon taught me how vain such a fancy is, how great the gulf between us must seem to you."

"Oh that miserable sermon!" she exclaimed, fairly crying now in her sympathy, "I wanted you not to hear it. What does he know of you? He has read in old musty books about your times, that is all. What do you care about him, to let yourself be vexed by anything he said? Isn't it anything to you, that we who know you feel differently? Don't you care more about what we think of you than what he does who never saw you? Oh, Mr. West! you don't know, you can't think, how it makes me feel to see you so forlorn. I can't have it so. What can I say to you? How can I convince you how different our feeling for you is from what you think?"

As before, in that other crisis of my fate when she had come to me, she extended her hands toward me in a gesture of helpfulness, and, as then, I caught and held them in my own; her bosom heaved with strong emotion, and little tremors in the fingers which I clasped emphasized the depth of her feeling. In her face, pity contended in a sort of divine spite against the obstacles which reduced it to impotence. Womanly compassion surely never wore a guise more lovely.

Such beauty and such goodness quite melted me, and it seemed that the only fitting response I could make was to tell her just the truth. Of course I had not a spark of hope, but on the other hand I had no fear that she would be angry. She was too pitiful for that. So I said presently, "It is very ungrateful in me not to be satisfied with such kindness as you have shown me, and are showing me now. But are you so blind as not to see why they are not enough to make me happy? Don't you see that it is because I have been mad enough to love you?"

At my last words she blushed deeply and her eyes fell before mine, but she made no effort to withdraw her hands from my clasp. For some moments she stood so, panting a little. Then blushing deeper than ever, but with a dazzling smile, she looked up.

"Are you sure it is not you who are blind?" she said.

That was all, but it was enough, for it told me that, unaccountable, incredible as it was, this radiant daughter of a golden age had bestowed upon me not alone her pity, but her love. Still, I half believed I must be under some blissful hallucination even as I clasped her in my arms. "If I am beside myself," I cried, "let me remain so."

"It is I whom you must think beside myself," she panted, escaping from my arms when I had barely tasted the sweetness of her lips. "Oh! oh! what must you think of me almost to throw myself in the arms of one I have known but a week? I did not mean that you should find it out so soon, but I was so sorry for you I forgot what I was saying. No, no; you must not touch me again till you know who I am. After that, sir, you shall apologize to me very humbly for thinking, as I know you do, that I have been over quick to fall in love with you. After you know who I am, you will be bound to confess that it was nothing less than my duty to fall in love with you at first sight, and that no girl of proper feeling in my place could do otherwise."

As may be supposed, I would have been quite content to waive explanations, but Edith was resolute that there should be no more kisses until she had been vindicated from all suspicion of precipitancy in the bestowal of her affections, and I was fain to follow the lovely enigma into the house. Having come where her mother was, she blushingly whispered something in her ear and ran away, leaving us together.

It then appeared that, strange as my experience had been, I was now first to know what was perhaps its strangest feature. From Mrs. Leete I learned that Edith was the great-granddaughter of no other than my lost love, Edith Bartlett. After mourning me for fourteen years, she had made a marriage of esteem, and left a son who had been Mrs. Leete's father. Mrs. Leete had never seen her grandmother, but had heard much of her, and, when her daughter was born, gave her the name of Edith. This fact might have tended to increase the interest which the girl took, as she grew up, in all that concerned her ancestress, and especially the tragic story of the supposed death of the lover, whose wife she expected to be, in the conflagration of his house. It was a tale well calculated to touch the sympathy of a romantic girl, and the fact that the blood of the unfortunate heroine was in her own veins naturally heightened Edith's interest in it. A portrait of Edith Bartlett and some of her papers, including a packet of my own letters, were among the family heirlooms. The picture represented a very beautiful young woman about whom it was easy to imagine all manner of tender and romantic things. My letters gave Edith some material for forming a distinct idea of my personality, and both together sufficed to make the sad old story very real to her. She used to tell her parents, half jestingly, that she would never marry till she found a lover like Julian West, and there were none such nowadays.

Now all this, of course, was merely the daydreaming of a girl whose mind had never been taken up by a love affair of her own, and would have had no serious consequence but for the discovery that morning of the buried vault in her father's garden and the revelation of the identity of its inmate. For when the apparently lifeless form had been borne into the house, the face in the locket found upon the breast was instantly recognized as that of Edith Bartlett, and by that fact, taken in connection with the other circumstances, they knew that I was no other than Julian West. Even had there been no thought, as at first there was not, of my resuscitation, Mrs. Leete said she believed that this event would have affected her daughter in a critical and life-long manner. The presumption of some subtle ordering of destiny, involving her fate with mine, would under all circumstances have possessed an irresistible fascination for almost any woman.

Whether when I came back to life a few hours afterward, and from the first seemed to turn to her with a peculiar dependence and to find a special solace in her company, she had been too quick in giving her love at the first sign of mine, I could now, her mother said, judge for myself. If I thought so, I must remember that this, after all, was the twentieth and not the nineteenth century, and love was, no doubt, now quicker in growth, as well as franker in utterance than then.

From Mrs. Leete I went to Edith. When I found her, it was first of all to take her by both hands and stand a long time in rapt contemplation of her face. As I gazed, the memory of that other Edith, which had been affected as with a benumbing shock by the tremendous experience that had parted us, revived, and my heart was dissolved with tender and pitiful emotions, but also very blissful ones. For she who brought to me so poignantly the sense of my loss was to make that loss good. It was as if from her eyes Edith Bartlett looked into mine, and smiled consolation to me. My fate was not alone the strangest, but the most fortunate that ever befell a man. A double miracle had been wrought for me. I had not been stranded upon the shore of this strange world to find myself alone and companionless. My love, whom I had dreamed lost, had been reembodied for my consolation. When at last, in an ecstasy of gratitude and tenderness, I folded the lovely girl in my arms, the two Ediths were blended in my thought, nor have they ever since been clearly distinguished. I was not long in finding that on Edith's part there was a corresponding confusion of identities. Never, surely, was there between freshly united lovers a stranger talk than ours that afternoon. She seemed more anxious to have me speak of Edith Bartlett than of herself, of how I had loved her than how I loved herself, rewarding my fond words concerning another woman with tears and tender smiles and pressures of the hand.

"You must not love me too much for myself," she said. "I shall be very jealous for her. I shall not let you forget her. I am going to tell you something which you may think strange. Do you not believe that spirits sometimes come back to the world to fulfill some work that lay near their hearts? What if I were to tell you that I have sometimes thought that her spirit lives in me—that Edith Bartlett, not Edith Leete, is my real name. I cannot know it; of course none of us can know who we really are; but I can feel it. Can you wonder that I have such a feeling, seeing how my life was affected by her and by you, even before you came. So you see you need not trouble to love me at all, if only you are true to her. I shall not be likely to be jealous."

Dr. Leete had gone out that afternoon, and I did not have an interview with him till later. He was not, apparently, wholly unprepared for the intelligence I conveyed, and shook my hand heartily.

"Under any ordinary circumstances, Mr. West, I should say that this step had been taken on rather short acquaintance; but these are decidedly not ordinary circumstances. In fairness, perhaps I ought to tell you," he added smilingly, "that while I cheerfully consent to the proposed arrangement, you must not feel too much indebted to me, as I judge my consent is a mere formality. From the moment the secret of the locket was out, it had to be, I fancy. Why, bless me, if Edith had not been there to redeem her great-grandmother's pledge, I really apprehend that Mrs. Leete's loyalty to me would have suffered a severe strain."

That evening the garden was bathed in moonlight, and till midnight Edith and I wandered to and fro there, trying to grow accustomed to our happiness.

"What should I have done if you had not cared for me?" she exclaimed. "I was afraid you were not going to. What should I have done then, when I felt I was consecrated to you! As soon as you came back to life, I was as sure as if she had told me that I was to be to you what she could not be, but that could only be if you would let me. Oh, how I wanted to tell you that morning, when you felt so terribly strange among us, who I was, but dared not open my lips about that, or let father or mother——"

"That must have been what you would not let your father tell me!" I exclaimed, referring to the conversation I had overheard as I came out of my trance.

"Of course it was," Edith laughed. "Did you only just guess that? Father being only a man, thought that it would make you feel among friends to tell you who we were. He did not think of me at all. But mother knew what I meant, and so I had my way. I could never have looked you in the face if you had known who I was. It would have been forcing myself on you quite too boldly. I am afraid you think I did that to-day, as it was. I am sure I did not mean to, for I know girls were expected to hide their feelings in your day, and I was dreadfully afraid of shocking you. Ah me, how hard it must have been for them to have always had to conceal their love like a fault. Why did they think it such a shame to love any one till they had been given permission? It is so odd to think of waiting for permission to fall in love. Was it because men in those days were angry when girls loved them? That is not the way women would feel, I am sure, or men either, I think, now. I don't understand it at all. That will be one of the curious things about the women of those days that you will have to explain to me. I don't believe Edith Bartlett was so foolish as the others."

After sundry ineffectual attempts at parting, she finally insisted that we must say good night. I was about to imprint upon her lips the positively last kiss, when she said, with an indescribable archness:

"One thing troubles me. Are you sure that you quite forgive Edith Bartlett for marrying any one else? The books that have come down to us make out lovers of your time more jealous than fond, and that is what makes me ask. It would be a great relief to me if I could feel sure that you were not in the least jealous of my great-grandfather for marrying your sweetheart. May I tell my great-grandmother's picture when I go to my room that you quite forgive her for proving false to you?"

Will the reader believe it, this coquettish quip, whether the speaker herself had any idea of it or not, actually touched and with the touching cured a preposterous ache of something like jealousy which I had been vaguely conscious of ever since Mrs. Leete had told me of Edith Bartlett's marriage. Even while I had been holding Edith Bartlett's great-granddaughter in my arms, I had not, till this moment, so illogical are some of our feelings, distinctly realized that but for that marriage I could not have done so. The absurdity of this frame of mind could only be equalled by the abruptness with which it dissolved as Edith's roguish query cleared the fog from my perceptions. I laughed as I kissed her.

"You may assure her of my entire forgiveness," I said, "although if it had been any man but your great-grandfather whom she married, it would have been a very different matter."

On reaching my chamber that night I did not open the musical telephone that I might be lulled to sleep with soothing tunes, as had become my habit. For once my thoughts made better music than even twentieth century orchestras discourse, and it held me enchanted till well toward morning, when I fell asleep.

Chapter 28

"It's a little after the time you told me to wake you, sir. You did not come out of it as quick as common, sir."

The voice was the voice of my man Sawyer. I started bolt upright in bed and stared around. I was in my underground chamber. The mellow light of the lamp which always burned in the room when I occupied it illumined the familiar walls and furnishings. By my bedside, with the glass of sherry in his hand which Dr. Pillsbury prescribed on first rousing from a mesmeric sleep, by way of awakening the torpid physical functions, stood Sawyer.

"Better take this right off, sir," he said, as I stared blankly at him. "You look kind of flushed like, sir, and you need it."

I tossed off the liquor and began to realize what had happened to me. It was, of course, very plain. All that about the twentieth century had been a dream. I had but dreamed of that enlightened and care-free race of men and their ingeniously simple institutions, of the glorious new Boston with its domes and pinnacles, its gardens and fountains, and its universal reign of comfort. The amiable family which I had learned to know so well, my genial host and Mentor, Dr. Leete, his wife, and their daughter, the second and more beauteous Edith, my betrothed—these, too, had been but figments of a vision.

For a considerable time I remained in the attitude in which this conviction had come over me, sitting up in bed gazing at vacancy, absorbed in recalling the scenes and incidents of my fantastic experience. Sawyer, alarmed at my looks, was meanwhile anxiously inquiring what was the matter with me. Roused at length by his importunities to a recognition of my surroundings, I pulled myself together with an effort and assured the faithful fellow that I was all right. "I have had an extraordinary dream, that's all, Sawyer," I said, "a most-ex-traor-dinary dream."

I dressed in a mechanical way, feeling light-headed and oddly uncertain of myself, and sat down to the coffee and rolls which Sawyer was in the habit of providing for my refreshment before I left the house. The morning newspaper lay by the plate. I took it up, and my eye fell on the date, May 31, 1887. I had known, of course, from the moment I opened my eyes that my long and detailed experience in another century had been a dream, and yet it was startling to have it so conclusively demonstrated that the world was but a few hours older than when I had lain down to sleep.

Glancing at the table of contents at the head of the paper, which reviewed the news of the morning, I read the following summary:

FOREIGN AFFAIRS.—The impending war between France and Germany. The French Chambers asked for new military credits to meet Germany's increase of her army. Probability that all Europe will be involved in case of war.—Great suffering among the unemployed in London. They demand work. Monster demonstration to be made. The authorities uneasy.—Great strikes in Belgium. The government preparing to repress outbreaks. Shocking facts in regard to the employment of girls in Belgium coal mines.—Wholesale evictions in Ireland.

"HOME AFFAIRS.—The epidemic of fraud unchecked. Embezzlement of half a million in New York.—Misappropriation of a trust fund by executors. Orphans left penniless.—Clever system of thefts by a bank teller; $50,000 gone.—The coal barons decide to advance the price of coal and reduce production.—Speculators engineering a great wheat corner at Chicago.—A clique forcing up the price of coffee.—Enormous land-grabs of Western syndicates.—Revelations of shocking corruption among Chicago officials. Systematic bribery.—The trials of the Boodle aldermen to go on at New York.—Large failures of business houses. Fears of a business crisis.—A large grist of burglaries and larcenies.—A woman murdered in cold blood for her money at New Haven.—A householder shot by a burglar in this city last night.—A man shoots himself in Worcester because he could not get work. A large family left destitute.—An aged couple in New Jersey commit suicide rather than go to the poor-house.—Pitiable destitution among the women wage-workers in the great cities.—Startling growth of illiteracy in Massachusetts.—More insane asylums wanted.—Decoration Day addresses. Professor Brown's oration on the moral grandeur of nineteenth century civilization."

It was indeed the nineteenth century to which I had awaked; there could be no kind of doubt about that. Its complete microcosm this summary of the day's news had presented, even to that last unmistakable touch of fatuous self-complacency. Coming after such a damning indictment of the age as that one day's chronicle of world-wide bloodshed, greed, and tyranny, was a bit of cynicism worthy of Mephistopheles, and yet of all whose eyes it had met this morning I was, perhaps, the only one who perceived the cynicism, and but yesterday I should have perceived it no more than the others. That strange dream it was which had made all the difference. For I know not how long, I forgot my surroundings after this, and was again in fancy moving in that vivid dream-world, in that glorious city, with its homes of simple comfort and its gorgeous public palaces. Around me were again faces unmarred by arrogance or servility, by envy or greed, by anxious care or feverish ambition, and stately forms of men and women who had never known fear of a fellow man or depended on his favor, but always, in the words of that sermon which still rang in my ears, had "stood up straight before God."

With a profound sigh and a sense of irreparable loss, not the less poignant that it was a loss of what had never really been, I roused at last from my reverie, and soon after left the house.

A dozen times between my door and Washington Street I had to stop and pull myself together, such power had been in that vision of the Boston of the future to make the real Boston strange. The squalor and malodorousness of the town struck me, from the moment I stood upon the street, as facts I had never before observed. But yesterday, moreover, it had seemed quite a matter of course that some of my fellow-citizens should wear silks, and others rags, that some should look well fed, and others hungry. Now on the contrary the glaring disparities in the dress and condition of the men and women who brushed each other on the sidewalks shocked me at every step, and yet more the entire indifference which the prosperous showed to the plight of the unfortunate. Were these human beings, who could behold the wretchedness of their fellows without so much as a change of countenance? And yet, all the while, I knew well that it was I who had changed, and not my contemporaries. I had dreamed of a city whose people fared all alike as children of one family and were one another's keepers in all things.

Another feature of the real Boston, which assumed the extraordinary effect of strangeness that marks familiar things seen in a new light, was the prevalence of advertising. There had been no personal advertising in the Boston of the twentieth century, because there was no need of any, but here the walls of the buildings, the windows, the broadsides of the newspapers in every hand, the very pavements, everything in fact in sight, save the sky, were covered with the appeals of individuals who sought, under innumerable pretexts, to attract the contributions of others to their support. However the wording might vary, the tenor of all these appeals was the same:

"Help John Jones. Never mind the rest. They are frauds. I, John Jones, am the right one. Buy of me. Employ me. Visit me. Hear me, John Jones. Look at me. Make no mistake, John Jones is the man and nobody else. Let the rest starve, but for God's sake remember John Jones!"

Whether the pathos or the moral repulsiveness of the spectacle most impressed me, so suddenly become a stranger in my own city, I know not. Wretched men, I was moved to cry, who, because they will not learn to be helpers of one another, are doomed to be beggars of one another from the least to the greatest! This horrible babel of shameless self-assertion and mutual depreciation, this stunning clamor of conflicting boasts, appeals, and adjurations, this stupendous system of brazen beggary, what was it all but the necessity of a society in which the opportunity to serve the world according to his gifts, instead of being secured to every man as the first object of social organization, had to be fought for!

I reached Washington Street at the busiest point, and there I stood and laughed aloud, to the scandal of the passers-by. For my life I could not have helped it, with such a mad humor was I moved at sight of the interminable rows of stores on either side, up and down the street so far as I could see—scores of them, to make the spectacle more utterly preposterous, within a stone's throw devoted to selling the same sort of goods. Stores! stores! stores! miles of stores! ten thousand stores to distribute the goods needed by this one city, which in my dream had been supplied with all things from a single warehouse, as they were ordered through one great store in every quarter, where the buyer, without waste of time or labor, found under one roof the world's assortment in whatever line he desired. There the labor of distribution had been so slight as to add but a scarcely perceptible fraction to the cost of commodities to the user. The cost of production was virtually all he paid. But here the mere distribution of the goods, their handling alone, added a fourth, a third, a half and more, to the cost. All these ten thousand plants must be paid for, their rent, their staffs of superintendence, their platoons of salesmen, their ten thousand sets of accountants, jobbers, and business dependents, with all they spent in advertising themselves and fighting one another, and the consumers must do the paying. What a famous process for beggaring a nation!

Were these serious men I saw about me, or children, who did their business on such a plan? Could they be reasoning beings, who did not see the folly which, when the product is made and ready for use, wastes so much of it in getting it to the user? If people eat with a spoon that leaks half its contents between bowl and lip, are they not likely to go hungry?

I had passed through Washington Street thousands of times before and viewed the ways of those who sold merchandise, but my curiosity concerning them was as if I had never gone by their way before. I took wondering note of the show windows of the stores, filled with goods arranged with a wealth of pains and artistic device to attract the eye. I saw the throngs of ladies looking in, and the proprietors eagerly watching the effect of the bait. I went within and noted the hawk-eyed floor-walker watching for business, overlooking the clerks, keeping them up to their task of inducing the customers to buy, buy, buy, for money if they had it, for credit if they had it not, to buy what they wanted not, more than they wanted, what they could not afford. At times I momentarily lost the clue and was confused by the sight. Why this effort to induce people to buy? Surely that had nothing to do with the legitimate business of distributing products to those who needed them. Surely it was the sheerest waste to force upon people what they did not want, but what might be useful to another. The nation was so much the poorer for every such achievement. What were these clerks thinking of? Then I would remember that they were not acting as distributors like those in the store I had visited in the dream Boston. They were not serving the public interest, but their immediate personal interest, and it was nothing to them what the ultimate effect of their course on the general prosperity might be, if but they increased their own hoard, for these goods were their own, and the more they sold and the more they got for them, the greater their gain. The more wasteful the people were, the more articles they did not want which they could be induced to buy, the better for these sellers. To encourage prodigality was the express aim of the ten thousand stores of Boston.

Nor were these storekeepers and clerks a whit worse men than any others in Boston. They must earn a living and support their families, and how were they to find a trade to do it by which did not necessitate placing their individual interests before those of others and that of all? They could not be asked to starve while they waited for an order of things such as I had seen in my dream, in which the interest of each and that of all were identical. But, God in heaven! what wonder, under such a system as this about me—what wonder that the city was so shabby, and the people so meanly dressed, and so many of them ragged and hungry!

Some time after this it was that I drifted over into South Boston and found myself among the manufacturing establishments. I had been in this quarter of the city a hundred times before, just as I had been on Washington Street, but here, as well as there, I now first perceived the true significance of what I witnessed. Formerly I had taken pride in the fact that, by actual count, Boston had some four thousand independent manufacturing establishments; but in this very multiplicity and independence I recognized now the secret of the insignificant total product of their industry.

If Washington Street had been like a lane in Bedlam, this was a spectacle as much more melancholy as production is a more vital function than distribution. For not only were these four thousand establishments not working in concert, and for that reason alone operating at prodigious disadvantage, but, as if this did not involve a sufficiently disastrous loss of power, they were using their utmost skill to frustrate one another's effort, praying by night and working by day for the destruction of one another's enterprises.

The roar and rattle of wheels and hammers resounding from every side was not the hum of a peaceful industry, but the clangor of swords wielded by foemen. These mills and shops were so many forts, each under its own flag, its guns trained on the mills and shops about it, and its sappers busy below, undermining them.

Within each one of these forts the strictest organization of industry was insisted on; the separate gangs worked under a single central authority. No interference and no duplicating of work were permitted. Each had his allotted task, and none were idle. By what hiatus in the logical faculty, by what lost link of reasoning, account, then, for the failure to recognize the necessity of applying the same principle to the organization of the national industries as a whole, to see that if lack of organization could impair the efficiency of a shop, it must have effects as much more disastrous in disabling the industries of the nation at large as the latter are vaster in volume and more complex in the relationship of their parts.

People would be prompt enough to ridicule an army in which there were neither companies, battalions, regiments, brigades, divisions, or army corps—no unit of organization, in fact, larger than the corporal's squad, with no officer higher than a corporal, and all the corporals equal in authority. And yet just such an army were the manufacturing industries of nineteenth century

Boston, an army of four thousand independent squads led by four thousand independent corporals, each with a separate plan of campaign.

Knots of idle men were to be seen here and there on every side, some idle because they could find no work at any price, others because they could not get what they thought a fair price. I accosted some of the latter, and they told me their grievances. It was very little comfort I could give them. "I am sorry for you," I said. "You get little enough, certainly, and yet the wonder to me is, not that industries conducted as these are do not pay you living wages, but that they are able to pay you any wages at all."

Making my way back again after this to the peninsular city, toward three o'clock I stood on State Street, staring, as if I had never seen them before, at the banks and brokers' offices, and other financial institutions, of which there had been in the State Street of my vision no vestige. Business men, confidential clerks, and errand boys were thronging in and out of the banks, for it wanted but a few minutes of the closing hour. Opposite me was the bank where I did business, and presently I crossed the street, and, going in with the crowd, stood in a recess of the wall looking on at the army of clerks handling money, and the cues of depositors at the tellers' windows. An old gentleman whom I knew, a director of the bank, passing me and observing my contemplative attitude, stopped a moment.

"Interesting sight, isn't it, Mr. West," he said. "Wonderful piece of mechanism; I find it so myself. I like sometimes to stand and look on at it just as you are doing. It's a poem, sir, a poem, that's what I call it. Did you ever think, Mr. West, that the bank is the heart of the business system? From it and to it, in endless flux and reflux, the life blood goes. It is flowing in now. It will flow out again in the morning"; and pleased with his little conceit, the old man passed on smiling.

Yesterday I should have considered the simile apt enough, but since then I had visited a world incomparably more affluent than this, in which money was unknown and without conceivable use. I had learned that it had a use in the world around me only because the work of producing the nation's livelihood, instead of being regarded as the most strictly public and common of all concerns, and as such conducted by the nation, was abandoned to the hap-hazard efforts of individuals. This original mistake necessitated endless exchanges to bring about any sort of general distribution of products. These exchanges money effected—how equitably, might be seen in a walk from the tenement house districts to the Back Bay—at the cost of an army of men taken from productive labor to manage it, with constant ruinous breakdowns of its machinery, and a generally debauching influence on mankind which had justified its description, from ancient time, as the "root of all evil."

Alas for the poor old bank director with his poem! He had mistaken the throbbing of an abscess for the beating of the heart. What he called "a wonderful piece of mechanism" was an imperfect device to remedy an unnecessary defect, the clumsy crutch of a self-made cripple.

After the banks had closed I wandered aimlessly about the business quarter for an hour or two, and later sat a while on one of the benches of the Common, finding an interest merely in watching the throngs that passed, such as one has in studying the populace of a foreign city, so strange since yesterday had my fellow citizens and their ways become to me. For thirty years I had lived among them, and yet I seemed to have never noted before how drawn and anxious were their faces, of the rich as of the poor, the refined, acute faces of the educated as well as the dull masks of the ignorant. And well it might be so, for I saw now, as never before I had seen so plainly, that each as he walked constantly turned to catch the whispers of a spectre at his ear, the spectre of Uncertainty. "Do your work never so well," the spectre was whispering—"rise early and toil till late, rob cunningly or serve faithfully, you shall never know security. Rich you may be now and still come to poverty at last. Leave never so much wealth to your children, you cannot buy the assurance that your son may not be the servant of your servant, or that your daughter will not have to sell herself for bread."

A man passing by thrust an advertising card in my hand, which set forth the merits of some new scheme of life insurance. The incident reminded me of the only device, pathetic in its admission of the universal need it so poorly supplied, which offered these tired and hunted men and women even a partial protection from uncertainty. By this means, those already well-to-do, I remembered, might purchase a precarious confidence that after their death their loved ones would not, for a while at least, be trampled under the feet of men. But this was all, and this was only for those who could pay well for it. What idea was possible to these wretched dwellers in the land of Ishmael, where every man's hand was against each and the hand of each against every other, of true life insurance as I had seen it among the people of that dream land, each of whom, by virtue merely of his membership in the national family, was guaranteed against need of any sort, by a policy underwritten by one hundred million fellow countrymen.

Some time after this it was that I recall a glimpse of myself standing on the steps of a building on Tremont Street, looking at a military parade. A regiment was passing. It was the first sight in that dreary day which had inspired me with any other emotions than wondering pity and amazement. Here at last were order and reason, an exhibition of what intelligent cooperation can accomplish. The people who stood looking on with kindling faces,—could it be that the sight had for them no more than but a spectacular interest? Could they fail to see that it was their perfect concert of action, their organization under one control, which made these men the tremendous engine they were, able to vanquish a mob ten times as numerous? Seeing this so plainly, could they fail to compare the scientific manner in which the nation went to war with the unscientific manner in which it went to work? Would they not query since what time the killing of men had been a task so much more important than feeding and clothing them, that a trained army should be deemed alone adequate to the former, while the latter was left to a mob?

It was now toward nightfall, and the streets were thronged with the workers from the stores, the shops, and mills. Carried along with the stronger part of the current, I found myself, as it began to grow dark, in the midst of a scene of squalor and human degradation such as only the South Cove tenement district could present. I had seen the mad wasting of human labor; here I saw in direst shape the want that waste had bred.

From the black doorways and windows of the rookeries on every side came gusts of fetid air. The streets and alleys reeked with the effluvia of a slave ship's between-decks. As I passed I had glimpses within of pale babies gasping out their lives amid sultry stenches, of hopeless-faced women deformed by hardship, retaining of womanhood no trait save weakness, while from the windows leered girls with brows of brass. Like the starving bands of mongrel curs that infest the streets of Moslem towns, swarms of half-clad brutalized children filled the air with shrieks and curses as they fought and tumbled among the garbage that littered the court-yards.

There was nothing in all this that was new to me. Often had I passed through this part of the city and witnessed its sights with feelings of disgust mingled with a certain philosophical wonder at the extremities mortals will endure and still cling to life. But not alone as regarded the economical follies of this age, but equally as touched its moral abominations, scales had fallen from my eyes since that vision of another century. No more did I look upon the woful dwellers in this Inferno with a callous curiosity as creatures scarcely human. I saw in them my brothers and sisters, my parents, my children, flesh of my flesh, blood of my blood. The festering mass of human wretchedness about me offended not now my senses merely, but pierced my heart like a knife, so that I could not repress sighs and groans. I not only saw but felt in my body all that I saw.

Presently, too, as I observed the wretched beings about me more closely, I perceived that they were all quite dead. Their bodies were so many living sepulchres. On each brutal brow was plainly written the hic jacet of a soul dead within.

As I looked, horror struck, from one death's head to another, I was affected by a singular hallucination. Like a wavering translucent spirit face superimposed upon each of these brutish masks I saw the ideal, the possible face that would have been the actual if mind and soul had lived. It was not till I was aware of these ghostly faces, and of the reproach that could not be gainsaid which was in their eyes, that the full piteousness of the ruin that had been wrought was revealed to me. I was moved with contrition as with a strong agony, for I had been one of those who had endured that these things should be. I had been one of those who, well knowing that they were, had not desired to hear or be compelled to think much of them, but had gone on as if they were not, seeking my own pleasure and profit. Therefore now I found upon my garments the blood of this great multitude of strangled souls of my brothers. The voice of their blood cried out against me from the ground. Every stone of the reeking pavements, every brick of the pestilential rookeries, found a tongue and called after me as I fled: What hast thou done with thy brother Abel?

I have no clear recollection of anything after this till I found myself standing on the carved stone steps of the magnificent home of my betrothed in Commonwealth Avenue. Amid the tumult of my thoughts that day, I had scarcely once thought of her, but now obeying some unconscious impulse my feet had found the familiar way to her door. I was told that the family were at dinner, but word was sent out that I should join them at table. Besides the family, I found several guests present, all known to me. The table glittered with plate and costly china. The ladies were sumptuously dressed and wore the jewels of queens. The scene was one of costly elegance and lavish luxury. The company was in excellent spirits, and there was plentiful laughter and a running fire of jests.

To me it was as if, in wandering through the place of doom, my blood turned to tears by its sights, and my spirit attuned to sorrow, pity, and despair, I had happened in some glade upon a merry party of roisterers. I sat in silence until Edith began to rally me upon my sombre looks, What ailed me? The others presently joined in the playful assault, and I became a target for quips and jests. Where had I been, and what had I seen to make such a dull fellow of me?

"I have been in Golgotha," at last I answered. "I have seen Humanity hanging on a cross! Do none of you know what sights the sun and stars look down on in this city, that you can think and talk of anything else? Do you not know that close to your doors a great multitude of men and women, flesh of your flesh, live lives that are one agony from birth to death? Listen! their dwellings are so near that if you hush your laughter you will hear their grievous voices, the piteous crying of the little ones that suckle poverty, the hoarse curses of men sodden in misery turned half-way back to brutes, the chaffering of an army of women selling themselves for bread. With what have you stopped your ears that you do not hear these doleful sounds? For me, I can hear nothing else."

Silence followed my words. A passion of pity had shaken me as I spoke, but when I looked around upon the company, I saw that, far from being stirred as I was, their faces expressed a cold and hard astonishment, mingled in Edith's with extreme mortification, in her father's with anger. The ladies were exchanging scandalized looks, while one of the gentlemen had put up his eyeglass and was studying me with an air of scientific curiosity. When I saw that things which were to me so intolerable moved them not at all, that words that melted my heart to speak had only offended them with the speaker, I was at first stunned and then overcome with a desperate sickness and faintness at the heart. What hope was there for the wretched, for the world, if thoughtful men and tender women were not moved by things like these! Then I bethought myself that it must be because I had not spoken aright. No doubt I had put the case badly. They were angry because they thought I was berating them, when God knew I was merely thinking of the horror of the fact without any attempt to assign the responsibility for it.

I restrained my passion, and tried to speak calmly and logically that I might correct this impression. I told them that I had not meant to accuse them, as if they, or the rich in general, were responsible for the misery of the world. True indeed it was, that the superfluity which they wasted would, otherwise bestowed, relieve much bitter suffering. These costly viands, these rich wines, these gorgeous fabrics and glistening jewels represented the ransom of many lives. They were verily not without the guiltiness of those who waste in a land stricken with famine. Nevertheless, all the waste of all the rich, were it saved, would go but a little way to cure the poverty of the world. There was so little to divide that even if the rich went share and share with the poor, there would be but a common fare of crusts, albeit made very sweet then by brotherly love.

The folly of men, not their hard-heartedness, was the great cause of the world's poverty. It was not the crime of man, nor of any class of men, that made the race so miserable, but a hideous, ghastly mistake, a colossal world-darkening blunder. And then I showed them how four fifths of the labor of men was utterly wasted by the mutual warfare, the lack of organization and concert among the workers. Seeking to make the matter very plain, I instanced the case of arid lands where the soil yielded the means of life only by careful use of the watercourses for irrigation. I showed how in such countries it was counted the most important function of the government to see that the water was not wasted by the selfishness or ignorance of individuals, since otherwise there would be famine. To this end its use was strictly regulated and systematized, and individuals of their mere caprice were not permitted to dam it or divert it, or in any way to tamper with it.

The labor of men, I explained, was the fertilizing stream which alone rendered earth habitable. It was but a scanty stream at best, and its use required to be regulated by a system which expended every drop to the best advantage, if the world were to be supported in abundance. But how far from any system was the actual practice! Every man wasted the precious fluid as he wished, animated only by the equal motives of saving his own crop and spoiling his neighbor's, that his might sell the better. What with greed and what with spite some fields were flooded while others were parched, and half the water ran wholly to waste. In such a land, though a few by strength or cunning might win the means of luxury, the lot of the great mass must be poverty, and of the weak and ignorant bitter want and perennial famine.

Let but the famine-stricken nation assume the function it had neglected, and regulate for the common good the course of the life-giving stream, and the earth would bloom like one garden, and none of its children lack any good thing. I described the physical felicity, mental enlightenment, and moral elevation which would then attend the lives of all men. With fervency I spoke of that new world, blessed with plenty, purified by justice and sweetened by brotherly kindness, the world of which I had indeed but dreamed, but which might so easily be made real. But when I had expected now surely the faces around me to light up with emotions akin to mine, they grew ever more dark, angry, and scornful. Instead of enthusiasm, the ladies showed only aversion and dread, while the men interrupted me with shouts of reprobation and contempt. "Madman!" "Pestilent fellow!" "Fanatic!" "Enemy of society!" were some of their cries, and the one who had before taken his eyeglass to me exclaimed, "He says we are to have no more poor. Ha! ha!"

"Put the fellow out!" exclaimed the father of my betrothed, and at the signal the men sprang from their chairs and advanced upon me.

It seemed to me that my heart would burst with the anguish of finding that what was to me so plain and so all important was to them meaningless, and that I was powerless to make it other. So hot had been my heart that I had thought to melt an iceberg with its glow, only to find at last the overmastering chill seizing my own vitals. It was not enmity that I felt toward them as they thronged me, but pity only, for them and for the world.

Although despairing, I could not give over. Still I strove with them. Tears poured from my eyes. In my vehemence I became inarticulate. I panted, I sobbed, I groaned, and immediately afterward found myself sitting upright in bed in my room in Dr. Leete's house, and the morning sun shining through the open window into my eyes. I was gasping. The tears were streaming down my face, and I quivered in every nerve.

As with an escaped convict who dreams that he has been recaptured and brought back to his dark and reeking dungeon, and opens his eyes to see the heaven's vault spread above him, so it was with me, as I realized that my return to the nineteenth century had been the dream, and my presence in the twentieth was the reality.

The cruel sights which I had witnessed in my vision, and could so well confirm from the experience of my former life, though they had, alas! once been, and must in the retrospect to the end of time move the compassionate to tears, were, God be thanked, forever gone by. Long ago oppressor and oppressed, prophet and scorner, had been dust. For generations, rich and poor had been forgotten words.

But in that moment, while yet I mused with unspeakable thankfulness upon the greatness of the world's salvation and my privilege in beholding it, there suddenly pierced me like a knife a pang of shame, remorse, and wondering self-reproach, that bowed my head upon my breast and made me wish the grave had hid me with my fellows from the sun. For I had been a man of that former time. What had I done to help on the deliverance whereat I now presumed to rejoice? I who had lived in those cruel, insensate days, what had I done to bring them to an end? I had been every whit as indifferent to the wretchedness of my brothers, as cynically incredulous of better things, as besotted a worshiper of Chaos and Old Night, as any of my fellows. So far as my personal influence went, it had been exerted rather to hinder than to help forward the enfranchisement of the race which was even then preparing. What right had I to hail a salvation which reproached me, to rejoice in a day whose dawning I had mocked?

"Better for you, better for you," a voice within me rang, "had this evil dream been the reality, and this fair reality the dream; better your part pleading for crucified humanity with a scoffing generation, than here, drinking of wells you digged not, and eating of trees whose husbandmen you stoned"; and my spirit answered, "Better, truly."

When at length I raised my bowed head and looked forth from the window, Edith, fresh as the morning, had come into the garden and was gathering flowers. I hastened to descend to her. Kneeling before her, with my face in the dust, I confessed with tears how little was my worth to breathe the air of this golden century, and how infinitely less to wear upon my breast its consummate flower. Fortunate is he who, with a case so desperate as mine, finds a judge so merciful.

EQUALITY

Preface.

Looking Backward was a small book, and I was not able to get into it all I wished to say on the subject. Since it was published what was left out of it has loomed up as so much more important than what it contained that I have been constrained to write another book. I have taken the date of Looking Backward, the year 2000, as that of Equality, and have utilized the framework of the former story as a starting point for this which I now offer. In order that those who have not read Looking Backward may be at no disadvantage, an outline of the essential features of that story is subjoined:

In the year 1887 Julian West was a rich young man living in Boston. He was soon to be married to a young lady of wealthy family named Edith Bartlett, and meanwhile lived alone with his man-servant Sawyer in the family mansion. Being a sufferer from insomnia, he had caused a chamber to be built of stone beneath the foundation of the house, which he used for a sleeping room. When even the silence and seclusion of this retreat failed to bring slumber, he sometimes called in a professional mesmerizer to put him into a hypnotic sleep, from which Sawyer knew how to arouse him at a fixed time. This habit, as well as the existence of the underground chamber, were secrets known only to Sawyer and the hypnotist who rendered his services. On the night of May 30, 1887, West sent for the latter, and was put to sleep as usual. The hypnotist had previously informed his patron that he was intending to leave the city permanently the same evening, and referred him to other practitioners. That night the house of Julian West took fire and was wholly destroyed. Remains identified as those of Sawyer were found and, though no vestige of West appeared, it was assumed that he of course had also perished.

One hundred and thirteen years later, in September, A. D. 2000, Dr. Leete, a physician of Boston, on the retired list, was conducting excavations in his garden for the foundations of a private laboratory, when the workers came on a mass of masonry covered with ashes and charcoal. On opening it, a vault, luxuriously fitted up in the style of a nineteenth-century bedchamber, was found, and on the bed the body of a young man looking as if he had just lain down to sleep. Although great trees had been growing above the vault, the unaccountable preservation of the youth's body tempted Dr. Leete to attempt resuscitation, and to his own astonishment his efforts proved successful. The sleeper returned to life, and after a short time to the full vigor of youth which his appearance had indicated. His shock on learning what had befallen him was so great as to have endangered his sanity but for the medical skill of Dr. Leete, and the not less sympathetic ministrations of the other members of the household, the doctor's wife, and Edith the beautiful daughter. Presently, however, the young man forgot to wonder at what had happened to himself in his astonishment on learning of the social transformation through which the world had passed while he lay sleeping. Step by step, almost as to a child, his hosts explained to him, who had known no other way of living except the struggle for existence, what were the simple principles of national co-operation for the promotion of the general welfare on which the new civilization rested. He learned that there were no longer any who were or could be richer or poorer than others, but that all were economic equals. He learned that no one any longer worked for another, either by compulsion or for hire, but that all alike were in the service of the nation working for the common fund, which all equally shared, and that even necessary personal attendance, as of the physician, was rendered as to the state like that of the military surgeon. All these wonders, it was explained, had very simply come about as the results of replacing private capitalism by public capitalism, and organizing the machinery of production and distribution, like the political government, as business of general concern to be carried on for the public benefit instead of private gain.

But, though it was not long before the young stranger's first astonishment at the institutions of the new world had passed into enthusiastic admiration and he was ready to admit that the race had for the first time learned how to live, he presently began to repine at a fate which had introduced him to the new world, only to leave him oppressed by a sense of hopeless loneliness which all the kindness of his new friends could not relieve, feeling, as he must, that it was dictated by pity only. Then it was that he first learned that his experience had been a yet more marvelous one than he had supposed. Edith Leete was no other than the great-granddaughter of Edith Bartlett, his betrothed, who, after long mourning her lost lover, had at last allowed herself to be consoled. The story of the tragical bereavement which had shadowed her early life was a family tradition, and among the family heirlooms were letters from Julian West, together with a photograph which represented so handsome a youth that Edith was illogically inclined to quarrel with her great-grandmother for ever marrying anybody else. As for the young man's picture, she kept it on her dressing table. Of course, it followed that the identity of the tenant of the subterranean chamber had been fully known to his rescuers from the moment of the discovery; but Edith, for reasons of her own, had insisted that he should not know who she was till she saw fit to tell him. When, at the proper time, she had seen fit to do this, there was no further question of loneliness for the young man, for how could destiny more unmistakably have indicated that two persons were meant for each other?

His cup of happiness now being full, he had an experience in which it seemed to be dashed from his lips. As he lay on his bed in Dr. Leete's house he was oppressed by a hideous nightmare. It seemed to him that he opened his eyes to find himself on his bed in the underground chamber where the mesmerizer had put him to sleep. Sawyer was just completing the passes used to break the hypnotic influence. He called for the morning paper, and read on the date line May 31, 1887. Then he knew that all this wonderful matter about the year 2000, its happy, care-free world of brothers and the fair girl he had met there were but fragments of a dream. His brain in a whirl, he went forth into the city. He saw everything with new eyes, contrasting it with what he had seen in the Boston of the year 2000. The frenzied folly of the competitive industrial system, the inhuman contrasts of luxury and woe--pride and abjectness--the boundless squalor, wretchedness, and madness of the whole scheme of things which met his eye at every turn, outraged his reason and made his heart sick. He felt like a sane man shut up by accident in a madhouse. After a day of this wandering he found himself at nightfall in a company of his former companions, who rallied him on his distraught appearance. He told them of his dream and what it had taught him of the possibilities of a juster, nobler, wiser social system. He reasoned with them, showing how easy it would be, laying aside the suicidal folly of competition, by means of fraternal co-operation, to make the actual world as blessed as that he had dreamed of. At first they derided him, but, seeing his earnestness, grew angry, and denounced him as a pestilent fellow, an anarchist, an enemy of society, and drove him from them. Then it was that, in an agony of weeping, he awoke, this time awaking really, not falsely, and found himself in his bed in Dr. Leete's house, with the morning sun of the twentieth century shining in his eyes. Looking from the window of his room, he saw Edith in the garden gathering flowers for the breakfast table, and hastened to descend to her and relate his experience. At this point we will leave him to continue the narrative for himself.

Contents.

Chapter
- I. A Sharp Cross-Examiner
- II. Why The Revolution Did Not Come Earlier
- III. I Acquire A Stake In The Country
- IV. A Twentieth-Century Bank Parlor
- V. I Experience A New Sensation
- VI. Honi Soit Qui Mal Y Pense
- VII. A String Of Surprises
- VIII. The Greatest Wonder Yet--Fashion Dethroned
- IX. Something That Had Not Changed
- X. A Midnight Plunge
- XI. Life The Basis Of The Right Of Property
- XII. How Inequality Of Wealth Destroys Liberty
- XIII. Private Capital Stolen From The Social Fund
- XIV. We Look Over My Collection Of Harnesses
- XV. What We Were Coming To But For The Revolution
- XVI. An Excuse That Condemned
- XVII. The Revolution Saves Private Property From Monopoly
- XVIII. An Echo Of The Past
- XIX. "Can A Maid Forget Her Ornaments?"
- XX. What The Revolution Did For Women
- XXI. At The Gymnasium
- XXII. Economic Suicide Of The Profit System
- XXIII. "The Parable Of The Water Tank"
- XXIV. I Am Shown All The Kingdoms Of The Earth
- XXV. The Strikers
- XXVI. Foreign Commerce Under Profits; Protection And Free Trade, Or Between The Devil And The Deep Sea
- XXVII. Hostility Of A System Of Vested Interests To Improvement
- XXVIII. How The Profit System Nullified The Benefit Of Inventions
- XXIX. I Receive An Ovation
- XXX. What Universal Culture Means
- XXXI. "Neither In This Mountain Nor At Jerusalem"
- XXXII. Eritis Sicut Deus
- XXXIII. Several Important Matters Overlooked
- XXXIV. What Started The Revolution
- XXXV. Why The Revolution Went Slow At First But Fast At Last
- XXXVI. Theater-Going In The Twentieth Century
- XXXVII. The Transition Period
- XXXVIII. The Book Of The Blind

CHAPTER I.

A Sharp Cross-Examiner.

With many expressions of sympathy and interest Edith listened to the story of my dream. When, finally, I had made an end, she remained musing.

"What are you thinking about?" I said.

"I was thinking," she answered, "how it would have been if your dream had been true."

"True!" I exclaimed. "How could it have been true?"

"I mean," she said, "if it had all been a dream, as you supposed it was in your nightmare, and you had never really seen our Republic of the Golden Rule or me, but had only slept a night and dreamed the whole thing about us. And suppose you had gone forth just as you did in your dream, and had passed up and down telling men of the terrible folly and wickedness of their way of life and how much nobler and happier a way there was. Just think what good you might have done, how you might have helped people in those days when they needed help so much. It seems to me you must be almost sorry you came back to us."

"You look as if you were almost sorry yourself," I said, for her wistful expression seemed susceptible of that interpretation.

"Oh, no," she answered, smiling. "It was only on your own account. As for me, I have very good reasons for being glad that you came back."

"I should say so, indeed. Have you reflected that if I had dreamed it all you would have had no existence save as a figment in the brain of a sleeping man a hundred years ago?"

"I had not thought of that part of it," she said smiling and still half serious; "yet if I could have been more useful to humanity as a fiction than as a reality, I ought not to have minded the--the inconvenience."

But I replied that I greatly feared no amount of opportunity to help mankind in general would have reconciled me to life anywhere or under any conditions after leaving her behind in a dream--a confession of shameless selfishness which she was pleased to pass over without special rebuke, in consideration, no doubt, of my unfortunate bringing up.

"Besides," I resumed, being willing a little further to vindicate myself, "it would not have done any good. I have just told you how in my nightmare last night, when I tried to tell my contemporaries and even my best friends about the nobler way men might live together, they derided me as a fool and madman. That is exactly what they would have done in reality had the dream been true and I had gone about preaching as in the case you supposed."

"Perhaps a few might at first have acted as you dreamed they did," she replied. "Perhaps they would not at once have liked the idea of economic equality, fearing that it might mean a leveling down for them, and not understanding that it would presently mean a leveling up of all together to a vastly higher plane of life and happiness, of material welfare and moral dignity than the most fortunate had ever enjoyed. But even if the rich had at first mistaken you for an enemy to their class, the poor, the great masses of the poor, the real nation, they surely from the first would have listened as for their lives, for to them your story would have meant glad tidings of great joy."

"I do not wonder that you think so," I answered, "but, though I am still learning the A B C of this new world, I knew my contemporaries, and I know that it would not have been as you fancy. The poor would have listened no better than the rich, for, though poor and rich in my day were at bitter odds in everything else, they were agreed in believing that there must always be rich and poor, and that a condition of material equality was impossible. It used to be commonly said, and it often seemed true, that the social reformer who tried to better the condition of the people found a more discouraging obstacle in the hopelessness of the masses he would raise than in the active resistance of the few, whose superiority was threatened. And indeed, Edith, to be fair to my own class, I am bound to say that with the best of the rich it was often as much this same hopelessness as deliberate selfishness that made them what we used to call conservative. So you see, it would have done no good even if I had gone to preaching as you fancied. The poor would have regarded my talk about the possibility of an equality of wealth as a fairy tale, not worth a laboring man's time to listen to. Of the rich, the baser sort would have mocked and the better sort would have sighed, but none would have given ear seriously."

But Edith smiled serenely.

"It seems very audacious for me to try to correct your impressions of your own contemporaries and of what they might be expected to think and do, but you see the peculiar circumstances give me a rather unfair advantage. Your knowledge of your times necessarily stops short with 1887, when you became oblivious of the course of events. I, on the other hand, having gone to school in the twentieth century, and been obliged, much against my will, to study nineteenth-century history, naturally know what happened after the date at which your knowledge ceased. I know, impossible as it may seem to you, that you had scarcely fallen into that long sleep before the American people began to be deeply and widely stirred with aspirations for an equal order such as we enjoy, and that very soon the political movement arose which, after various mutations, resulted early in the twentieth century in overthrowing the old system and setting up the present one."

This was indeed interesting information to me, but when I began to question Edith further, she sighed and shook her head.

"Having tried to show my superior knowledge, I must now confess my ignorance. All I know is the bare fact that the revolutionary movement began, as I said, very soon after you fell asleep. Father must tell you the rest. I might as well admit while I am about it, for you would soon find it out, that I know almost nothing either as to the Revolution or nineteenth-century matters generally. You have no idea how hard I have been trying to post myself on the subject so as to be able to talk intelligently with you, but I fear it is of no use. I could not understand it in school and can not seem to understand it any better now. More than ever this morning I am sure that I never shall. Since you have been telling me how the old world appeared to you in that dream, your talk has brought those days so terribly near that I can almost see them, and yet I can not say that they seem a bit more intelligible than before."

"Things were bad enough and black enough certainly," I said; "but I don't see what there was particularly unintelligible about them. What is the difficulty?"

"The main difficulty comes from the complete lack of agreement between the pretensions of your contemporaries about the way their society was organized and the actual facts as given in the histories."

"For example?" I queried.

"I don't suppose there is much use in trying to explain my trouble," she said. "You will only think me stupid for my pains, but I'll try to make you see what I mean. You ought to be able to clear up the matter if anybody can. You have just been telling me about the shockingly unequal conditions of the people, the contrasts of waste and want, the pride and power of the rich, the abjectness and servitude of the poor, and all the rest of the dreadful story."

"Yes."

"It appears that these contrasts were almost as great as at any previous period of history."

"It is doubtful," I replied, "if there was ever a greater disparity between the conditions of different classes than you would find in a half hour's walk in Boston, New York, Chicago, or any other great city of America in the last quarter of the nineteenth century."

"And yet," said Edith, "it appears from all the books that meanwhile the Americans' great boast was that they differed from all other and former nations in that they were free and equal. One is constantly coming upon this phrase in the literature of the day. Now, you have made it clear that they were neither free nor equal in any ordinary sense of the word, but were divided as mankind had always been before into rich and poor, masters and servants. Won't you please tell me, then, what they meant by calling themselves free and equal?"

"It was meant, I suppose, that they were all equal before the law."

"That means in the courts. And were the rich and poor equal in the courts? Did they receive the same treatment?"

"I am bound to say," I replied, "that they were nowhere else more unequal. The law applied in terms to all alike, but not in fact. There was more difference in the position of the rich and the poor man before the law than in any other respect. The rich were practically above the law, the poor under its wheels."

"In what respect, then, were the rich and poor equal?"

"They were said to be equal in opportunities."

"Opportunities for what?"

"For bettering themselves, for getting rich, for getting ahead of others in the struggle for wealth."

"It seems to me that only meant, if it were true, not that all were equal, but that all had an equal chance to make themselves unequal. But was it true that all had equal opportunities for getting rich and bettering themselves?"

"It may have been so to some extent at one time when the country was new," I replied, "but it was no more so in my day. Capital had practically monopolized all economic opportunities by that time; there was no opening in business enterprise for those without large capital save by some extraordinary fortune."

"But surely," said Edith, "there must have been, in order to give at least a color to all this boasting about equality, some one respect in which the people were really equal?"

"Yes, there was. They were political equals. They all had one vote alike, and the majority was the supreme lawgiver."

"So the books say, but that only makes the actual condition of things more absolutely unaccountable."

"Why so?"

"Why, because if these people all had an equal voice in the government--these toiling, starving, freezing, wretched masses of the poor--why did they not without a moment's delay put an end to the inequalities from which they suffered?"

"Very likely," she added, as I did not at once reply, "I am only showing how stupid I am by saying this. Doubtless I am overlooking some important fact, but did you not say that all the people, at least all the men, had a voice in the government?"

"Certainly; by the latter part of the nineteenth century manhood suffrage had become practically universal in America."

"That is to say, the people through their chosen agents made all the laws. Is that what you mean?"

"Certainly."

"But I remember you had Constitutions of the nation and of the States. Perhaps they prevented the people from doing quite what they wished."

"No; the Constitutions were only a little more fundamental sort of laws. The majority made and altered them at will. The people were the sole and supreme final power, and their will was absolute."

"If, then, the majority did not like any existing arrangement, or think it to their advantage, they could change it as radically as they wished?"

"Certainly; the popular majority could do anything if it was large and determined enough."

"And the majority, I understand, were the poor, not the rich--the ones who had the wrong side of the inequalities that prevailed?"

"Emphatically so; the rich were but a handful comparatively."

"Then there was nothing whatever to prevent the people at any time, if they just willed it, from making an end of their sufferings and organizing a system like ours which would guarantee their equality and prosperity?"

"Nothing whatever."

"Then once more I ask you to kindly tell me why, in the name of common sense, they didn't do it at once and be happy instead of making a spectacle of themselves so woeful that even a hundred years after it makes us cry?"

"Because," I replied, "they were taught and believed that the regulation of industry and commerce and the production and distribution of wealth was something wholly outside of the proper province of government."

"But, dear me, Julian, life itself and everything that meanwhile makes life worth living, from the satisfaction of the most primary physical needs to the gratification of the most refined tastes, all that belongs to the development of mind as well as body, depend first, last, and always on the manner in which the production and distribution of wealth is regulated. Surely that must have been as true in your day as ours."

"Of course."

"And yet you tell me, Julian, that the people, after having abolished the rule of kings and taken the supreme power of regulating their affairs into their own hands, deliberately consented to exclude from their jurisdiction the control of the most important, and indeed the only really important, class of their interests."

"Do not the histories say so?"

"They do say so, and that is precisely why I could never believe them. The thing seemed so incomprehensible I thought there must be some way of explaining it. But tell me, Julian, seeing the people did not think that they could trust themselves to regulate their own industry and the distribution of the product, to whom did they leave the responsibility?"

"To the capitalists."

"And did the people elect the capitalists?"

"Nobody elected them."

"By whom, then, were they appointed?"

"Nobody appointed them."

"What a singular system! Well, if nobody elected or appointed them, yet surely they must have been accountable to somebody for the manner in which they exercised powers on which the welfare and very existence of everybody depended."

"On the contrary, they were accountable to nobody and nothing but their own consciences."

"Their consciences! Ah, I see! You mean that they were so benevolent, so unselfish, so devoted to the public good, that people tolerated their usurpation out of gratitude. The people nowadays would not endure the irresponsible rule even of demigods, but probably it was different in your day."

"As an ex-capitalist myself, I should be pleased to confirm your surmise, but nothing could really be further from the fact. As to any benevolent interest in the conduct of industry and commerce, the capitalists expressly disavowed it. Their only object was to secure the greatest possible gain for themselves without any regard whatever to the welfare of the public."

"Dear me! Dear me! Why you make out these capitalists to have been even worse than the kings, for the kings at least professed to govern for the welfare of their people, as fathers acting for children, and the good ones did try to. But the capitalists, you say, did not even pretend to feel any responsibility for the welfare of their subjects?"

"None whatever."

"And, if I understand," pursued Edith, "this government of the capitalists was not only without moral sanction of any sort or plea of benevolent intentions, but was practically an economic failure--that is, it did not secure the prosperity of the people."

"What I saw in my dream last night," I replied, "and have tried to tell you this morning, gives but a faint suggestion of the misery of the world under capitalist rule."

Edith meditated in silence for some moments. Finally she said: "Your contemporaries were not madmen nor fools; surely there is something you have not told me; there must be some explanation or at least color of excuse why the people not only abdicated the power of controlling their most vital and important interests, but turned them over to a class which did not even pretend any interest in their welfare, and whose government completely failed to secure it."

"Oh, yes," I said, "there was an explanation, and a very fine-sounding one. It was in the name of individual liberty, industrial freedom, and individual initiative that the economic government of the country was surrendered to the capitalists."

"Do you mean that a form of government which seems to have been the most irresponsible and despotic possible was defended in the name of liberty?"

"Certainly; the liberty of economic initiative by the individual."

"But did you not just tell me that economic initiative and business opportunity in your day were practically monopolized by the capitalists themselves?"

"Certainly. It was admitted that there was no opening for any but capitalists in business, and it was rapidly becoming so that only the greatest of the capitalists themselves had any power of initiative."

"And yet you say that the reason given for abandoning industry to capitalist government was the promotion of industrial freedom and individual initiative among the people at large."

"Certainly. The people were taught that they would individually enjoy greater liberty and freedom of action in industrial matters under the dominion of the capitalists than if they collectively conducted the industrial system for their own benefit; that the capitalists would, moreover, look out for their welfare more wisely and kindly than they could possibly do it themselves, so that they would be able to provide for themselves more bountifully out of such portion of their product as the capitalists might be disposed to give them than they possibly could do if they became their own employers and divided the whole product among themselves."

"But that was mere mockery; it was adding insult to injury."

"It sounds so, doesn't it? But I assure you it was considered the soundest sort of political economy in my time. Those who questioned it were set down as dangerous visionaries."

"But I suppose the people's government, the government they voted for, must have done something. There must have been some odds and ends of things which the capitalists left the political government to attend to."

"Oh, yes, indeed. It had its hands full keeping the peace among the people. That was the main part of the business of political governments in my day."

"Why did the peace require such a great amount of keeping? Why didn't it keep itself, as it does now?"

"On account of the inequality of conditions which prevailed. The strife for wealth and desperation of want kept in quenchless blaze a hell of greed and envy, fear, lust, hate, revenge, and every foul passion of the pit. To keep this general frenzy in some restraint, so that the entire social system should not resolve itself into a general massacre, required an army of soldiers, police, judges, and jailers, and endless law-making to settle the quarrels. Add to these elements of discord a horde of outcasts degraded and desperate, made enemies of society by their sufferings and requiring to be kept in check, and you will readily admit there was enough for the people's government to do."

"So far as I can see," said Edith, "the main business of the people's government was to struggle with the social chaos which resulted from its failure to take hold of the economic system and regulate it on a basis of justice."

"That is exactly so. You could not state the whole case more adequately if you wrote a book."

"Beyond protecting the capitalist system from its own effects, did the political government do absolutely nothing?"

"Oh, yes, it appointed postmasters and tidewaiters, maintained an army and navy, and picked quarrels with foreign countries."

"I should say that the right of a citizen to have a voice in a government limited to the range of functions you have mentioned would scarcely have seemed to him of much value."

"I believe the average price of votes in close elections in America in my time was about two dollars."

"Dear me, so much as that!" said Edith. "I don't know exactly what the value of money was in your day, but I should say the price was rather extortionate."

"I think you are right," I answered. "I used to give in to the talk about the pricelessness of the right of suffrage, and the denunciation of those whom any stress of poverty could induce to sell it for money, but from the point of view to which you have brought me this morning I am inclined to think that the fellows who sold their votes had a far clearer idea of the sham of our so-called popular government, as limited to the class of functions I have described, than any of the rest of us did, and that if they were wrong it was, as you suggest, in asking too high a price."

"But who paid for the votes?"

"You are a merciless cross-examiner," I said. "The classes which had an interest in controling the government--that is, the capitalists and the office-seekers--did the buying. The capitalists advanced the money necessary to procure the election of the office-seekers on the understanding that when elected the latter should do what the capitalists wanted. But I ought not to give you the impression that the bulk of the votes were bought outright. That would have been too open a confession of the sham of popular government as well as too expensive. The money contributed by the capitalists to procure the election of the office-seekers was mainly expended to influence the people by indirect means. Immense sums under the name of campaign funds were raised for this purpose and used in innumerable devices, such as fireworks, oratory, processions, brass bands, barbecues, and all sorts of devices, the object of which was to galvanize the people to a sufficient degree of interest in the election to go through the motion of voting. Nobody who has not actually witnessed a nineteenth-century American election could even begin to imagine the grotesqueness of the spectacle."

"It seems, then," said Edith, "that the capitalists not only carried on the economic government as their special province, but also practically managed the machinery of the political government as well."

"Oh, yes, the capitalists could not have got along at all without control of the political government. Congress, the Legislatures, and the city councils were quite necessary as instruments for putting through their schemes. Moreover, in order to protect themselves and their property against popular outbreaks, it was highly needful that they should have the police, the courts, and the soldiers devoted to their interests, and the President, Governors, and mayors at their beck."

"But I thought the President, the Governors, and Legislatures represented the people who voted for them."

"Bless your heart! no, why should they? It was to the capitalists and not to the people that they owed the opportunity of officeholding. The people who voted had little choice for whom they should vote. That question was determined by the political party organizations, which were beggars to the capitalists for pecuniary support. No man who was opposed to capitalist interests was permitted the opportunity as a candidate to appeal to the people. For a public official to support the people's interest as against that of the capitalists would be a sure way of sacrificing his career. You must remember, if you would understand how absolutely the capitalists controlled the Government, that a President, Governor, or mayor, or member of the municipal, State, or national council, was only temporarily a servant of the people or dependent on their favour. His public position he held only from election to election, and rarely long. His permanent, lifelong, and all-controling interest, like that of us all, was his livelihood, and that was dependent, not on the applause of the people, but the favor and patronage of capital, and this he could not afford to imperil in the pursuit of the bubbles of popularity. These circumstances, even if there had been no instances of direct bribery, sufficiently explained why our politicians and officeholders with few exceptions were vassals and tools of the capitalists. The lawyers, who, on account of the complexities of our system, were almost the only class competent for public business, were especially and directly dependent upon the patronage of the great capitalistic interests for their living."

"But why did not the people elect officials and representatives of their own class, who would look out for the interests of the masses?"

"There was no assurance that they would be more faithful. Their very poverty would make them the more liable to money temptation; and the poor, you must remember, although so much more pitiable, were not morally any better than the rich. Then, too--and that was the most important reason why the masses of the people, who were poor, did not send men of their class to represent them--poverty as a rule implied ignorance, and therefore practical inability, even where the intention was good. As soon as the poor man developed intelligence he had every temptation to desert his class and seek the patronage of capital."

Edith remained silent and thoughtful for some moments.

"Really," she said, finally, "it seems that the reason I could not understand the so-called popular system of government in your day is that I was trying to find out what part the people had in it, and it appears that they had no part at all."

"You are getting on famously," I exclaimed. "Undoubtedly the confusion of terms in our political system is rather calculated to puzzle one at first, but if you only grasp firmly the vital point that the rule of the rich, the supremacy of capital and its interests, as against those of the people at large, was the central principle of our system, to which every other interest was made subservient, you will have the key that clears up every mystery."

CHAPTER II.

Why The Revolution Did Not Come Earlier.

Absorbed in our talk, we had not heard the steps of Dr. Leete as he approached.

"I have been watching you for ten minutes from the house," he said, "until, in fact, I could no longer resist the desire to know what you find so interesting."

"Your daughter," said I, "has been proving herself a mistress of the Socratic method. Under a plausible pretext of gross ignorance, she has been asking me a series of easy questions, with the result that I see as I never imagined it before the colossal sham of our pretended popular government in America. As one of the rich I knew, of course, that we had a great deal of power in the state, but I did not before realize how absolutely the people were without influence in their own government."

"Aha!" exclaimed the doctor in great glee, "so my daughter gets up early in the morning with the design of supplanting her father in his position of historical instructor?"

Edith had risen from the garden bench on which we had been seated and was arranging her flowers to take into the house. She shook her head rather gravely in reply to her father's challenge.

"You need not be at all apprehensive," she said; "Julian has quite cured me this morning of any wish I might have had to inquire further into the condition of our ancestors. I have always been dreadfully sorry for the poor people of that day on account of the misery they endured from poverty and the oppression of the rich. Henceforth, however, I wash my hands of them and shall reserve my sympathy for more deserving objects."

"Dear me!" said the doctor, "what has so suddenly dried up the fountains of your pity? What has Julian been telling you?"

"Nothing, really, I suppose, that I had not read before and ought to have known, but the story always seemed so unreasonable and incredible that I never quite believed it until now. I thought there must be some modifying facts not set down in the histories."

"But what is this that he has been telling you?"

"It seems," said Edith, "that these very people, these very masses of the poor, had all the time the supreme control of the Government and were able, if determined and united, to put an end at any moment to all the inequalities and oppressions of which they complained and to equalize things as we have done. Not only did they not do this, but they gave as a reason for enduring their bondage that their liberties would be endangered unless they had irresponsible masters to manage their interests, and that to take charge of their own affairs would imperil their freedom. I feel that I have been cheated out of all the tears I have shed over the sufferings of such people. Those who tamely endure wrongs which they have the power to end deserve not compassion but contempt. I have felt a little badly that Julian should have been one of the oppressor class, one of the rich. Now that I really understand the matter, I am glad. I fear that, had he been one of the poor, one of the mass of real masters, who with supreme power in their hands consented to be bondsmen, I should have despised him."

Having thus served formal notice on my contemporaries that they must expect no more sympathy from her, Edith went into the house, leaving me with a vivid impression that if the men of the twentieth century should prove incapable of preserving their liberties, the women might be trusted to do so.

"Really, doctor," I said, "you ought to be greatly obliged to your daughter. She has saved you lots of time and effort."

"How so, precisely?"

"By rendering it unnecessary for you to trouble yourself to explain to me any further how and why you came to set up your nationalized industrial system and your economic equality. If you have ever seen a desert or sea mirage, you remember that, while the picture in the sky is very clear and distinct in itself, its unreality is betrayed by a lack of detail, a sort of blur, where it blends with the foreground on which you are standing. Do you know that this new social order of which I have so strangely become a witness has hitherto had something of this mirage effect? In itself it is a scheme precise, orderly, and very reasonable, but I could see no way by which it could have naturally grown out of the utterly different conditions of the nineteenth century. I could only imagine that this world transformation must have been the result of new ideas and forces that had come into action since my day. I had a volume of questions all ready to ask you on the subject, but now we shall be able to use the time in talking of other things, for Edith has shown me in ten minutes' time that the only wonderful thing about your organization of the industrial system as public business is not that it has taken place, but that it waited so long before taking place, that a nation of rational beings consented to remain economic serfs of irresponsible masters for more than a century after coming into possession of absolute power to change at pleasure all social institutions which inconvenienced them."

"Really," said the doctor, "Edith has shown herself a very efficient teacher, if an involuntary one. She has succeeded at one stroke in giving you the modern point of view as to your period. As we look at it, the immortal preamble of the American Declaration of Independence, away back in 1776, logically contained the entire statement of the doctrine of universal economic equality guaranteed by the nation collectively to its members individually. You remember how the words run:

"'We hold these truths to be self-evident; that all men are created equal, with certain inalienable rights; that among these are life, liberty, and the pursuit of happiness; that to secure these rights governments are instituted among men, deriving their just powers from the consent of the governed; that whenever any form of government becomes destructive of these rights it is the right of the people to alter or to abolish it and institute a new government, laying its foundations on such principles and organizing its powers in such form as may seem most likely to effect their safety and happiness.'

"Is it possible, Julian, to imagine any governmental system less adequate than ours which could possibly realize this great ideal of what a true people's government should be? The corner stone of our state is economic equality, and is not that the obvious, necessary, and only adequate pledge of these three birthrights--life, liberty, and happiness? What is life without its material basis, and what is an equal right to life but a right to an equal material basis for it? What is liberty? How can men be free who must ask the right to labor and to live from their fellow-men and seek their bread from the hands of others? How else can any government guarantee liberty to men save by providing them a means of labor and of life coupled with independence; and how could that be done unless the government conducted the economic system upon which employment and maintenance depend? Finally, what is implied in the equal right of all to the pursuit of happiness? What form of happiness, so far as it depends at all on material facts, is not bound up with economic conditions; and how shall an equal opportunity for the pursuit of happiness be guaranteed to all save by a guarantee of economic equality?"

"Yes," I said, "it is indeed all there, but why were we so long in seeing it?"

"Let us make ourselves comfortable on this bench," said the doctor, "and I will tell you what is the modern answer to the very interesting question you raise. At first glance, certainly the delay of the world in general, and especially of the American people, to realize that democracy logically meant the substitution of popular government for the rule of the rich in regulating the production and distribution of wealth seems incomprehensible, not only because it was so plain an inference from the idea of popular government, but also because it was one which the masses of the people were so directly interested in carrying out. Edith's conclusion that people who were not capable of so simple a process of reasoning as that did not deserve much sympathy for the afflictions they might so easily have remedied, is a very natural first impression.

"On reflection, however, I think we shall conclude that the time taken by the world in general and the Americans in particular in finding out the full meaning of democracy as an economic as well as a political proposition was not greater than might have been expected, considering the vastness of the conclusions involved. It is the democratic idea that all human beings are peers in rights and dignity, and that the sole just excuse and end of human governments is, therefore, the maintenance and furtherance of the common welfare on equal terms. This idea was the greatest social conception that the human mind had up to that time ever formed. It contained, when first conceived, the promise and potency of a complete transformation of all then existing social institutions, one and all of which had hitherto been based and formed on the principle of personal and class privilege and authority and the domination and selfish use of the many by the few. But it was simply inconsistent with the limitations of the human intellect that the implications of an idea so prodigious should at once have been taken in. The idea must absolutely have time to grow. The entire present order of economic democracy and equality was indeed logically bound up in the first full statement of the democratic idea, but only as the full-grown tree is in the seed: in the one case, as in the other, time was an essential element in the evolution of the result.

"We divide the history of the evolution of the democratic idea into two broadly contrasted phases. The first of these we call the phase of negative democracy. To understand it we must consider how the democratic idea originated. Ideas are born of previous ideas and are long in outgrowing the characteristics and limitations impressed on them by the circumstances under which they came into existence. The idea of popular government, in the case of America as in previous republican experiments in general, was a protest against royal government and its abuses. Nothing is more certain than that the signers of the immortal Declaration had no idea that democracy necessarily meant anything more than a device for getting along without kings. They conceived of it as a change in the forms of government only, and not at all in the principles and purposes of government.

"They were not, indeed, wholly without misgivings lest it might some time occur to the sovereign people that, being sovereign, it would be a good idea to use their sovereignty to improve their own condition. In fact, they seem to have given some serious thought to that possibility, but so little were they yet able to appreciate the logic and force of the democratic idea that they believed it possible by ingenious clauses in paper Constitutions to prevent the people from using their power to help themselves even if they should wish to.

"This first phase of the evolution of democracy, during which it was conceived of solely as a substitute for royalty, includes all the so-called republican experiments up to the beginning of the twentieth century, of which, of course, the American Republic was the most important. During this period the democratic idea remained a mere protest against a previous form of government, absolutely without any new positive or vital principle of its own. Although the people had deposed the king as driver of the social chariot, and taken the reins into their own hands, they did not think as yet of anything but keeping the vehicle in the old ruts and naturally the passengers scarcely noticed the change.

"The second phase in the evolution of the democratic idea began with the awakening of the people to the perception that the deposing of kings, instead of being the main end and mission of democracy, was merely preliminary to its real programme, which was the use of the collective social machinery for the indefinite promotion of the welfare of the people at large.

"It is an interesting fact that the people began to think of applying their political power to the improvement of their material condition in Europe earlier than in America, although democratic forms had found much less acceptance there. This was, of course, on account of the perennial economic distress of the masses in the old countries, which prompted them to think first about the bearing any new idea might have on the question of livelihood. On the other hand, the general prosperity of the masses in America and the comparative ease of making a living up to the beginning of the last quarter of the nineteenth century account for the fact that it was not till then that the American people began to think seriously of improving their economic condition by collective action.

"During the negative phase of democracy it had been considered as differing from monarchy only as two machines might differ, the general use and purpose of which were the same. With the evolution of the democratic idea into the second or positive phase, it was recognized that the transfer of the supreme power from king and nobles to people meant not merely a change in the forms of government, but a fundamental revolution in the whole idea of government, its motives, purposes, and functions--a revolution equivalent to a reversal of polarity of the entire social system, carrying, so to speak, the entire compass card with it, and making north south, and east west. Then was seen what seems so plain to us that it is hard to understand why it was not always seen, that instead of its being proper for the sovereign people to confine themselves to the functions which the kings and classes had discharged when they were in power, the presumption was, on the contrary, since the interest of kings and classes had always been exactly opposed to those of the people, that whatever the previous governments had done, the people as rulers ought not to do, and whatever the previous governments had not done, it would be presumably for the interest of the people to do; and that the main use and function of popular government was properly one which no previous government had ever paid any attention to, namely, the use of the power of the social organization to raise the material and moral welfare of the whole body of the sovereign people to the highest possible point at which the same degree of welfare could be secured to all--that is to say, an equal level. The democracy of the second or positive phase triumphed in the great Revolution, and has since been the only form of government known in the world."

"Which amounts to saying," I observed, "that there never was a democratic government properly so called before the twentieth century."

"Just so," assented the doctor. "The so-called republics of the first phase we class as pseudo-republics or negative democracies. They were not, of course, in any sense, truly popular governments at all, but merely masks for plutocracy, under which the rich were the real though irresponsible rulers! You will readily see that they could have been nothing else. The masses from the beginning of the world had been the subjects and servants of the rich, but the kings had been above the rich, and constituted a check on their dominion. The overthrow of the kings left no check at all on the power of the rich, which became supreme. The people, indeed, nominally were sovereigns; but as these sovereigns were individually and as a class the economic serfs of the rich, and lived at their mercy, the so-called popular government became the mere stalking-horse of the capitalists.

"Regarded as necessary steps in the evolution of society from pure monarchy to pure democracy, these republics of the negative phase mark a stage of progress; but if regarded as finalities they were a type far less admirable on the whole than decent monarchies. In respect especially to their susceptibility to corruption and plutocratic subversion they were the worst kind of government possible. The nineteenth century, during which this crop of pseudo-democracies ripened for the sickle of the great Revolution, seems to the modern view nothing but a dreary interregnum of nondescript, *faineant* government intervening between the decadence of virile monarchy in the eighteenth century and the rise of positive democracy in the twentieth. The period may be compared to that of the minority of a king, during which the royal power is abused by wicked stewards. The people had been proclaimed as sovereign, but they had not yet assumed the sceptre."

"And yet," said I, "during the latter part of the nineteenth century, when, as you say, the world had not yet seen a single specimen of popular government, our wise men were telling us that the democratic system had been fully tested and was ready to be judged on its results. Not a few of them, indeed, went so far as to say that the democratic experiment had proved a failure when, in point of fact, it seems that no experiment in democracy, properly understood, had as yet ever been so much as attempted."

The doctor shrugged his shoulders.

"It is a very sympathetic task," he said, "to explain the slowness of the masses in feeling their way to a comprehension of all that the democratic idea meant for them, but it is one equally difficult and thankless to account for the blank failure of the philosophers, historians, and statesmen of your day to arrive at an intelligent estimate of the logical content of democracy and to forecast its outcome. Surely the very smallness of the practical results thus far achieved by the democratic movement as compared with the magnitude of its proposition and the forces behind it ought to have suggested to them that its evolution was yet but in the first stage. How could intelligent men delude themselves with the notion that the most portentous and revolutionary idea of all time had exhausted its influence and fulfilled its mission in changing the title of the executive of a nation from king to President, and the name of the national Legislature from Parliament to Congress? If your pedagogues, college professors and presidents, and others who were responsible for your education, had been worth their salt, you would have found nothing in the present order of economic equality that would in the least have surprised you. You would have said at once that it was just what you had been taught must necessarily be the next phase in the inevitable evolution of the democratic idea."

Edith beckoned from the door and we rose from our seat.

"The revolutionary party in the great Revolution," said the doctor, as we sauntered toward the house, "carried on the work of agitation and propaganda under various names more or less grotesque and ill-fitting as political party names were apt to be, but the one word democracy, with its various equivalents and derivatives, more accurately and completely expressed, explained, and justified their method, reason, and purpose than a library of books could do. The American people fancied that they had set up a popular government when they separated from England, but they were deluded. In conquering the political power formerly exercised by the king, the people had but taken the outworks of the fortress of tyranny. The economic system which was the citadel and commanded every part of the social structure remained in possession of private and irresponsible rulers, and so long as it was so held, the possession of the outworks was of no use to the people, and only retained by the sufferance of the garrison of the citadel. The Revolution came when the people saw that they must either take the citadel or evacuate the outworks. They must either complete the work of establishing popular government which had been barely begun by their fathers, or abandon all that their fathers had accomplished."

CHAPTER III.

I Acquire A Stake In The Country.

On going into breakfast the ladies met us with a highly interesting piece of intelligence which they had found in the morning's news. It was, in fact, nothing less than an announcement of action taken by the United States Congress in relation to myself. A resolution had, it appeared, been unanimously passed which, after reciting the facts of my extraordinary return to life, proceeded to clear up any conceivable question that might arise as to my legal status by declaring me an American citizen in full standing and entitled to all a citizen's rights and immunities, but at the same time a guest of the nation, and as such free of the duties and services incumbent upon citizens in general except as I might choose to assume them.

Secluded as I had been hitherto in the Leete household, this was almost the first intimation I had the public in my case. That interest, I was now informed, had passed beyond my personality and was already producing a general revival of the study of nineteenth-century literature and politics, and especially of the history and philosophy of the transition period, when the old order passed into the new.

"The fact is," said the doctor, "the nation has only discharged a debt of gratitude in making you its guest, for you have already done more for our educational interests by promoting historical study than a regiment of instructors could achieve in a lifetime."

Recurring to the topic of the congressional resolution, the doctor said that, in his opinion, it was superfluous, for though I had certainly slept on my rights as a citizen rather an extraordinary length of time, there was no ground on which I could be argued to have forfeited any of them. However that might be, seeing the resolution left no doubt as to my status, he suggested that the first thing we did after breakfast should be to go down to the National Bank and open my citizen's account.

"Of course," I said, as we left the house, "I am glad to be relieved of the necessity of being a pensioner on you any longer, but I confess I feel a little cheap about accepting as a gift this generous provision of the nation."

"My dear Julian," replied the doctor, "it is sometimes a little difficult for me to quite get your point of view of our institutions."

"I should think it ought to be easy enough in this case. I feel as if I were an object of public charity."

"Ah!" said the doctor, "you feel that the nation has done you a favor, laid you under an obligation. You must excuse my obtuseness, but the fact is we look at this matter of the economic provision for citizens from an entirely different standpoint. It seems to us that in claiming and accepting your citizen's maintenance you perform a civic duty, whereby you put the nation--that is, the general body of your fellow-citizens--under rather more obligation than you incur."

I turned to see if the doctor were not jesting, but he was evidently quite serious.

"I ought by this time to be used to finding that everything goes by contraries in these days," I said, "but really, by what inversion of common sense, as it was understood in the nineteenth century, do you make out that by accepting a pecuniary provision from the nation I oblige it more than it obliges me?"

"I think it will be easy to make you see that," replied the doctor, "without requiring you to do any violence to the methods of reasoning to which your contemporaries were accustomed. You used to have, I believe, a system of gratuitous public education maintained by the state."

"Yes."

"What was the idea of it?"

"That a citizen was not a safe voter without education."

"Precisely so. The state therefore at great expense provided free education for the people. It was greatly for the advantage of the citizen to accept this education just as it is for you to accept this provision, but it was still more for the interest of the state that the citizen should accept it. Do you see the point?"

"I can see that it is the interest of the state that I should accept an education, but not exactly why it is for the state's interest that I should accept a share of the public wealth."

"Nevertheless it is the same reason, namely, the public interest in good government. We hold it to be a self-evident principle that every one who exercises the suffrage should not only be educated, but should have a stake in the country, in order that self-interest may be identified with public interest. As the power exercised by every citizen through the suffrage is the same, the economic stake should be the same, and so you see we come to the reason why the public safety requires that you should loyally accept your equal stake in the country quite apart from the personal advantage you derive by doing so."

"Do you know," I said, "that this idea of yours, that every one who votes should have an economic stake in the country, is one which our rankest Tories were very fond of insisting on, but the practical conclusion they drew from it was diametrically opposed to that which you draw? They would have agreed with you on the axiom that political power and economic stake in the country should go together, but the practical application they made of it was negative instead of positive. You argue that because an economic interest in the country should go with the suffrage, all who have the suffrage should have that interest guaranteed them. They argued, on the contrary, that from all who had not the economic stake the suffrage should be taken away. There were not a few of my friends who maintained that some such limitation of the suffrage was needed to save the democratic experiment from failure."

"That is to say," observed the doctor, "it was proposed to save the democratic experiment by abandoning it. It was an ingenious thought, but it so happened that democracy was not an experiment which could be abandoned, but an evolution which must be fulfilled. In what a striking manner does that talk of your contemporaries about limiting the suffrage to correspond with the economic position of citizens illustrate the failure of even the most intelligent classes in your time to grasp the full significance of the democratic faith which they professed! The primal principle of democracy is the worth and dignity of the individual. That dignity, consisting in the quality of human nature, is essentially the same in all individuals, and therefore equality is the vital principle of democracy. To this intrinsic and equal dignity of the individual all material conditions must be made subservient, and personal accidents and attributes subordinated. The raising up of the human being without respect of persons is the constant and only rational motive of the democratic policy. Contrast with this conception that precious notion of your contemporaries as to restricting suffrage. Recognizing the material disparities in the circumstances of individuals, they proposed to conform the rights and dignities of the individual to his material circumstances instead of conforming the material circumstances to the essential and equal dignity of the man."

"In short," said I, "while under our system we conformed men to things, you think it more reasonable to conform things to men?"

"That is, indeed," replied the doctor, "the vital difference between the old and the new orders."

We walked in silence for some moments. Presently the doctor said: "I was trying to recall an expression you just used which suggested a wide difference between the sense in which the same phrase was understood in your day and now is. I was saying that we thought everybody who voted ought to have a property stake in the country, and you observed that some people had the same idea in your time, but according to our view of what a stake in the country is no one had it or could have it under your economic system."

"Why not?" I demanded. "Did not men who owned property in a country--a millionaire, for instance, like myself--have a stake in it?"

"In the sense that his property was geographically located in the country it might be perhaps called a stake within the country but not a stake in the country. It was the exclusive ownership of a piece of the country or a portion of the wealth in the country, and all it prompted the owner to was devotion to and care for that specific portion without regard to the rest. Such a separate stake or the ambition to obtain it, far from making its owner or seeker a citizen devoted to the common weal, was quite as likely to make him a dangerous one, for his selfish interest was to aggrandize his separate stake at the expense of his fellow-citizens and of the public interest. Your millionaires--with no personal reflection upon yourself, of course--appear to have been the most dangerous class of citizens you had, and that is just what might be expected from their having what you called but what we should not call a stake in the country. Wealth owned in that way could only be a divisive and antisocial influence.

"What we mean by a stake in the country is something which nobody could possibly have until economic solidarity had replaced the private ownership of capital. Every one, of course, has his own house and piece of land if he or she desires them, and always his or her own income to use at pleasure; but these are allotments for use only, and, being always equal, can furnish no ground for dissension. The capital of the nation, the source of all this consumption, is indivisibly held by all in common, and it is impossible that there should be any dispute on selfish grounds as to the administration of this common interest on which all private interests depend, whatever differences of judgment there may be. The citizen's share in this common fund is a sort of stake in the country that makes it impossible to hurt another's interest without hurting one's own, or to help one's own interest without promoting equally all other interests. As to its economic bearings it may be said that it makes the Golden Rule an automatic principle of government. What we would do for ourselves we must of necessity do also for others. Until economic solidarity made it possible to carry out in this sense the idea that every citizen ought to have a stake in the country, the democratic system never had a chance to develop its genius."

"It seems," I said, "that your foundation principle of economic equality which I supposed was mainly suggested and intended in the interest of the material well-being of the people, is quite as much a principle of political policy for safeguarding the stability and wise ordering of government."

"Most assuredly," replied the doctor. "Our economic system is a measure of statesmanship quite as much as of humanity. You see, the first condition of efficiency or stability in any government is that the governing power should have a direct, constant, and supreme interest in the general welfare--that is, in the prosperity of the whole state as distinguished from any part of it. It had been the strong point of monarchy that the king, for selfish reasons as proprietor of the country, felt this interest. The autocratic form of government, solely on that account, had always a certain rough sort of efficiency. It had been, on the other hand, the fatal weakness of democracy, during its negative phase previous to the great Revolution, that the people, who were the rulers, had individually only an indirect and sentimental interest in the state as a whole, or its machinery--their real, main, constant, and direct interest being concentrated upon their personal fortunes, their private stakes, distinct from and adverse to the general stake. In moments of enthusiasm they might rally to the support of the commonwealth, but for the most part that had no custodian, but was at the mercy of designing men and factions who sought to plunder the commonwealth and use the machinery of government for personal or class ends. This was the structural weakness of democracies, by the effect of which, after passing their first youth, they became invariably, as the inequality of wealth developed, the most corrupt and worthless of all forms of government and the most susceptible to misuse and perversion for selfish, personal, and class purposes. It was a weakness incurable so long as the capital of the country, its economic interests, remained in private hands, and one that could be remedied only by the radical abolition of private capitalism and the unification of the nation's capital under collective control. This done, the same economic motive--which, while the capital remained in private hands, was a divisive influence tending to destroy that public spirit which is the breath of life in a democracy--became the most powerful of cohesive forces, making popular government not only ideally the most just but practically the most successful and efficient of political systems. The citizen, who before had been the champion of a part against the rest, became by this change a guardian of the whole."

CHAPTER IV.

A Twentieth-Century Bank Parlor.

The formalities at the bank proved to be very simple. Dr. Leete introduced me to the superintendent, and the rest followed as a matter of course, the whole process not taking three minutes. I was informed that the annual credit of the adult citizen for that year was $4,000, and that the portion due me for the remainder of the year, it being the latter part of September, was $1,075.41. Taking vouchers to the amount of $300, I left the rest on deposit precisely as I should have done at one of the nineteenth-century banks in drawing money for present use. The transaction concluded, Mr. Chapin, the superintendent, invited me into his office.

"How does our banking system strike you as compared with that of your day?" he asked.

"It has one manifest advantage from the point of view of a penniless *revenant* like myself," I said--"namely, that one receives a credit without having made a deposit; otherwise I scarcely know enough of it to give an opinion."

"When you come to be more familiar with our banking methods," said the superintendent. "I think you will be struck with their similarity to your own. Of course, we have no money and nothing answering to money, but the whole science of banking from its inception was preparing the way for the abolition of money. The only way, really, in which our system differs from yours is that every one starts the year with the same balance to his credit and that this credit is not transferable. As to requiring deposits before accounts are opened, we are necessarily quite as strict as your bankers were, only in our case the people, collectively, make the deposit for all at once. This collective deposit is made up of such provisions of different commodities and such installations for the various public services as are expected to be necessary. Prices or cost estimates are put on these commodities and services, and the aggregate sum of the prices being divided by the population gives the amount of the citizen's personal credit, which is simply his aliquot share of the commodities and services available for the year. No doubt, however, Dr. Leete has told you all about this."

"But I was not here to be included in the estimate of the year," I said. "I hope that my credit is not taken out of other people's."

"You need feel no concern," replied the superintendent. "While it is astonishing how variations in demand balance one another when great populations are concerned, yet it would be impossible to conduct so big a business as ours without large margins. It is the aim in the production of perishable things, and those in which fancy often changes, to keep as little ahead of the demand as possible, but in all the important staples such great surpluses are constantly carried that a two years' drought would not affect the price of non-perishable produce, while an unexpected addition of several millions to the population could be taken care of at any time without disturbance."

"Dr. Leete has told me," I said, "that any part of the credit not used by a citizen during the year is canceled, not being good for the next year. I suppose that is to prevent the possibility of hoarding, by which the equality of your economic condition might be undermined."

"It would have the effect to prevent such hoarding, certainly," said the superintendent, "but it is otherwise needful to simplify the national bookkeeping and prevent confusion. The annual credit is an order on a specific provision available during a certain year. For the next year a new calculation with somewhat different elements has to be made, and to make it the books must be balanced and all orders canceled that have not been presented, so that we may know just where we stand."

"What, on the other hand, will happen if I run through my credit before the year is out?"

The superintendent smiled. "I have read," he said, "that the spendthrift evil was quite a serious one in your day. Our system has the advantage over yours that the most incorrigible spendthrift can not trench on his principal, which consists in his indivisible equal share in the capital of the nation. All he can at most do is to waste the annual dividend. Should you do this, I have no doubt your friends will take care of you, and if they do not you may be sure the nation will, for we have not the strong stomachs that enabled our forefathers to enjoy plenty with hungry people about them. The fact is, we are so squeamish that the knowledge that a single individual in the nation was in want would keep us all awake nights. If you insisted on being in need, you would have to hide away for the purpose.

"Have you any idea," I asked, "how much this credit of $4,000 would have been equal to in purchasing power in 1887?"

"Somewhere about $6,000 or $7,000, I should say," replied Mr. Chapin. "In estimating the economic position of the citizen you must consider that a great variety of services and commodities are now supplied gratuitously on public account, which formerly individuals had to pay for, as, for example, water, light, music, news, the theatre and opera, all sorts of postal and electrical communications, transportation, and other things too numerous to detail."

"Since you furnish so much on public or common account, why not furnish everything in that way? It would simplify matters, I should say."

"We think, on the contrary, that it would complicate the administration, and certainly it would not suit the people as well. You see, while we insist on equality we detest uniformity, and seek to provide free play to the greatest possible variety of tastes in our expenditure."

Thinking I might be interested in looking them over, the superintendent had brought into the office some of the books of the bank. Without having been at all expert in nineteenth-century methods of bookkeeping, I was much impressed with the extreme simplicity of these accounts compared with any I had been familiar with. Speaking of this, I added that it impressed me the more, as I had received an impression that, great as were the superiorities of the national co-operative system over our way of doing business, it must involve a great increase in the amount of bookkeeping as compared with what was necessary under the old system. The superintendent and Dr. Leete looked at each other and smiled.

"Do you know, Mr. West," said the former, "it strikes us as very odd that you should have that idea? We estimate that under our system one accountant serves where dozens were needed in your day."

"But," said I, "the nation has now a separate account with or for every man, woman, and child in the country."

"Of course," replied the superintendent, "but did it not have the same in your day? How else could it have assessed and collected taxes or exacted a dozen other duties from citizens? For example, your tax system alone with its inquisitions, appraisements, machinery of collection and penalties was vastly more complex than the accounts in these books before you, which consist, as you see, in giving to every person the same credit at the beginning of the year, and afterward simply recording the withdrawals without calculations of interest or other incidents whatever. In fact, Mr.

West, so simple and invariable are the conditions that the accounts are kept automatically by a machine, the accountant merely playing on a keyboard."

"But I understand that every citizen has a record kept also of his services as the basis of grading and regrading."

"Certainly, and a most minute one, with most careful guards against error or unfairness. But it is a record having none of the complications of one of your money or wages accounts for work done, but is rather like the simple honor records of your educational institutions by which the ranking of the students was determined."

"But the citizen also has relations with the public stores from which he supplies his needs?"

"Certainly, but not a relation of account. As your people would have said, all purchases are for cash only--that is, on the credit card."

"There remains," I persisted, "the accounting for goods and services between the stores and the productive departments and between the several departments."

"Certainly; but the whole system being under one head and all the parts working together with no friction and no motive for any indirection, such accounting is child's work compared with the adjustment of dealings between the mutually suspicious private capitalists, who divided among themselves the field of business in your day, and sat up nights devising tricks to deceive, defeat, and overreach one another."

"But how about the elaborate statistics on which you base the calculations that guide production? There at least is need of a good deal of figuring."

"Your national and State governments," replied Mr. Chapin, "published annually great masses of similar statistics, which, while often very inaccurate, must have cost far more trouble to accumulate, seeing that they involved an unwelcome inquisition into the affairs of private persons instead of a mere collection of reports from the books of different departments of one great business. Forecasts of probable consumption every manufacturer, merchant, and storekeeper had to make in your day, and mistakes meant ruin. Nevertheless, he could but guess, because he had no sufficient data. Given the complete data that we have, and a forecast is as much increased in certainty as it is simplified in difficulty."

"Kindly spare me any further demonstration of the stupidity of my criticism."

"Dear me, Mr. West, there is no question of stupidity. A wholly new system of things always impresses the mind at first sight with an effect of complexity, although it may be found on examination to be simplicity itself. But please do not stop me just yet, for I have told you only one side of the matter. I have shown you how few and simple are the accounts we keep compared with those in corresponding relations kept by you; but the biggest part of the subject is the accounts you had to keep which we do not keep at all. Debit and credit are no longer known; interest, rents, profits, and all the calculations based on them no more have any place in human affairs. In your day everybody, besides his account with the state, was involved in a network of accounts with all about him. Even the humblest wage-earner was on the books of half a dozen tradesmen, while a man of substance might be down in scores or hundreds, and this without speaking of men not engaged in commerce. A fairly nimble dollar had to be set down so many times in so many places, as it went from hand to hand, that we calculate in about five years it must have cost itself in ink, paper, pens, and clerk hire, let alone fret and worry. All these forms of private and business accounts have now been done away with. Nobody owes anybody, or is owed by anybody, or has any contract with anybody, or any account of any sort with anybody, but is simply beholden to everybody for such kindly regard as his virtues may attract."

CHAPTER V.

I Experience A New Sensation.

"Doctor," said I as we came out of the bank, "I have a most extraordinary feeling."

"What sort of a feeling?"

"It is a sensation which I never had anything like before," I said, "and never expected to have. I feel as if I wanted to go to work. Yes, Julian West, millionaire, loafer by profession, who never did anything useful in his life and never wanted to, finds himself seized with an overmastering desire to roll up his sleeves and do something toward rendering an equivalent for his living."

"But," said the doctor, "Congress has declared you the guest of the nation, and expressly exempted you from the duty of rendering any sort of public service."

"That is all very well, and I take it kindly, but I begin to feel that I should not enjoy knowing that I was living on other people."

"What do you suppose it is," said the doctor, smiling, "that has given you this sensitiveness about living on others which, as you say, you never felt before?"

"I have never been much given to self-analysis," I replied, "but the change of feeling is very easily explained in this case. I find myself surrounded by a community every member of which not physically disqualified is doing his or her own part toward providing the material prosperity which I share. A person must be of remarkably tough sensibilities who would not feel ashamed under such circumstances if he did not take hold with the rest and do his part. Why didn't I feel that way about the duty of working in the nineteenth century? Why, simply because there was no such system then for sharing work, or indeed any system at all. For the reason that there was no fair play or suggestion of justice in the distribution of work, everybody shirked it who could, and those who could not shirk it cursed the luckier ones and got even by doing as bad work as they could. Suppose a rich young fellow like myself had a feeling that he would like to do his part. How was he going to go about it? There was absolutely no social organization by which labor could be shared on any principle of justice. There was no possibility of co-operation. We had to choose between taking advantage of the economic system to live on other people or have them take advantage of it to live on us. We had to climb on their backs as the only way of preventing them from climbing on our backs. We had the alternative of profiting by an unjust system or being its victims. There being no more moral satisfaction in the one alternative than the other, we naturally preferred the first. By glimpses all the more decent of us realized the ineffable meanness of sponging our living out of the toilers, but our consciences were completely bedeviled by an economic system which seemed a hopeless muddle that nobody could see through or set right or do right under. I will undertake to say that there was not a man of my set, certainly not of my friends, who, placed just as I am this morning in presence of an absolutely simple, just, and equal system for distributing the industrial burden, would not feel just as I do the impulse to roll up his sleeves and take hold."

"I am quite sure of it," said the doctor. "Your experience strikingly confirms the chapter of revolutionary history which tells us that when the present economic order was established those who had been under the old system the most irreclaimable loafers and vagabonds, responding to the absolute justice and fairness of the new arrangements, rallied to the service of the state with enthusiasm. But talking of what you are to do, why was not my former suggestion a good one, that you should tell our people in lectures about the nineteenth century?"

"I thought at first that it would be a good idea," I replied, "but our talk in the garden this morning has about convinced me that the very last people who had any intelligent idea of the nineteenth century, what it meant, and what it was leading to, were just myself and my contemporaries of that time. After I have been with you a few years I may learn enough about my own period to discuss it intelligently."

"There is something in that," replied the doctor. "Meanwhile, you see that great building with the dome just across the square? That is our local Industrial Exchange. Perhaps, seeing that we are talking of what you are to do to make yourself useful, you may be interested in learning a little of the method by which our people choose their occupations."

I readily assented, and we crossed the square to the exchange.

"I have given you thus far," said the doctor, "only a general outline of our system of universal industrial service. You know that every one of either sex, unless for some reason temporarily or permanently exempt, enters the public industrial service in the twenty-first year, and after three years of a sort of general apprenticeship in the unclassified grades elects a special occupation, unless he prefers to study further for one of the scientific professions. As there are a million youth, more or less, who thus annually elect their occupations, you may imagine that it must be a complex task to find a place for each in which his or her own taste shall be suited as well as the needs of the public service."

I assured the doctor that I had indeed made this reflection.

"A very few moments will suffice," he said, "to disabuse your mind of that notion and to show you how wonderfully a little rational system has simplified the task of finding a fitting vocation in life which used to be so difficult a matter in your day and so rarely was accomplished in a satisfactory manner."

Finding a comfortable corner for us near one of the windows of the central hall, the doctor presently brought a lot of sample blanks and schedules and proceeded to explain them to me. First he showed me the annual statement of exigencies by the General Government, specifying in what proportion the force of workers that was to become available that year ought to be distributed among the several occupations in order to carry on the industrial service. That was the side of the subject which represented the necessities of the public service that must be met. Next he showed me the volunteering or preference blank, on which every youth that year graduating from the unclassified service indicated, if he chose to, the order of his preference as to the various occupations making up the public service, it being inferred, if he did not fill out the blank, that he or she was willing to be assigned for the convenience of the service.

"But," said I, "locality of residence is often quite as important as the kind of one's occupation. For example, one might not wish to be separated from parents, and certainly would not wish to be from a sweetheart, however agreeable the occupation assigned might be in other respects."

"Very true," said the doctor. "If, indeed, our industrial system undertook to separate lovers and friends, husbands and wives, parents and children, without regard to their wishes, it certainly would not last long. You see this column of localities. If you make your cross against Boston in that column, it becomes imperative upon the administration to provide you employment somewhere in this district. It is one of the rights of every citizen to demand employment within his home district. Otherwise, as you say, ties of love and friendship might be rudely broken. But, of course, one can not have his cake and eat it too; if you make work in the home district imperative, you may have to take an occupation to which you would have preferred some other that might have been open to you had you been willing to leave home. However, it is not common that one needs to sacrifice a chosen career to the ties of affection. The country is divided into industrial districts or circles, in each of which there is intended to be as nearly as possible a complete system of industry, wherein all the important arts and occupations are represented. It is in this way made possible for most of us to find an opportunity in a chosen occupation without separation from friends. This is the more simply done, as the modern means of communication have so far abolished distance that the man who lives in Boston and works in Springfield, one hundred miles away, is quite as near his place of business as was the average workingman of your day. One who, living in Boston, should work two hundred miles away (in Albany), would be far better situated than the average suburbanite doing business in Boston a century ago. But while a great number desire to find occupations at home, there are also many who from love of change much prefer to leave the scenes of their childhood. These, too, indicate their preferences by marking the number of the district to which they prefer to be assigned. Second or third preferences may likewise be indicated, so that it would go hard indeed if one could not obtain a location in at least the part of the country he desired, though the locality preference is imperative only when the person desires to stay in the home district. Otherwise it is consulted so far as consistent with conflicting claims. The volunteer having thus filled out his preference blank, takes it to the proper registrar and has his ranking officially stamped upon it."

"What is the ranking?" I asked.

"It is the figure which indicates his previous standing in the schools and during his service as an unclassified worker, and is supposed to give the best attainable criterion thus far of his relative intelligence, efficiency, and devotion to duty. Where there are more volunteers for particular occupations than there is room for, the lowest in ranking have to be content with a second or third preference. The preference blanks are finally handed in at the local exchange, and are collated at the central office of the industrial district. All who have made home work imperative are first provided for in accordance with rank. The blanks of those preferring work in other districts are forwarded to the national bureau and there collated with those from other districts, so that the volunteers may be provided for as nearly as may be according to their wishes, subject, where conflict of claim arises, to their relative ranking right. It has always been observed that the personal eccentricities of individuals in great bodies have a wonderful tendency to balance and mutually complement one another, and this principle is strikingly illustrated in our system of choice of occupation and locality. The preference blanks are filled out in June, and by the first of August everybody knows just where he or she is to report for service in October.

"However, if any one has received an assignment which is decidedly unwelcome either as to location or occupation, it is not even then, or indeed at any time, too late to endeavor to find another. The administration has done its best to adjust the individual aptitude and wishes of each worker to the needs of the public service, but its machinery is at his service for any further attempts he may wish to make to suit himself better."

And then the doctor took me to the Transfer Department and showed me how persons who were dissatisfied either with their assignment of occupation or locality could put themselves in communication with all others in any part of the country who were similarly dissatisfied, and arrange, subject to liberal regulations, such exchanges as might be mutually agreeable.

"If a person is not absolutely unwilling to do anything at all," he said, "and does not object to all parts of the country equally, he ought to be able sooner or later to provide himself both with pretty nearly the occupation and locality he desires. And if, after all, there should be any one so dull that he can not hope to succeed in his occupation or make a better exchange with another, yet there is no occupation now tolerated by the state which would not have been as to its conditions a godsend to the most fortunately situated workman of your day. There is none in which peril to life or health is not reduced to a minimum, and the dignity and rights of the worker absolutely guaranteed. It is a constant study of the administration so to bait the less attractive occupations with special advantages as to leisure and otherwise always to keep the balance of preference between them as nearly true as possible; and if, finally, there were any occupation which, after all, remained so distasteful as to attract no volunteers, and yet was necessary, its duties would be performed by all in rotation."

"As, for example," I said, "the work of repairing and cleansing the sewers."

"If that sort of work were as offensive as it must have been in your day, I dare say it might have to be done by a rotation in which all would take their turn," replied the doctor, "but our sewers are as clean as our streets. They convey only water which has been chemically purified and deodorized before it enters them by an apparatus connected with every dwelling. By the same apparatus all solid sewage is electrically cremated, and removed in the form of ashes. This improvement in the sewer system, which followed the great Revolution very closely, might have waited a hundred years before introduction but for the Revolution, although the necessary scientific knowledge and appliances had long been available. The case furnishes merely one instance out of a thousand of the devices for avoiding repulsive and perilous sorts of work which, while simple enough, the world would never have troubled itself to adopt so long as the rich had in the poor a race of uncomplaining economic serfs on which to lay all their burdens. The effect of economic equality was to make it equally the interest of all to avoid, so far as possible, the more unpleasant tasks, since henceforth they must be shared by all. In this way, wholly apart from the moral aspects of the matter, the progress of chemical, sanitary, and mechanical science owes an incalculable debt to the Revolution."

"Probably," I said, "you have sometimes eccentric persons--'crooked sticks' we used to call them--who refuse to adapt themselves to the social order on any terms or admit any such thing as social duty. If such a person should flatly refuse to render any sort of industrial or useful service on any terms, what would be done with him? No doubt there is a compulsory side to your system for dealing with such persons?"

"Not at all," replied the doctor. "If our system can not stand on its merits as the best possible arrangement for promoting the highest welfare of all, let it fall. As to the matter of industrial service, the law is simply that if any one shall refuse to do his or her part toward the maintenance of the social order he shall not be allowed to partake of its benefits. It would obviously not be fair to the rest that he should do so. But as to compelling him to work against his will by force, such an idea would be abhorrent to our people. The service of society is, above all, a service of honor, and all its associations are what you used to call chivalrous. Even as in your day soldiers would not serve with skulkers, but drummed cowards out of the camp, so would our workers refuse the companionship of persons openly seeking to evade their civic duty."

"But what do you do with such persons?"

"If an adult, being neither criminal nor insane, should deliberately and fixedly refuse to render his quota of service in any way, either in a chosen occupation or, on failure to choose, in an assigned one, he would be furnished with such a collection of seeds and tools as he might choose and turned loose on a reservation expressly prepared for such persons, corresponding a little perhaps with the reservations set apart for such Indians in your day as were unwilling to accept civilization. There he would be left to work out a better solution of the problem of existence than our society offers, if he could do so. We think we have the best possible social system, but if there is a better we want to know it, so that we may adopt it. We encourage the spirit of experiment."

"And are there really cases," I said, "of individuals who thus voluntarily abandon society in preference to fulfilling their social duty?"

"There have been such cases, though I do not know that there are any at the present time. But the provision for them exists."

CHAPTER VI.

Honi Soit Qui Mal Y Pense.

When we reached the house the doctor said:

"I am going to leave you to Edith this morning. The fact is, my duties as mentor, while extremely to my taste, are not quite a sinecure. The questions raised in our talks frequently suggest the necessity of refreshing my general knowledge of the contrasts between your day and this by looking up the historical authorities. The conversation this morning has indicated lines of research which will keep me busy in the library the rest of the day."

I found Edith in the garden, and received her congratulations upon my fully fledged citizenship. She did not seem at all surprised on learning my intention promptly to find a place in the industrial service.

"Of course you will want to enter the service as soon as you can," she said. "I knew you would. It is the only way to get in touch with the people and feel really one of the nation. It is the great event we all look forward to from childhood."

"Talking of industrial service," I said, "reminds me of a question it has a dozen times occurred to me to ask you. I understand that everyone who is able to do so, women as well as men, serves the nation from twenty-one to forty-five years of age in some useful occupation; but so far as I have seen, although you are the picture of health and vigor, you have no employment, but are quite like young ladies of elegant leisure in my day, who spent their time sitting in the parlor and looking handsome. Of course, it is highly agreeable to me that you should be so free, but how, exactly, is so much leisure on your part squared with the universal obligation of service?"

Edith was greatly amused. "And so you thought I was shirking? Had it not occurred to you that there might probably be such things as vacations or furloughs in the industrial service, and that the rather unusual and interesting guest in our household might furnish a natural occasion for me to take an outing if I could get it?"

"And can you take your vacation when you please?"

"We can take a portion of it when we please, always subject, of course, to the needs of the service."

"But what do you do when you are at work--teach school, paint china, keep books for the Government, stand behind a counter in the public stores, or operate a typewriter or telegraph wire?"

"Does that list exhaust the number of women's occupations in your day?"

"Oh, no; those were only some of their lighter and pleasanter occupations. Women were also the scrubbers, the washers, the servants of all work. The most repulsive and humiliating kinds of drudgery were put off upon the women of the poorer class; but I suppose, of course, you do not do any such work."

"You may be sure that I do my part of whatever unpleasant things there are to do, and so does every one in the nation; but, indeed, we have long ago arranged affairs so that there is very little such work to do. But, tell me, were there no women in your day who were machinists, farmers, engineers, carpenters, iron workers, builders, engine drivers, or members of the other great crafts?"

"There were no women in such occupations. They were followed by men only."

"I suppose I knew that," she said; "I have read as much; but it is strange to talk with a man of the nineteenth century who is so much like a man of to-day and realize that the women were so different as to seem like another order of beings."

"But, really," said I, "I don't understand how in these respects the women can do very differently now unless they are physically much stronger. Most of these occupations you have just mentioned were too heavy for their strength, and for that reason, largely, were limited to men, as I should suppose they must still be."

"There is not a trade or occupation in the whole list," replied Edith, "in which women do not take part. It is partly because we are physically much more vigorous than the poor creatures of your time that we do the sorts of work that were too heavy for them, but it is still more an account of the perfection of machinery. As we have grown stronger, all sorts of work have grown lighter. Almost no heavy work is done directly now; machines do all, and we only need to guide them, and the lighter the hand that guides, the better the work done. So you see that nowadays physical qualities have much less to do than mental with the choice of occupations. The mind is constantly getting nearer to the work, and father says some day we may be able to work by sheer will power directly and have no need of hands at all. It is said that there are actually more women than men in great machine works. My mother was first lieutenant in a great iron works. Some have a theory that the sense of power which one has in controlling giant engines appeals to women's sensibilities even more than to men's. But really it is not quite fair to make you guess what my occupation is, for I have not fully decided on it."

"But you said you were already at work."

"Oh, yes, but you know that before we choose our life occupation we are three years in the unclassified or miscellaneous class of workers. I am in my second year in that class."

"What do you do?"

"A little of everything and nothing long. The idea is to give us during that period a little practical experience in all the main departments of work, so that we may know better how and what to choose as an occupation. We are supposed to have got through with the schools before we enter this class, but really I have learned more since I have been at work than in twice the time spent in school. You can not imagine how perfectly delightful this grade of work is. I don't wonder some people prefer to stay in it all their lives for the sake of the constant change in tasks, rather than elect a regular occupation. Just now I am among the agricultural workers on the great farm near Lexington. It is delightful, and I have about made up my mind to choose farm work as an occupation. That is what I had in mind when I asked you to guess my trade. Do you think you would ever have guessed that?"

"I don't think I ever should, and unless the conditions of farm work have greatly changed since my day I can not imagine how you could manage it in a woman's costume."

Edith regarded me for a moment with an expression of simple surprise, her eyes growing large. Then her glance fell to her dress, and when she again looked up her expression had changed to one which was at once meditative, humorous, and wholly inscrutable. Presently she said:

"Have you not observed, my dear Julian, that the dress of the women you see on the streets is different from that which women wore in the nineteenth century?"

"I have noticed, of course, that they generally wear no skirts, but you and your mother dress as women did in my day."

"And has it not occurred to you to wonder why our dress was not like theirs--why we wear skirts and they do not?"

"Possibly that has occurred to me among the thousand other questions that every day arise in my mind, only to be driven out by a thousand others before I can ask them; but I think in this case I should have rather wondered why these other women did not dress as you do instead of why you did not dress as they do, for your costume, being the one I was accustomed to, naturally struck me as the normal type, and this other style as a variation for some special or local reason which I should later learn about. You must not think me altogether stupid. To tell the truth, these other women have as yet scarcely impressed me as being very real. You were at first the only person about whose reality I felt entirely sure. All the others seemed merely parts of a fantastic farrago of wonders, more or less possible, which is only just beginning to become intelligible and coherent. In time I should doubtless have awakened to the fact that there were other women in the world besides yourself and begun to make inquiries about them."

As I spoke of the absoluteness with which I had depended on her during those first bewildering days for the assurance even of my own identity the quick tears rushed to my companion's eyes, and--well, for a space the other women were more completely forgotten than ever.

Presently she said: "What were we talking about? Oh, yes, I remember--about those other women. I have a confession to make. I have been guilty toward you all this time of a sort of fraud, or at least of a flagrant suppression of the truth, which ought not to be kept up a moment longer. I sincerely hope you will forgive me, in consideration of my motive, and not----"

"Not what?"

"Not be too much startled."

"You make me very curious," I said. "What is this mystery? I think I can stand the disclosure."

"Listen, then," she said. "That wonderful night when we saw you first, of course our great thought was to avoid agitating you when you should recover full consciousness by any more evidence of the amazing things that had happened since your day than it was necessary you should see. We knew that in your time the use of long skirts by women was universal, and we reflected that to see mother and me in the modern dress would no doubt strike you very strangely. Now, you see, although skirtless costumes are the general--indeed, almost universal--wear for most occasions, all possible costumes, ancient and modern, of all races, ages, and civilizations, are either provided or to be obtained on the shortest possible notice at the stores. It was therefore very easy for us to furnish ourselves with the old-style dress before father introduced you to us. He said people had in your day such strange ideas of feminine modesty and propriety that it would be the best way to do. Can you forgive us, Julian, for taking such an advantage of your ignorance?"

"Edith," I said, "there were a great many institutions of the nineteenth century which we tolerated because we did not know how to get rid of them, without, however, having a bit better opinion of them than you have, and one of them was the costume by means of which our women used to disguise and cripple themselves."

"I am delighted!" exclaimed Edith. "I perfectly detest these horrible bags, and will not wear them a moment longer!" And bidding me wait where I was, she ran into the house.

Five minutes, perhaps, I waited there in the arbor, where we had been sitting, and then, at a light step on the grass, looked up to see Edith with eyes of smiling challenge standing before me in modern dress. I have seen her in a hundred varieties of that costume since then, and have grown familiar with the exhaustless diversity of its adaptations, but I defy the imagination of the greatest artist to devise a scheme of color and fabric that would again produce upon me the effect of enchanting surprise which I received from that quite simple and hasty toilet.

I don't know how long I stood looking at her without a thought of words, my eyes meanwhile no doubt testifying eloquently enough how adorable I found her. She seemed, however, to divine more than that in my expression, for presently she exclaimed:

"I would give anything to know what you are thinking down in the bottom of your mind! It must be something awfully funny. What are you turning so red for?"

"I am blushing for myself," I said, and that is all I would tell her, much as she teased me. Now, at this distance of time I may tell the truth. My first sentiment, apart from overwhelming admiration, had been a slight astonishment at her absolute ease and composure of bearing under my gaze. This is a confession that may well seem incomprehensible to twentieth-century readers, and God forbid that they should ever catch the point of view which would enable them to understand it better! A woman of my day, unless professionally accustomed to use this sort of costume, would have seemed embarrassed and ill at ease, at least for a time, under a gaze so intent as mine, even though it were a brother's or a father's. I, it seems, had been prepared for at least some slight appearance of discomposure on Edith's part, and was consciously surprised at a manner which simply expressed an ingenuous gratification at my admiration. I refer to this momentary experience because it has always seemed to me to illustrate in a particularly vivid way the change that has taken place not only in the customs but in the mental attitude of the sexes as to each other since my former life. In justice to myself I must hasten to add that this first feeling of surprise vanished even as it arose, in a moment, between two heart-beats. I caught from her clear, serene eyes the view point of the modern man as to woman, never again to lose it. Then it was that I flushed red with shame for myself. Wild horses could not have dragged from me the secret of that blush at the time, though I have told her long ago.

"I was thinking," I said, and I was thinking so, too, "that we ought to be greatly obliged to twentieth-century women for revealing for the first time the artistic possibilities of the masculine dress."

"The masculine dress," she repeated, as if not quite comprehending my meaning. "Do you mean my dress?"

"Why, yes; it is a man's dress I suppose, is it not?"

"Why any more than a woman's?" she answered rather blankly. "Ah, yes, I actually forgot for a moment whom I was talking to. I see; so it was considered a man's dress in your day, when the women masqueraded as mermaids. You may think me stupid not to catch your idea more quickly, but I told you I was dull at history. It is now two full generations since women as well as men have worn this dress, and the idea of associating it with men more than women would occur to no one but a professor of history. It strikes us merely as the only natural and convenient solution of the dress necessity, which is essentially the same for both sexes, since their bodily conformation is on the same general lines."

CHAPTER VII.

A String Of Surprises.

The extremely delicate tints of Edith's costume led me to remark that the color effects of the modern dress seemed to be in general very light as compared with those which prevailed in my day.

"The result," I said, "is extremely pleasing, but if you will excuse a rather prosaic suggestion, it occurs to me that with the whole nation given over to wearing these delicate schemes of color, the accounts for washing must be pretty large. I should suppose they would swamp the national treasury if laundry bills are anything like what they used to be."

This remark, which I thought a very sensible one, set Edith to laughing. "Doubtless we could not do much else if we washed our clothes," she said; "but you see we do not wash them."

"Not wash them!--why not?"

"Because we don't think it nice to wear clothes again after they have been so much soiled as to need washing."

"Well, I won't say that I am surprised," I replied; "in fact, I think I am no longer capable of being surprised at anything; but perhaps you will kindly tell me what you do with a dress when it becomes soiled."

"We throw it away--that is, it goes back to the mills to be made into something else."

"Indeed! To my nineteenth-century intellect, throwing away clothing would seem even more expensive than washing it."

"Oh, no, much less so. What do you suppose, now, this costume of mine cost?"

"I don't know, I am sure. I never had a wife to pay dressmaker's bills for, but I should say certainly it cost a great deal of money."

"Such costumes cost from ten to twenty cents," said Edith. "What do you suppose it is made of?"

I took the edge of her mantle between my fingers.

"I thought it was silk or fine linen," I replied, "but I see it is not. Doubtless it is some new fiber."

"We have discovered many new fibers, but it is rather a question of process than material that I had in mind. This is not a textile fabric at all, but paper. That is the most common material for garments nowadays."

"But--but," I exclaimed, "what if it should come on to rain on these paper clothes? Would they not melt, and at a little strain would they not part?"

"A costume such as this," said Edith, "is not meant for stormy weather, and yet it would by no means melt in a rainstorm, however severe. For storm-garments we have a paper that is absolutely impervious to moisture on the outer surface. As to toughness, I think you would find it as hard to tear this paper as any ordinary cloth. The fabric is so strengthened with fiber as to hold together very stoutly."

"But in winter, at least, when you need warmth, you must have to fall back on our old friend the sheep."

"You mean garments made of sheep's hair? Oh, no, there is no modern use for them. Porous paper makes a garment quite as warm as woolen could, and vastly lighter than the clothes you had. Nothing but eider down could have been at once so warm and light as our winter coats of paper."

"And cotton!--linen! Don't tell me that they have been given up, like wool?"

"Oh, no; we weave fabrics of these and other vegetable products, and they are nearly as cheap as paper, but paper is so much lighter and more easily fashioned into all shapes that it is generally preferred for garments. But, at any rate, we should consider no material fit for garments which could not be thrown away after being soiled. The idea of washing and cleaning articles of bodily use and using them over and over again would be quite intolerable. For this reason, while we want beautiful garments, we distinctly do not want durable ones. In your day, it seems, even worse than the practice of washing garments to be used again you were in the habit of keeping your outer garments without washing at all, not only day after day, but week after week, year after year, sometimes whole lifetimes, when they were specially valuable, and finally, perhaps, giving them away to others. It seems that women sometimes kept their wedding dresses long enough for their daughters to wear at their weddings. That would seem shocking to us, and yet, even your fine ladies did such things. As for what the poor had to do in the way of keeping and wearing their old clothes till they went to rags, that is something which won't bear thinking of."

"It is rather startling," I said, "to find the problem of clean clothing solved by the abolition of the wash tub, although I perceive that that was the only radical solution. 'Warranted to wear and wash' used to be the advertisement of our clothing merchants, but now it seems, if you would sell clothing, you must warrant the goods neither to wear nor to wash."

"As for wearing," said Edith, "our clothing never gets the chance to show how it would wear before we throw it away, any more than the other fabrics, such as carpets, bedding, and hangings that we use about our houses."

"You don't mean that they are paper-made also!" I exclaimed.

"Not always made of paper, but always of some fabric so cheap that they can be rejected after the briefest period of using. When you would have swept a carpet we put in a new one. Where you would wash or air bedding we renew it, and so with all the hangings about our houses so far as we use them at all. We upholster with air or water instead of feathers. It is more than I can understand how you ever endured your musty, fusty, dusty rooms with the filth and disease germs of whole generations stored in the woolen and hair fabrics that furnished them. When we clean out a room we turn the hose on ceiling, walls, and floor. There is nothing to harm--nothing but tiled or other hard-finished surfaces. Our hygienists say that the change in customs in these matters relating to the purity of our clothing and dwellings, has done more than all our other improvements to eradicate the germs of contagious and other diseases and relegate epidemics to ancient history.

"Talking of paper," said Edith, extending a very trim foot by way of attracting attention to its gear, "what do you think of our modern shoes?"

"Do you mean that they also are made of paper?" I exclaimed.

"Of course."

"I noticed the shoes your father gave me were very light as compared with anything I had ever worn before. Really that is a great idea, for lightness in foot wear is the first necessity. Scamp shoemakers used to put paper soles in shoes in my day. It is evident that instead of prosecuting them for rascals we should have revered them as unconscious prophets. But, for that matter, how do you prepare soles of paper that will last?"

"There are plenty of solutions which will make paper as hard as iron."

"And do not these shoes leak in winter?"

"We have different kinds for different weathers. All are seamless, and the wet-weather sort are coated outside with a lacquer impervious to moisture."

"That means, I suppose, that rubbers too as articles of wear have been sent to the museum?"

"We use rubber, but not for wear. Our waterproof paper is much lighter and better every way."

"After all this it is easy to believe that your hats and caps are also paper-made."

"And so they are to a great extent," said Edith; "the heavy headgear that made your men bald ours would not endure. We want as little as possible on our heads, and that as light as may be."

"Go on!" I exclaimed. "I suppose I am next to be told that the delicious but mysterious articles of food which come by the pneumatic carrier from the restaurant or are served there are likewise made out of paper. Proceed--I am prepared to believe it!"

"Not quite so bad as that," laughed my companion, "but really the next thing to it, for the dishes you eat them from are made of paper. The crash of crockery and glass, which seems to have been a sort of running accompaniment to housekeeping in your day, is no more heard in the land. Our dishes and kettles for eating or cooking, when they need cleaning are thrown away, or rather, as in the case of all these rejected materials I have spoken of, sent back to the factories to be reduced again to pulp and made over into other forms."

"But you certainly do not use paper kettles? Fire will still burn, I fancy, although you seem to have changed most of the other rules we went by."

"Fire will still burn, indeed, but the electrical heat has been adopted for cooking as well as for all other purposes. We no longer heat our vessels from without but from within, and the consequence is that we do our cooking in paper vessels on wooden stoves, even as the savages used to do it in birch-bark vessels with hot stones, for, so the philosophers say, history repeats itself in an ever-ascending spiral."

And now Edith began to laugh at my perplexed expression. She declared that it was clear my credulity had been taxed with these accounts of modern novelties about as far as it would be prudent to try it without furnishing some further evidence of the truth of the statements she had made. She proposed accordingly, for the balance of the morning, a visit to some of the great paper-process factories.

CHAPTER VIII.

The Greatest Wonder Yet--Fashion Dethroned.

"You surely can not form the slightest idea of the bodily ecstasy it gives me to have done with that horrible masquerade in mummy clothes," exclaimed my companion as we left the house. "To think this is the first time we have actually been walking together!"

"Surely you forget," I replied; "we have been out together several times."

"Out together, yes, but not walking," she answered; "at least I was not walking. I don't know what would be the proper zoological term to describe the way I got over the ground inside of those bags, but it certainly was not walking. The women of your day, you see, were trained from childhood in that mode of progression, and no doubt acquired some skill in it; but I never had skirts on in my life except once, in some theatricals. It was the hardest thing I ever tried, and I doubt if I ever again give you so strong a proof of my regard. I am astonished that you did not seem to notice what a distressful time I was having."

But if, being accustomed, as I had been, to the gait of women hampered by draperies, I had not observed anything unusual in Edith's walk when we had been out on previous occasions, the buoyant grace of her carriage and the elastic vigor of her step as she strode now by my side was a revelation of the possibilities of an athletic companionship which was not a little intoxicating.

To describe in detail what I saw in my tour that day through the paper-process factories would be to tell an old story to twentieth-century readers; but what far more impressed me than all the ingenuity and variety of mechanical adaptations was the workers themselves and the conditions of their labor. I need not tell my readers what the great mills are in these days--lofty, airy halls, walled with beautiful designs in tiles and metal, furnished like palaces, with every convenience, the machinery running almost noiselessly, and every incident of the work that might be offensive to any sense reduced by ingenious devices to the minimum. Neither need I describe to you the princely workers in these palaces of industry, the strong and splendid men and women, with their refined and cultured faces, prosecuting with the enthusiasm of artists their self-chosen tasks of combining use and beauty. You all know what your factories are to-day; no doubt you find them none too pleasant or convenient, having been used to such things all your lives. No doubt you even criticise them in various ways as falling short of what they might be, for such is human nature; but if you would understand how they seem to me, shut your eyes a moment and try to conceive in fancy what our cotton and woolen and paper mills were like a hundred years ago.

Picture low rooms roofed with rough and grimy timbers and walled with bare or whitewashed brick. Imagine the floor so crammed with machinery for economy of space as to allow bare room for the workers to writhe about among the flying arms and jaws of steel, a false motion meaning death or mutilation. Imagine the air space above filled, instead of air, with a mixture of stenches of oil and filth, unwashed human bodies, and foul clothing. Conceive a perpetual clang and clash of machinery like the screech of a tornado.

But these were only the material conditions of the scene. Shut your eyes once more, that you may see what I would fain forget I had ever seen--the interminable rows of women, pallid, hollow-cheeked, with faces vacant and stolid but for the accent of misery, their clothing tattered, faded, and foul; and not women only, but multitudes of little children, weazen-faced and ragged--children whose mother's milk was barely out of their blood, their bones yet in the gristle.

Edith introduced me to the superintendent of one of the factories, a handsome woman of perhaps forty years. She very kindly showed us about and explained matters to me, and was much interested in turn to know what I thought of the modern factories and their points of contrast with those of former days. Naturally, I told her that I had been impressed, far more than by anything in the new mechanical appliances, with the transformation in the condition of the workers themselves.

"Ah, yes," she said, "of course you would say so; that must indeed be the great contrast, though the present ways seem so entirely a matter of course to us that we forget it was not always so. When the workers settle how the work shall be done, it is not wonderful that the conditions should be the pleasantest possible. On the other hand, when, as in your day, a class like your private capitalists, who did not share the work, nevertheless settled how it should be done it is not surprising that the conditions of industry should have been as barbarous as they were, especially when the operation of the competitive system compelled the capitalists to get the most work possible out of the workers on the cheapest terms."

"Do I understand." I asked, "that the workers in each trade regulate for themselves the conditions of their particular occupation?"

"By no means. The unitary character of our industrial administration is the vital idea of it, without which it would instantly become impracticable. If the members of each trade controlled its conditions, they would presently be tempted to conduct it selfishly and adversely to the general interest of the community, seeking, as your private capitalists did, to get as much and give as little as possible. And not only would every distinctive class of workers be tempted to act in this manner, but every subdivision of workers in the same trade would presently be pursuing the same policy, until the whole industrial system would become disintegrated, and we should have to call the capitalists from their graves to save us. When I said that the workers regulated the conditions of work, I meant the workers as a whole--that is, the people at large, all of whom are nowadays workers, you know. The regulation and mutual adjustment of the conditions of the several branches of the industrial system are wholly done by the General Government. At the same time, however, the regulation of the conditions of work in any occupation is effectively, though indirectly, controlled by the workers in it through the right we all have to choose and change our occupations. Nobody would choose an occupation the conditions of which were not satisfactory, so they have to be made and kept satisfactory."

While we were at the factory the noon hour came, and I asked the superintendent and Edith to go out to lunch with me. In fact, I wanted to ascertain whether my newly acquired credit card was really good for anything or not.

"There is one point about your modern costumes," I said, as we sat at our table in the dining hall, "about which I am rather curious. Will you tell me who or what sets the fashions?"

"The Creator sets the only fashion which is now generally followed," Edith answered.

"And what is that?"

"The fashion of our bodies," she answered.

"Ah, yes, very good," I replied, "and very true, too, of your costumes, as it certainly was not of ours; but my question still remains. Allowing that you have a general theory of dress, there are a thousand differences in details, with possible variations of style, shape, color, material, and what not. Now, the making of garments is carried on, I suppose, like all your other industries, as public business, under collective management, is it not?"

"Certainly. People, of course, can make their own clothes if they wish to, just as they can make anything else, but it would be a great waste of time and energy."

"Very well. The garments turned out by the factories have to be made up on some particular design or designs. In my day the question of designs of garments was settled by society leaders, fashion journals, edicts from Paris, or the Lord knows how; but at any rate the question was settled for us, and we had nothing to do but to obey. I don't say it was a good way; on the contrary, it was detestable; but what I want to know is, What system have you instead, for I suppose you have now no society leaders, fashion journals, or Paris edicts? Who settles the question what you shall wear?"

"We do," replied the superintendent.

"You mean, I suppose, that you determine it collectively by democratic methods. Now, when I look around me in this dining hall and see the variety and beauty of the costumes, I am bound to say that the result of your system seems satisfactory, and yet I think it would strike even the strongest believer in the principle of democracy that the rule of the majority ought scarcely to extend to dress. I admit that the yoke of fashion which we bowed to was very onerous, and yet it was true that if we were brave enough, as few indeed were, we might defy it; but with the style of dress determined by the administration, and only certain styles made, you must either follow the taste of the majority or lie abed. Why do you laugh? Is it not so?"

"We were smiling," replied the superintendent, "on account of a slight misapprehension on your part. When I said that we regulated questions of dress, I meant that we regulated them not collectively, by majority, but individually, each for himself or herself."

"But I don't see how you can," I persisted. "The business of producing fabrics and of making them into garments is carried on by the Government. Does not that imply, practically, a governmental control or initiative in fashions of dress?"

"Dear me, no!" exclaimed the superintendent. "It is evident, Mr. West, as indeed the histories say, that governmental action carried with it in your day an arbitrary implication which it does not now. The Government is actually now what it nominally was in the America of your day--the servant, tool, and instrument by which the people give effect to their will, itself being without will. The popular will is expressed in two ways, which are quite distinct and relate to different provinces: First, collectively, by majority, in regard to blended, mutually involved interests, such as the large economic and political concerns of the community; second, personally, by each individual for himself or herself in the furtherance of private and self-regarding matters. The Government is not more absolutely the servant of the collective will in regard to the blended interests of the community than it is of the individual convenience in personal matters. It is at once the august representative of all in general concerns, and everybody's agent, errand boy, and factotum for all private ends. Nothing is too high or too low, too great or too little, for it to do for us.

"The dressmaking department holds its vast provision of fabrics and machinery at the absolute disposition of the whims of every man or woman in the nation. You can go to one of the stores and order any costume of which a historical description exists, from the days of Eve to yesterday, or you can furnish a design of your own invention for a brand-new costume, designating any material at present existing, and it will be sent home to you in less time than any nineteenth-century dressmaker ever even promised to fill an order. Really, talking of this, I want you to see our garment-making machines in operation. Our paper garments, of course, are seamless, and made wholly by machinery. The apparatus being adjustable to any measure, you can have a costume turned out for you complete while you are looking over the machine. There are, of course, some general styles and shapes that are usually popular, and the stores keep a supply of them on hand, but that is for the convenience of the people, not of the department, which holds itself always ready to follow the initiative of any citizen and provide anything ordered in the least possible time."

"Then anybody can set the fashion?" I said.

"Anybody can set it, but whether it is followed depends on whether it is a good one, and really has some new point in respect of convenience or beauty; otherwise it certainly will not become a fashion. Its vogue will be precisely proportioned to the merit the popular taste recognizes in it, just as if it were an invention in mechanics. If a new idea in dress has any merit in it, it is taken up with great promptness, for our people are extremely interested in enhancing personal beauty by costume, and the absence of any arbitrary standards of style such as fashion set for you leaves us on the alert for attractions and novelties in shape and color. It is in variety of effect that our mode of dressing seems indeed to differ most from yours. Your styles were constantly being varied by the edicts of fashion, but as only one style was tolerated at a time, you had only a successive and not a simultaneous variety, such as we have. I should imagine that this uniformity of style, extending, as I understand it often did, to fabric, color, and shape alike, must have caused your great assemblages to present a depressing effect of sameness.

"That was a fact fully admitted in my day," I replied. "The artists were the enemies of fashion, as indeed all sensible people were, but resistance was in vain. Do you know, if I were to return to the nineteenth century, there is perhaps nothing else I could tell my contemporaries of the changes you have made that would so deeply impress them as the information that you had broken the scepter of fashion, that there were no longer any arbitrary standards in dress recognized, and that no style had any other vogue that might be given it by individual recognition of its merits. That most of the other yokes humanity wore might some day be broken, the more hopeful of us believed, but the yoke of fashion we never expected to be freed from, unless perhaps in heaven."

"The reign of fashion, as the history books call it, always seemed to me one of the most utterly incomprehensible things about the old order," said Edith. "It would seem that it must have had some great force behind it to compel such abject submission to a rule so tyrannical. And yet there seems to have been no force at all used. Do tell us what the secret was, Julian?"

"Don't ask me," I protested. "It seemed to be some fell enchantment that we were subject to--that is all I know. Nobody professed to understand why we did as we did. Can't you tell us," I added, turning to the superintendent--"how do you moderns diagnose the fashion mania that made our lives such a burden to us?"

"Since you appeal to me," replied our companion, "I may say that the historians explain the dominion of fashion in your age as the natural result of a disparity of economic conditions prevailing in a community in which rigid distinctions of caste had ceased to exist. It resulted from two factors: the desire of the common herd to imitate the superior class, and the desire of the superior class to protect themselves from that imitation and preserve distinction of appearance. In times and countries where class was caste, and fixed by law or iron custom, each caste had its distinctive dress, to imitate which was not allowed to another class. Consequently fashions were stationary. With the rise of democracy, the legal protection of class distinctions was abolished, while the actual disparity in social ranks still existed, owing to the persistence of economic inequalities. It was now free for all to imitate the superior class, and thus seem at least to be as good as it, and no kind of imitation was so natural and easy as dress. First, the socially ambitious led off in this imitation; then presently the less pretentious were constrained to follow their example, to avoid an apparent confession of social inferiority; till, finally, even the philosophers had to follow the herd and conform to the fashion, to avoid being conspicuous by an exceptional appearance."

"I can see," said Edith, "how social emulation should make the masses imitate the richer and superior class, and how the fashions should in this way be set; but why were they changed so often, when it must have been so terribly expensive and troublesome to make the changes?"

"For the reason," answered the superintendent, "that the only way the superior class could escape their imitators and preserve their distinction in dress was by adopting constantly new fashions, only to drop them for still newer ones as soon as they were imitated.--Does it seem to you, Mr. West, that this explanation corresponds with the facts as you observed them?"

"Entirely so," I replied. "It might be added, too, that the changes in fashions were greatly fomented and assisted by the self-interest of vast industrial and commercial interests engaged in purveying the materials of dress and personal belongings. Every change, by creating a demand for new materials and rendering those in use obsolete, was what we called good for trade, though if tradesmen were unlucky enough to be caught by a sudden change of fashion with a lot of goods on hand it meant ruin to them. Great losses of this sort, indeed, attended every change in fashion."

"But we read that there were fashions in many things besides dress," said Edith.

"Certainly," said the superintendent. "Dress was the stronghold and main province of fashion because imitation was easiest and most effective through dress, but in nearly everything that pertained to the habits of living, eating, drinking, recreation, to houses, furniture, horses and carriages, and servants, to the manner of bowing even, and shaking hands, to the mode of eating food and taking tea, and I don't know what else--there were fashions which must be followed, and were changed as soon as they were followed. It was indeed a sad, fantastic race, and, Mr. West's contemporaries appear to have fully realized it; but as long as society was made up of unequals with no caste barriers to prevent imitation, the inferiors were bound to ape the superiors, and the superiors were bound to baffle imitation, so far as possible, by seeking ever-fresh devices for expressing their superiority."

"In short," I said, "our tedious sameness in dress and manners appears to you to have been the logical result of our lack of equality in conditions."

"Precisely so," answered the superintendent. "Because you were not equal, you made yourself miserable and ugly in the attempt to seem so. The aesthetic equivalent of the moral wrong of inequality was the artistic abomination of uniformity. On the other hand, equality creates an atmosphere which kills imitation, and is pregnant with originality, for every one acts out himself, having nothing to gain by imitating any one else."

CHAPTER IX.

Something That Had Not Changed.

When we parted with the superintendent of the paper-process factory I said to Edith that I had taken in since that morning about all the new impressions and new philosophies I could for the time mentally digest, and felt great need of resting my mind for a space in the contemplation of something--if indeed there were anything--which had not changed or been improved in the last century.

After a moment's consideration Edith exclaimed: "I have it! Ask no questions, but just come with me."

Presently, as we were making our way along the route she had taken, she touched my arm, saying, "Let us hurry a little."

Now, hurrying was the regulation gait of the nineteenth century. "Hurry up!" was about the most threadbare phrase in the English language, and rather than "*E pluribus unum*" should especially have been the motto of the American people, but it was the first time the note of haste had impressed my consciousness since I had been living twentieth-century days. This fact, together with the touch of my companion upon my arm as she sought to quicken my pace, caused me to look around, and in so doing to pause abruptly.

"What is this?" I exclaimed.

"It is too bad!" said my companion. "I tried to get you past without seeing it."

But indeed, though I had asked what was this building we stood in presence of, nobody could know so well as I what it was. The mystery was how it had come to be there for in the midst of this splendid city of equals, where poverty was an unknown word, I found myself face to face with a typical nineteenth-century tenement house of the worst sort--one of the rookeries, in fact, that used to abound in the North End and other parts of the city. The environment was indeed in strong enough contrast with that of such buildings in my time, shut in as they generally were by a labyrinth of noisome alleys and dark, damp courtyards which were reeking reservoirs of foetid odors, kept in by lofty, light-excluding walls. This building stood by itself, in the midst of an open square, as if it had been a palace or other show place. But all the more, indeed, by this fine setting was the dismal squalor of the grimy structure emphasized. It seemed to exhale an atmosphere of gloom and chill which all the bright sunshine of the breezy September afternoon was unable to dominate. One would not have been surprised, even at noonday, to see ghosts at the black windows. There was an inscription over the door, and I went across the square to read it, Edith reluctantly following me. These words I read, above the central doorway:

"THIS HABITATION OF CRUELTY IS PRESERVED AS A MEMENTO TO COMING GENERATIONS OF THE RULE OF THE RICH."

"This is one of the ghost buildings," said Edith, "kept to scare the people with, so that they may never risk anything that looks like bringing back the old order of things by allowing any one on any plea to obtain an economic advantage over another. I think they had much better be torn down, for there is no more danger of the world's going back to the old order than there is of the globe reversing its rotation."

A band of children, accompanied by a young woman, came across the square as we stood before the building, and filed into the doorway and up the black and narrow stairway. The faces of the little ones were very serious, and they spoke in whispers.

"They are school children." said Edith. "We are all taken through this building, or some other like it, when we are in the schools, and the teacher explains what manner of things used to be done and endured there. I remember well when I was taken through this building as a child. It was long afterward before I quite recovered from the terrible impression I received. Really, I don't think it is a good idea to bring young children here, but it is a custom that became settled in the period after the Revolution, when the horror of the bondage they had escaped from was yet fresh in the minds of the people, and their great fear was that by some lack of vigilance the rule of the rich might be restored.

"Of course," she continued, "this building and the others like it, which were reserved for warnings when the rest were razed to the ground, have been thoroughly cleaned and strengthened and made sanitary and safe every way, but our artists have very cunningly counterfeited all the old effects of filth and squalor, so that the appearance of everything is just as it was. Tablets in the rooms describe how many human beings used to be crowded into them, and the horrible conditions of their lives. The worst about it is that the facts are all taken from historical records, and are absolutely true. There are some of these places in which the inhabitants of the buildings as they used to swarm in them are reproduced in wax or plaster with every detail of garments, furniture, and all the other features based on actual records or pictures of the time. There is something indescribably dreadful in going through the buildings fitted out in that way. The dumb figures seem to appeal to you to help them. It was so long ago, and yet it makes one feel conscience-stricken not to be able to do anything."

"But, Julian, come away. It was just a stupid accident my bringing you past here. When I undertook to show you something that had not changed since your day, I did not mean to mock you."

Thanks to modern rapid transit, ten minutes later we stood on the ocean shore, with the waves of the Atlantic breaking noisily at our feet and its blue floor extending unbroken to the horizon. Here indeed was something that had not been changed--a mighty existence, to which a thousand years were as one day and one day as a thousand years. There could be no tonic for my case like the inspiration of this great presence, this unchanging witness of all earth's mutations. How petty seemed the little trick of time that had been played on me as I stood in the presence of this symbol of everlastingness which made past, present, and future terms of little meaning!

In accompanying Edith to the part of the beach where we stood I had taken no note of directions, but now, as I began to study the shore, I observed with lively emotion that she had unwittingly brought me to the site of my old seaside place at Nahant. The buildings were indeed gone, and the growth of trees had quite changed the aspect of the landscape, but the shore line remained unaltered, and I knew it at once. Bidding her follow me, I led the way around a point to a little strip of beach between the sea and a wall of rock which shut off all sight or sound of the land behind. In my former life the spot had been a favorite resort when I visited the shore. Here in that life so long ago, and yet recalled as if of yesterday, I had been used from a lad to go to do my day dreaming. Every feature of the little nook was as familiar to me as my bedroom and all was quite unchanged. The sea in front, the sky above, the islands and the blue headlands of the distant coast--all, indeed, that filled the view was the same in every detail. I threw myself upon the warm sand by the margin of the sea, as I had been wont to do, and in a moment the flood of familiar associations had so completely carried me back to my old life that all the marvels that had happened to me, when presently I began to recall them, seemed merely as a day dream that had come to me like so many others before it in that spot by the shore. But what a dream it had been, that vision of the world to be; surely of all the dreams that had come to me there by the sea the weirdest!

There had been a girl in the dream, a maiden much to be desired. It had been ill if I had lost her; but I had not, for this was she, the girl in this strange and graceful garb, standing by my side and smiling down at me. I had by some great hap brought her back from dreamland, holding her by the very strength of my love when all else of the vision had dissolved at the opening of the eyes.

Why not? What youth has not often been visited in his dreams by maidenly ideals fairer than walk on earth, whom, waking, he has sighed for and for days been followed by the haunting beauty of their half-remembered faces? I, more fortunate than they, had baffled the jealous warder at the gates of sleep and brought my queen of dreamland through.

When I proceeded to state to Edith this theory to account for her presence, she professed to find it highly reasonable, and we proceeded at much length to develop the idea. Falling into the conceit that she was an anticipation of the twentieth-century woman instead of my being an excavated relic of the nineteenth-century man, we speculated what we should do for the summer. We decided to visit the great pleasure resorts, where, no doubt, she would under the circumstances excite much curiosity and at the same time have an opportunity of studying what to her twentieth-century mind would seem even more astonishing types of humanity than she would seem to them--namely, people who, surrounded by a needy and anguished world, could get their own consent to be happy in a frivolous and wasteful idleness. Afterward we would go to Europe and inspect such things there as might naturally be curiosities to a girl out of the year 2000, such as a Rothschild, an emperor, and a few specimens of human beings, some of which were at that time still extant in Germany, Austria, and Russia, who honestly believed that God had given to certain fellow-beings a divine title to reign over them.

CHAPTER X.

A Midnight Plunge.

It was after dark when we reached home, and several hours later before we had made an end of telling our adventures. Indeed, my hosts seemed at all times unable to hear too much of my impressions of modern things, appearing to be as much interested in what I thought of them as I was in the things themselves.

"It is really, you see," Edith's mother had said, "the manifestation of vanity on our part. You are a sort of looking-glass to us, in which we can see how we appear from a different point of view from our own. If it were not for you, we should never have realized what remarkable people we are, for to one another, I assure you, we seem very ordinary."

To which I replied that in talking with them I got the same looking-glass effect as to myself and my contemporaries, but that it was one which by no means ministered to my vanity.

When, as we talked, the globe of the color clock turning white announced that it was midnight, some one spoke of bed, but the doctor had another scheme.

"I propose," said he, "by way of preparing a good night's rest for us all, that we go over to the natatorium and take a plunge."

"Are there any public baths open so late as this?" I said. "In my day everything was shut up long before now."

Then and there the doctor gave me the information which, matter of course as it is to twentieth-century readers, was surprising enough to me, that no public service or convenience is ever suspended at the present day, whether by day or night, the year round; and that, although the service provided varies in extent, according to the demand, it never varies in quality.

"It seems to us," said the doctor, "that among the minor inconveniences of life in your day none could have been more vexing than the recurrent interruption of all, or of the larger part of all, public services every night. Most of the people, of course, are asleep then, but always a portion of them have occasion to be awake and about, and all of us sometimes, and we should consider it a very lame public service that did not provide for the night workers as good a service as for the day workers. Of course, you could not do it, lacking any unitary industrial organization, but it is very easy with us. We have day and night shifts for all the public services--the latter, of course, much the smaller."

"How about public holidays; have you abandoned them?"

"Pretty generally. The occasional public holidays in your time were prized by the people, as giving them much-needed breathing spaces. Nowadays, when the working day is so short and the working year so interspersed with ample vacations, the old-fashioned holiday has ceased to serve any purpose, and would be regarded as a nuisance. We prefer to choose and use our leisure time as we please."

It was to the Leander Natatorium that we had directed our steps. As I need not remind Bostonians, this is one of the older baths, and considered quite inferior to the modern structures. To me, however, it was a vastly impressive spectacle. The lofty interior glowing with light, the immense swimming tank, the four great fountains filling the air with diamond-dazzle and the noise of falling water, together with the throng of gayly dressed and laughing bathers, made an exhilarating and magnificent scene, which was a very effective introduction to the athletic side of the modern life. The loveliest thing of all was the great expanse of water made translucent by the light reflected from the white tiled bottom, so that the swimmers, their whole bodies visible, seemed as if floating on a pale emerald cloud, with an effect of buoyancy and weightlessness that was as startling as charming. Edith was quick to tell me, however, that this was as nothing to the beauty of some of the new and larger baths, where, by varying the colors of the tiling at the bottom, the water is made to shade through all the tints of the rainbow while preserving the same translucent appearance.

I had formed an impression that the water would be fresh, but the green hue, of course, showed it to be from the sea.

"We have a poor opinion of fresh water for swimming when we can get salt," said the doctor. "This water came in on the last tide from the Atlantic."

"But how do you get it up to this level?"

"We make it carry itself up," laughed the doctor; "it would be a pity if the tidal force that raises the whole harbor fully seven feet, could not raise what little we want a bit higher. Don't look at it so suspiciously," he added. "I know that Boston Harbor water was far from being clean enough for bathing in your day, but all that is changed. Your sewerage systems, remember, are forgotten abominations, and nothing that can defile is allowed to reach sea or river nowadays. For that reason we can and do use sea water, not only for all the public baths, but provide it as a distinct service for our home baths and also for all the public fountains, which, thus inexhaustibly supplied, can be kept always playing. But let us go in."

"Certainly, if you say so," said I, with a shiver, "but are you sure that it is not a trifle cool? Ocean water was thought by us to be chilly for bathing in late September."

"Did you think we were going to give you your death?" said the doctor. "Of course, the water is warmed to a comfortable temperature; these baths are open all winter."

"But, dear me! how can you possibly warm such great bodies of water, which are so constantly renewed, especially in winter?"

"Oh, we have no conscience at all about what we make the tides do for us," replied the doctor. "We not only make them lift the water up here, but heat it, too. Why, Julian, cold or hot are terms without real meaning, mere coquettish airs which Nature puts on, indicating that she wants to be wooed a little. She would just as soon warm you as freeze you, if you will approach her rightly. The blizzards which used to freeze your generation might just as well have taken the place of your coal mines. You look incredulous, but let me tell you now, as a first step toward the understanding of modern conditions, that power, with all its applications of light, heat, and energy, is to-day practically exhaustless and costless, and scarcely enters as an element into mechanical calculation. The uses of the tides, winds, and waterfalls are indeed but crude methods of drawing on Nature's resources of strength compared with others that are employed by which boundless power is developed from natural inequalities of temperature."

A few moments later I was enjoying the most delicious sea bath that ever up to that time had fallen to my lot; the pleasure of the pelting under the fountains was to me a new sensation in life.

"You'll make a first-rate twentieth-century Bostonian," said the doctor, laughing at my delight. "It is said that a marked feature of our modern civilization is that we are tending to revert to the amphibious type of our remote ancestry; evidently you will not object to drifting with the tide."

It was one o'clock when we reached home.

"I suppose," said Edith, as I bade her good-night, "that in ten minutes you will be back among your friends of the nineteenth century if you dream as you did last night. What would I not give to take the journey with you and see for myself what the world was like!"

"And I would give as much to be spared a repetition of the experience," I said, "unless it were in your company."

"Do you mean that you really are afraid you will dream of the old times again?"

"So much afraid," I replied, "that I have a good mind to sit up all night to avoid the possibility of another such nightmare."

"Dear me! you need not do that," she said. "If you wish me to, I will see that you are troubled no more in that way."

"Are you, then, a magician?"

"If I tell you not to dream of any particular matter, you will not," she said.

"You are easily the mistress of my waking thoughts," I said; "but can you rule my sleeping mind as well?"

"You shall see," she said, and, fixing her eyes upon mine, she said quietly, "Remember, you are not to dream of anything to-night which belonged to your old life!" and, as she spoke, I knew in my mind that it would be as she said.

CHAPTER XI.

Life The Basis Of The Right Of Property.

Among the pieces of furniture in the subterranean bedchamber where Dr. Leete had found me sleeping was one of the strong boxes of iron cunningly locked which in my time were used for the storage of money and valuables. The location of this chamber so far underground, its solid stone construction and heavy doors, had not only made it impervious to noise but equally proof against thieves, and its very existence being, moreover, a secret, I had thought that no place could be safer for keeping the evidences of my wealth.

Edith had been very curious about the safe, which was the name we gave to these strong boxes, and several times when we were visiting the vault had expressed a lively desire to see what was inside. I had proposed to open it for her, but she had suggested that, as her father and mother would be as much interested in the process as herself, it would be best to postpone the treat till all should be present.

As we sat at breakfast the day after the experiences narrated in the previous chapters, she asked why that morning would not be a good time to show the inside of the safe, and everybody agreed that there could be no better.

"What is in the safe?" asked Edith's mother.

"When I last locked it in the year 1887," I replied, "there were in it securities and evidences of value of various sorts representing something like a million dollars. When we open it this morning we shall find, thanks to the great Revolution, a fine collection of waste paper.--I wonder, by the way, doctor, just what your judges would say if I were to take those securities to them and make a formal demand to be reinstated in the possessions which they represented? Suppose I said: 'Your Honors, these properties were once mine and I have never voluntarily parted with them. Why are they not mine now, and why should they not be returned to me?' You understand, of course, that I have no desire to start a revolt against the present order, which I am very ready to admit is much better than the old arrangements, but I am quite curious to know just what the judges would reply to such a demand, provided they consented to entertain it seriously. I suppose they would laugh me out of court. Still, I think I might argue with some plausibility that, seeing I was not present when the Revolution divested us capitalists of our wealth, I am at least entitled to a courteous explanation of the grounds on which that course was justified at the time. I do not want my million back, even if it were possible to return it, but as a matter of rational satisfaction I should like to know on just what plea it was appropriated and is retained by the community."

"Really Julian," said the doctor, "it would be an excellent idea if you were to do just what you have suggested--that is, bring a formal suit against the nation for reinstatement in your former property. It would arouse the liveliest popular interest and stimulate a discussion of the ethical basis of our economic equality that would be of great educational value to the community. You see the present order has been so long established that it does not often occur to anybody except historians that there ever was any other. It would be a good thing for the people to have their minds stirred up on the subject and be compelled to do some fundamental thinking as to the merits of the differences between the old and the new order and the reasons for the present system. Confronting the court with those securities in your hand, you would make a fine dramatic situation. It would be the nineteenth century challenging the twentieth, the old civilization, demanding an accounting of the new. The judges, you may be sure, would treat you with the greatest consideration. They would at once admit your rights under the peculiar circumstances to have the whole question of wealth distribution and the rights of property reopened from the beginning, and be ready to discuss it in the broadest spirit."

"No doubt," I answered, "but it is just an illustration, I suppose, of the lack of unselfish public spirit among my contemporaries that I do not feel disposed to make myself a spectacle even in the cause of education. Besides, what is the need? You can tell me as well as the judges could what the answer would be, and as it is the answer I want and not the property that will do just as well."

"No doubt," said the doctor, "I could give you the general line of reasoning they would follow."

"Very well. Let us suppose, then, that you are the court. On what ground would you refuse to return me my million, for I assume that you would refuse?"

"Of course it would be the same ground," replied the doctor, "that the nation proceeded upon in nationalizing the property which that same million represented at the time of the great Revolution."

"I suppose so; that is what I want to get at. What is that ground?"

"The court would say that to allow any person to withdraw or withhold from the public administration for the common use any larger portion of capital than the equal portion allotted to all for personal use and consumption would in so far impair the ability of society to perform its first duty to its members."

"What is this first duty of society to its members, which would be interfered with by allowing particular citizens to appropriate more than an equal proportion of the capital of the country?"

"The duty of safeguarding the first and highest right of its members--the right of life."

"But how is the duty of society to safeguard the lives of its members interfered with when one person, has more capital than another?"

"Simply," answered the doctor, "because people have to eat in order to live, also to be clothed and to consume a mass of necessary and desirable things, the sum of which constitutes what we call wealth or capital. Now, if the supply of these things was always unlimited, as is the air we need to breathe, it would not be necessary to see that each one had his share, but the supply of wealth being, in fact, at any one time limited, it follows that if some have a disproportionate share, the rest will not have enough and may be left with nothing, as was indeed the case of millions all over the world until the great Revolution established economic equality. If, then, the first right of the citizen is protection to life and the first duty of society is to furnish it, the state must evidently see to it that the means of life are not unduly appropriated by particular individuals, but are distributed so as to meet the needs of all. Moreover, in order to secure the means of life to all, it is not merely necessary that the state should see that the wealth available for consumption is properly distributed at any given time; for, although all might in that case fare well for to-day, tomorrow all might starve unless, meanwhile, new wealth were being produced. The duty of society to guarantee the life of the citizen implies, therefore, not merely the equal distribution of wealth for consumption, but its employment as capital to the best possible advantage for all in the production of more wealth. In both ways, therefore, you will readily see that society would fail in its first and greatest function in proportion as it were to permit individuals beyond the equal allotment to withdraw wealth, whether for consumption or employment as capital, from the public administration in the common interest."

"The modern ethics of ownership is rather startlingly simple to a representative of the nineteenth century," I observed. "Would not the judges even ask me by what right or title of ownership I claimed my wealth?"

"Certainly not. It is impossible that you or any one could have so strong a title to material things as the least of your fellow-citizens have to their lives, or could make so strong a plea for the use of the collective power to enforce your right to things as they could make that the collective power should enforce their right to life against your right to things at whatever point the two claims might directly or indirectly conflict. The effect of the disproportionate possession of the wealth of a community by some of its members to curtail and threaten the living of the rest is not in any way affected by the means by which that wealth was obtained. The means may have constituted, as in past times they often did by their iniquity, an added injury to the community; but the fact of the disproportion, however resulting, was a continuing injury, without regard to its beginnings. Our ethics of wealth is indeed, as you say, extremely simple. It consists merely in the law of self-preservation, asserted in the name of all against the encroachments of any. It rests upon a principle which a child can understand as well as a philosopher, and which no philosopher ever attempted to refute--namely, the supreme right of all to live, and consequently to insist that society shall be so organized as to secure that right.

"But, after all," said the doctor, "what is there in our economic application of this principle which need impress a man of your time with any other sensation than one of surprise that it was not earlier made? Since what you were wont to call modern civilization existed, it has been a principle subscribed to by all governments and peoples that it is the first and supreme duty of the state to protect the lives of the citizens. For the purpose of doing this the police, the courts, the army, and the greater part of the machinery of governments has existed. You went so far as to hold that a state which did not at any cost and to the utmost of its resources safeguard the lives of its citizens forfeited all claim to their allegiance.

"But while professing this principle so broadly in words, you completely ignored in practice half and vastly the greater half of its meaning. You wholly overlooked and disregarded the peril to which life is exposed on the economic side--the hunger, cold, and thirst side. You went on the theory that it was only by club, knife, bullet, poison, or some other form of physical violence that life could be endangered, as if hunger, cold, and thirst--in a word, economic want--were not a far more constant and more deadly foe to existence than all the forms of violence together. You overlooked the plain fact that anybody who by any means, however indirect or remote, took away or curtailed one's means of subsistence attacked his life quite as dangerously as it could be done with knife or bullet--more so, indeed, seeing that against direct attack he would have a better chance of defending himself. You failed to consider that no amount of police, judicial, and military protection would prevent one from perishing miserably if he had not enough to eat and wear."

"We went on the theory," I said, "that it was not well for the state to intervene to do for the individual or to help him to do what he was able to do for himself. We held that the collective organization should only be appealed to when the power of the individual was manifestly unequal to the task of self-defense."

"It was not so bad a theory if you had lived up to it," said the doctor, "although the modern theory is far more rational that whatever can be done better by collective than individual action ought to be so undertaken, even if it could, after a more imperfect fashion, be individually accomplished. But don't you think that under the economic conditions which prevailed in America at the end of the nineteenth century, not to speak of Europe, the average man armed with a good revolver would have found the task of protecting himself and family against violence a far easier one than that of protecting them against want? Were not the odds against him far greater in the latter struggle than they could have been, if he were a tolerably good shot, in the former? Why, then, according to your own maxim, was the collective force of society devoted without stint to safeguarding him against violence, which he could have done for himself fairly well, while he was left to struggle against hopeless odds for the means of a decent existence? What hour, of what day of what year ever passed in which the number of deaths, and the physical and moral anguish resulting from the anarchy of the economic struggle and the crushing odds against the poor, did not outweigh as a hundred to one that same hour's record of death or suffering resulting from violence? Far better would society have fulfilled its recognized duty of safeguarding the lives of its members if, repealing every criminal law and dismissing every judge and policeman, it had left men to protect themselves as best they might against physical violence, while establishing in place of the machinery of criminal justice a system of economic administration whereby all would have been guaranteed against want. If, indeed, it had but substituted this collective economic organization for the criminal and judicial system it presently would have had as little need of the latter as we do, for most of the crimes that plagued you were direct or indirect consequences of your unjust economic conditions, and would have disappeared with them.

"But excuse my vehemence. Remember that I am arraigning your civilization and not you. What I wanted to bring out is that the principle that the first duty of society is to safeguard the lives of its members was as fully admitted by your world as by ours, and that in failing to give the principle an economic as well as police, judicial, and military interpretation, your world convicted itself of an inconsistency as glaring in logic as it was cruel in consequences. We, on the other hand, in assuming as a nation the responsibility of safeguarding the lives of the people on the economic side, have merely, for the first time, honestly carried out a principle as old as the civilized state."

"That is clear enough," I said. "Any one, on the mere statement of the case, would of course be bound to admit that the recognized duty of the state to guarantee the life of the citizen against the action of his fellows does logically involve responsibility to protect him from influences attacking the economic basis of life quite as much as from direct forcible assaults. The more advanced governments of my day, by their poor laws and pauper systems, in a dim way admitted this responsibility, although the kind of provision they made for the economically unfortunate was so meager and accompanied with such conditions of ignominy that men would ordinarily rather die than accept it. But grant that the sort of recognition we gave of the right of the citizen to be guaranteed a subsistence was a mockery more brutal than its total denial would have been, and that a far larger interpretation of its duty in this respect was incumbent on the state, yet how does it logically follow that society is bound to guarantee or the citizen to demand an absolute economic equality?"

"It is very true, as you say," answered the doctor, "that the duty of society to guarantee every member the economic basis of his life might be after some fashion discharged short of establishing economic equality. Just so in your day might the duty of the state to safeguard the lives of citizens from physical violence have been discharged after a nominal fashion if it had contented itself with preventing outright murders, while leaving the people to suffer from one another's wantonness all manner of violence not directly deadly; but tell me, Julian, were governments in your day content with so construing the limit of their duty to protect citizens from violence, or would the citizens have been content with such a limitation?"

"Of course not."

"A government which in your day," continued the doctor, "had limited its undertaking to protect citizens from violence to merely preventing murders would not have lasted a day. There were no people so barbarous as to have tolerated it. In fact, not only did all civilized governments undertake to protect citizens from assaults against their lives, but from any and every sort of physical assault and offense, however petty. Not only might not a man so much as lay a finger on another in anger, but if he only wagged his tongue against him maliciously he was laid by the heels in jail. The law undertook to protect men in their dignity as well as in their mere bodily integrity, rightly recognizing that to be insulted or spit upon is as great a grievance as any assault upon life itself.

"Now, in undertaking to secure the citizen in his right to life on the economic side, we do but studiously follow your precedents in safeguarding him from direct assault. If we did but secure his economic basis so far as to avert death by direct effect of hunger and cold as your pauper laws made a pretense of doing, we should be like a State in your day which forbade outright murder but permitted every kind of assault that fell short of it. Distress and deprivation resulting from economic want falling short of actual starvation precisely correspond to the acts of minor violence against which your State protected citizens as carefully as against murder. The right of the citizen to have his life secured him on the economic side can not therefore be satisfied by any provision for bare subsistence, or by anything less than the means for the fullest supply of every need which it is in the power of the nation by the thriftiest stewardship of the national resources to provide for all.

"That is to say, in extending the reign of law and public justice to the protection and security of men's interests on the economic side, we have merely followed, as we were reasonably bound to follow, your much-vaunted maxim of 'equality before the law.' That maxim meant that in so far as society collectively undertook any governmental function, it must act absolutely without respect of persons for the equal benefit of all. Unless, therefore, we were to reject the principle of 'equality before the law,' it was impossible that society, having assumed charge of the production and distribution of wealth as a collective function, could discharge it on any other principle than equality."

"If the court please," I said, "I should like to be permitted at this point to discontinue and withdraw my suit for the restoration of my former property. In my day we used to hold on to all we had and fight for all we could get with a good stomach, for our rivals were as selfish as we, and represented no higher right or larger view. But this modern social system with its public stewardship of all capital for the general welfare quite changes the situation. It puts the man who demands more than his share in the light of a person attacking the livelihood and seeking to impair the welfare of everybody else in the nation. To enjoy that attitude anybody must be a good deal better convinced of the justice of his title than I ever was even in the old days."

CHAPTER XII.

How Inequality Of Wealth Destroys Liberty.

"Nevertheless," said the doctor, "I have stated only half the reason the judges would give wherefore they could not, by returning your wealth, permit the impairment of our collective economic system and the beginnings of economic inequality in the nation. There is another great and equal right of all men which, though strictly included under the right of life, is by generous minds set even above it: I mean the right of liberty--that is to say, the right not only to live, but to live in personal independence of one's fellows, owning only those common social obligations resting on all alike.

"Now, the duty of the state to safeguard the liberty of citizens was recognized in your day just as was its duty to safeguard their lives, but with the same limitation, namely, that the safeguard should apply only to protect from attacks by violence. If it were attempted to kidnap a citizen and reduce him by force to slavery, the state would interfere, but not otherwise. Nevertheless, it was true in your day of liberty and personal independence, as of life, that the perils to which they were chiefly exposed were not from force or violence, but resulted from economic causes, the necessary consequences of inequalities of wealth. Because the state absolutely ignored this side, which was incomparably the largest side of the liberty question, its pretense of defending the liberties of citizens was as gross a mockery as that of guaranteeing their lives. Nay, it was a yet more absolute mockery and on a far vaster scale.

"For, although I have spoken of the monopolization of wealth and of the productive machinery by a portion of the people as being first of all a threat to the lives of the rest of the community and to be resisted as such, nevertheless the main practical effect of the system was not to deprive the masses of mankind of life outright, but to force them, through want, to buy their lives by the surrender of their liberties. That is to say, they accepted servitude to the possessing class and became their serfs on condition of receiving the means of subsistence. Although multitudes were always perishing from lack of subsistence, yet it was not the deliberate policy of the possessing class that they should do so. The rich had no use for dead men; on the other hand, they had endless use for human beings as servants, not only to produce more wealth, but as the instruments of their pleasure and luxury.

"As I need not remind you who were familiar with it, the industrial system of the world before the great Revolution was wholly based upon the compulsory servitude of the mass of mankind to the possessing class, enforced by the coercion of economic need."

"Undoubtedly," I said, "the poor as a class were in the economic service of the rich, or, as we used to say, labor was dependent on capital for employment, but this service and employment had become in the nineteenth century an entirely voluntary relation on the part of the servant or employee. The rich had no power to compel the poor to be their servants. They only took such as came voluntarily to ask to be taken into service, and even begged to be, with tears. Surely a service so sought after could scarcely be called compulsory."

"Tell us, Julian," said the doctor, "did the rich go to one another and ask the privilege of being one another's servants or employees?"

"Of course not."

"But why not?"

"Because, naturally, no one could wish to be another's servant or subject to his orders who could get along without it."

"I should suppose so, but why, then, did the poor so eagerly seek to serve the rich when the rich refused with scorn to serve one another? Was it because the poor so loved the rich?"

"Scarcely."

"Why then?"

"It was, of course, for the reason that it was the only way the poor could get a living."

"You mean that it was only the pressure of want or the fear of it that drove the poor to the point of becoming the servants of the rich?"

"That is about it."

"And would you call that voluntary service? The distinction between forced service and such service as that would seem quite imperceptible to us. If a man may be said to do voluntarily that which only the pressure of bitter necessity compels him to elect to do, there has never been any such thing as slavery, for all the acts of a slave are at the last the acceptance of a less evil for fear of a worse. Suppose, Julian, you or a few of you owned the main water supply, or food supply, clothing supply, land supply, or main industrial opportunities in a community and could maintain your ownership, that fact alone would make the rest of the people your slaves, would it not, and that, too, without any direct compulsion on your part whatever?"

"No doubt."

"Suppose somebody should charge you with holding the people under compulsory servitude, and you should answer that you laid no hand on them but that they willingly resorted to you and kissed your hands for the privilege of being allowed to serve you in exchange for water, food, or clothing, would not that be a very transparent evasion on your part of the charge of slaveholding?"

"No doubt it would be."

"Well, and was not that precisely the relation the capitalists or employers as a class held toward the rest of the community through their monopolization of wealth and the machinery of production?"

"I must say that it was."

"There was a great deal said by the economists of your day," the doctor went on, "about the freedom of contract--the voluntary, unconstrained agreement of the laborer with the employer as to the terms of his employment. What hypocrisy could have been so brazen as that pretense when, as a matter of fact, every contract made between the capitalist who had bread and could keep it and the laborer who must have it or die would have been declared void, if fairly judged, even under your laws as a contract made under duress of hunger, cold, and nakedness, nothing less than the threat of death! If you own the things men must have, you own the men who must have them."

"But the compulsion of want," said I, "meaning hunger and cold, is a compulsion of Nature. In that sense we are all under compulsory servitude to Nature."

"Yes, but not to one another. That is the whole difference between slavery and freedom. To-day no man serves another, but all the common good in which we equally share. Under your system the compulsion of Nature through the appropriation by the rich of the means of supplying Nature's demands was turned into a club by which the rich made the poor pay Nature's debt of labor not only for themselves but for the rich also, with a vast overcharge besides for the needless waste of the system."

"You make out our system to have been little better than slavery. That is a hard word."

"It is a very hard word, and we want above all things to be fair. Let us look at the question. Slavery exists where there is a compulsory using of men by other men for the benefit of the users. I think we are quite agreed that the poor man in your day worked for the rich only because his necessities compelled him to. That compulsion varied in force according to the degree of want the worker was in. Those who had a little economic means would only render the lighter kinds of service on more or less easy and honorable conditions, while those who had less means or no means at all would do anything on any terms however painful or degrading. With the mass of the workers the compulsion of necessity was of the sharpest kind. The chattel slave had the choice between working for his master and the lash. The wage-earner chose between laboring for an employer or starving. In the older, cruder forms of slavery the masters had to be watching constantly to prevent the escape of their slaves, and were troubled with the charge of providing for them. Your system was more convenient, in that it made Nature your taskmaster, and depended on her to keep your servants to the task. It was a difference between the direct exercise of coercion, in which the slave was always on the point of rebellion, and an indirect coercion by which the same industrial result was obtained, while the slave, instead of rebelling against his master's authority, was grateful for the opportunity of serving him."

"But," said I, "the wage-earner received wages and the slave received nothing."

"I beg your pardon. The slave received subsistence--clothing and shelter--and the wage-earner who could get more than these out of his wages was rarely fortunate. The rate of wages, except in new countries and under special conditions and for skilled workers, kept at about the subsistence point, quite as often dropping below as rising above. The main difference was that the master expended the subsistence wage of the chattel slave for him while the earner expended it for himself. This was better for the worker in some ways; in others less desirable, for the master out of self-interest usually saw that the chattel, children had enough; while the employer, having no stake in the life or health of the wage-earner, did not concern himself as to whether he lived or died. There were never any slave quarters so vile as the tenement houses of the city slums where the wage-earners were housed."

"But at least," said I, "there was this radical difference between the wage-earner of my day and the chattel slave: the former could leave his employer at will, the latter could not."

"Yes, that is a difference, but one surely that told not so much in favor of as against the wage-earner. In all save temporarily fortunate countries with sparse population the laborer would have been glad indeed to exchange the right to leave his employer for a guarantee that he would not be discharged by him. Fear of losing his opportunity to work--his job, as you called it--was the nightmare of the laborer's life as it was reflected in the literature of your period. Was it not so?"

I had to admit that it was even so.

"The privilege of leaving one employer for another," pursued the doctor, "even if it had not been more than balanced by the liability to discharge, was of very little worth to the worker, in view of the fact that the rate of wages was at about the same point wherever he might go, and the change would be merely a choice between the personal dispositions of different masters, and that difference was slight enough, for business rules controlled the relations of masters and men."

I rallied once more.

"One point of real superiority at least you must admit the wage-earner had over the chattel slave. He could by merit rise out of his condition and become himself an employer, a rich man."

"Surely, Julian, you forget that there has rarely been a slave system under which the more energetic, intelligent, and thrifty slaves could and did not buy their freedom or have it given them by their masters. The freedmen in ancient Rome rose to places of importance and power quite as frequently as did the born proletarian of Europe or America get out of his condition."

I did not think of anything to reply at the moment, and the doctor, having compassion on me, pursued: "It is an old illustration of the different view points of the centuries that precisely this point which you make of the possibility of the wage-earner rising, although it was getting to be a vanishing point in your day, seems to us the most truly diabolical feature of the whole system. The prospect of rising as a motive to reconcile the wage-earner or the poor man in general to his subjection, what did it amount to? It was but saying to him, 'Be a good slave, and you, too, shall have slaves of your own.' By this wedge did you separate the cleverer of the wage-workers from the mass of them and dignify treason to humanity by the name of ambition. No true man should wish to rise save to raise others with him."

"One point of difference, however, you must at least admit," I said. "In chattel slavery the master had a power over the persons of his slaves which the employer did not have over even the poorest of his employees: he could not lay his hand upon them in violence."

"Again, Julian," said the doctor, "you have mentioned a point of difference that tells in favor of chattel slavery as a more humane industrial method than the wage system. If here and there the anger of the chattel slave owner made him forget his self-restraint so far as to cripple or maim his slaves, yet such cases were on the whole rare, and such masters were held to an account by public opinion if not by law; but under the wage system the employer had no motive of self-restraint to spare life or limb of his employees, and he escaped responsibility by the fact of the consent and even eagerness of the needy people to undertake the most perilous and painful tasks for the sake of bread. We read that in the United States every year at least two hundred thousand men, women, and children were done to death or maimed in the performance of their industrial duties, nearly forty thousand alone in the single branch of the steam railroad service. No estimate seems to have ever been attempted of the many times greater number who perished more indirectly through the injurious effects of bad industrial conditions. What chattel-slave system ever made a record of such wastefulness of human life, as that?

"Nay, more, the chattel-slave owner, if he smote his slave, did it in anger and, as likely as not, with some provocation; but these wholesale slaughters of wage-earners that made your land red were done in sheer cold-bloodedness, without any other motive on the part of the capitalists, who were responsible, save gain.

"Still again, one of the more revolting features of chattel slavery has always been considered the subjection of the slave women to the lust of their masters. How was it in this respect under the rule of the rich? We read in our histories that great armies of women in your day were forced by poverty to make a business of submitting their bodies to those who had the means of furnishing them a little bread. The books say that these armies amounted in your great cities to bodies of thirty or forty thousand women. Tales come down to us of the magnitude of the maiden tribute levied upon the poorer classes for the gratification of the lusts of those who could pay, which the annals of antiquity could scarcely match for horror. Am I saying too much, Julian?"

"You have mentioned nothing but facts which stared me in the face all my life," I replied, "and yet it appears I have had to wait for a man of another century to tell me what they meant."

"It was precisely because they stared you and your contemporaries so constantly in the face, and always had done so, that you lost the faculty of judging their meaning. They were, as we might say, too near the eyes to be seen aright. You are far enough away from the facts now to begin to see them clearly and to realize their significance. As you shall continue to occupy this modern view point, you will more and more completely come to see with us that the most revolting aspect of the human condition before the great Revolution was not the suffering from physical privation or even the outright starvation of multitudes which directly resulted from the unequal distribution of wealth, but the indirect effect of that inequality to reduce almost the total human race to a state of degrading bondage to their fellows. As it seems to us, the offense of the old order against liberty was even greater than the offense to life; and even if it were conceivable that it could have satisfied the right of life by guaranteeing abundance to all, it must just the same have been destroyed, for, although the collective administration of the economic system had been unnecessary to guarantee life, there could be no such thing as liberty so long as by the effect of inequalities of wealth and the private control of the means of production the opportunity of men to obtain the means of subsistence depended on the will of other men."

CHAPTER XIII.

Private Capital Stolen From The Social Fund.

"I observe," pursued the doctor, "that Edith is getting very impatient with these dry disquisitions, and thinks it high time we passed from wealth in the abstract to wealth in the concrete, as illustrated by the contents of your safe. I will delay the company only while I say a very few words more; but really this question of the restoration of your million, raised half in jest as it was, so vitally touches the central and fundamental principle of our social order that I want to give you at least an outline idea of the modern ethics of wealth distribution.

"The essential difference between the new and the old point of view you fully possess by this time. The old ethics conceived of the question of what a man might rightfully possess as one which began and ended with the relation of individuals to things. Things have no rights as against moral beings, and there was no reason, therefore, in the nature of the case as thus stated, why individuals should not acquire an unlimited ownership of things so far as their abilities permitted. But this view absolutely ignored the social consequences which result from an unequal distribution of material things in a world where everybody absolutely depends for life and all its uses on their share of those things. That is to say, the old so-called ethics of property absolutely overlooked the whole ethical side of the subject--namely, its bearing on human relations. It is precisely this consideration which furnishes the whole basis of the modern ethics of property. All human beings are equal in rights and dignity, and only such a system of wealth distribution can therefore be defensible as respects and secures those equalities. But while this is the principle which you will hear most generally stated as the moral ground of our economic equality, there is another quite sufficient and wholly different ground on which, even if the rights of life and liberty were not involved, we should yet maintain that equal sharing of the total product of industry was the only just plan, and that any other was robbery.

"The main factor in the production of wealth among civilized men is the social organism, the machinery of associated labor and exchange by which hundreds of millions of individuals provide the demand for one another's product and mutually complement one another's labors, thereby making the productive and distributive systems of a nation and of the world one great machine. This was true even under private capitalism, despite the prodigious waste and friction of its methods; but of course it is a far more important truth now when the machinery of co-operation runs with absolute smoothness and every ounce of energy is utilized to the utmost effect. The element in the total industrial product which is due to the social organism is represented by the difference between the value of what one man produces as a worker in connection with the social organization and what he could produce in a condition of isolation. Working in concert with his fellows by aid of the social organism, he and they produce enough to support all in the highest luxury and refinement. Toiling in isolation, human experience has proved that he would be fortunate if he could at the utmost produce enough to keep himself alive. It is estimated, I believe, that the average daily product of a worker in America to-day is some fifty dollars. The product of the same man working in isolation would probably be highly estimated on the same basis of calculation if put at a quarter of a dollar. Now tell me, Julian, to whom belongs the social organism, this vast machinery of human association, which enhances some two hundredfold the product of every one's labor?"

"Manifestly," I replied, "it can belong to no one in particular, but to nothing less than society collectively. Society collectively can be the only heir to the social inheritance of intellect and discovery, and it is society collectively which furnishes the continuous daily concourse by which alone that inheritance is made effective."

"Exactly so. The social organism, with all that it is and all it makes possible, is the indivisible inheritance of all in common. To whom, then, properly belongs that two hundredfold enhancement of the value of every one's labor which is owing to the social organism?"

"Manifestly to society collectively--to the general fund."

"Previous to the great Revolution," pursued the doctor. "Although there seems to have been a vague idea of some such social fund as this, which belonged to society collectively, there was no clear conception of its vastness, and no custodian of it, or possible provision to see that it was collected and applied for the common use. A public organization of industry, a nationalized economic system, was necessary before the social fund could be properly protected and administered. Until then it must needs be the subject of universal plunder and embezzlement. The social machinery was seized upon by adventurers and made a means of enriching themselves by collecting tribute from the people to whom it belonged and whom it should have enriched. It would be one way of describing the effect of the Revolution to say that it was only the taking possession by the people collectively of the social machinery which had always belonged to them, thenceforth to be conducted as a public plant, the returns of which were to go to the owners as the equal proprietors and no longer to buccaneers.

"You will readily see," the doctor went on, "how this analysis of the product of industry must needs tend to minimize the importance of the personal equation of performance as between individual workers. If the modern man, by aid of the social machinery, can produce fifty dollars' worth of product where he could produce not over a quarter of a dollar's worth without society, then forty-nine dollars and three quarters out of every fifty dollars must be credited to the social fund to be equally distributed. The industrial efficiency of two men working without society might have differed as two to one--that is, while one man was able to produce a full quarter dollar's worth of work a day, the other could produce only twelve and a half cents' worth. This was a very great difference under those circumstances, but twelve and a half cents is so slight a proportion of fifty dollars as not to be worth mentioning. That is to say, the difference in individual endowments between the two men would remain the same, but that difference would be reduced to relative unimportance by the prodigious equal addition made to the product of both alike by the social organism. Or again, before gunpowder was invented one man might easily be worth two as a warrior. The difference between the men as individuals remained what it was; yet the overwhelming factor added to the power of both alike by the gun practically equalized them as fighters. Speaking of guns, take a still better illustration--the relation of the individual soldiers in a square of infantry to the formation. There might be large differences in the fighting power of the individual soldiers singly outside the ranks. Once in the ranks, however, the formation added to the fighting efficiency of every soldier equally an element so overwhelming as to dwarf the difference between the individual efficiency of different men. Say, for instance, that the formation added ten to the fighting force of every member, then the man who outside the ranks was as two to one in power compared with his comrade would, when they both stood in the ranks, compare with him only as twelve to eleven--an inconsiderable difference.

"I need scarcely point out to you, Julian, the bearing of the principle of the social fund on economic equality when the industrial system was nationalized. It made it obvious that even if it were possible to figure out in a satisfactory manner the difference in the industrial products which in an accounting with the social fund could be respectively credited to differences in individual performance, the result would not be worth the trouble. Even the worker of special ability, who might hope to gain most by it, could not hope to gain so much as he would lose in common with others by sacrificing the increased efficiency of the industrial machinery that would result from the sentiment of solidarity and public spirit among the workers arising from a feeling of complete unity of interest."

"Doctor," I exclaimed, "I like that idea of the social fund immensely! It makes me understand, among other things, the completeness with which you seem to have outgrown the wages notion, which in one form or other was fundamental to all economic thought in my day. It is because you are accustomed to regarding the social capital rather than your day-to-day specific exertions as the main source of your wealth. It is, in a word, the difference between the attitude of the capitalist and the proletarian."

"Even so," said the doctor. "The Revolution made us all capitalists, and the idea of the dividend has driven out that of the stipend. We take wages only in honor. From our point of view as to the collective ownership of the economic machinery of the social system, and the absolute claim of society collectively to its product, there is something amusing in the laborious disputations by which your contemporaries used to try to settle just how much or little wages or compensation for services this or that individual or group was entitled to. Why, dear me, Julian, if the cleverest worker were limited to his own product, strictly separated and distinguished from the elements by which the use of the social machinery had multiplied it, he would fare no better than a half-starved savage. Everybody is entitled not only to his own product, but to vastly more--namely, to his share of the product of the social organism, in addition to his personal product, but he is entitled to this share not on the grab-as-grab-can plan of your day, by which some made themselves millionaires and others were left beggars, but on equal terms with all his fellow-capitalists."

"The idea of an unearned increment given to private properties by the social organism was talked of in my day," I said, "but only, as I remember, with reference to land values. There were reformers who held that society had the right to take in taxes all increase in value of land that resulted from social factors, such as increased population or public improvements, but they seemed to think the doctrine applicable to land only."

"Yes," said the doctor, "and it is rather odd that, having hold of the clew, they did not follow it up."

CHAPTER XIV.

We Look Over My Collection Of Harnesses.

Wires for light and heat had been put into the vault, and it was as warm and bright and habitable a place as it had been a century before, when it was my sleeping chamber. Kneeling before the door of the safe, I at once addressed myself to manipulating the dial, my companions meanwhile leaning over me in attitudes of eager interest.

It had been one hundred years since I locked the safe the last time, and under ordinary circumstances that would have been long enough for me to forget the combination several times over, but it was as fresh in my mind as if I had devised it a fortnight before, that being, in fact, the entire length of the intervening period so far as my conscious life was concerned.

"You observe," I said, "that I turn this dial until the letter 'K' comes opposite the letter 'R.' Then I move this other dial till the number '9' comes opposite the same point. Now the safe is practically unlocked. All I have to do to open it is to turn this knob, which moves the bolts, and then swing the door open, as you see."

But they did not see just then, for the knob would not turn, the lock remaining fast. I knew that I had made no mistake about the combination. Some of the tumblers in the lock had failed to fall. I tried it over again several times and thumped the dial and the door, but it was of no use. The lock remained stubborn. One might have said that its memory was not as good as mine. It had forgotten the combination. A materialistic explanation somewhat more probable was that the oil in the lock had been hardened by time so as to offer a slight resistance. The lock could not have rusted, for the atmosphere of the room had been absolutely dry. Otherwise I should not have survived.

"I am sorry to disappoint you," I said, "but we shall have to send to the headquarters of the safe manufacturers for a locksmith. I used to know just where in Sudbury Street to go, but I suppose the safe business has moved since then."

"It has not merely moved," said the doctor, "it has disappeared; there are safes like this at the historical museum, but I never knew how they were opened until now. It is really very ingenious."

"And do you mean to say that there are actually no locksmiths to-day who could open this safe?"

"Any machinist can cut the steel like cardboard," replied the doctor; "but really I don't believe there is a man in the world who could pick the lock. We have, of course, simple locks to insure privacy and keep children out of mischief, but nothing calculated to offer serious resistance either to force or cunning. The craft of the locksmith is extinct."

At this Edith, who was impatient to see the safe opened, exclaimed that the twentieth century had nothing to boast of if it could not solve a puzzle which any clever burglar of the nineteenth century was equal to.

"From the point of view of an impatient young woman it may seem so," said the doctor. "But we must remember that lost arts often are monuments of human progress, indicating outgrown limitations and necessities, to which they ministered. It is because we have no more thieves that we have no more locksmiths. Poor Julian had to go to all this pains to protect the papers in that safe, because if he lost them he would be left a beggar, and, from being one of the masters of the many, would have become one of the servants of the few, and perhaps be tempted to turn burglar himself. No wonder locksmiths were in demand in those days. But now you see, even supposing any one in a community enjoying universal and equal wealth could wish to steal anything, there is nothing that he could steal with a view to selling it again. Our wealth consists in the guarantee of an equal share in the capital and income of the nation--a guarantee that is personal and can not be taken from us nor given away, being vested in each one at birth, and divested only by death. So you see the locksmith and safe-maker would be very useless persons."

As we talked, I had continued to work the dial in the hope that the obstinate tumbler might be coaxed to act, and presently a faint click rewarded my efforts and I swung the door open.

"Faugh!" exclaimed Edith at the musty gust of confined air which followed. "I am sorry for your people if that is a fair sample of what you had to breathe."

"It is probably about the only sample left, at any rate," observed the doctor.

"Dear me! what a ridiculous little box it turns out to be for such a pretentious outside!" exclaimed Edith's mother.

"Yes," said I. "The thick walls are to make the contents fireproof as well as burglar-proof--and, by the way, I should think you would need fireproof safes still."

"We have no fires, except in the old structures," replied the doctor. "Since building was undertaken by the people collectively, you see we could not afford to have them, for destruction of property means to the nation a dead loss, while under private capitalism the loss might be shuffled off on others in all sorts of ways. They could get insured, but the nation has to insure itself."

Opening the inner door of the safe, I took out several drawers full of securities of all sorts, and emptied them on the table in the room.

"Are these stuffy-looking papers what you used to call wealth?" said Edith, with evident disappointment.

"Not the papers in themselves," I said, "but what they represented."

"And what was that?" she asked.

"The ownership of land, houses, mills, ships, railroads, and all manner of other things," I replied, and went on as best I could to explain to her mother and herself about rents, profits, interest, dividends, etc. But it was evident, from the blank expression of their countenances, that I was not making much headway.

Presently the doctor looked up from the papers which he was devouring with the zeal of an antiquarian, and chuckled.

"I am afraid, Julian, you are on the wrong tack. You see economic science in your day was a science of things; in our day it is a science of human beings. We have nothing at all answering to your rent, interest, profits, or other financial devices, and the terms expressing them have no meaning now except to students. If you wish Edith and her mother to understand you, you must translate these money terms into terms of men and women and children, and the plain facts of their relations as affected by your system. Shall you consider it impertinent if I try to make the matter a little clearer to them?"

"I shall be much obliged to you," I said; "and perhaps you will at the same time make it clearer to me."

"I think," said the doctor, "that we shall all understand the nature and value of these documents much better if, instead of speaking of them as titles of ownership in farms, factories, mines, railroads, etc., we state plainly that they were evidences that their possessors were the masters of various groups of men, women, and children in different parts of the country. Of course, as Julian says, the documents nominally state his title to things only, and say nothing about men and women.

But it is the men and women who went with the lands, the machines, and various other things, and were bound to them by their bodily necessities, which gave all the value to the possession of the things.

"But for the implication that there were men who, because they must have the use of the land, would submit to labor for the owner of it in return for permission to occupy it, these deeds and mortgages would have been of no value. So of these factory shares. They speak only of water power and looms, but they would be valueless but for the thousands of human workers bound to the machines by bodily necessities as fixedly as if they were chained there. So of these coal-mine shares. But for the multitude of wretched beings condemned by want to labor in living graves, of what value would have been these shares which yet make no mention of them? And see again how significant is the fact that it was deemed needless to make mention of and to enumerate by name these serfs of the field, of the loom, of the mine! Under systems of chattel slavery, such as had formerly prevailed, it was necessary to name and identify each chattel, that he might be recovered in case of escape, and an account made of the loss in case of death. But there was no danger of loss by the escape or the death of the serfs transferred by these documents. They would not run away, for there was nothing better to run to or any escape from the world-wide economic system which enthralled them; and if they died, that involved no loss to their owners, for there were always plenty more to take their places. Decidedly, it would have been a waste of paper to enumerate them.

"Just now at the breakfast table," continued the doctor, "I was explaining the modern view of the economic system of private capitalism as one based on the compulsory servitude of the masses to the capitalists, a servitude which the latter enforced by monopolizing the bulk of the world's resources and machinery, leaving the pressure of want to compel the masses to accept their yoke, the police and soldiers meanwhile defending them in their monopolies. These documents turn up in a very timely way to illustrate the ingenious and effectual methods by which the different sorts of workers were organized for the service of the capitalists. To use a plain illustration, these various sorts of so-called securities may be described as so many kinds of human harness by which the masses, broken and tamed by the pressure of want, were yoked and strapped to the chariots of the capitalists.

"For instance, here is a bundle of farm mortgages on Kansas farms. Very good; by virtue of the operation of this security certain Kansas farmers worked for the owner of it, and though they might never know who he was nor he who they were, yet they were as securely and certainly his thralls as if he had stood over them with a whip instead of sitting in his parlor at Boston, New York, or London. This mortgage harness was generally used to hitch in the agricultural class of the population. Most of the farmers of the West were pulling in it toward the end of the nineteenth century.--Was it not so, Julian? Correct me if I am wrong."

"You are stating the facts very accurately," I answered. "I am beginning to understand more clearly the nature of my former property."

"Now let us see what this bundle is," pursued the doctor. "Ah! yes; these are shares in New England cotton factories. This sort of harness was chiefly used for women and children, the sizes ranging away down so as to fit girls and boys of eleven and twelve. It used to be said that it was only the margin of profit furnished by the almost costless labor of the little children that made these factories paying properties. The population of New England was largely broken in at a very tender age to work in this style of harness.

"Here, now, is a little different sort. These are railroad, gas, and water-works shares. They were a sort of comprehensive harness, by which not only a particular class of workers but whole communities were hitched in and made to work for the owner of the security.

"And, finally, we have here the strongest harness of all, the Government bond. This document, you see, is a bond of the United States Government. By it seventy million people--the whole nation, in fact--were harnessed to the coach of the owner of this bond; and, what was more, the driver in this case was the Government itself, against which the team would find it hard to kick. There was a great deal of kicking and balking in the other sorts of harness, and the capitalists were often inconvenienced and temporarily deprived of the labor of the men they had bought and paid for with good money. Naturally, therefore, the Government bond was greatly prized by them as an investment. They used every possible effort to induce the various governments to put more and more of this sort of harness on the people, and the governments, being carried on by the agents of the capitalists, of course kept on doing so, up to the very eve of the great Revolution, which was to turn the bonds and all the other harnesses into waste paper."

"As a representative of the nineteenth century," I said, "I can not deny the substantial correctness of your rather startling way of describing our system of investments. Still, you will admit that, bad as the system was and bitter as was the condition of the masses under it, the function performed by the capitalists in organizing and directing such industry as we had was a service to the world of some value."

"Certainly, certainly," replied the doctor. "The same plea might be urged, and has been, in defense of every system by which men have ever made other men their servants from the beginning. There was always some service, generally valuable and indispensable, which the oppressors could urge and did urge as the ground and excuse of the servitude they enforced. As men grew wiser they observed that they were paying a ruinous price for the services thus rendered. So at first they said to the kings: 'To be sure, you help defend the state from foreigners and hang thieves, but it is too much to ask us to be your serfs in exchange; we can do better.' And so they established republics. So also, presently, the people said to the priests: 'You have done something for us, but you have charged too much for your services in asking us to submit our minds to you; we can do better.' And so they established religious liberty.

"And likewise, in this last matter we are speaking of, the people finally said to the capitalists: 'Yes, you have organized our industry, but at the price of enslaving us. We can do better.' And substituting national co-operation for capitalism, they established the industrial republic based on economic democracy. If it were true, Julian, that any consideration of service rendered to others, however valuable, could excuse the benefactors for making bondmen of the benefited, then there never was a despotism or slave system which could not excuse itself."

"Haven't you some real money to show us," said Edith, "something besides these papers--some gold and silver such as they have at the museum?"

It was not customary in the nineteenth century for people to keep large supplies of ready money in their houses, but for emergencies I had a little stock of it in my safe, and in response to Edith's request I took out a drawer containing several hundred dollars in gold and emptied it on the table.

"How pretty they are!" exclaimed Edith, thrusting her hands in the pile of yellow coins and clinking them together. "And is it really true that if you only had enough of these things, no matter how or where you got them, men and women would submit themselves to you and let you make what use you pleased of them?"

"Not only would they let you use them as you pleased, but they would be extremely grateful to you for being so good as to use them instead of others. The poor fought each other for the privilege of being the servants and underlings of those who had the money."

"Now I see," said Edith, "what the Masters of the Bread meant."

"What is that about Masters of the Bread?" I asked. "Who were they?"

"It was a name given to the capitalists in the revolutionary period," replied the doctor. "This thing Edith speaks of is a scrap of the literature of that time, when the people first began to fully wake up to the fact that class monopoly of the machinery of production meant slavery for the mass."

"Let me see if I can recall it," said Edith. "It begins this way: 'Everywhere men, women, and children stood in the market-place crying to the Masters of the Bread to take them to be their servants, that they might have bread. The strong men said: "O Lords of the Bread, feel our thews and sinews, our arms and our legs; see how strong we are. Take us and use us. Let us dig for you. Let us hew for you. Let us go down in the mine and delve for you. Let us freeze and starve in the forecastles of your ships. Send us into the hells of your steamship stokeholes. Do what you will with us, but let us serve you, that we may eat and not die!"

"'Then spoke up also the learned men, the scribes and the lawyers, whose strength was in their brains and not in their bodies: "O Masters of the Bread," they said, "take us to be your servants and to do your will. See how fine is our wit, how great our knowledge; our minds are stored with the treasures of learning and the subtlety of all the philosophies. To us has been given clearer vision than to others, and the power of persuasion that we should be leaders of the people, voices to the voiceless, and eyes to the blind. But the people whom we should serve have no bread to give us. Therefore, Masters of the Bread, give us to eat, and we will betray the people to you, for we must live. We will plead for you in the courts against the widow and the fatherless. We will speak and write in your praise, and with cunning words confound those who speak against you and your power and state. And nothing that you require of us shall seem too much. But because we sell not only our bodies, but our souls also, give us more bread than these laborers receive, who sell their bodies only."

"'And the priests and Levites also cried out as the Lords of the Bread passed through the market-place: "Take us, Masters, to be your servants and to do your will, for we also must eat, and you only have the bread. We are the guardians of the sacred oracles, and the people hearken unto us and reply not, for our voice to them is as the voice of God. But we must have bread to eat like others. Give us therefore plentifully of your bread, and we will speak to the people, that they be still and trouble you not with their murmurings because of hunger. In the name of God the Father will we forbid them to claim the rights of brothers, and in the name of the Prince of Peace will we preach your law of competition."

"'And above all the clamor of the men were heard the voices of a multitude of women crying to the Masters of the Bread: "Pass us not by, for we must also eat. The men are stronger than we, but they eat much bread while we eat little, so that though we be not so strong yet in the end you shall not lose if you take us to be your servants instead of them. And if you will not take us for our labor's sake, yet look upon us: we are women, and should be fair in your eyes. Take us and do with us according to your pleasure, for we must eat."

"'And above all the chaffering of the market, the hoarse voices of the men, and the shrill voices of the women, rose the piping treble of the little children, crying: "Take us to be your servants, for the breasts of our mothers are dry and our fathers have no bread for us, and we hunger. We are weak, indeed, but we ask so little, so very little, that at last we shall be cheaper to you than the men, our fathers, who eat so much, and the women, our mothers, who eat more than we."

"'And the Masters of the Bread, having taken for their use or pleasure such of the men, the women, and the little ones as they saw fit, passed by. And there was left a great multitude in the market-place for whom there was no bread.'"

"Ah!" said the doctor, breaking the silence which followed the ceasing of Edith's voice, "it was indeed the last refinement of indignity put upon human nature by your economic system that it compelled men to seek the sale of themselves. Voluntary in a real sense the sale was not, of course, for want or the fear of it left no choice as to the necessity of selling themselves to somebody, but as to the particular transaction there was choice enough to make it shameful. They had to seek those to whom to offer themselves and actively to procure their own purchase. In this respect the submission of men to other men through the relation of hire was more abject than under a slavery resting directly on force. In that case the slave might be compelled to yield to physical duress, but he could still keep a mind free and resentful toward his master; but in the relation of hire men sought for their masters and begged as a favor that they would use them, body and mind, for their profit or pleasure. To the view of us moderns, therefore, the chattel slave was a more dignified and heroic figure than the hireling of your day who called himself a free worker.

"It was possible for the slave to rise in soul above his circumstances and be a philosopher in bondage like Epictetus, but the hireling could not scorn the bonds he sought. The abjectness of his position was not merely physical but mental. In selling himself he had necessarily sold his independence of mind also. Your whole industrial system seems in this point of view best and most fitly described by a word which you oddly enough reserved to designate a particular phase of self-selling practiced by women.

"Labor for others in the name of love and kindness, and labor with others for a common end in which all are mutually interested, and labor for its own joy, are alike honorable, but the hiring out of our faculties to the selfish uses of others, which was the form labor generally took in your day, is unworthy of human nature. The Revolution for the first time in history made labor truly honorable by putting it on the basis of fraternal co-operation for a common and equally shared result. Until then it was at best but a shameful necessity."

Presently I said: "When you have satisfied your curiosity as to these papers I suppose we might as well make a bonfire of them, for they seem to have no more value now than a collection of heathen fetiches after the former worshipers have embraced Christianity."

"Well, and has not such a collection a value to the student of history?" said the doctor. "Of course, these documents are scarcely now valuable in the sense they were, but in another they have much value. I see among them several varieties which are quite scarce in the historical collections, and if you feel disposed to present the whole lot to our museum I am sure the gift will be much appreciated. The fact is, the great bonfire our grandfathers made, while a very natural and excusable expression of jubilation over broken bondage, is much to be regretted from an archaeological point of view."

"What do you mean by the great bonfire?" I inquired.

"It was a rather dramatic incident at the close of the great Revolution. When the long struggle was ended and economic equality, guaranteed by the public administration of capital, had been established, the people got together from all parts of the land enormous collections of what you used to call the evidences of value, which, while purporting to be certificates of property in things, had been really certificates of the ownership of men, deriving, as we have seen, their whole value from the serfs attached to the things by the constraint of bodily necessities. These it pleased the people--exalted, as you may well imagine, by the afflatus of liberty--to collect in a vast mass on the site of the New York Stock Exchange, the great altar of Plutus, whereon millions of human beings had been sacrificed to him, and there to make a bonfire of them. A great pillar stands on the spot to-day, and from its summit a mighty torch of electric flame is always streaming, in commemoration of that event and as a testimony forever to the ending of the parchment bondage that was heavier than the scepters of kings. It is estimated that certificates of ownership in human beings, or, as you called them, titles to property, to the value of forty billion dollars, together with hundreds of millions of paper money, went up in that great blaze, which we devoutly consider must have been, of all the innumerable burnt sacrifices which have been offered up to God from the beginning, the one that pleased him best.

"Now, if I had been there, I can easily imagine that I should have rejoiced over that conflagration as much as did the most exultant of those who danced about it; but from the calmer point of view of the present I regret the destruction of a mass of historic material. So you see that your bonds and deeds and mortgages and shares of stock are really valuable still."

CHAPTER XV.

What We Were Coming To But For The Revolution.

"We read in the histories," said Edith's mother, "much about the amazing extent to which particular individuals and families succeeded in concentrating in their own hands the natural resources, industrial machinery, and products of the several countries. Julian had only a million dollars, but many individuals or families had, we are told, wealth amounting to fifty, a hundred, and even two or three hundred millions. We read of infants who in the cradle were heirs of hundreds of millions. Now, something I never saw mentioned in the books was the limit, for there must have been some limit fixed, to which one individual might appropriate the earth's surface and resources, the means of production, and the products of labor."

"There was no limit," I replied.

"Do you mean," exclaimed Edith, "that if a man were only clever and unscrupulous enough he might appropriate, say, the entire territory of a country and leave the people actually nothing to stand on unless by his consent?"

"Certainly," I replied. "In fact, in many countries of the Old World individuals owned whole provinces, and in the United States even vaster tracts had passed and were passing into private and corporate hands. There was no limit whatever to the extent of land which one person might own, and of course this ownership implied the right to evict every human being from the territory unless the owner chose to let individuals remain on payment of tribute."

"And how about other things besides land?" asked Edith.

"It was the same," I said. "There was no limit to the extent to which an individual might acquire the exclusive ownership of all the factories, shops, mines, and means of industry, and commerce of every sort, so that no person could find an opportunity to earn a living except as the servant of the owner and on his terms."

"If we are correctly informed," said the doctor, "the concentration of the ownership of the machinery of production and distribution, trade and industry, had already, before you fell asleep, been carried to a point in the United States through trusts and syndicates which excited general alarm."

"Certainly," I replied. "It was then already in the power of a score of men in New York city to stop at will every car-wheel in the United States, and the combined action of a few other groups of capitalists would have sufficed practically to arrest the industries and commerce of the entire country, forbid employment to everybody, and starve the entire population. The self-interest of these capitalists in keeping business going on was the only ground of assurance the rest of the people had for their livelihood from day to day. Indeed, when the capitalists desired to compel the people to vote as they wished, it was their regular custom to threaten to stop the industries of the country and produce a business crisis if the election did not go to suit them."

"Suppose, Julian, an individual or family or group of capitalists, having become sole owners of all the land and machinery of one nation, should wish to go on and acquire the sole ownership of all the land and economic means and machinery of the whole earth, would that have been inconsistent with your law of property?"

"Not at all. If one individual, as you suggest, through the effect of cunning and skill combined with inheritances, should obtain a legal title to the whole globe, it would be his to do what he pleased with as absolutely as if it were a garden patch, according to our law of property. Nor is your supposition about one person or family becoming owner of the whole earth a wholly fanciful one. There was, when I fell asleep, one family of European bankers whose world-wide power and resources were so vast and increasing at such a prodigious and accelerating rate that they had already an influence over the destinies of nations wider than perhaps any monarch ever exercised."

"And if I understand your system, if they had gone on and attained the ownership of the globe to the lowest inch of standing room at low tide, it would have been the legal right of that family or single individual, in the name of the sacred right of property, to give the people of the human race legal notice to move off the earth, and in case of their failure to comply with the requirement of the notice, to call upon them in the name of the law to form themselves into sheriffs' *posses* and evict themselves from the earth's surface?"

"Unquestionably."

"O father," exclaimed Edith, "you and Julian are trying to make fun of us. You must think we will believe anything if you only keep straight faces. But you are going too far."

"I do not wonder you think so," said the doctor. "But you can easily satisfy yourself from the books that we have in no way exaggerated the possibilities of the old system of property. What was called under that system the right of property meant the unlimited right of anybody who was clever enough to deprive everybody else of any property whatever."

"It would seem, then," said Edith, "that the dream of world conquest by an individual, if ever realized, was more likely under the old *regime* to be realized by economic than by military means."

"Very true," said the doctor. "Alexander and Napoleon mistook their trade; they should have been bankers, not soldiers. But, indeed, the time was not in their day ripe for a world-wide money dynasty, such as we have been speaking of. Kings had a rude way of interfering with the so-called rights of property when they conflicted with royal prestige or produced dangerous popular discontent. Tyrants themselves, they did not willingly brook rival tyrants in their dominions. It was not till the kings had been shorn of power and the interregnum of sham democracy had set in, leaving no virile force in the state or the world to resist the money power, that the opportunity for a world-wide plutocratic despotism arrived. Then, in the latter part of the nineteenth century, when international trade and financial relations had broken down national barriers and the world had become one field of economic enterprise, did the idea of a universally dominant and centralized money power become not only possible, but, as Julian has said, had already so far materialized itself as to cast its shadow before. If the Revolution had not come when it did, we can not doubt that something like this universal plutocratic dynasty or some highly centered oligarchy, based upon the complete monopoly of all property by a small body, would long before this time have become the government of the world. But of course the Revolution must have come when it did, so we need not talk of what would have happened if it had not come."

CHAPTER XVI.

An Excuse That Condemned.

"I have read," said Edith, "that there never was a system of oppression so bad that those who benefited by it did not recognize the moral sense so far as to make some excuse for themselves. Was the old system of property distribution, by which the few held the many in servitude through fear of starvation, an exception to this rule? Surely the rich could not have looked the poor in the face unless they had some excuse to offer, some color of reason to give for the cruel contrast between their conditions."

"Thanks for reminding us of that point," said the doctor. "As you say, there never was a system so bad that it did not make an excuse for itself. It would not be strictly fair to the old system to dismiss it without considering the excuse made for it, although, on the other hand, it would really be kinder not to mention it, for it was an excuse that, far from excusing, furnished an additional ground of condemnation for the system which it undertook to justify."

"What was the excuse?" asked Edith.

"It was the claim that, as a matter of justice, every one is entitled to the effect of his qualities-- that is to say, the result of his abilities, the fruit of his efforts. The qualities, abilities, and efforts of different persons being different, they would naturally acquire advantages over others in wealth seeking as in other ways; but as this was according to Nature, it was urged that it must be right, and nobody had any business to complain, unless of the Creator.

"Now, in the first place, the theory that a person has a right in dealing with his fellows to take advantage of his superior abilities is nothing other than a slightly more roundabout expression of the doctrine that might is right. It was precisely to prevent their doing this that the policeman stood on the corner, the judge sat on the bench, and the hangman drew his fees. The whole end and amount of civilization had indeed been to substitute for the natural law of superior might an artificial equality by force of statute, whereby, in disregard of their natural differences, the weak and simple were made equal to the strong and cunning by means of the collective force lent them.

"But while the nineteenth-century moralists denied as sharply as we do men's right to take advantage of their superiorities in direct dealings by physical force, they held that they might rightly do so when the dealings were indirect and carried on through the medium of things. That is to say, a man might not so much as jostle another while drinking a cup of water lest he should spill it, but he might acquire the spring of water on which the community solely depended and make the people pay a dollar a drop for water or go without. Or if he filled up the spring so as to deprive the population of water on any terms, he was held to be acting within his right. He might not by force take away a bone from a beggar's dog, but he might corner the grain supply of a nation and reduce millions to starvation.

"If you touch a man's living you touch him, would seem to be about as plain a truth as could be put in words; but our ancestors had not the least difficulty in getting around it. 'Of course,' they said, 'you must not touch the man; to lay a finger on him would be an assault punishable by law. But his living is quite a different thing. That depends on bread, meat, clothing, land, houses, and other material things, which you have an unlimited right to appropriate and dispose of as you please without the slightest regard to whether anything is left for the rest of the world.'

"I think I scarcely need dwell on the entire lack of any moral justification for the different rule which our ancestors followed in determining what use you might rightly make of your superior powers in dealing with your neighbor directly by physical force and indirectly by economic duress. No one can have any more or other right to take away another's living by superior economic skill or financial cunning than if he used a club, simply because no one has any right to take advantage of any one else or to deal with him otherwise than justly by any means whatever. The end itself being immoral, the means employed could not possibly make any difference. Moralists at a pinch used to argue that a good end might justify bad means, but none, I think, went so far as to claim that good means justified a bad end; yet this was precisely what the defenders of the old property system did in fact claim when they argued that it was right for a man to take away the living of others and make them his servants, if only his triumph resulted from superior talent or more diligent devotion to the acquisition of material things.

"But indeed the theory that the monopoly of wealth could be justified by superior economic ability, even if morally sound, would not at all have fitted the old property system, for of all conceivable plans for distributing property, none could have more absolutely defied every notion of desert based on economic effort. None could have been more utterly wrong if it were true that wealth ought to be distributed according to the ability and industry displayed by individuals."

"All this talk started with the discussion of Julian's fortune. Now tell us, Julian, was your million dollars the result of your economic ability, the fruit of your industry?"

"Of course not," I replied. "Every cent of it was inherited. As I have often told you, I never lifted a finger in a useful way in my life."

"And were you the only person whose property came to him by descent without effort of his own?"

"On the contrary, title by descent was the basis and backbone of the whole property system. All land, except in the newest countries, together with the bulk of the more stable kinds of property, was held by that title."

"Precisely so. We hear what Julian says. While the moralists and the clergy solemnly justified the inequalities of wealth and reproved the discontent of the poor on the ground that those inequalities were justified by natural differences in ability and diligence, they knew all the time, and everybody knew who listened to them, that the foundation principle of the whole property system was not ability, effort, or desert of any kind whatever, but merely the accident of birth, than which no possible claim could more completely mock at ethics."

"But, Julian," exclaimed Edith, "you must surely have had some way of excusing yourself to your conscience for retaining in the presence of a needy world such an excess of good things as you had!"

"I am afraid," I said, "that you can not easily imagine how callous was the cuticle of the nineteenth-century conscience. There may have been some of my class on the intellectual plane of little Jack Horner in Mother Goose, who concluded he must be a good boy because he pulled out a plum, but I did not at least belong to that grade. I never gave much thought to the subject of my right to an abundance which I had done nothing to earn in the midst of a starving world of toilers, but occasionally, when I did think of it, I felt like craving pardon of the beggar who asked alms for being in a position to give to him."

"It is impossible to get up any sort of a quarrel with Julian," said the doctor; "but there were others of his class less rational. Cornered as to their moral claim to their possessions, they fell back on that of their ancestors. They argued that these ancestors, assuming them to have had a right by merit to their possessions, had as an incident of that merit the right to give them to others. Here, of course, they absolutely confused the ideas of legal and moral right. The law might indeed give a person power to transfer a legal title to property in any way that suited the lawmakers, but the meritorious right to the property, resting as it did on personal desert, could not in the nature of moral things be transferred or ascribed to any one else. The cleverest lawyer would never have pretended that he could draw up a document that would carry over the smallest tittle of merit from one person to another, however close the tie of blood.

"In ancient times it was customary to hold children responsible for the debts of their fathers and sell them into slavery to make satisfaction. The people of Julian's day found it unjust thus to inflict upon innocent offspring the penalty of their ancestors' faults. But if these children did not deserve the consequences of their ancestors' sloth, no more had they any title to the product of their ancestors' industry. The barbarians who insisted on both sorts of inheritance were more logical than Julian's contemporaries, who, rejecting one sort of inheritance, retained the other. Will it be said that at least the later theory of inheritance was more humane, although one-sided? Upon that point you should have been able to get the opinion of the disinherited masses who, by reason of the monopolizing of the earth and its resources from generation to generation by the possessors of inherited property, were left no place to stand on and no way to live except by permission of the inheriting class."

"Doctor," I said, "I have nothing to offer against all that. We who inherited our wealth had no moral title to it, and that we knew as well as everybody else did, although it was not considered polite to refer to the fact in our presence. But if I am going to stand up here in the pillory as a representative of the inheriting class, there are others who ought to stand beside me. We were not the only ones who had no right to our money. Are you not going to say anything about the money makers, the rascals who raked together great fortunes in a few years by wholesale fraud and extortion?"

"Pardon me, I was just coming to them," said the doctor. "You ladies must remember," he continued, "that the rich, who in Julian's day possessed nearly everything of value in every country, leaving the masses mere scraps and crumbs, were of two sorts: those who had inherited their wealth, and those who, as the saying was, had made it. We have seen how far the inheriting class were justified in their holdings by the principle which the nineteenth century asserted to be the excuse for wealth--namely, that individuals were entitled to the fruit of their labors. Let us next inquire how far the same principle justified the possessions of these others whom Julian refers to, who claimed that they had made their money themselves, and showed in proof lives absolutely devoted from childhood to age without rest or respite to the piling up of gains. Now, of course, labor in itself, however arduous, does not imply moral desert. It may be a criminal activity. Let us see if these men who claimed that they made their money had any better title to it than Julian's class by the rule put forward as the excuse for unequal wealth, that every one has a right to the product of his labor. The most complete statement of the principle of the right of property, as based on economic effort, which has come down to us, is this maxim: 'Every man is entitled to his own product, his whole product, and nothing but his product.' Now, this maxim had a double edge, a negative as well as a positive, and the negative edge is very sharp. If everybody was entitled to his own product, nobody else was entitled to any part of it, and if any one's accumulation was found to contain any product not strictly his own, he stood condemned as a thief by the law he had invoked.

If in the great fortunes of the stockjobbers, the railroad kings, the bankers, the great landlords, and the other moneyed lords who boasted that they had begun life with a shilling--if in these great fortunes of mushroom rapidity of growth there was anything that was properly the product of the efforts of any one but the owner, it was not his, and his possession of it condemned him as a thief. If he would be justified, he must not be more careful to obtain all that was his own product than to avoid taking anything that was not his product. If he insisted upon the pound of flesh awarded him by the letter of the law, he must stick to the letter, observing the warning of Portia to Shylock:

> Nor cut thou less nor more
> But just a pound of flesh; if thou tak'st more
> Or less than a just pound, be it so much
> As makes light or heavy in the substance,
> Or the division of the twentieth part
> Of one poor scruple; nay, if the scale do turn
> But in the estimation of a hair,
> Thou diest, and thy goods are confiscate.

How many of the great fortunes heaped up by the self-made men of your day, Julian, would have stood that test?"

"It is safe to say," I replied, "that there was not one of the lot whose lawyer would not have advised him to do as Shylock did, and resign his claim rather than try to push it at the risk of the penalty. Why, dear me, there never would have been any possibility of making a great fortune in a lifetime if the maker had confined himself to his own product. The whole acknowledged art of wealth-making on a large scale consisted in devices for getting possession of other people's product without too open breach of the law. It was a current and a true saying of the times that nobody could honestly acquire a million dollars. Everybody knew that it was only by extortion, speculation, stock gambling, or some other form of plunder under pretext of law that such a feat could be accomplished. You yourselves can not condemn the human cormorants who piled up these heaps of ill-gotten gains more bitterly than did the public opinion of their own time. The execration and contempt of the community followed the great money-getters to their graves, and with the best of reason. I have had nothing to say in defense of my own class, who inherited our wealth, but actually the people seemed to have more respect for us than for these others who claimed to have made their money. For if we inheritors had confessedly no moral right to the wealth we had done nothing to produce or acquire, yet we had committed no positive wrong to obtain it."

"You see," said the doctor, "what a pity it would have been if we had forgotten to compare the excuse offered by the nineteenth century for the unequal distribution of wealth with the actual facts of that distribution. Ethical standards advance from age to age, and it is not always fair to judge the systems of one age by the moral standards of a later one. But we have seen that the property system of the nineteenth century would have gained nothing by way of a milder verdict by appealing from the moral standards of the twentieth to those of the nineteenth century. It was not necessary, in order to justify its condemnation, to invoke the modern ethics of wealth which deduce the rights of property from the rights of man. It was only necessary to apply to the actual realities of the system the ethical plea put forth in its defense--namely, that everybody was entitled to the fruit of his own labor, and was not entitled to the fruit of anybody's else--to leave not one stone upon another of the whole fabric."

"But was there, then, absolutely no class under your system," said Edith's mother, "which even by the standards of your time could claim an ethical as well as a legal title to their possessions?"

"Oh, yes," I replied, "we have been speaking of the rich. You may set it down as a rule that the rich, the possessors of great wealth, had no moral right to it as based upon desert, for either their fortunes belonged to the class of inherited wealth, or else, when accumulated in a lifetime, necessarily represented chiefly the product of others, more or less forcibly or fraudulently obtained. There were, however, a great number of modest competencies, which were recognized by public opinion as being no more than a fair measure of the service rendered by their possessors to the community. Below these there was the vast mass of well-nigh wholly penniless toilers, the real people. Here there was indeed abundance of ethical title to property, for these were the producers of all; but beyond the shabby clothing they wore, they had little or no property."

"It would seem," said Edith, "that, speaking generally, the class which chiefly had the property had little or no right to it, even according to the ideas of your day, while the masses which had the right had little or no property."

"Substantially that was the case," I replied. "That is to say, if you took the aggregate of property held by the merely legal title of inheritance, and added to it all that had been obtained by means which public opinion held to be speculative, extortionate, fraudulent, or representing results in excess of services rendered, there would be little property left, and certainly none at all in considerable amounts."

"From the preaching of the clergy in Julian's time," said the doctor, "you would have thought the corner stone of Christianity was the right of property, and the supreme crime was the wrongful appropriation of property. But if stealing meant only taking that from another to which he had a sound ethical title, it must have been one of the most difficult of all crimes to commit for lack of the requisite material. When one took away the possessions of the poor it was reasonably certain that he was stealing, but then they had nothing to take away."

"The thing that seems to me the most utterly incredible about all this terrible story," said Edith, "is that a system which was such a disastrous failure in its effects on the general welfare, which, by disinheriting the great mass of the people, had made them its bitter foes, and which finally even people like Julian, who were its beneficiaries, did not attempt to defend as having any ground of fairness, could have maintained itself a day."

"No wonder it seems incomprehensible to you, as now, indeed, it seems to me as I look back," I replied. "But you can not possibly imagine, as I myself am fast losing the power to do, in my new environment, how benumbing to the mind was the prestige belonging to the immemorial antiquity of the property system as we knew it and of the rule of the rich based on it. No other institution, no other fabric of power ever known to man, could be compared with it as to duration. No different economic order could really be said ever to have been known. There had been changes and fashions in all other human institutions, but no radical change in the system of property. The procession of political, social, and religious systems, the royal, imperial, priestly, democratic epochs, and all other great phases of human affairs, had been as passing cloud shadows, mere fashions of a day, compared with the hoary antiquity of the rule of the rich. Consider how profound and how widely ramified a root in human prejudices such a system must have had, how overwhelming the presumption must have been with the mass of minds against the possibility of making an end of an order that had never been known to have a beginning! What need for excuses or defenders had a system so deeply based in usage and antiquity as this? It is not too much to say that to the mass of mankind in my day the division of the race into rich and poor, and the subjection of the latter to the former, seemed almost as much a law of Nature as the succession of the seasons--something that might not be agreeable, but was certainly unchangeable. And just here, I can well understand, must have come the hardest as well as, necessarily, the first task of the revolutionary leaders--that is, of overcoming the enormous dead weight of immemorial inherited prejudice against the possibility of getting rid of abuses which had lasted so long, and opening people's eyes to the fact that the system of wealth distribution was merely a human institution like others, and that if there is any truth in human progress, the longer an institution had endured unchanged, the more completely it was likely to have become out of joint with the world's progress, and the more radical the change must be which, should bring it into correspondence with other lines of social evolution."

"That is quite the modern view of the subject," said the doctor. "I shall be understood in talking with a representative of the century which invented poker if I say that when the revolutionists attacked the fundamental justice of the old property system, its defenders were able on account of its antiquity to meet them with a tremendous bluff--one which it is no wonder should have been for a time almost paralyzing. But behind the bluff there was absolutely nothing. The moment public opinion could be nerved up to the point of calling it, the game was up. The principle of inheritance, the backbone of the whole property system, at the first challenge of serious criticism abandoned all ethical defense and shriveled into a mere convention established by law, and as rightfully to be disestablished by it in the name of anything fairer. As for the buccaneers, the great money-getters, when the light was once turned on their methods, the question was not so much of saving their booty as their bacon.

"There is historically a marked difference," the doctor went on, "between the decline and fall of the systems of royal and priestly power and the passing of the rule of the rich. The former systems were rooted deeply in sentiment and romance, and for ages after their overthrow retained a strong hold on the hearts and imaginations of men. Our generous race has remembered without rancor all the oppressions it has endured save only the rule of the rich. The dominion of the money power had always been devoid of moral basis or dignity, and from the moment its material supports were destroyed, it not only perished, but seemed to sink away at once into a state of putrescence that made the world hurry to bury it forever out of sight and memory."

CHAPTER XVII.

The Revolution Saves Private Property From Monopoly.

"Really," said her mother, "Edith touched the match to quite a large discussion when she suggested that you should open the safe for us."

To which I added that I had learned more that morning about the moral basis of economic equality and the grounds for the abolition of private property than in my entire previous experience as a citizen of the twentieth century.

"The abolition of private property!" exclaimed the doctor. "What is that you say?"

"Of course," I said, "I am quite ready to admit that you have something--very much better in its place, but private property you have certainly abolished--have you not? Is not that what we have been talking about?"

The doctor turned as if for sympathy to the ladies. "And this young man," he said, "who thinks that we have abolished private property has at this moment in his pocket a card of credit representing a private annual income, for strictly personal use, of four thousand dollars, based upon a share of stock in the wealthiest and soundest corporation in the world, the value of his share, calculating the income on a four-per-cent basis, coming to one hundred thousand dollars."

I felt a little silly at being convicted so palpably of making a thoughtless observation, but the doctor hastened to say that he understood perfectly what had been in my mind. I had, no doubt, heard it a hundred times asserted by the wise men of my day that the equalization of human conditions as to wealth would necessitate destroying the institution of private property, and, without having given special thought to the subject, had naturally assumed that the equalization of wealth having been effected, private property must have been abolished, according to the prediction.

"Thanks," I said; "that is it exactly."

"The Revolution," said the doctor, "abolished private capitalism--that is to say, it put an end to the direction of the industries and commerce of the people by irresponsible persons for their own benefit and transferred that function to the people collectively to be carried on by responsible agents for the common benefit. The change created an entirely new system of property holding, but did not either directly or indirectly involve any denial of the right of private property. Quite on the contrary, the change in system placed the private and personal property rights of every citizen upon a basis incomparably more solid and secure and extensive than they ever before had or could have had while private capitalism lasted. Let us analyze the effects of the change of systems and see if it was not so."

"Suppose you and a number of other men of your time, all having separate claims in a mining region, formed a corporation to carry on as one mine your consolidated properties, would you have any less private property than you had when you owned your claims separately? You would have changed the mode and tenure of your property, but if the arrangement were a wise one that would be wholly to your advantage, would it not?"

"No doubt."

"Of course, you could no longer exercise the personal and complete control over the consolidated mine which you exercised over your separate claim. You would have, with your fellow-corporators, to intrust the management of the combined property to a board of directors chosen by yourselves, but you would not think that meant a sacrifice of your private property, would you?"

"Certainly not. That was the form under which a very large part, if not the largest part, of private property in my day was invested and controlled."

"It appears, then," said the doctor, "that it is not necessary to the full possession and enjoyment of private property that it should be in a separate parcel or that the owner should exercise a direct and personal control over it. Now, let us further suppose that instead of intrusting the management of your consolidated property to private directors more or less rascally, who would be constantly trying to cheat the stockholders, the nation undertook to manage the business for you by agents chosen by and responsible to you; would that be an attack on your property interests?"

"On the contrary, it would greatly enhance the value of the property. It would be as if a government guarantee were obtained for private bonds."

"Well, that is what the people in the Revolution did with private property. They simply consolidated the property in the country previously held in separate parcels and put the management of the business into the hands of a national agency charged with paying over the dividends to the stockholders for their individual use. So far, surely, it must be admitted the Revolution did not involve any abolition of private property."

"That is true," said I, "except in one particular. It is or used to be a usual incident to the ownership of property that it may be disposed of at will by the owner. The owner of stock in a mine or mill could not indeed sell a piece of the mine or mill, but he could sell his stock in it; but the citizen now can not dispose of his share in the national concern. He can only dispose of the dividend."

"Certainly," replied the doctor; "but while the power of alienating the principal of one's property was a usual incident of ownership in your time, it was very far from being a necessary incident or one which was beneficial to the owner, for the right of disposing of property involved the risk of being dispossessed of it by others. I think there were few property owners in your day who would not very gladly have relinquished the right to alienate their property if they could have had it guaranteed indefeasibly to them and their children. So to tie up property by trusts that the beneficiary could not touch the principal was the study of rich people who desired best to protect their heirs. Take the case of entailed estates as another illustration of this idea. Under that mode of holding property the possessor could not sell it, yet it was considered the most desirable sort of property on account of that very fact. The fact you refer to--that the citizen can not alienate his share in the national corporation which forms the basis of his income--tends in the same way to make it a more and not a less valuable sort of property. Certainly its quality as a strictly personal and private sort of property is intensified by the very indefeasibleness with which it is attached to the individual. It might be said that the reorganization of the property system which we are speaking of amounted to making the United States an entailed estate for the equal benefit of the citizens thereof and their descendants forever."

"You have not yet mentioned" I said, "the most drastic measure of all by which the Revolution affected private property, namely, the absolute equalizing of the amount of property to be held by each. Here was not perhaps any denial of the principle itself of private property, but it was certainly a prodigious interference with property holders."

"The distinction is well made. It is of vital importance to a correct apprehension of this subject. History has been full of just such wholesale readjustments of property interests by spoliation, conquest, or confiscation. They have been more or less justifiable, but when least so they were never thought to involve any denial of the idea of private property in itself, for they went right on to reassert it under a different form. Less than any previous readjustment of property relations could the general equalizing of property in the Revolution be called a denial of the right of property. On the precise contrary it was an assertion and vindication of that right on a scale never before dreamed of. Before the Revolution very few of the people had any property at all and no economic provision save from day to day. By the new system all were assured of a large, equal, and fixed share in the total national principal and income. Before the Revolution even those who had secured a property were likely to have it taken from them or to slip from them by a thousand accidents. Even the millionaire had no assurance that his grandson might not become a homeless vagabond or his granddaughter be forced to a life of shame. Under the new system the title of every citizen to his individual fortune became indefeasible, and he could lose it only when the nation became bankrupt. The Revolution, that is to say, instead of denying or abolishing the institution of private property, affirmed it in an incomparably more positive, beneficial, permanent, and general form than had ever been known before.

"Of course, Julian, it was in the way of human nature quite a matter of course that your contemporaries should have cried out against the idea of a universal right of property as an attack on the principle of property. There was never a prophet or reformer who raised his voice for a purer, more spiritual, and perfect idea of religion whom his contemporaries did not accuse of seeking to abolish religion; nor ever in political affairs did any party proclaim a juster, larger, wiser ideal of government without being accused of seeking to abolish government. So it was quite according to precedent that those who taught the right of all to property should be accused of attacking the right of property. But who, think you, were the true friends and champions of private property? those who advocated a system under which one man if clever enough could monopolize the earth--and a very small number were fast monopolizing it--turning the rest of the race into proletarians, or, on the other hand, those who demanded a system by which all should become property holders on equal terms?"

"It strikes me," I said, "that as soon as the revolutionary leaders succeeded in opening the eyes of the people to this view of the matter, my old friends the capitalists must have found their cry about 'the sacred right of property' turned into a most dangerous sort of boomerang."

"So they did. Nothing could have better served the ends of the Revolution, as we have seen, than to raise the issue of the right of property. Nothing was so desirable as that the people at large should be led to give a little serious consideration on rational and moral grounds to what that right was as compared with what it ought to be. It was very soon, then, that the cry of 'the sacred right of property,' first raised by the rich in the name of the few, was re-echoed with overwhelming effect by the disinherited millions in the name of all."

CHAPTER XVIII.

An Echo Of The Past.

"Ah!" exclaimed Edith, who with her mother had been rummaging the drawers of the safe as the doctor and I talked, "here are some letters, if I am not mistaken. It seems, then, you used safes for something besides money."

It was, in fact, as I noted with quite indescribable emotion, a packet of letters and notes from Edith Bartlett, written on various occasions during our relation as lovers, that Edith, her great-granddaughter, held in her hand. I took them from her, and opening one, found it to be a note dated May 30, 1887, the very day on which I parted with her forever. In it she asked me to join her family in their Decoration-day visit to the grave at Mount Auburn where her brother lay, who had fallen in the civil war.

"I do not expect, Julian," she had written, "that you will adopt all my relations as your own because you marry me--that would be too much--but my hero brother I want you to take for yours, and that is why I would like you to go with us to-day."

The gold and parchments, once so priceless, now carelessly scattered about the chamber, had lost their value, but these tokens of love had not parted with their potency through lapse of time. As by a magic power they called up in a moment a mist of memories which shut me up in a world of my own--a world in which the present had no part. I do not know for how long I sat thus tranced and oblivious of the silent, sympathizing group around me. It was by a deep involuntary sigh from my own lips that I was at last roused from my abstraction, and returned from the dream world of the past to a consciousness of my present environment and its conditions.

"These are letters," I said, "from the other Edith--Edith Bartlett, your great-grandmother. Perhaps you would be interested in looking them over. I don't know who has a nearer or better claim to them after myself than you and your mother."

Edith took the letters and began to examine them with reverent curiosity.

"They will be very interesting," said her mother, "but I am afraid, Julian, we shall have to ask you to read them for us."

My countenance no doubt expressed the surprise I felt at this confession of illiteracy on the part of such highly cultivated persons.

"Am I to understand," I finally inquired, "that handwriting, and the reading of it, like lock-making, is a lost art?"

"I am afraid it is about so," replied the doctor, "although the explanation here is not, as in the other case, economic equality so much as the progress of invention. Our children are still taught to write and to read writing, but they have so little practice in after-life that they usually forget their acquirements pretty soon after leaving school; but really Edith ought still to be able to make out a nineteenth-century letter.--My dear, I am a little ashamed of you."

"Oh, I can read this, papa," she exclaimed, looking up, with brows still corrugated, from a page she had been studying. "Don't you remember I studied out those old letters of Julian's to Edith Bartlett, which mother had?--though that was years ago, and I have grown rusty since. But I have read nearly two lines of this already. It is really quite plain. I am going to work it all out without any help from anybody except mother."

"Dear me, dear me!" said I, "don't you write letters any more?"

"Well, no," replied the doctor, "practically speaking, handwriting has gone out of use. For correspondence, when we do not telephone, we send phonographs, and use the latter, indeed, for all purposes for which you employed handwriting. It has been so now so long that it scarcely occurs to us that people ever did anything else. But surely this is an evolution that need surprise you little: you had the phonograph, and its possibilities were patent enough from the first. For our important records we still largely use types, of course, but the printed matter is transcribed from phonographic copy, so that really, except in emergencies, there is little use for handwriting. Curious, isn't it, when one comes to think of it, that the riper civilization has grown, the more perishable its records have become? The Chaldeans and Egyptians used bricks, and the Greeks and Romans made more or less use of stone and bronze, for writing. If the race were destroyed to-day and the earth should be visited, say, from Mars, five hundred years later or even less, our books would have perished, and the Roman Empire be accounted the latest and highest stage of human civilization."

CHAPTER XIX.

"Can A Maid Forget Her Ornaments?"

Presently Edith and her mother went into the house to study out the letters, and the doctor being so delightfully absorbed with the stocks and bonds that it would have been unkind not to leave him alone, it struck me that the occasion was favorable for the execution of a private project for which opportunity had hitherto been lacking.

From the moment of receiving my credit card I had contemplated a particular purchase which I desired to make on the first opportunity. This was a betrothal ring for Edith. Gifts in general, it was evident, had lost their value in this age when everybody had everything he wanted, but this was one which, for sentiment's sake, I was sure would still seem as desirable to a woman as ever.

Taking advantage, therefore, of the unusual absorption of my hosts in special interests, I made my way to the great store Edith had taken me to on a former occasion, the only one I had thus far entered. Not seeing the class of goods which I desired indicated by any of the placards over the alcoves, I presently asked one of the young women attendants to direct me to the jewelry department.

"I beg your pardon," she said, raising her eyebrows a little, "what did I understand you to ask for?"

"The jewelry department," I repeated. "I want to look at some rings."

"Rings," she repeated, regarding me with a rather blank expression. "May I ask what kind of rings, for what sort of use?"

"Finger rings," I repeated, feeling that the young woman could not be so intelligent as she looked.

At the word she glanced at my left hand, on one of the fingers of which I wore a seal ring after a fashion of my day. Her countenance took on an expression at once of intelligence and the keenest interest.

"I beg your pardon a thousand times!" she exclaimed. "I ought to have understood before. You are Julian West?"

I was beginning to be a little nettled with so much mystery about so simple a matter.

"I certainly am Julian West," I said; "but pardon me if I do not see the relevancy of that fact to the question I asked you."

"Oh, you must really excuse me," she said, "but it is most relevant. Nobody in America but just yourself would ask for finger rings. You see they have not been used for so long a period that we have quite ceased to keep them in stock; but if you would like one made to order you have only to leave a description of what you want and it will be at once manufactured."

I thanked her, but concluded that I would not prosecute the undertaking any further until I had looked over the ground a little more thoroughly.

I said nothing about my adventure at home, not caring to be laughed at more than was necessary; but when after dinner I found the doctor alone in his favorite outdoor study on the housetop, I cautiously sounded him on the subject.

Remarking, as if quite in a casual way, that I had not noticed so much as a finger ring worn by any one, I asked him whether the wearing of jewelry had been disused, and, if so, what was the explanation of the abandonment of the custom?

The doctor said that it certainly was a fact that the wearing of jewelry had been virtually an obsolete custom for a couple of generations if not more. "As for the reasons for the fact," he continued, "they really go rather deeply into the direct and indirect consequences of our present economic system. Speaking broadly, I suppose the main and sufficient reason why gold and silver and precious stones have ceased to be prized as ornaments is that they entirely lost their commercial value when the nation organized wealth distribution on the basis of the indefeasible economic equality of all citizens. As you know, a ton of gold or a bushel of diamonds would not secure a loaf of bread at the public stores, nothing availing there except or in addition to the citizen's credit, which depends solely on his citizenship, and is always equal to that of every other citizen. Consequently nothing is worth anything to anybody nowadays save for the use or pleasure he can personally derive from it. The main reason why gems and the precious metals were formerly used as ornaments seems to have been the great convertible value belonging to them, which made them symbols of wealth and importance, and consequently a favorite means of social ostentation. The fact that they have entirely lost this quality would account, I think, largely for their disuse as ornaments, even if ostentation itself had not been deprived of its motive by the law of equality."

"Undoubtedly," I said; "yet there were those who thought them pretty quite apart from their value."

"Well, possibly," replied the doctor. "Yes, I suppose savage races honestly thought so, but, being honest, they did not distinguish between precious stones and glass beads so long as both were equally shiny. As to the pretension of civilized persons to admire gems or gold for their intrinsic beauty apart from their value, I suspect that was a more or less unconscious sham. Suppose, by any sudden abundance, diamonds of the first water had gone down to the value of bottle glass, how much longer do you think they would have been worn by anybody in your day?"

I was constrained to admit that undoubtedly they would have disappeared from view promptly and permanently.

"I imagine," said the doctor, "that good taste, which we understand even in your day rather frowned on the use of such ornaments, came to the aid of the economic influence in promoting their disuse when once the new order of things had been established. The loss by the gems and precious metals of the glamour that belonged to them as forms of concentrated wealth left the taste free to judge of the real aesthetic value of ornamental effects obtained by hanging bits of shining stones and plates and chains and rings of metal about the face and neck and fingers, and the view seems to have been soon generally acquiesced in that such combinations were barbaric and not really beautiful at all."

"But what has become of all the diamonds and rubies and emeralds, and gold and silver jewels?" I exclaimed.

"The metals, of course--silver and gold--kept their uses, mechanical and artistic. They are always beautiful in their proper places, and are as much used for decorative purposes as ever, but those purposes are architectural, not personal, as formerly. Because we do not follow the ancient practice of using paints on our faces and bodies, we use them not the less in what we consider their proper places, and it is just so with gold and silver. As for the precious stones, some of them have found use in mechanical applications, and there are, of course, collections of them in museums here and there. Probably there never were more than a few hundred bushels of precious stones in existence, and it is easy to account for the disappearance and speedy loss of so small a quantity of such minute objects after they had ceased to be prized."

"The reasons you give for the passing of jewelry," I said, "certainly account for the fact, and yet you can scarcely imagine what a surprise I find in it. The degradation of the diamond to the rank of the glass bead, save for its mechanical uses, expresses and typifies as no other one fact to me the completeness of the revolution which at the present time has subordinated things to humanity. It would not be so difficult, of course, to understand that men might readily have dispensed with jewel-wearing, which indeed was never considered in the best of taste as a masculine practice except in barbarous countries, but it would have staggered the prophet Jeremiah to have his query 'Can a maid forget her ornaments?' answered in the affirmative."

The doctor laughed.

"Jeremiah was a very wise man," he said, "and if his attention had been drawn to the subject of economic equality and its effect upon the relation of the sexes, I am sure he would have foreseen as one of its logical results the growth of a sentiment of quite as much philosophy concerning personal ornamentation on the part of women as men have ever displayed. He would not have been surprised to learn that one effect of that equality as between men and women had been to revolutionize women's attitude on the whole question of dress so completely that the most bilious of misogynists--if indeed any were left--would no longer be able to accuse them of being more absorbed in that interest than are men."

"Doctor, doctor, do not ask me to believe that the desire to make herself attractive has ceased to move woman!"

"Excuse me, I did not mean to say anything of the sort," replied the doctor. "I spoke of the disproportionate development of that desire which tends to defeat its own end by over-ornament and excess of artifice. If we may judge from the records of your time, this was quite generally the result of the excessive devotion to dress on the part of your women; was it not so?"

"Undoubtedly. Overdressing, overexertion to be attractive, was the greatest drawback to the real attractiveness of women in my day."

"And how was it with the men?"

"That could not be said of any men worth calling men. There were, of course, the dandies, but most men paid too little attention to their appearance rather than too much."

"That is to say, one sex paid too much attention to dress and the other too little?"

"That was it."

"Very well; the effect of economic equality of the sexes and the consequent independence of women at all times as to maintenance upon men is that women give much less thought to dress than in your day and men considerably more. No one would indeed think of suggesting that either sex is nowadays more absorbed in setting off its personal attractions than the other. Individuals differ as to their interest in this matter, but the difference is not along the line of sex."

"But why do you attribute this miracle," I exclaimed, "for miracle it seems, to the effect of economic equality on the relation of men and women?"

"Because from the moment that equality became established between them it ceased to be a whit more the interest of women to make themselves attractive and desirable to men than for men to produce the same impression upon women."

"Meaning thereby that previous to the establishment of economic equality between men and women it was decidedly more the interest of the women to make themselves personally attractive than of the men."

"Assuredly," said the doctor. "Tell me to what motive did men in your day ascribe the excessive devotion of the other sex to matters of dress as compared with men's comparative neglect of the subject?"

"Well, I don't think we did much clear thinking on the subject. In fact, anything which had any sexual suggestion about it was scarcely ever treated in any other than a sentimental or jesting tone."

"That is indeed," said the doctor, "a striking trait of your age, though explainable enough in view of the utter hypocrisy underlying the entire relation of the sexes, the pretended chivalric deference to women on the one hand, coupled with their practical suppression on the other, but you must have had some theory to account for women's excessive devotion to personal adornment."

"The theory, I think, was that handed down from the ancients--namely, that women were naturally vainer than men. But they did not like to hear that said: so the polite way of accounting for the obvious fact that they cared so much more for dress than did men was that they were more sensitive to beauty, more unselfishly desirous of pleasing, and other agreeable phrases."

"And did it not occur to you that the real reason why woman gave so much thought to devices for enhancing her beauty was simply that, owing to her economic dependence on man's favor, a woman's face was her fortune, and that the reason men were so careless for the most part as to their personal appearance was that their fortune in no way depended on their beauty; and that even when it came to commending themselves to the favor of the other sex their economic position told more potently in their favor than any question of personal advantages? Surely this obvious consideration fully explained woman's greater devotion to personal adornment, without assuming any difference whatever in the natural endowment of the sexes as to vanity."

"And consequently," I put in, "when women ceased any more to depend for their economic welfare upon men's favor, it ceased to be their main aim in life to make themselves attractive to men's eyes?"

"Precisely so, to their unspeakable gain in comfort, dignity, and freedom of mind for more important interests."

"But to the diminution, I suspect, of the picturesqueness of the social panorama?"

"Not at all, but most decidedly to its notable advantage. So far as we can judge, what claim the women of your period had to be regarded as attractive was achieved distinctly in spite of their efforts to make themselves so. Let us recall that we are talking about that excessive concern of women for the enhancement of their charms which led to a mad race after effect that for the most part defeated the end sought. Take away the economic motive which made women's attractiveness to men a means of getting on in life, and there remained Nature's impulse to attract the admiration of the other sex, a motive quite strong enough for beauty's end, and the more effective for not being too strong."

"It is easy enough to see," I said, "why the economic independence of women should have had the effect of moderating to a reasonable measure their interest in personal adornment; but why should it have operated in the opposite direction upon men, in making them more attentive to dress and personal appearance than before?"

"For the simple reason that their economic superiority to women having disappeared, they must henceforth depend wholly upon personal attractiveness if they would either win the favor of women or retain it when won."

CHAPTER XX.

What The Revolution Did For Women.

"It occurs to me, doctor," I said, "that it would have been even better worth the while of a woman of my day to have slept over till now than for me, seeing that the establishment of economic equality seems to have meant for more for women than for men."

"Edith would perhaps not have been pleased with the substitution," said the doctor; "but really there is much in what you say, for the establishment of economic equality did in fact mean incomparably more for women than for men. In your day the condition of the mass of men was abject as compared with their present state, but the lot of women was abject as compared with that of the men. The most of men were indeed the servants of the rich, but the woman was subject to the man whether he were rich or poor, and in the latter and more common case was thus the servant of a servant. However low down in poverty a man might be, he had one or more lower even than he in the persons of the women dependent on him and subject to his will. At the very bottom of the social heap, bearing the accumulated burden of the whole mass, was woman. All the tyrannies of soul and mind and body which the race endured, weighed at last with cumulative force upon her. So far beneath even the mean estate of man was that of woman that it would have been a mighty uplift for her could she have only attained his level. But the great Revolution not merely lifted her to an equality with man but raised them both with the same mighty upthrust to a plane of moral dignity and material welfare as much above the former state of man as his former state had been above that of woman. If men then owe gratitude to the Revolution, how much greater must women esteem their debt to it! If to the men the voice of the Revolution was a call to a higher and nobler plane of living, to woman it was as the voice of God calling her to a new creation."

"Undoubtedly," I said, "the women of the poor had a pretty abject time of it, but the women of the rich certainly were not oppressed."

"The women of the rich," replied the doctor, "were numerically too insignificant a proportion of the mass of women to be worth considering in a general statement of woman's condition in your day. Nor, for that matter, do we consider their lot preferable to that of their poorer sisters. It is true that they did not endure physical hardship, but were, on the contrary, petted and spoiled by their men protectors like over-indulged children; but that seems to us not a sort of life to be desired. So far as we can learn from contemporary accounts and social pictures, the women of the rich lived in a hothouse atmosphere of adulation and affectation, altogether less favorable to moral or mental development than the harder conditions of the women of the poor. A woman of to-day, if she were doomed to go back to live in your world, would beg at least to be reincarnated as a scrub woman rather than as a wealthy woman of fashion. The latter rather than the former seems to us the sort of woman which most completely typified the degradation of the sex in your age."

As the same thought had occurred to me, even in my former life, I did not argue the point.

"The so-called woman movement, the beginning of the great transformation in her condition," continued the doctor, "was already making quite a stir in your day. You must have heard and seen much of it, and may have even known some of the noble women who were the early leaders."

"Oh, yes." I replied. "There was a great stir about women's rights, but the programme then announced was by no means revolutionary. It only aimed at securing the right to vote, together with various changes in the laws about property-holding by women, the custody of children in divorces, and such details. I assure you that the women no more than the men had at that time any notion of revolutionizing the economic system."

"So we understand," replied the doctor. "In that respect the women's struggle for independence resembled revolutionary movements in general, which, in their earlier stages, go blundering and stumbling along in such a seemingly erratic and illogical way that it takes a philosopher to calculate what outcome to expect. The calculation as to the ultimate outcome of the women's movement was, however, as simple as was the same calculation in the case of what you called the labor movement. What the women were after was independence of men and equality with them, while the workingmen's desire was to put an end to their vassalage to capitalists. Now, the key to the fetters the women wore was the same that locked the shackles of the workers. It was the economic key, the control of the means of subsistence. Men, as a sex, held that power over women, and the rich as a class held it over the working masses. The secret of the sexual bondage and of the industrial bondage was the same--namely, the unequal distribution of the wealth power, and the change which was necessary to put an end to both forms of bondage must obviously be economic equalization, which in the sexual as in the industrial relation would at once insure the substitution of co-operation for coercion.

"The first leaders of the women's revolt were unable to see beyond the ends of their noses, and consequently ascribed their subject condition and the abuses they endured to the wickedness of man, and appeared to believe that the only remedy necessary was a moral reform on his part. This was the period during which such expressions as the 'tyrant man' and 'man the monster' were watchwords of the agitation. The champions of the women fell into precisely the same mistake committed by a large proportion of the early leaders of the workingmen, who wasted good breath and wore out their tempers in denouncing the capitalists as the willful authors of all the ills of the proletarian. This was worse than idle rant; it was misleading and blinding. The men were essentially no worse than the women they oppressed nor the capitalists than the workmen they exploited. Put workingmen in the places of the capitalists and they would have done just as the capitalists were doing. In fact, whenever workingmen did become capitalists they were commonly said to make the hardest sort of masters. So, also, if women could have changed places with the men, they would undoubtedly have dealt with the men precisely as the men had dealt with them. It was the system which permitted human beings to come into relations of superiority and inferiority to one another which was the cause of the whole evil. Power over others is necessarily demoralizing to the master and degrading to the subject. Equality is the only moral relation between human beings. Any reform which should result in remedying the abuse of women by men, or workingmen by capitalists, must therefore be addressed to equalizing their economic condition. Not till the women, as well as the workingmen, gave over the folly of attacking the consequences of economic inequality and attacked the inequality itself, was there any hope for the enfranchisement of either class.

"The utterly inadequate idea which the early leaders of the women had of the great salvation they must have, and how it must come, are curiously illustrated by their enthusiasm for the various so-called temperance agitations of the period for the purpose of checking drunkenness among men. The special interest of the women as a class in this reform in men's manners--for women as a rule did not drink intoxicants--consisted in the calculation that if the men drank less they would be less likely to abuse them, and would provide more liberally for their maintenance; that is to say, their highest aspirations were limited to the hope that, by reforming the morals of their masters, they might secure a little better treatment for themselves. The idea of abolishing the mastership had not yet occurred to them as a possibility.

"This point, by the way, as to the efforts of women in your day to reform men's drinking habits by law rather strikingly suggests the difference between the position of women then and now in their relation to men. If nowadays men were addicted to any practice which made them seriously and generally offensive to women, it would not occur to the latter to attempt to curb it by law. Our spirit of personal sovereignty and the rightful independence of the individual in all matters mainly self-regarding would indeed not tolerate any of the legal interferences with the private practices of individuals so common in your day. But the women would not find force necessary to correct the manners of the men. Their absolute economic independence, whether in or out of marriage, would enable them to use a more potent influence. It would presently be found that the men who made themselves offensive to women's susceptibilities would sue for their favor in vain. But it was practically impossible for women of your day to protect themselves or assert their wills by assuming that attitude. It was economically a necessity for a woman to marry, or at least of so great advantage to her that she could not well dictate terms to her suitors, unless very fortunately situated, and once married it was the practical understanding that in return for her maintenance by her husband she must hold herself at his disposal."

"It sounds horribly," I said, "at this distance of time, but I beg you to believe that it was not always quite as bad as it sounds. The better men exercised their power with consideration, and with persons of refinement the wife virtually retained her self-control, and for that matter in many families the woman was practically the head of the house."

"No doubt, no doubt," replied the doctor. "So it has always been under every form of servitude. However absolute the power of a master, it has been exercised with a fair degree of humanity in a large proportion of instances, and in many cases the nominal slave, when of strong character, has in reality exercised a controlling influence over the master. This observed fact is not, however, considered a valid argument for subjecting human beings to the arbitrary will of others. Speaking generally, it is undoubtedly true that both the condition of women when subjected to men, as well as that of the poor in subjection to the rich, were in fact far less intolerable than it seems to us they possibly could have been. As the physical life of man can be maintained and often thrive in any climate from the poles to the equator, so his moral nature has shown its power to live and even put forth fragrant flowers under the most terrible social conditions."

"In order to realize the prodigious debt of woman to the great Revolution," resumed the doctor, "we must remember that the bondage from which it delivered her was incomparably more complete and abject than any to which men had ever been subjected by their fellow-men. It was enforced not by a single but by a triple yoke. The first yoke was the subjection to the personal and class rule of the rich, which the mass of women bore in common with the mass of men. The other two yokes were peculiar to her. One of them was her personal subjection not only in the sexual relation, but in all her behavior to the particular man on whom she depended for subsistence. The third yoke was an intellectual and moral one, and consisted in the slavish conformity exacted of her in all her thinking, speaking, and acting to a set of traditions and conventional standards calculated to repress all that was spontaneous and individual, and impose an artificial uniformity upon both the inner and outer life.

"The last was the heaviest yoke of the three, and most disastrous in its effects both upon women directly and indirectly upon mankind through the degradation of the mothers of the race. Upon the woman herself the effect was so soul-stifling and mind-stunting as to be made a plausible excuse for treating her as a natural inferior by men not philosophical enough to see that what they would make an excuse for her subjection was itself the result of that subjection. The explanation of woman's submission in thought and action to what was practically a slave code--a code peculiar to her sex and scorned and derided by men--was the fact that the main hope of a comfortable life for every woman consisted in attracting the favorable attention of some man who could provide for her. Now, under your economic system it was very desirable for a man who sought employment to think and talk as his employer did if he was to get on in life. Yet a certain degree of independence of mind and conduct was conceded to men by their economic superiors under most circumstances, so long as they were not actually offensive, for, after all, what was mainly wanted of them was their labor. But the relation of a woman to the man who supported her was of a very different and much closer character. She must be to him *persona grata*, as your diplomats used to say. To attract him she must be personally pleasing to him, must not offend his tastes or prejudices by her opinions or conduct. Otherwise he would be likely to prefer some one else. It followed from this fact that while a boy's training looked toward fitting him to earn a living, a girl was educated with a chief end to making her, if not pleasing, at least not displeasing to men.

"Now, if particular women had been especially trained to suit particular men's tastes--trained to order, so to speak--while that would have been offensive enough to any idea of feminine dignity, yet it would have been far less disastrous, for many men would have vastly preferred women of independent minds and original and natural opinions. But as it was not known beforehand what particular men would support particular women, the only safe way was to train girls with a view to a negative rather than a positive attractiveness, so that at least they might not offend average masculine prejudices. This ideal was most likely to be secured by educating a girl to conform herself to the customary traditional and fashionable habits of thinking, talking, and behaving--in a word, to the conventional standards prevailing at the time. She must above all things avoid as a contagion any new or original ideas or lines of conduct in any important respect, especially in religious, political, and social matters. Her mind, that is to say, like her body, must be trained and dressed according to the current fashion plates. By all her hopes of married comfort she must not be known to have any peculiar or unusual or positive notions on any subject more important than embroidery or parlor decoration. Conventionality in the essentials having been thus secured, the brighter and more piquant she could be in small ways and frivolous matters the better for her chances. Have I erred in describing the working of your system in this particular, Julian?"

"No doubt," I replied, "you have described to the life the correct and fashionable ideal of feminine education in my time, but there were, you must understand, a great many women who were persons of entirely original and serious minds, who dared to think and speak for themselves."

"Of course there were. They were the prototypes of the universal woman of to-day. They represented the coming woman, who to-day has come. They had broken for themselves the conventional trammels of their sex, and proved to the world the potential equality of women with men in every field of thought and action. But while great minds master their circumstances, the mass of minds are mastered by them and formed by them. It is when we think of the bearing of the system upon this vast majority of women, and how the virus of moral and mental slavery through their veins entered into the blood of the race, that we realize how tremendous is the indictment of humanity against your economic arrangements on account of woman, and how vast a benefit to mankind was the Revolution that gave free mothers to the race-free not merely from physical but from moral and intellectual fetters.

"I referred a moment ago," pursued the doctor, "to the close parallelism existing in your time between the industrial and the sexual situation, between the relations of the working masses to the capitalists, and those of the women to men. It is strikingly illustrated in yet another way.

"The subjection of the workingmen to the owners of capital was insured by the existence at all times of a large class of the unemployed ready to underbid the workers and eager to get employment at any price and on any terms. This was the club with which the capitalist kept down the workers. In like manner it was the existence of a body of unappropriated women which riveted the yoke of women's subjection to men. When maintenance was the difficult problem it was in your day there were many men who could not maintain themselves, and a vast number who could not maintain women in addition to themselves. The failure of a man to marry might cost him happiness, but in the case of women it not only involved loss of happiness, but, as a rule, exposed them to the pressure or peril of poverty, for it was a much more difficult thing for women than for men to secure an adequate support by their own efforts. The result was one of the most shocking spectacles the world has ever known--nothing less, in fact, than a state of rivalry and competition among women for the opportunity of marriage. To realize how helpless were women in your day, to assume toward men an attitude of physical, mental, or moral dignity and independence, it is enough to remember their terrible disadvantage in what your contemporaries called with brutal plainness the marriage market.

"And still woman's cup of humiliation was not full. There was yet another and more dreadful form of competition by her own sex to which she was exposed. Not only was there a constant vast surplus of unmarried women desirous of securing the economic support which marriage implied, but beneath these there were hordes of wretched women, hopeless of obtaining the support of men on honorable terms, and eager to sell themselves for a crust. Julian, do you wonder that, of all the aspects of the horrible mess you called civilization in the nineteenth century, the sexual relation reeks worst?"

"Our philanthropists were greatly disturbed over what we called the social evil," said I--"that is, the existence of this great multitude of outcast women--but it was not common to diagnose it as a part of the economic problem. It was regarded rather as a moral evil resulting from the depravity of the human heart, to be properly dealt with by moral and religious influences."

"Yes, yes, I know. No one in your day, of course, was allowed to intimate that the economic system was radically wicked, and consequently it was customary to lay off all its hideous consequences upon poor human nature. Yes, I know there were, people who agreed that it might be possible by preaching to lessen the horrors of the social evil while yet the land contained millions of women in desperate need, who had no other means of getting bread save by catering to the desires of men. I am a bit of a phrenologist, and have often wished for the chance of examining the cranial developments of a nineteenth-century philanthropist who honestly believed this, if indeed any of them honestly did."

"By the way," I said, "high-spirited women, even in my day, objected to the custom that required them to take their husbands' names on marriage. How do you manage that now?"

"Women's names are no more affected by marriage than men's."

"But how about the children?"

"Girls take the mother's last name with the father's as a middle name, while with boys it is just the reverse."

"It occurs to me," I said, "that it would be surprising if a fact so profoundly affecting woman's relations with man as her achievement of economic independence, had not modified the previous conventional standards of sexual morality in some respects."

"Say rather," replied the doctor, "that the economic equalization of men and women for the first time made it possible to establish their relations on a moral basis. The first condition of ethical action in any relation is the freedom of the actor. So long as women's economic dependence upon men prevented them from being free agents in the sexual relation, there could be no ethics of that relation. A proper ethics of sexual conduct was first made possible when women became capable of independent action through the attainment of economic equality."

"It would have startled the moralists of my day," I said, "to be told that we had no sexual ethics. We certainly had a very strict and elaborate system of 'thou shalt nots.'"

"Of course, of course," replied my companion. "Let us understand each other exactly at this point, for the subject is highly important. You had, as you say, a set of very rigid rules and regulations as to the conduct of the sexes--that is, especially as to women--but the basis of it, for the most part, was not ethical but prudential, the object being the safeguarding of the economic interests of women in their relations with men. Nothing could have been more important to the protection of women on the whole, although so often bearing cruelly upon them individually, than these rules. They were the only method by which, so long as woman remained an economically helpless and dependent person, she and her children could be even partially guarded from masculine abuse and neglect. Do not imagine for a moment that I would speak lightly of the value of this social code to the race during the time it was necessary. But because it was entirely based upon considerations not suggested by the natural sanctities of the sexual relation in itself, but wholly upon prudential considerations affecting economic results, it would be an inexact use of terms to call it a system of ethics. It would be more accurately described as a code of sexual economics--that is to say, a set of laws and customs providing for the economic protection of women and children in the sexual and family relation.

"The marriage contract was embellished by a rich embroidery of sentimental and religious fancies, but I need not remind you that its essence in the eyes of the law and of society was its character as a contract, a strictly economic *quid-pro-quo* transaction. It was a legal undertaking by the man to maintain the woman and future family in consideration of her surrender of herself to his exclusive disposal--that is to say, on condition of obtaining a lien on his property, she became a part of it. The only point which the law or the social censor looked to as fixing the morality or immorality, purity or impurity, of any sexual act was simply the question whether this bargain had been previously executed in accordance with legal forms. That point properly attended to, everything that formerly had been regarded as wrong and impure for the parties became rightful and chaste. They might have been persons unfit to marry or to be parents; they might have been drawn together by the basest and most sordid motives; the bride may have been constrained by need to accept a man she loathed; youth may have been sacrificed to decrepitude, and every natural propriety outraged; but according to your standard, if the contract had been legally executed, all that followed was white and beautiful. On the other hand, if the contract had been neglected, and a woman had accepted a lover without it, then, however great their love, however fit their union in every natural way, the woman was cast out as unchaste, impure, and abandoned, and consigned to the living death of social ignominy. Now let me repeat that we fully recognize the excuse for this social law under your atrocious system as the only possible way of protecting the economic interests of women and children, but to speak of it as ethical or moral in its view of the sex relation is certainly about as absurd a misuse of words as could be committed. On the contrary, we must say that it was a law which, in order to protect women's material interests, was obliged deliberately to disregard all the laws that are written on the heart touching such matters.

"It seems from the records that there was much talk in your day about the scandalous fact that there were two distinct moral codes in sexual matters, one for men and another for women--men refusing to be bound by the law imposed on women, and society not even attempting to enforce it against them. It was claimed by the advocates of one code for both sexes that what was wrong or right for woman was so for man, and that there should be one standard of right and wrong, purity and impurity, morality and immorality, for both. That was obviously the correct view of the matter; but what moral gain would there have been for the race even if men could have been induced to accept the women's code--a code so utterly unworthy in its central idea of the ethics of the sexual relation? Nothing but the bitter duress of their economic bondage had forced women to accept a law against which the blood of ten thousand stainless Marguerites, and the ruined lives of a countless multitude of women, whose only fault had been too tender loving, cried to God perpetually. Yes, there should doubtless be one standard of conduct for both men and women as there is now, but it was not to be the slave code, with its sordid basis, imposed upon the women by their necessities. The common and higher code for men and women which the conscience of the race demanded would first become possible, and at once thereafter would become assured when men and women stood over against each other in the sexual relation, as in all others, in attitudes of absolute equality and mutual independence."

"After all, doctor," I said, "although at first it startled me a little to hear you say that we had no sexual ethics, yet you really say no more, nor use stronger words, than did our poets and satirists in treating the same theme. The complete divergence between our conventional sexual morality and the instinctive morality of love was a commonplace with us, and furnished, as doubtless you well know, the motive of a large part of our romantic and dramatic literature."

"Yes," replied the doctor, "nothing could be added to the force and feeling with which your writers exposed the cruelty and injustice of the iron law of society as to these matters--a law made doubly cruel and unjust by the fact that it bore almost exclusively on women. But their denunciations were wasted, and the plentiful emotions they evoked were barren of result, for the reason that they failed entirely to point out the basic fact that was responsible for the law they attacked, and must be abolished if the law were ever to be replaced by a just ethics. That fact, as we have seen, was the system of wealth distribution, by which woman's only hope of comfort and security was made to depend on her success in obtaining a legal guarantee of support from some man as the price of her person."

"It seems to me," I observed, "that when the women, once fairly opened their eyes to what the revolutionary programme meant for their sex by its demand of economic equality for all, self-interest must have made them more ardent devotees of the cause than even the men."

"It did indeed," replied the doctor. "Of course the blinding, binding influence of conventionality, tradition, and prejudice, as well as the timidity bred of immemorial servitude, for a long while prevented the mass of women from understanding the greatness of the deliverance which was offered them; but when once they did understand it they threw themselves into the revolutionary movement with a unanimity and enthusiasm that had a decisive effect upon the struggle. Men might regard economic equality with favor or disfavor, according to their economic positions, but every woman, simply because she was a woman, was bound to be for it as soon as she got it through her head what it meant for her half of the race."

CHAPTER XXI.

At The Gymnasium.

Edith had come up on the house top in time to hear the last of our talk, and now she said to her father:

"Considering what you have been telling Julian about women nowadays as compared with the old days, I wonder if he would not be interested in visiting the gymnasium this afternoon and seeing something of how we train ourselves? There are going to be some foot races and air races, and a number of other tests. It is the afternoon when our year has the grounds, and I ought to be there anyway."

To this suggestion, which was eagerly accepted, I owe one of the most interesting and instructive experiences of those early days during which I was forming the acquaintance of the twentieth-century civilization.

At the door of the gymnasium Edith left us to join her class in the amphitheater.

"Is she to compete in anything?" I asked.

"All her year--that is, all of her age--in this ward will be entered in more or less events."

"What is Edith's specialty?" I asked.

"As to specialties," replied the doctor, "our people do not greatly cultivate them. Of course, privately they do what they please, but the object of our public training is not so much to develop athletic specialties as to produce an all-around and well-proportioned physical development. We aim first of all to secure a certain standard of strength and measurement for legs, thighs, arms, loins, chest, shoulders, neck, etc. This is not the highest point of perfection either of physique or performance. It is the necessary minimum. All who attain it may be regarded as sound and proper men and women. It is then left to them as they please individually to develop themselves beyond that point in special directions.

"How long does this public gymnastic education last?"

"It is as obligatory as any part of the educational course until the body is set, which we put at the age of twenty-four; but it is practically kept up through life, although, of course, that is according to just how one feels."

"Do you mean that you take regular exercise in a gymnasium?"

"Why should I not? It is no less of an object to me to be well at sixty than it was at twenty."

"Doctor," said I, "if I seem surprised you must remember that in my day it was an adage that no man over forty-five ought to allow himself to run for a car, and as for women, they stopped running at fifteen, when their bodies were put in a vise, their legs in bags, their toes in thumbscrews, and they bade farewell to health."

"You do indeed seem to have disagreed terribly with your bodies," said the doctor. "The women ignored theirs altogether, and as for the men, so far as I can make out, up to forty they abused their bodies, and after forty their bodies abused them, which, after all, was only fair. The vast mass of physical misery caused by weakness and sickness, resulting from wholly preventable causes, seems to us, next to the moral aspect of the subject, to be one of the largest single items chargeable to your system of economic inequality, for to that primal cause nearly every feature of the account appears directly or indirectly traceable. Neither souls nor bodies could be considered by your men in their mad struggle for a living, and for a grip on the livelihood of others, while the complicated system of bondage under which the women were held perverted mind and body alike, till it was a wonder if there were any health left in them."

On entering the amphitheater we saw gathered at one end of the arena some two or three hundred young men and women talking and lounging. These, the doctor told me, were Edith's companions of the class of 1978, being all those of twenty-two years of age, born in that ward or since coming there to live. I viewed with admiration the figures of these young men and women, all strong and beautiful as the gods and goddesses of Olympus.

"Am I to understand," I asked, "that this is a fair sample of your youth, and not a picked assembly of the more athletic?"

"Certainly," he replied; "all the youth in their twenty-third year who live in this ward are here today, with perhaps two or three exceptions on account of some special reason."

"But where are the cripples, the deformed, the feeble, the consumptive?"

"Do you see that young man yonder in the chair with so many of the others about him?" asked the doctor.

"Ah! there is then at least one invalid?"

"Yes," replied my companion: "he met with an accident, and will never be vigorous. He is the only sickly one of the class, and you see how much the others make of him. Your cripples and sickly were so many that pity itself grew weary and spent of tears, and compassion callous with use; but with us they are so few as to be our pets and darlings."

At that moment a bugle sounded, and some scores of young men and women dashed by us in a foot race. While they ran, the bugle continued to sound a nerve-bracing strain. The thing that astonished me was the evenness of the finish, in view of the fact that the contestants were not specially trained for racing, but were merely the group which in the round of tests had that day come to the running test. In a race of similarly unselected competitors in my day, they would have been strung along the track from the finish to the half, and the most of them nearest that.

"Edith, I see, was third in," said the doctor, reading from the signals. "She will be pleased to have done so well, seeing you were here."

The next event was a surprise. I had noticed a group of youths on a lofty platform at the far end of the amphitheater making some sort of preparations, and wondered what they were going to do. Now suddenly, at the sound of a trumpet, I saw them leap forward over the edge of the platform. I gave an involuntary cry of horror, for it was a deadly distance to the ground below.

"It's all right," laughed the doctor, and the next moment I was staring up at a score of young men and women charging through the air fifty feet above the race course.

Then followed contests in ball-throwing and putting the shot.

"It is plain where your women get their splendid chests and shoulders," said I.

"You have noticed that, then!" exclaimed the doctor.

"I have certainly noticed," was my answer, "that your modern women seem generally to possess a vigorous development and appearance of power above the waist which were only occasionally seen in our day."

"You will be interested, no doubt," said the doctor, "to have your impression corroborated by positive evidence. Suppose we leave the amphitheater for a few minutes and step into the anatomical rooms. It is indeed a rare fortune for an anatomical enthusiast like myself to have a pupil so well qualified to be appreciative, to whom to point out the effect our principle of social equality, and the best opportunities of culture for all, have had in modifying toward perfection the human form in general, and especially the female figure. I say especially the female figure, for that had been most perverted in your day by the influences which denied woman a full life. Here are a group of plaster statues, based on the lines handed down to us by the anthropometric experts of the last decades of the nineteenth century, to whom we are vastly indebted. You will observe, as your remark just now indicated that you had observed, that the tendency was to a spindling and inadequate development above the waist and an excessive development below. The figure seemed a little as if it had softened and run down like a sugar cast in warm weather. See, the front breadth flat measurement of the hips is actually greater than across the shoulders, whereas it ought to be an inch or two less, and the bulbous effect must have been exaggerated by the bulging mass of draperies your women accumulated about the waist."

At his words I raised my eyes to the stony face of the woman figure, the charms of which he had thus disparaged, and it seemed to me that the sightless eyes rested on mine with an expression of reproach, of which my heart instantly confessed the justice. I had been the contemporary of this type of women, and had been indebted to the light of their eyes for all that made life worth living. Complete or not, as might be their beauty by modern standards, through them I had learned to know the stress of the ever-womanly, and been made an initiate of Nature's sacred mysteries. Well might these stony eyes reproach me for consenting by my silence to the disparagement of charms to which I owed so much, by a man of another age.

"Hush, doctor, hush!" I exclaimed. "No doubt you are right, but it is not for me to hear these words."

I could not find the language to explain what was in my mind, but it was not necessary. The doctor understood, and his keen gray eyes glistened as he laid his hand on my shoulder.

"Right, my boy, quite right! That is the thing for you to say, and Edith would like you the better for your words, for women nowadays are jealous for one another's honor, as I judge they were not in your day. But, on the other hand, if there were present in this room disembodied shades of those women of your day, they would rejoice more than any others could at the fairer, ampler temples liberty has built for their daughters' souls to dwell in.

"Look!" he added, pointing to another figure; "this is the typical woman of to-day, the lines not ideal, but based on an average of measurements for the purpose of scientific comparison. First, you will observe that the figure is over two inches taller than the other. Note the shoulders! They have gained two inches in width relatively to the hips, as compared with the figure we have been examining. On the other hand, the girth at the hips is greater, showing more powerful muscular development. The chest is an inch and a half deeper, while the abdominal measure is fully two inches deeper. These increased developments are all over and above what the mere increase in stature would call for. As to the general development of the muscular system, you will see there is simply no comparison.

"Now, what is the explanation? Simply the effect upon woman of the full, free, untrammeled physical life to which her economic independence opened the way. To develop the shoulders, arms, chest, loins, legs, and body generally, exercise is needed--not mild and gentle, but vigorous, continuous exertion, undertaken not spasmodically but regularly. There is no dispensation of Providence that will or ever would give a woman physical development on any other terms than those by which men have acquired their development. But your women had recourse to no such means. Their work had been confined for countless ages to a multiplicity of petty tasks--hand work and finger work--tasks wearing to body and mind in the extreme, but of a sort wholly failing to provoke that reaction of the vital forces which builds up and develops the parts exercised. From time immemorial the boy had gone out to dig and hunt with his father, or contend for the mastery with other youths while the girl stayed at home to spin and bake. Up to fifteen she might share with her brother a few of his more insipid sports, but with the beginnings of womanhood came the end of all participation in active physical outdoor life. What could be expected save what resulted--a dwarfed and enfeebled physique and a semi-invalid existence? The only wonder is that, after so long a period of bodily repression and perversion, the feminine physique should have responded, by so great an improvement in so brief a period, to the free life opened up to woman within the last century."

"We had very many beautiful women; physically perfect they seemed at least to us," I said.

"Of course you did, and no doubt they were the perfect types you deemed them," replied the doctor. "They showed you what Nature meant the whole sex to be. But am I wrong in assuming that ill health was a general condition among your women? Certainly the records tell us so. If we may believe them, four fifths of the practice of doctors was among women, and it seemed to do them mighty little good either, although perhaps I ought not to reflect on my own profession. The fact is, they could not do anything, and probably knew they couldn't, so long as the social customs governing women remained unchanged."

"Of course you are right enough as to the general fact," I replied. "Indeed, a great writer had given currency to a generally accepted maxim when he said that invalidism was the normal condition of woman."

"I remember that expression. What a confession it was of the abject failure of your civilization to solve the most fundamental proposition of happiness for half the race! Woman's invalidism was one of the great tragedies of your civilization, and her physical rehabilitation is one of the greatest single elements in the total increment of happiness which economic equality has brought the human race. Consider what is implied in the transformation of the woman's world of sighs and tears and suffering, as you know it, into the woman's world of to-day, with its atmosphere of cheer and joy and overflowing vigor and vitality!"

"But," said I, "one thing is not quite clear to me. Without being a physician, or knowing more of such matters than a young man might be supposed to, I have yet understood in a general way that the weakness and delicacy of women's physical condition had their causes in certain natural disabilities of the sex."

"Yes, I know it was the general notion in your day that woman's physical constitution doomed her by its necessary effect to be sick, wretched, and unhappy, and that at most her condition could not be rendered more than tolerable in a physical sense. A more blighting blasphemy against Nature never found expression. No natural function ought to cause constant suffering or disease; and if it does, the rational inference is that something is wrong in the circumstances. The Orientals invented the myth of Eve and the apple, and the curse pronounced upon her, to explain the sorrows and infirmities of the sex, which were, in fact, a consequence, not of God's wrath, but of man-made conditions and customs. If you once admit that these sorrows and infirmities are inseparable from woman's natural constitution, why, then there is no logical explanation but to accept that myth as a matter of history. There were, however, plentiful illustrations already in your day of the great differences in the physical conditions of women under different circumstances and different social environments to convince unprejudiced minds that thoroughly healthful conditions which should be maintained a sufficiently long period would lead to a physical rehabilitation for woman that would quite redeem from its undeserved obloquy the reputation of her Creator."

"Am I to understand that maternity now is unattended with risk or suffering?"

"It is not nowadays an experience which is considered at all critical either in its actual occurrence or consequences. As to the other supposed natural disabilities which your wise men used to make so much of as excuses for keeping women in economic subjection, they have ceased to involve any physical disturbance whatever.

"And the end of this physical rebuilding of the feminine physique is not yet in view. While men still retain superiority in certain lines of athletics, we believe the sexes will yet stand on a plane of entire physical equality, with differences only as between individuals."

"There is one question," said I, "which this wonderful physical rebirth of woman suggests. You say that she is already the physical equal of man, and that your physiologists anticipate in a few generations more her evolution to a complete equality with him. That amounts to saying, does it not, that normally and potentially she always has been man's physical equal and that nothing but adverse circumstances and conditions have ever made her seem less than his equal?"

"Certainly."

"How, then, do you account for the fact that she has in all ages and countries since the dawn of history, with perhaps a few doubtful and transient exceptions, been his physical subject and thrall? If she ever was his equal, why did she cease to become so, and by a rule so universal? If her inferiority since historic times may be ascribed to unfavorable man-made conditions, why, if she was his equal, did she permit those conditions to be imposed upon her? A philosophical theory as to how a condition is to cease should contain a rational suggestion as to how it arose."

"Very true indeed," replied the doctor. "Your question is practical. The theory of those who hold that woman will yet be man's full equal in physical vigor necessarily implies, as you suggest, that she must probably once have been his actual equal, and calls for an explanation of the loss of that equality. Suppose man and woman actual physical equals at some point of the past. There remains a radical difference in their relation as sexes--namely, that man can passionally appropriate woman against her will if he can overpower her, while woman can not, even if disposed, so appropriate man without his full volition, however great her superiority of force. I have often speculated as to the reason of this radical difference, lying as it does at the root of all the sex tyranny of the past, now happily for evermore replaced by mutuality. It has sometimes seemed to me that it was Nature's provision to keep the race alive in periods of its evolution when life was not worth living save for a far-off posterity's sake. This end, we may say, she shrewdly secured by vesting the aggressive and appropriating power in the sex relation in that sex which had to bear the least part of the consequences resultant on its exercise. We may call the device a rather mean one on Nature's part, but it was well calculated to effect the purpose. But for it, owing to the natural and rational reluctance of the child-bearing sex to assume a burden so bitter and so seemingly profitless, the race might easily have been exposed to the risk of ceasing utterly during the darker periods of its upward evolution.

"But let us come back to the specific question we were talking about. Suppose man and woman in some former age to have been, on the whole, physically equal, sex for sex. Nevertheless, there would be many individual variations. Some of each sex would be stronger than others of their own sex. Some men would be stronger than some women, and as many women be stronger than some men. Very good; we know that well within historic times the savage method of taking wives has been by forcible capture. Much more may we suppose force to have been used wherever possible in more primitive periods. Now, a strong woman would have no object to gain in making captive a weaker man for any sexual purpose, and would not therefore pursue him. Conversely, however, strong men would have an object in making captive and keeping as their wives women weaker than themselves. In seeking to capture wives, men would naturally avoid the stronger women, whom they might have difficulty in dominating, and prefer as mates the weaker individuals, who would be less able to resist their will. On the other hand, the weaker of the men would find it relatively difficult to capture any mates at all, and would be consequently less likely to leave progeny. Do you see the inference?"

"It is plain enough," I replied. "You mean that the stronger women and the weaker men would both be discriminated against, and that the types which survived would be the stronger of the men and the weaker of the women."

"Precisely so. Now, suppose a difference in the physical strength of the sexes to have become well established through this process in prehistoric times, before the dawn of civilization, the rest of the story follows very simply. The now confessedly dominant sex would, of course, seek to retain and increase its domination and the now fully subordinated sex would in time come to regard the inferiority to which it was born as natural, inevitable, and Heaven-ordained. And so it would go on as it did go on, until the world's awakening, at the end of the last century, to the necessity and possibility of a reorganization of human society on a moral basis, the first principle of which must be the equal liberty and dignity of all human beings. Since then women have been reconquering, as they will later fully reconquer, their pristine physical equality with men."

"A rather alarming notion occurs to me," said I. "What if woman should in the end not only equal but excel man in physical and mental powers, as he has her in the past, and what if she should take as mean an advantage of that superiority as he did?"

The doctor laughed. "I think you need not be apprehensive that such a superiority, even if attained, would be abused. Not that women, as such, are any more safely to be trusted with irresponsible power than men, but for the reason that the race is rising fast toward the plane already in part attained in which spiritual forces will fully dominate all things, and questions of physical power will cease to be of any importance in human relations. The control and leading of humanity go already largely, and are plainly destined soon to go wholly, to those who have the largest souls-- that is to say, to those who partake most of the Spirit of the Greater Self; and that condition is one which in itself is the most absolute guarantee against the misuse of that power for selfish ends, seeing that with such misuse it would cease to be a power."

"The Greater Self--what does that mean?" I asked.

"It is one of our names for the soul and for God," replied the doctor, "but that is too great a theme to enter on now."

CHAPTER XXII.

Economic Suicide Of The Profit System.

The morning following, Edith received a call to report at her post of duty for some special occasion. After she had gone, I sought out the doctor in the library and began to ply him with questions, of which, as usual, a store had accumulated in my mind overnight.

"If you desire to continue your historical studies this morning," he said presently, "I am going to propose a change of teachers."

"I am very well satisfied with the one whom Providence assigned to me," I answered, "but it is quite natural you should want a little relief from such persistent cross-questioning."

"It is not that at all," replied the doctor. "I am sure no one could conceivably have a more inspiring task than mine has been, nor have I any idea of giving it up as yet. But it occurred to me that a little change in the method and medium of instruction this morning might be agreeable."

"Who is to be the new teacher?" I asked.

"There are to be a number of them, and they are not teachers at all, but pupils."

"Come, doctor," I protested, "don't you think a man in my position has enough riddles to guess, without making them up for him?"

"It sounds like a riddle, doesn't it? But it is not. However, I will hasten to explain. As one of those citizens to whom for supposed public services the people have voted the blue ribbon, I have various honorary functions as to public matters, and especially educational affairs. This morning I have notice of an examination at ten o'clock of the ninth grade in the Arlington School. They have been studying the history of the period before the great Revolution, and are going to give their general impressions of it. I thought that perhaps, by way of a change, you might be interested in listening to them, especially in view of the special topic they are going to discuss."

I assured the doctor that no programme could promise more entertainment. "What is the topic they discuss?" I inquired.

"The profit system as a method of economic suicide is their theme," replied the doctor. "In our talks hitherto we have chiefly touched on the moral wrongfulness of the old economic order. In the discussion we shall listen to this morning there will be no reference unless incidentally to moral considerations. The young people will endeavor to show us that there were certain inherent and fatal defects in private capitalism as a machine for producing wealth which, quite apart from its ethical character, made its abolition necessary if the race was ever to get out of the mire of poverty."

"That is a very different doctrine from the preaching I used to hear," I said. "The clergy and moralists in general assured us that there were no social evils for which moral and religious medicine was not adequate. Poverty, they said, was in the end the result of human depravity, and would disappear if everybody would only be good."

"So we read," said the doctor. "How far the clergy and the moralists preached this doctrine with a professional motive as calculated to enhance the importance of their services as moral instructors, how far they merely echoed it as an excuse for mental indolence, and how far they may really have been sincere, we can not judge at this distance, but certainly more injurious nonsense was never taught. The industrial and commercial system by which the labor of a great population is organized and directed constitutes a complex machine. If the machine is constructed unscientifically, it will result in loss and disaster, without the slightest regard to whether the managers are the rarest of saints or the worst of sinners. The world always has had and will have need of all the virtue and true religion that men can be induced to practice; but to tell farmers that personal religion will take the place of a scientific agriculture, or the master of an unseaworthy ship that the practice of good morals will bring his craft to shore, would be no greater childishness than the priests and moralists of your day committed in assuring a world beggared by a crazy economic system that the secret of plenty was good works and personal piety. History gives a bitter chapter to these blind guides, who, during the revolutionary period, did far more harm than those who openly defended the old order, because, while the brutal frankness of the latter repelled good men, the former misled them and long diverted from the guilty system the indignation which otherwise would have sooner destroyed it.

"And just here let me say, Julian, as a most important point for you to remember in the history of the great Revolution, that it was not until the people had outgrown this childish teaching and saw the causes of the world's want and misery, not primarily in human depravity, but in the economic madness of the profit system on which private capitalism depended, that the Revolution began to go forward in earnest."

Now, although the doctor had said that the school we were to visit was in Arlington, which I knew to be some distance out of the city, and that the examination would take place at ten o'clock, he continued to sit comfortably in his chair, though the time was five minutes of ten.

"Is this Arlington the same town that was a suburb of the city in my time?" I presently ventured to inquire.

"Certainly."

"It was then ten or twelve miles from the city," I said.

"It has not been moved, I assure you," said the doctor.

"Then if not, and if the examination is to begin in five minutes, are we not likely to be late?" I mildly observed.

"Oh, no," replied the doctor, "there are three or four minutes left yet."

"Doctor," said I, "I have been introduced within the last few days to many new and speedy modes of locomotion, but I can't see how you are going to get me to Arlington from here in time for the examination that begins three minutes hence, unless you reduce me to an electrified solution, send me by wire, and have me precipitated back to my shape at the other end of the line; and even in that case I should suppose we had no time to waste."

"We shouldn't have, certainly, if we were intending to go to Arlington even by that process. It did not occur to me that you would care to go, or we might just as well have started earlier. It is too bad!"

"I did not care about visiting Arlington." I replied, "but I assumed that it would be rather necessary to do so if I were to attend an examination at that place. I see my mistake. I ought to have learned by this time not to take for granted that any of what we used to consider the laws of Nature are still in force."

"The laws of Nature are all right," laughed the doctor. "But is it possible that Edith has not shown you the electroscope?"

"What is that?" I asked.

"It does for vision what the telephone does for hearing," replied the doctor, and, leading the way to the music room, he showed me the apparatus.

"It is ten o'clock," he said, "and we have no time for explanations now. Take this chair and adjust the instrument as you see me do. Now!"

Instantly, without warning, or the faintest preparation for what was coming, I found myself looking into the interior of a large room. Some twenty boys and girls, thirteen to fourteen years of age, occupied a double row of chairs arranged in the form of a semicircle about a desk at which a young man was seated with his back to us. The rows of students were facing us, apparently not twenty feet away. The rustling of their garments and every change of expression in their mobile faces were as distinct to my eyes and ears as if we had been directly behind the teacher, as indeed we seemed to be. At the moment the scene had flashed upon me I was in the act of making some remark to the doctor. As I checked myself, he laughed. "You need not be afraid of interrupting them," he said. "They don't see or hear us, though we both see and hear them so well. They are a dozen miles away."

"Good heavens!" I whispered--for, in spite of his assurance, I could not realize that they did not hear me--"are we here or there?"

"We are here certainly," replied the doctor, "but our eyes and ears are there. This is the electroscope and telephone combined. We could have heard the examination just as well without the electroscope, but I thought you would be better entertained if you could both see and hear. Fine-looking young people, are they not? We shall see now whether they are as intelligent as they are handsome."

HOW PROFITS CUT DOWN CONSUMPTION.

"Our subject this morning," said the teacher briskly, "is 'The Economic Suicide of Production for Profit,' or 'The Hopelessness of the Economic Outlook of the Race under Private Capitalism.'-- Now, Frank, will you tell us exactly what this proposition means?"

At these words one of the boys of the class rose to his feet.

"It means," he said, "that communities which depended--as they had to depend, so long as private capitalism lasted--upon the motive of profit making for the production of the things by which they lived, must always suffer poverty, because the profit system, by its necessary nature, operated to stop limit and cripple production at the point where it began to be efficient."

"By what is the possible production of wealth limited?"

"By its consumption."

"May not production fall short of possible consumption? May not the demand for consumption exceed the resources of production?"

"Theoretically it may, but not practically--that is, speaking of demand as limited to rational desires, and not extending to merely fanciful objects. Since the division of labor was introduced, and especially since the great inventions multiplied indefinitely the powers of man, production has been practically limited only by the demand created by consumption."

"Was this so before the great Revolution?"

"Certainly. It was a truism among economists that either England, Germany, or the United States alone could easily have supplied the world's whole consumption of manufactured goods. No country began to produce up to its capacity in any line."

"Why not?"

"On account of the necessary law of the profit system, by which it operated to limit production."

"In what way did this law operate?"

"By creating a gap between the producing and consuming power of the community, the result of which was that the people were not able to consume as much as they could produce."

"Please tell us just how the profit system led to this result."

"There being under the old order of things," replied the boy Frank, "no collective agency to undertake the organization of labor and exchange, that function naturally fell into the hands of enterprising individuals who, because the undertaking called for much capital, had to be capitalists. They were of two general classes--the capitalist who organized labor for production; and the traders, the middlemen, and storekeepers, who organized distribution, and having collected all the varieties of products in the market, sold them again to the general public for consumption. The great mass of the people--nine, perhaps, out of ten--were wage-earners who sold their labor to the producing capitalists; or small first-hand producers, who sold their personal product to the middlemen. The farmers were of the latter class. With the money the wage-earners and farmers received in wages, or as the price of their produce, they afterward went into the market, where the products of all sorts were assembled, and bought back as much as they could for consumption. Now, of course, the capitalists, whether engaged in organizing production or distribution, had to have some inducement for risking their capital and spending their time in this work. That inducement was profit."

"Tell us how the profits were collected."

"The manufacturing or employing capitalists paid the people who worked for them, and the merchants paid the farmers for their products in tokens called money, which were good to buy back the blended products of all in the market. But the capitalists gave neither the wage-earner nor the farmer enough of these money tokens to buy back the equivalent of the product of his labor. The difference which the capitalists kept back for themselves was their profit. It was collected by putting a higher price on the products when sold in the stores than the cost of the product had been to the capitalists."

"Give us an example."

"We will take then, first, the manufacturing capitalist, who employed labor. Suppose he manufactured shoes. Suppose for each pair of shoes he paid ten cents to the tanner for leather, twenty cents for the labor of putting, the shoe together, and ten cents for all other labor in any way entering into the making of the shoe, so that the pair cost him in actual outlay forty cents. He sold the shoes to a middleman for, say, seventy-five cents. The middleman sold them to the retailer for a dollar, and the retailer sold them over his counter to the consumer for a dollar and a half. Take next the case of the farmer, who sold not merely his labor like the wage-earner, but his labor blended with his material. Suppose he sold his wheat to the grain merchant for forty cents a bushel. The grain merchant, in selling it to the flouring mill, would ask, say, sixty cents a bushel. The flouring mill would sell it to the wholesale flour merchant for a price over and above the labor cost of milling at a figure which would include a handsome profit for him. The wholesale flour merchant would add another profit in selling to the retail grocer, and the last yet another in selling to the consumer. So that finally the equivalent of the bushel of wheat in finished flour as bought back by the original farmer for consumption would cost him, on account of profit charges alone, over and above the actual labor cost of intermediate processes, perhaps twice what he received for it from the grain merchant."

"Very well," said the teacher. "Now for the practical effect of this system."

"The practical effect," replied the boy, "was necessarily to create a gap between the producing and consuming power of those engaged in the production of the things upon which profits were charged. Their ability to consume would be measured by the value of the money tokens they received for producing the goods, which by the statement was less than the value put upon those goods in the stores. That difference would represent a gap between what they could produce and what they could consume."

MARGARET TELLS ABOUT THE DEADLY GAP.

"Margaret," said the teacher, "you may now take up the subject where Frank leaves it, and tell us what would be the effect upon the economic system of a people of such a gap between its consuming and producing power as Frank shows us was caused by profit taking."

"The effect," said the girl who answered to the name of Margaret, "would depend on two factors: first, on how numerous a body were the wage-earners and first producers, on whose products the profits were charged; and, second, how large was the rate of profit charged, and the consequent discrepancy between the producing and consuming power of each individual of the working body. If the producers on whose product a profit was charged were but a handful of the people, the total effect of their inability to buy back and consume more than a part of their product would create but a slight gap between the producing and consuming power of the community as a whole. If, on the other hand, they constituted a large proportion of the whole population, the gap would be correspondingly great, and the reactive effect to check production would be disastrous in proportion."

"And what was the actual proportion of the total population made up by the wage-earners and original producers, who by the profit system were prevented from consuming as much as they produced?"

"It constituted, as Frank has said, at least nine tenths of the whole people, probably more. The profit takers, whether they were organizers of production or of distribution, were a group numerically insignificant, while those on whose product the profits were charged constituted the bulk of the community."

"Very well. We will now consider the other factor on which the size of the gap between the producing and consuming power of the community created by the profit system was dependent--namely, the rate of profits charged. Tell us, then, what was the rule followed by the capitalists in charging profits. No doubt, as rational men who realized the effect of high profits to prevent consumption, they made a point of making their profits as low as possible."

"On the contrary, the capitalists made their profits as high as possible. Their maxim was, 'Tax the traffic all it will bear.'"

"Do you mean that instead of trying to minimize the effect of profit charging to diminish consumption, they deliberately sought to magnify it to the greatest possible degree?"

"I mean that precisely," replied Margaret. "The golden rule of the profit system, the great motto of the capitalists, was, 'Buy in the Cheapest Market, and sell in the Dearest.'"

"What did that mean?"

"It meant that the capitalist ought to pay the least possible to those who worked for him or sold him their produce, and on the other hand should charge the highest possible price for their product when he offered it for sale to the general public in the market."

"That general public," observed the teacher, "being chiefly composed of the workers to whom he and his fellow-capitalists had just been paying as nearly nothing as possible for creating the product which they were now expected to buy back at the highest possible price."

"Certainly."

"Well, let us try to realize the full economic wisdom of this rule as applied to the business of a nation. It means, doesn't it, Get something for nothing, or as near nothing as you can. Well, then, if you can get it for absolutely nothing, you are carrying out the maxim to perfection. For example, if a manufacturer could hypnotize his workmen so as to get them to work for him for no wages at all, he would be realizing the full meaning of the maxim, would he not?"

"Certainly; a manufacturer who could do that, and then put the product of his unpaid workmen on the market at the usual price, would have become rich in a very short time."

"And the same would be true, I suppose, of a grain merchant who was able to take such advantage of the farmers as to obtain their grain for nothing, afterward selling it at the top price."

"Certainly. He would become a millionaire at once."

"Well, now, suppose the secret of this hypnotizing process should get abroad among the capitalists engaged in production and exchange, and should be generally applied by them so that all of them were able to get workmen without wages, and buy produce without paying anything for it, then doubtless all the capitalists at once would become fabulously rich."

"Not at all."

"Dear me! why not?"

"Because if the whole body of wage-earners failed to receive any wages for their work, and the farmers received nothing for their produce, there would be nobody to buy anything, and the market would collapse entirely. There would be no demand for any goods except what little the capitalists themselves and their friends could consume. The working people would then presently starve, and the capitalists be left to do their own work."

"Then it appears that what would be good for the particular capitalist, if he alone did it, would be ruinous to him and everybody else if all the capitalists did it. Why was this?"

"Because the particular capitalist, in expecting to get rich by underpaying his employees, would calculate on selling his produce, not to the particular group of workmen he had cheated, but to the community at large, consisting of the employees of other capitalists not so successful in cheating their workmen, who therefore would have something to buy with. The success of his trick depended on the presumption that his fellow-capitalists would not succeed in practicing the same trick. If that presumption failed, and all the capitalists succeeded at once in dealing with their employees, as all were trying to do, the result would be to stop the whole industrial system outright."

"It appears, then, that in the profit system we have an economic method, of which the working rule only needed to be applied thoroughly enough in order to bring the system to a complete standstill and that all which kept the system going was the difficulty found in fully carrying out the working rule.

"That was precisely so," replied the girl; "the individual capitalist grew rich fastest who succeeded best in beggaring those whose labor or produce he bought; but obviously it was only necessary for enough capitalists to succeed in so doing in order to involve capitalists and people alike in general ruin. To make the sharpest possible bargain with the employer or producer, to give him the least possible return for his labor or product, was the ideal every capitalist must constantly keep before him, and yet it was mathematically certain that every such sharp bargain tended to undermine the whole business fabric, and that it was only necessary that enough capitalists should succeed in making enough such sharp bargains to topple the fabric over."

"One question more. The bad effects of a bad system are always aggravated by the willfulness of men who take advantage of it, and so, no doubt, the profit system was made by selfish men to work worse than it might have done. Now, suppose the capitalists had all been fair-minded men and not extortioners, and had made their charges for their services as small as was consistent with reasonable gains and self-protection, would that course have involved such a reduction of profit charges as would have greatly helped the people to consume their products and thus to promote production?"

"It would not," replied the girl. "The antagonism of the profit system to effective wealth production arose from causes inherent in and inseparable from private capitalism; and so long as private capitalism was retained, those causes must have made the profit system inconsistent with any economic improvement in the condition of the people, even if the capitalists had been, angels. The root of the evil was not moral, but strictly economic."

"But would not the rate of profits have been much reduced in the case supposed?"

"In some instances temporarily no doubt, but not generally, and in no case permanently. It is doubtful if profits, on the whole, were higher than they had to be to encourage capitalists to undertake production and trade."

"Tell us why the profits had to be so large for this purpose."

"Legitimate profits under private capitalism," replied the girl Margaret--"that is, such profits as men going into production or trade must in self-protection calculate upon, however well disposed toward the public--consisted of three elements, all growing out of conditions inseparable from private capitalism, none of which longer exist. First, the capitalist must calculate on at least as large a return on the capital he was to put into the venture as he could obtain by lending it on good security--that is to say, the ruling rate of interest. If he were not sure of that, he would prefer to lend his capital. But that was not enough. In going into business he risked the entire loss of his capital, as he would not if it were lent on good security. Therefore, in addition to the ruling rate of interest on capital, his profits must cover the cost of insurance on the capital risked--that is, there must be a prospect of gains large enough in case the venture succeeded to cover the risk of loss of capital in case of failure. If the chances of failure, for instance, were even, he must calculate on more than a hundred per cent profit in case of success. In point of fact, the chances of failure in business and loss of capital in those days were often far more than even. Business was indeed little more than a speculative risk, a lottery in which the blanks greatly outnumbered the prizes. The prizes to tempt investment must therefore be large. Moreover, if a capitalist were personally to take charge of the business in which he invested his capital, he would reasonably have expected adequate wages of superintendence--compensation, in other words, for his skill and judgment in navigating the venture through the stormy waters of the business sea, compared with which, as it was in that day, the North Atlantic in midwinter is a mill pond. For this service he would be considered justified in making a large addition to the margin of profit charged."

"Then you conclude, Margaret, that, even if disposed to be fair toward the community, a capitalist of those days would not have been able safely to reduce his rate of profits sufficiently to bring the people much nearer the point of being able to consume their products than they were."

"Precisely so. The root of the evil lay in the tremendous difficulties, complexities, mistakes, risks, and wastes with which private capitalism necessarily involved the processes of production and distribution, which under public capitalism have become so entirely simple, expeditious, and certain."

"Then it seems it is not necessary to consider our capitalist ancestors moral monsters in order to account for the tragical outcome of their economic methods."

"By no means. The capitalists were no doubt good and bad, like other people, but probably stood up as well as any people could against the depraving influences of a system which in fifty years would have turned heaven itself into hell."

MARION EXPLAINS OVER-PRODUCTION.

"That will do, Margaret," said the teacher. "We will next ask you, Marion, to assist us in further elucidating the subject. If the profit system worked according to the description we have listened to, we shall be prepared to learn that the economic situation was marked by the existence of large stores of consumable goods in the hands of the profit takers which they would be glad to sell, and, on the other hand, by a great population composed of the original producers of the goods, who were in sharp need of the goods but unable to purchase them. How does this theory agree with the facts stated in the histories?"

"So well," replied Marion, "that one might almost think you had been reading them." At which the class smiled, and so did I.

"Describe, without unnecessary infusion of humor--for the subject was not humorous to our ancestors--the condition of things to which you refer. Did our great-grandfathers recognize in this excess of goods over buyers a cause of economic disturbance?"

"They recognized it as the great and constant cause of such disturbance. The perpetual burden of their complaints was dull times, stagnant trade, glut of products. Occasionally they had brief periods of what they called good times, resulting from a little brisker buying, but in the best of what they called good times the condition of the mass of the people was what we should call abjectly wretched."

"What was the term by which they most commonly described the presence in the market of more products than could be sold?"

"Overproduction."

"Was it meant by this expression that there had been actually more food, clothing, and other good things produced than the people could use?"

"Not at all. The mass of the people were in great need always, and in more bitter need than ever precisely at the times when the business machine was clogged by what they called overproduction. The people, if they could have obtained access to the overproduced goods, would at any time have consumed them in a moment and loudly called for more. The trouble was, as has been said, that the profits charged by the capitalist manufacturers and traders had put them out of the power of the original producers to buy back with the price they had received for their labor or products."

"To what have our historians been wont to compare the condition of the community under the profit system?"

"To that of a victim of the disease of chronic dyspepsia so prevalent among our ancestors."

"Please develop the parallel."

"In dyspepsia the patient suffered from inability to assimilate food. With abundance of dainties at hand he wasted away from the lack of power to absorb nutriment. Although unable to eat enough to support life, he was constantly suffering the pangs of indigestion, and while actually starving for want of nourishment, was tormented by the sensation of an overloaded stomach. Now, the economic condition of a community under the profit system afforded a striking analogy to the plight of such a dyspeptic. The masses of the people were always in bitter need of all things, and were abundantly able by their industry to provide for all their needs, but the profit system would not permit them to consume even what they produced, much less produce what they could. No sooner did they take the first edge off of their appetite than the commercial system was seized with the pangs of acute indigestion and all the symptoms of an overloaded system, which nothing but a course of starvation would relieve, after which the experience would be repeated with the same result, and so on indefinitely."

"Can you explain why such an extraordinary misnomer as overproduction, should be applied to a situation that would better be described as famine; why a condition should be said to result from glut when it was obviously the consequence of enforced abstinence? Surely, the mistake was equivalent to diagnosing a case of starvation as one of gluttony."

"It was because the economists and the learned classes, who alone had a voice, regarded the economic question entirely from the side of the capitalists and ignored the interest of the people. From the point of view of the capitalist it was a case of overproduction when he had charged profits on products which took them beyond the power of the people to buy, and so the economist writing in his interest called it. From the point of view of the capitalist, and consequently of the economist, the only question was the condition of the market, not of the people. They did not concern themselves whether the people were famished or glutted; the only question was the condition of the market. Their maxim that demand governed supply, and supply would always meet demand, referred in no way to the demand representing human need, but wholly to an artificial thing called the market, itself the product of the profit system."

"What was the market?"

"The market was the number of those who had money to buy with. Those who had no money were non-existent so far as the market was concerned, and in proportion as people had little money they were a small part of the market. The needs of the market were the needs of those who had the money to supply their needs with. The rest, who had needs in plenty but no money, were not counted, though they were as a hundred to one of the moneyed. The market was supplied when those who could buy had enough, though the most of the people had little and many had nothing. The market was glutted when the well-to-do were satisfied, though starving and naked mobs might riot in the streets."

"Would such a thing be possible nowadays as full storehouses and a hungry and naked people existing at the same time?"

"Of course not. Until every one was satisfied there could be no such thing as overproduct now. Our system is so arranged that there can be too little nowhere so long as there is too much anywhere. But the old system had no circulation of the blood."

"What name did our ancestors give to the various economic disturbances which they ascribed to overproduction?"

"They called them commercial crises. That is to say, there was a chronic state of glut which might be called a chronic crisis, but every now and then the arrears resulting from the constant discrepancy between consumption and production accumulated to such a degree as to nearly block business. When this happened they called it, in distinction from the chronic glut, a crisis or panic, on account of the blind terror which it caused."

"To what cause did they ascribe the crises?"

"To almost everything besides the perfectly plain reason. An extensive literature seems to have been devoted to the subject. There are shelves of it up at the museum which I have been trying to go through, or at least to skim over, in connection with this study. If the books were not so dull in style they would be very amusing, just on account of the extraordinary ingenuity the writers display in avoiding the natural and obvious explanation of the facts they discuss. They even go into astronomy."

"What do you mean?"

"I suppose the class will think I am romancing, but it is a fact that one of the most famous of the theories by which our ancestors accounted for the periodical breakdowns of business resulting from the profit system was the so-called 'sun-spot theory.' During the first half of the nineteenth century it so happened that there were severe crises at periods about ten or eleven years apart. Now, it happened that sun spots were at a maximum about every ten years, and a certain eminent English economist concluded that these sun spots caused the panics. Later on it seems this theory was found unsatisfactory, and gave place to the lack-of-confidence explanation."

"And what was that?"

"I could not exactly make out, but it seemed reasonable to suppose that there must have developed a considerable lack of confidence in an economic system which turned out such results."

"Marion, I fear you do not bring a spirit of sympathy to the study of the ways of our forefathers, and without sympathy we can not understand others."

"I am afraid they are a little too other, for me to understand."

The class tittered, and Marion was allowed to take her seat.

JOHN TELLS ABOUT COMPETITION.

"Now, John," said the teacher, "we will ask you a few questions. We have seen by what process a chronic glut of goods in the market resulted from the operation of the profit system to put products out of reach of the purchasing power of the people at large. Now, what notable characteristic and main feature of the business system of our forefathers resulted from the glut thus produced?"

"I suppose you refer to competition?" said the boy.

"Yes. What was competition and what caused it, referring especially to the competition between capitalists?"

"It resulted, as you intimate, from the insufficient consuming power of the public at large, which in turn resulted from the profit system. If the wage-earners and first-hand producers had received purchasing power sufficient to enable them to take up their numerical proportion of the total product offered in the market, it would have been cleared of goods without any effort on the part of sellers, for the buyers would have sought the sellers and been enough to buy all. But the purchasing power of the masses, owing to the profits charged on their products, being left wholly inadequate to take those products out of the market, there naturally followed a great struggle between the capitalists engaged in production and distribution to divert the most possible of the all too scanty buying each in his own direction. The total buying could not of course be increased a dollar without relatively, or absolutely increasing the purchasing power in the people's hands, but it was possible by effort to alter the particular directions in which it should be expended, and this was the sole aim and effect of competition. Our forefathers thought it a wonderfully fine thing. They called it the life of trade, but, as we have seen, it was merely a symptom of the effect of the profit system to cripple consumption."

"What were the methods which the capitalists engaged in production and exchange made use of to bring trade their way, as they used to say?"

"First was direct solicitation of buyers and a shameless vaunting of every one's wares by himself and his hired mouthpieces, coupled with a boundless depreciation of rival sellers and the wares they offered. Unscrupulous and unbounded misrepresentation was so universally the rule in business that even when here and there a dealer told the truth he commanded no credence. History indicates that lying has always been more or less common, but it remained for the competitive system as fully developed in the nineteenth century to make it the means of livelihood of the whole world. According to our grandfathers--and they certainly ought to have known--the only lubricant which was adapted to the machinery of the profit system was falsehood, and the demand for it was unlimited."

"And all this ocean of lying, you say, did not and could not increase the total of goods consumed by a dollar's worth."

"Of course not. Nothing, as I said, could increase that save an increase in the purchasing power of the people. The system of solicitation or advertising, as it was called, far from increasing the total sale, tended powerfully to decrease it."

"How so?"

"Because it was prodigiously expensive and the expense had to be added to the price of the goods and paid by the consumer, who therefore could buy just so much less than if he had been left in peace and the price of the goods had been reduced by the saving in advertising."

"You say that the only way by which consumption could have been increased was by increasing the purchasing power in the hands of the people relatively to the goods to be bought. Now, our forefathers claimed that this was just what competition did. They claimed that it was a potent means of reducing prices and cutting down the rate of profits, thereby relatively increasing the purchasing power of the masses. Was this claim well based?"

"The rivalry of the capitalists among themselves," replied the lad, "to tempt the buyers' custom certainly prompted them to undersell one another by nominal reductions of prices, but it was rarely that these nominal reductions, though often in appearance very large, really represented in the long run any economic benefit to the people at large, for they were generally effected by means which nullified their practical value."

"Please make that clear."

"Well, naturally, the capitalist would prefer to reduce the prices of his goods in such a way, if possible, as not to reduce his profits, and that would be his study. There were numerous devices which he employed to this end. The first was that of reducing the quality and real worth of the goods on which the price was nominally cut down. This was done by adulteration and scamped work, and the practice extended in the nineteenth century to every branch of industry and commerce and affected pretty nearly all articles of human consumption. It came to that point, as the histories tell us, that no one could ever depend on anything he purchased being what it appeared or was represented. The whole atmosphere of trade was mephitic with chicane. It became the policy of the capitalists engaged in the most important lines of manufacture to turn out goods expressly made with a view to wearing as short a time as possible, so as to need the speedier renewal. They taught their very machines to be dishonest, and corrupted steel and brass. Even the purblind people of that day recognized the vanity of the pretended reductions in price by the epithet 'cheap and nasty,' with which they characterized cheapened goods. All this class of reductions, it is plain, cost the consumer two dollars for every one it professed to save him. As a single illustration of the utterly deceptive character of reductions in price under the profit system, it may be recalled that toward the close of the nineteenth century in America, after almost magical inventions for reducing the cost of shoemaking, it was a common saying that although the price of shoes was considerably lower than fifty years before, when they were made by hand, yet that later-made shoes were so much poorer in quality as to be really quite as expensive as the earlier."

"Were adulteration and scamped work the only devices by which sham reductions of prices was effected?"

"There were two other ways. The first was where the capitalist saved his profits while reducing the price of goods by taking the reduction out of the wages he had paid his employees. This was the method by which the reductions in price were very generally brought about. Of course, the process was one which crippled the purchasing power of the community by the amount of the lowered wages. By this means the particular group of capitalists cutting down wages might quicken their sales for a time until other capitalists likewise cut wages. In the end nobody was helped, not even the capitalist. Then there was the third of the three main kinds of reductions in price to be credited to competition--namely, that made on account of labor-saving machinery or other inventions which enabled the capitalist to discharge his laborers. The reduction in price on the goods was here based, as in the former case, on the reduced amount of wages paid out, and consequently meant a reduced purchasing power on the part of the community, which, in the total effect, usually nullified the advantage of reduced price, and often more than nullified it."

"You have shown," said the teacher, "that most of the reductions of price effected by competition were reductions at the expense of the original producers or of the final consumers, and not reductions in profits. Do you mean to say that the competition of capitalists for trade never operated to reduce profits?"

"Undoubtedly it did so operate in countries where from the long operation of the profit system surplus capital had accumulated so as to compete under great pressure for investment; but under such circumstances reductions in prices, even though they might come from sacrifices of profits, usually came too late to increase the consumption of the people."

"How too late?"

"Because the capitalist had naturally refrained from sacrificing his profits in order to reduce prices so long as he could take the cost of the reduction out of the wages of his workmen or out of the first-hand producer. That is to say, it was only when the working masses had been reduced to pretty near the minimum subsistence point that the capitalist would decide to sacrifice a portion of his profits. By that time it was too late for the people to take advantage of the reduction. When a population had reached that point, it had no buying power left to be stimulated. Nothing short of giving commodities away freely could help it. Accordingly, we observe that in the nineteenth century it was always in the countries where the populations were most hopelessly poor that the prices were lowest. It was in this sense a bad sign for the economic condition of a community when the capitalist found it necessary to make a real sacrifice of profits, for it was a clear indication that the working masses had been squeezed until they could be squeezed no longer."

"Then, on the whole, competition was not a palliative of the profit system?"

"I think that it has been made apparent that it was a grievous aggravation of it. The desperate rivalry of the capitalists for a share in the scanty market which their own profit taking had beggared drove them to the practice of deception and brutality, and compelled a hard-heartedness such as we are bound to believe human beings would not under a less pressure have been guilty of."

"What was the general economic effect of competition?"

"It operated in all fields of industry, and in the long run for all classes, the capitalists as well as the non-capitalists, as a steady downward pull as irresistible and universal as gravitation. Those felt it first who had least capital, the wage-earners who had none, and the farmer proprietors who, having next to none, were under almost the same pressure to find a prompt market at any sacrifice of their product, as were the wage-earners to find prompt buyers for their labor. These classes were the first victims of the competition to sell in the glutted markets of things and of men. Next came the turn of the smaller capitalists, till finally only the largest were left, and these found it necessary for self-preservation to protect themselves against the process of competitive decimation by the consolidation of their interests. One of the signs of the times in the period preceding the Revolution was this tendency among the great capitalists to seek refuge from the destructive efforts of competition through the pooling of their undertakings in great trusts and syndicates."

"Suppose the Revolution had not come to interrupt that process, would a system under which capital and the control of all business had been consolidated in a few hands have been worse for the public interest than the effect of competition?"

"Such a consolidated system would, of course, have been an intolerable despotism, the yoke of which, once assumed, the race might never have been able to break. In that respect private capitalism under a consolidated plutocracy, such as impended at the time of the Revolution, would have been a worse threat to the world's future than the competitive system; but as to the immediate bearings of the two systems on human welfare, private capital in the consolidated form might have had some points of advantage. Being an autocracy, it would have at least given some chance to a benevolent despot to be better than the system and to ameliorate a little the conditions of the people, and that was something competition did not allow the capitalists to do."

"What do you mean?"

"I mean that under competition there was no free play whatever allowed for the capitalist's better feelings even if he had any. He could not be better than the system. If he tried to be, the system would crush him. He had to follow the pace set by his competitors or fail in business. Whatever rascality or cruelty his rivals might devise, he must imitate or drop out of the struggle. The very wickedest, meanest, and most rascally of the competitors, the one who ground his employees lowest, adulterated his goods most shamefully, and lied about them most skillfully, set the pace for all the rest."

"Evidently, John, if you had lived in the early part of the revolutionary agitation you would have had scant sympathy with those early reformers whose fear was lest the great monopolies would put an end to competition."

"I can't say whether I should have been wiser than my contemporaries in that case," replied the lad, "but I think my gratitude to the monopolists for destroying competition would have been only equaled by my eagerness to destroy the monopolists to make way for public capitalism."

ROBERT TELLS ABOUT THE GLUT OF MEN.

"Now, Robert," said the teacher, "John has told us how the glut of products resulting from the profit system caused a competition among capitalists to sell goods and what its consequences were. There was, however, another sort of glut besides that of goods which resulted from the profit system. What was that?"

"A glut of men," replied the boy Robert. "Lack of buying power on the part of the people, whether from lack of employment or lowered wages, meant less demand for products, and that meant less work for producers. Clogged storehouses meant closed factories and idle populations of workers who could get no work--that is to say, the glut in the goods market caused a corresponding glut in the labor or man market. And as the glut in the goods market stimulated competition among the capitalists to sell their goods, so likewise did the glut in the labor market stimulate an equally desperate competition among the workers to sell their labor. The capitalists who could not find buyers for their goods lost their money indeed, but those who had nothing to sell but their strength and skill, and could find none to buy, must perish. The capitalist, unless his goods were perishable, could wait for a market, but the workingman must find a buyer for his labor at once or die. And in respect to this inability to wait for a market, the farmer, while technically a capitalist, was little better off than the wage-earner, being, on account of the smallness of his capital, almost as unable to withhold his product as the workingman his labor. The pressing necessity of the wage-earner to sell his labor at once on any terms and of the small capitalist to dispose of his product was the means by which the great capitalists were able steadily to force down the rate of wages and the prices paid for their product to the first producers."

"And was it only among the wage-earners and the small producers that this glut of men existed?"

"On the contrary, every trade, every occupation, every art, and every profession, including the most learned ones, was similarly overcrowded, and those in the ranks of each regarded every fresh recruit with jealous eyes, seeing in him one more rival in the struggle for life, making it just so much more difficult than it had been before. It would seem that in those days no man could have had any satisfaction in his labor, however self-denying and arduous, for he must always have been haunted by the feeling that it would have been kinder to have stood aside and let another do the work and take the pay, seeing that there was not work and pay for all."

"Tell us, Robert, did not our ancestors recognize the facts of the situation you have described? Did they not see that this glut of men indicated something out of order in the social arrangements?"

"Certainly. They professed to be much distressed over it. A large literature was devoted to discussing why there was not enough work to go around in a world in which so much more work evidently needed to be done as indicated by its general poverty. The Congresses and Legislatures were constantly appointing commissions of learned men to investigate and report on the subject."

"And did these learned men ascribe it to its obvious cause as the necessary effect of the profit system to maintain and constantly increase a gap between the consuming and producing power of the community?"

"Dear me, no! To have criticised the profit system would have been flat blasphemy. The learned men called it a problem--the problem of the unemployed--and gave it up as a conundrum. It was a favorite way our ancestors had of dodging questions which they could not answer without attacking vested interests to call them problems and give them up as insolvable mysteries of Divine Providence."

"There was one philosopher, Robert--an Englishman--who went to the bottom of this difficulty of the glut of men resulting from the profit system. He stated the only way possible to avoid the glut, provided the profit system was retained. Do you remember his name?"

"You mean Malthus, I suppose."

"Yes. What was his plan?"

"He advised poor people, as the only way to avoid starvation, not to get born--that is, I mean he advised poor people not to have children. This old fellow, as you say, was the only one of the lot who went to the root of the profit system, and saw that there was not room for it and for mankind on the earth. Regarding the profit system as a God-ordained necessity, there could be no doubt in his mind that it was mankind which must, under the circumstances, get off the earth. People called Malthus a cold-blooded philosopher. Perhaps he was, but certainly it was only common humanity that, so long as the profit system lasted, a red flag should be hung out on the planet, warning souls not to land except at their own risk."

EMILY SHOWS THE NECESSITY OF WASTE PIPES.

"I quite agree with you, Robert," said the teacher, "and now, Emily, we will ask you to take us in charge as we pursue a little further this interesting, if not very edifying theme. The economic system of production and distribution by which a nation lives may fitly be compared to a cistern with a supply pipe, representing production, by which water is pumped in; and an escape pipe, representing consumption, by which the product is disposed of. When the cistern is scientifically constructed the supply pipe and escape pipe correspond in capacity, so that the water may be drawn off as fast as supplied, and none be wasted by overflow. Under the profit system of our ancestors, however, the arrangement was different. Instead of corresponding in capacity with the supply pipe representing production, the outlet representing consumption was half or two thirds shut off by the water-gate of profits, so that it was not able to carry off more than, say, a half or a third of the supply that was pumped into the cistern through the feed pipe of production. Now, Emily, what would be the natural effect of such a lack of correspondence between the inlet and the outlet capacity of the cistern?"

"Obviously," replied the girl who answered to the name of Emily, "the effect would be to clog the cistern, and compel the pumps to slow down to half or one third of their capacity--namely, to the capacity of the escape pipe."

"But," said the teacher, "suppose that in the case of the cistern used by our ancestors the effect of slowing down the pump of production was to diminish still further the capacity of the escape pipe of consumption, already much too small, by depriving the working masses of even the small purchasing power they had before possessed in the form of wages for labor or prices for produce."

"Why, in that case," replied the girl, "it is evident that since slowing down production only checked instead of hastening relief by consumption, there would be no way to avoid a stoppage of the whole service except to relieve the pressure in the cistern by opening waste pipes."

"Precisely so. Well, now, we are in a position to appreciate how necessary a part the waste pipes played in the economic system of our forefathers. We have seen that under that system the bulk of the people sold their labor or produce to the capitalists, but were unable to buy back and consume but a small part of the result of that labor or produce in the market, the rest remaining in the hands of the capitalists as profits. Now, the capitalists, being a very small body numerically, could consume upon their necessities but a petty part of these accumulated profits, and yet, if they did not get rid of them somehow, production would stop, for the capitalists absolutely controlled the initiative in production, and would have no motive to increase accumulations they could not dispose of. In proportion, moreover, as the capitalists from lack of use for more profits should slacken production, the mass of the people, finding none to hire them, or buy their produce to sell again, would lose what little consuming power they had before, and a still larger accumulation of products be left on the capitalists' hands. The question then is, How did the capitalists, after consuming all they could of their profits upon their own necessities, dispose of the surplus, so as to make room for more production?"

"Of course," said the girl Emily, "if the surplus products were to be so expended as to relieve the glut, the first point was that they must be expended in such ways that there should be no return, for them. They must be absolutely wasted--like water poured into the sea. This was accomplished by the use of the surplus products in the support of bodies of workers employed in unproductive kinds of labor. This waste labor was of two sorts--the first was that employed in wasteful industrial and commercial competition; the second was that employed in the means and services of luxury."

"Tell us about the wasteful expenditure of labor in competition."

"That was through the undertaking of industrial and commercial enterprises which were not called for by any increase in consumption, their object being merely the displacement of the enterprises of one capitalist by those of another."

"And was this a very large cause of waste?"

"Its magnitude may be inferred from the saying current at the time that ninety-five per cent of industrial and commercial enterprises failed, which merely meant that in this proportion of instances capitalists wasted their investments in trying to fill a demand which either did not exist or was supplied already. If that estimate were even a remote suggestion of the truth, it would serve to give an idea of the enormous amounts of accumulated profits which were absolutely wasted in competitive expenditure. And it must be remembered also that when a capitalist succeeded in displacing another and getting away his business the total waste of capital was just as great as if he failed, only in the one case it was the capital of the previous investor that was destroyed instead of the capital of the newcomer. In every country which had attained any degree of economic development there were many times more business enterprises in every line than there was business for, and many times as much capital already invested as there was a return for. The only way in which new capital could be put into business was by forcing out and destroying old capital already invested. The ever-mounting aggregation of profits seeking part of a market that was prevented from increasing by the effect of those very profits, created a pressure of competition among capitalists which, by all accounts that come down to us, must have been like a conflagration in its consuming effects upon capital.

"Now tell us something about the other great waste of profits by which the pressure in the cistern was sufficiently relieved to permit production to go on--that is to say, the expenditure of profits for the employment of labor in the service of luxury. What was luxury?"

"The term luxury, in referring to the state of society before the Revolution, meant the lavish expenditure of wealth by the rich to gratify a refined sensualism, while the masses of the people were suffering lack of the primary necessities."

"What were some of the modes of luxurious expenditure indulged in by the capitalists?"

"They were unlimited in variety, as, for example, the construction of costly palaces for residence and their decoration in royal style, the support of great retinues of servants, costly supplies for the table, rich equipages, pleasure ships, and all manner of boundless expenditure in fine raiment and precious stones. Ingenuity was exhausted in contriving devices by which the rich might waste the abundance the people were dying for. A vast army of laborers was constantly engaged in manufacturing an infinite variety of articles and appliances of elegance and ostentation which mocked the unsatisfied primary necessities of those who toiled to produce them."

"What have you to say of the moral aspect of this expenditure for luxury?"

"If the entire community had arrived at that stage of economic prosperity which would enable all alike to enjoy the luxuries equally," replied the girl, "indulgence in them would have been merely a question of taste. But this waste of wealth by the rich in the presence of a vast population suffering lack of the bare necessaries of life was an illustration of inhumanity that would seem incredible on the part of civilized people were not the facts so well substantiated. Imagine a company of persons sitting down with enjoyment to a banquet, while on the floors and all about the corners of the banquet hall were groups of fellow-beings dying with want and following with hungry eyes every morsel the feasters lifted to their mouths. And yet that precisely describes the way in which the rich used to spend their profits in the great cities of America, France, England, and Germany before the Revolution, the one difference being that the needy and the hungry, instead of being in the banquet room itself, were just outside on the street."

"It was claimed, was it not, by the apologists of the luxurious expenditure of the capitalists that they thus gave employment to many who would otherwise have lacked it?"

"And why would they have lacked employment? Why were the people glad to find employment in catering to the luxurious pleasures and indulgences of the capitalists, selling themselves to the most frivolous and degrading uses? It was simply because the profit taking of these same capitalists, by reducing the consuming power of the people to a fraction of its producing power, had correspondingly limited the field of productive employment, in which under a rational system there must always have been work for every hand until all needs were satisfied, even as there is now. In excusing their luxurious expenditure on the ground you have mentioned, the capitalists pleaded the results of one wrong to justify the commission of another."

"The moralists of all ages," said the teacher, "condemned the luxury of the rich. Why did their censures effect no change?"

"Because they did not understand the economics of the subject. They failed to see that under the profit system the absolute waste of the excess of profits in unproductive expenditure was an economic necessity, if production was to proceed, as you showed in comparing it with the cistern. The waste of profits in luxury was an economic necessity, to use another figure, precisely as a running sore is a necessary vent in some cases for the impurities of a diseased body. Under our system of equal sharing, the wealth of a community is freely and equally distributed among its members as is the blood in a healthy body. But when, as under the old system, that wealth was concentrated in the hands of a portion of the community, it lost its vitalizing quality, as does the blood when congested in particular organs, and like that becomes an active poison, to be got rid of at any cost. Luxury in this way might be called an ulcer, which must be kept open if the profit system was to continue on any terms."

"You say," said the teacher, "that in order that production should go on it was absolutely necessary to get the excess of profits wasted in some sort of unproductive expenditure. But might not the profit takers have devised some way of getting rid of the surplus more intelligent than mere competition to displace one another, and more consistent with humane feeling than wasting wealth upon refinements of sensual indulgence in the presence of a needy multitude?"

"Certainly. If the capitalists had cared at all about the humane aspect of the matter, they could have taken a much less demoralizing method in getting rid of the obstructive surplus. They could have periodically made a bonfire of it as a burnt sacrifice to the god Profit, or, if they preferred, it might have been carried out in scows beyond soundings and dumped there."

"It is easy to see," said the teacher, "that from a moral point of view such a periodical bonfire or dump would have been vastly more edifying to gods and men than was the actual practice of expending it in luxuries which mocked the bitter want of the mass. But how about the economic operation of this plan?"

"It would have been as advantageous economically as morally. The process of wasting the surplus profits in competition and luxury was slow and protracted, and meanwhile productive industry languished and the workers waited in idleness and want for the surplus to be so far reduced as to make room for more production. But if the surplus at once, on being ascertained, were destroyed, productive industry would go right on."

"But how about the workmen employed by the capitalists in ministering to their luxuries? Would they not have been thrown out of work if luxury had been given up?"

"On the contrary, under the bonfire system there would have been a constant demand for them in productive employment to provide material for the blaze, and that surely would have been a far more worthy occupation than helping the capitalists to consume in folly the product of their brethren employed in productive industry. But the greatest advantage of all which would have resulted from the substitution of the bonfire for luxury remains to be mentioned. By the time the nation had made a few such annual burnt offerings to the principle of profit, perhaps even after the first one, it is likely they would begin to question, in the light of such vivid object lessons, whether the moral beauties of the profit system were sufficient compensation for so large an economic sacrifice."

CHARLES REMOVES AN APPREHENSION.

"Now, Charles," said the teacher, "you shall help us a little on a point of conscience. We have, one and another, told a very bad story about the profit system, both in its moral and its economic aspects. Now, is it not possible that we have done it injustice? Have we not painted too black a picture? From an ethical point of view we could indeed scarcely have done so, for there are no words strong enough to justly characterize the mock it made of all the humanities. But have we not possibly asserted too strongly its economic imbecility and the hopelessness of the world's outlook for material welfare so long as it should be tolerated? Can you reassure us on this point?"

"Easily," replied the lad Charles. "No more conclusive testimony to the hopelessness of the economic outlook under private capitalism could be desired than is abundantly given by the nineteenth-century economists themselves. While they seemed quite incapable of imagining anything different from private capitalism as the basis of an economic system, they cherished no illusions as to its operation. Far from trying to comfort mankind by promising that if present ills were bravely borne matters would grow better, they expressly taught that the profit system must inevitably result at some time not far ahead in the arrest of industrial progress and a stationary condition of production."

"How did they make that out?"

"They recognized, as we do, the tendency under private capitalism of rents, interest, and profits to accumulate as capital in the hands of the capitalist class, while, on the other hand, the consuming power of the masses did not increase, but either decreased or remained practically stationary. From this lack of equilibrium between production and consumption it followed that the difficulty of profitably employing capital in productive industry must increase as the accumulations of capital so disposable should grow. The home market having been first, glutted with products and afterward the foreign market, the competition of the capitalists to find productive employment for their capital would lead them, after having reduced wages to the lowest possible point, to bid for what was left of the market by reducing their own profits to the minimum point at which it was worth while to risk capital. Below this point more capital would not be invested in business. Thus the rate of wealth production would cease to advance, and become stationary."

"This, you say, is what the nineteenth-century economists themselves taught concerning the outcome of the profit system?"

"Certainly. I could, quote from their standard books any number of passages foretelling this condition of things, which, indeed, it required no prophet to foretell."

"How near was the world--that is, of course, the nations whose industrial evolution had gone farthest--to this condition when the Revolution came?"

"They were apparently on its verge. The more economically advanced countries had generally exhausted their home markets and were struggling desperately for what was left of foreign markets. The rate of interest, which indicated the degree to which capital had become glutted, had fallen in England to two per cent and in America within thirty years had sunk from seven and six to five and three and four per cent, and was falling year by year. Productive industry had become generally clogged, and proceeded by fits and starts. In America the wage-earners were becoming proletarians, and the farmers fast sinking into the state of a tenantry. It was indeed the popular discontent caused by these conditions, coupled with apprehension of worse to come, which finally roused the people at the close of the nineteenth century to the necessity of destroying private capitalism for good and all."

"And do I understand, then, that this stationary condition, after which no increase in the rate of wealth production could be looked for, was setting in while yet the primary needs of the masses remained unprovided for?"

"Certainly. The satisfaction of the needs of the masses, as we have abundantly seen, was in no way recognized as a motive for production under the profit system. As production approached the stationary point the misery of the people would, in fact, increase as a direct result of the competition among capitalists to invest their glut of capital in business. In order to do so, as has already been shown, they sought to reduce the prices of products, and that meant the reduction of wages to wage-earners and prices to first producers to the lowest possible point before any reduction in the profits of the capitalist was considered. What the old economists called the stationary condition of production meant, therefore, the perpetuation indefinitely of the maximum degree of hardship endurable by the people at large."

"That will do, Charles; you have said enough to relieve any apprehension that possibly we were doing injustice to the profit system. Evidently that could not be done to a system of which its own champions foretold such an outcome as you have described. What, indeed, could be added to the description they give of it in these predictions of the stationary condition as a programme of industry confessing itself at the end of its resources in the midst of a naked and starving race? This was the good time coming, with the hope of which the nineteenth-century economists cheered the cold and hungry world of toilers--a time when, being worse off than ever, they must abandon forever even the hope of improvement. No wonder our forefathers described their so-called political economy as a dismal science, for never was there a pessimism blacker, a hopelessness more hopeless than it preached. Ill indeed had it been for humanity if it had been truly a science.

ESTHER COUNTS THE COST OF THE PROFIT SYSTEM.

"Now, Esther," the teacher pursued, "I am going to ask you to do a little estimating as to about how much the privilege of retaining the profit system cost our forefathers. Emily has given us an idea of the magnitude of the two great wastes of profits--the waste of competition and the waste of luxury. Now, did the capital wasted in these two ways represent all that the profit system cost the people?"

"It did not give a faint idea of it, much less represent it," replied the girl Esther. "The aggregate wealth wasted respectively in competition and luxury, could it have been distributed equally for consumption among the people, would undoubtedly have considerably raised the general level of comfort. In the cost of the profit system to a community, the wealth wasted by the capitalists was, however, an insignificant item. The bulk of that cost consisted in the effect of the profit system to prevent wealth from being produced, in holding back and tying down the almost boundless wealth-producing power of man. Imagine the mass of the population, instead of being sunk in poverty and a large part of them in bitter want, to have received sufficient to satisfy all their needs and give them ample, comfortable lives, and estimate the amount of additional wealth which it would have been necessary to produce to meet this standard of consumption. That will give you a basis for calculating the amount of wealth which the American people or any people of those days might and would have produced but for the profit system. You may estimate that this would have meant a fivefold, sevenfold, or tenfold increase of production, as you please to guess.

"But tell us this: Would it have been possible for the people of America, say, in the last quarter of the nineteenth century, to have multiplied their production at such a rate if consumption had demanded it?"

"Nothing is more certain than that they could easily have done so. The progress of invention had been so great in the nineteenth century as to multiply from twentyfold to many hundredfold the productive power of industry. There was no time during the last quarter of the century in America or in any of the advanced countries when the existing productive plants could not have produced enough in six months to have supplied the total annual consumption as it actually was. And those plants could have been multiplied indefinitely. In like manner the agricultural product of the country was always kept far within its possibility, for a plentiful crop under the profit system meant ruinous prices to the farmers. As has been said, it was an admitted proposition of the old economists that there was no visible limit to production if only sufficient demand for consumption could be secured."

"Can you recall any instance in history in which it can be argued that a people paid so large a price in delayed and prevented development for the privilege of retaining any other tyranny as they did for keeping the profit system?"

"I am sure there never was such another instance, and I will tell you why I think so. Human progress has been delayed at various stages by oppressive institutions, and the world has leaped forward at their overthrow. But there was never before a time when the conditions had been so long ready and waiting for so great and so instantaneous a forward movement all along the line of social improvement as in the period preceding the Revolution. The mechanical and industrial forces, held in check by the profit system, only required to be unleashed to transform the economic condition of the race as by magic. So much for the material cost of the profit system to our forefathers; but, vast as that was, it is not worth considering for a moment in comparison with its cost in human happiness. I mean the moral cost in wrong and tears and black negations and stifled moral possibilities which the world paid for every day's retention of private capitalism: there are no words adequate to express the sum of that."

NO POLITICAL ECONOMY BEFORE THE REVOLUTION.

"That will do, Esther.--Now, George, I want you to tell us just a little about a particular body among the learned class of the nineteenth century, which, according to the professions of its members, ought to have known and to have taught the people all that we have so easily perceived as to the suicidal character of the profit system and the economic perdition it meant for mankind so long as it should be tolerated. I refer to the political economists."

"There were no political economists before the Revolution," replied the lad.

"But there certainly was a large class of learned men who called themselves political economists."

"Oh, yes; but they labeled themselves wrongly."

"How do you make that out?"

"Because there was not, until the Revolution--except, of course, among those who sought to bring it to pass--any conception whatever of what political economy is."

"What is it?"

"Economy," replied the lad, "means the wise husbandry of wealth in production and distribution. Individual economy is the science of this husbandry when conducted in the interest of the individual without regard to any others. Family economy is this husbandry carried on for the advantage of a family group without regard to other groups. Political economy, however, can only mean the husbandry of wealth for the greatest advantage of the political or social body, the whole number of the citizens constituting the political organization. This sort of husbandry necessarily implies a public or political regulation of economic affairs for the general interest. But before the Revolution there was no conception of such an economy, nor any organization to carry it out. All systems and doctrines of economy previous to that time were distinctly and exclusively private and individual in their whole theory and practice. While in other respects our forefathers did in various ways and degrees recognize a social solidarity and a political unity with proportionate rights and duties, their theory and practice as to all matters touching the getting and sharing of wealth were aggressively and brutally individualistic, antisocial, and unpolitical."

"Have you ever looked over any of the treatises which our forefathers called political economies, at the Historical Library?"

"I confess," the boy answered, "that the title of the leading work under that head was enough for me. It was called The Wealth of Nations. That would be an admirable title for a political economy nowadays, when the production and distribution of wealth are conducted altogether by and for the people collectively; but what meaning could it conceivably have had as applied to a book written nearly a hundred years before such a thing as a national economic organization was thought of, with the sole view of instructing capitalists how to get rich at the cost of, or at least in total disregard of, the welfare of their fellow-citizens? I noticed too that quite a common subtitle used for these so-called works on political economy was the phrase 'The Science of Wealth.' Now what could an apologist of private capitalism and the profit system possibly have to say about the science of wealth? The A B C of any science of wealth production is the necessity of co-ordination and concert of effort; whereas competition, conflict, and endless cross-purposes were the sum and substance of the economic methods set forth by these writers."

"And yet," said the teacher, "the only real fault of these so-called books on Political Economy consists in the absurdity of the title. Correct that, and their value as documents of the times at once becomes evident. For example, we might call them 'Examinations into the Economic and Social Consequences of trying to get along without any Political Economy.' A title scarcely less fit would perhaps be 'Studies into the Natural Course of Economic Affairs when left to Anarchy by the Lack of any Regulation in the General Interest.' It is, when regarded in this light, as painstaking and conclusive expositions of the ruinous effects of private capitalism upon the welfare of communities, that we perceive the true use and value of these works. Taking up in detail the various phenomena of the industrial and commercial world of that day, with their reactions upon the social status, their authors show how the results could not have been other than they were, owing to the laws of private capitalism, and that it was nothing but weak sentimentalism to suppose that while those laws continued in operation any different results could be obtained, however good men's intentions. Although somewhat heavy in style for popular reading, I have often thought that during the revolutionary period no documents could have been better calculated to convince rational men who could be induced to read them, that it was absolutely necessary to put an end to private capitalism if humanity were ever to get forward.

"The fatal and quite incomprehensible mistake of their authors was that they did not themselves see this, conclusion and preach it. Instead of that they committed the incredible blunder of accepting a set of conditions that were manifestly mere barbaric survivals as the basis of a social science when they ought easily to have seen that the very idea of a scientific social order suggested the abolition of those conditions as the first step toward its realization.

"Meanwhile, as to the present lesson, there are two or three points to clear up before leaving it. We have been talking altogether of profit taking, but this was only one of the three main methods by which the capitalists collected the tribute from the toiling world by which their power was acquired and maintained. What were the other two?"

"Rent and interest."

"What was rent?"

"In those days," replied George, "the right to a reasonable and equal allotment of land for private uses did not belong as a matter of course to every person as it does now. No one was admitted to have any natural right to land at all. On the other hand, there was no limit to the extent of land, though it were a whole province, which any one might not legally possess if he could get hold of it. By natural consequence of this arrangement the strong and cunning had acquired most of the land, while the majority of the people were left with none at all. Now, the owner of the land had the right to drive any one off his land and have him punished for entering on it. Nevertheless, the people who owned n required to have it and to use it and must needs go to the capitalists for it. Rent was the price charged by capitalists for not driving people off their land."

"Did this rent represent any economic service of any sort rendered to the community by the rent receiver?"

"So far as regards the charge for the use of the land itself apart from improvements it represented no service of any sort, nothing but the waiver for a price of the owner's legal right of ejecting the occupant. It was not a charge for doing anything, but for not doing something."

"Now tell us about interest; what was that?"

"Interest was the price paid for the use of money. Nowadays the collective administration directs the industrial forces of the nation for the general welfare, but in those days all economic enterprises were for private profit, and their projectors had to hire the labor they needed with money. Naturally, the loan of so indispensable a means as this commanded a high price; that price was interest."

"And did interest represent any economic service to the community on the part of the interest taker in lending his money?"

"None whatever. On the contrary, it was by the very nature of the transaction, a waiver on the part of the lender of the power of action in favor of the borrower. It was a price charged for letting some one else do what the lender might have done but chose not to. It was a tribute levied by inaction upon action."

"If all the landlords and money lenders had died over night, would it have made any difference to the world?"

"None whatever, so long as they left the land and the money behind. Their economic role was a passive one, and in strong contrast with that of the profit-seeking capitalists, which, for good or bad, was at least active."

"What was the general effect of rent and interest upon the consumption and consequently the production of wealth by the community?"

"It operated to reduce both."

"How?"

"In the same way that profit taking did. Those who received rent were very few, those who paid it were nearly all. Those who received interest were few, and those who paid it many. Rent and interest meant, therefore, like profits, a constant drawing away of the purchasing power of the community at large and its concentration in the hands of a small part of it."

"What have you to say of these three processes as to their comparative effect in destroying the consuming power of the masses, and consequently the demand for production?"

"That differed in different ages and countries according to the stage of their economic development. Private capitalism has been compared to a three-horned bull, the horns being rent, profit, and interest, differing in comparative length and strength according to the age of the animal. In the United States, at the time covered by our lesson, profits were still the longest of the three horns, though the others were growing terribly fast."

"We have seen, George," said his teacher, "that from a period long before the great Revolution it was as true as it is now that the only limit to the production of wealth in society was its consumption. We have seen that what kept the world in poverty under private capitalism was the effect of profits, aided by rent and interest to reduce consumption and thus cripple production, by concentrating the purchasing power of the people in the hands of a few. Now, that was the wrong way of doing things. Before leaving the subject I want you to tell us in a word what is the right way. Seeing that production is limited by consumption, what rule must be followed in distributing the results of production to be consumed in order to develop consumption to the highest possible point, and thereby in turn to create the greatest possible demand for production."

"For that purpose the results of production must be distributed equally among all the members of the producing community."

"Show why that is so."

"It is a self-evident mathematical proposition. The more people a loaf of bread or any given thing is divided among, and the more equally it is divided, the sooner it will be consumed and more bread be called for. To put it in a more formal way, the needs of human beings result from the same natural constitution and are substantially the same. An equal distribution of the things needed by them is therefore that general plan by which the consumption of such things will be at once enlarged to the greatest possible extent and continued on that scale without interruption to the point of complete satisfaction for all. It follows that the equal distribution of products is the rule by which the largest possible consumption can be secured, and thus in turn the largest production be stimulated."

"What, on the other hand, would be the effect on consumption of an unequal division of consumable products?"

"If the division were unequal, the result would be that some would have more than they could consume in a given time, and others would have less than they could have consumed in the same time, the result meaning a reduction of total consumption below what it would have been for that time with an equal division of products. If a million dollars were equally divided among one thousand men, it would presently be wholly expended in the consumption of needed things, creating a demand for the production of as much more; but if concentrated in one man's hands, not a hundredth part of it, however great his luxury, would be likely to be so expended in the same period. The fundamental general law in the science of social wealth is, therefore, that the efficiency of a given amount of purchasing power to promote consumption is in exact proportion to its wide distribution, and is most efficient when equally distributed among the whole body of consumers because that is the widest possible distribution."

"You have not called attention to the fact that the formula of the greatest wealth production--namely, equal sharing of the product among the community--is also that application of the product which will cause the greatest sum of human happiness."

"I spoke strictly of the economic side of the subject."

"Would it not have startled the old economists to hear that the secret of the most efficient system of wealth production was conformity on a national scale to the ethical idea of equal treatment for all embodied by Jesus Christ in the golden rule?"

"No doubt, for they falsely taught that there were two kinds of science dealing with human conduct--one moral, the other economic; and two lines of reasoning as to conduct--the economic, and the ethical; both right in different ways. We know better. There can be but one science of human conduct in whatever field, and that is ethical. Any economic proposition which can not be stated in ethical terms is false. Nothing can be in the long run or on a large scale sound economics which is not sound ethics. It is not, therefore, a mere coincidence, but a logical necessity, that the supreme word of both ethics and economics should be one and the same--equality. The golden rule in its social application is as truly the secret of plenty as of peace."

CHAPTER XXIII.

"The Parable Of The Water Tank."

"That will do, George. We will close the session here. Our discussion, I find, has taken a broader range than I expected, and to complete the subject we shall need to have a brief session this afternoon.--And now, by way of concluding the morning, I propose to offer a little contribution of my own. The other day, at the museum, I was delving among the relics of literature of the great Revolution, with a view to finding something that might illustrate our theme. I came across a little pamphlet of the period, yellow and almost undecipherable, which, on examination, I found to be a rather amusing skit or satirical take-off on the profit system. It struck me that probably our lesson might prepare us to appreciate it, and I made a copy. It is entitled "The Parable of the Water Tank," and runs this way:

"'There was a certain very dry land, the people whereof were in sore need of water. And they did nothing but to seek after water from morning until night, and many perished because they could not find it.

"'Howbeit, there were certain men in that land who were more crafty and diligent than the rest, and these had gathered stores of water where others could find none, and the name of these men was called capitalists. And it came to pass that the people of the land came unto the capitalists and prayed them that they would give them of the water they had gathered that they might drink, for their need was sore. But the capitalists answered them and said:

"'"Go to, ye silly people! why should we give you of the water which we have gathered, for then we should become even as ye are, and perish with you? But behold what we will do unto you. Be ye our servants and ye shall have water."

"'And the people said, "Only give us to drink and we will be your servants, we and our children." And it was so.

"'Now, the capitalists were men of understanding, and wise in their generation. They ordered the people who were their servants in bands with captains and officers, and some they put at the springs to dip, and others did they make to carry the water, and others did they cause to seek for new springs. And all the water was brought together in one place, and there did the capitalists make a great tank for to hold it, and the tank was called the Market, for it was there that the people, even the servants of the capitalists, came to get water. And the capitalists said unto the people:

"'"For every bucket of water that ye bring to us, that we may pour it into the tank, which is the Market, behold! we will give you a penny, but for every bucket that we shall draw forth to give unto you that ye may drink of it, ye and your wives and your children, ye shall give to us two pennies, and the difference shall be our profit, seeing that if it were not for this profit we would not do this thing for you, but ye should all perish."

"'And it was good in the people's eyes, for they were dull of understanding, and they diligently brought water unto the tank for many days, and for every bucket which they did bring the capitalists gave them every man a penny; but for every bucket that the capitalists drew forth from the tank to give again unto the people, behold! the people rendered to the capitalists two pennies.

"'And after many days the water tank, which was the Market, overflowed at the top, seeing that for every bucket the people poured in they received only so much as would buy again half of a bucket. And because of the excess that was left of every bucket, did the tank overflow, for the people were many, but the capitalists were few, and could drink no more than others. Therefore did the tank overflow.

'"And when the capitalists saw that the water overflowed, they said to the people:

'"''See ye not the tank, which is the Market, doth overflow? Sit ye down, therefore and be patient, for ye shall bring us no more water till the tank be empty."

'"But when the people no more received the pennies of the capitalists for the water they brought, they could buy no more water from the capitalists, having naught wherewith to buy. And when the capitalists saw that they had no more profit because no man bought water of them, they were troubled. And they sent forth men in the highways, the byways, and the hedges, crying, "If any thirst let him come to the tank and buy water of us, for it doth overflow." For they said among themselves, "Behold, the times are dull; we must advertise."

'"But the people answered, saying: "How can we buy unless ye hire us, for how else shall we have wherewithal to buy? Hire ye us, therefore, as before, and we will gladly buy water, for we thirst, and ye will have no need to advertise." But the capitalists said to the people: "Shall we hire you to bring water when the tank, which is the Market, doth already overflow? Buy ye, therefore, first water, and when the tank is empty, through your buying, will we hire you again." And so it was because the capitalists hired them no more to bring water that the people could not buy the water they had brought already, and because the people could not buy the water they had brought already, the capitalists no more hired them to bring water. And the saying went abroad, "It is a crisis."

'"And the thirst of the people was great, for it was not now as it had been in the days of their fathers, when the land was open before them, for every one to seek water for himself, seeing that the capitalists had taken all the springs, and the wells, and the water wheels, and the vessels and the buckets, so that no man might come by water save from the tank, which was the Market. And the people murmured against the capitalists and said: "Behold, the tank runneth over, and we die of thirst. Give us, therefore, of the water, that we perish not."

'"But the capitalists answered: "Not so. The water is ours. Ye shall not drink thereof unless ye buy it of us with pennies." And they confirmed it with an oath, saying, after their manner, "Business is business."

'"But the capitalists were disquieted that the people bought no more water, whereby they had no more any profits, and they spake one to another, saying: "It seemeth that our profits have stopped our profits, and by reason of the profits we have made, we can make no more profits. How is it that our profits are become unprofitable to us, and our gains do make us poor? Let us therefore send for the soothsayers, that they may interpret this thing unto us," and they sent for them.

'"Now, the soothsayers were men learned in dark sayings, who joined themselves to the capitalists by reason of the water of the capitalists, that they might have thereof and live, they and their children. And they spake for the capitalists unto the people, and did their embassies for them, seeing that the capitalists were not a folk quick of understanding neither ready of speech.

'"And the capitalists demanded of the soothsayers that they should interpret this thing unto them, wherefore it was that the people bought no more water of them, although the tank was full. And certain of the soothsayers answered and said, "It is by reason of overproduction," and some said, "It is glut"; but the signification of the two words is the same. And others said, "Nay, but this thing is by reason of the spots on the sun." And yet others answered, saying, "It is neither by reason of glut, nor yet of spots on the sun that this evil hath come to pass, but because of lack of confidence."

"'And while the soothsayers contended among themselves, according to their manner, the men of profit did slumber and sleep, and when they awoke they said to the soothsayers: "It is enough. Ye have spoken comfortably unto us. Now go ye forth and speak comfortably likewise unto this people, so that they be at rest and leave us also in peace."

"'But the soothsayers, even the men of the dismal science--for so they were named of some--were loath to go forth to the people lest they should be stoned, for the people loved them not. And they said to the capitalists:

"'"Masters, it is a mystery of our craft that if men be full and thirst not but be at rest, then shall they find comfort in our speech even as ye. Yet if they thirst and be empty, find they no comfort therein but rather mock us, for it seemeth that unless a man be full our wisdom appeareth unto him but emptiness." But the capitalists said: "Go ye forth. Are ye not our men to do our embassies?"

"'And the soothsayers went forth to the people and expounded to them the mystery of overproduction, and how it was that they must needs perish of thirst because there was overmuch water, and how there could not be enough because there was too much. And likewise spoke they unto the people concerning the sun spots, and also wherefore it was that these things had come upon them by reason of lack of confidence. And it was even as the soothsayers had said, for to the people their wisdom seemed emptiness. And the people reviled them, saying: "Go up, ye bald-heads! Will ye mock us? Doth plenty breed famine? Doth nothing come out of much?" And they took up stones to stone them.

"'And when the capitalists saw that the people still murmured and would not give ear to the soothsayers, and because also they feared lest they should come upon the tank and take of the water by force, they brought forth to them certain holy men (but they were false priests), who spake unto the people that they should be quiet and trouble not the capitalists because they thirsted. And these holy men, who were false priests, testified to the people that this affliction was sent to them of God for the healing of their souls, and that if they should bear it in patience and lust not after the water, neither trouble the capitalists, it would come to pass that after they had given up the ghost they would come to a country where there should be no capitalists but an abundance of water. Howbeit, there were certain true prophets of God also, and these had compassion on the people and would not prophesy for the capitalists, but rather spake constantly against them.

"'Now, when the capitalists saw that the people still murmured and would not be still, neither for the words of the soothsayers nor of the false priests, they came forth themselves unto them and put the ends of their fingers in the water that overflowed in the tank and wet the tips thereof, and they scattered the drops from the tips of their fingers abroad upon the people who thronged the tank, and the name of the drops of water was charity, and they were exceeding bitter.

"'And when the capitalists saw yet again that neither for the words of the soothsayers, nor of the holy men who were false priests, nor yet for the drops that were called charity, would the people be still, but raged the more, and crowded upon the tank as if they would take it by force, then took they counsel together and sent men privily forth among the people. And these men sought out the mightiest among the people and all who had skill in war, and took them apart and spake craftily with them, saying:

"'"Come, now, why cast ye not your lot in with the capitalists? If ye will be their men and serve them against the people, that they break not in upon the tank, then shall ye have abundance of water, that ye perish not, ye and your children."

"'And the mighty men and they who were skilled in war hearkened unto this speech and suffered themselves to be persuaded, for their thirst constrained them, and they went within unto the capitalists and became their men, and staves and swords were put in their hands and they became a defense unto the capitalists and smote the people when they thronged upon the tank.

"'And after many days the water was low in the tank, for the capitalists did make fountains and fish ponds of the water thereof, and did bathe therein, they and their wives and their children, and did waste the water for their pleasure.

"'And when the capitalists saw that the tank was empty, they said, "The crisis is ended"; and they sent forth and hired the people that they should bring water to fill it again. And for the water that the people brought to the tank they received for every bucket a penny, but for the water which the capitalists drew forth from the tank to give again to the people they received two pennies, that they might have their profit. And after a time did the tank again overflow even as before.

"'And now, when many times the people had filled the tank until it overflowed and had thirsted till the water therein had been wasted by the capitalists, it came to pass that there arose in the land certain men who were called agitators, for that they did stir up the people. And they spake to the people, saying that they should associate, and then would they have no need to be servants of the capitalists and should thirst no more for water. And in the eyes of the capitalists were the agitators pestilent fellows, and they would fain have crucified them, but durst not for fear of the people.

"'And the words of the agitators which they spake to the people were on this wise:

"'"Ye foolish people, how long will ye be deceived by a lie and believe to your hurt that which is not? for behold all these things that have been said unto you by the capitalists and by the soothsayers are cunningly devised fables. And likewise the holy men, who say that it is the will of God that ye should always be poor and miserable and athirst, behold! they do blaspheme God and are liars, whom he will bitterly judge though he forgive all others. How cometh it that ye may not come by the water in the tank? Is it not because ye have no money? And why have ye no money? Is it not because ye receive but one penny for every bucket that ye bring to the tank, which is the Market, but must render two pennies for every bucket ye take out, so that the capitalists may have their profit? See ye not how by this means the tank must overflow, being filled by that ye lack and made to abound out of your emptiness? See ye not also that the harder ye toil and the more diligently ye seek and bring the water, the worse and not the better it shall be for you by reason of the profit, and that forever?"

"'After this manner spake the agitators for many days unto the people, and none heeded them, but it was so that after a time the people hearkened. And they answered and said unto the agitators:

"'"Ye say truth. It is because of the capitalists and of their profits that we want, seeing that by reason of them and their profits we may by no means come by the fruit of our labor, so that our labor is in vain, and the more we toil to fill the tank the sooner doth it overflow, and we may receive nothing because there is too much, according to the words of the soothsayers. But behold, the capitalists are hard men and their tender mercies are cruel. Tell us if ye know any way whereby we may deliver ourselves out of our bondage unto them. But if ye know of no certain way of deliverance we beseech you to hold your peace and let us alone, that we may forget our misery."

"'And the agitators answered and said, "We know a way."

"'And the people said: "Deceive us not, for this thing hath been from the beginning, and none hath found a way of deliverance until now, though many have sought it carefully with tears. But if ye know a way, speak unto us quickly."

"'Then the agitators spake unto the people of the way. And they said:

"'"Behold, what need have ye at all of these capitalists, that ye should yield them profits upon your labor? What great thing do they wherefore ye render them this tribute? Lo! it is only because they do order you in bands and lead you out and in and set your tasks and afterward give you a little of the water yourselves have brought and not they. Now, behold the way out of this bondage! Do ye for yourselves that which is done by the capitalists--namely, the ordering of your labor, and the marshaling of your bands, and the dividing of your tasks. So shall ye have no need at all of the capitalists and no more yield to them any profit, but all the fruit of your labor shall ye share as brethren, every one having the same; and so shall the tank never overflow until every man is full, and would not wag the tongue for more, and afterward shall ye with the overflow make pleasant fountains and fish ponds to delight yourselves withal even as did the capitalists; but these shall be for the delight of all."

"'And the people answered, "How shall we go about to do this thing, for it seemeth good to us?"

"'And the agitators answered: "Choose ye discreet men to go in and out before you and to marshal your bands and order your labor, and these men shall be as the capitalists were; but, behold, they shall not be your masters as the capitalists are, but your brethren and officers who do your will, and they shall not take any profits, but every man his share like the others, that there may be no more masters and servants among you, but brethren only. And from time to time, as ye see fit, ye shall choose other discreet men in place of the first to order the labor."

"'And the people hearkened, and the thing was very good to them. Likewise seemed it not a hard thing. And with one voice they cried out, "So let it be as ye have said, for we will do it!"

"'And the capitalists heard the noise of the shouting and what the people said, and the soothsayers heard it also, and likewise the false priests and the mighty men of war, who were a defense unto the capitalists; and when they heard they trembled exceedingly, so that their knees smote together, and they said one to another, "It is the end of us!"

"'Howbeit, there were certain true priests of the living God who would not prophesy for the capitalists, but had compassion on the people; and when they heard the shouting of the people and what they said, they rejoiced with exceeding great joy, and gave thanks to God because of the deliverance.

"'And the people went and did all the things that were told them of the agitators to do. And it came to pass as the agitators had said, even according to all their words. And there was no more any thirst in that land, neither any that was ahungered, nor naked, nor cold, nor in any manner of want; and every man said unto his fellow, "My brother," and every woman said unto her companion, "My sister," for so were they with one another as brethren and sisters which do dwell together in unity. And the blessing of God rested upon that land forever.'"

CHAPTER XXIV.

I Am Shown All The Kingdoms Of The Earth.

The boys and girls of the political-economy class rose to their feet at the teacher's word of dismissal, and in the twinkling of an eye the scene which had been absorbing my attention disappeared, and I found myself staring at Dr. Leete's smiling countenance and endeavoring to imagine how I had come to be where I was. During the greater part and all the latter part of the session of the class so absolute had been the illusion of being actually present in the schoolroom, and so absorbing the interest of the theme, that I had quite forgotten the extraordinary device by which I was enabled to see and hear the proceedings. Now, as I recalled it, my mind reverted with an impulse of boundless curiosity to the electroscope and the processes by which it performed its miracles.

Having given me some explanation of the mechanical operation of the apparatus and the way in which it served the purpose of a prolonged optic nerve, the doctor went on to exhibit its powers on a large scale. During the following hour, without leaving my chair, I made the tour of the earth, and learned by the testimony of my senses that the transformation which had come over Boston since my former life was but a sample of that which the whole world of men had undergone. I had but to name a great city or a famous locality in any country to be at once present there so far as sight and hearing were concerned. I looked down on modern New York, then upon Chicago, upon San Francisco, and upon New Orleans, finding each of these cities quite unrecognizable but for the natural features which constituted their setting. I visited London. I heard the Parisians talk French and the Berlinese talk German, and from St. Petersburg went to Cairo by way of Delhi. One city would be bathed in the noonday sun; over the next I visited, the moon, perhaps, was rising and the stars coming out; while over the third the silence of midnight brooded. In Paris, I remember, it was raining hard, and in London fog reigned supreme. In St. Petersburg there was a snow squall. Turning from the contemplation of the changing world of men to the changeless face of Nature, I renewed my old-time acquaintance with the natural wonders of the earth--the thundering cataracts, the stormy ocean shores, the lonely mountain tops, the great rivers, the glittering splendors of the polar regions, and the desolate places of the deserts.

Meanwhile the doctor explained to me that not only the telephone and electroscope were always connected with a great number of regular stations commanding all scenes of special interest, but that whenever in any part of the world there occurred a spectacle or accident of particular interest, special connections were instantly made, so that all mankind could at once see what the situation was for themselves without need of actual or alleged special artists on the spot.

With all my conceptions of time and space reduced to chaos, and well-nigh drunk with wonder, I exclaimed at last:

"I can stand no more of this just now! I am beginning to doubt seriously whether I am in or out of the body."

As a practical way of settling that question the doctor proposed a brisk walk, for we had not been out of the house that morning.

"Have we had enough of economics for the day?" he asked as we left the house, "or would you like to attend the afternoon session the teacher spoke of?"

I replied that I wished to attend it by all means.

"Very good," said the doctor; "it will doubtless be very short, and what do you say to attending it this time in person? We shall have plenty of time for our walk and can easily get to the school before the hour by taking a car from any point. Seeing this is the first time you have used the electroscope, and have no assurance except its testimony that any such school or pupils really exist, perhaps it would help to confirm any impressions you may have received to visit the spot in the body."

CHAPTER XXV.

The Strikers.

Presently, as we were crossing Boston Common, absorbed in conversation, a shadow fell athwart the way, and looking up, I saw towering above us a sculptured group of heroic size.

"Who are these?" I exclaimed.

"You ought to know if any one," said the doctor. "They are contemporaries of yours who were making a good deal of disturbance in your day."

But, indeed, it had only been as an involuntary expression of surprise that I had questioned what the figures stood for.

Let me tell you, readers of the twentieth century, what I saw up there on the pedestal, and you will recognize the world-famous group. Shoulder to shoulder, as if rallied to resist assault, were three figures of men in the garb of the laboring class of my time. They were bareheaded, and their coarse-textured shirts, rolled above the elbow and open at the breast, showed the sinewy arms and chest. Before them, on the ground, lay a pair of shovels and a pickaxe. The central figure, with the right hand extended, palm outward, was pointing to the discarded tools. The arms of the other two were folded on their breasts. The faces were coarse and hard in outline and bristled with unkempt beards. Their expression was one of dogged defiance, and their gaze was fixed with such scowling intensity upon the void space before them that I involuntarily glanced behind me to see what they were looking at. There were two women also in the group, as coarse of dress and features as the men. One was kneeling before the figure on the right, holding up to him with one arm an emaciated, half-clad infant, while with the other she indicated the implements at his feet with an imploring gesture. The second of the women was plucking by the sleeve the man on the left as if to draw him back, while with the other hand she covered her eyes. But the men heeded the women not at all, or seemed, in their bitter wrath, to know that they were there.

"Why," I exclaimed, "these are strikers!"

"Yes," said the doctor, "this is The Strikers, Huntington's masterpiece, considered the greatest group of statuary in the city and one of the greatest in the country."

"Those people are alive!" I said.

"That is expert testimony," replied the doctor. "It is a pity Huntington died too soon to hear it. He would have been pleased."

Now, I, in common with the wealthy and cultured class generally, of my day, had always held strikers in contempt and abhorrence, as blundering, dangerous marplots, as ignorant of their own best interests as they were reckless of other people's, and generally as pestilent fellows, whose demonstrations, so long as they were not violent, could not unfortunately be repressed by force, but ought always to be condemned, and promptly put down with an iron hand the moment there was an excuse for police interference. There was more or less tolerance among the well-to-do, for social reformers, who, by book or voice, advocated even very radical economic changes so long as they observed the conventionalities of speech, but for the striker there were few apologists. Of course, the capitalists emptied on him the vials of their wrath and contempt, and even people who thought they sympathized with the working class shook their heads at the mention of strikes, regarding them as calculated rather to hinder than help the emancipation of labor. Bred as I was in these prejudices, it may not seem strange that I was taken aback at finding such unpromising subjects selected for the highest place in the city.

"There is no doubt as to the excellence of the artist's work," I said, "but what was there about the strikers that has made you pick them out of our generation as objects of veneration?"

"We see in them," replied the doctor, "the pioneers in the revolt against private capitalism which brought in the present civilization. We honor them as those who, like Winkelried, 'made way for liberty, and died.' We revere in them the protomartyrs of co-operative industry and economic equality."

"But I can assure you, doctor, that these fellows, at least in my day, had not the slightest idea of revolting against private capitalism as a system. They were very ignorant and quite incapable of grasping so large a conception. They had no notion of getting along without capitalists. All they imagined as possible or desirable was a little better treatment by their employers, a few cents more an hour, a few minutes less working time a day, or maybe merely the discharge of an unpopular foreman. The most they aimed at was some petty improvement in their condition, to attain which they did not hesitate to throw the whole industrial machine into disorder."

"All which we moderns know quite well," replied the doctor. "Look at those faces. Has the sculptor idealized them? Are they the faces of philosophers? Do they not bear out your statement that the strikers, like the working-men generally, were, as a rule, ignorant, narrow-minded men, with no grasp of large questions, and incapable of so great an idea as the overthrow of an immemorial economic order? It is quite true that until some years after you fell asleep they did not realize that their quarrel was with private capitalism and not with individual capitalists. In this slowness of awakening to the full meaning of their revolt they were precisely on a par with the pioneers of all the great liberty revolutions. The minutemen at Concord and Lexington, in 1775, did not realize that they were pointing their guns at the monarchical idea. As little did the third estate of France, when it entered the Convention in 1789, realize that its road lay over the ruins of the throne. As little did the pioneers of English freedom, when they began to resist the will of Charles I, foresee that they would be compelled, before they got through, to take his head. In none of these instances, however, has posterity considered that the limited foresight of the pioneers as to the full consequences of their action lessened the world's debt to the crude initiative, without which the fuller triumph would never have come. The logic of the strike meant the overthrow of the irresponsible conduct of industry, whether the strikers knew it or not, and we can not rejoice in the consequences of that overthrow without honoring them in a way which very likely, as you intimate, would surprise them, could they know of it, as much as it does you. Let me try to give you the modern point of view as to the part played by their originals." We sat down upon one of the benches before the statue, and the doctor went on:

"My dear Julian, who was it, pray, that first roused the world of your day to the fact that there was an industrial question, and by their pathetic demonstrations of passive resistance to wrong for fifty years kept the public attention fixed on that question till it was settled? Was it your statesmen, perchance your economists, your scholars, or any other of your so-called wise men? No. It was just those despised, ridiculed, cursed, and hooted fellows up there on that pedestal who with their perpetual strikes would not let the world rest till their wrong, which was also the whole world's wrong, was righted. Once more had God chosen the foolish things of this world to confound the wise, the weak things to confound the mighty.

"In order to realize how powerfully these strikes operated to impress upon the people the intolerable wickedness and folly of private capitalism, you must remember that events are what teach men, that deeds have a far more potent educating influence than any amount of doctrine, and especially so in an age like yours, when the masses had almost no culture or ability to reason. There were not lacking in the revolutionary period many cultured men and women, who, with voice and pen, espoused the workers' cause, and showed them the way out; but their words might well have availed little but for the tremendous emphasis with which they were confirmed by the men up there, who starved to prove them true. Those rough-looking fellows, who probably could not have constructed a grammatical sentence, by their combined efforts, were demonstrating the necessity of a radically new industrial system by a more convincing argument than any rhetorician's skill could frame. When men take their lives in their hands to resist oppression, as those men did, other men are compelled to give heed to them. We have inscribed on the pedestal yonder, where you see the lettering, the words, which the action of the group above seems to voice:

"'We can bear no more. It is better to starve than live on the terms you give us. Our lives, the lives of our wives and of our children, we set against your gains. If you put your foot upon our neck, we will bite your heel!'

"This was the cry," pursued the doctor, "of men made desperate by oppression, to whom existence through suffering had become of no value. It was the same cry that in varied form but in one sense has been the watchword of every revolution that has marked an advance of the race-- 'Give us liberty, or give us death!' and never did it ring out with a cause so adequate, or wake the world to an issue so mighty, as in the mouths of these first rebels against the folly and the tyranny of private capital.

"In your age, I know, Julian," the doctor went on in a gentler tone, "it was customary to associate valor with the clang of arms and the pomp and circumstance of war. But the echo of the fife and drum comes very faintly up to us, and moves us not at all. The soldier has had his day, and passed away forever with the ideal of manhood which he illustrated. But that group yonder stands for a type of self-devotion that appeals to us profoundly. Those men risked their lives when they flung down the tools of their trade, as truly as any soldiers going into battle, and took odds as desperate, and not only for themselves, but for their families, which no grateful country would care for in case of casualty to them. The soldier went forth cheered with music, and supported by the enthusiasm of the country, but these others were covered with ignominy and public contempt, and their failures and defeats were hailed with general acclamation. And yet they sought not the lives of others, but only that they might barely live; and though they had first thought of the welfare of themselves, and those nearest them, yet not the less were they fighting the fight of humanity and posterity in striking in the only way they could, and while yet no one else dared strike at all, against the economic system that had the world by the throat, and would never relax its grip by dint of soft words, or anything less than disabling blows. The clergy, the economists and the pedagogues, having left these ignorant men to seek as they might the solution of the social problem, while they themselves sat at ease and denied that there was any problem, were very voluble in their criticisms of the mistakes of the workingmen, as if it were possible to make any mistake in seeking a way out of the social chaos, which could be so fatuous or so criminal as the mistake of not trying to seek any. No doubt, Julian, I have put finer words in the mouths of those men up there than their originals might have even understood, but if the meaning was not in their words it was in their deeds. And it is for what they did, not for what they said, that we honor them as protomartyrs of the industrial republic of to-day, and bring our children, that they may kiss in gratitude the rough-shod feet of those who made the way for us."

My experiences since I waked up in this year 2000 might be said to have consisted of a succession of instantaneous mental readjustments of a revolutionary character, in which what had formerly seemed evil to me had become good, and what had seemed wisdom had become foolishness. Had this conversation about the strikers taken place anywhere else, the entirely new impression I had received of the part played by them in the great social revolution of which I shared the benefit would simply have been one more of these readjustments, and the process entirely a mental one. But the presence of this wondrous group, the lifelikeness of the figures growing on my gaze as I listened to the doctor's words, imparted a peculiar personal quality--if I may use the term--to the revulsion of feeling that I experienced. Moved by an irresistible impulse, I rose to my feet, and, removing my hat, saluted the grim forms whose living originals I had joined my contemporaries in reviling.

The doctor smiled gravely.

"Do you know, my boy," he said, "it is not often that the whirligig of Time brings round his revenges in quite so dramatic a way as this?"

CHAPTER XXVI.

Foreign Commerce Under Profits; Protection And Free Trade, Or Between The Devil And The Deep Sea.

We arrived at the Arlington School some time before the beginning of the recitation which we were to attend, and the doctor took the opportunity to introduce me to the teacher. He was extremely interested to learn that I had attended the morning session, and very desirous to know something of my impressions. As to the forthcoming recitation, he suggested that if the members of the class were aware that they had so distinguished an auditor, it would be likely to embarrass them, and he should therefore say nothing about my presence until the close of the session, when he should crave the privilege of presenting his pupils to me personally. He hoped I would permit this, as it would be for them the event of a lifetime which their grandchildren would never tire of hearing them describe. The entrance of the class interrupted our conversation, and the doctor and myself, having taken our seats in a gallery, where we could hear and see without being seen, the session at once began.

"This morning," said the teacher, "we confined ourselves for the sake of clearness to the effects of the profit system upon a nation or community considered as if it were alone in the world and without relations to other communities. There is no way in which such outside relations operated to negative any of the laws of profit which were brought out this morning, but they did operate to extend the effect of those laws in many interesting ways, and without some reference to foreign commerce our review of the profit system would be incomplete.

"In the so-called political economies of our forefathers we read a vast deal about the advantages to a country of having an international trade. It was supposed to be one of the great secrets of national prosperity, and a chief study of the nineteenth-century statesmen seems to have been to establish and extend foreign commerce.--Now, Paul, will you tell us the economic theory as to the advantages of foreign commerce?"

"It is based on the fact," said the lad Paul, "that countries differ in climate, natural resources, and other conditions, so that in some it is wholly impossible or very difficult to produce certain needful things, while it is very easy to produce certain other things in greater abundance than is needed. In former times also there were marked differences in the grade of civilization and the condition of the arts in different countries, which still further modified their respective powers in the production of wealth. This being so, it might obviously be for the mutual advantage of countries to exchange with one another what they could produce against what they could not produce at all or only with difficulty, and not merely thus secure many things which otherwise they must go without, but also greatly increase the total effectiveness of their industry by applying it to the sorts of production best fitted to their conditions. In order, however, that the people of the respective countries should actually derive this advantage or any advantage from foreign exchange, it would be necessary that the exchanges should be carried on in the general interest for the purpose of giving the people at large the benefit of them, as is done at the present day, when foreign commerce, like other economic undertakings, is carried on by the governments of the several countries. But there was, of course, no national agency to carry on foreign commerce in that day. The foreign trade, just like the internal processes of production and distribution, was conducted by the capitalists on the profit system. The result was that all the benefits of this fair sounding theory of foreign commerce were either totally nullified or turned into curses, and the international trade relations of the countries constituted merely a larger field for illustrating the baneful effects of the profit system and its power to turn good to evil and 'shut the gates of mercy on mankind.'"

HOW PROFITS NULLIFIED THE BENEFIT OF COMMERCE.

"Illustrate, please, the operation of the profit system in international trade."

"Let us suppose," said the boy Paul, "that America could produce grain and other food stuffs with great cheapness and in greater quantities than the people needed. Suppose, on the contrary, that England could produce food stuffs only with difficulty and in small quantities. Suppose, however, that England, on account of various conditions, could produce clothing and hardware much more cheaply and abundantly than America. In such a case it would seem that both countries would be gainers if Americans exchanged the food stuffs which it was so easy for them to produce for the clothing and hardware which it was so easy for the English to produce. The result would appear to promise a clear and equal gain for both people. But this, of course, is on the supposition that the exchange should be negotiated by a public agency for the benefit of the respective populations at large. But when, as in those days, the exchange was negotiated wholly by private capitalists competing for private profits at the expense of the communities, the result was totally different.

"The American grain merchant who exported grain to the English would be impelled, by the competition of other American grain merchants, to put his price to the English as low as possible, and to do that he would beat down to the lowest possible figure the American farmer who produced the grain. And not only must the American merchant sell as low as his American rivals, but he must also undersell the grain merchants of other grain-producing countries, such as Russia, Egypt, and India. And now let us see how much benefit the English people received from the cheap American grain. We will say that, owing to the foreign food supply, the cost of living declined one half or a third in England. Here would seem a great gain surely; but look at the other side of it. The English must pay for their grain by supplying the Americans with cloth and hardware. The English manufacturers of these things were rivals just as the American grain merchants were--each one desirous of capturing as large a part of the American market as he could. He must therefore, if possible, undersell his home rivals. Moreover, like the American grain merchant, the English manufacturer must contend with foreign rivals. Belgium and Germany made hardware and cloth very cheaply, and the Americans would exchange their grain for these commodities with the Belgians and the Germans unless the English sold cheaper. Now, the main element in the cost of making cloth and hardware was the wages paid for labor. A pressure was accordingly sure to be brought to bear by every English manufacturer upon his workmen to compel them to accept lower wages so that he might undersell his English rivals, and also cut under the German and Belgian manufacturers, who were trying to get the American trade. Now can the English workman live on less wages than before? Plainly he can, for his food supply has been greatly cheapened. Presently, therefore, he finds his wages forced down by as much as the cheaper food supply has cheapened his living, and so finds himself just where he was to start with before the American trade began. And now look again at the American farmer. He is now getting his imported clothing and tools much cheaper than before, and consequently the lowest living price at which he can afford to sell grain is considerably lower than before the English trade began--lower by so much, in fact, as he has saved on his tools and clothing. Of this, the grain merchant, of course, took prompt advantage, for unless he put his grain into the English market lower than other grain merchants, he would lose his trade, and Russia, Egypt, and India stood ready to flood England with grain if the Americans could not bid below them, and then farewell to cheap cloth and tools! So down presently went the price the American farmer received for his grain, until the reduction absorbed all that he had gained by the cheaper imported fabrics and hardware, and he, like his fellow-victim across the sea--the English iron worker or factory operative--was no better off than he was before English trade had been suggested.

"But was he as well off? Was either the American or the English worker as well off as before this interchange of products began, which, if rightly conducted, would have been so greatly beneficial to both? On the contrary, both alike were in important ways distinctly worse off. Each had indeed done badly enough before, but the industrial system on which they depended, being limited by the national borders, was comparatively simple and uncomplex, self-sustaining, and liable only to local and transient disturbances, the effect of which could be to some extent estimated, possibly remedied. Now, however, the English operatives and the American farmer had alike become dependent upon the delicate balance of a complex set of international adjustments liable at any moment to derangements that might take away their livelihood, without leaving them even the small satisfaction of understanding what hurt them. The prices of their labor or their produce were no longer dependent as before upon established local customs and national standards of living, but had become subject to determination by the pitiless necessities of a world-wide competition in which the American farmer and the English artisan were forced into rivalship with the Indian ryot, the Egyptian fellah, the half-starved Belgian miner, or the German weaver. In former ages, before international trade had become general, when one nation was down another was up, and there was always hope in looking over seas; but the prospect which the unlimited development of international commerce upon the profit system was opening to mankind the latter part of the nineteenth century was that of a world-wide standard of living fixed by the rate at which life could be supported by the worst-used races. International trade was already showing itself to be the instrumentality by which the world-wide plutocracy would soon have established its sway if the great Revolution had tarried."

"In the case of the supposed reciprocal trade between England and America, which you have used as an illustration," said the teacher, "you have assumed that the trade relation was an exchange of commodities on equal terms. In such a case it appears that the effect of the profit system was to leave the masses of both countries somewhat worse off than they would have been without foreign trade, the gain on both the American and English side inuring wholly to the manufacturing and trading capitalists. But in fact both countries in a trade relation were not usually on equal terms. The capitalists of one were often far more powerful than those of another, and had a stronger or older economic organization at their service. In that case what was the result?"

"The overwhelming competition of the capitalists of the stronger country crushed out the enterprises of the capitalists of the weaker country, the people of which consequently became wholly dependent upon the foreign capitalists for many productions which otherwise would have been produced at home to the profit of home capitalists, and in proportion as the capitalists of the dependent country were thus rendered economically incapable of resistance the capitalists of the stronger country regulated at their pleasure the terms of trade. The American colonies, in 1776, were driven to revolt against England by the oppression resulting from such a relation. The object of founding colonies, which was one of the main ends of seventeenth, eighteenth, and nineteenth century statesmanship, was to bring new communities into this relation of economic vassalage to the home capitalists, who, having beggared the home market by their profit, saw no prospect of making more except by fastening their suckers upon outside communities. Great Britain, whose capitalists were strongest of all, was naturally the leader in this policy, and the main end of her wars and her diplomacy for many centuries before the great Revolution was to obtain such colonies, and to secure from weaker nations trade concessions and openings--peaceably if possible, at the mouth of the cannon if necessary."

"How about the condition of the masses in a country thus reduced to commercial vassalage to the capitalists of another country? Was it necessarily worse than the condition of the masses of the superior country?"

"That did not follow at all. We must constantly keep in mind that the interests of the capitalists and of the people were not identical. The prosperity of the capitalists of a country by no means implied prosperity on the part of the population, nor the reverse. If the masses of the dependent country had not been exploited by foreign capitalists, they would have been by domestic capitalists. Both they and the working masses of the superior country were equally the tools and slaves of the capitalists, who did not treat workingmen any better on account of being their fellow countrymen than if they had been foreigners. It was the capitalists of the dependent country rather than the masses who suffered by the suppression of independent business enterprises."

BETWEEN THE DEVIL AND THE DEEP SEA.

"That will do, Paul.--We will now ask some information from you, Helen, as to a point which Paul's last words have suggested. During the eighteenth and nineteenth centuries a bitter controversy raged among our ancestors between two parties in opinion and politics, calling themselves, respectively, the Protectionists and the Free Traders, the former of whom held that it was well to shut out the competition of foreign capitalists in the market of a country by a tariff upon imports, while the latter held that no impediment should be allowed to the entirely free course of trade. What have you to say as to the merits of this controversy?"

"Merely," replied the girl called Helen, "that the difference between the two policies, so far as it affected the people at large, reduced itself to the question whether they preferred being fleeced by home or foreign capitalists. Free trade was the cry of the capitalists who felt themselves able to crush those of rival nations if allowed the opportunity to compete with them. Protection was the cry of the capitalists who felt themselves weaker than those of other nations, and feared that their enterprises would be crushed and their profits taken away if free competition were allowed. The Free Traders were like a man who, seeing his antagonist is no match for him, boldly calls for a free fight and no favor, while the Protectionist was the man who, seeing himself overmatched, called for the police. The Free Trader held that the natural, God-given right of the capitalist to shear the people anywhere he found them was superior to considerations of race, nationality, or boundary lines. The Protectionist, on the contrary, maintained the patriotic right of the capitalist to the exclusive shearing of his own fellow-countrymen without interference of foreign capitalists. As to the mass of the people, the nation at large, it was, as Paul has just said, a matter of indifference whether they were fleeced by the capitalists of their own country under protection or the capitalists of foreign countries under free trade. The literature of the controversy between Protectionists and Free Traders makes this very clear. Whatever else the Protectionists failed to prove, they were able to demonstrate that the condition of the people in free-trade countries was quite as bad as anywhere else, and, on the other hand, the Free Traders were equally conclusive in the proofs they presented that the people in protected countries, other things being equal, were no better off than those in free-trade lands. The question of Protection or Free Trade interested the capitalists only. For the people, it was the choice between the devil and the deep sea."

"Let us have a concrete illustration." said the teacher. "Take the case of England. She was beyond comparison the country of all others in the nineteenth century which had most foreign trade and commanded most foreign markets. If a large volume of foreign trade under conditions practically dictated by its capitalists was under the profit system a source of national prosperity to a country, we should expect to see the mass of the British people at the end of the nineteenth century enjoying an altogether extraordinary felicity and general welfare as compared with that of other peoples or any former people, for never before did a nation develop so vast a foreign commerce. What were the facts?"

"It was common," replied the girl, "for our ancestors in the vague and foggy way in which they used the terms 'nation' and 'national' to speak of Great Britain as rich. But it was only her capitalists, some scores of thousands of individuals among some forty million people, who were rich. These indeed had incredible accumulations, but the remainder of the forty millions--the whole people, in fact, save an infinitesimal fraction--were sunk in poverty. It is said that England had a larger and more hopeless pauper problem than any other civilized nation. The condition of her working masses was not only more wretched than that of many contemporary people, but was worse, as proved by the most careful economic comparisons, than it had been in the fifteenth century, before foreign trade was thought of. People do not emigrate from a land where they are well off, but the British people, driven out by want, had found the frozen Canadas and the torrid zone more hospitable than their native land. As an illustration of the fact that the welfare of the working masses was in no way improved when the capitalists of a country commanded foreign markets, it is interesting to note the fact that the British emigrant was able to make a better living in English colonies whose markets were wholly dominated by English capitalists than he had been at home as the employee of those capitalists. We shall remember also that Malthus, with his doctrine that it was the best thing that could happen to a workingman not to be born, was an Englishman, and based his conclusions very logically upon his observation of the conditions of life for the masses in that country which had been more successful than any other in any age in monopolizing the foreign markets of the world by its commerce.

"Or," the lad went on, "take Belgium, that old Flemish land of merchants, where foreign trade had been longer and more steadily used than in any other European country. In the latter part of the nineteenth century the mass of the Belgian people, the hardest-worked population in the world, was said to have been, as a rule, without adequate food--to be undergoing, in short, a process of slow starvation. They, like the people of England and the people of Germany, are proved, by statistical calculations upon the subject that have come down to us, to have been economically very much better off during the fifteenth and early part of the sixteenth century, when foreign trade was hardly known, than they were in the nineteenth. There was a possibility before foreign trade for profit began that a population might obtain some share of the richness of a bountiful land just from the lack of any outlet for it. But with the beginning of foreign commerce, under the profit system, that possibility vanished. Thenceforth everything good or desirable, above what might serve for the barest subsistence of labor, was systematically and exhaustively gathered up by the capitalists, to be exchanged in foreign lands for gold and gems, silks, velvets, and ostrich plumes for the rich. As Goldsmith had it:

"Around the world each needful product flies
For all the luxuries the world supplies."

"To what has the struggle of the nations for foreign markets in the nineteenth century been aptly compared?"

"To a contest between galleys manned by slaves, whose owners were racing for a prize."

"In such a race, which crew was likely to fare worse, that of the winning or the losing galley?"

"That of the winning galley, by all means," replied the girl, "for the supposition is that, other conditions being equal, it was the more sorely scourged."

"Just so," said the teacher, "and on the same principle, when the capitalists of two countries contended for the supplying of a foreign market it was the workers subject to the successful group of capitalists who were most to be pitied, for, other conditions being equal, they were likely to be those whose wages had been cut lowest and whose general condition was most degraded."

"But tell us," said the teacher, "were there not instances of a general poverty in countries having no foreign trade as great as prevailed in the countries you have mentioned?"

"Dear me, yes!" replied the girl. "I have not meant to convey any impression that because the tender mercies of the foreign capitalists were cruel, those of the domestic capitalist were any less so. The comparison is merely between the operation of the profit system on a larger or smaller scale. So long as the profit system was retained, it would be all one in the end, whether you built a wall around a country and left the people to be exploited exclusively by home capitalists, or threw the wall down and let in the foreigners."

CHAPTER XXVII.

Hostility Of A System Of Vested Interests To Improvement.

"Now, Florence," said the teacher, "with your assistance we will take up the closing topic in our consideration of the economic system of our fathers--namely, its hostility to invention and improvement. It has been our painful duty to point out numerous respects in which our respected ancestors were strangely blind to the true character and effects of their economic institutions, but no instance perhaps is more striking than this. Far from seeing the necessary antagonism between private capitalism and the march of improvement which is so plain to us, they appear to have sincerely believed that their system was peculiarly favorable to the progress of invention, and that its advantage in this respect was so great as to be an important set-off to its admitted ethical defects. Here there is decidedly a broad difference in opinion, but fortunately the facts are so well authenticated that we shall have no difficulty in concluding which view is correct.

"The subject divides itself into two branches: First, the natural antagonism of the old system to economic changes; and, second, the effect of the profit principle to minimize if not wholly to nullify the benefit of such economic improvements as were able to overcome that antagonism so far as to get themselves introduced.--Now, Florence, tell us what there was about the old economic system, the system of private capitalism, which made it constitutionally opposed to changes in methods."

"It was," replied the girl, "the fact that it consisted of independent vested interests without any principle of coordination or combination, the result being that the economic welfare of every individual or group was wholly dependent upon his or its particular vested interest without regard to others or to the welfare of the whole body."

"Please bring out your meaning by comparing our modern system in the respect you speak of with private capitalism."

"Our system is a strictly integrated one--that is to say, no one has any economic interest in any part or function of the economic organization which is distinct from his interest in every other part and function. His only interest is in the greatest possible output of the whole. We have our several occupations, but only that we may work the more efficiently for the common fund. We may become very enthusiastic about our special pursuit, but as a matter of sentiment only, for our economic interests are no more dependent upon our special occupation than upon any other. We share equally in the total product, whatever it is."

"How does the integrated character of the economic system affect our attitude toward improvements or inventions of any sort in economic processes?"

"We welcome them with eagerness. Why should we not? Any improvement of this sort must necessarily redound to the advantage of every one in the nation and to every one's advantage equally. If the occupation affected by the invention happens to be our particular employment we lose nothing, though it should make that occupation wholly superfluous. We might in that case feel a little sentimental regret over the passing away of old habits, but that is all. No one's substantial interests are in any way more identified with one pursuit than another. All are in the service of the nation, and it is the business and interest of the nation to see that every one is provided with other work as soon as his former occupation becomes unnecessary to the general weal, and under no circumstances is his rate of maintenance affected. From its first production every improvement in economic processes is therefore an unalloyed blessing to all. The inventor comes bringing a gift of greater wealth or leisure in his hand for every one on earth, and it is no wonder that the people's gratitude makes his reward the most enviable to be won by a public benefactor."

"Now, Florence, tell us in what way the multitude of distinct vested interests which made up private capitalism operated to produce an antagonism toward economic inventions and improvements."

HOW PROGRESS ANTAGONIZED VESTED INTERESTS.

"As I have said," replied the girl, "everybody's interest was wholly confined to and bound up with the particular occupation he was engaged in. If he was a capitalist, his capital was embarked in it; if he was an artisan, his capital was the knowledge of some particular craft or part of a craft, and he depended for his livelihood on the demand for the sort of work he had learned how to do. Neither as capitalist or artisan, as employer or employee, had he any economic interest or dependence outside of or larger than his special business. Now, the effect of any new idea, invention, or discovery for economic application is to dispense more or less completely with the process formerly used in that department, and so far to destroy the economic basis of the occupations connected with that business. Under our system, as I have said, that means no loss to anybody, but simply a shifting of workers, with a net gain in wealth or leisure to all; but then it meant ruin to those involved in the change. The capitalist lost his capital, his plant, his investments more or less totally, and the workingmen lost their means of livelihood and were thrown on what you well called the cold charity of the world--a charity usually well below zero; and this loss without any rebate or compensation whatever from the public at large on account of any general benefit that might be received from the invention. It was complete. Consequently, the most beneficent of inventions was cruel as death to those who had been dependent for living or for profit on the particular occupations it affected. The capitalists grew gray from fear of discoveries which in a day might turn their costly plants to old iron fit only for the junkshop, and the nightmare of the artisan was some machine which should take bread from his children's mouths by enabling his employer to dispense with his services.

"Owing to this division of the economic field into a set of vested personal and group interests wholly without coherency or integrating idea, each standing or falling by and for itself, every step in the advance of the arts and sciences was gained only at the cost of an amount of loss and ruin to particular portions of the community such as would be wrought by a blight or pestilence. The march of invention was white with the bleaching bones of innumerable hecatombs of victims. The spinning jenny replaced the spinning wheel, and famine stalked through English villages. The railroad supplanted the stagecoach, and a thousand hill towns died while as many sprang up in the valleys, and the farmers of the East were pauperized by the new agriculture of the West. Petroleum succeeded whale-oil, and a hundred seaports withered. Coal and iron were found in the South, and the grass grew in the streets of the Northern centers of iron-making. Electricity succeeded steam, and billions of railroad property were wiped out. But what is the use of lengthening a list which might be made interminable? The rule was always the same: every important invention brought uncompensated disaster to some portion of the people. Armies of bankrupts, hosts of workers forced into vagabondage, a sea of suffering of every sort, made up the price which our ancestors paid for every step of progress.

"Afterward, when the victims had been buried or put out of the way, it was customary with our fathers to celebrate these industrial triumphs, and on such occasions a common quotation in the mouths of the orators was a line of verse to the effect that--

"Peace hath her victories not less renowned than those of war.

The orators were not wont to dwell on the fact that these victories of what they so oddly called peace were usually purchased at a cost in human life and suffering quite as great as--yes, often greater than--those of so-called war. We have all read of Tamerlane's pyramid at Damascus made of seventy thousand skulls of his victims. It may be said that if the victims of the various inventions connected with the introduction of steam had consented to contribute their skulls to a monument in honor of Stevenson or Arkwright it would dwarf Tamerlane's into insignificance. Tamerlane was a beast, and Arkwright was a genius sent to help men, yet the hideous juggle of the old-time economic system made the benefactor the cause of as much human suffering as the brutal conqueror. It was bad enough when men stoned and crucified those who came to help them, but private capitalism did them a worse outrage still in turning the gifts they brought into curses."

"And did the workers and the capitalists whose interests were threatened by the progress of invention take practical means of resisting that progress and suppressing the inventions and the inventors?"

"They did all they could in that way. If the working-men had been strong enough they would have put an absolute veto on inventions of any sort tending to diminish the demand for crude hand labor in their respective crafts. As it was, they did all it was possible for them to accomplish in that direction by trades-union dictation and mob violence; nor can any one blame the poor fellows for resisting to the utmost improvements which improved them out of the means of livelihood. A machine gun would have been scarcely more deadly if turned upon the workingmen of that day than a labor-saving machine. In those bitter times a man thrown out of the employment he had fitted himself for might about as well have been shot, and if he were not able to get any other work, as so many were not, he would have been altogether better off had he been killed in battle with the drum and fife to cheer him and the hope of a pension for his family. Only, of course, it was the system of private capitalism and not the labor-saving machine which the workingmen should have attacked, for with a rational economic system the machine would have been wholly beneficent."

"How did the capitalists resist inventions?"

"Chiefly by negative means, though much more effective ones than the mob violence which the workingmen used. The initiative in everything belonged to the capitalists. No inventor could introduce an invention, however excellent, unless he could get capitalists to take it up, and this usually they would not do unless the inventor relinquished to them most of his hopes of profit from the discovery. A much more important hindrance to the introduction of inventions resulted from the fact that those who would be interested in taking them up were those already carrying on the business the invention applied to, and their interest was in most cases to suppress an innovation which threatened to make obsolete the machinery and methods in which their capital was invested. The capitalist had to be fully assured not only that the invention was a good one in itself, but that it would be so profitable to himself personally as to make up for all the damage to his existing capital before he would touch it. When inventions wholly did away with processes which had been the basis of profit-charging it was often suicidal for the capitalist to adopt them. If they could not suppress such inventions in any other way, it was their custom to buy them up and pigeonhole them. After the Revolution there were found enough of these patents which had been bought up and pigeonholed in self-protection by the capitalists to have kept the world in novelties for ten years if nothing more had been discovered. One of the most tragical chapters in the history of the old order is made up of the difficulties, rebuffs, and lifelong disappointments which inventors had to contend with before they could get their discoveries introduced, and the frauds by which in most cases they were swindled out of the profits of them by the capitalists through whom their introduction was obtained. These stories seem, indeed, well-nigh incredible nowadays, when the nation is alert and eager to foster and encourage every stirring of the inventive spirit, and every one with any sort of new idea can command the offices of the administration without cost to safeguard his claim to priority and to furnish him all possible facilities of information, material, and appliances to perfect his conception."

"Considering," said the teacher, "that these facts as to the resistance offered by vested interests to the march of improvement must have been even more obvious to our ancestors than to us, how do you account for the belief they seem to have sincerely held that private capitalism as a system was favorable to invention?"

"Doubtless," replied the girl, "it was because they saw that whenever an invention was introduced it was under the patronage of capitalists. This was, of course, necessarily so because all economic initiative was confined to the capitalists. Our forefathers, observing that inventions when introduced at all were introduced through the machinery of private capitalism, overlooked the fact that usually it was only after exhausting its power as an obstruction to invention that capital lent itself to its advancement. They were in this respect like children who, seeing the water pouring over the edge of a dam and coming over nowhere else, should conclude that the dam was an agency for aiding the flow of the river instead of being an obstruction which let it over only when it could be kept back no longer."

"Our lesson," said the teacher, "relates in strictness only to the economic results of the old order, but at times the theme suggests aspects of former social conditions too important to pass without mention. We have seen how obstructive was the system of vested interests which underlaid private capitalism to the introduction of improvements and inventions in the economic field. But there was another field in which the same influence was exerted with effects really far more important and disastrous.--Tell us, Florence, something of the manner in which the vested interest system tended to resist the advance of new ideas in the field of thought, of morals, science, and religion."

"Previous to the great Revolution," the girl replied, "the highest education not being universal as with us, but limited to a small body, the members of this body, known as the learned and professional classes, necessarily became the moral and intellectual teachers and leaders of the nation. They molded the thoughts of the people, set them their standards, and through the control of their minds dominated their material interests and determined the course of civilization. No such power is now monopolized by any class, because the high level of general education would make it impossible for any class of mere men to lead the people blindly. Seeing, however, that such a power was exercised in that day and limited to so small a class, it was a most vital point that this class should be qualified to discharge so responsible a duty in a spirit of devotion to the general weal unbiased by distracting motives. But under the system of private capitalism, which made every person and group economically dependent upon and exclusively concerned in the prosperity of the occupation followed by himself and his group, this ideal was impossible of attainment. The learned class, the teachers, the preachers, writers, and professional men were only tradesmen after all, just like the shoemakers and the carpenters, and their welfare was absolutely bound up with the demand for the particular sets of ideas and doctrines they represented and the particular sorts of professional services they got their living by rendering. Each man's line of teaching or preaching was his vested interest--the means of his livelihood. That being so, the members of the learned and professional class were bound to be affected by innovations in their departments precisely as shoemakers or carpenters by inventions affecting their trades. It necessarily followed that when any new idea was suggested in religion, in medicine, in science, in economics, in sociology, and indeed in almost any field of thought, the first question which the learned body having charge of that field and making a living out of it would ask itself was not whether the idea was good and true and would tend to the general welfare, but how it would immediately and directly affect the set of doctrines, traditions, and institutions, with the prestige of which their own personal interests were identified. If it was a new religious conception that had been suggested, the clergyman considered, first of all, how it would affect his sect and his personal standing in it. If it were a new medical idea, the doctor asked first how it would affect the practice of the school he was identified with. If it was a new economic or social theory, then all those whose professional capital was their reputation as teachers in that branch questioned first how the new idea agreed with the doctrines and traditions constituting their stock in trade. Now, as any new idea, almost as a matter of course, must operate to discredit previous ideas in the same field, it followed that the economic self-interest of the learned classes would instinctively and almost invariably be opposed to reform or advance of thought in their fields.

"Being human, they were scarcely more to be blamed for involuntarily regarding new ideas in their specialties with aversion than the weaver or the brickmaker for resisting the introduction of inventions calculated to take the bread out of his mouth. And yet consider what a tremendous, almost insurmountable, obstacle to human progress was presented by the fact that the intellectual leaders of the nations and the molders of the people's thoughts, by their economic dependence upon vested interests in established ideas, were biased against progress by the strongest motives of self-interest. When we give due thought to the significance of this fact, we shall find ourselves wondering no longer at the slow rate of human advance in the past, but rather that there should have been any advance at all."

CHAPTER XXVIII.

How The Profit System Nullified The Benefit Of Inventions.

"The general subject of the hostility of private capitalism to progress," pursued the teacher, "divides itself, as I said, into two branches. First, the constitutional antagonism between a system of distinct and separate vested interests and all unsettling changes which, whatever their ultimate effect, must be directly damaging to those interests. We will now ask you, Harold, to take up the second branch of the subject--namely, the effect of the profit principle to minimize, if not wholly to nullify, the benefit to the community of such inventions and improvements as were able to overcome the antagonism of vested interests so far as to get themselves introduced. The nineteenth century, including the last quarter of the eighteenth, was marked by an astonishing and absolutely unprecedented number of great inventions in economic processes. To what was this outburst of inventive genius due?"

"To the same cause," replied the boy, "which accounts for the rise of the democratic movement and the idea of human equality during the same period--that is to say, the diffusion of intelligence among the masses, which, for the first time becoming somewhat general, multiplied ten-thousandfold the thinking force of mankind, and, in the political aspect of the matter, changed the purpose of that thinking from the interest of the few to that of the many."

"Our ancestors," said the teacher, "seeing that this outburst of invention took place under private capitalism, assumed that there must be something in that system peculiarly favorable to the genius of invention. Have you anything to say on that point beyond what has been said?"

"Nothing," replied the boy, "except that by the same rule we ought to give credit to the institutions of royalty, nobility, and plutocracy for the democratic idea which under their fostering influence during the same period grew to flowering in the great Revolution."

"I think that will do on that point," answered the teacher. "We will now ask you to tell us something more particularly of this great period of invention which began in the latter part of the eighteenth century."

HAROLD STATES THE FACTS.

"From the times of antiquity up to the last quarter of the eighteenth century," said the lad, "there had been almost no progress in the mechanical sciences save as to shipbuilding and arms. From 1780, or thereabouts, dates the beginning of a series of discoveries of sources of power, and their application by machinery to economic purposes, which, during the century following, completely revolutionized the conditions of industry and commerce. Steam and coal meant a multiplication of human energy in the production of wealth which was almost incalculable. For industrial purposes it is not too much to say that they transformed man from a pygmy to a Titan. These were, of course, only the greatest factors in a countless variety of discoveries by which prodigious economies of labor were effected in every detail of the arts by which human life is maintained and ministered to. In agriculture, where Nature, which can not be too much hurried, is a large partner, and wherein, therefore, man's part is less controlling than in other industries, it might be expected that the increase of productive energy through human invention would be least. Yet here it was estimated that agricultural machinery, as most perfectly developed in America, had multiplied some fifteenfold the product of the individual worker. In most sorts of production less directly dependent upon Nature, invention during this period had multiplied the efficiency of labor in a much greater degree, ranging from fifty and a hundred-fold to several thousand-fold, one man being able to accomplish as much as a small army in all previous ages."

"That is to say," said the teacher, "it would seem that while the needs of the human race had not increased, its power to supply those needs had been indefinitely multiplied. This prodigious increase in the potency of labor was a clear net economic gain for the world, such as the previous history of the race furnished nothing comparable to. It was as if God had given to man his power of attorney in full, to command all the forces of the universe to serve him. Now, Harold, suppose you had merely been told as much as you have told us concerning the hundredfold multiplication of the wealth-producing power of the race which took place at this period, and were left, without further information, to infer for yourself how great a change for the better in the condition of mankind would naturally follow, what would it seem reasonable to suppose?"

"It would seem safe to take for granted at the least," replied the boy, "that every form of human unhappiness or imperfection resulting directly or indirectly from economic want would be absolutely banished from the earth. That the very meaning of the word poverty would have been forgotten would seem to be a matter-of-course assumption to begin with. Beyond that we might go on and fancy almost anything in the way of universal diffusion of luxury that we pleased. The facts given as the basis of the speculation would justify the wildest day-dreams of universal happiness, so far as material abundance could directly or indirectly minister to it."

"Very good, Harold. We know now what to expect when you shall go on to tell us what the historical facts are as to the degree of improvement in the economic condition of the mass of the race, which actually did result from the great inventions of the eighteenth and nineteenth centuries. Take the condition of the mass of the people in the advanced countries at the close of the nineteenth century, after they had been enjoying the benefits of coal and steam, and the most of the other great inventions for a century, more or less, and comparing it with their condition, say, in 1780, give us some idea of the change for the better which had taken place in their economic welfare. Doubtless it was something marvelous."

"It was a subject of much nice debate and close figuring," replied the boy, "whether in the most advanced countries there had been, taking one class with another, and disregarding mere changes in fashions, any real improvement at all in the economic basis of the great majority of the people."

"Is it possible that the improvement had been so small that there could be a question raised whether there had been any at all?"

"Precisely so. As to the English people in the nineteenth century, Florence has given us the facts in speaking of the effects of foreign commerce. The English had not only a greater foreign commerce than any other nation, but had also made earlier and fuller use of the great inventions than any other. She has told us that the sociologists of the time had no difficulty in proving that the economic condition of the English people was more wretched in the latter part of the nineteenth century than it had been centuries previous, before steam had been thought of, and that this was equally true of the peoples of the Low Countries, and the masses of Germany. As to the working masses of Italy and Spain, they had been in much better economic condition during periods of the Roman Empire than they were in the nineteenth century. If the French were a little better off in the nineteenth than in the eighteenth century, it was owing wholly to the distribution of land effected by the French Revolution, and in no way to the great inventions."

"How was it in the United States?"

"If America," replied the lad, "had shown a notable improvement in the condition of the people, it would not be necessary to ascribe it to the progress of invention, for the wonderful economic opportunities of a new country had given them a vast though necessarily temporary advantage over other nations. It does not appear, however, that there was any more agreement of testimony as to whether the condition of the masses had on the whole improved in America than in the Old World. In the last decade of the nineteenth century, with a view to allaying the discontent of the wage-earners and the farmers, which was then beginning to swell to revolutionary volume, agents of the United States Government published elaborate comparisons of wages and prices, in which they argued out a small percentage of gain on the whole in the economic condition of the American artisans during the century. At this distance we can not, of course, criticise these calculations in detail, but we may base a reasonable doubt of the conclusion that the condition of the masses had very greatly improved upon the existence of the popular discontent which they were published in the vain hope of moderating. It seems safe to assume that the people were better acquainted with their own condition than the sociologists, and it is certain that it was the growing conviction of the American masses during the closing decades of the nineteenth century that they were losing ground economically and in danger of sinking into the degraded condition of the proletariat and peasantry of the ancient and contemporary European world. Against the laborious tabulations of the apologists of capitalism we may adduce, as far superior and more convincing evidence of the economic tendency of the American people during the latter part of the nineteenth century, such signs of the times as the growth of beggary and vagabondage to Old World proportions, the embittered revolts of the wage-earners which kept up a constant industrial war, and finally the condition of bankruptcy into which the farming population was sinking."

"That will do as to that point," said the teacher. "In such a comparison as this small margins and nice points of difference are impertinent. It is enough that if the indefinite multiplication of man's wealth-producing power by inventive progress had been developed and distributed with any degree of intelligence for the general interest, poverty would have disappeared and comfort if not luxury have become the universal condition. This being a fact as plain and large as the sun, it is needless to consider the hairsplitting debates of the economists as to whether the condition of this or that class of the masses in this or that country was a grain better or two grains worse than it had been. It is enough for the purpose of the argument that nobody anywhere in any country pretended that there had been an improvement noticeable enough to make even a beginning toward that complete transformation in the human condition for the better, of which the great inventions by universal admission had contained the full and immediate promise and potency.

"And now tell us, Harold, what our ancestors had to say as to this astonishing fact--a fact more marvelous than the great inventions themselves, namely, their failure to prove of any considerable benefit to mankind. Surely a phenomenon at once so amazing in itself and involving so prodigious a defeat to the hopes of human happiness must have set a world of rational beings to speculating in a very impassioned way as to what the explanation might be. One would suppose that the facts of this failure with which our ancestors were confronted would have been enough to convince them that there must be something radically and horribly wrong about any economic system which was responsible for it or had permitted it, and that no further argument would have been wanted to induce them to make a radical change in it."

"One would think so, certainly," said the boy, "but it did not seem to occur to our great-grandfathers to hold their economic system to any responsibility for the result. As we have seen, they recognized, however they might dispute as to percentages, that the great inventions had failed to make any notable improvement in the human condition, but they never seemed to get so far as to inquire seriously why this was so. In the voluminous works of the economists of the period we find no discussions, much less any attempt to explain, a fact which to our view absolutely overshadows all the other features of the economic situation before the Revolution. And the strangest thing about it all is that their failure to derive any benefit worth speaking of from the progress of invention in no way seemed to dampen the enthusiasm of our ancestors about the inventions. They seemed fairly intoxicated with the pride of their achievements, barren of benefit as they had been, and their day dreams were of further discoveries that to a yet more amazing degree should put the forces of the universe at their disposal. None of them apparently paused to reflect that though God might empty his treasure house for their benefit of its every secret of use and of power, the race would not be a whit the better off for it unless they devised some economic machinery by which these discoveries might be made to serve the general welfare more effectually than they had done before. They do not seem to have realized that so long as poverty remained, every new invention which multiplied the power of wealth production was but one more charge in the indictment against their economic system as guilty of an imbecility as great as its iniquity. They appear to have wholly overlooked the fact that until their mighty engines should be devoted to increasing human welfare they were and would continue mere curious scientific toys of no more real worth or utility to the race than so many particularly ingenious jumping-jacks. This craze for more and more and ever greater and wider inventions for economic purposes, coupled with apparent complete indifference as to whether mankind derived any ultimate benefit from them or not, can only be understood by regarding it as one of those strange epidemics of insane excitement which have been known to affect whole populations at certain periods, especially of the middle ages. Rational explanation it has none."

"You may well say so," exclaimed the teacher. "Of what use indeed was it that coal had been discovered, when there were still as many fireless homes as ever? Of what use was the machinery by which one man could weave as much cloth as a thousand a century before when there were as many ragged, shivering human beings as ever? Of what use was the machinery by which the American farmer could produce a dozen times as much food as his grandfather when there were more cases of starvation and a larger proportion of half-fed and badly fed people in the country than ever before, and hordes of homeless, desperate vagabonds traversed the land, begging for bread at every door? They had invented steamships, these ancestors of ours, that were miracles, but their main business was transporting paupers from lands where they had been beggared in spite of labor-saving machinery to newer lands where, after a short space, they would inevitably be beggared again. About the middle of the nineteenth century the world went wild over the invention of the sewing-machine and the burden it was to lift from the shoulders of the race. Yet, fifty years after, the business of garment-making, which it had been expected to revolutionize for the better, had become a slavery both in America and Europe which, under the name of the 'sweating system,' scandalized even that tough generation. They had lucifer matches instead of flint and steel, kerosene and electricity instead of candles and whale-oil, but the spectacles of squalor, misery, and degradation upon which the improved light shone were the same and only looked the worse for it. What few beggars there had been in America in the first quarter of the nineteenth century went afoot, while in the last quarter they stole their transportation on trains drawn by steam engines, but there were fifty times as many beggars. The world traveled sixty miles an hour instead of five or ten at the beginning of the century, but it had not gained an inch on poverty, which clung to it as the shadow to the racer."

HELEN GIVES THE EXPLANATION OF THE FACTS.

"Now, Helen," pursued the teacher, "we want you to explain the facts that Harold has so clearly brought out. We want you to tell us why it was that the economic condition of humanity derived but a barely perceptible advantage at most, if indeed any at all, from an inventive progress which by its indefinite multiplication of productive energy should by every rule of reason have completely transformed for the better the economic condition of the race and wholly banished want from earth. What was there about the old system of private capitalism to account for a *fiasco* so tremendous?"

"It was the operation of the profit principle," replied the girl Helen.

"Please proceed with the explanation."

"The great economic inventions which Harold has been talking about," said the girl, "were of the class of what were called labor-saving machines and devices--that is to say, they enabled one man to produce more than before with the same labor, or to produce the same as before with less labor. Under a collective administration of industry in the equal general interest like ours, the effect of any such invention would be to increase the total output to be shared equally among all, or, if the people preferred and so voted, the output would remain what it was, and the saving of labor be appropriated as a dividend of leisure to be equally enjoyed by all. But under the old system there was, of course, no collective administration. Capitalists were the administrators, being the only persons who were able to carry on extensive operations or take the initiative in economic enterprises, and in what they did or did not do they had no regard to the public interest or the general gain, but to their own profit only. The only motive which could induce a capitalist to adopt an invention was the idea of increasing his profits either by getting a larger product at the same labor cost, or else getting the same product at a reduced labor cost. We will take the first case. Suppose a capitalist in adopting labor-saving machinery calculated to keep all his former employees and make his profit by getting a larger product with the same labor cost. Now, when a capitalist proposed to increase his output without the aid of a machine he had to hire more workers, who must be paid wages to be afterward expended in purchasing products in the market. In this case, for every increase of product there was some increase, although not at all an equal one, in the buying power of the community. But when the capitalist increased his output by the aid of machinery, with no increase in the number of workers employed, there was no corresponding increase of purchasing power on the part of the community to set off against the increased product. A certain amount of purchasing power went, indeed, in wages to the mechanics who constructed the labor-saving machines, but it was small in comparison with the increase in the output which the capitalist expected to make by means of the machinery, otherwise it would have been no object to him to buy the machine. The increased product would therefore tend directly to glut yet more the always glutted market; and if any considerable number of capitalists should introduce machinery in the same way, the glut would become intensified into a crisis and general stoppage of production.

"In order to avert or minimize such a disaster, the capitalists could take one or two courses. They could, if they chose, reduce the price of their increased machine product so that the purchasing power of the community, which had remained stationary, could take it up at least as nearly as it had taken up the lesser quantity of higher-priced product before the machinery was introduced. But if the capitalists did this, they would derive no additional profit whatever from the adoption of the machinery, the whole benefit going to the community. It is scarcely necessary to say that this was not what the capitalists were in business for. The other course before them was to keep their product where it was before introducing the machine, and to realize their profit by discharging the workers, thus saving on the labor cost of the output. This was the course most commonly taken, because the glut of goods was generally so threatening that, except when inventions opened up wholly new fields, capitalists were careful not greatly to increase outputs. For example, if the machine enabled one man to do two men's work, the capitalist would discharge half of his force, put the saving in labor cost in his pocket, and still produce as many goods as ever. Moreover, there was another advantage about this plan. The discharged workers swelled the numbers of the unemployed, who were underbidding one another for the opportunity to work. The increased desperation of this competition made it possible presently for the capitalist to reduce the wages of the half of his former force which he still retained. That was the usual result of the introduction of labor-saving machinery: First, the discharge of workers, then, after more or less time, reduced wages for those who were retained."

"If I understand you, then," said the teacher, "the effect of labor-saving inventions was either to increase the product without any corresponding increase in the purchasing power of the community, thereby aggravating the glut of goods, or else to positively decrease the purchasing power of the community, through discharges and wage reductions, while the product remained the same as before. That is to say, the net result of labor-saving machinery was to increase the difference between the production and consumption of the community which remained in the hands of the capitalists as profit."

"Precisely so. The only motive of the capitalist in introducing labor-saving machinery was to retain as profit a larger share of the product than before by cutting down the share of labor--that is to say, labor-saving machinery which should have banished poverty from the world became the means under the profit system of impoverishing the masses more rapidly than ever."

"But did not the competition among the capitalists compel them to sacrifice a part of these increased profits in reductions of prices in order to get rid of their goods?"

"Undoubtedly; but such reductions in price would not increase the consuming power of the people except when taken out of profits, and, as John explained to us this morning, when capitalists were forced by competition to reduce their prices they saved their profits as long as possible by making up for the reductions in price by debasing the quality of the goods or cutting down wages until the public and the wage-earners could be cheated and squeezed no longer. Then only did they begin to sacrifice profits, and it was then too late for the impoverished consumers to respond by increasing consumption. It was always, as John told us, in the countries where the people were poorest that the prices were lowest, but without benefit to the people."

THE AMERICAN FARMER AND MACHINERY.

"And now," said the teacher, "I want to ask you something about the effect of labor-saving inventions upon a class of so-called capitalists who made up the greater half of the American people--I mean the farmers. In so far as they owned their farms and tools, however encumbered by debts and mortgages, they were technically capitalists, although themselves quite as pitiable victims of the capitalists as were the proletarian artisans. The agricultural labor-saving inventions of the nineteenth century in America were something simply marvelous, enabling, as we have been told, one man to do the work of fifteen a century before. Nevertheless, the American farmer was going straight to the dogs all the while these inventions were being introduced. Now, how do you account for that? Why did not the farmer, as a sort of capitalist, pile up his profits on labor-saving machinery like the other capitalists?"

"As I have said," replied the girl, "the profits made by labor-saving machinery resulted from the increased productiveness of the labor employed, thus enabling the capitalist either to turn out a greater product with the same labor cost or an equal product with a less labor cost, the workers supplanted by the machine being discharged. The amount of profits made was therefore dependent on the scale of the business carried on--that is, the number of workers employed and the consequent figure which labor cost made in the business. When farming was carried on upon a very large scale, as were the so-called bonanza farms in the United States of that period, consisting of twenty to thirty thousand acres of land, the capitalists conducting them did for a time make great profits, which were directly owing to the labor-saving agricultural machines, and would have been impossible without them. These machines enabled them to put a greatly increased product on the market with small increase of labor cost or else the same product at a great decrease of labor cost. But the mass of the American farmers operated on a small scale only and employed very little labor, doing largely their own work. They could therefore make little profit, if any, out of labor-saving machinery by discharging employees. The only way they could utilize it was not by cutting down the expense of their output but by increasing the amount of the output through the increased efficiency of their own labor. But seeing that there had been no increase meanwhile in the purchasing power of the community at large, there was no more money demand for their products than before, and consequently if the general body of farmers through labor-saving machinery increased their output, they could dispose of the greater aggregate only at a reduced price, so that in the end they would get no more for the greater output than for the less. Indeed, they would not get so much, for the effect of even a small surplus when held by weak capitalists who could not keep it back, but must press for sale, had an effect to reduce the market price quite out of proportion to the amount of the surplus. In the United States the mass of these small farmers was so great and their pressure to sell so desperate that in the latter part of the century they destroyed the market not only for themselves but finally even for the great capitalists who conducted the great farms."

"The conclusion is, then, Helen," said the teacher, "that the net effect of labor-saving machinery upon the mass of small farmers in the United States was ruinous."

"Undoubtedly," replied the girl. "This is a case in which the historical facts absolutely confirm the rational theory. Thanks to the profit system, inventions which multiplied the productive power of the farmer fifteenfold made a bankrupt of him, and so long as the profit system was retained there was no help for him."

"Were farmers the only class of small capitalists who were injured rather than helped by labor-saving machinery?"

"The rule was the same for all small capitalists whatever business they were engaged in. Its basis, as I have said, was the fact that the advantage to be gained by the capitalists from introducing labor-saving machinery was in proportion to the amount of labor which the machinery enabled them to dispense with--that is to say, was dependent upon the scale of their business. If the scale of the capitalist's operations was so small that he could not make a large saving in reduced labor cost by introducing machinery, then the introduction of such machinery put him at a crushing disadvantage as compared with larger capitalists. Labor-saving machinery was in this way one of the most potent of the influences which toward the close of the nineteenth century made it impossible for the small capitalists in any field to compete with the great ones, and helped to concentrate the economic dominion of the world in few and ever fewer hands."

"Suppose, Helen, that the Revolution had not come, that labor-saving machinery had continued to be invented as fast as ever, and that the consolidation of the great capitalists' interests, already foreshadowed, had been completed, so that the waste of profits in competition among themselves had ceased, what would have been the result?"

"In that case," replied the girl, "all the wealth that had been wasted in commercial rivalry would have been expended in luxury in addition to what had been formerly so expended. The new machinery year by year would have gone on making it possible for a smaller and ever smaller fraction of the population to produce all the necessaries for the support of mankind, and the rest of the world, including the great mass of the workers, would have found employment in unproductive labor to provide the materials of luxury for the rich or in personal services to them. The world would thus come to be divided into three classes: a master caste, very limited in numbers; a vast body of unproductive workers employed in ministering to the luxury and pomp of the master caste; and a small body of strictly productive workers, which, owing to the perfection of machinery, would be able to provide for the needs of all. It is needless to say that all save the masters would be at the minimum point as to means of subsistence. Decaying empires in ancient times have often presented such spectacles of imperial and aristocratic splendor, to the supply and maintenance of which the labor of starving nations was devoted. But no such spectacle ever presented in the past would have been comparable to that which the twentieth century would have witnessed if the great Revolution had permitted private capitalism to complete its evolution. In former ages the great mass of the population has been necessarily employed in productive labor to supply the needs of the world, so that the portion of the working force available for the service of the pomp and pleasures of the masters as unproductive laborers has always been relatively small. But in the plutocratic empire we are imagining, the genius of invention, through labor-saving machinery, would have enabled the masters to devote a greater proportion of the subject population to the direct service of their state and luxury than had been possible under any of the historic despotisms. The abhorrent spectacles of men enthroned as gods above abject and worshiping masses, which Assyria, Egypt, Persia, and Rome exhibited in their day, would have been eclipsed."

"That will do, Helen," said the teacher. "With your testimony we will wind up our review of the economic system of private capitalism which the great Revolution abolished forever. There are of course a multitude of other aspects and branches of the subject which we might take up, but the study would be as unprofitable as depressing. We have, I think, covered the essential points. If you understand why and how profits, rent, and interest operated to limit the consuming power of most of the community to a fractional part of its productive power, thereby in turn correspondingly crippling the latter, you have the open secret of the poverty of the world before the Revolution, and of the impossibility of any important or lasting improvement from any source whatever in the economic circumstances of mankind, until and unless private capitalism, of which the profit system with rent and interest were necessary and inseparable parts, should be put an end to."

CHAPTER XXIX.

I Receive An Ovation.

"And now," the teacher went on, glancing at the gallery where the doctor and I had been sitting unseen, "I have a great surprise for you. Among those who have listened to your recitation to-day, both in the forenoon and afternoon, has been a certain personage whose identity you ought to be able to infer when I say that, of all persons now on earth, he is absolutely the one best able, and the only one fully able, to judge how accurate your portrayal of nineteenth-century conditions has been. Lest the knowledge should disturb your equanimity, I have refrained from telling you, until the present moment, that we have present with us this afternoon a no less distinguished visitor than Julian West, and that with great kindness he has consented to permit me to present you to him."

I had assented, rather reluctantly, to the teacher's request, not being desirous of exposing myself unnecessarily to curious staring. But I had yet to make the acquaintance of twentieth-century boys and girls. When they came around me it was easy to see in the wistful eyes of the girls and the moved faces of the boys how deeply their imaginations were stirred by the suggestions of my presence among them, and how far their sentiment was from one of common or frivolous curiosity. The interest they showed in me was so wholly and delicately sympathetic that it could not have offended the most sensitive temperament.

This had indeed been the attitude of all the persons of mature years whom I had met, but I had scarcely expected the same considerateness from school children. I had not, it seemed, sufficiently allowed for the influence upon manners of the atmosphere of refinement which surrounds the child of to-day from the cradle. These young people had never seen coarseness, rudeness, or brusqueness on the part of any one. Their confidence had never been abused, their sympathy wounded, or their suspicion excited. Having never imagined such a thing as a person socially superior or inferior to themselves, they had never learned but one sort of manners. Having never had any occasion to create a false or deceitful impression or to accomplish anything by indirection, it was natural that they should not know what affectation was.

Truly, it is these secondary consequences, these moral and social reactions of economic equality to create a noble atmosphere of human intercourse, that, after all, have been the greatest contribution which the principle has made to human happiness.

At once I found myself talking and jesting with the young people as easily as if I had always known them, and what with their interest in what I told them of the old-time schools, and my delight in their naive comments, an hour slipped away unnoticed. Youth is always inspiring, and the atmosphere of these fresh, beautiful, ingenuous lives was like a wine bath.

Florence! Esther! Helen! Marion! Margaret! George! Robert! Harold! Paul!--Never shall I forget that group of star-eyed girls and splendid lads, in whom I first made acquaintance with the boys and girls of the twentieth century. Can it be that God sends sweeter souls to earth now that the world is so much fitter for them?

CHAPTER XXX.

What Universal Culture Means.

It was one of those Indian summer afternoons when it seems sinful waste of opportunity to spend a needless hour within. Being in no sort of hurry, the doctor and I chartered a motor-carriage for two at the next station, and set forth in the general direction of home, indulging ourselves in as many deviations from the route as pleased our fancy. Presently, as we rolled noiselessly over the smooth streets, leaf-strewn from the bordering colonnades of trees, I began to exclaim about the precocity of school children who at the age of thirteen or fourteen were able to handle themes usually reserved in my day for the college and university. This, however, the doctor made light of.

"Political economy," he said, "from the time the world adopted the plan of equal sharing of labor and its results, became a science so simple that any child who knows the proper way to divide an apple with his little brothers has mastered the secret of it. Of course, to point out the fallacies of a false political economy is a very simple matter also, when one has only to compare it with the true one.

"As to intellectual precocity in general," pursued the doctor, "I do not think it is particularly noticeable in our children as compared with those of your day. We certainly make no effort to develop it. A bright school child of twelve in the nineteenth century would probably not compare badly as to acquirements with the average twelve-year-old in our schools. It would be as you compared them ten years later that the difference in the educational systems would show its effect. At twenty-one or twenty-two the average youth would probably in your day have been little more advanced in education than at fourteen, having probably left school for the factory or farm at about that age or a couple of years later unless perhaps he happened to be one of the children of the rich minority. The corresponding child under our system would have continued his or her education without break, and at twenty-one have acquired what you used to call a college education."

"The extension of the educational machinery necessary to provide the higher education for all must have been enormous," I said. "Our primary-school system provided the rudiments for nearly all children, but not one in twenty went as far as the grammar school, not one in a hundred as far as the high school, and not one in a thousand ever saw a college. The great universities of my day--Harvard, Yale, and the rest--must have become small cities in order to receive the students flocking to them."

"They would need to be very large cities certainly," replied the doctor, "if it were a question of their undertaking the higher education of our youth, for every year we graduate not the thousands or tens of thousands that made up your annual grist of college graduates, but millions. For that very reason--that is, the numbers to be dealt with--we can have no centers of the higher education any more than you had of the primary education. Every community has its university just as formerly its common schools, and has in it more students from the vicinage than one of your great universities could collect with its drag net from the ends of the earth."

"But does not the reputation of particular teachers attract students to special universities?"

"That is a matter easily provided for," replied the doctor. "The perfection of our telephone and electroscope systems makes it possible to enjoy at any distance the instruction of any teacher. One of much popularity lectures to a million pupils in a whisper, if he happens to be hoarse, much easier than one of your professors could talk to a class of fifty when in good voice."

"Really, doctor," said I, "there is no fact about your civilization that seems to open so many vistas of possibility and solve beforehand so many possible difficulties in the arrangement and operation of your social system as this universality of culture. I am bound to say that nothing that is rational seems impossible in the way of social adjustments when once you assume the existence of that condition. My own contemporaries fully recognized in theory, as you know, the importance of popular education to secure good government in a democracy; but our system, which barely at best taught the masses to spell, was a farce indeed compared with the popular education of to-day."

"Necessarily so," replied the doctor. "The basis of education is economic, requiring as it does the maintenance of the pupil without economic return during the educational period. If the education is to amount to anything, that period must cover the years of childhood and adolescence to the age of at least twenty. That involves a very large expenditure, which not one parent in a thousand was able to support in your day. The state might have assumed it, of course, but that would have amounted to the rich supporting the children of the poor, and naturally they would not hear to that, at least beyond the primary grades of education. And even if there had been no money question, the rich, if they hoped to retain their power, would have been crazy to provide for the masses destined to do their dirty work--a culture which would have made them social rebels. For these two reasons your economic system was incompatible with any popular education worthy of the name. On the other hand, the first effect of economic equality was to provide equal educational advantages for all and the best the community could afford. One of the most interesting chapters in the history of the Revolution is that which tells how at once after the new order was established the young men and women under twenty-one years of age who had been working in fields or factories, perhaps since childhood, left their work and poured back into the schools and colleges as fast as room could be made for them, so that they might as far as possible repair their early loss. All alike recognized, now that education had been made economically possible for all, that it was the greatest boon the new order had brought. It recorded also in the books that not only the youth, but the men and women, and even the elderly who had been without educational advantages, devoted all the leisure left from their industrial duties to making up, so far as possible, for their lack of earlier advantages, that they might not be too much ashamed in the presence of a rising generation to be composed altogether of college graduates.

"In speaking of our educational system as it is at present," the doctor went on, "I should guard you against the possible mistake of supposing that the course which ends at twenty-one completes the educational curriculum of the average individual. On the contrary, it is only the required minimum of culture which society insists that all youth shall receive during their minority to make them barely fit for citizenship. We should consider it a very meager education indeed that ended there. As we look at it, the graduation from the schools at the attainment of majority means merely that the graduate has reached an age at which he can be presumed to be competent and has the right as an adult to carry on his further education without the guidance or compulsion of the state. To provide means for this end the nation maintains a vast system of what you would call elective post-graduate courses of study in every branch of science, and these are open freely to every one to the end of life to be pursued as long or as briefly, as constantly or as intermittently, as profoundly or superficially, as desired.

"The mind is really not fit for many most important branches of knowledge, the taste for them does not awake, and the intellect is not able to grasp them, until mature life, when a month of application will give a comprehension of a subject which years would have been wasted in trying to impart to a youth. It is our idea, so far as possible, to postpone the serious study of such branches to the post-graduate schools. Young people must get a smattering of things in general, but really theirs is not the time of life for ardent and effective study. If you would see enthusiastic students to whom the pursuit of knowledge is the greatest joy of life you must seek them among the middle-aged fathers and mothers in the post-graduate schools.

"For the proper use of these opportunities for the lifelong pursuit of knowledge we find the leisure of our lives, which seems to you so ample, all too small. And yet that leisure, vast as it is, with half of every day and half of every year and the whole latter half of life sacred to personal uses--even the aggregate of these great spaces, growing greater with every labor-saving invention, which are reserved for the higher uses of life, would seem to us of little value for intellectual culture, but for a condition commanded by almost none in your day but secured to all by our institutions. I mean the moral atmosphere of serenity resulting from an absolute freedom of mind from disturbing anxieties and carking cares concerning our material welfare or that of those dear to us. Our economic system puts us in a position where we can follow Christ's maxim, so impossible for you, to 'take no thought for the morrow.' You must not understand, of course, that all our people are students or philosophers, but you may understand that we are more or less assiduous and systematic students and school-goers all our lives."

"Really, doctor," I said, "I do not remember that you have ever told me anything that has suggested a more complete and striking contrast between your age and mine than this about the persistent and growing development of the purely intellectual interests through life. In my day there was, after all, only six or eight years' difference in the duration of the intellectual life of the poor man's son drafted into the factory at fourteen and the more fortunate youth's who went to college. If that of the one stopped at fourteen, that of the other ceased about as completely at twenty-one or twenty-two. Instead of being in a position to begin his real education on graduating from college, that event meant the close of it for the average student, and was the high-water mark of his life, so far as concerned the culture and knowledge of the sciences and humanities. In these respects the average college man never afterward knew so much as on his graduation day. For immediately thereafter, unless of the richest class, he must needs plunge into the turmoil and strife of business life and engage in the struggle for the material means of existence. Whether he failed or succeeded, made little difference as to the effect to stunt and wither his intellectual life. He had no time and could command no thought for anything else. If he failed, or barely avoided failure, perpetual anxiety ate out his heart; and if he succeeded, his success usually made him a grosser and more hopelessly self-satisfied materialist than if he had failed. There was no hope for his mind or soul either way. If at the end of life his efforts had won him a little breathing space, it could be of no high use to him, for the spiritual and intellectual parts had become atrophied from disuse, and were no longer capable of responding to opportunity.

"And this apology for an existence," said the doctor, "was the life of those whom you counted most fortunate and most successful--of those who were reckoned to have won the prizes of life. Can you be surprised that we look back to the great Revolution as a sort of second creation of man, inasmuch as it added the conditions of an adequate mind and soul life to the bare physical existence under more or less agreeable conditions, which was about all the life the most of human being's, rich or poor, had up to that time known? The effect of the struggle for existence in arresting, with its engrossments, the intellectual development at the very threshold of adult life would have been disastrous enough had the character of the struggle been morally unobjectionable. It is when we come to consider that the struggle was one which not only prevented mental culture, but was utterly withering to the moral life, that we fully realize the unfortunate condition of the race before the Revolution. Youth is visited with noble aspirations and high dreams of duty and perfection. It sees the world as it should be, not as it is; and it is well for the race if the institutions of society are such as do not offend these moral enthusiasms, but rather tend to conserve and develop them through life. This, I think, we may fully claim the modern social order does. Thanks to an economic system which illustrates the highest ethical idea in all its workings, the youth going forth into the world finds it a practice school for all the moralities. He finds full room and scope in its duties and occupations for every generous enthusiasm, every unselfish aspiration he ever cherished. He can not possibly have formed a moral idea higher or completer than that which dominates our industrial and commercial order.

"Youth was as noble in your day as now, and dreamed the same great dreams of life's possibilities. But when the young man went forth into the world of practical life it was to find his dreams mocked and his ideals derided at every turn. He found himself compelled, whether he would or not, to take part in a fight for life, in which the first condition of success was to put his ethics on the shelf and cut the acquaintance of his conscience. You had various terms with which to describe the process whereby the young man, reluctantly laying aside his ideals, accepted the conditions of the sordid struggle. You described it as a 'learning to take the world as it is,' 'getting over romantic notions,' 'becoming practical,' and all that. In fact, it was nothing more nor less than the debauching of a soul. Is that too much to say?

"It is no more than the truth, and we all knew it," I answered.

"Thank God, that day is over forever! The father need now no longer instruct the son in cynicism lest he should fail in life, nor the mother her daughter in worldly wisdom as a protection from generous instinct. The parents are worthy of their children and fit to associate with them, as it seems to us they were not and could not be in your day. Life is all the way through as spacious and noble as it seems to the ardent child standing on the threshold. The ideals of perfection, the enthusiasms of self-devotion, honor, love, and duty, which thrill the boy and girl, no longer yield with advancing years to baser motives, but continue to animate life to the end. You remember what Wordsworth said:

"Heaven lies about us in our infancy.
Shades of the prison house begin to close
Upon the growing boy.

I think if he were a partaker of our life he would not have been moved to extol childhood at the expense of maturity, for life grows ever wider and higher to the last."

CHAPTER XXXI.

"Neither In This Mountain Nor At Jerusalem."

The next morning, it being again necessary for Edith to report at her post of duty, I accompanied her to the railway station. While we stood waiting for the train my attention was drawn to a distinguished-looking man who alighted from an incoming car. He appeared by nineteenth-century standards about sixty years old, and was therefore presumably eighty or ninety, that being about the rate of allowance I have found it necessary to make in estimating the ages of my new contemporaries, owing to the slower advent of signs of age in these times. On speaking to Edith of this person I was much interested when she informed me that he was no other than Mr. Barton, whose sermon by telephone had so impressed me on the first Sunday of my new life, as set forth in Looking Backward. Edith had just time to introduce me before taking the train.

As we left the station together I said to my companion that if he would excuse the inquiry I should be interested to know what particular sect or religious body he represented.

"My dear Mr. West," was the reply, "your question suggests that my friend Dr. Leete has not probably said much to you about the modern way of regarding religious matters."

"Our conversation has turned but little on that subject," I answered, "but it will not surprise me to learn that your ideas and practices are quite different from those of my day. Indeed, religious ideas and ecclesiastical institutions were already at that time undergoing such rapid and radical decomposition that it was safe to predict if religion were to survive another century it would be under very different forms from any the past had known."

"You have suggested a topic," said my companion, "of the greatest possible interest to me. If you have nothing else to do, and would like to talk a little about it, nothing would give me more pleasure."

Upon receiving the assurance that I had absolutely no occupation except to pick up information about the twentieth century, Mr. Barton said:

"Let us then go into this old church, which you will no doubt have already recognized as a relic of your time. There we can sit comfortably while we talk, amid surroundings well fitted to our theme."

I then perceived that we stood before one of the last-century church buildings which have been preserved as historical monuments, and, moreover, as it oddly enough fell out, that this particular church was no other than the one my family had always attended, and I as well--that is, whenever I attended any church, which was not often.

"What an extraordinary coincidence!" exclaimed Mr. Barton, when I told him this; "who would have expected it? Naturally, when you revisit a spot so fraught with affecting associations, you will wish to be alone. You must pardon my involuntary indiscretion in proposing to turn in here."

"Really," I replied, "the coincidence is interesting merely, not at all affecting. Young men of my day did not, as a rule, take their church relations very seriously. I shall be interested to see how the old place looks. Let us go in, by all means."

The interior proved to be quite unchanged in essential particulars since the last time I had been within its walls, more than a century before. That last occasion, I well remembered, had been an Easter service, to which I had escorted some pretty country cousins who wanted to hear the music and see the flowers. No doubt the processes of decay had rendered necessary many restorations, but they had been carried out so as to preserve completely the original effects.

Leading the way down the main aisle, I paused in front of the family pew.

"This, Mr. Barton," I said, "is, or was, my pew. It is true that I am a little in arrears on pew rent, but I think I may venture to invite you to sit with me."

I had truly told Mr. Barton that there was very little sentiment connected with such church relations as I had maintained. They were indeed merely a matter of family tradition and social propriety. But in another way I found myself not a little moved, as, dropping into my accustomed place at the head of the pew, I looked about the dim and silent interior. As my eye roved from pew to pew, my imagination called back to life the men and women, the young men and maidens, who had been wont of a Sunday, a hundred years before, to sit in those places. As I recalled their various activities, ambitions, hopes, fears, envies, and intrigues, all dominated, as they had been, by the idea of money possessed, lost, or lusted after, I was impressed not so much with the personal death which had come to these my old acquaintances as by the thought of the completeness with which the whole social scheme in which they had lived and moved and had their being had passed away. Not only were they gone, but their world was gone, and its place knew it no more. How strange, how artificial, how grotesque that world had been!--and yet to them and to me, while I was one of them, it had seemed the only possible mode of existence.

Mr. Barton, with delicate respect for my absorption, waited for me to break the silence.

"No doubt," I said, "since you preserve our churches as curiosities, you must have better ones of your own for use?"

"In point of fact," my companion replied, "we have little or no use for churches at all."

"Ah, yes! I had forgotten for the moment that it was by telephone I heard your sermon. The telephone, in its present perfection, must indeed have quite dispensed with the necessity of the church as an audience room."

"In other words," replied Mr. Barton, "when we assemble now we need no longer bring our bodies with us. It is a curious paradox that while the telephone and electroscope, by abolishing distance as a hindrance to sight and hearing, have brought mankind into a closeness of sympathetic and intellectual rapport never before imagined, they have at the same time enabled individuals, although keeping in closest touch with everything going on in the world, to enjoy, if they choose, a physical privacy, such as one had to be a hermit to command in your day. Our advantages in this respect have so far spoiled us that being in a crowd, which was the matter-of-course penalty you had to pay for seeing or hearing anything interesting, would seem too dear a price to pay for almost any enjoyment."

"I can imagine," I said, "that ecclesiastical institutions must have been affected in other ways besides the disuse of church buildings, by the general adaptation of the telephone system to religious teaching. In my day, the fact that no speaker could reach by voice more than a small group of hearers made it necessary to have a veritable army of preachers--some fifty thousand, say, in the United States alone--in order to instruct the population. Of these, not one in many hundreds was a person who had anything to utter really worth hearing. For example, we will say that fifty thousand clergymen preached every Sunday as many sermons to as many congregations. Four fifths of these sermons were poor, half of the rest perhaps fair, some of the others good, and a few score, possibly, out of the whole really of a fine class. Now, nobody, of course, would hear a poor discourse on any subject when he could just as easily hear a fine one, and if we had perfected the telephone system to the point you have, the result would have been, the first Sunday after its introduction, that everybody who wanted to hear a sermon would have connected with the lecture rooms or churches of the few widely celebrated preachers, and the rest would have had no hearers at all, and presently have been obliged to seek new occupations."

Mr. Barton was amused. "You have, in fact, hit," he said, "upon the mechanical side of one of the most important contrasts between your times and ours--namely, the modern suppression of mediocrity in teaching, whether intellectual or religious. Being able to pick from the choicest intellects, and most inspired moralists and seers of the generation, everybody of course agrees in regarding it a waste of time to listen to any who have less weighty messages to deliver. When you consider that all are thus able to obtain the best inspiration the greatest minds can give, and couple this with the fact that, thanks to the universality of the higher education, all are at least pretty good judges of what is best, you have the secret of what might be called at once the strongest safeguard of the degree of civilization we have attained, and the surest pledge of the highest possible rate of progress toward ever better conditions--namely, the leadership of moral and intellectual genius. To one like you, educated according to the ideas of the nineteenth century as to what democracy meant, it may seem like a paradox that the equalizing of economic and educational conditions, which has perfected democracy, should have resulted in the most perfect aristocracy, or government by the best, that could be conceived; yet what result could be more matter-of-course? The people of to-day, too intelligent to be misled or abused for selfish ends even by demigods, are ready, on the other hand, to comprehend and to follow with enthusiasm every better leading. The result is, that our greatest men and women wield to-day an unselfish empire, more absolute than your czars dreamed of, and of an extent to make Alexander's conquests seem provincial. There are men in the world who when they choose to appeal to their fellow-men, by the bare announcement are able to command the simultaneous attention of one to five or eight hundred millions of people. In fact, if the occasion be a great one, and the speaker worthy of it, a world-wide silence reigns as in their various places, some beneath the sun and others under the stars, some by the light of dawn and others at sunset, all hang on the lips of the teacher. Such power would have seemed, perhaps, in your day dangerous, but when you consider that its tenure is conditional on the wisdom and unselfishness of its exercise, and would fail with the first false note, you may judge that it is a dominion as safe as God's."

"Dr. Leete," I said, "has told me something of the way in which the universality of culture, combined with your scientific appliances, has made physically possible this leadership of the best; but, I beg your pardon, how could a speaker address numbers so vast as you speak of unless the pentecostal miracle were repeated? Surely the audience must be limited at least by the number of those understanding one language."

"Is it possible that Dr. Leete has not told you of our universal language?"

"I have heard no language but English."

"Of course, everybody talks the language of his own country with his countrymen, but with the rest of the world he talks the general language--that is to say, we have nowadays to acquire but two languages to talk to all peoples--our own, and the universal. We may learn as many more as we please, and we usually please to learn many, but these two are alone needful to go all over the world or to speak across it without an interpreter. A number of the smaller nations have wholly abandoned their national tongue and talk only the general language. The greater nations, which have fine literature embalmed in their languages, have been more reluctant to abandon them, and in this way the smaller folks have actually had a certain sort of advantage over the greater. The tendency, however, to cultivate but one language as a living tongue and to treat all the others as dead or moribund is increasing at such a rate that if you had slept through another generation you might have found none but philological experts able to talk with you."

"But even with the universal telephone and the universal language," I said, "there still remains the ceremonial and ritual side of religion to be considered. For the practice of that I should suppose the piously inclined would still need churches to assemble in, however able to dispense with them for purposes of instruction."

"If any feel that need, there is no reason why they should not have as many churches as they wish and assemble as often as they see fit. I do not know but there are still those who do so. But with a high grade of intelligence become universal the world was bound to outgrow the ceremonial side of religion, which with its forms and symbols, its holy times and places, its sacrifices, feasts, fasts, and new moons, meant so much in the child-time of the race. The time has now fully come which Christ foretold in that talk with the woman by the well of Samaria when the idea of the Temple and all it stood for would give place to the wholly spiritual religion, without respect of times or places, which he declared most pleasing to God.

"With the ritual and ceremonial side of religion outgrown," said I, "with church attendance become superfluous for purposes of instruction, and everybody selecting his own preacher on personal grounds, I should say that sectarian lines must have pretty nearly disappeared."

"Ah, yes!" said Mr. Barton, "that reminds me that our talk began with your inquiry as to what religious sect I belonged to. It is a very long time since it has been customary for people to divide themselves into sects and classify themselves under different names on account of variations of opinion as to matters of religion."

"Is it possible," I exclaimed, "that you mean to say people no longer quarrel over religion? Do you actually tell me that human beings have become capable of entertaining different opinions about the next world without becoming enemies in this? Dr. Leete has compelled me to believe a good many miracles, but this is too much."

"I do not wonder that it seems rather a startling proposition, at first statement, to a man of the nineteenth century," replied Mr. Barton. "But, after all, who was it who started and kept up the quarreling over religion in former days?"

"It was, of course, the ecclesiastical bodies--the priests and preachers."

"But they were not many. How were they able to make so much trouble?"

"On account of the masses of the people who, being densely ignorant, were correspondingly superstitious and bigoted, and were tools in the hands of the ecclesiastics."

"But there was a minority of the cultured. Were they bigoted also? Were they tools of the ecclesiastics?"

"On the contrary, they always held a calm and tolerant attitude on religious questions and were independent of the priesthoods. If they deferred to ecclesiastical influence at all, it was because they held it needful for the purpose of controlling the ignorant populace."

"Very good. You have explained your miracle. There is no ignorant populace now for whose sake it is necessary for the more intelligent to make any compromises with truth. Your cultured class, with their tolerant and philosophical view of religious differences, and the criminal folly of quarreling about them, has become the only class there is."

"How long is it since people ceased to call themselves Catholics, Protestants, Baptists, Methodists, and so on?"

"That kind of classification may be said to have received a fatal shock at the time of the great Revolution, when sectarian demarcations and doctrinal differences, already fallen into a good deal of disregard, were completely swept away and forgotten in the passionate impulse of brotherly love which brought men together for the founding of a nobler social order. The old habit might possibly have revived in time had it not been for the new culture, which, during the first generation subsequent to the Revolution, destroyed the soil of ignorance and superstition which had supported ecclesiastical influence, and made its recrudescence impossible for evermore.

"Although, of course," continued my companion, "the universalizing of intellectual culture is the only cause that needs to be considered in accounting for the total disappearance of religious sectarianism, yet it will give you a more vivid realization of the gulf fixed between the ancient and the modern usages as to religion if you consider certain economic conditions, now wholly passed away, which in your time buttressed the power of ecclesiastical institutions in very substantial ways. Of course, in the first place, church buildings were needful to preach in, and equally so for the ritual and ceremonial side of religion. Moreover, the sanction of religious teaching, depending chiefly on the authority of tradition instead of its own reasonableness, made it necessary for any preacher who would command hearers to enter the service of some of the established sectarian organizations. Religion, in a word, like industry and politics, was capitalized by greater or smaller corporations which exclusively controlled the plant and machinery, and conducted it for the prestige and power of the firms. As all those who desired to engage in politics or industry were obliged to do so in subjection to the individuals and corporations controlling the machinery, so was it in religious matters likewise. Persons desirous of entering on the occupation of religious teaching could do so only by conforming to the conditions of some of the organizations controlling the machinery, plant, and good will of the business--that is to say, of some one of the great ecclesiastical corporations. To teach religion outside of these corporations, when not positively illegal, was a most difficult undertaking, however great the ability of the teacher--as difficult, indeed, as it was to get on in politics without wearing a party badge, or to succeed in business in opposition to the great capitalists. The would-be religious teacher had to attach himself, therefore, to some one or other of the sectarian organizations, whose mouthpiece he must consent to be, as the condition of obtaining any hearing at all. The organization might be hierarchical, in which case he took his instructions from above, or it might be congregational, in which case he took his orders from below. The one method was monarchical, the other democratic, but one as inconsistent as the other with the office of the religious teacher, the first condition of which, as we look at it, should be absolute spontaneity of feeling and liberty of utterance.

"It may be said that the old ecclesiastical system depended on a double bondage: first, the intellectual subjection of the masses through ignorance to their spiritual directors; and, secondly, the bondage of the directors themselves to the sectarian organizations, which as spiritual capitalists monopolized the opportunities of teaching. As the bondage was twofold, so also was the enfranchisement--a deliverance alike of the people and of their teachers, who, under the guise of leaders, had been themselves but puppets. Nowadays preaching is as free as hearing, and as open to all. The man who feels a special calling to talk to his fellows upon religious themes has no need of any other capital than something worth saying. Given this, without need of any further machinery than the free telephone, he is able to command an audience limited only by the force and fitness of what he has to say. He now does not live by his preaching. His business is not a distinct profession. He does not belong to a class apart from other citizens, either by education or occupation. It is not needful for any purpose that he should do so. The higher education which he shares with all others furnishes ample intellectual equipment, while the abundant leisure for personal pursuits with which our life is interfused, and the entire exemption from public duty after forty-five, give abundant opportunity for the exercise of his vocation. In a word, the modern religious teacher is a prophet, not a priest. The sanction of his words lies not in any human ordination or ecclesiastical *exequatur*, but, even as it was with the prophets of old, in such response as his words may have power to evoke from human hearts."

"If people," I suggested, "still retaining a taste for the old-time ritual and ceremonial observances and face-to-face preaching, should desire to have churches and clergy for their special service, is there anything to prevent it?"

"No, indeed. Liberty is the first and last word of our civilization. It is perfectly consistent with our economic system for a group of individuals, by contributing out of their incomes, not only to rent buildings for group purposes, but by indemnifying the nation for the loss of an individual's public service to secure him as their special minister. Though the state will enforce no private contracts of any sort, it does not forbid them. The old ecclesiastical system was, for a time after the Revolution, kept up by remnants in this way, and might be until now if anybody had wished. But the contempt into which the hireling relation had fallen at once after the Revolution soon made the position of such hired clergymen intolerable, and presently there were none who would demean themselves by entering upon so despised a relation, and none, indeed, who would have spiritual service, of all others, on such terms."

"As you tell the story," I said, "it seems very plain how it all came about, and could not have been otherwise; but you can perhaps hardly imagine how a man of the nineteenth century, accustomed to the vast place occupied by the ecclesiastical edifice and influence in human affairs, is affected by the idea of a world getting on without anything of the sort."

"I can imagine something of your sensation," replied my companion, "though doubtless not adequately. And yet I must say that no change in the social order seems to us to have been more distinctly foreshadowed by the signs of the times in your day than precisely this passing away of the ecclesiastical system. As you yourself observed, just before we came into this church, there was then going on a general deliquescence of dogmatism which made your contemporaries wonder what was going to be left. The influence and authority of the clergy were rapidly disappearing, the sectarian lines were being obliterated, the creeds were falling into contempt, and the authority of tradition was being repudiated. Surely if anything could be safely predicted it was that the religious ideas and institutions of the world were approaching some great change."

"Doubtless," said I, "if the ecclesiastics of my day had regarded the result as merely depending on the drift of opinion among men, they would have been inclined to give up all hope of retaining their influence, but there was another element in the case which gave them courage."

"And what was that?"

"The women. They were in my day called the religious sex. The clergy generally were ready to admit that so far as the interest of the cultured class of men, and indeed of the men generally, in the churches went, they were in a bad way, but they had faith that the devotion of the women would save the cause. Woman was the sheet anchor of the Church. Not only were women the chief attendants at religious functions, but it was largely through their influence on the men that the latter tolerated, even so far as they did, the ecclesiastical pretensions. Now, were not our clergymen justified in counting on the continued support of women, whatever the men might do?"

"Certainly they would have been if woman's position was to remain unchanged, but, as you are doubtless by this time well aware, the elevation and enlargement of woman's sphere in all directions was perhaps the most notable single aspect of the Revolution. When women were called the religious sex it would have been indeed a high ascription if it had been meant that they were the more spiritually minded, but that was not at all what the phrase signified to those who used it; it was merely intended to put in a complimentary way the fact that women in your day were the docile sex. Less educated, as a rule, than men, unaccustomed to responsibility, and trained in habits of subordination and self-distrust, they leaned in all things upon precedent and authority. Naturally, therefore, they still held to the principle of authoritative teaching in religion long after men had generally rejected it. All that was changed with the Revolution, and indeed began to change long before it. Since the Revolution there has been no difference in the education of the sexes nor in the independence of their economic and social position, in the exercise of responsibility or experience in the practical conduct of affairs. As you might naturally infer, they are no longer, as formerly, a peculiarly docile class, nor have they any more toleration for authority, whether in religion, politics, or economics, than their brethren. In every pursuit of life they join with men on equal terms, including the most important and engrossing of all our pursuits--the search after knowledge concerning the nature and destiny of man and his relation to the spiritual and material infinity of which he is a part."

CHAPTER XXXII.

Eritis Sicut Deus.

"I infer, then," I said, "that the disappearance of religious divisions and the priestly caste has not operated to lessen the general interest in religion."

"Should you have supposed that it would so operate?"

"I don't know. I never gave much thought to such matters. The ecclesiastical class represented that they were very essential to the conservation of religion, and the rest of us took it for granted that it was so."

"Every social institution which has existed for a considerable time," replied Mr. Barton, "has doubtless performed some function which was at the time more or less useful and necessary. Kings, ecclesiastics, and capitalists--all of them, for that matter, merely different sorts of capitalists--have, no doubt, in their proper periods, performed functions which, however badly discharged, were necessary and could not then have been discharged in any better manner. But just as the abolition of royalty was the beginning of decent government, just as the abolition of private capitalism was the beginning of effective wealth production, so the disappearance of church organization and machinery, or ecclesiastical capitalism, was the beginning of a world-awakening of impassioned interest in the vast concerns covered by the word religion.

"Necessary as may have been the subjection of the race to priestly authority in the course of human evolution, it was the form of tutelage which, of all others, was most calculated to benumb and deaden the faculties affected by it, and the collapse of ecclesiasticism presently prepared the way for an enthusiasm of interest in the great problems of human nature and destiny which would have been scarcely conceivable by the worthy ecclesiastics of your day who with such painful efforts and small results sought to awake their flocks to spiritual concerns. The lack of general interest in these questions in your time was the natural result of their monopoly as the special province of the priestly class whose members stood as interpreters between man and the mystery about him, undertaking to guarantee the spiritual welfare of all who would trust them. The decay of priestly authority left every soul face to face with that mystery, with the responsibility of its interpretation upon himself. The collapse of the traditional theologies relieved the whole subject of man's relation with the infinite from the oppressive effect of the false finalities of dogma which had till then made the most boundless of sciences the most cramped and narrow. Instead of the mind-paralyzing worship of the past and the bondage of the present to that which is written, the conviction took hold on men that there was no limit to what they might know concerning their nature and destiny and no limit to that destiny. The priestly idea that the past was diviner than the present, that God was behind the race, gave place to the belief that we should look forward and not backward for inspiration, and that the present and the future promised a fuller and more certain knowledge concerning the soul and God than any the past had attained."

"Has this belief," I asked, "been thus far practically confirmed by any progress actually made in the assurance of what is true as to these things? Do you consider that you really know more about them than we did, or that you know more positively the things which we merely tried to believe?"

Mr. Barton paused a moment before replying.

"You remarked a little while ago," he said, "that your talks with Dr. Leete had as yet turned little on religious matters. In introducing you to the modern world it was entirely right and logical that he should dwell at first mainly upon the change in economic systems, for that has, of course, furnished the necessary material basis for all the other changes that have taken place. But I am sure that you will never meet any one who, being asked in what direction the progress of the race during the past century has tended most to increase human happiness, would not reply that it had been in the science of the soul and its relation to the Eternal and Infinite.

"This progress has been the result not merely of a more rational conception of the subject and complete intellectual freedom in its study, but largely also of social conditions which have set us almost wholly free from material engrossments. We have now for nearly a century enjoyed an economic welfare which has left nothing to be wished for in the way of physical satisfactions, especially as in proportion to the increase of this abundance there has been through culture a development of simplicity in taste which rejects excess and surfeit and ever makes less and less of the material side of life and more of the mental and moral. Thanks to this co-operation of the material with the moral evolution, the more we have the less we need. Long ago it came to be recognized that on the material side the race had reached the goal of its evolution. We have practically lost ambition for further progress in that direction. The natural result has been that for a long period the main energies of the intellect have been concentrated upon the possibilities of the spiritual evolution of mankind for which the completion of its material evolution has but prepared the beginning. What we have so far learned we are convinced is but the first faint inkling of the knowledge we shall attain to; and yet if the limitations of this earthly state were such that we might never hope here to know more than now we should not repine, for the knowledge we have has sufficed to turn the shadow of death into a bow of promise and distill the saltness out of human tears. You will observe, as you shall come to know more of our literature, that one respect in which it differs from yours is the total lack of the tragic note. This has very naturally followed, from a conception of our real life, as having an inaccessible security, 'hid in God,' as Paul said, whereby the accidents and vicissitudes of the personality are reduced to relative triviality.

"Your seers and poets in exalted moments had seen that death was but a step in life, but this seemed to most of you to have been a hard saying. Nowadays, as life advances toward its close, instead of being shadowed by gloom, it is marked by an access of impassioned expectancy which would cause the young to envy the old, but for the knowledge that in a little while the same door will be opened to them. In your day the undertone of life seems to have been one of unutterable sadness, which, like the moaning of the sea to those who live near the ocean, made itself audible whenever for a moment the noise and bustle of petty engrossments ceased. Now this undertone is so exultant that we are still to hear it."

"If men go on," I said, "growing at this rate in the knowledge of divine things and the sharing of the divine life, what will they yet come to?"

Mr. Barton smiled.

"Said not the serpent in the old story, 'If you eat of the fruit of the tree of knowledge you shall be as gods'? The promise was true in words, but apparently there was some mistake about the tree. Perhaps it was the tree of selfish knowledge, or else the fruit was not ripe. The story is obscure. Christ later said the same thing when he told men that they might be the sons of God. But he made no mistake as to the tree he showed them, and the fruit was ripe. It was the fruit of love, for universal love is at once the seed and fruit, cause and effect, of the highest and completest knowledge. Through boundless love man becomes a god, for thereby is he made conscious of his oneness with God, and all things are put under his feet. It has been only since the great Revolution brought in the era of human brotherhood that mankind has been able to eat abundantly of this fruit of the true tree of knowledge, and thereby grow more and more into the consciousness of the divine soul as the essential self and the true hiding of our lives. Yes, indeed, we shall be gods. The motto of the modern civilization is '*Eritis sicut Deus*.'"

"You speak of Christ. Do I understand that this modern religion is considered by you to be the same doctrine Christ taught?"

"Most certainly. It has been taught from the beginning of history and doubtless earlier, but Christ's teaching is that which has most fully and clearly come down to us. It was the doctrine that he taught, but the world could not then receive it save a few, nor indeed has it ever been possible for the world in general to receive it or even to understand it until this present century."

"Why could not the world receive earlier the revelation it seems to find so easy of comprehension now?"

"Because," replied Mr. Barton, "the prophet and revealer of the soul and of God, which are the same, is love, and until these latter days the world refused to hear love, but crucified him. The religion of Christ, depending as it did upon the experience and intuitions of the unselfish enthusiasms, could not possibly be accepted or understood generally by a world which tolerated a social system based upon fratricidal struggle as the condition of existence. Prophets, messiahs, seers, and saints might indeed for themselves see God face to face, but it was impossible that there should be any general apprehension of God as Christ saw him until social justice had brought in brotherly love. Man must be revealed to man as brother before God could be revealed to him as father. Nominally, the clergy professed to accept and repeat Christ's teaching that God is a loving father, but of course it was simply impossible that any such idea should actually germinate and take root in hearts as cold and hard as stone toward their fellow-beings and sodden with hate and suspicion of them. 'If a man love not his brother whom he hath seen, how shall he love God whom he hath not seen?' The priests deafened their flocks with appeals to love God, to give their hearts to him. They should have rather taught them, as Christ did, to love their fellow-men and give their hearts to them. Hearts so given the love of God would presently enkindle, even as, according to the ancients, fire from heaven might be depended on to ignite a sacrifice fitly prepared and laid.

"From the pulpit yonder, Mr. West, doubtless you have many times heard these words and many like them repeated: 'If we love one another God dwelleth in us and his love is perfected in us.' 'He that loveth his brother dwelleth in the light.' 'If any man say I love God, and hateth his brother, he is a liar.' 'He that loveth not his brother, abideth in death.' 'God is love and he that dwelleth in love dwelleth in God.' 'Every one that loveth knoweth God.' 'He that loveth not knoweth not God.'

"Here is the very distillation of Christ's teaching as to the conditions of entering on the divine life. In this we find the sufficient explanation why the revelation which came to Christ so long ago and to other illumined souls could not possibly be received by mankind in general so long as an inhuman social order made a wall between man and God, and why, the moment that wall was cast down, the revelation flooded the earth like a sunburst.

"'If we love one another God dwelleth in us,' and mark how the words were made good in the way by which at last the race found God! It was not, remember, by directly, purposely, or consciously seeking God. The great enthusiasm of humanity which overthrew the old order and brought in the fraternal society was not primarily or consciously a godward aspiration at all. It was essentially a humane movement. It was a melting and flowing forth of men's hearts toward one another, a rush of contrite, repentant tenderness, an impassioned impulse of mutual love and self-devotion to the common weal. But 'if we love one another God dwelleth in us,' and so men found it. It appears that there came a moment, the most transcendent moment in the history of the race of man, when with the fraternal glow of this world of new-found embracing brothers there seems to have mingled the ineffable thrill of a divine participation, as if the hand of God were clasped over the joined hands of men. And so it has continued to this day and shall for evermore."

CHAPTER XXXIII.

Several Important Matters Overlooked.

After dinner the doctor said that he had an excursion to suggest for the afternoon.

"It has often occurred to me," he went on, "that when you shall go out into the world and become familiar with its features by your own observation, you will, in looking back on these preparatory lessons I have tried to give you, form a very poor impression of my talent as a pedagogue. I am very much dissatisfied myself with the method in which I have developed the subject, which, instead of having been philosophically conceived as a plan of instruction, has been merely a series of random talks, guided rather by your own curiosity than any scheme on my part."

"I am very thankful, my dear friend and teacher," I replied, "that you have spared me the philosophical method. Without boasting that I have acquired so soon a complete understanding of your modern system, I am very sure that I know a good deal more about it than I otherwise should, for the very reason that you have so good-naturedly followed the lead of my curiosity instead of tying me to the tailboard of a method."

"I should certainly like to believe," said the doctor, "that our talks have been as instructive to you as they have been delightful to me, and if I have made mistakes it should be remembered that perhaps no instructor ever had or is likely to have a task quite so large as mine, or one so unexpectedly thrust upon him, or, finally, one which, being so large, the natural curiosity of his pupil compelled him to cover in so short a time."

"But you were speaking of an excursion for this afternoon."

"Yes," said the doctor. "It is a suggestion in the line of an attempt to remedy some few of my too probable omissions of important things in trying to acquaint you with how we live now. What do you say to chartering an air car this afternoon for the purpose of taking a bird's-eye view of the city and environs, and seeing what its various aspects may suggest in the way of features of present-day civilization which we have not touched upon?"

The idea struck me as admirable, and we at once proceeded to put it in execution.

In these brief and fragmentary reminiscences of my first experiences in the modern world it is, of course, impossible that I should refer to one in a hundred of the startling things which happened to me. Still, even with that limitation, it may seem strange to my readers that I have not had more to say of the wonder excited in my mind by the number and character of the great mechanical inventions and applications unknown in my day, which contribute to the material fabric and actuate the mechanism of your civilization. For example, although this was very far from being my first air trip, I do not think that I have before referred to a sort of experience which, to a representative of the last century, must naturally have been nothing less than astounding. I can only say, by way of explanation of this seeming indifference to the mechanical wonders of this age, that had they been ten times more marvelous, they would still have impressed me with infinitely less astonishment than the moral revolution illustrated by your new social order.

This, I am sure, is what would be the experience of any man of my time under my circumstances. The march of scientific discovery and mechanical invention during the last half of the nineteenth century had already been so great and was proceeding so rapidly that we were prepared to expect almost any amount of development in the same lines in the future. Your submarine shipping we had distinctly anticipated and even partially realized. The discovery of the electrical powers had made almost any mechanical conception seem possible. As to navigation of the air, we fully expected that would be somehow successfully solved by our grandchildren if not by our children. If, indeed, I had not found men sailing the air I should have been distinctly disappointed.

But while we were prepared to expect well-nigh anything of man's intellectual development and the perfecting of his mastery over the material world, we were utterly skeptical as to the possibility of any large moral improvement on his part. As a moral being, we believed that he had got his growth, as the saying was, and would never in this world at least attain to a nobler stature. As a philosophical proposition, we recognized as fully as you do that the golden rule would afford the basis of a social life in which every one would be infinitely happier than anybody was in our world, and that the true interest of all would be furthered by establishing such a social order; but we held at the same time that the moral baseness and self-blinding selfishness of man would forever prevent him from realizing such an ideal. In vain, had he been endowed with a godlike intellect; it would not avail him for any of the higher uses of life, for an ineradicable moral perverseness would always hinder him from doing as well as he knew and hold him in hopeless subjection to the basest and most suicidal impulses of his nature.

"Impossible; it is against human nature!" was the cry which met and for the most part overbore and silenced every prophet or teacher who sought to rouse the world to discontent with the reign of chaos and awaken faith in the possibility of a kingdom of God on earth.

Is it any wonder, then, that one like me, bred in that atmosphere of moral despair, should pass over with comparatively little attention the miraculous material achievements of this age, to study with ever-growing awe and wonder the secret of your just and joyous living?

As I look back I see now how truly this base view of human nature was the greatest infidelity to God and man which the human race ever fell into, but, alas! it was not the infidelity which the churches condemned, but rather a sort which their teachings of man's hopeless depravity were calculated to implant and confirm.

This very matter of air navigation of which I was speaking suggests a striking illustration of the strange combination on the part of my contemporaries of unlimited faith in man's material progress with total unbelief in his moral possibilities. As I have said, we fully expected that posterity would achieve air navigation, but the application of the art most discussed was its use in war to drop dynamite bombs in the midst of crowded cities. Try to realize that if you can. Even Tennyson, in his vision of the future, saw nothing more. You remember how he

Heard the heavens fill with shouting,
And there rained a ghastly dew
From the nations airy navies,
Grappling in the central blue.

HOW THE PEOPLE HOLD THE REINS.

"And now," said the doctor, as he checked the rise of our car at an altitude of about one thousand feet, "let us attend to our lesson. What do you see down there to suggest a question?"

"Well, to begin with," I said, as the dome of the Statehouse caught my eye, "what on earth have you stuck up there? It looks for all the world like one of those self-steering windmills the farmers in my day used to pump up water with. Surely that is an odd sort of ornament for a public building."

"It is not intended as an ornament, but a symbol," replied the doctor. "It represents the modern ideal of a proper system of government. The mill stands for the machinery of administration, the wind that drives it symbolizes the public will, and the rudder that always keeps the vane of the mill before the wind, however suddenly or completely the wind may change, stands for the method by which the administration is kept at all times responsive and obedient to every mandate of the people, though it be but a breath.

"I have talked to you so much on that subject that I need enlarge no further on the impossibility of having any popular government worthy of the name which is not based upon the economic equality of the citizens with its implications and consequences. No constitutional devices or cleverness of parliamentary machinery could have possibly made popular government anything but a farce, so long as the private economic interest of the citizen was distinct from and opposed to the public interest, and the so-called sovereign people ate their bread from the hand of capitalists. Given, on the other hand, economic unity of private interests with public interest, the complete independence of every individual on every other, and universal culture to cap all, and no imperfection of administrative machinery could prevent the government from being a good one. Nevertheless, we have improved the machinery as much as we have the motive force. You used to vote once a year, or in two years, or in six years, as the case might be, for those who were to rule over you till the next election, and those rulers, from the moment of their election to the term of their offices, were as irresponsible as czars. They were far more so, indeed, for the czar at least had a supreme motive to leave his inheritance unimpaired to his son, while these elected tyrants had no interest except in making the most they could out of their power while they held it.

"It appears to us that it is an axiom of democratic government that power should never be delegated irrevocably for an hour, but should always be subject to recall by the delegating power. Public officials are nowadays chosen for a term as a matter of convenience, but it is not a term positive. They are liable to have their powers revoked at any moment by the vote of their principals; neither is any measure of more than merely routine character ever passed by a representative body without reference back to the people. The vote of no delegate upon any important measure can stand until his principals--or constituents, as you used to call them--have had the opportunity to cancel it. An elected agent of the people who offended the sentiment of the electors would be displaced, and his act repudiated the next day. You may infer that under this system the agent is solicitous to keep in contact with his principals. Not only do these precautions exist against irresponsible legislation, but the original proposition of measures comes from the people more often than from their representatives.

"So complete through our telephone system has the most complicated sort of voting become, that the entire nation is organized so as to be able to proceed almost like one parliament if needful. Our representative bodies, corresponding to your former Congresses, Legislatures, and Parliaments, are under this system reduced to the exercise of the functions of what you used to call congressional committees. The people not only nominally but actually govern. We have a democracy in fact.

"We take pains to exercise this direct and constant supervision of our affairs not because we suspect or fear our elected agents. Under our system of indefeasible, unchangeable, economic equality there is no motive or opportunity for venality. There is no motive for doing evil that could be for a moment set against the overwhelming motive of deserving the public esteem, which is indeed the only possible object that nowadays could induce any one to accept office. All our vital interests are secured beyond disturbance by the very framework of society. We could safely turn over to a selected body of citizens the management of the public affairs for their lifetime. The reason we do not is that we enjoy the exhilaration of conducting the government of affairs directly. You might compare us to a wealthy man of your day who, though having in his service any number of expert coachmen, preferred to handle the reins himself for the pleasure of it. You used to vote perhaps once a year, taking five minutes for it, and grudging the time at that as lost from your private business, the pursuit of which you called, I believe, 'the main chance.' Our private business is the public business, and we have no other of importance. Our 'main chance' is the public welfare, and we have no other chance. We vote a hundred times perhaps in a year, on all manner of questions, from the temperature of the public baths or the plan to be selected for a public building, to the greatest questions of the world union, and find the exercise at once as exhilarating as it is in the highest sense educational.

"And now, Julian, look down again and see if you do not find some other feature of the scene to hang a question on."

THE LITTLE WARS AND THE GREAT WAR.

"I observe," I said, "that the harbor forts are still there. I suppose you retain them, like the specimen tenement houses, as historical evidences of the barbarism of your ancestors, my contemporaries."

"You must not be offended," said the doctor, "if I say that we really have to keep a full assortment of such exhibits, for fear the children should flatly refuse to believe the accounts the books give of the unaccountable antics of their great-grandfathers."

"The guarantee of international peace which the world union has brought," I said, "must surely be regarded by your people as one of the most signal achievements of the new order, and yet it strikes me I have heard you say very little about it."

"Of course," said the doctor, "it is a great thing in itself, but so incomparably less important than the abolition of the economic war between man and man that we regard it as merely incidental to the latter. Nothing is much more astonishing about the mental operations of your contemporaries than the fuss they made about the cruelty of your occasional international wars while seemingly oblivious to the horrors of the battle for existence in which you all were perpetually involved. From our point of view, your wars, while of course very foolish, were comparatively humane and altogether petty exhibitions as contrasted with the fratricidal economic struggle. In the wars only men took part--strong, selected men, comprising but a very small part of the total population. There were no women, no children, no old people, no cripples allowed to go to war. The wounded were carefully looked after, whether by friends or foes, and nursed back to health. The rules of war forbade unnecessary cruelty, and at any time an honorable surrender, with good treatment, was open to the beaten. The battles generally took place on the frontiers, out of sight and sound of the masses. Wars were also very rare, often not one in a generation. Finally, the sentiments appealed to in international conflicts were, as a rule, those of courage and self-devotion. Often, indeed generally, the causes of the wars were unworthy of the sentiments of self-devotion which the fighting called out, but the sentiments themselves belonged to the noblest order.

"Compare with warfare of this character the conditions of the economic struggle for existence. That was a war in which not merely small selected bodies of combatants took part, but one in which the entire population of every country, excepting the inconsiderable groups of the rich, were forcibly enlisted and compelled to serve. Not only did women, children, the aged and crippled have to participate in it, but the weaker the combatants the harder the conditions under which they must contend. It was a war in which there was no help for the wounded, no quarter for the vanquished. It was a war not on far frontiers, but in every city, every street, and every house, and its wounded, broken, and dying victims lay underfoot everywhere and shocked the eye in every direction that it might glance with some new form of misery. The ear could not escape the lamentations of the stricken and their vain cries for pity. And this war came not once or twice in a century, lasting for a few red weeks or months or years, and giving way again to peace, as did the battles of the soldiers, but was perennial and perpetual, truceless, lifelong. Finally, it was a war which neither appealed to nor developed any noble, any generous, any honorable sentiment, but, on the contrary, set a constant premium on the meanest, falsest, and most cruel propensities of human nature.

"As we look back upon your era, the sort of fighting those old forts down there stood for seems almost noble and barely tragical at all, as compared with the awful spectacle of the struggle for existence.

"We even are able to sympathize with the declaration of some of the professional soldiers of your age that occasional wars, with their appeals, however false, to the generous and self-devoting passions, were absolutely necessary to prevent your society, otherwise so utterly sordid and selfish in its ideals, from dissolving into absolute putrescence."

"It is to be feared," I was moved to observe, "that posterity has not built so high a monument to the promoters of the universal peace societies of my day as they expected."

"They were well meaning enough so far as they saw, no doubt," said the doctor, "but seem to have been a dreadfully short-sighted and purblind set of people. Their efforts to stop wars between nations, while tranquilly ignoring the world-wide economic struggle for existence which cost more lives and suffering in any one month than did the international wars of a generation, was a most striking case of straining at a gnat and swallowing a camel.

"As to the gain to humanity which has come from the abolition of all war or possibility of war between nations of to-day, it seems to us to consist not so much in the mere prevention of actual bloodshed as in the dying out of the old jealousies and rancors which used to embitter peoples against one another almost as much in peace as in war, and the growth in their stead of a fraternal sympathy and mutual good will, unconscious of any barrier of race or country."

THE OLD PATRIOTISM AND THE NEW.

As the doctor was speaking, the waving folds of a flag floating far below caught my eye. It was the Star-Spangled Banner. My heart leaped at the sight and my eyes grew moist.

"Ah!" I exclaimed, "it is Old Glory!" for so it had been a custom to call the flag in the days of the civil war and after.

"Yes," replied my companion, as his eyes followed my gaze, "but it wears a new glory now, because nowhere in the land it floats over is there found a human being oppressed or suffering any want that human aid can relieve.

"The Americans of your day," he continued, "were extremely patriotic after their fashion, but the difference between the old and the new patriotism is so great that it scarcely seems like the same sentiment. In your day and ever before, the emotions and associations of the flag were chiefly of the martial sort. Self-devotion to the nation in war with other nations was the idea most commonly conveyed by the word 'patriotism' and its derivatives. Of course, that must be so in ages when the nations had constantly to stand ready to fight one another for their existence. But the result was that the sentiment of national solidarity was arrayed against the sentiment of human solidarity. A lesser social enthusiasm was set in opposition to a greater, and the result was necessarily full of moral contradictions. Too often what was called love of country might better have been described as hate and jealousy of other countries, for no better reason than that there were other, and bigoted prejudices against foreign ideas and institutions--often far better than domestic ones--for no other reason than that they were foreign. This sort of patriotism was a most potent hindrance for countless ages to the progress of civilization, opposing to the spread of new ideas barriers higher than mountains, broader than rivers, deeper than seas.

"The new patriotism is the natural outcome of the new social and international conditions which date from the great Revolution. Wars, which were already growing infrequent in your day, were made impossible by the rise of the world union, and for generations have now been unknown. The old blood-stained frontiers of the nations have become scarcely more than delimitations of territory for administrative convenience, like the State lines in the American Union. Under these circumstances international jealousies, suspicions, animosities, and apprehensions have died a natural death. The anniversaries of battles and triumphs over other nations, by which the antique patriotism was kept burning, have been long ago forgotten. In a word, patriotism is no longer a martial sentiment and is quite without warlike associations. As the flag has lost its former significance as an emblem of outward defiance, it has gained a new meaning as the supreme symbol of internal concord and mutuality; it has become the visible sign of the social solidarity in which the welfare of all is equally and impregnably secured. The American, as he now lifts his eyes to the ensign of the nation, is not reminded of its military prowess as compared with other nations, of its past triumphs in battle and possible future victories. To him the waving folds convey no such suggestions. They recall rather the compact of brotherhood in which he stands pledged with all his countrymen mutually to safeguard the equal dignity and welfare of each by the might of all.

"The idea of the old-time patriots was that foreigners were the only people at whose hands the flag could suffer dishonor, and the report of any lack of etiquette toward it on their part used to excite the people to a patriotic frenzy. That sort of feeling would be simply incomprehensible now. As we look at it, foreigners have no power to insult the flag, for they have nothing to do with it, nor with what it stands for. Its honor or dishonor must depend upon the people whose plighted faith one to another it represents, to maintain the social contract. To the old-time patriot there was nothing incongruous in the spectacle of the symbol of the national unity floating over cities reeking with foulest oppressions, full of prostitution, beggary, and dens of nameless misery. According to the modern view, the existence of a single instance in any corner of the land where a citizen had been deprived of the full enjoyment of equality would turn the flag into a flaunting lie, and the people would demand with indignation that it should be hauled down and not raised again till the wrong was remedied."

"Truly," I said, "the new glory which Old Glory wears is a greater than the old glory."

MORE FOREIGN TRAVEL BUT LESS FOREIGN TRADE.

As we had talked, the doctor had allowed our car to drift before the westerly breeze till now we were over the harbor, and I was moved to exclaim at the scanty array of shipping it contained.

"It does not seem to me," I said, "that there are more vessels here than in my day, much less the great fleets one might expect to see after a century's development in population and resources."

"In point of fact," said the doctor, "the new order has tended to decrease the volume of foreign trade, though on the other hand there is a thousandfold more foreign travel for instruction and pleasure."

"In just what way," I asked, "did the new order tend to decrease exchanges with foreign countries?"

"In two ways," replied the doctor. "In the first place, as you know, the profit idea is now abolished in foreign trade as well as in domestic distribution. The International Council supervises all exchanges between nations, and the price of any product exported by one nation to another must not be more than that at which the exporting nation provides its own people with the same. Consequently there is no reason why a nation should care to produce goods for export unless and in so far as it needs for actual consumption products of another country which it can not itself so well produce.

"Another yet more potent effect of the new order in limiting foreign exchange is the general equalization of all nations which has long ago come about as to intelligence and the knowledge and practice of sciences and arts. A nation of to-day would be humiliated to have to import any commodity which insuperable natural conditions did not prevent the production of at home. It is consequently to such productions that commerce is now limited, and the list of them grows ever shorter as with the progress of invention man's conquest of Nature proceeds. As to the old advantage of coal-producing countries in manufacturing, that disappeared nearly a century ago with the great discoveries which made the unlimited development of electrical power practically costless.

"But you should understand that it is not merely on economic grounds or for self-esteem's sake that the various peoples desire to do everything possible for themselves rather than depend on people at a distance. It is quite as much for the education and mind-awakening influence of a diversified industrial system within a small space. It is our policy, so far as it can be economically carried out in the grouping of industries, not only to make the system of each nation complete, but so to group the various industries within each particular country that every considerable district shall present within its own limits a sort of microcosm of the industrial world. We were speaking of that, you may remember, the other morning, in the Labor Exchange."

THE MODERN DOCTOR'S EASY TASK.

The doctor had some time before reversed our course, and we were now moving westward over the city.

"What is that building which we are just passing over that has so much glass about it?" I asked.

"That is one of the sanitariums," replied the doctor, "which people go to who are in bad health and do not wish to change their climate, as we think persons in serious chronic ill health ought to do and as all can now do if they desire. In these buildings everything is as absolutely adapted to the condition of the patient as if he were for the time being in a world in which his disease were the normal type."

"Doubtless there have been great improvements in all matters relating to your profession-- medicine, hygiene, surgery, and the rest--since my day."

"Yes," replied the doctor, "there have been great improvements in two ways--negative and positive--and the more important of the two is perhaps the negative way, consisting in the disappearance of conditions inimical to health, which physicians formerly had to combat with little chance of success in many cases. For example, it is now two full generations since the guarantee of equal maintenance for all placed women in a position of economic independence and consequent complete control of their relations to men. You will readily understand how, as one result of this, the taint of syphilis has been long since eliminated from the blood of the race. The universal prevalence now for three generations of the most cleanly and refined conditions of housing, clothing, heating, and living generally, with the best treatment available for all in case of sickness, have practically--indeed I may say completely--put an end to the zymotic and other contagious diseases. To complete the story, add to these improvements in the hygienic conditions of the people the systematic and universal physical culture which is a part of the training of youth, and then as a crowning consideration think of the effect of the physical rehabilitation--you might almost call it the second creation of woman in a bodily sense--which has purified and energized the stream of life at its source."

"Really, doctor, I should say that, without going further, you have fairly reasoned your profession out of its occupation."

"You may well say so," replied the doctor. "The progress of invention and improvement since your day has several times over improved the doctors out of their former occupations, just as it has every other sort of workers, but only to open new and higher fields of finer work.

"Perhaps," my companion resumed, "a more important negative factor in the improvement in medical and hygienic conditions than any I have mentioned is the fact that people are no longer in the state of ignorance as to their own bodies that they seem formerly to have been. The progress of knowledge in that respect has kept pace with the march of universal culture. It is evident from what we read that even the cultured classes in your day thought it no shame to be wholly uninformed as to physiology and the ordinary conditions of health and disease. They appear to have left their physical interests to the doctors, with much the same spirit of cynical resignation with which they turned over their souls to the care of the clergy. Nowadays a system of education would be thought farcical which did not impart a sufficient knowledge of the general principles of physiology, hygiene, and medicine to enable a person to treat any ordinary physical disturbance without recourse to a physician. It is perhaps not too much to say that everybody nowadays knows as much about the treatment of disease as a large proportion of the members of the medical profession did in your time. As you may readily suppose, this is a situation which, even apart from the general improvement in health, would enable the people to get on with one physician where a score formerly found business. We doctors are merely specialists and experts on subjects that everybody is supposed to be well grounded in. When we are called in, it is really only in consultation, to use a phrase of the profession in your day, the other parties being the patient and his friends.

"But of all the factors in the advance of medical science, one of the most important has been the disappearance of sectarianism, resulting largely from the same causes, moral and economic, which banished it from religion. You will scarcely need to be reminded that in your day medicine, next to theology, suffered most of all branches of knowledge from the benumbing influence of dogmatic schools. There seems to have been well-nigh as much bigotry as to the science of curing the body as the soul, and its influence to discourage original thought and retard progress was much the same in one field as the other.

"There are really no conditions to limit the course of physicians. The medical education is the fullest possible, but the methods of practice are left to the doctor and patient. It is assumed that people as cultured as ours are as competent to elect the treatment for their bodies as to choose that for their souls. The progress in medical science which has resulted from this complete independence and freedom of initiative on the part of the physician, stimulated by the criticism and applause of a people well able to judge of results, has been unprecedented. Not only in the specific application of the preserving and healing arts have innumerable achievements been made and radically new principles discovered, but we have made advances toward a knowledge of the central mystery of life which in your day it would have been deemed almost sacrilegious to dream of. As to pain, we permit it only for its symptomatic indications, and so far only as we need its guidance in diagnosis."

"I take it, however, that you have not abolished death."

"I assure you," laughed the doctor, "that if perchance any one should find out the secret of that, the people would mob him and burn up his formula. Do you suppose we want to be shut up here forever?"

"HOW COULD WE INDEED?"

Applying myself again to the study of the moving panorama below us, I presently remarked to the doctor that we must be pretty nearly over what was formerly called Brighton, a suburb of the city at which the live stock for the food supply of the city had mainly been delivered.

"I see the old cattle-sheds are gone," I said. "Doubtless you have much better arrangements. By the way, now that everybody is well-to-do, and can afford the best cuts of beef, I imagine the problem of providing a big city with fresh meats must be much more difficult than in my day, when the poor were able to consume little flesh food, and that of the poorest sort."

The doctor looked over the side of the car for some moments before answering.

"I take it," he said, "that you have not spoken to any one before on this point."

"Why, I think not. It has not before occurred to me."

"It is just as well," said the doctor. "You see, Julian, in the transformation in customs and habits of thought and standards of fitness since your day, it could scarcely have happened but that in some cases the changes should have been attended with a decided revulsion in sentiment against the former practices. I hardly know how to express myself, but I am rather glad that you first spoke of this matter to me."

A light dawned on me, and suddenly brought out the significance of numerous half-digested observations which I had previously made.

"Ah!" I exclaimed, "you mean you don't eat the flesh of animals any more."

"Is it possible you have not guessed that? Had you not noticed that you were offered no such food?"

"The fact is," I replied, "the cooking is so different in all respects from that of my day that I have given up all attempt to identify anything. But I have certainly missed no flavor to which I have been accustomed, though I have been delighted by a great many novel ones."

"Yes," said the doctor, "instead of the one or two rude processes inherited from primitive men by which you used to prepare food and elicit its qualities, we have a great number and variety. I doubt if there was any flavor you had which we do not reproduce, besides the great number of new ones discovered since your time."

"But when was the use of animals for food discontinued?"

"Soon after the great Revolution."

"What caused the change? Was it a conviction that health would be favored by avoiding flesh?"

"It does not seem to have been that motive which chiefly led to the change. Undoubtedly the abandonment of the custom of eating animals, by which we inherited all their diseases, has had something to do with the great physical improvement of the race, but people did not apparently give up eating animals mainly for health's sake any more than cannibals in more ancient times abandoned eating their fellow-men on that account. It was, of course, a very long time ago, and there was perhaps no practice of the former order of which the people, immediately after giving it up, seem to have become so much ashamed. This is doubtless why we find such meager information in the histories of the period as to the circumstances of the change. There appears, however, to be no doubt that the abandonment of the custom was chiefly an effect of the great wave of humane feeling, the passion of pity and compunction for all suffering--in a word, the impulse of tender-heartedness--which was really the great moral power behind the Revolution. As might be expected, this outburst did not affect merely the relations of men with men, but likewise their relations with the whole sentient world. The sentiment of brotherhood, the feeling of solidarity, asserted itself not merely toward men and women, but likewise toward the humbler companions of our life on earth and sharers of its fortunes, the animals. The new and vivid light thrown on the rights and duties of men to one another brought also into view and recognition the rights of the lower orders of being. A sentiment against cruelty to animals of every kind had long been growing in civilized lands, and formed a distinct feature of the general softening of manners which led up to the Revolution. This sentiment now became an enthusiasm. The new conception of our relation to the animals appealed to the heart and captivated the imagination of mankind. Instead of sacrificing the weaker races to our use or pleasure, with no thought for their welfare, it began to be seen that we should rather, as elder brothers in the great family of Nature, be, so far as possible, guardians and helpers to the weaker orders whose fate is in our hands and to which we are as gods. Do you not see, Julian, how the prevalence of this new view might soon have led people to regard the eating of their fellow-animals as a revolting practice, almost akin to cannibalism?"

"That is, of course, very easily understood. Indeed, doctor, you must not suppose that my contemporaries were wholly without feeling on this subject. Long before the Revolution was dreamed of there were a great many persons of my acquaintance who owned to serious qualms over flesh-eating, and perhaps the greater part of refined persons were not without pangs of conscience at various times over the practice. The trouble was, there really seemed nothing else to do. It was just like our economic system. Humane persons generally admitted that it was very bad and brutal, and yet very few could distinctly see what the world was going to replace it with. You people seem to have succeeded in perfecting a *cuisine* without using flesh, and I admit it is every way more satisfactory than ours was, but you can not imagine how absolutely impossible the idea of getting on without the use of animal food looked in my day, when as yet nothing definite had been suggested to take its place which offered any reasonable amount of gratification to the palate, even if it provided the means of aliment."

"I can imagine the difficulty to some extent. It was, as you say, like that which so long hindered the change of economic systems. People could not clearly realize what was to take its place. While one's mouth is full of one flavor it is difficult to imagine another. That lack of constructive imagination on the part of the mass is the obstacle that has stood in the way of removing every ancient evil, and made necessary a wave of revolutionary force to do the work. Such a wave of feeling as I have described was needful in this case to do away with the immemorial habit of flesh-eating. As soon as the new attitude of men's minds took away their taste for flesh, and there was a demand that had to be satisfied for some other and adequate sort of food, it seems to have been very promptly met."

"From what source?"

"Of course," replied the doctor, "chiefly from the vegetable world, though by no means wholly. There had never been any serious attempt before to ascertain what its provisions for food actually were, still less what might be made of them by scientific treatment. Nor, as long as there was no objection to killing some animal and appropriating without trouble the benefit of its experiments, was there likely to be. The rich lived chiefly on flesh. As for the working masses, which had always drawn their vigor mainly from vegetables, nobody of the influential classes cared to make their lot more agreeable. Now, however, all with one consent set about inquiring what sort of a table Nature might provide for men who had forsworn murder.

"Just as the crude and simple method of slavery, first chattel slavery and afterward wage slavery, had, so long as it prevailed, prevented men from seeking to replace its crude convenience by a scientific industrial system, so in like manner the coarse convenience of flesh for food had hitherto prevented men from making a serious perquisition of Nature's edible resources. The delay in this respect is further accounted for by the fact that the preparation of food, on account of the manner of its conduct as an industry, had been the least progressive of all the arts of life."

"What is that?" I said. "The least progressive of arts? Why so?"

"Because it had always been carried on as an isolated household industry, and as such chiefly left to servants or women, who in former times were the most conservative and habit-bound class in the communities. The rules of the art of cookery had been handed down little changed in essentials since the wife of the Aryan cowherd dressed her husband's food for him.

"Now, it must remain very doubtful how immediately successful the revolt against animal food would have proved if the average family cook, whether wife or hireling, had been left each for herself in her private kitchen to grapple with the problem of providing for the table a satisfactory substitute for flesh. But, thanks to the many-sided character of the great Revolution, the juncture of time at which the growth of humane feeling created a revolt against animal food coincided with the complete breakdown of domestic service and the demand of women for a wider life, facts which compelled the placing of the business of providing and preparing food on a co-operative basis, and the making of it a branch of the public service. So it was that as soon as men, losing appetite for their fellow-creatures, began to ask earnestly what else could be eaten, there was already being organized a great governmental department commanding all the scientific talent of the nation, and backed by the resources of the country, for the purpose of solving the question. And it is easy to believe that none of the new departments was stimulated in its efforts by a keener public interest than this which had in charge the preparation of the new national bill of fare. These were the conditions for which alimentation had waited from the beginnings of the race to become a science.

"In the first place, the food materials and methods of preparing them actually extant, and used in the different nations, were, for the first time in history, collected and collated. In presence of the cosmopolitan variety and extent of the international *menu* thus presented, every national *cuisine* was convicted of having until then run in a rut. It was apparent that in nothing had the nations been more provincial, more stupidly prejudiced against learning from one another, than in matters of food and cooking. It was discovered, as observing travelers had always been aware, that every nation and country, often every province, had half a dozen gastronomic secrets that had never crossed the border, or at best on very brief excursions.

"It is well enough to mention, in passing, that the collation of this international bill of fare was only one illustration of the innumerable ways in which the nations, as soon as the new order put an end to the old prejudices, began right and left to borrow and adopt the best of one another's ideas and institutions, to the great general enrichment.

"But the organization of a scientific system of alimentation did not cease with utilizing the materials and methods already existing. The botanist and the chemist next set about finding new food materials and new methods of preparing them. At once it was discovered that of the natural products capable of being used as food by man, but a petty proportion had ever been utilized; only those, and a small part even of that class, which readily lent themselves to the single primitive process whereby the race hitherto had attempted to prepare food--namely, the application of dry or wet heat. To this, manifold other processes suggested by chemistry were now added, with effects that our ancestors found as delightful as novel. It had hitherto been with the science of cooking as with metallurgy when simple fire remained its only method.

"It is written that the children of Israel, when practicing an enforced vegetarian diet in the wilderness, yearned after the flesh-pots of Egypt, and probably with good reason. The experience of our ancestors appears to have been in this respect quite different. It would seem that the sentiments with which, after a very short period had elapsed, they looked back upon the flesh-pots they had left behind were charged with a feeling quite the reverse of regret. There is an amusing cartoon of the period, which suggests how brief a time it took for them to discover what a good thing they had done for themselves in resolving to spare the animals. The cartoon, as I remember it, is in two parts. The first shows Humanity, typified by a feminine figure regarding a group of animals consisting of the ox, the sheep, and the hog. Her face expresses the deepest compunction, while she tearfully exclaims, 'Poor things! How could we ever bring ourselves to eat you?' The second part reproduces the same group, with the heading 'Five Years After.' But here the countenance of Humanity as she regards the animals expresses not contrition or self-reproach, but disgust and loathing, while she exclaims in nearly identical terms, but very different emphasis, 'How could we, indeed?'"

WHAT BECAME OF THE GREAT CITIES.

Continuing to move westward toward the interior, we had now gradually left behind the more thickly settled portions of the city, if indeed any portion of these modern cities, in which every home stands in its own inclosure, can be called thickly settled. The groves and meadows and larger woods had become numerous, and villages occurred at frequent intervals. We were out in the country.

"Doctor," said I, "it has so happened, you will remember, that what I have seen of twentieth-century life has been mainly its city side. If country life has changed since my day as much as city life, it will be very interesting to make its acquaintance again. Tell me something about it."

"There are few respects, I suppose," replied the doctor, "in which the effect of the nationalization of production and distribution on the basis of economic equality has worked a greater transformation than in the relations of city and country, and it is odd we should not have chanced to speak of this before now."

"When I was last in the world of living people," I said, "the city was fast devouring the country. Has that process gone on, or has it possibly been reversed?"

"Decidedly the latter," replied the doctor, "as indeed you will at once see must have been the case when you consider that the enormous growth of the great cities of the past was entirely an economic consequence of the system of private capitalism, with its necessary dependence upon individual initiative, and the competitive system."

"That is a new idea to me," I said.

"I think you will find it a very obvious one upon reflection," replied the doctor. "Under private capitalism, you see, there was no public or governmental system for organizing productive effort and distributing its results. There was no general and unfailing machinery for bringing producers and consumers together. Everybody had to seek his own occupation and maintenance on his own account, and success depended on his finding an opportunity to exchange his labor or possessions for the possessions or labor of others. For this purpose the best place, of course, was where there were many people who likewise wanted to buy or sell their labor or goods. Consequently, when, owing either to accident or calculation, a mass of people were drawn together, others flocked to them, for every such aggregation made a market place where, owing simply to the number of persons desiring to buy and sell, better opportunities for exchange were to be found than where fewer people were, and the greater the number of people the larger and better the facilities for exchange. The city having thus taken a start, the larger it became, the faster it was likely to grow by the same logic that accounted for its first rise. The laborer went there to find the largest and steadiest market for his muscle, and the capitalist--who, being a conductor of production, desired the largest and steadiest labor market--went there also. The capitalist trader went there to find the greatest group of consumers of his goods within least space.

"Although at first the cities rose and grew, mainly because of the facilities for exchange among their own citizens, yet presently the result of the superior organization of exchange facilities made them centers of exchange for the produce of the surrounding country. In this way those who lived in the cities had not only great opportunities to grow rich by supplying the needs of the dense resident population, but were able also to levy a tribute upon the products of the people in the country round about by compelling those products to pass through their hands on the way to the consumers, even though the consumers, like the producers, lived in the country, and might be next door neighbors.

"In due course," pursued the doctor, "this concentration of material wealth in the cities led to a concentration there of all the superior, the refined, the pleasant, and the luxurious ministrations of life. Not only did the manual laborers flock to the cities as the market where they could best exchange their labor for the money of the capitalists, but the professional and learned class resorted thither for the same purpose. The lawyers, the pedagogues, the doctors, the rhetoricians, and men of special skill in every branch, went there as the best place to find the richest and most numerous employers of their talents, and to make their careers.

"And in like manner all who had pleasure to sell--the artists, the players, the singers, yes, and the courtesans also--flocked to the cities for the same reasons. And those who desired pleasure and had wealth to buy it, those who wished to enjoy life, either as to its coarse or refined gratifications, followed the pleasure-givers. And, finally, the thieves and robbers, and those pre-eminent in the wicked arts of living on their fellow-men, followed the throng to the cities, as offering them also the best field for their talents. And so the cities became great whirlpools, which drew to themselves all that was richest and best, and also everything that was vilest, in the whole land.

"Such, Julian, was the law of the genesis and growth of the cities, and it was by necessary consequence the law of the shrinkage, decay, and death of the country and country life. It was only necessary that the era of private capitalism in America should last long enough for the rural districts to have been reduced to what they were in the days of the Roman Empire, and of every empire which achieved full development--namely, regions whence all who could escape had gone to seek their fortune in the cities, leaving only a population of serfs and overseers.

"To do your contemporaries justice, they seemed themselves to realize that the swallowing up of the country by the city boded no good to civilization, and would apparently have been glad to find a cure for it, but they failed entirely to observe that, as it was a necessary effect of private capitalism, it could only be remedied by abolishing that."

"Just how," said I, "did the abolition of private capitalism and the substitution of a nationalized economic system operate to stop the growth of the cities?"

"By abolishing the need of markets for the exchange of labor and commodities," replied the doctor. "The facilities of exchange organized in the cities under the private capitalists were rendered wholly superfluous and impertinent by the national organization of production and distribution. The produce of the country was no longer handled by or distributed through the cities, except so far as produced or consumed there. The quality of goods furnished in all localities, and the measure of industrial service required of all, was the same. Economic equality having done away with rich and poor, the city ceased to be a place where greater luxury could be enjoyed or displayed than the country. The provision of employment and of maintenance on equal terms to all took away the advantages of locality as helps to livelihood. In a word, there was no longer any motive to lead a person to prefer city to country life, who did not like crowds for the sake of being crowded. Under these circumstances you will not find it strange that the growth of the cities ceased, and their depopulation began from the moment the effects of the Revolution became apparent."

"But you have cities yet!" I exclaimed.

"Certainly--that is, we have localities where population still remains denser than in other places. None of the great cities of your day have become extinct, but their populations are but small fractions of what they were."

"But Boston is certainly a far finer-looking city than in my day."

"All the modern cities are far finer and fairer in every way than their predecessors and infinitely fitter for human habitation, but in order to make them so it was necessary to get rid of their surplus population. There are in Boston to-day perhaps a quarter as many people as lived in the same limits in the Boston of your day, and that is simply because there were four times as many people within those limits as could be housed and furnished with environments consistent with the modern idea of healthful and agreeable living. New York, having been far worse crowded than Boston, has lost a still larger proportion of its former population. Were you to visit Manhattan Island I fancy your first impression would be that the Central Park of your day had been extended all the way from the Battery to Harlem River, though in fact the place is rather thickly built up according to modern notions, some two hundred and fifty thousand people living there among the groves and fountains."

"And you say this amazing depopulation took place at once after the Revolution?"

"It began then. The only way in which the vast populations of the old cities could be crowded into spaces so small was by packing them like sardines in tenement houses. As soon as it was settled that everybody must be provided with really and equally good habitations, it followed that the cities must lose the greater part of their population. These had to be provided with dwellings in the country. Of course, so vast a work could not be accomplished instantly, but it proceeded with all possible speed. In addition to the exodus of people from the cities because there was no room for them to live decently, there was also a great outflow of others who, now there had ceased to be any economic advantages in city life, were attracted by the natural charms of the country; so that you may easily see that it was one of the great tasks of the first decade after the Revolution to provide homes elsewhere for those who desired to leave the cities. The tendency countryward continued until the cities having been emptied of their excess of people, it was possible to make radical changes in their arrangements. A large proportion of the old buildings and all the unsightly, lofty, and inartistic ones were cleared away and replaced with structures of the low, broad, roomy style adapted to the new ways of living. Parks, gardens, and roomy spaces were multiplied on every hand and the system of transit so modified as to get rid of the noise and dust, and finally, in a word, the city of your day was changed into the modern city. Having thus been made as pleasant places to live in as was the country itself, the outflow of population from the cities ceased and an equilibrium became established."

"It strikes me," I observed, "that under any circumstances cities must still, on account of their greater concentration of people, have certain better public services than small villages, for naturally such conveniences are least expensive where a dense population is to be supplied."

"As to that," replied the doctor, "if a person desires to live in some remote spot far away from neighbors he will have to put up with some inconveniences. He will have to bring his supplies from the nearest public store and dispense with various public services enjoyed by those who live nearer together; but in order to be really out of reach of these services he must go a good way off. You must remember that nowadays the problems of communication and transportation both by public and private means have been so entirely solved that conditions of space which were prohibitive in your day are unimportant now. Villages five and ten miles apart are as near together for purposes of social intercourse and economic administration as the adjoining wards of your cities. Either on their own account or by group combinations with other communities dwellers in the smallest villages enjoy installations of all sorts of public services as complete as exist in the cities. All have public stores and kitchens with telephone and delivery systems, public baths, libraries, and institutions of the highest education. As to the quality of the services and commodities provided, they are of absolutely equal excellence wherever furnished. Finally, by telephone and electroscope the dwellers in any part of the country, however deeply secluded among the forests or the mountains, may enjoy the theater, the concert, and the orator quite as advantageously as the residents of the largest cities."

THE REFORESTING.

Still we swept on mile after mile, league after league, toward the interior, and still the surface below presented the same parklike aspect that had marked the immediate environs of the city. Every natural feature appeared to have been idealized and all its latent meaning brought out by the loving skill of some consummate landscape artist, the works of man blending with the face of Nature in perfect harmony. Such arrangements of scenery had not been uncommon in my day, when great cities prepared costly pleasure grounds, but I had never imagined anything on a scale like this.

"How far does this park extend?" I demanded at last. "There seems no end to it."

"It extends to the Pacific Ocean," said the doctor.

"Do you mean that the whole United States is laid out in this way?"

"Not precisely in this way by any means, but in a hundred different ways according to the natural suggestions of the face of the country and the most effective way of co-operating with them. In this region, for instance, where there are few bold natural features, the best effect to be obtained was that of a smiling, peaceful landscape with as much diversification in detail as possible. In the mountainous regions, on the contrary, where Nature has furnished effects which man's art could not strengthen, the method has been to leave everything absolutely as Nature left it, only providing the utmost facilities for travel and observation. When you visit the White Mountains or the Berkshire Hills you will find, I fancy, their slopes shaggier, the torrents wilder, the forests loftier and more gloomy than they were a hundred years ago. The only evidences of man's handiwork to be found there are the roadways which traverse every gorge and top every summit, carrying the traveler within reach of all the wild, rugged, or beautiful bits of Nature."

"As far as forests go, it will not be necessary for me to visit the mountains in order to perceive that the trees are not only a great deal loftier as a rule, but that there are vastly more of them than formerly."

"Yes," said the doctor, "it would be odd if you did not notice that difference in the landscape. There are said to be five or ten trees nowadays where there was one in your day, and a good part of those you see down there are from seventy-five to a hundred years old, dating from the reforesting."

"What was the reforesting?" I asked.

"It was the restoration of the forests after the Revolution. Under private capitalism the greed or need of individuals had led to so general a wasting of the woods that the streams were greatly reduced and the land was constantly plagued with droughts. It was found after the Revolution that one of the things most urgent to be done was to reforest the country. Of course, it has taken a long time for the new plantings to come to maturity, but I believe it is now some twenty-five years since the forest plan reached its full development and the last vestiges of the former ravages disappeared."

"Do you know," I said presently, "that one feature which is missing from the landscape impresses me quite as much as any that it presents?"

"What is it that is missing?"

"The hayfield."

"Ah! yes, no wonder you miss it," said the doctor. "I understand that in your day hay was the main crop of New England?"

"Altogether so," I replied, "and now I suppose you have no use for hay at all. Dear me, in what a multitude of important ways the passing of the animals out of use both for food and work must have affected human occupations and interests!"

"Yes, indeed," said the doctor, "and always to the notable improvement of the social condition, though it may sound ungrateful to say so. Take the case of the horse, for example. With the passing of that long-suffering servant of man to his well earned reward, smooth, permanent, and clean roadways first became possible; dust, dirt, danger, and discomfort ceased to be necessary incidents of travel.

"Thanks to the passing of the horse, it was possible to reduce the breadth of roadways by half or a third, to construct them of smooth concrete from grass to grass, leaving no soil to be disturbed by wind or water, and such ways once built, last like Roman roads, and can never be overgrown by vegetation. These paths, penetrating every nook and corner of the land, have, together with the electric motors, made travel such a luxury that as a rule we make all short journeys, and when time does not press even very long ones, by private conveyance. Had land travel remained in the condition it was in when it depended on the horse, the invention of the air-car would have strongly tempted humanity to treat the earth as the birds do--merely as a place to alight on between flights. As it is, we consider the question an even one whether it is pleasanter to swim through the air or to glide over the ground, the motion being well-nigh as swift, noiseless, and easy in one case as in the other."

"Even before 1887," I said, "the bicycle was coming into such favor and the possibilities of electricity were beginning so to loom up that prophetic people began to talk about the day of the horse as almost over. But it was believed that, although dispensed with for road purposes, he must always remain a necessity for the multifarious purposes of farm work, and so I should have supposed. How is it about that?"

TWENTIETH-CENTURY FARMING.

"Wait a moment," replied the doctor; "when we have descended a little I will give you a practical answer."

After we had dropped from an altitude of perhaps a thousand feet to a couple of hundred, the doctor said:

"Look down there to the right."

I did so, and saw a large field from which the crops had been cut. Over its surface was moving a row of great machines, behind which the earth surged up in brown and rigid billows. On each machine stood or sat in easy attitude a young man or woman with quite the air of persons on a pleasure excursion.

"Evidently," I said, "these are plows, but what drives them?"

"They are electric plows," replied the doctor. "Do you see that snakelike cord trailing away over the broken ground behind each machine? That is the cable by which the force is supplied. Observe those posts at regular intervals about the field. It is only necessary to attach one of those cables to a post to have a power which, connected with any sort of agricultural machine, furnishes energy graduated from a man's strength to that of a hundred horses, and requiring for its guidance no other force than the fingers of a child can supply."

And not only this, but it was further explained to me that by this system of flexible cables of all sizes the electric power was applied not only to all the heavy tasks formerly done by animals, but also to the hand instruments--the spade, the shovel, and the fork--which the farmer in my time must bend his own back to, however well supplied he might be with horse power. There was, indeed, no tool, however small, the doctor explained, whether used in agriculture or any other art, to which this motor was not applicable, leaving to the worker only the adjustment and guiding of the instrument.

"With one of our shovels," said the doctor, "an intelligent boy can excavate a trench or dig a mile of potatoes quicker than a gang of men in your day, and with no more effort than he would use in wheeling a barrow."

I had been told several times that at the present day farm work was considered quite as desirable as any other occupation, but, with my impressions as to the peculiar arduousness of the earth worker's task, I had not been able to realize how this could really be so. It began to seem possible.

The doctor suggested that perhaps I would like to land and inspect some of the arrangements of a modern farm, and I gladly assented. But first he took advantage of our elevated position to point out the network of railways by which all the farm transportation was done and whereby the crops when gathered could, if desirable, be shipped directly, without further handling, to any point in the country. Having alighted from our car, we crossed the field toward the nearest of the great plows, the rider of which was a dark-haired young woman daintily costumed, such a figure certainly as no nineteenth-century farm field ever saw. As she sat gracefully upon the back of the shining metal monster which, as it advanced, tore up the earth with terrible horns, I could but be reminded of Europa on her bull. If her prototype was as charming as this young woman, Jupiter certainly was excusable for running away with her.

As we approached, she stopped the plow and pleasantly returned our greeting. It was evident that she recognized me at the first glance, as, thanks doubtless to the diffusion of my portrait, everybody seemed to do. The interest with which she regarded me would have been more flattering had I not been aware that I owed it entirely to my character as a freak of Nature and not at all to my personality.

When I asked her what sort of a crop they were expecting to plant at this season, she replied that this was merely one of the many annual plowings given to all soil to keep it in condition.

"We use, of course, abundant fertilizers," she said, "but consider the soil its own best fertilizer if kept moving."

"Doubtless," said I, "labor is the best fertilizer of the soil. So old an authority as Aesop taught us that in his fable of 'The Buried Treasure,' but it was a terribly expensive sort of fertilizer in my day when it had to come out of the muscles of men and beasts. One plowing a year was all our farmers could manage, and that nearly broke their backs."

"Yes," she said, "I have read of those poor men. Now you see it is different. So long as the tides rise and fall twice a day, let alone the winds and waterfalls, there is no reason why we should not plow every day if it were desirable. I believe it is estimated that about ten times the amount of power is nowadays given to the working of every acre of land that it was possible to apply in former times."

We spent some time inspecting the farm. The doctor explained the drainage and pumping systems by which both excess and deficiency of rain are guarded against, and gave me opportunity to examine in detail some of the wonderful tools he had described, which make practically no requisition on the muscle of the worker, only needing a mind behind them.

Connected with the farm was one of the systems of great greenhouse establishments upon which the people depend for fresh vegetables in the winter, and this, too, we visited. The wonders of intensive culture which I saw in that great structure would of course astonish none of my readers, but to me the revelation of what could be done with plants when all the conditions of light, heat, moisture, and soil ingredients were absolutely to be commanded, was a never-to-be-forgotten experience. It seemed to me that I had stolen into the very laboratory of the Creator, and found him at the task of fashioning with invisible hands the dust of the earth and the viewless air into forms of life. I had never seen plants actually grow before and had deemed the Indian juggler's trick an imposture. But here I saw them lifting their heads, putting forth their buds, and opening their flowers by movements which the eye could follow. I confess that I fairly listened to hear them whisper.

"In my day, greenhouse culture of vegetables out of season had been carried on only to an extent to meet the demands of a small class of very rich. The idea of providing such supplies at moderate prices for the entire community, according to the modern practice, was of course quite undreamed of."

When we left the greenhouse the afternoon had worn away and the sun was setting. Rising swiftly to a height where its rays still warmed us, we set out homeward.

Strongest of all the impressions of that to me so wonderful afternoon there lingered most firmly fixed in my mind the latest--namely, the object lesson I had received of the transformation in the conditions of agriculture, the great staple human occupation from the beginning, and the basis of every industrial system. Presently I said:

"Since you have so successfully done away with the first of the two main drawbacks of the agricultural occupation as known in my day--namely, its excessive laboriousness--you have no doubt also known how to eliminate the other, which was the isolation, the loneliness, the lack of social intercourse and opportunity of social culture which were incident to the farmer's life."

"Nobody would certainly do farm work," replied the doctor, "if it had continued to be either more lonesome or more laborious than other sorts of work. As regards the social surroundings of the agriculturist, he is in no way differently situated from the artisan or any other class of workers. He, like the others, lives where he pleases, and is carried to and fro just as they are between the place of his residence and occupation by the lines of swift transit with which the country is threaded. Work on a farm no longer implies life on a farm, unless for those who like it."

"One of the conditions of the farmer's life, owing to the variations of the season," I said, "has always been the alternation of slack work and periods of special exigency, such as planting and harvesting, when the sudden need of a multiplied labor force has necessitated the severest strain of effort for a time. This alternation of too little with too much work, I should suppose, would still continue to distinguish agriculture from other occupations."

"No doubt," replied the doctor, "but this alternation, far from involving either a wasteful relaxation of effort or an excessive strain on the worker, furnishes occasions of recreation which add a special attraction to the agricultural occupation. The seasons of planting and harvesting are of course slightly or largely different in the several districts of a country so extensive as this. The fact makes it possible successively to concentrate in each district as large an extra contingent of workers drawn from other districts as is needed. It is not uncommon on a few days' notice to throw a hundred thousand extra workers into a region where there is a special temporary demand for labor. The inspiration of these great mass movements is remarkable, and must be something like that which attended in your day the mobilizing and marching of armies to war."

We drifted on for a space in silence through the darkening sky.

"Truly, Julian," said the doctor at length, "no industrial transformation since your day has been so complete, and none surely has affected so great a proportion of the people, as that which has come over agriculture. The poets from Virgil up and down have recognized in rural pursuits and the cultivation of the earth the conditions most favorable to a serene and happy life. Their fancies in this respect have, however, until the present time, been mocked by the actual conditions of agriculture, which have combined to make the lot of the farmer, the sustainer of all the world, the saddest, most difficult, and most hopeless endured by any class of men. From the beginning of the world until the last century the tiller of the soil has been the most pathetic figure in history. In the ages of slavery his was the lowest class of slaves. After slavery disappeared his remained the most anxious, arduous, and despairing of occupations. He endured more than the poverty of the wage-earner without his freedom from care, and all the anxiety of the capitalist without his hope of compensating profits. On the one side he was dependent for his product, as was no other class, upon the caprices of Nature, while on the other in disposing of it he was more completely at the mercy of the middleman than any other producer. Well might he wonder whether man or Nature were the more heartless. If the crops failed, the farmer perished; if they prospered, the middleman took the profit. Standing as a buffer between the elemental forces and human society, he was smitten by the one only to be thrust back by the other. Bound to the soil, he fell into a commercial serfdom to the cities well-nigh as complete as the feudal bondage had been. By reason of his isolated and unsocial life he was uncouth, unlettered, out of touch with culture, without opportunities for self-improvement, even if his bitter toil had left him energy or time for it. For this reason the dwellers in the towns looked down upon him as one belonging to an inferior race. In all lands, in all ages, the countryman has been considered a proper butt by the most loutish townsman. The starving proletarian of the city pavement scoffed at the farmer as a boor. Voiceless, there was none to speak for him, and his rude, inarticulate complaints were met with jeers. Baalam was not more astonished when the ass he was riding rebuked him than the ruling classes of America seem to have been when the farmers, toward the close of the last century, undertook to have something to say about the government of the country.

"From time to time in the progress of history the condition of the farmer has for brief periods been tolerable. The yeoman of England was once for a little while one who looked nobles in the face. Again, the American farmer, up to the middle of the nineteenth century, enjoyed the golden age of agriculture. Then for a space, producing chiefly for use and not for sale to middlemen, he was the most independent of men and enjoyed a rude abundance. But before the nineteenth century had reached its last third, American agriculture had passed through its brief idyllic period, and, by the inevitable operation of private capitalism, the farmer began to go down hill toward the condition of serfdom, which in all ages before had been his normal state, and must be for evermore, so long as the economic exploitation of men by men should continue. While in one sense economic equality brought an equal blessing to all, two classes had especial reason to hail it as bringing to them a greater elevation from a deeper degradation than to any others. One of these classes was the women, the other the farmers."

CHAPTER XXXIV.

What Started The Revolution.

What did I say to the theater for that evening? was the question with which Edith met me when we reached home. It seemed that a celebrated historical drama of the great Revolution was to be given in Honolulu that afternoon, and she had thought I might like to see it.

"Really you ought to attend," she said, "for the presentation of the play is a sort of compliment to you, seeing that it is revived in response to the popular interest in revolutionary history which your presence has aroused."

No way of spending the evening could have been more agreeable to me, and it was agreed that we should make up a family theater party.

"The only trouble," I said, as we sat around the tea table, "is that I don't know enough yet about the Revolution to follow the play very intelligently. Of course, I have heard revolutionary events referred to frequently, but I have no connected idea of the Revolution as a whole."

"That will not matter," said Edith. "There is plenty of time before the play for father to tell you what is necessary. The matinee does not begin till three in the afternoon at Honolulu, and as it is only six now the difference in time will give us a good hour before the curtain rises."

"That's rather a short time, as well as a short notice, for so big a task as explaining the great Revolution," the doctor mildly protested, "but under the circumstances I suppose I shall have to do the best I can."

"Beginnings are always misty," he said, when I straightway opened at him with the question when the great Revolution began. "Perhaps St. John disposed of that point in the simplest way when he said that 'in the beginning was God.' To come down nearer, it might be said that Jesus Christ stated the doctrinal basis and practical purpose of the great Revolution when he declared that the golden rule of equal and the best treatment for all was the only right principle on which people could live together. To speak, however, in the language of historians, the great Revolution, like all important events, had two sets of causes--first, the general, necessary, and fundamental cause which must have brought it about in the end, whatever the minor circumstances had been; and, second, the proximate or provoking causes which, within certain limits, determined when it actually did take place, together with the incidental features. These immediate or provoking causes were, of course, different in different countries, but the general, necessary, and fundamental cause was the same in all countries, the great Revolution being, as you know, world-wide and nearly simultaneous, as regards the more advanced nations.

"That cause, as I have often intimated in our talks, was the growth of intelligence and diffusion of knowledge among the masses, which, beginning with the introduction of printing, spread slowly through the sixteenth, seventeenth, and eighteenth centuries, and much more rapidly during the nineteenth, when, in the more favored countries, it began, to be something like general. Previous to the beginning of this process of enlightenment the condition of the mass of mankind as to intelligence, from the most ancient times, had been practically stationary at a point little above the level of the brutes. With no more thought or will of their own than clay in the hands of the potter, they were unresistingly molded to the uses of the more intelligent and powerful individuals and groups of their kind. So it went on for innumerable ages, and nobody dreamed of anything else until at last the conditions were ripe for the inbreathing of an intellectual life into these inert and senseless clods. The process by which this awakening took place was silent, gradual, imperceptible, but no previous event or series of events in the history of the race had been comparable to it in the effect it was to have upon human destiny. It meant that the interest of the many instead of the few, the welfare of the whole instead of that of a part, were henceforth to be the paramount purpose of the social order and the goal of its evolution.

"Dimly your nineteenth-century philosophers seem to have perceived that the general diffusion of intelligence was a new and large fact, and that it introduced a very important force into the social evolution, but they were wall-eyed in their failure to see the certainty with which it foreshadowed a complete revolution of the economic basis of society in the interest of the whole body of the people as opposed to class interest or partial interest of every sort. Its first effect was the democratic movement by which personal and class rule in political matters was overthrown in the name of the supreme interest and authority of the people. It is astonishing that there should have been any intelligent persons among you who did not perceive that political democracy was but the pioneer corps and advance guard of economic democracy, clearing the way and providing the instrumentality for the substantial part of the programme--namely, the equalization of the distribution of work and wealth. So much for the main, general, and necessary cause and explanation of the great Revolution--namely, the progressive diffusion of intelligence among the masses from the sixteenth to the end of the nineteenth centuries. Given this force in operation, and the revolution of the economic basis of society must sooner or later have been its outcome everywhere: whether a little sooner or later and in just what way and with just what circumstances, the differing conditions of different countries determined.

"In the case of America, the period of revolutionary agitation which resulted in the establishment of the present order began almost at once upon the close of the civil war. Some historians date the beginning of the Revolution from 1873."

"Eighteen seventy-three!" I exclaimed; "why, that was more than a dozen years before I fell asleep! It seems, then, that I was a contemporary and witness of at least a part of the Revolution, and yet I saw no Revolution. It is true that we recognized the highly serious condition of industrial confusion and popular discontent, but we did not realize that a Revolution was on."

"It was to have been expected that you would not," replied the doctor. "It is very rarely that the contemporaries of great revolutionary movements have understood their nature until they have nearly run their course. Following generations always think that they would have been wiser in reading the signs of the times, but that is not likely."

"But what was there," I said, "about 1873 which has led historians to take it as the date from which to reckon the beginning of the Revolution?"

"Simply the fact that it marked in a rather distinct way the beginning of a period of economic distress among the American people, which continued, with temporary and partial alleviations, until the overthrow of private capitalism. The popular discontent resulting from this experience was the provoking cause of the Revolution. It awoke Americans from their self-complacent dream that the social problem had been solved or could be solved by a system of democracy limited to merely political forms, and set them to seeking the true solution.

"The economic distress beginning at the last third of the century, which was the direct provocation of the Revolution, was very slight compared with that which had been the constant lot and ancient heritage of other nations. It represented merely the first turn or two of the screw by which capitalism in due time squeezed dry the masses always and everywhere. The unexampled space and richness of their new land had given Americans a century's respite from the universal fate. Those advantages had passed, the respite was ended, and the time had come when the people must adapt their necks to the yoke all peoples before had worn. But having grown high-spirited from so long an experience of comparative welfare, the Americans resisted the imposition, and, finding mere resistance vain, ended by making a revolution. That in brief is the whole story of the way the great Revolution came on in America. But while this might satisfy a languid twentieth-century curiosity as to a matter so remote in time, you will naturally want a little more detail. There is a particular chapter in Storiot's History of the Revolution explaining just how and why the growth of the power of capital provoked the great uprising, which deeply impressed me in my school days, and I don't think I can make a better use of a part of our short time than by reading a few paragraphs from it."

And Edith having brought the book from the library--for we still sat at the tea table--the doctor read:

"'With reference to the evolution of the system of private capitalism to the point where it provoked the Revolution by threatening the lives and liberties of the people, historians divide the history of the American Republic, from its foundation in 1787 to the great Revolution which made it a true republic, into three periods.

"'The first comprises the decades from the foundation of the republic to about the end of the first third of the nineteenth century--say, up to the thirties or forties. This was the period during which the power of capital in private hands had not as yet shown itself seriously aggressive. The moneyed class was small and the accumulations of capital petty. The vastness of the natural resources of the virgin country defied as yet the lust of greed. The ample lands to be had for the taking guaranteed independence to all at the price of labor. With this resource no man needed to call another master. This may be considered the idyllic period of the republic, the time when De Tocqueville saw and admired it, though not without prescience of the doom that awaited it. The seed of death was in the state in the principle of private capitalism, and was sure in time to grow and ripen, but as yet the conditions were not favorable to its development. All seemed to go well, and it is not strange that the American people indulged in the hope that their republic had indeed solved the social question.

"'From about 1830 or 1840, speaking of course in a general way as to date, we consider the republic to have entered on its second phase--namely, that in which the growth and concentration of capital began to be rapid. The moneyed class now grew powerful, and began to reach out and absorb the natural resources of the country and to organize for its profit the labor of the people. In a word, the growth of the plutocracy became vigorous. The event which gave the great impulse to this movement, and fixed the time of the transition from the first to the second period in the history of the nation, was of course the general application of steam to commerce and industry. The transition may indeed be said to have begun somewhat earlier, with the introduction of the factory system. Of course, if neither steam nor the inventions which made the factory system possible had ever been introduced, it would have been merely a question of a longer time before the capitalist class, proceeding in this case by landlordism and usury, would have reduced the masses to vassalage, and overthrown democracy even as in the ancient republics, but the great inventions amazingly accelerated the plutocratic conquest. For the first time in history the capitalist in the subjugation of his fellows had machinery for his ally, and a most potent one it was. This was the mighty factor which, by multiplying the power of capital and relatively dwarfing the importance of the workingman, accounts for the extraordinary rapidity with which, during the second and third periods the conquest of the republic by the plutocracy was carried out.

"'It is a fact creditable to Americans that they appear to have begun to realize as early as the forties that new and dangerous tendencies were affecting the republic and threatening to falsify its promise of a wide diffusion of welfare. That decade is notable in American history for the popular interest taken in the discussion of the possibility of a better social order, and for the numerous experiments undertaken to test the feasibility of dispensing with the private capitalist by co-operative industry. Already the more intelligent and public-spirited citizens were beginning to observe that their so-called popular government did not seem to interfere in the slightest degree with the rule of the rich and the subjection of the masses to economic masters, and to wonder, if that were to continue to be so, of exactly how much value the so-called republican institutions were on which they had so prided themselves.

"'This nascent agitation of the social question on radical lines was, however, for the time destined to prove abortive by force of a condition peculiar to America--namely, the existence on a vast scale of African chattel slavery in the country. It was fitting in the evolution of complete human liberty that this form of bondage, cruder and more brutal, if not on the whole more cruel, than wage slavery, should first be put out of the way. But for this necessity and the conditions that produced it, we may believe that the great Revolution would have occurred in America twenty-five years earlier. From the period of 1840 to 1870 the slavery issue, involving as it did a conflict of stupendous forces, absorbed all the moral and mental as well as physical energies of the nation.

"'During the thirty or forty years from the serious beginning of the antislavery movement till the war was ended and its issues disposed of, the nation had no thought to spare for any other interests. During this period the concentration of capital in few hands, already alarming to the far-sighted in the forties, had time, almost unobserved and quite unresisted, to push its conquest of the country and the people. Under cover of the civil war, with its preceding and succeeding periods of agitation over the issues of the war, the capitalists may be said to have stolen a march upon the nation and intrenched themselves in a commanding position.

"'Eighteen seventy-three is the point, as near as any date, at which the country, delivered at last from the distracting ethical, and sectional issues of slavery, first began to open its eyes to the irrepressible conflict which the growth of capitalism had forced--a conflict between the power of wealth and the democratic idea of the equal right of all to life, liberty, and happiness. From about this time we date, therefore, the beginning of the final or revolutionary period of the pseudo-American Republic which resulted in the establishment of the present system.

"'History had furnished abundant previous illustrations of the overthrow of republican societies by the growth and concentration of private wealth, but never before had it recorded a revolution in the economic basis of a great nation at once so complete and so swiftly effected. In America before the war, as we have seen, wealth had been distributed with a general effect of evenness never previously known in a large community. There had been few rich men and very few considerable fortunes. It had been in the power neither of individuals nor a class, through the possession of overwhelming capital, to exercise oppression upon the rest of the community. In the short space of twenty-five to thirty years these economic conditions had been so completely reversed as to give America in the seventies and eighties the name of the land of millionaires, and make it famous to the ends of the earth as the country of all others where the vastest private accumulations of wealth existed. The consequences of this amazing concentration of wealth formerly so equally diffused, as it had affected the industrial, the social, and the political interests of the people, could not have been other than revolutionary.

"'Free competition in business had ceased to exist. Personal initiative in industrial enterprises, which formerly had been open to all, was restricted to the capitalists, and to the larger capitalists at that. Formerly known all over the world as the land of opportunities, America had in the time of a generation become equally celebrated as the land of monopolies. A man no longer counted chiefly for what he was, but for what he had. Brains and industry, if coupled with civility, might indeed win an upper servant's place in the employ of capital, but no longer could command a career.

"'The concentration of the economic administration of the country in the hands of a comparatively small body of great capitalists had necessarily consolidated and centralized in a corresponding manner all the functions of production and distribution. Single great concerns, backed by enormous aggregations of capital, had appropriated tracts of the business field formerly occupied by innumerable smaller concerns. In this process, as a matter of course, swarms of small businesses were crushed like flies, and their former independent proprietors were fortunate to find places as underlings in the great establishments which had supplanted them. Straight through the seventies and eighties, every month, every week, every day saw some fresh province of the economic state, some new branch of industry or commerce formerly open to the enterprise of all, captured by a combination of capitalists and turned into an intrenched camp of monopoly. The words *syndicate* and *trust* were coined to describe these monstrous growths, for which the former language of the business world had no name.

"'Of the two great divisions of the working masses it would be hard to say whether the wage-earner or the farmer had suffered most by the changed order. The old personal relationship and kindly feeling between employee and employer had passed away. The great aggregations of capital which had taken the place of the former employers were impersonal forces, which knew the worker no longer as a man, but as a unit of force. He was merely a tool in the employ of a machine, the managers of which regarded him as a necessary nuisance, who must unfortunately be retained at the least possible expense, until he could be invented wholly out of existence by some new mechanical contrivance.

"'The economic function and possibilities of the farmer had similarly been dwarfed or cut off as a result of the concentration of the business system of the country in the hands of a few. The railroads and the grain market had, between them, absorbed the former profits of farming, and left the farmer only the wages of a day laborer in case of a good crop, and a mortgage debt in case of a bad one; and all this, moreover, coupled with the responsibilities of a capitalist whose money was invested in his farm. This latter responsibility, however, did not long continue to trouble the farmer, for, as naturally might be supposed, the only way he could exist from year to year under such conditions was by contracting debts without the slightest prospect of paying them, which presently led to the foreclosure of his land, and his reduction from the once proud estate of an American farmer to that of a tenant on his way to become a peasant.

"'From 1873 to 1896 the histories quote some six distinct business crises. The periods of rallying between them were, however, so brief that we may say a continuous crisis existed during a large part of that period. Now, business crises had been numerous and disastrous in the early and middle epoch of the republic, but the business system, resting at that time on a widely extended popular initiative, had shown itself quickly and strongly elastic, and the rallies that promptly followed the crashes had always led to a greater prosperity than that before enjoyed. But this elasticity, with the cause of it, was now gone. There was little or slow reaction after the crises of the seventies, eighties, and early nineties, but, on the contrary, a scarcely interrupted decline of prices, wages, and the general prosperity and content of the farming and wage-earning masses.

"'There could not be a more striking proof of the downward tendency in the welfare of the wage-earner and the farmer than the deteriorating quality and dwindling volume of foreign immigration which marked the period. The rush of European emigrants to the United States as the land of promise for the poor, since its beginning half a century before, had continued with increasing volume, and drawn to us a great population from the best stocks of the Old World. Soon after the war the character of the immigration began to change, and during the eighties and nineties came to be almost entirely made up of the lowest, most wretched, and barbarous races of Europe--the very scum of the continent. Even to secure these wretched recruits the agents of the transatlantic steamers and the American land syndicates had to send their agents all over the worst districts of Europe and flood the countries with lying circulars. Matters had come to the point that no European peasant or workingman, who was yet above the estate of a beggar or an exile, could any longer afford to share the lot of the American workingman and farmer, so little time before the envy of the toiling world.

"'While the politicians sought, especially about election time, to cheer the workingman with the assurance of better times just ahead, the more serious economic writers seem to have frankly admitted that the superiority formerly enjoyed by American workingmen over those of other countries could not be expected to last longer, that the tendency henceforward was to be toward a world-wide level of prices and wages--namely, the level of the country where they were lowest. In keeping with this prediction we note that for the first time, about the beginning of the nineties, the American employer began to find himself, through the reduced cost of production in which wages were the main element, in a position to undersell in foreign markets the products of the slave gangs of British, Belgian, French, and German capitalists.

"'It was during this period, when the economic distress of the masses was creating industrial war and making revolutionists of the most contented and previously prosperous agricultural population in history, that the vastest private fortunes in the history of the world were being accumulated. The millionaire, who had been unknown before the war and was still an unusual and portentous figure in the early seventies, was presently succeeded by the multimillionaire, and above the multimillionaires towered yet a new race of economic Titans, the hundred millionaires, and already the coming of the billionaire was being discussed. It is not difficult, nor did the people of the time find it so, to see, in view of this comparison, where the wealth went which the masses were losing. Tens of thousands of modest competencies disappeared, to reappear in colossal fortunes in single hands. Visibly as the body of the spider swells as he sucks the juices of his victims, had these vast aggregations grown in measure as the welfare of the once prosperous people had shrunk away.

"'The social consequences of so complete an overthrow of the former economic equilibrium as had taken place could not have been less than revolutionary. In America, before the war, the accumulations of wealth were usually the result of the personal efforts of the possessor and were consequently small and correspondingly precarious. It was a saying of the time that there were usually but three generations from shirt-sleeves to shirt-sleeves--meaning that if a man accumulated a little wealth, his son generally lost it, and the grandson was again a manual laborer. Under these circumstances the economic disparities, slight at most and constantly fluctuating, entirely failed to furnish a basis for class distinctions. There were recognized no laboring class as such, no leisure class, no fixed classes of rich and poor. Riches or poverty, the condition of being at leisure or obliged to work were considered merely temporary accidents of fortune and not permanent conditions. All this was now changed. The great fortunes of the new order of things by their very magnitude were stable acquisitions, not easily liable to be lost, capable of being handed down from generation to generation with almost as much security as a title of nobility. On the other hand, the monopolization of all the valuable economic opportunities in the country by the great capitalists made it correspondingly impossible for those not of the capitalist class to attain wealth. The hope of becoming rich some day, which before the war every energetic American had cherished, was now practically beyond the horizon of the man born to poverty. Between rich and poor the door was henceforth shut. The way up, hitherto the social safety valve, had been closed, and the bar weighted with money bags.

"'A natural reflex of the changed social conditions of the country is seen in the new class terminology, borrowed from the Old World, which soon after the war crept into use in the United States. It had been the boast of the former American that everybody in this country was a workingman; but now that term we find more and more frankly employed to distinguish the poor from the well-to-do. For the first time in American literature we begin to read of the lower classes, the upper classes, and the middle classes--terms which would have been meaningless in America before the war, but now corresponded so closely with the real facts of the situation that those who detested them most could not avoid their use.

"'A prodigious display of luxury such as Europe could not rival had begun to characterize the manner of life of the possessors of the new and unexampled fortunes. Spectacles of gilded splendor, of royal pomp and boundless prodigality mocked the popular discontent and brought out in dazzling light the width and depth of the gulf that was being fixed between the masters and the masses.

"'Meanwhile the money kings took no pains to disguise the fullness of their conviction that the day of democracy was passing and the dream of equality nearly at an end. As the popular feeling in America had grown bitter against them they had responded with frank indications of their dislike of the country and disgust with its democratic institutions. The leading American millionaires had become international personages, spending the greater part of their time and their revenue in European countries, sending their children there for education and in some instances carrying their preference for the Old World to the extent of becoming subjects of foreign powers. The disposition on the part of the greater American capitalists to turn their backs upon democracy and ally themselves with European and monarchical institutions was emphasized in a striking manner by the long list of marriages arranged during this period between great American heiresses and foreign noblemen. It seemed to be considered that the fitting destiny for the daughter of an American multimillionaire was such a union. These great capitalists were very shrewd in money matters, and their investments of vast sums in the purchase of titles for their posterity was the strongest evidence they could give of a sincere conviction that the future of the world, like its past, belonged not to the people but to class and privilege.

"'The influence exercised over the political government by the moneyed class under the convenient euphemism of "the business interests," which merely meant the interests of the rich, had always been considerable, and at times caused grave scandals. In measure as the wealth of the country had become concentrated and allied, its influence in the government had naturally increased, and during the seventies, eighties, and nineties it became a scarcely veiled dictatorship. Lest the nominal representatives of the people should go astray in doing the will of the capitalists, the latter were represented by bodies of picked agents at all the places of government. These agents closely followed the conduct of all public officials, and wherever there was any wavering in their fidelity to the capitalists, were able to bring to bear influences of intimidation or bribery which were rarely unsuccessful. These bodies of agents had a recognized semi-legal place in the political system of the day under the name of lobbyists.

"'The history of government contains few more shameful chapters than that which records how during this period the Legislatures--municipal, State, and national--seconded by the Executives and the courts, vied with each other by wholesale grants of land, privileges, franchises, and monopolies of all kinds, in turning over the country, its resources, and its people to the domination of the capitalists, their heirs and assigns forever. The public lands, which a few decades before had promised a boundless inheritance to future generations, were ceded in vast domains to syndicates and individual capitalists, to be held against the people as the basis of a future territorial aristocracy with tributary populations of peasants. Not only had the material substance of the national patrimony been thus surrendered to a handful of the people, but in the fields of commerce and of industry all the valuable economic opportunities had been secured by franchises to monopolies, precluding future generations from opportunity of livelihood or employment, save as the dependents and liegemen of a hereditary capitalist class. In the chronicles of royal misdoings there have been many dark chapters recording how besotted or imbecile monarchs have sold their people into bondage and sapped the welfare of their realms to enrich licentious favorites, but the darkest of those chapters is bright beside that which records the sale of the heritage and hopes of the American people to the highest bidder by the so-called democratic State, national, and local governments during the period of which we are speaking.

"'Especially necessary had it become for the plutocracy to be able to use the powers of government at will, on account of the embittered and desperate temper of the working masses.

"'The labor strikes often resulted in disturbances too extensive to be dealt with by the police, and it became the common practice of the capitalists, in case of serious strikes, to call on the State and national governments to furnish troops to protect their property interest. The principal function of the militia of the States had become the suppression of strikes with bullet or bayonet, or the standing guard over the plants of the capitalists, till hunger compelled the insurgent workmen to surrender.

"'During the eighties the State governments entered upon a general policy of preparing the militia for this new and ever-enlarging field of usefulness. The National Guard was turned into a Capitalist Guard. The force was generally reorganized, increased in numbers, improved in discipline, and trained with especial reference to the business of shooting riotous workingmen. The drill in street firing--a quite new feature in the training of the American militiaman, and a most ominous one--became the prominent test of efficiency. Stone and brick armories, fortified against attack, loopholed for musketry and mounted with guns to sweep the streets, were erected at the strategic points of the large cities. In some instances the militia, which, after all, was pretty near the people, had, however, shown such unwillingness to fire on strikers and such symptoms of sympathy for their grievances, that the capitalists did not trust them fully, but in serious cases preferred to depend on the pitiless professional soldiers of the General Government, the regulars. Consequently, the Government, upon request of the capitalists, adopted the policy of establishing fortified camps near the great cities, and posting heavy garrisons in them. The Indian wars were ceasing at about this time, and the troops that had been stationed on the Western plains to protect the white settlements from the Indians were brought East to protect the capitalists from the white settlements. Such was the evolution of private capitalism.

"'The extent and practical character of the use to which the capitalists intended to put the military arm of the Government in their controvery with the workingmen may be judged from the fact that in single years of the early nineties armies of eight and ten thousand men were on the march, in New York and Pennsylvania, to suppress strikes. In 1892 the militia of five States, aided by the regulars, were under arms against strikers simultaneously, the aggregate force of troops probably making a larger body than General Washington ever commanded. Here surely was civil war already.

"'Americans of the former days had laughed scornfully at the bayonet-propped monarchies of Europe, saying rightly that a government which needed to be defended by force from its own people was a self-confessed failure. To this pass, however, the industrial system of the United States was fast coming--it was becoming a government by bayonets.

"'Thus briefly, and without attempt at detail, may be recapitulated some of the main aspects of the transformation in the condition of the American people, resulting from the concentration of the wealth of the country, which first began to excite serious alarm at the close of the civil war.

"'It might almost be said that the citizen armies of the North had returned from saving the republic from open foes, to find that it had been stolen from them by more stealthy but far more dangerous enemies whom they had left at home. While they had been putting down caste rule based on race at the South, class rule based on wealth had been set up at the North, to be in time extended over South and North alike. While the armies of the people had been shedding rivers of blood in the effort to preserve the political unity of the nation, its social unity, upon which the very life of a republic depends, had been attacked by the beginnings of class divisions, which could only end by splitting the once coherent nation into mutually suspicious and inimical bodies of citizens, requiring the iron bands of despotism to hold them together in a political organization. Four million negroes had indeed been freed from chattel slavery, but meanwhile a nation of white men had passed under the yoke of an economic and social vassalage which, though the common fate of European peoples and of the ancient world, the founders of the republic had been proudly confident their posterity would never wear.'"

The doctor closed the book from which he had been reading and laid it down.

"Julian," he said, "this story of the subversion of the American Republic by the plutocracy is an astounding one. You were a witness of the situation it describes, and are able to judge whether the statements are exaggerated."

"On the contrary," I replied, "I should think you had been reading aloud from a collection of newspapers of the period. All the political, social, and business facts and symptoms to which the writer has referred were matters of public discussion and common notoriety. If they did not impress me as they do now, it is simply because I imagine I never heard them grouped and marshaled with the purpose of bringing out their significance."

Once more the doctor asked Edith to bring him a book from the library. Turning the pages until he had found the desired place, he said:

"Lest you should fancy that the force of Storiot's statement of the economic situation in the United States during the last third of the nineteenth century owes anything to the rhetorical arrangement, I want to give you just a few hard, cold statistics as to the actual distribution of property during that period, showing the extent to which its ownership had been concentrated. Here is a volume made up of information on this subject based upon analyses of census reports, tax assessments, the files of probate courts, and other official documents. I will give you three sets of calculations, each prepared by a separate authority and based upon a distinct line of investigation, and all agreeing with a closeness which, considering the magnitude of the calculation, is astounding, and leaves no room to doubt the substantial accuracy of the conclusions.

"From the first set of tables, which was prepared in 1893 by a census official from the returns of the United States census, we find it estimated that out of sixty-two billions of wealth in the country a group of millionaires and multimillionaires, representing three one-hundredths of one per cent of the population, owned twelve billions, or one fifth. Thirty-three billions of the rest was owned by a little less than nine per cent of the American people, being the rich and well-to-do class less than millionaires. That is, the millionaires, rich, and well-to-do, making altogether but nine per cent of the whole nation, owned forty-five billions of the total national valuation of sixty-two billions. The remaining ninety-one per cent of the whole nation, constituting the bulk of the people, were classed as the poor, and divided among themselves the remaining seventeen million dollars.

"A second table, published in 1894 and based upon the surrogates' records of estates in the great State of New York, estimates that one per cent of the people, one one-hundredth of the nation, possessed over half, or fifty-five per cent, of its total wealth. It finds that a further fraction of the population, including the well-to-do, and amounting to eleven per cent, owned over thirty-two per cent of the total wealth, so that twelve per cent of the whole nation, including the very rich and the well-to-do, monopolized eighty-seven per cent of the total wealth of the country, leaving but thirteen per cent of that wealth to be shared among the remaining eighty-eight per cent of the nation. This eighty-eight per cent of the nation was subdivided into the poor and the very poor. The last, constituting fifty per cent out of the eighty-eight, or half the entire nation, had too little wealth to be estimated at all, apparently living a hand-to-mouth existence.

"The estimates of a third computator whom I shall quote, although taken from quite different data, agree remarkably with the others, representing as they do about the same period. These last estimates, which were published in 1889 and 1891, and like the others produced a strong impression, divide the nation into three classes--the rich, the middle, and the working class. The rich, being one and four tenths per cent of the population, are credited with seventy per cent of the total wealth. The middle class, representing nine and two tenths per cent of the population, is credited with twelve per cent of the total wealth, the rich and middle classes, together, representing ten and six tenths per cent of the population, having therefore eighty-two per cent of the total wealth, leaving to the working class, which constituted eighty-nine and four tenths of the nation, but eighteen per cent of the wealth, to share among them."

"Doctor," I exclaimed, "I knew things were pretty unequally divided in my day, but figures like these are overwhelming. You need not take the trouble to tell me anything further by way of explaining why the people revolted against private capitalism. These figures were enough to turn the very stones into revolutionists."

"I thought you would say so," replied the doctor. "And please remember also that these tremendous figures represent only the progress made toward the concentration of wealth mainly within the period of a single generation. Well might Americans say to themselves 'If such things are done in the green tree, what shall be done in the dry?' If private capitalism, dealing with a community in which had previously existed a degree of economic equality never before known, could within a period of some thirty years make such a prodigious stride toward the complete expropriation of the rest of the nation for the enrichment of a class, what was likely to be left to the people at the end of a century? What was to be left even to the next generation?"

CHAPTER XXXV.

Why The Revolution Went Slow At First But Fast At Last.

"So much for the causes of the Revolution in America, both the general fundamental cause, consisting in the factor newly introduced into social evolution by the enlightenment of the masses and irresistibly tending to equality, and the immediate local causes peculiar to America, which account for the Revolution having come at the particular time it did and for its taking the particular course it did. Now, briefly as to that course:

"The pinching of the economic shoe resulting from the concentration of wealth was naturally first felt by the class with least reserves, the wage-earners, and the Revolution may be said to have begun with their revolt. In 1869 the first great labor organization in America was formed to resist the power of capital. Previous to the war the number of strikes that had taken place in the country could be counted on the fingers. Before the sixties were out they were counted by hundreds, during the seventies by thousands, and during the eighties the labor reports enumerate nearly ten thousand, involving two or three million workers. Many of these strikes were of continental scope, shaking the whole commercial fabric and causing general panics.

"Close after the revolt of the wage earners came that of the farmers--less turbulent in methods but more serious and abiding in results. This took the form of secret leagues and open political parties devoted to resisting what was called the money power. Already in the seventies these organizations threw State and national politics into confusion, and later became the nucleus of the revolutionary party.

"Your contemporaries of the thinking classes can not be taxed with indifference to these signs and portents. The public discussion and literature of the time reflect the confusion and anxiety with which the unprecedented manifestations of popular discontent had affected all serious persons. The old-fashioned Fourth-of-July boastings had ceased to be heard in the land. All agreed that somehow republican forms of government had not fulfilled their promise as guarantees of the popular welfare, but were showing themselves impotent to prevent the recrudescence in the New World of all the Old World's evils, especially those of class and caste, which it had been supposed could never exist in the atmosphere of a republic. It was recognized on all sides that the old order was changing for the worse, and that the republic and all it had been thought to stand for was in danger. It was the universal cry that something must be done to check the ruinous tendency. Reform was the word in everybody's mouth, and the rallying cry, whether in sincerity or pretense, of every party. But indeed, Julian, I need waste no time describing this state of affairs to you, for you were a witness of it till 1887."

"It was all quite as you describe it, the industrial and political warfare and turmoil, the general sense that the country was going wrong, and the universal cry for some sort of reform. But, as I said before, the agitation, while alarming enough, was too confused and purposeless to seem revolutionary. All agreed that something ailed the country, but no two agreed what it was or how to cure it."

"Just so," said the doctor. "Our historians divide the entire revolutionary epoch--from the close of the war, or the beginning of the seventies, to the establishment of the present order early in the twentieth century--into two periods, the incoherent and the rational. The first of these is the period of which we have been talking, and with which Storiot deals with in the paragraphs I have read--the period with which you were, for the most part, contemporary. As we have seen, and you know better than we can, it was a time of terror and tumult, of confused and purposeless agitation, and a Babel of contradictory clamor. The people were blindly kicking in the dark against the pricks of capitalism, without any clear idea of what they were kicking against.

"The two great divisions of the toilers, the wage-earners and the farmers, were equally far from seeing clear and whole the nature of the situation and the forces of which they were the victims. The wage-earners' only idea was that by organizing the artisans and manual workers their wages could be forced up and maintained indefinitely. They seem to have had absolutely no more knowledge than children of the effect of the profit system always and inevitably to keep the consuming power of the community indefinitely below its producing power and thus to maintain a constant state of more or less aggravated glut in the goods and labor markets, and that nothing could possibly prevent the constant presence of these conditions so long as the profit system was tolerated, or their effect finally to reduce the wage-earner to the subsistence point or below as profits tended downward. Until the wage-earners saw this and no longer wasted their strength in hopeless or trivial strikes against individual capitalists which could not possibly affect the general result, and united to overthrow the profit system, the Revolution must wait, and the capitalists had no reason to disturb themselves.

"As for the farmers, as they were not wage-earners, they took no interest in the plans of the latter, which aimed merely to benefit the wage-earning class, but devoted themselves to equally futile schemes for their class, in which, for the same reason that they were merely class remedies, the wage-earners took no interest. Their aim was to obtain aid from the Government to improve their condition as petty capitalists oppressed by the greater capitalists who controlled the traffic and markets of the country; as if any conceivable device, so long as private capitalism should be tolerated, would prevent its natural evolution, which was the crushing of the smaller capitalists by the larger.

"Their main idea seems to have been that their troubles as farmers were chiefly if not wholly to be accounted for by certain vicious acts of financial legislation, the effect of which they held had been to make money scarce and dear. What they demanded as the sufficient cure of the existing evils was the repeal of the vicious legislation and a larger issue of currency. This they believed would be especially beneficial to the farming class by reducing the interest on their debts and raising the price of their product.

"Undoubtedly the currency and the coinage and the governmental financial system in general had been shamelessly abused by the capitalists to corner the wealth of the nation in their hands, but their misuse of this part of the economic machinery had been no worse than their manipulation of the other portions of the system. Their trickery with the currency had only helped them to monopolize the wealth of the people a little faster than they would have done it had they depended for their enrichment on what were called the legitimate operations of rent, interest, and profits. While a part of their general policy of economic subjugation of the people, the manipulation of the currency had not been essential to that policy, which would have succeeded just as certainly had it been left out. The capitalists were under no necessity to juggle with the coinage had they been content to make a little more leisurely process of devouring the lands and effects of the people. For that result no particular form of currency system was necessary, and no conceivable monetary system would have prevented it. Gold, silver, paper, dear money, cheap money, hard money, bad money, good money--every form of token from cowries to guineas--had all answered equally well in different times and countries for the designs of the capitalist, the details of the game being only slightly modified according to the conditions.

"To have convinced himself of the folly of ascribing the economic distress to which his class as well as the people at large had been reduced, to an act of Congress relating to the currency, the American farmer need only have looked abroad to foreign lands, where he would have seen that the agricultural class everywhere was plunged in a misery greater than his own, and that, too, without the slightest regard to the nature of the various monetary systems in use.

"Was it indeed a new or strange phenomenon in human affairs that the agriculturists were going to the wall, that the American farmer should seek to account for the fact by some new and peculiarly American policy? On the contrary, this had been the fate of the agricultural class in all ages, and what was now threatening the American tiller of the soil was nothing other than the doom which had befallen his kind in every previous generation and in every part of the world. Manifestly, then, he should seek the explanation not in any particular or local conjunction of circumstances, but in some general and always operative cause. This general cause, operative in all lands and times and among all races, he would presently see when he should interrogate history, was the irresistible tendency by which the capitalist class in the evolution of any society through rent, interest, and profits absorbs to itself the whole wealth of the country, and thus reduces the masses of the people to economic, social, and political subjection, the most abject class of all being invariably the tillers of the soil. For a time the American population, including the farmers, had been enabled, thanks to the vast bounty of a virgin and empty continent, to evade the operation of this universal law, but the common fate was now about to overtake them, and nothing would avail to avert it save the overthrow of the system of private capitalism of which it always had been and always must be the necessary effect.

"Time would fail even to mention the innumerable reform nostrums offered for the cure of the nation by smaller bodies of reformers. They ranged from the theory of the prohibitionists that the chief cause of the economic distress--from which the teetotal farmers of the West were the worst sufferers--was the use of intoxicants, to that of the party which agreed that the nation was being divinely chastised because there was no formal recognition of the Trinity in the Constitution. Of course, these were extravagant persons, but even those who recognized the concentration of wealth as the cause of the whole trouble quite failed to see that this concentration was itself the natural evolution of private capitalism, and that it was not possible to prevent it or any of its consequences unless and until private capitalism itself should be put an end to.

"As might be expected, efforts at resistance so ill calculated as these demonstrations of the wage-earners and farmers, not to speak of the host of petty sects of so-called reformers during the first phase of the Revolution, were ineffectual. The great labor organizations which had sprung up shortly after the war as soon as the wage-earners felt the necessity of banding themselves to resist the yoke of concentrated capital, after twenty-five years of fighting, had demonstrated their utter inability to maintain, much less to improve, the condition of the workingman. During this period ten or fifteen thousand recorded strikes and lock-outs had taken place, but the net result of the industrial civil war, protracted through so long a period, had been to prove to the dullest of workingmen the hopelessness of securing any considerable amelioration of their lot by class action or organization, or indeed of even maintaining it against encroachments. After all this unexampled suffering and fighting, the wage-earners found themselves worse off than ever. Nor had the farmers, the other great division of the insurgent masses, been any more successful in resisting the money power. Their leagues, although controlling votes by the million, had proved even more impotent if possible than the wage-earners' organizations to help their members. Even where they had been apparently successful and succeeded in capturing the political control of states, they found the money power still able by a thousand indirect influences to balk their efforts and turn their seeming victories into apples of Sodom, which became ashes in the hands of those who would pluck them.

"Of the vast, anxious, and anguished volume of public discussion as to what should be done, what after twenty-five years had been the practical outcome? Absolutely nothing. If here and there petty reforms had been introduced, on the whole the power of the evils against which those reforms were directed had vastly increased. If the power of the plutocracy in 1873 had been as the little finger of a man, in 1895 it was thicker than his loins. Certainly, so far as superficial and material indications went, it looked as if the battle had been going thus far steadily, swiftly, and hopelessly against the people, and that the American capitalists who expended their millions in buying titles of nobility for their children were wiser in their generation than the children of light and better judges of the future.

"Nevertheless, no conclusion could possibly have been more mistaken. During these decades of apparently unvaried failure and disaster the revolutionary movement for the complete overthrow of private capitalism had made a progress which to rational minds should have presaged its complete triumph in the near future."

"Where had the progress been?" I said; "I don't see any."

"In the development among, the masses of the people of the necessary revolutionary temper," replied the doctor; "in the preparation of the popular mind by the only process that could have prepared it, to accept the programme of a radical reorganization of the economic system from the ground up. A great revolution, you must remember, which is to profoundly change a form of society, must accumulate a tremendous moral force, an overwhelming weight of justification, so to speak, behind it before it can start. The processes by which and the period during which this accumulation of impulse is effected are by no means so spectacular as the events of the subsequent period when the revolutionary movement, having obtained an irresistible momentum, sweeps away like straws the obstacles that so long held it back only to swell its force and volume at last. But to the student the period of preparation is the more truly interesting and critical field of study. It was absolutely necessary that the American people, before they would seriously think of undertaking so tremendous a reformation as was implied in the substitution of public for private capitalism, should be fully convinced not by argument only, but by abundant bitter experience and convincing object lessons, that no remedy for the evils of the time less complete or radical would suffice. They must become convinced by numerous experiments that private capitalism had evolved to a point where it was impossible to amend it before they would listen to the proposition to end it. This painful but necessary experience the people were gaining during the earlier decades of the struggle. In this way the innumerable defeats, disappointments, and fiascoes which met their every effort at curbing and reforming the money power during the seventies, eighties, and early nineties, contributed far more than as many victories would have done to the magnitude and completeness of the final triumph of the people. It was indeed necessary that all these things should come to pass to make the Revolution possible. It was necessary that the system of private and class tyranny called private capitalism should fill up the measure of its iniquities and reveal all it was capable of, as the irreconcilable enemy of democracy, the foe of life and liberty and human happiness, in order to insure that degree of momentum to the coming uprising against it which was necessary to guarantee its complete and final overthrow. Revolutions which start too soon stop too soon, and the welfare of the race demanded that this revolution should not cease, nor pause, until the last vestige of the system by which men usurped power over the lives and liberties of their fellows through economic means was destroyed. Therefore not one outrage, not one act of oppression, not one exhibition of conscienceless rapacity, not one prostitution of power on the part of Executive, Legislature, or judiciary, not one tear of patriotic shame over the degradation of the national name, not one blow of the policeman's bludgeon, not a single bullet or bayonet thrust of the soldiery, could have been spared. Nothing but just this discipline of failure, disappointment, and defeat on the part of the earlier reformers could have educated the people to the necessity of attacking the system of private capitalism in its existence instead of merely in its particular manifestations.

"We reckon the beginning of the second part of the revolutionary movement to which we give the name of the coherent or rational phase, from the time when there became apparent a clear conception, on the part of at least a considerable body of the people, of the true nature of the issue as one between the rights of man and the principle of irresponsible power embodied in private capitalism, and the realization that its outcome, if the people were to triumph, must be the establishment of a wholly new economic system which should be based upon the public control in the public interest of the system of production and distribution hitherto left to private management."

"At about what date," I asked, "do you consider that the revolutionary movement began to pass from the incoherent into the logical phase?"

"Of course," replied the doctor, "it was not the case of an immediate outright change of character, but only of the beginning of a new spirit and intelligence. The confusion and incoherence and short-sightedness of the first period long overlapped the time when the infusion of a more rational spirit and adequate ideal began to appear, but from about the beginning of the nineties we date the first appearance of an intelligent purpose in the revolutionary movement and the beginning of its development from a mere formless revolt against intolerable conditions into a logical and self-conscious evolution toward the order of to-day."

"It seems I barely missed it."

"Yes," replied the doctor, "if you had been able to keep awake only a year or two longer you would not have been so wholly surprised by our industrial system, and especially by the economic equality for and by which it exists, for within a couple of years after your supposed demise the possibility that such a social order might be the outcome of the existing crisis was being discussed from one end of America to the other.

"Of course," the doctor went on, "the idea of an integrated economic system co-ordinating the efforts of all for the common welfare, which is the basis of the modern state, is as old as philosophy. As a theory it dates back to Plato at least, and nobody knows how much further, for it is a conception of the most natural and obvious order. Not, however, until popular government had been made possible by the diffusion of intelligence was the world ripe for the realization of such a form of society. Until that time the idea, like the soul waiting for a fit incarnation, must remain without social embodiment. Selfish rulers thought of the masses only as instruments for their own aggrandizement, and if they had interested themselves in a more exact organization of industry it would only have been with a view of making that organization the means of a more complete tyranny. Not till the masses themselves became competent to rule was a serious agitation possible or desirable for an economic organization on a co-operative basis. With the first stirrings of the democratic spirit in Europe had come the beginning of earnest discussion as to the feasibility of such a social order. Already, by the middle of the century, this agitation in the Old World had become, to discerning eyes, one of the signs of the times, but as yet America, if we except the brief and abortive social experiments in the forties, had remained wholly unresponsive to the European movement.

"I need not repeat that the reason, of course, was the fact that the economic conditions in America had been more satisfactory to the masses than ever before, or anywhere else in the world. The individualistic method of making a living, every man for himself, had answered the purpose on the whole so well that the people did not care to discuss other methods. The powerful motive necessary to rouse the sluggish and habit-bound minds of the masses and interest them in a new and revolutionary set of ideas was lacking. Even during the early stage of the revolutionary period it had been found impossible to obtain any hearing for the notions of a new economic order which were already agitating Europe. It was not till the close of the eighties that the total and ridiculous failure of twenty years of desperate efforts to reform the abuses of private capitalism had prepared the American people to give serious attention to the idea of dispensing with the capitalist altogether by a public organization of industry to be administered like other common affairs in the common interest.

"The two great points of the revolutionary programme--the principle of economic equality and a nationalized industrial system as its means and pledge--the American people were peculiarly adapted to understand and appreciate. The lawyers had made a Constitution of the United States, but the true American constitution--the one written on the people's hearts--had always remained the immortal Declaration with its assertion of the inalienable equality of all men. As to the nationalization of industry, while it involved a set of consequences which would completely transform society, the principle on which the proposition was based, and to which it appealed for justification, was not new to Americans in any sense, but, on the contrary, was merely a logical development of the idea of popular self-government on which the American system was founded. The application of this principle to the regulation of the economic administration was indeed a use of it which was historically new, but it was one so absolutely and obviously implied in the content of the idea that, as soon as it was proposed, it was impossible that any sincere democrat should not be astonished that so plain and common-sense a corollary of popular government had waited so long for recognition. The apostles of a collective administration of the economic system in the common interest had in Europe a twofold task: first, to teach the general doctrine of the absolute right of the people to govern, and then to show the economic application of that right. To Americans, however, it was only necessary to point out an obvious although hitherto overlooked application of a principle already fully accepted as an axiom.

"The acceptance of the new ideal did not imply merely a change in specific programmes, but a total facing about of the revolutionary movement. It had thus far been an attempt to resist the new economic conditions being imposed by the capitalists by bringing back the former economic conditions through the restoration of free competition as it had existed before the war. This was an effort of necessity hopeless, seeing that the economic changes which had taken place were merely the necessary evolution of any system of private capitalism, and could not be successfully resisted while the system was retained.

"'Face about!' was the new word of command. 'Fight forward, not backward! March with the course of economic evolution, not against it. The competitive system can never be restored, neither is it worthy of restoration, having been at best an immoral, wasteful, brutal scramble for existence. New issues demand new answers. It is in vain to pit the moribund system of competition against the young giant of private monopoly; it must rather be opposed by the greater giant of public monopoly. The consolidation of business in private interests must be met with greater consolidation in the public interest, the trust and the syndicate with the city, State, and nation, capitalism with nationalism. The capitalists have destroyed the competitive system. Do not try to restore it, but rather thank them for the work, if not the motive, and set about, not to rebuild the old village of hovels, but to rear on the cleared place the temple humanity so long has waited for.'

"By the light of the new teaching the people began to recognize that the strait place into which the republic had come was but the narrow and frowning portal of a future of universal welfare and happiness such as only the Hebrew prophets had colors strong enough to paint.

"By the new philosophy the issue which had arisen between the people and the plutocracy was seen not to be a strange and unaccountable or deplorable event, but a necessary phase in the evolution of a democratic society in passing from a lower to an incomparably higher plane, an issue therefore to be welcomed not shunned, to be forced not evaded, seeing that its outcome in the existing state of human enlightenment and world-wide democratic sentiment could not be doubtful. By the road by which every republic had toiled upward from the barren lowlands of early hardship and poverty, just at the point where the steepness of the hill had been overcome and a prospect opened of pleasant uplands of wealth and prosperity, a sphinx had ever stood, propounding the riddle, 'How shall a state combine the preservation of democratic equality with the increase of wealth?' Simple indeed had been the answer, for it was only needful that the people should so order their system of economy that wealth should be equally shared as it increased, in order that, however great the increase, it should in no way interfere with the equalities of the people; for the great justice of equality is the well of political life everlasting for peoples, whereof if a nation drink it may live forever. Nevertheless, no republic before had been able to answer the riddle, and therefore their bones whitened the hilltop, and not one had ever survived to enter on the pleasant land in view. But the time had now come in the evolution of human intelligence when the riddle so often asked and never answered was to be answered aright, the sphinx made an end of, and the road freed forever for all the nations.

"It was this note of perfect assurance, of confident and boundless hope, which distinguished the new propaganda, and was the more commanding and uplifting from its contrast with the blank pessimism on the one side of the capitalist party, and the petty aims, class interests, short vision, and timid spirit of the reformers who had hitherto opposed them.

"With a doctrine to preach of so compelling force and beauty, promising such good things to men in so great want of them, it might seem that it would require but a brief time to rally the whole people to its support. And so it would doubtless have been if the machinery of public information and direction had been in the hands of the reformers or in any hands that were impartial, instead of being, as it was, almost wholly in those of the capitalists. In previous periods the newspapers had not represented large investments of capital, having been quite crude affairs. For this very reason, however, they were more likely to represent the popular feeling. In the latter part of the nineteenth century a great newspaper with large circulation necessarily required a vast investment of capital, and consequently the important newspapers of the country were owned by capitalists and of course carried on in the owners' interests. Except when the capitalists in control chanced to be men of high principle, the great papers were therefore upon the side of the existing order of things and against the revolutionary movement. These papers monopolized the facilities of gathering and disseminating public intelligence and thereby exercised a censorship, almost as effective as that prevailing at the same time in Russia or Turkey, over the greater part of the information which reached the people.

"Not only the press but the religious instruction of the people was under the control of the capitalists. The churches were the pensioners of the rich and well-to-do tenth of the people, and abjectly dependent on them for the means of carrying on and extending their work. The universities and institutions of higher learning were in like manner harnessed to the plutocratic chariot by golden chains. Like the churches, they were dependent for support and prosperity upon the benefactions of the rich, and to offend them would have been suicidal. Moreover, the rich and well-to-do tenth of the population was the only class which could afford to send children to institutions of the secondary education, and they naturally preferred schools teaching a doctrine comfortable to the possessing class.

"If the reformers had been put in possession of press, pulpit, and university, which the capitalists controlled, whereby to set home their doctrine to the heart and mind and conscience of the nation, they would have converted and carried the country in a month.

"Feeling how quickly the day would be theirs if they could but reach the people, it was natural that they should chafe bitterly at the delay, confronted as they were by the spectacle of humanity daily crucified afresh and enduring an illimitable anguish which they knew was needless. Who indeed would not have been impatient in their place, and cried as they did, 'How long, O Lord, how long?' To men so situated, each day's postponement of the great deliverance might well have seemed like a century. Involved as they were in the din and dust of innumerable petty combats, it was as difficult for them as for soldiers in the midst of a battle to obtain an idea of the general course of the conflict and the operation of the forces which would determine its issue. To us, however, as we look back, the rapidity of the process by which during the nineties the American people were won over to the revolutionary programme seems almost miraculous, while as to the ultimate result there was, of course, at no time the slightest ground of question.

"From about the beginning of the second phase of the revolutionary movement, the literature of the times begins to reflect in the most extraordinary manner a wholly new spirit of radical protest against the injustices of the social order. Not only in the serious journals and books of public discussion, but in fiction and in belles-lettres, the subject of social reform becomes prominent and almost commanding. The figures that have come down to us of the amazing circulation of some of the books devoted to the advocacy of a radical social reorganization are almost enough in themselves to explain the revolution. The antislavery movement had one Uncle Tom's Cabin; the anticapitalist movement had many.

"A particularly significant fact was the extraordinary unanimity and enthusiasm with which the purely agricultural communities of the far West welcomed the new gospel of a new and equal economic system. In the past, governments had always been prepared for revolutionary agitation among the proletarian wage-earners of the cities, and had always counted on the stolid conservatism of the agricultural class for the force to keep the inflammable artisans down. But in this revolution it was the agriculturists who were in the van. This fact alone should have sufficiently foreshadowed the swift course and certain issue of the struggle. At the beginning of the battle the capitalists had lost their reserves.

"At about the beginning of the nineties the revolutionary movement first prominently appears in the political field. For twenty years after the close of the civil war the surviving animosities between North and South mainly determined party lines, and this fact, together with the lack of agreement on a definite policy, had hitherto prevented the forces of industrial discontent from making any striking political demonstration. But toward the close of the eighties the diminished bitterness of feeling between North and South left the people free to align themselves on the new issue, which had been steadily looming up ever since the war, as the irrepressible conflict of the near future--the struggle to the death between democracy and plutocracy, between the rights of man and the tyranny of capital in irresponsible hands.

"Although the idea of the public conduct of economic enterprises by public agencies had never previously attracted attention or favor in America, yet already in 1890, almost as soon as it began to be talked about, political parties favoring its application to important branches of business had polled heavy votes. In 1892 a party, organized in nearly every State in the Union, cast a million votes in favor of nationalizing at least the railroads, telegraphs, banking system, and other monopolized businesses. Two years later the same party showed large gains, and in 1896 its platform was substantially adopted by one of the great historic parties of the country, and the nation divided nearly equally on the issue.

"The terror which this demonstration of the strength of the party of social discontent caused among the possessing class seems at this distance rather remarkable, seeing that its demands, while attacking many important capitalist abuses, did not as yet directly assail the principle of the private control of capital as the root of the whole social evil. No doubt, what alarmed the capitalists even more than the specific propositions of the social insurgents were the signs of a settled popular exasperation against them and all their works, which indicated that what was now called for was but the beginning of what would be demanded later. The antislavery party had not begun with demanding the abolition of slavery, but merely its limitation. The slaveholders were not, however, deceived as to the significance of the new political portent, and the capitalists would have been less wise in their generation than their predecessors had they not seen in the political situation the beginning of a confrontation of the people and the capitalists--the masses and the classes, as the expression of the day was--which threatened an economic and social revolution in the near future."

"It seems to me," I said, "that by this stage of the revolutionary movement American capitalists capable of a dispassionate view of the situation ought to have seen the necessity of making concessions if they were to preserve any part of their advantages."

"If they had," replied the doctor, "they would have been the first beneficiaries of a tyranny who in presence of a rising flood of revolution ever realized its force or thought of making concessions until it was hopelessly too late. You see, tyrants are always materialists, while the forces behind great revolutions are moral. That is why the tyrants never foresee their fate till it is too late to avert it."

"We ought to be in our chairs pretty soon," said Edith. "I don't want Julian to miss the opening scene."

"There are a few minutes yet," said the doctor, "and seeing that I have been rather unintentionally led into giving this sort of outline sketch of the course of the Revolution, I want to say a word about the extraordinary access of popular enthusiasm which made a short story of its later stages, especially as it is that period with which the play deals that we are to attend.

"There had been many, you must know, Julian, who, while admitting that a system of co-operation, must eventually take the place of private capitalism in America and everywhere, had expected that the process would be a slow and gradual one, extending over several decades, perhaps half a century, or even more. Probably that was the more general opinion. But those who held it failed to take account of the popular enthusiasm which would certainly take possession of the movement and drive it irresistibly forward from the moment that the prospect of its success became fairly clear to the masses. Undoubtedly, when the plan of a nationalized industrial system, and an equal sharing of results, with its promise of the abolition of poverty and the reign of universal comfort, was first presented to the people, the very greatness of the salvation it offered operated to hinder its acceptance. It seemed too good to be true. With difficulty the masses, sodden in misery and inured to hopelessness, had been able to believe that in heaven there would be no poor, but that it was possible here and now in this everyday America to establish such an earthly paradise was too much to believe.

"But gradually, as the revolutionary propaganda diffused a knowledge of the clear and unquestionable grounds on which this great assurance rested, and as the growing majorities of the revolutionary party convinced the most doubtful that the hour of its triumph was at hand, the hope of the multitude grew into confidence, and confidence flamed into a resistless enthusiasm. By the very magnitude of the promise which at first appalled them they were now transported. An impassioned eagerness seized upon them to enter into the delectable land, so that they found every day's, every hour's delay intolerable. The young said, 'Let us make haste, and go in to the promised land while we are young, that we may know what living is': and the old said, 'Let us go in ere we die, that we may close our eyes in peace, knowing that it will be well with our children after us.' The leaders and pioneers of the Revolution, after having for so many years exhorted and appealed to a people for the most part indifferent or incredulous, now found themselves caught up and borne onward by a mighty wave of enthusiasm which it was impossible for them to check, and difficult for them to guide, had not the way been so plain.

"Then, to cap the climax, as if the popular mind were not already in a sufficiently exalted frame, came 'The Great Revival,' touching this enthusiasm with religious emotion."

"We used to have what were called revivals of religion in my day," I said, "sometimes quite extensive ones. Was this of the same nature?"

"Scarcely," replied the doctor. "The Great Revival was a tide of enthusiasm for the social, not the personal, salvation, and for the establishment in brotherly love of the kingdom of God on earth which Christ bade men hope and work for. It was the general awakening of the people of America in the closing years of the last century to the profoundly ethical and truly religious character and claims of the movement for an industrial system which should guarantee the economic equality of all the people.

"Nothing, surely, could be more self-evident than the strictly Christian inspiration of the idea of this guarantee. It contemplated nothing less than a literal fulfillment, on a complete social scale, of Christ's inculcation that all should feel the same solicitude and make the same effort for the welfare of others as for their own. The first effect of such a solicitude must needs be to prompt effort to bring about an equal material provision for all, as the primary condition of welfare. One would certainly think that a nominally Christian people having some familiarity with the New Testament would have needed no one to tell them these things, but that they would have recognized on its first statement that the programme of the revolutionists was simply a paraphrase of the golden rule expressed in economic and political terms. One would have said that whatever other members of the community might do, the Christian believers would at once have flocked to the support of such a movement with their whole heart, soul, mind, and might. That they were so slow to do so must be ascribed to the wrong teaching and non-teaching of a class of persons whose express duty, above all other persons and classes, was to prompt them to that action--namely, the Christian clergy.

"For many ages--almost, indeed, from the beginning of the Christian era--the churches had turned their backs on Christ's ideal of a kingdom of God to be realized on earth by the adoption of the law of mutual helpfulness and fraternal love. Giving up the regeneration of human society in this world as a hopeless undertaking, the clergy, in the name of the author of the Lord's Prayer, had taught the people not to expect God's will to be done on earth. Directly reversing the attitude of Christ toward society as an evil and perverse order of things needing to be made over, they had made themselves the bulwarks and defenses of existing social and political institutions, and exerted their whole influence to discourage popular aspirations for a more just and equal order. In the Old World they had been the champions and apologists of power and privilege and vested rights against every movement for freedom and equality. In resisting the upward strivings of their people, the kings and emperors had always found the clergy more useful servants than the soldiers and the police. In the New World, when royalty, in the act of abdication, had passed the scepter behind its back to capitalism, the ecclesiastical bodies had transferred their allegiance to the money power, and as formerly they had preached the divine right of kings to rule their fellow-men, now preached the divine right of ruling and using others which inhered in the possession of accumulated or inherited wealth, and the duty of the people to submit without murmuring to the exclusive appropriation of all good things by the rich.

"The historical attitude of the churches as the champions and apologists of power and privilege in every controversy with the rights of man and the idea of equality had always been a prodigious scandal, and in every revolutionary crisis had not failed to cost them great losses in public respect and popular following. Inasmuch as the now impending crisis between the full assertion of human equality and the existence of private capitalism was incomparably the most radical issue of the sort that had ever arisen, the attitude of the churches was likely to have a critical effect upon their future. Should they make the mistake of placing themselves upon the unpopular side in this tremendous controversy, it would be for them a colossal if not a fatal mistake--one that would threaten the loss of their last hold as organizations on the hearts and minds of the people. On the other hand, had the leaders of the churches been able to discern the full significance of the great turning of the world's heart toward Christ's ideal of human society, which marked the closing of the nineteenth century, they might have hoped by taking the right side to rehabilitate the churches in the esteem and respect of the world, as, after all, despite so many mistakes, the faithful representatives of the spirit and doctrine of Christianity. Some there were indeed--yes, many, in the aggregate--among the clergy who did see this and sought desperately to show it to their fellows, but, blinded by clouds of vain traditions, and bent before the tremendous pressure of capitalism, the ecclesiastical bodies in general did not, with these noble exceptions, awake to their great opportunity until it had passed by. Other bodies of learned men there were which equally failed to discern the irresistible force and divine sanction of the tidal wave of humane enthusiasm that was sweeping over the earth, and to see that it was destined to leave behind it a transformed and regenerated world. But the failure of these others, however lamentable, to discern the nature of the crisis, was not like the failure of the Christian clergy, for it was their express calling and business to preach and teach the application to human relations of the Golden Rule of equal treatment for all which the Revolution came to establish, and to watch for the coming of this very kingdom of brotherly love, whose advent they met with anathemas.

"The reformers of that time were most bitter against the clergy for their double treason to humanity and Christianity, in opposing instead of supporting the Revolution; but time has tempered harsh judgments of every sort, and it is rather with deep pity than with indignation that we look back on these unfortunate men, who will ever retain the tragic distinction of having missed the grandest opportunity of leadership ever offered to men. Why add reproach to the burden of such a failure as that?

"While the influence of ecclesiastical authority in America, on account of the growth of intelligence, had at this time greatly shrunken from former proportions, the generally unfavorable or negative attitude of the churches toward the programme of equality had told heavily to hold back the popular support which the movement might reasonably have expected from professedly Christian people. It was, however, only a question of time, and the educating influence of public discussion, when the people would become acquainted for themselves with the merits of the subject. 'The Great Revival' followed, when, in the course of this process of education, the masses of the nation reached the conviction that the revolution against which the clergy had warned them as unchristian was, in fact, the most essentially and intensely Christian movement that had ever appealed to men since Christ called his disciples, and as such imperatively commanded the strongest support of every believer or admirer of Christ's doctrine.

"The American people appear to have been, on the whole, the most intelligently religious of the large populations of the world--as religion was understood at that time--and the most generally influenced by the sentiment of Christianity. When the people came to recognize that the ideal of a world of equal welfare, which had been represented to them by the clergy as a dangerous delusion, was no other than the very dream of Christ; when they realized that the hope which led on the advocates of the new order was no baleful *ignis fatuus*, as the churches had taught, but nothing less nor other than the Star of Bethlehem, it is not to be wondered at that the impulse which the revolutionary movement received should have been overwhelming. From that time on it assumes more and more the character of a crusade, the first of the many so-called crusades of history which had a valid and adequate title to that name and right to make the cross its emblem. As the conviction took hold on the always religious masses that the plan of an equalized human welfare was nothing less than the divine design, and that in seeking their own highest happiness by its adoption they were also fulfilling God's purpose for the race, the spirit of the Revolution became a religious enthusiasm. As to the preaching of Peter the Hermit, so now once more the masses responded to the preaching of the reformers with the exultant cry, 'God wills it!' and none doubted any longer that the vision would come to pass. So it was that the Revolution, which had begun its course under the ban of the churches, was carried to its consummation upon a wave of moral and religious emotion."

"But what became of the churches and the clergy when the people found out what blind guides they had been?" I asked.

"No doubt," replied the doctor, "it must have seemed to them something like the Judgment Day when their flocks challenged them with open Bibles and demanded why they had hid the Gospel all these ages and falsified the oracles of God which they had claimed to interpret. But so far as appears, the joyous exultation of the people over the great discovery that liberty, equality, and fraternity were nothing less than the practical meaning and content of Christ's religion seems to have left no room in their heart for bitterness toward any class. The world had received a crowning demonstration that was to remain conclusive to all time of the untrustworthiness of ecclesiastical guidance; that was all. The clergy who had failed in their office of guides had not done so, it is needless to say, because they were not as good as other men, but on account of the hopeless falsity of their position as the economic dependents of those they assumed to lead. As soon as the great revival had fairly begun they threw themselves into it as eagerly as any of the people, but not now with any pretensions of leadership. They followed the people whom they might have led.

"From the great revival we date the beginning of the era of modern religion--a religion which has dispensed with the rites and ceremonies, creeds and dogmas, and banished from this life fear and concern for the meaner self; a religion of life and conduct dominated by an impassioned sense of the solidarity of humanity and of man with God; the religion of a race that knows itself divine and fears no evil, either now or hereafter."

"I need not ask," I said, "as to any subsequent stages of the Revolution, for I fancy its consummation did not tarry long after 'The Great Revival.'"

"That was indeed the culminating impulse," replied the doctor; "but while it lent a momentum to the movement for the immediate realization of an equality of welfare which no obstacle could have resisted, it did its work, in fact, not so much by breaking down opposition as by melting it away. The capitalists, as you who were one of them scarcely need to be told, were not persons of a more depraved disposition than other people, but merely, like other classes, what the economic system had made them. Having like passions and sensibilities with other men, they were as incapable of standing out against the contagion of the enthusiasm of humanity, the passion of pity, and the compulsion of humane tenderness which The Great Revival had aroused, as any other class of people. From the time that the sense of the people came generally to recognize that the fight of the existing order to prevent the new order was nothing more nor less than a controversy between the almighty dollar and the Almighty God, there was substantially but one side to it. A bitter minority of the capitalist party and its supporters seems indeed to have continued its outcry against the Revolution till the end, but it was of little importance. The greater and all the better part of the capitalists joined with the people in completing the installation of the new order which all had now come to see was to redound to the benefit of all alike."

"And there was no war?"

"War! Of course not. Who was there to fight on the other side? It is odd how many of the early reformers seem to have anticipated a war before private capitalism could be overthrown. They were constantly referring to the civil war in the United States and to the French Revolution as precedents which justified their fear, but really those were not analogous cases. In the controversy over slavery, two geographical sections, mutually impenetrable to each other's ideas were opposed and war was inevitable. In the French Revolution there would have been no bloodshed in France but for the interference of the neighboring nations with their brutal kings and brutish populations. The peaceful outcome of the great Revolution in America was, moreover, potently favored by the lack as yet of deep class distinctions, and consequently of rooted class hatred. Their growth was indeed beginning to proceed at an alarming rate, but the process had not yet gone far or deep and was ineffectual to resist the glow of social enthusiasm which in the culminating years of the Revolution blended the whole nation in a common faith and purpose.

"You must not fail to bear in mind that the great Revolution, as it came in America, was not a revolution at all in the political sense in which all former revolutions in the popular interest had been. In all these instances the people, after making up their minds what they wanted changed, had to overthrow the Government and seize the power in order to change it. But in a democratic state like America the Revolution was practically done when the people had made up their minds that it was for their interest. There was no one to dispute their power and right to do their will when once resolved on it. The Revolution as regards America and in other countries, in proportion as their governments were popular, was more like the trial of a case in court than a revolution of the traditional blood-and-thunder sort. The court was the people, and the only way that either contestant could win was by convincing the court, from which there was no appeal.

"So far as the stage properties of the traditional revolution were concerned, plots, conspiracies, powder-smoke, blood and thunder, any one of the ten thousand squabbles in the mediaeval, Italian, and Flemish towns, furnishes far more material to the romancer or playwright than did the great Revolution in America."

"Am I to understand that there was actually no violent doings in connection with this great transformation?"

"There were a great number of minor disturbances and collisions, involving in the aggregate a considerable amount of violence and bloodshed, but there was nothing like the war with pitched lines which the early reformers looked for. Many a petty dispute, causeless and resultless, between nameless kings in the past, too small for historical mention, has cost far more violence and bloodshed than, so far as America is concerned, did the greatest of all revolutions."

"And did the European nations fare as well when they passed through the same crisis?"

"The conditions of none of them were so favorable to peaceful social revolution as were those of the United States, and the experience of most was longer and harder, but it may be said that in the case of none of the European peoples were the direful apprehensions of blood and slaughter justified which the earlier reformers seem to have entertained. All over the world the Revolution was, as to its main factors, a triumph of moral forces."

CHAPTER XXXVI.

Theater-Going In The Twentieth Century.

"I am sorry to interrupt," said Edith, "but it wants only five minutes of the time for the rising of the curtain, and Julian ought not to miss the first scene."

On this notice we at once betook ourselves to the music room, where four easy chairs had been cozily arranged for our convenience. While the doctor was adjusting the telephone and electroscope connections for our use, I expatiated to my companion upon the contrasts between the conditions of theater-going in the nineteenth and in the twentieth centuries--contrasts which the happy denizens of the present world can scarcely, by any effort of imagination, appreciate. "In my time, only the residents of the larger cities, or visitors to them, were ever able to enjoy good plays or operas, pleasures which were by necessary consequence forbidden and unknown to the mass of the people. But even those who as to locality might enjoy these recreations were obliged, in order to do so, to undergo and endure such prodigious fuss, crowding, expense, and general derangement of comfort that for the most part they preferred to stay at home. As for enjoying the great artists of other countries, one had to travel to do so or wait for the artists to travel. To-day, I need not tell you how it is: you stay at home and send your eyes and ears abroad to see and hear for you. Wherever the electric connection is carried--and there need be no human habitation however remote from social centers, be it the mid-air balloon or mid-ocean float of the weather watchman, or the ice-crusted hut of the polar observer, where it may not reach--it is possible in slippers and dressing gown for the dweller to take his choice of the public entertainments given that day in every city of the earth. And remember, too, although you can not understand it, who have never seen bad acting or heard bad singing, how this ability of one troupe to play or sing to the whole earth at once has operated to take away the occupation of mediocre artists, seeing that everybody, being able to see and hear the best, will hear them and see them only."

"There goes the bell for the curtain," said the doctor, and in another moment I had forgotten all else in the scene upon the stage. I need not sketch the action of a play so familiar as "The Knights of the Golden Rule." It is enough for this purpose to recall the fact that the costumes and setting were of the last days of the nineteenth century, little different from what they had been when I looked last on the world of that day. There were a few anachronisms and inaccuracies in the setting which the theatrical administration has since done me the honor to solicit my assistance in correcting, but the best tribute to the general correctness of the scheme was its effect to make me from the first moment oblivious of my actual surroundings. I found myself in presence of a group of living contemporaries of my former life, men and women dressed as I had seen them dressed, talking and acting, as till within a few weeks I had always seen people talk and act; persons, in short, of like passions, prejudices, and manners to my own, even to minute mannerisms ingeniously introduced by the playwright, which even more than the larger traits of resemblance affected my imagination. The only feeling that hindered my full acceptance of the idea that I was attending a nineteenth-century show was a puzzled wonder why I should seem to know so much more than the actors appeared to about the outcome of the social revolution they were alluding to as in progress.

When the curtain fell on the first scene, and I looked about and saw Edith, her mother and father, sitting about me in the music room, the realization of my actual situation came with a shock that earlier in my twentieth-century career would have set my brain swimming. But I was too firm on my new feet now for anything of that sort, and for the rest of the play the constant sense of the tremendous experience which had made me at once a contemporary of two ages so widely apart, contributed an indescribable intensity to my enjoyment of the play.

After the curtain fell, we sat talking of the drama, and everything else, till the globe of the color clock, turning from bottle-green to white, warned us of midnight, when the ladies left the doctor and myself to our own devices.

CHAPTER XXXVII.

The Transition Period.

"It is pretty late," I said, "but I want very much to ask you just a few more questions about the Revolution. All that I have learned leaves me quite as puzzled as ever to imagine any set of practical measures by which the substitution of public for private capitalism could have been effected without a prodigious shock. We had in our day engineers clever enough to move great buildings from one site to another, keeping them meanwhile so steady and upright as not to interfere with the dwellers in them, or to cause an interruption of the domestic operations. A problem something like this, but a millionfold greater and more complex, must have been raised when it came to changing the entire basis of production and distribution and revolutionizing the conditions of everybody's employment and maintenance, and doing it, moreover, without meanwhile seriously interrupting the ongoing of the various parts of the economic machinery on which the livelihood of the people from day to day depended. I should be greatly interested to have you tell me something about how this was done."

"Your question," replied the doctor, "reflects a feeling which had no little influence during the revolutionary period to prolong the toleration extended by the people to private capitalism despite the mounting indignation against its enormities. A complete change of economic systems seemed to them, as it does to you, such a colossal and complicated undertaking that even many who ardently desired the new order and fully believed in its feasibility when once established, shrank back from what they apprehended would be the vast confusion and difficulty of the transition process. Of course, the capitalists, and champions of things as they were, made the most of this feeling, and apparently bothered the reformers not a little by calling on them to name the specific measures by which they would, if they had the power, proceed to substitute for the existing system a nationalized plan of industry managed in the equal interest of all.

"One school of revolutionists declined to formulate or suggest any definite programme whatever for the consummating or constructive stage of the Revolution. They said that the crisis would suggest the method for dealing with it, and it would be foolish and fanciful to discuss the emergency before it arose. But a good general makes plans which provide in advance for all the main eventualities of his campaign. His plans are, of course, subject to radical modifications or complete abandonment, according to circumstances, but a provisional plan he ought to have. The reply of this school of revolutionists was not, therefore, satisfactory, and, so long as no better one could be made, a timid and conservative community inclined to look askance at the revolutionary programme.

"Realizing the need of something more positive as a plan of campaign, various schools of reformers suggested more or less definite schemes. One there was which argued that the trades unions might develop strength enough to control the great trades, and put their own elected officers in place of the capitalists, thus organizing a sort of federation of trades unions. This, if practicable, would have brought in a system of group capitalism as divisive and antisocial, in the large sense, as private capitalism itself, and far more dangerous to civil order. This idea was later heard little of, as it became evident that the possible growth and functions of trade unionism were very limited.

"There was another school which held that the solution was to be found by the establishment of great numbers of voluntary colonies, organized on co-operative principles, which by their success would lead to the formation of more and yet more, and that, finally, when most of the population had joined such groups they would simply coalesce and form one. Many noble and enthusiastic souls devoted themselves to this line of effort, and the numerous colonies that were organized in the United States during the revolutionary period were a striking indication of the general turning of men's hearts toward a better social order. Otherwise such experiments led, and could lead, to nothing. Economically weak, held together by a sentimental motive, generally composed of eccentric though worthy persons, and surrounded by a hostile environment which had the whole use and advantage of the social and economic machinery, it was scarcely possible that such enterprises should come to anything practical unless under exceptional leadership or circumstances.

"There was another school still which held that the better order was to evolve gradually out of the old as the result of an indefinite series of humane legislation, consisting of factory acts, short-hour laws, pensions for the old, improved tenement houses, abolition of slums, and I don't know how many other poultices for particular evils resultant from the system of private capitalism. These good people argued that when at some indefinitely remote time all the evil consequences of capitalism had been abolished, it would be time enough and then comparatively easy to abolish capitalism itself--that is to say, after all the rotten fruit of the evil tree had been picked by hand, one at a time, off the branches, it would be time enough to cut down the tree. Of course, an obvious objection to this plan was that, so long as the tree remained standing, the evil fruit would be likely to grow as fast as it was plucked. The various reform measures, and many others urged by these reformers, were wholly humane and excellent, and only to be criticised when put forward as a sufficient method of overthrowing capitalism. They did not even tend toward such a result, but were quite as likely to help capitalism to obtain a longer lease of life by making it a little less abhorrent. There was really a time after the revolutionary movement had gained considerable headway when judicious leaders felt considerable apprehension lest it might be diverted from its real aim, and its force wasted in this programme of piecemeal reforms.

"But you have asked me what was the plan of operation by which the revolutionists, when they finally came into power, actually overthrew private capitalism. It was really as pretty an illustration of the military manoeuvre that used to be called flanking as the history of war contains. Now, a flanking operation is one by which an army, instead of attacking its antagonist directly in front, moves round one of his flanks in such a way that without striking a blow it forces the enemy to leave his position. That is just the strategy the revolutionists used in the final issue with capitalism.

"The capitalists had taken for granted that they were to be directly assaulted by wholesale forcible seizure and confiscation of their properties. Not a bit of it. Although in the end, of course, collective ownership was wholly substituted for the private ownership of capital, yet that was not done until after the whole system of private capitalism had broken down and fallen to pieces, and not as a means of throwing it down. To recur to the military illustration, the revolutionary army did not directly attack the fortress of capitalism at all, but so manoeuvred as to make it untenable, and to compel its evacuation.

"Of course, you will understand that this policy was not suggested by any consideration for the rights of the capitalists. Long before this time the people had been educated to see in private capitalism the source and sum of all villainies, convicting mankind of deadly sin every day that it was tolerated. The policy of indirect attack pursued by the revolutionists was wholly dictated by the interest of the people at large, which demanded that serious derangements of the economic system should be, so far as possible, avoided during the transition from the old order to the new.

"And now, dropping figures of speech, let me tell you plainly what was done--that is, so far as I remember the story. I have made no special study of the period since my college days, and very likely when you come to read the histories you will find that I have made many mistakes as to the details of the process. I am just trying to give you a general idea of the main course of events, to the best of my remembrance. I have already explained that the first step in the programme of political action adopted by the opponents of private capitalism had been to induce the people to municipalize and nationalize various quasi-public services, such as waterworks, lighting plants, ferries, local railroads, the telegraph and telephone systems, the general railroad system, the coal mines and petroleum production, and the traffic in intoxicating liquors. These being a class of enterprises partly or wholly non-competitive and monopolistic in character, the assumption of public control over them did not directly attack the system of production and distribution in general, and even the timid and conservative viewed the step with little apprehension. This whole class of natural or legal monopolies might indeed have been taken under public management without logically involving an assault on the system of private capitalism as a whole. Not only was this so, but even if this entire class of businesses was made public and run at cost, the cheapening in the cost of living to the community thus effected would presently be swallowed up by reductions of wages and prices, resulting from the remorseless operation of the competitive profit system.

"It was therefore chiefly as a means to an ulterior end that the opponent of capitalism favored the public operation of these businesses. One part of that ulterior end was to prove to the people the superior simplicity, efficiency, and humanity of public over private management of economic undertakings. But the principal use which this partial process of nationalization served was to prepare a body of public employees sufficiently large to furnish a nucleus of consumers when the Government should undertake the establishment of a general system of production and distribution on a non-profit basis. The employees of the nationalized railroads alone numbered nearly a million, and with their dependent women and children represented some 4,000,000 people. The employees in the coal mines, iron mines, and other businesses taken charge of by the Government as subsidiary to the railroads, together with the telegraph and telephone workers, also in the public service, made some hundreds of thousands more persons with their dependents. Previous to these additions there had been in the regular civil service of the Government nearly 250,000 persons, and the army and navy made some 50,000 more. These groups with their dependents amounted probably to a million more persons, who, added to the railroad, mining, telegraph, and other employees, made an aggregate of something like 5,000,000 persons dependent on the national employment. Besides these were the various bodies of State and municipal employees in all grades, from the Governors of States down to the street-cleaners.

THE PUBLIC-SERVICE STORES.

"The first step of the revolutionary party when it came to power, with the mandate of a popular majority to bring in the new order, was to establish in all important centers public-service stores, where public employees could procure at cost all provisions of necessity or luxury previously bought at private stores. The idea was the less startling for not being wholly new. It had been the custom of various governments to provide for certain of the needs of their soldiers and sailors by establishing service stores at which everything was of absolutely guaranteed quality and sold strictly at cost. The articles thus furnished were proverbial for their cheapness and quality compared with anything that could be bought elsewhere, and the soldier's privilege of obtaining such goods was envied by the civilian, left to the tender mercies of the adulterating and profit-gorging retailer. The public stores now set up by the Government were, however, on a scale of completeness quite beyond any previous undertakings, intended as they were to supply all the consumption of a population large enough for a small-sized nation.

"At first the goods in these stores were of necessity bought by the Government of the private capitalists, producers, or importers. On these the public employee saved all the middlemen's and retailers' profits, getting them at perhaps half or two thirds of what they must have paid at private stores, with the guarantee, moreover, of a careful Government inspection as to quality. But these substantial advantages were but a foretaste of the prosperity he enjoyed when the Government added the function of production to that of distribution, and proceeded as rapidly as possible to manufacture products, instead of buying them of capitalists.

"To this end great food and cotton farms were established in all sections of the country and innumerable shops and factories started, so that presently the Government had in public employ not only the original 5,000,000, but as many more--farmers, artisans, and laborers of all sorts. These, of course, also had the right to be provided for at the public stores, and the system had to be extended correspondingly. The buyers in the public stores now saved not only the profits of the middleman and the retailer, but those as well of the manufacturer, the producer, and the importer.

"Still further, not only did the public stores furnish the public employees with every kind of goods for consumption, but the Government likewise organized all sorts of needful services, such as cooking, laundry work, housework agencies, etc., for the exclusive benefit of public employees--all, of course, conducted absolutely at cost. The result was that the public employee was able to be supplied at home or in restaurants with food prepared by the best skill out of the best material and in the greatest possible variety, and more cheaply than he had ever been able to provide himself with even the coarsest provisions."

"How did the Government acquire the lands and manufacturing plants it needed?" I inquired. "Did it buy them of the owners, or as to the plants did it build them?"

"It co erected them without affecting the success of the programme, but that was generally needless. As to land, the farmers by millions were only too glad to turn over their farms to the Government and accept employment on them, with the security of livelihood which that implied for them and theirs. The Government, moreover, took for cultivation all unoccupied lands that were convenient for the purpose, remitting the taxes for compensation.

"It was much the same with the factories and shops which the national system called for. They were standing idle by thousands in all parts of the country, in the midst of starving populations of the unemployed. When these plants were suited to the Government requirements they were taken possession of, put in operation, and the former workers provided with employment. In most instances former superintendents and foremen as well as the main body of operatives were glad to keep their old places, with the nation as employer. The owners of such plants, if I remember rightly, received some allowance, equal to a very low rate of interest, for the use of their property until such time as the complete establishment of the new order should make the equal maintenance of all citizens the subject of a national guarantee. That this was to be the speedy and certain outcome of the course of events was now no longer doubted, and pending that result the owners of idle plants were only too glad to get anything at all for their use.

"The manufacturing plants were not the only form of idle capital which the Government on similar terms made use of. Considerable quantities of foreign imports were required to supply the public stores; and to avoid the payment of profits to capitalists on these, the Government took possession of idle shipping, building what it further needed, and went into foreign trade, exporting products of the public industries, and bringing home in exchange the needed foreign goods. Fishing fleets flying the national flag also brought home the harvest of the seas. These peace fleets soon far outnumbered the war ships which up to that time exclusively had borne the national commission. On these fleets the sailor was no more a slave.

HOW MONEY LOST ITS VALUE.

"And now consider the effect of another feature of the public-store system, namely, the disuse of money in its operations. Ordinary money was not received in the public stores, but a sort of scrip canceled on use and good for a limited time only. The public employee had the right of exchanging the money he received for wages, at par, into this scrip. While the Government issued it only to public employees, it was accepted at the public stores from any who presented it, the Government being only careful that the total amount did not exceed the wages exchanged into such scrip by the public employees. It thus became a currency which commanded three, four, and five hundred per cent premium over money which would only buy the high-priced and adulterated goods for sale in the remaining stores of the capitalists. The gain of the premium went, of course, to the public employees. Gold, which had been worshiped by the capitalists as the supreme and eternal type of money, was no more receivable than silver, copper, or paper currency at the public stores, and people who desired the best goods were fortunate to find a public employee foolish enough to accept three or four dollars in gold for one in scrip.

"The effect to make money a drug in the market, of this sweeping reduction in its purchasing utility, was greatly increased by its practically complete disuse by the large and ever-enlarging proportion of the people in the public service. The demand for money was still further lessened by the fact that nobody wanted to borrow it now for use in extending business, seeing that the field of enterprise open to private capital was shrinking every hour, and evidently destined presently to disappear. Neither did any one desire money to hoard it, for it was more evident every day that it would soon become worthless. I have spoken of the public-store scrip commanding several hundred per cent premium over money, but that was in the earlier stages of the transition period. Toward the last the premium mounted to ever-dizzier altitudes, until the value of money quite disappeared, it being literally good for nothing as money.

"If you would imagine the complete collapse of the entire monetary and financial system with all its standards and influences upon human relations and conditions, you have only to fancy what the effect would have been upon the same interests and relations in your day if positive and unquestioned information had become general that the world was to be destroyed within a few weeks or months, or at longest within a year. In this case indeed the world was not to be destroyed, but to be rejuvenated and to enter on an incomparably higher and happier and more vigorous phase of evolution; but the effect on the monetary system and all dependent on it was quite the same as if the world were to come to an end, for the new world would have no use for money, nor recognize any human rights or relations as measured by it."

"It strikes me," said I, "that as money grew valueless the public taxes must have failed to bring in anything to support the Government."

"Taxes," replied the doctor, "were an incident of private capitalism and were to pass away with it. Their use had been to give the Government a means of commanding labor under the money system. In proportion as the nation collectively organized and directly applied the whole labor of the people as the public welfare required it, had no need and could make no use of taxes any more than of money in other respects. Taxation went to pieces in the culminating stage of the Revolution, in measure as the organization of the capital and labor of the people for public purposes put an end to its functions."

HOW THE REST OF THE PEOPLE CAME IN.

"It seems to me that about this time, if not before, the mass of the people outside of the public service must have begun to insist pretty loudly upon being let in to share these good things."

"Of course they did," replied the doctor; "and of course that was just what they were expected to do and what it had been arranged they should do as soon as the nationalized system of production and distribution was in full running order. The previously existing body of public employees had merely been utilized as furnishing a convenient nucleus of consumers to start with, which might be supplied without deranging meantime any more than necessary the outside wage or commodity markets. As soon as the system was in working order the Government undertook to receive into the public service not merely selected bodies of workers, but all who applied. From that time the industrial army received its recruits by tens and fifties of thousands a day till within a brief time the people as a whole were in the public service.

"Of course, everybody who had an occupation or trade was kept right on at it at the place where he had formerly been employed, and the labor exchanges, already in full use, managed the rest. Later on, when all was going smoothly, would be time enough for the changings and shiftings about that would seem desirable."

"Naturally," I said, "under the operation of the public employment programme, the working people must have been those first brought into the system, and the rich and well-to-do must probably have remained outside longest, and come in, so to speak, all in a batch, when they did."

"Evidently so," replied the doctor. "Of course, the original nucleus of public employees, for whom the public stores were first opened, were all working people, and so were the bodies of people successively taken into the public service, as farmers, artisans, and tradesmen of all sorts. There was nothing to prevent a capitalist from joining the service, but he could do so only as a worker on a par with the others. He could buy in the public stores only to the extent of his pay as a worker. His other money would not be good there. There were many men and women of the rich who, in the humane enthusiasm of the closing days of the Revolution, abandoned their lands and mills to the Government and volunteered in the public service at anything that could be given them to do; but on the whole, as might be expected, the idea of going to work for a living on an economic equality with their former servants was not one that the rich welcomed, and they did not come to it till they had to."

"And were they then, at last, enlisted by force?" I asked.

"By force!" exclaimed the doctor; "dear me! no. There was no sort of constraint brought to bear upon them any more than upon anybody else, save that created by the growing difficulty and final impossibility of hiring persons for private employment, or obtaining the necessities of life except from the public stores with the new scrip. Before the Government entered on the policy of receiving into the public service every one who applied, the unemployed had thronged upon the capitalists, seeking to be hired. But immediately afterward the rich began to find it impossible to obtain men and women to serve them in field, factory, or kitchen. They could offer no inducements in the depreciated money which alone they possessed that were enough to counterbalance the advantages of the public service. Everybody knew also that there was no future for the wealthy class, and nothing to be gained through their favor.

"Moreover, as you may imagine, there was already a strong popular feeling of contempt for those who would abase themselves to serve others for hire when they might serve the nation of which they were citizens; and, as you may well imagine, this growing sentiment made the position of a private servant or employee of any sort intolerable. And not only did the unfortunate capitalists find it impossible to induce people to cook for them, wash for them, to black their boots, to sweep their rooms, or drive their coaches, but they were put to straits to obtain in the dwindling private markets, where alone their money was good, the bare necessities of life, and presently found even that impossible. For a while, it would seem, they struggled against a relentless fate, sullenly supporting life on crusts in the corners of their lonesome palaces; but at last, of course, they all had to follow their former servants into the new nation, for there was no way of living save by connection with the national economic organization. Thus strikingly was illustrated, in the final exit of the capitalists from the human stage, how absolute was and always had been the dependence of capital upon the labor it despised and tyrannized over."

"And do I understand that there was no compulsion upon anybody to join the public service?"

"None but what was inherent in the circumstances I have named," replied the doctor. "The new order had no need or use for unwilling recruits. In fact, it needed no one, but every one needed it. If any one did not wish to enter the public service and could live outside of it without stealing or begging, he was quite welcome to. The books say that the woods were full of self-exiled hermits for a while, but one by one they tired of it and came into the new social house. Some isolated communities, however, remained outside for years."

"The mill seems, indeed, to have been calculated to grind to an exceeding fineness all opposition to the new order," I observed, "and yet it must have had its own difficulties, too, in the natural refractoriness of the materials it had to make grist of. Take, for example, my own class of the idle rich, the men and women whose only business had been the pursuit of pleasure. What useful work could have been got out of such people as we were, however well disposed we might have become to render service? Where could we have been fitted into any sort of industrial service without being more hindrance than help?"

"The problem might have been serious if the idle rich of whom you speak had been a very large proportion of the population, but, of course, though very much in evidence, they were in numbers insignificant compared with the mass of useful workers. So far as they were educated persons--and quite generally they had some smattering of knowledge--there was an ample demand for their services as teachers. Of course, they were not trained teachers, or capable of good pedagogical work; but directly after the Revolution, when the children and youth of the former poor were turned back by millions from the field and factories to the schools, and when the adults also of the working classes passionately demanded some degree of education to correspond with the improved conditions of life they had entered on, there was unlimited call for the services as instructors of everybody who was able to teach anything, even one of the primary branches, spelling, writing, geography, or arithmetic in the rudiments. The women of the former wealthy class, being mostly well educated, found in this task of teaching the children of the masses, the new heirs of the world, an employment in which I fancy they must have tasted more real happiness in the feeling of being useful to their kind than all their former frivolous existences could have given them. Few, indeed, were there of any class who did not prove to have some physical or mental quality by which they might with pleasure to themselves be serviceable to their kind."

WHAT WAS DONE WITH THE VICIOUS AND CRIMINAL.

"There was another class of my contemporaries," I said, "which I fancy must have given the new order more trouble to make anything out of than the rich, and those were the vicious and criminal idle. The rich were at least intelligent and fairly well behaved, and knew enough to adapt themselves to a new state of things and make the best of the inevitable, but these others must have been harder to deal with. There was a great floating population of vagabond criminals, loafers, and vicious of every class, male and female, in my day, as doubtless you well know. Admit that our vicious form of society was responsible for them; nevertheless, there they were, for the new society to deal with. To all intents and purposes they were dehumanized, and as dangerous as wild beasts. They were barely kept in some sort of restraint by an army of police and the weapons of criminal law, and constituted a permanent menace to law and order. At times of unusual agitation, and especially at all revolutionary crises, they were wont to muster in alarming force and become aggressive. At the crisis you are describing they must doubtless have made themselves extremely turbulent. What did the new order do with them? Its just and humane propositions would scarcely appeal to the members of the criminal class. They were not reasonable beings; they preferred to live by lawless violence, rather than by orderly industry, on terms however just. Surely the new nation must have found this class of citizens a very tough morsel for its digestion."

"Not nearly so tough," replied the doctor, "as the former society had found it. In the first place, the former society, being itself based on injustice, was wholly without moral prestige or ethical authority in dealing with the criminal and lawless classes. Society itself stood condemned in their presence for the injustice which had been the provocation and excuse of their revolt. This was a fact which made the whole machinery of so-called criminal justice in your day a mockery. Every intelligent man knew in his heart that the criminal and vicious were, for the most part, what they were on account of neglect and injustice, and an environment of depraving influences for which a defective social order was responsible, and that if righteousness were done, society, instead of judging them, ought to stand with them in the dock before a higher justice, and take upon itself the heavier condemnation. This the criminals themselves felt in the bottom of their hearts, and that feeling forbade them to respect the law they feared. They felt that the society which bade them reform was itself in yet greater need of reformation. The new order, on the other hand, held forth to the outcasts hands purged of guilt toward them. Admitting the wrong that they had suffered in the past, it invited them to a new life under new conditions, offering them, on just and equal terms, their share in the social heritage. Do you suppose that there ever was a human heart so base that it did not at least know the difference between justice and injustice, and to some extent respond to it?

"A surprising number of the cases you speak of, who had been given up as failures by your civilization, while in fact they had been proofs of its failure, responded with alacrity to the first fair opportunity to be decent men and women which had ever come to them. There was, of course, a large residuum too hopelessly perverted, too congenitally deformed, to have the power of leading a good life, however assisted. Toward these the new society, strong in the perfect justice of its attitude, proceeded with merciful firmness. The new society was not to tolerate, as the old had done, a criminal class in its midst any more than a destitute class. The old society never had any moral right to forbid stealing or to punish robbers, for the whole economic system was based on the appropriation, by force or fraud on the part of a few, of the earth and its resources and the fruit of the toil of the poor. Still less had it any right to forbid beggary or to punish violence, seeing that the economic system which it maintained and defended necessarily operated to make beggars and to provoke violence. But the new order, guaranteeing an equality of plenty to all, left no plea for the thief and robber, no excuse for the beggar, no provocation for the violent. By preferring their evil courses to the fair and honorable life offered them, such persons would henceforth pronounce sentence on themselves as unfit for human intercourse. With a good conscience, therefore, the new society proceeded to deal with all vicious and criminal persons as morally insane, and to segregate them in places of confinement, there to spend their lives--not, indeed, under punishment, or enduring hardships of any sort beyond enough labor for self-support, but wholly secluded from the world--and absolutely prevented from continuing their kind. By this means the race, in the first generation after the Revolution, was able to leave behind itself forever a load of inherited depravity and base congenital instincts, and so ever since it has gone on from generation to generation, purging itself of its uncleanness."

THE COLORED RACE AND THE NEW ORDER.

"In my day," I said, "a peculiar complication of the social problem in America was the existence in the Southern States of many millions of recently freed negro slaves, but partially as yet equal to the responsibility of freedom. I should be interested to know just how the new order adapted itself to the condition of the colored race in the South."

"It proved," replied the doctor, "the prompt solution of a problem which otherwise might have continued indefinitely to plague the American people. The population of recent slaves was in need of some sort of industrial regimen, at once firm and benevolent, administered under conditions which should meanwhile tend to educate, refine, and elevate its members. These conditions the new order met with ideal perfection. The centralized discipline of the national industrial army, depending for its enforcement not so much on force as on the inability of any one to subsist outside of the system of which it was a part, furnished just the sort of a control--gentle yet resistless--which was needed by the recently emancipated bondsman. On the other hand, the universal education and the refinements and amenities of life which came with the economic welfare presently brought to all alike by the new order, meant for the colored race even more as a civilizing agent than it did to the white population which relatively had been further advanced."

"There would have been in some parts," I remarked, "a strong prejudice on the part of the white population against any system which compelled a closer commingling of the races."

"So we read, but there was absolutely nothing in the new system to offend that prejudice. It related entirely to economic organization, and had nothing more to do then than it has now with social relations. Even for industrial purposes the new system involved no more commingling of races than the old had done. It was perfectly consistent with any degree of race separation in industry which the most bigoted local prejudices might demand."

HOW THE TRANSITION MIGHT HAVE BEEN HASTENED.

"There is just one point about the transition stage that I want to go back to," I said. "In the actual case, as you have stated it, it seems that the capitalists held on to their capital and continued to conduct business as long as they could induce anybody to work for them or buy of them. I suppose that was human nature--capitalist human nature anyway; but it was also convenient for the Revolution, for this course gave time to get the new economic system perfected as a framework before the strain of providing for the whole people was thrown on it. But it was just possible, I suppose, that the capitalists might have taken a different course. For example, suppose, from the moment the popular majority gave control of the national Government to the revolutionists the capitalists had with one accord abandoned their functions and refused to do business of any kind. This, mind you, would have been before the Government had any time to organize even the beginnings of the new system. That would have made a more difficult problem to deal with, would it not?"

"I do not think that the problem would have been more difficult," replied the doctor, "though it would have called for more prompt and summary action. The Government would have had two things to do and to do at once: on the one hand, to take up and carry on the machinery of productive industry abandoned by the capitalists, and simultaneously to provide maintenance for the people pending the time when the new product should become available. I suppose that as to the matter of providing for the maintenance of the people the action taken would be like that usually followed by a government when by flood, famine, siege, or other sudden emergency the livelihood of a whole community has been endangered. No doubt the first step would have been to requisition, for public use all stores of grain, clothing, shoes, and commodities in general throughout the country, excepting of course reasonable stocks in strictly private use. There was always in any civilized country a supply ahead of these necessities sufficient for several months or a year which would be many times more than would be needful to bridge over the gap between the stoppage of the wheels of production under private management and their getting into full motion under public administration. Orders on the public stores for food and clothing would have been issued to all citizens making application and enrolling themselves in the public industrial service. Meanwhile the Government would have immediately resumed the operation of the various productive enterprises abandoned by the capitalists. Everybody previously employed in them would simply have kept on, and employment would have been as rapidly as possible provided for those who had formerly been without it. The new product, as fast as made, would be turned into the public stores and the process would, in fact, have been just the same as that I have described, save that it would have gone through in much quicker time. If it did not go quite so smoothly on account of the necessary haste, on the other hand it would have been done with sooner, and at most we can hardly imagine that the inconvenience and hardship to the people would have been greater than resulted from even a mild specimen of the business crises which your contemporaries thought necessary every seven years, and toward the last of the old order became perpetual.

HOW CAPITALIST COERCION OF EMPLOYEES WAS MET.

"Your question, however," continued the doctor, "reminds me of another point which I had forgotten to mention--namely, the provisional methods of furnishing employment for the unemployed before the organization of the complete national system of industry. What your contemporaries were pleased to call 'the problem of the unemployed'--namely, the necessary effect of the profit system to create and perpetuate an unemployed class--had been increasing in magnitude from the beginning of the revolutionary period, and toward the close of the century the involuntary idlers were numbered by millions. While this state of things on the one hand furnished a powerful argument for the revolutionary propaganda by the object lesson it furnished of the incompetence of private capitalism to solve the problem of national maintenance, on the other hand, in proportion as employment became hard to get, the hold of the employers over the actual and would-be employees became strengthened. Those who had employment and feared to lose it, and those who had it not but hoped to get it, became, through fear and hope, very puppets in the hands of the employing class and cast their votes at their bidding. Election after election was carried in this way by the capitalists through their power to compel the workingman to vote the capitalist ticket against his own convictions, from the fear of losing or hope of obtaining an opportunity to work.

"This was the situation which made it necessary previous to the conquest of the General Government by the revolutionary party, in order that the workingmen should be made free to vote for their own deliverance, that at least a provisional system of employment should be established whereby the wage-earner might be insured a livelihood when unable to find a private employer.

"In different States of the Union, as the revolutionary party came into power, slightly different methods were adopted for meeting this emergency. The crude and wasteful makeshift of indiscriminate employment on public works, which had been previously adopted by governments in dealing with similar emergencies, would not stand the criticism of the new economic science. A more intelligent method was necessary and easily found. The usual plan, though varied in different localities, was for the State to guarantee to every citizen who applied therefor the means of maintenance, to be paid for in his or her labor, and to be taken in the form of commodities and lodgings, these commodities and lodgings being themselves produced and maintained by the sum of the labor of those, past and present, who shared them. The necessary imported commodities or raw materials were obtained by the sale of the excess of product at market rates, a special market being also found in the consumption of the State prisons, asylums, etc. This system, whereby the State enabled the otherwise unemployed mutually to maintain themselves by merely furnishing the machinery and superintendence, came very largely into use to meet the emergencies of the transition period, and played an important part in preparing the people for the new order, of which it was in an imperfect way a sort of anticipation. In some of these State establishments for the unemployed the circle of industries was remarkably complete, and the whole product of their labor above expenses being shared among the workers, they enjoyed far better fare than when in private employment, together with a sense of security then impossible. The employer's power to control his workmen by the threat of discharge was broken from the time these co-operative systems began to be established, and when, later, the national industrial organization was ready to absorb them, they merely melted into it."

HOW ABOUT THE WOMEN?

"How about the women?" I said. "Do I understand that, from the first organization of the industrial public service on a complete scale, the women were expected, like the men, if physically able, to take their places in the ranks?"

"Where women were sufficiently employed already in housework in their own families," replied the doctor, "they were recognized as rendering public service until the new co-operative housekeeping was sufficiently systematized to do away with the necessity of separate kitchens and other elaborate domestic machinery for each family. Otherwise, except as occasions for exemption existed, women took their place from the beginning of the new order as units in the industrial state on the same basis with men.

"If the Revolution had come a hundred years before, when as yet women had no other vocation but housework, the change in customs might have been a striking one, but already at that time women had made themselves a place in the industrial and business world, and by the time the Revolution came it was rather exceptional when unmarried women not of the rich and idle class did not have some regular occupation outside the home. In recognizing women as equally eligible and liable to public service with men, the new order simply confirmed to the women workers the independence they had already won."

"But how about the married women?"

"Of course," replied the doctor, "there would be considerable periods during which married women and mothers would naturally be wholly exempt from the performance of any public duty. But except at such times there seems to be nothing in the nature of the sexual relation constituting a reason why a married woman should lead a more secluded and useless life than a man. In this matter of the place of women under the new order, you must understand that it was the women themselves, rather than the men, who insisted that they must share in full the duties as well as the privileges of citizenship. The men would not have demanded it of them. In this respect you must remember that during its whole course the Revolution had been contemporary with a movement for the enlargement and greater freedom of women's lives, and their equalization as to rights and duties with men. The women, married as well as unmarried, had become thoroughly tired of being effaced, and were in full revolt against the headship of man. If the Revolution had not guaranteed the equality and comradeship with him which she was fast conquering under the old order, it could never have counted on her support."

"But how about the care of children, of the home, etc.?"

"Certainly the mothers could have been trusted to see that nothing interfered with the welfare of their children, nor was there anything in the public service expected of them that need do so. There is nothing in the maternal function which establishes such a relation between mother and child as need permanently interfere with her performance of social and public duties, nor indeed does it appear that it was allowed to do so in your day by women of sufficient economic means to command needed assistance. The fact that women of the masses so often found it necessary to abandon an independent existence, and cease to live any more for themselves the moment they had children, was simply a mark of the imperfection of your social arrangements, and not a natural or moral necessity. So, too, as to what you call caring for a home. As soon as co-operative methods were applied to housekeeping, and its various departments were systematized as branches of the public service, the former housewife had perforce to find another vocation in order to keep herself busy."

THE LODGINGS QUESTION.

"Talking about housework," I said, "how did they manage about houses? There were, of course, not enough good lodgings to go around, now that all were economic equals. How was it settled who should have the good houses and who the poor?"

"As I have said," replied the doctor, "the controlling idea of the revolutionary policy at the climax of the Revolution was not to complicate the general readjustment by making any changes at that time not necessary to its main purpose. For the vast number of the badly housed the building of better houses was one of the first and greatest tasks of the nation. As to the habitable houses, they were all assessed at a graduated rental according to size and desirability, which their former occupants, if they desired to keep them, were expected to pay out of their new incomes as citizens. For a modest house the rent was nominal, but for a great house--one of the palaces of the millionaires, for instance--the rent was so large that no individual could pay it, and indeed no individual without a host of servants would be able to occupy it, and these, of course, he had no means of employing. Such buildings had to be used as hotels, apartment houses, or for public purposes. It would appear that nobody changed dwellings except the very poor, whose houses were unfit for habitation, and the very rich, who could make no use of their former habitation under the changed condition of things."

WHEN ECONOMIC EQUALITY WAS FULLY REALIZED.

"There is one point not quite clear in my mind," I said, "and that is just when the guarantee of equal maintenance for all citizens went into effect."

"I suppose," replied the doctor, "that it must have been when, after the final collapse of what was left of private capitalism, the nation assumed the responsibility of providing for all the people. Until then the organization of the public service had been on the wage basis, which indeed was the only practicable way of initiating the plan of universal public employment while yet the mass of business was conducted by the capitalists, and the new and rising system had to be accommodated at so many points to the existing order of things. The tremendous rate at which the membership of the national industrial army was growing from week to week during the transition period would have made it impossible to find any basis of equal distribution that would hold good for a fortnight. The policy of the Government had, however, been to prepare the workers for equal sharing by establishing, as far as possible, a level wage for all kinds of public employees. This it was possible to do, owing to the cheapening of all sorts of commodities by the abolition of profits, without reducing any one's income.

"For example, suppose one workman had received two dollars a day, and another a dollar and a half. Owing to the cheapening of goods in the public stores, these wages presently purchased twice as much as before. But, instead of permitting the virtual increase of wages to operate by multiplication, so as to double the original discrepancy between the pay of the two, it was applied by equal additions to the account of each. While both alike were better off than before, the disproportion in their welfare was thus reduced. Nor could the one previously more highly paid object to this as unfair, because the increased value of his wages was not the result of his own efforts, but of the new public organization, from which he could only ask an equal benefit with all others. Thus by the time the nation was ready for equal sharing, a substantially level wage, secured by leveling up, not leveling down, had already been established. As to the high salaries of special employees, out of all proportion to workmen's wages, which obtained under private capitalism, they were ruthlessly cut down in the public service from the inception of the revolutionary policy.

"But of course the most radical innovation in establishing universal economic equality was not the establishment of a level wage as between the workers, but the admission of the entire population, both of workers and of those unable to work or past the working age, to an equal share in the national product. During the transition period the Government had of necessity proceeded like a capitalist in respect to recognizing and dealing only with effective workers. It took no more cognizance of the existence of the women, except when workers, or the children, or the old, or the infirm, crippled, or sick, or other dependents on the workers than the capitalists had been in the habit of doing. But when the nation gathered into its hands the entire economic resources of the country it proceeded to administer them on the principle--proclaimed, indeed, in the great Declaration, but practically mocked by the former republic--that all human beings have an equal right to liberty, life, and happiness, and that governments rightfully exist only for the purpose of making good that right--a principle of which the first practical consequence ought to be the guarantee to all on equal terms of the economic basis. Thenceforth all adult persons who could render any useful service to the nation were required to do so if they desired to enjoy the benefits of the economic system; but all who acknowledged the new order, whether they were able or unable to render any economic service, received an equal share with all others of the national product, and such provision was made for the needs of children as should absolutely safeguard their interests from the neglect or caprice of selfish parents.

"Of course, the immediate effect must have been that the active workers received a less income than when they had been the only sharers; but if they had been good men and distributed their wages as they ought among those dependent on them, they still had for their personal use quite as much as before. Only those wage-earners who had formerly had none dependent on them or had neglected them suffered any curtailment of income, and they deserved to. But indeed there was no question of curtailment for more than a very short time for any; for, as soon as the now completed economic organization was fairly in motion, everybody was kept too busy devising ways to expend his or her own allowance to give any thought to that of others. Of course, the equalizing of the economic maintenance of all on the basis of citizenship put a final end to the employment of private servants, even if the practice had lasted till then, which is doubtful; for if any one desired a personal servant he must henceforth pay him as much as he could receive in the public service, which would be equivalent to the whole income of the would-be employer, leaving him nothing for himself."

THE FINAL SETTLEMENT WITH THE CAPITALISTS.

"There is one point," I said, "on which I should like to be a little more clearly informed. When the nation finally took possession absolutely in perpetuity of all the lands, machinery, and capital after the final collapse of private capitalism, there must have been doubtless some sort of final settling and balancing of accounts between the people and the capitalists whose former properties had been nationalized. How was that managed? What was the basis of final settlement?"

"The people waived a settlement," replied the doctor. "The guillotine, the gallows, and the firing platoon played no part in the consummation of the great Revolution. During the previous phases of the revolutionary agitation there had indeed been much bitter talk of the reckoning which the people in the hour of their triumph would demand of the capitalists for the cruel past; but when the hour of triumph came, the enthusiasm of humanity which glorified it extinguished the fires of hate and took away all desire of barren vengeance. No, there was no settlement demanded; the people forgave the past."

"Doctor," I said, "you have sufficiently--in fact, overwhelmingly--answered my question, and all the more so because you did not catch my meaning. Remember that I represent the mental and moral condition of the average American capitalist in 1887. What I meant was to inquire what compensation the people made to the capitalists for nationalizing what had been their property. Evidently, however, from the twentieth-century point of view, if there were to be any final settlement between the people and the capitalists it was the former who had the bill to present."

"I rather pride myself," replied the doctor, "in keeping track of your point of view and distinguishing it from ours, but I confess that time I fairly missed the cue. You see, as we look back upon the Revolution, one of its most impressive features seems to be the vast magnanimity of the people at the moment of their complete triumph in according a free quittance to their former oppressors.

"Do you not see that if private capitalism was right, then the Revolution was wrong; but, on the other hand, if the Revolution was right, then private capitalism was wrong, and the greatest wrong that ever existed; and in that case it was the capitalists who owed reparation to the people they had wronged, rather than the people who owed compensation to the capitalists for taking from them the means of that wrong? For the people to have consented on any terms to buy their freedom from their former masters would have been to admit the justice of their former bondage. When insurgent slaves triumph, they are not in the habit of paying their former masters the price of the shackles and fetters they have broken; the masters usually consider themselves fortunate if they do not have their heads broken with them. Had the question of compensating the capitalists been raised at the time we are speaking of, it would have been an unfortunate issue for them. To their question, Who was to pay them for what the people had taken from them? the response would have been, Who was to pay the people for what the capitalist system had taken from them and their ancestors, the light of life and liberty and happiness which it had shut off from unnumbered generations? That was an accounting which would have gone so deep and reached back so far that the debtors might well be glad to waive it. In taking possession of the earth and all the works of man that stood upon it, the people were but reclaiming their own heritage and the work of their own hands, kept back from them by fraud. When the rightful heirs come to their own, the unjust stewards who kept them out of their inheritance may deem themselves mercifully dealt with if the new masters are willing to let bygones be bygones.

"But while the idea of compensating the capitalists for putting an end to their oppression would have been ethically absurd, you will scarcely get a full conception of the situation without considering that any such compensation was in the nature of the case impossible. To have compensated the capitalists in any practical way--that is, any way which would have preserved to them under the new order any economic equivalent for their former holdings--would have necessarily been to set up private capitalism over again in the very act of destroying it, thus defeating and stultifying the Revolution in the moment of its triumph.

"You see that this last and greatest of revolutions in the nature of the case absolutely differed from all former ones in the finality and completeness of its work. In all previous instances in which governments had abolished or converted to public use forms of property in the hands of citizens it had been possible to compensate them in some other kind of property through which their former economic advantage should be perpetuated under a different form. For example, in condemning lands it was possible to pay for them in money, and in abolishing property in men it was possible to pay for the slaves, so that the previous superiority or privilege held by the property owner was not destroyed outright, but merely translated, so to speak, into other terms. But the great Revolution, aiming as it did at the final destruction of all forms of advantage, dominion, or privilege among men, left no guise or mode possible under which the capitalist could continue to exercise his former superiority. All the modes under which in past time men had exercised dominion over their fellows had been by one revolution after another reduced to the single form of economic superiority, and now that this last incarnation of the spirit of selfish dominion was to perish there was no further refuge for it. The ultimate mask torn off, it was left to wither in the face of the sun."

"Your explanation leaves me nothing further to ask as to the matter of a final settling between the people and the capitalists," I said. "Still, I have understood that in the first steps toward the substitution of public business management for private capitalism, consisting in the nationalizing or municipalizing of quasi-public services, such as gas works, railroads, telegraphs, etc., some theory of compensation was followed. Public opinion, at that stage not having accepted the whole revolutionary programme, must probably have insisted upon this practice. Just when was it discontinued?'

"You will readily perceive," replied the doctor, "that in measure as it became generally recognized that economic equality was at hand, it began to seem farcical to pay the capitalists for their possessions in forms of wealth which must presently, as all knew, become valueless. So it was that, as the Revolution approached its consummation, the idea of buying the capitalists out gave place to plans for safeguarding them from unnecessary hardships pending the transition period. All the businesses of the class you speak of which were taken over by the people in the early stages of the revolutionary agitation, were paid for in money or bonds, and usually at prices most favorable to the capitalists. As to the greater plants, which were taken over later, such as railroads and the mines, a different course was followed. By the time public opinion was ripe for these steps, it began to be recognized by the dullest that it was possible, even if not probable, that the revolutionary programme would go completely through, and all forms of monetary value or obligation become waste paper. With this prospect the capitalists owning the properties were naturally not particularly desirous of taking national bonds for them which would have been the natural form of compensation had they been bought outright. Even if the capitalists had been willing to take the bonds, the people would never have consented to increase the public debt by the five or six billions of bonds that would have been necessary to carry out the purchase. Neither the railroads nor the mines were therefore purchased at all. It was their management, not their ownership, which had excited the public indignation and created the demand for their nationalization. It was their management, therefore, which was nationalized, their ownership remaining undisturbed.

"That is to say, the Government, on the high ground of public policy and for the correction of grievances that had become intolerable, assumed the exclusive and perpetual management and operation of the railroad lines. An honest valuation of the plants having been made, the earnings, if any, up to a reasonable percentage, were paid over to the security holders. This arrangement answered the purpose of delivering the people and the security holders alike from the extortions and mismanagement of the former private operators, and at the same time brought a million railroad employees into the public service and the enjoyment of all its benefits quite as effectively as if the lines had been bought outright. A similar plan was followed with the coal and other mines. This combination of private ownership with public management continued until, the Revolution having been consummated, all the capital of the country was nationalized by comprehensive enactment.

"The general principle which governed the revolutionary policy in dealing with property owners of all sorts was that while the distribution of property was essentially unjust and existing property rights morally invalid, and as soon as possible a wholly new system should be established, yet that, until the new system of property could as a whole replace the existing one, the legal rights of property owners ought to be respected, and when overruled in the public interest proper provision should be made to prevent hardship. The means of private maintenance should not, that is to say, be taken away from any one until the guarantee of maintenance from public sources could take its place. The application of this principle by the revolutionists seems to have been extremely logical, clean cut, and positive. The old law of property, bad as it was, they did not aim to abolish in the name of license, spoliation, and confusion, but in the name of a stricter and more logical as well as more righteous law. In the most nourishing days of capitalism, stealing, so called, was never repressed more sternly than up to the very eve of the complete introduction of the new system.

"To sum up the case in a word," I suggested, "it seems that in passing from the old order into the new it necessarily fared with the rich as it did when they passed out of this world into the next. In one case, as in the other, they just absolutely had to leave their money behind them."

"The illustration is really very apt," laughed the doctor, "except in one important particular. It has been rumored that the change which Dives made from this world to the next was an unhappy one for him; but within half a dozen years after the new economic system had been in operation there was not an ex-millionaire of the lot who was not ready to admit that life had been made as much better worth living for him and his class as for the rest of the community."

"Did the new order get into full running condition so quickly as that?" I asked.

"Of course, it could not get into perfect order as you see it now for many years. The *personnel* of any community is the prime factor in its economic efficiency, and not until the first generation born under the new order had come to maturity--a generation of which every member had received the highest intellectual and industrial training--did the economic order fully show what it was capable of. But not ten nor two years had elapsed from the time when the national Government took all the people into employment on the basis of equal sharing in the product before the system showed results which overwhelmed the world with amazement. The partial system of public industries and public stores which the Government had already undertaken had given the people some intimation of the cheapening of products and improvement in their quality which might follow from the abolition of profits even under a wage system, but not until the entire economic system had been nationalized and all co-operated for a common weal was it possible completely to pool the product and share it equally. No previous experience had therefore prepared the public for the prodigious efficiency of the new economic enginery. The people had thought the reformers made rather large promises as to what the new system would do in the way of wealth-making, but now they charged them of keeping back the truth. And yet the result was one that need not have surprised any one who had taken the trouble to calculate the economic effect of the change in systems. The incalculable increase of wealth which but for the profit system the great inventions of the century would long before have brought the world, was being reaped in a long-postponed but overwhelming harvest.

"The difficulty under the profit system had been to avoid producing too much; the difficulty under the equal sharing system was how to produce enough. The smallness of demand had before limited supply, but supply had now set to it an unlimited task. Under private capitalism demand had been a dwarf and lame at that, and yet this cripple had been pace-maker for the giant production. National cooperation had put wings on the dwarf and shod the cripple with Mercury's sandals. Henceforth the giant would need all his strength, all his thews of steel and sinews of brass even, to keep him in sight as he flitted on before.

"It would be difficult to give you an idea of the tremendous burst of industrial energy with which the rejuvenated nation on the morrow of the Revolution threw itself into the task of uplifting the welfare of all classes to a level where the former rich man might find in sharing the common lot nothing to regret. Nothing like the Titanic achievement by which this result was effected had ever before been known in human history, and nothing like it seems likely ever to occur again. In the past there had not been work enough for the people. Millions, some rich, some poor, some willingly, some unwillingly, had always been idle, and not only that, but half the work that was done was wasted in competition or in producing luxuries to gratify the secondary wants of the few, while yet the primary wants of the mass remained unsatisfied. Idle machinery equal to the power of other millions of men, idle land, idle capital of every sort, mocked the need of the people. Now, all at once there were not hands enough in the country, wheels enough in the machinery, power enough in steam and electricity, hours enough in the day, days enough in the week, for the vast task of preparing the basis of a comfortable existence for all. For not until all were well-to-do, well housed, well clothed, well fed, might any be so under the new order of things.

"It is said that in the first full year after the new order was established the total product of the country was tripled, and in the second the first year's product was doubled, and every bit of it consumed.

"While, of course, the improvement in the material welfare of the nation was the most notable feature in the first years after the Revolution, simply because it was the place at which any improvement must begin, yet the ennobling and softening of manners and the growth of geniality in social intercourse are said to have been changes scarcely less notable. While the class differences inherited from the former order in point of habits, education, and culture must, of course, continue to mark and in a measure separate the members of the generation then on the stage, yet the certain knowledge that the basis of these differences had passed away forever, and that the children of all would mingle not only upon terms of economic equality, but of moral, intellectual, and social sympathy, and entire community of interest, seems to have had a strong anticipatory influence in bringing together in a sentiment of essential brotherhood those who were too far on in life to expect to see the full promise of the Revolution realized.

"One other matter is worth speaking of, and that is the effect almost at once of the universal and abounding material prosperity which the nation had entered on to make the people forget all about the importance they had so lately attached to petty differences in pay and wages and salary. In the old days of general poverty, when a sufficiency was so hard to come by, a difference in wages of fifty cents or a dollar had seemed so great to the artisan that it was hard for him to accept the idea of an economic equality in which such important distinctions should disappear. It was quite natural that it should be so. Men fight for crusts when they are starving, but they do not quarrel over bread at a banquet table. Somewhat so it befell when in the years after the Revolution material abundance and all the comforts of life came to be a matter of course for every one, and storing for the future was needless. Then it was that the hunger motive died out of human nature and covetousness as to material things, mocked to death by abundance, perished by atrophy, and the motives of the modern worker, the love of honor, the joy of beneficence, the delight of achievement, and the enthusiasm of humanity, became the impulses of the economic world. Labor was glorified, and the cringing wage-slave of the nineteenth century stood forth transfigured as the knight of humanity."

CHAPTER XXXVIII.

The Book Of The Blind.

If the reader were to judge merely from what has been set down in these pages he would be likely to infer that my most absorbing interest during these days I am endeavoring to recall was the study of the political economy and social philosophy of the modern world, which I was pursuing under the direction of Dr. Leete. That, however, would be a great mistake. Full of wonder and fascination as was that occupation, it was prosaic business compared with the interest of a certain old story which his daughter and I were going over together, whereof but slight mention has been made, because it is a story which all know or ought to know for themselves. The dear doctor, being aware of the usual course of such stories, no doubt realized that this one might be expected presently to reach a stage of interest where it would be likely, for a time at least, wholly to distract my attention from other themes. No doubt he had been governed by this consideration in trying to give to our talks a range which should result in furnishing me with a view of the institutions of the modern world and their rational basis that would be as symmetrical and rounded out as was at all consistent with the vastness of the subject and the shortness of the time. It was some days after he had told me the story of the transition period before we had an opportunity for another long talk, and the turn he gave to our discourse on that occasion seemed to indicate that he intended it as a sort of conclusion of the series, as indeed it proved to be.

Edith and I had come home rather late that evening, and when she left me I turned into the library, where a light showed that the doctor was still sitting. As I entered he was turning over the leaves of a very old and yellow-looking volume, the title of which, by its oddity, caught my eye.

"Kenloe's Book of the Blind," I said. "That is an odd title."

"It is the title of an odd book," replied the doctor. "The Book of the Blind is nearly a hundred years old, having been compiled soon after the triumph of the Revolution. Everybody was happy, and the people in their joy were willing to forgive and forget the bitter opposition of the capitalists and the learned class, which had so long held back the blessed change. The preachers who had preached, the teachers who had taught, and the writers who had written against the Revolution, were now the loudest in its praise, and desired nothing so much as to have their previous utterances forgotten. But Kenloe, moved by a certain crabbed sense of justice, was bound that they should not be forgotten. Accordingly, he took the pains to compile, with great care as to authenticity, names, dates, and places, a mass of excerpts from speeches, books, sermons, and newspapers, in which the apologists of private capitalism had defended that system and assailed the advocates of economic equality during the long period of revolutionary agitation. Thus he proposed to pillory for all time the blind guides who had done their best to lead the nation and the world into the ditch. The time would come, he foresaw, as it has come, when it would seem incredible to posterity that rational men and, above all, learned men should have opposed in the name of reason a measure which, like economic equality obviously meant nothing more nor less than the general diffusion of happiness. Against that time he prepared this book to serve as a perpetual testimony. It was dreadfully hard on the men, all alive at the time and desiring the past to be forgotten, on whom he conferred this most undesirable immortality. One can imagine how they must have anathematized him when the book came out. Nevertheless it must be said that if men ever deserved to endure perpetual obloquy those fellows did.

"When I came across this old volume on the top shelf of the library the other day it occurred to me that it might be helpful to complete your impression of the great Revolution by giving you an idea of the other side of the controversy--the side of your own class, the capitalists, and what sort of reasons they were able to give against the proposition to equalize the basis of human welfare."

I assured the doctor that nothing would interest me more. Indeed, I had become so thoroughly naturalized as a twentieth-century American that there was something decidedly piquant in the idea of having my former point of view as a nineteenth-century capitalist recalled to me.

"Anticipating that you would take that view," said the doctor, "I have prepared a little list of the main heads of objection from Kenloe's collection, and we will go over them, if you like, this evening. Of course, there are many more than I shall quote, but the others are mainly variations of these, or else relate to points which have been covered in our talks."

I made myself comfortable, and the doctor proceeded:

THE PULPIT OBJECTION.

"The clergy in your day assumed to be the leaders of the people, and it is but respectful to their pretensions to take up first what seems to have been the main pulpit argument against the proposed system of economic equality collectively guaranteed. It appears to have been rather in the nature of an excuse for not espousing the new social ideal than a direct attack on it, which indeed it would have been rather difficult for nominal Christians to make, seeing that it was merely the proposal to carry out the golden rule.

"The clergy reasoned that the fundamental cause of social misery was human sin and depravity, and that it was vain to expect any great improvement in the social condition through mere improvements in social forms and institutions unless there was a corresponding moral improvement in men. Until that improvement took place it was therefore of no use to introduce improved social systems, for they would work as badly as the old ones if those who were to operate them were not themselves better men and women.

"The element of truth in this argument is the admitted fact that the use which individuals or communities are able to make of any idea, instrument, or institution depends on the degree to which they have been educated up to the point of understanding and appreciating it.

"On the other hand, however, it is equally true, as the clergy must at once have admitted, that from the time a people begins to be morally and intellectually educated up to the point of understanding and appreciating better institutions, their adoption is likely to be of the greatest benefit to them. Take, for example, the ideas of religious liberty and of democracy. There was a time when the race could not understand or fitly use either, and their adoption as formal institutions would have done no good. Afterward there came a time when the world was ready for the ideas, and then their realization by means of new social institutions constituted great forward steps in civilization.

"That is to say, if, on the one hand, it is of no use to introduce an improved institution before people begin to be ready for it, on the other hand great loss results if there be a delay or refusal to adopt the better institution as soon as the readiness begins to manifest itself.

"This being the general law of progress, the practical question is, How are we to determine as to any particular proposed improvement in institutions whether the world is yet ready to make a good use of it or whether it is premature?

"The testimony of history is that the only test of the fitness of people at any time for a new institution is the volume and earnestness of the popular demand for the change. When the peoples began in earnest to cry out for religious liberty and freedom of conscience, it was evident that they were ready for them. When nations began strongly to demand popular government, it was proof that they were ready for that. It did not follow that they were entirely able at once to make the best possible use of the new institution; that they could only learn to do by experience, and the further development which they would attain through the use of the better institution and could not otherwise attain at all. What was certain was that after the people had reached this state of mind the old institution had ceased to be serviceable, and that however badly for a time the new one might work, the interest of the race demanded its adoption, and resistance to the change was resistance to progress.

"Applying this test to the situation toward the close of the nineteenth century, what evidence was there that the world was beginning to be ready for a radically different and more humane set of social institutions? The evidence was the volume, earnestness, and persistence of the popular demand for it which at that period had come to be the most widespread, profound, and powerful movement going on in the civilized world. This was the tremendous fact which should have warned the clergy who withstood the people's demand for better things to beware lest haply they be found fighting even against God. What more convincing proof could be asked that the world had morally and intellectually outgrown the old economic order than the detestation and denunciation of its cruelties and fatuities which had become the universal voice? What stronger evidence could there be that the race was ready at least to attempt the experiment of social life on a nobler plane than the marvelous development during this period of the humanitarian and philanthropic spirit, the passionate acceptance by the masses of the new idea of social solidarity and the universal brotherhood of man?

"If the clergymen who objected to the Revolution on the ground that better institutions would be of no utility without a better spirit had been sincere in that objection, they would have found in a survey of the state and tendencies of popular feeling the most striking proof of the presence of the very conditions in extraordinary measure which they demanded as necessary to insure the success of the experiment.

"But indeed it is to be greatly feared that they were not sincere. They pretended to hold Christ's doctrine that hatred of the old life and a desire to lead a better one is the only vocation necessary to enter upon such a life. If they had been sincere in professing this doctrine, they would have hailed with exultation the appeal of the masses to be delivered from their bondage to a wicked social order and to be permitted to live together on better, kinder, juster terms. But what they actually said to the people was in substance this: It is true, as you complain, that the present social and economic system is morally abominable and thoroughly antichristian, and that it destroys men's souls and bodies. Nevertheless, you must not think of trying to change it for a better system, because you are not yet good enough to try to be better. It is necessary that you should wait until you are more righteous before you attempt to leave off doing evil. You must go on stealing and fighting until you shall become fully sanctified.

"How would the clergy have been scandalized to hear that a Christian minister had in like terms attempted to discourage an individual penitent who professed loathing for his former life and a desire to lead a better! What language shall we find then that is strong enough fitly to characterize the attitude of these so-called ministers of Christ, who in his name rebuked and derided the aspirations of a world weary of social wrong and seeking for a better way?"

THE LACK OF INCENTIVE OBJECTION.

"But, after all," pursued the doctor, turning the pages of Kenloe, "let us not be too hard on these unfortunate clergymen, as if they were more blinded or bigoted in their opposition to progress than were other classes of the learned men of the day, as, for example, the economists. One of the main arguments--perhaps the leading one--of the nineteenth-century economists against the programme of economic equality under a nationalized economic system was that the people would not prove efficient workers owing to the lack of sufficiently sharp personal incentives to diligence.

"Now, let us look at this objection. Under the old system there were two main incentives to economic exertion: the one chiefly operative on the masses, who lived from hand to mouth, with no hope of more than a bare subsistence; the other operating to stimulate the well-to-do and rich to continue their efforts to accumulate wealth. The first of these motives, the lash that drove the masses to their tasks, was the actual pressure or imminent fear of want. The second of the motives, that which spurred the already rich, was the desire to be ever richer, a passion which we know increased with what it fed on. Under the new system every one on easy conditions would be sure of as good a maintenance as any one else and be quite relieved from the pressure or fear of want. No one, on the other hand, by any amount of effort, could hope to become the economic superior of another. Moreover, it was said, since every one looked to his share in the general result rather than to his personal product, the nerve of zeal would be cut. It was argued that the result would be that everybody would do as little as he could and keep within the minimum requirement of the law, and that therefore, while the system might barely support itself, it could never be an economic success."

"That sounds very natural," I said. "I imagine it is just the sort of argument that I should have thought very powerful."

"So your friends the capitalists seem to have regarded it, and yet the very statement of the argument contains a confession of the economic imbecility of private capitalism which really leaves nothing to be desired as to completeness. Consider, Julian, what is implied as to an economic system by the admission that under it the people never escape the actual pressure of want or the immediate dread of it. What more could the worst enemy of private capitalism allege against it, or what stronger reason could he give for demanding that some radically new system be at least given a trial, than the fact which its defenders stated in this argument for retaining it--namely, that under it the masses were always hungry? Surely no possible new system could work any worse than one which confessedly depended upon the perpetual famine of the people to keep it going."

"It was a pretty bad giving away of their case," I said, "when you come to think of it that way. And yet at first statement it really had a formidable sound."

"Manifestly," said the doctor, "the incentives to wealth-production under a system confessedly resulting in perpetual famine must be ineffectual, and we really need consider them no further; but your economists praised so highly the ambition to get rich as an economic motive and objected so strongly to economic equality because it would shut it off, that a word may be well as to the real value of the lust of wealth as an economic motive. Did the individual pursuit of riches under your system necessarily tend to increase the aggregate wealth of the community? The answer is significant. It tended to increase the aggregate wealth only when it prompted the production of new wealth. When, on the other hand, it merely prompted individuals to get possession of wealth already produced and in the hands of others, it tended only to change the distribution without at all increasing the total of wealth. Not only, indeed, did the pursuit of wealth by acquisition, as distinguished from production, not tend to increase the total, but greatly to decrease it by wasteful strife. Now, I will leave it to you, Julian, whether the successful pursuers of wealth, those who illustrated most strikingly the force of this motive of accumulation, usually sought their wealth by themselves producing it or by getting hold of what other people had produced or supplanting other people's enterprises and reaping the field others had sown."

"By the latter processes, of course," I replied. "Production was slow and hard work. Great wealth could not be gained that way, and everybody knew it. The acquisition of other people's product and the supplanting of their enterprises were the easy and speedy and royal ways to riches for those who were clever enough, and were the basis of all large and rapid accumulations."

"So we read," said the doctor; "but the desire of getting rich also stimulated capitalists to more or less productive activity which was the source of what little wealth you had. This was called production for profit, but the political-economy class the other morning showed us that production for profit was economic suicide, tending inevitably, by limiting the consuming power of a community, to a fractional part of its productive power to cripple production in turn, and so to keep the mass of mankind in perpetual poverty. And surely this is enough to say about the incentives to wealth-making which the world lost in abandoning private capitalism, first general poverty, and second the profit system, which caused that poverty. Decidedly we can dispense with those incentives.

"Under the modern system it is indeed true that no one ever imagined such a thing as coming to want unless he deliberately chose to, but we think that fear is on the whole the weakest as well as certainly the cruelest of incentives. We would not have it on any terms were it merely for gain's sake. Even in your day your capitalists knew that the best man was not he who was working for his next dinner, but he who was so well off that no immediate concern for his living affected his mind. Self-respect and pride in achievement made him a far better workman than he who was thinking of his day's pay. But if those motives were as strong then, think how much more powerful they are now! In your day when two men worked side by side for an employer it was no concern of the one, however the other might cheat or loaf. It was not his loss, but the employer's. But now that all work for the common fund, the one who evades or scamps his work robs every one of his fellows. A man had better hang himself nowadays than get the reputation of a shirk.

"As to the notion of these objectors that economic equality would cut the nerve of zeal by denying the individual the reward of his personal achievements, it was a complete misconception of the effects of the system. The assumption that there would be no incentives to impel individuals to excel one another in industry merely because these incentives would not take a money form was absurd. Every one is as directly and far more certainly the beneficiary of his own merits as in your day, save only that the reward is not in what you called 'cash.' As you know, the whole system of social and official rank and headship, together with the special honors of the state, are determined by the relative value of the economic and other services of individuals to the community. Compared with the emulation aroused by this system of nobility by merit, the incentives to effort offered under the old order of things must have been slight indeed.

"The whole of this subject of incentive taken by your contemporaries seems, in fact, to have been based upon the crude and childish theory that the main factor in diligence or execution of any kind is external, whereas it is wholly internal. A person is congenitally slothful or energetic. In the one case no opportunity and no incentive can make him work beyond a certain minimum of efficiency, while in the other case he will make his opportunity and find his incentives, and nothing but superior force can prevent his doing the utmost possible. If the motive force is not in the man to start with, it can not be supplied from without, and there is no substitute for it. If a man's mainspring is not wound up when he is born, it never can be wound up afterward. The most that any industrial system can do to promote diligence is to establish such absolutely fair conditions as shall promise sure recognition for all merit in its measure. This fairness, which your system, utterly unjust in all respects, wholly failed to secure, ours absolutely provides. As to the unfortunates who are born lazy, our system has certainly no miraculous power to make them energetic, but it does see to it with absolute certainty that every able-bodied person who receives economic maintenance of the nation shall render at least the minimum of service. The laziest is sure to pay his cost. In your day, on the other hand, society supported millions of able-bodied loafers in idleness, a dead weight on the world's industry. From the hour of the consummation of the great Revolution, this burden ceased to be borne."

"Doctor," I said, "I am sure my old friends could do better than that. Let us have another of their objections."

AFRAID THAT EQUALITY WOULD MAKE EVERYBODY ALIKE.

"Here, then, is one which they seem to have thought a great deal of. They argued that the effect of economic equality would be to make everybody just alike, as if they had been sawed off to one measure, and that consequently life would become so monotonous that people would all hang themselves at the end of a month. This objection is beautifully typical of an age when everything and everybody had been reduced to a money valuation. It having been proposed to equalize everybody's supply of money, it was at once assumed, as a matter of course, that there would be left no points of difference between individuals that would be worth considering. How perfectly does this conclusion express the philosophy of life held by a generation in which it was the custom to sum up men as respectively 'worth' so many thousands, hundred thousands, or millions of dollars! Naturally enough, to such people it seemed that human beings would become well-nigh indistinguishable if their bank accounts were the same.

"But let us be entirely fair to your contemporaries. Possibly those who used this argument against economic equality would have felt aggrieved to have it made out the baldly sordid proposition it seems to be. They appear, to judge from the excerpts collected in this book, to have had a vague but sincere apprehension that in some quite undefined way economic equality would really tend to make people monotonously alike, tediously similar, not merely as to bank accounts, but as to qualities in general, with the result of obscuring the differences in natural endowments, the interaction of which lends all the zest to social intercourse. It seems almost incredible that the obvious and necessary effect of economic equality could be apprehended in a sense so absolutely opposed to the truth. How could your contemporaries look about them without seeing that it is always inequality which prompts the suppression of individuality by putting a premium on servile imitation of superiors, and, on the other hand, that it is always among equals that one finds independence? Suppose, Julian, you had a squad of recruits and wanted to ascertain at a glance their difference in height, what sort of ground would you select to line them up on?"

"The levelest piece I could find, of course."

"Evidently; and no doubt these very objectors would have done the same in a like case, and yet they wholly failed to see that this was precisely what economic equality would mean for the community at large. Economic equality with the equalities of education and opportunity implied in it was the level standing ground, the even floor, on which the new order proposed to range all alike, that they might be known for what they were, and all their natural inequalities be brought fully out. The charge of abolishing and obscuring the natural differences between men lay justly not against the new order, but against the old, which, by a thousand artificial conditions and opportunities arising from economic inequality, made it impossible to know how far the apparent differences in individuals were natural, and how far they were the result of artificial conditions. Those who voiced the objection to economic equality as tending to make men all alike were fond of calling it a leveling process. So it was, but it was not men whom the process leveled, but the ground they stood on. From its introduction dates the first full and clear revelation of the natural and inherent varieties in human endowments. Economic equality, with all it implies, is the first condition of any true anthropometric or man-measuring system."

"Really," I said, "all these objections seem to be of the boomerang pattern, doing more damage to the side that used them than to the enemy."

"For that matter," replied the doctor, "the revolutionists would have been well off for ammunition if they had used only that furnished by their opponents' arguments. Take, for example, another specimen, which we may call the aesthetic objection to economic equality, and might regard as a development of the one just considered. It was asserted that the picturesqueness and amusement of the human spectacle would suffer without the contrast of conditions between the rich and poor. The question first suggested by this statement is: To whom, to what class did these contrasts tend to make life more amusing? Certainly not to the poor, who made up the mass of the race. To them they must have been maddening. It was then in the interest of the mere handful of rich and fortunate that this argument for retaining poverty was urged. Indeed this appears to have been quite a fine ladies' argument. Kenloe puts it in the mouths of leaders of polite society. As coolly as if it had been a question of parlor decoration, they appear to have argued that the black background of the general misery was a desirable foil to set off the pomp of the rich. But, after all, this objection was not more brutal than it was stupid. If here and there might be found some perverted being who relished his luxuries the more keenly for the sight of others' want, yet the general and universal rule is that happiness is stimulated by the sight of the happiness of others. As a matter of fact, far from desiring to see or be even reminded of squalor and poverty, the rich seem to have tried to get as far as possible from sight or sound of them, and to wish to forget their existence.

"A great part of the objections to economic equality in this book seems to have been based on such complete misapprehensions of what the plan implied as to have no sort of relevancy to it. Some of these I have passed over. One of them, by way of illustration, was based on the assumption that the new social order would in some way operate to enforce, by law, relations of social intimacy of all with all, without regard to personal tastes or affinities. Quite a number of Kenloe's subjects worked themselves up to a frenzy, protesting against the intolerable effects of such a requirement. Of course, they were fighting imaginary foes. There was nothing under the old social order which compelled men to associate merely because their bank accounts or incomes were the same, and there was nothing under the new order that would any more do so. While the universality of culture and refinement vastly widens the circle from which one may choose congenial associates, there is nothing to prevent anybody from living a life as absolutely unsocial as the veriest cynic of the old time could have desired.

OBJECTION THAT EQUALITY WOULD END THE COMPETITIVE SYSTEM.

"The theory of Kenloe," continued the doctor, "that unless he carefully recorded and authenticated these objections to economic equality, posterity would refuse to believe that they had ever been seriously offered, is specially justified by the next one on the list. This is an argument against the new order because it would abolish the competitive system and put an end to the struggle for existence. According to the objectors, this would be to destroy an invaluable school of character and testing process for the weeding out of inferiority, and the development and survival as leaders of the best types of humanity. Now, if your contemporaries had excused themselves for tolerating the competitive system on the ground that, bad and cruel as it was, the world was not ripe for any other, the attitude would have been intelligible, if not rational; but that they should defend it as a desirable institution in itself, on account of its moral results, and therefore not to be dispensed with even if it could be, seems hard to believe. For what was the competitive system but a pitiless, all-involving combat for the means of life, the whole zest of which depended on the fact that there was not enough to go round, and the losers must perish or purchase bare existence by becoming the bondmen of the successful? Between a fight for the necessary means of life like this and a fight for life itself with sword and gun, it is impossible to make any real distinction. However, let us give the objection a fair hearing.

"In the first place, let us admit that, however dreadful were the incidents of the fight for the means of life called competition, yet, if it were such a school of character and testing process for developing the best types of the race as these objectors claimed, there would be something to have been said in favor of its retention. But the first condition of any competition or test, the results of which are to command respect or possess any value, is the fairness and equality of the struggle. Did this first and essential condition of any true competitive struggle characterize the competitive system of your day?"

"On the contrary," I replied, "the vast majority of the contestants were hopelessly handicapped at the start by ignorance and lack of early advantages, and never had even the ghost of a chance from the word go. Differences in economic advantages and backing, moreover, gave half the race at the beginning to some, leaving the others at a distance which only extraordinary endowments might overcome. Finally, in the race for wealth all the greatest prizes were not subject to competition at all, but were awarded without any contest according to the accident of birth."

"On the whole, then, it would appear," resumed the doctor, "that of all the utterly unequal, unfair, fraudulent, sham contests, whether in sport or earnest, that were ever engaged in, the so-called competitive system was the ghastliest farce. It was called the competitive system apparently for no other reason than that there was not a particle of genuine competition in it, nothing but brutal and cowardly slaughter of the unarmed and overmatched by bullies in armor; for, although we have compared the competitive struggle to a foot race, it was no such harmless sport as that, but a struggle to the death for life and liberty, which, mind you, the contestants did not even choose to risk, but were forced to undertake, whatever their chances. The old Romans used to enjoy the spectacle of seeing men fight for their lives, but they at least were careful to pair their gladiators as nearly as possible. The most hardened attendants at the Coliseum would have hissed from the arena a performance in which the combatants were matched with such utter disregard of fairness as were those who fought for their lives in the so-called competitive struggle of your day."

"Even you, doctor," I said, "though you know these things so well through the written record, can not realize how terribly true your words are."

"Very good. Now tell me what it would have been necessary to do by way of equalizing the conditions of the competitive struggle in order that it might be called, without mockery, a fair test of the qualities of the contestants."

"It would have been necessary, at least," I said, "to equalize their educational equipment, early advantages, and economic or money backing."

"Precisely so; and that is just what economic equality proposed to do. Your extraordinary contemporaries objected to economic equality because it would destroy the competitive system, when, in fact, it promised the world the first and only genuine competitive system it ever had."

"This objection seems the biggest boomerang yet," I said.

"It is a double-ended one," said the doctor, "and we have yet observed but one end. We have seen that the so-called competitive system under private capitalism was not a competitive system at all, and that nothing but economic equality could make a truly competitive system possible. Grant, however, for the sake of the argument, that the old system was honestly competitive, and that the prizes went to the most proficient under the requirements of the competition; the question would remain whether the qualities the competition tended to develop were desirable ones. A training school in the art of lying, for example, or burglary, or slander, or fraud, might be efficient in its method and the prizes might be fairly distributed to the most proficient pupils, and yet it would scarcely be argued that the maintenance of the school was in the public interest. The objection we are considering assumes that the qualities encouraged and rewarded under the competitive system were desirable qualities, and such as it was for the public policy to develop. Now, if this was so, we may confidently expect to find that the prize-winners in the competitive struggle, the great money-makers of your age, were admitted to be intellectually and morally the finest types of the race at the time. How was that?"

"Don't be sarcastic, doctor."

"No, I will not be sarcastic, however great the temptation, but just talk straight on. What did the world, as a rule, think of the great fortune-makers of your time? What sort of human types did they represent? As to intellectual culture, it was held as an axiom that a college education was a drawback to success in business, and naturally so, for any knowledge of the humanities would in so far have unmanned men for the sordid and pitiless conditions of the fight for wealth. We find the great prize takers in the competitive struggle to have generally been men who made it a boast that they had never had any mental education beyond the rudiments. As a rule, the children and grandchildren, who gladly inherited their wealth, were ashamed of their appearance and manners as too gross for refined surroundings.

"So much for the intellectual qualities that marked the victors in the race for wealth under the miscalled competitive system; what of the moral? What were the qualities and practices which the successful seeker after great wealth must systematically cultivate and follow? A lifelong habit of calculating upon and taking advantage of the weaknesses, necessities, and mistakes of others, a pitiless insistence upon making the most of every advantage which one might gain over another, whether by skill or accident, the constant habit of undervaluing and depreciating what one would buy, and overvaluing what one would sell; finally, such a lifelong study to regulate every thought and act with sole reference to the pole star of self-interest in its narrowest conception as must needs presently render the man incapable of every generous or self-forgetting impulse. That was the condition of mind and soul which the competitive pursuit of wealth in your day tended to develop, and which was naturally most brilliantly exemplified in the cases of those who carried away the great prizes of the struggle.

"But, of course, these winners of the great prizes were few, and had the demoralizing influence of the struggle been limited to them it would have involved the moral ruin of a small number. To realize how wide and deadly was the depraving influence of the struggle for existence, we must remember that it was not confined to its effect upon the characters of the few who succeeded, but demoralized equally the millions who failed, not on account of a virtue superior to that of the few winners, or any unwillingness to adopt their methods, but merely through lack of the requisite ability or fortune. Though not one in ten thousand might succeed largely in the pursuit of wealth, yet the rules of the contest must be followed as closely to make a bare living as to gain a fortune, in bargaining for a bag of old rags as in buying a railroad. So it was that the necessity equally upon all of seeking their living, however humble, by the methods of competition, forbade the solace of a good conscience as effectually to the poor man as to the rich, to the many losers at the game as to the few winners. You remember the familiar legend which represents the devil as bargaining with people for their souls, with the promise of worldly success as the price. The bargain was in a manner fair as set forth in the old story. The man always received the price agreed on. But the competitive system was a fraudulent devil, which, while requiring everybody to forfeit their souls, gave in return worldly success to but one in a thousand.

"And now, Julian, just let us glance at the contrast between what winning meant under the old false competitive system and what it means under the new and true competitive system, both to the winner and to the others. The winners then were those who had been most successful in getting away the wealth of others. They had not even pretended to seek the good of the community or to advance its interest, and if they had done so, that result had been quite incidental. More often than otherwise their wealth represented the loss of others. What wonder that their riches became a badge of ignominy and their victory their shame? The winners in the competition of to-day are those who have done most to increase the general wealth and welfare. The losers, those who have failed to win the prizes, are not the victims of the winners, but those whose interest, together with the general interest, has been served by them better than they themselves could have served it. They are actually better off because a higher ability than theirs was developed in the race, seeing that this ability redounded wholly to the common interest. The badges of honor and rewards of rank and office which are the tangible evidence of success won in the modern competitive struggle are but expressions of the love and gratitude of the people to those who have proved themselves their most devoted and efficient servants and benefactors."

"It strikes me," I said, "so far as you have gone, that if some one had been employed to draw up a list of the worst and weakest aspects of private capitalism, he could not have done better than to select the features of the system on which its champions seem to have based their objections to a change."

OBJECTION THAT EQUALITY WOULD DISCOURAGE INDEPENDENCE AND ORIGINALITY.

"That is an impression," said the doctor, "which you will find confirmed as we take up the next of the arguments on our list against economic equality. It was asserted that to have an economic maintenance on simple and easy terms guaranteed to all by the nation would tend to discourage originality and independence of thought and conduct on the part of the people, and hinder the development of character and individuality. This objection might be regarded as a branch of the former one that economic equality would make everybody just alike, or it might be considered a corollary of the argument we have just disposed of about the value of competition as a school of character. But so much seems to have been made of it by the opponents of the Revolution that I have set it down separately.

"The objection is one which, by the very terms necessary to state it, seems to answer itself, for it amounts to saying that a person will be in danger of losing independence of feeling by gaining independence of position. If I were to ask you what economic condition was regarded as most favorable to moral and intellectual independence in your day, and most likely to encourage a man to act out himself without fear or favor, what would you say?"

"I should say, of course, that a secure and independent basis of livelihood was that condition."

"Of course. Now, what the new order promised to give and guarantee everybody was precisely this absolute independence and security of livelihood. And yet it was argued that the arrangement would be objectionable, as tending to discourage independence of character. It seems to us that if there is any one particular in which the influence upon humanity of economic equality has been more beneficent than any other, it has been the effect which security of economic position has had to make every one absolute lord of himself and answerable for his opinions, speech, and conduct to his own conscience only.

"That is perhaps enough to say in answer to an objection which, as I remarked, really confutes itself, but the monumental audacity of the defenders of private capitalism in arguing that any other possible system could be more unfavorable than itself to human dignity and independence tempts a little comment, especially as this is an aspect of the old order on which I do not remember that we have had much talk. As it seems to us, perhaps the most offensive feature of private capitalism, if one may select among so many offensive features, was its effect to make cowardly, time-serving, abject creatures of human beings, as a consequence of the dependence for a living, of pretty nearly everybody upon some individual or group.

"Let us just glance at the spectacle which the old order presented in this respect. Take the women in the first place, half the human race. Because they stood almost universally in a relation of economic dependence, first upon men in general and next upon some man in particular, they were all their lives in a state of subjection both to the personal dictation of some individual man, and to a set of irksome and mind-benumbing conventions representing traditional standards of opinion as to their proper conduct fixed in accordance with the masculine sentiment. But if the women had no independence at all, the men were not so very much better off. Of the masculine half of the world, the greater part were hirelings dependent for their living upon the favor of employers and having the most direct interest to conform so far as possible in opinions and conduct to the prejudices of their masters, and, when they could not conform, to be silent. Look at your secret ballot laws. You thought them absolutely necessary in order to enable workingmen to vote freely. What a confession is that fact of the universal intimidation of the employed by the employer! Next there were the business men, who held themselves above the workingmen. I mean the tradesmen, who sought a living by persuading the people to buy of them. But here our quest of independence is even more hopeless than among the workingmen, for, in order to be successful in attracting the custom of those whom they cringingly styled their patrons, it was necessary for the merchant to be all things to all men, and to make an art of obsequiousness.

"Let us look yet higher. We may surely expect to find independence of thought and speech among the learned classes in the so-called liberal professions if nowhere else. Let us see how our inquiry fares there. Take the clerical profession first--that of the religious ministers and teachers. We find that they were economic servants and hirelings either of hierarchies or congregations, and paid to voice the opinions of their employers and no others. Every word that dropped from their lips was carefully weighed lest it should indicate a trace of independent thinking, and if it were found, the clergyman risked his living. Take the higher branches of secular teaching in the colleges and professions. There seems to have been some freedom allowed in teaching the dead languages; but let the instructor take up some living issue and handle it in a manner inconsistent with the capitalist interest, and you know well enough what became of him. Finally, take the editorial profession, the writers for the press, who on the whole represented the most influential branch of the learned class. The great nineteenth-century newspaper was a capitalistic enterprise as purely commercial in its principle as a woolen factory, and the editors were no more allowed to write their own opinions than the weavers to choose the patterns they wove. They were employed to advocate the opinions and interests of the capitalists owning the paper and no others. The only respect in which the journalists seem to have differed from the clergy was in the fact that the creeds which the latter were employed to preach were more or less fixed traditions, while those which the editors must preach changed with the ownership of the paper. This, Julian, is the truly exhilarating spectacle of abounding and unfettered originality, of sturdy moral and intellectual independence and rugged individuality, which it was feared by your contemporaries might be endangered by any change in the economic system. We may agree with them that it would have been indeed a pity if any influence should operate to make independence any rarer than it was, but they need not have been apprehensive; it could not be."

"Judging from these examples of the sort of argumentative opposition which the revolutionists had to meet," I observed, "it strikes me that they must have had a mighty easy time of it."

"So far as rational argument was concerned," replied the doctor, "no great revolutionary movement ever had to contend with so little opposition. The cause of the capitalists was so utterly bad, either from the point of view of ethics, politics, or economic science, that there was literally nothing that could be said for it that could not be turned against it with greater effect. Silence was the only safe policy for the capitalists, and they would have been glad enough to follow it if the people had not insisted that they should make some sort of a plea to the indictment against them. But because the argumentative opposition which the revolutionists had to meet was contemptible in quality, it did not follow that their work was an easy one. Their real task--and it was one for giants--was not to dispose of the arguments against their cause, but to overcome the moral and intellectual inertia of the masses and rouse them to do just a little clear thinking for themselves.

POLITICAL CORRUPTION AS AN OBJECTION TO NATIONALIZING INDUSTRY.

"The next objection--there are only two or three more worth mentioning--is directed not so much against economic equality in itself as against the fitness of the machinery by which the new industrial system was to be carried on. The extension of popular government over industry and commerce involved of course the substitution of public and political administration on a large scale for the previous irresponsible control of private capitalists. Now, as I need not tell you, the Government of the United States--municipal, State, and national--in the last third of the nineteenth century had become very corrupt. It was argued that to intrust any additional functions to governments so corrupt would be nothing short of madness."

"Ah!" I exclaimed, "that is perhaps the rational objection we have been waiting for. I am sure it is one that would have weighed heavily with me, for the corruption of our governmental system smelled to heaven."

"There is no doubt," said the doctor, "that there was a great deal of political corruption and that it was a very bad thing, but we must look a little deeper than these objectors did to see the true bearing of this fact on the propriety of nationalizing industry.

"An instance of political corruption was one where the public servant abused his trust by using the administration under his control for purposes of private gain instead of solely for the public interest--that is to say, he managed his public trust just as if it were his private business and tried to make a profit out of it. A great outcry was made, and very properly, when any such conduct was suspected; and therefore the corrupt officers operated under great difficulties, and were in constant danger of detection and punishment. Consequently, even in the worst governments of your period the mass of business was honestly conducted, as it professed to be, in the public interest, comparatively few and occasional transactions being affected by corrupt influences.

"On the other hand, what were the theory and practice pursued by the capitalists in carrying on the economic machinery which were under their control? They did not profess to act in the public interest or to have any regard for it. The avowed object of their whole policy was so to use the machinery of their position as to make the greatest personal gains possible for themselves out of the community. That is to say, the use of his control of the public machinery for his personal gain--which on the part of the public official was denounced and punished as a crime, and for the greater part prevented by public vigilance--was the avowed policy of the capitalist. It was the pride of the public official that he left office as poor as when he entered it, but it was the boast of the capitalist that he made a fortune out of the opportunities of his position. In the case of the capitalist these gains were not called corrupt, as they were when made by public officials in the discharge of public business. They were called profits, and regarded as legitimate; but the practical point to consider as to the results of the two systems was that these profits cost the people they came out of just as much as if they had been called political plunder.

"And yet these wise men in Kenloe's collection taught the people, and somebody must have listened to them, that because in some instances public officials succeeded in spite of all precautions in using the public administration for their own gain, it would not be safe to put any more public interests under public administration, but would be safer to leave them to private capitalists, who frankly proposed as their regular policy just what the public officials were punished whenever caught doing--namely, taking advantage of the opportunities of their position to enrich themselves at public expense. It was precisely as if the owner of an estate, finding it difficult to secure stewards who were perfectly faithful, should be counseled to protect himself by putting his affairs in the hands of professional thieves."

"You mean," I said, "that political corruption merely meant the occasional application to the public administration of the profit-seeking principle on which all private business was conducted."

"Certainly. A case of corruption in office was simply a case where the public official forgot his oath and for the occasion took a businesslike view of the opportunities of his position--that is to say, when the public official fell from grace he only fell to the normal level on which all private business was admittedly conducted. It is simply astonishing, Julian, how completely your contemporaries overlooked this obvious fact. Of course, it was highly proper that they should be extremely critical of the conduct of their public officials; but it is unaccountable that they should fail to see that the profits of private capitalists came out of the community's pockets just as certainly as did the stealings of dishonest officials, and that even in the most corrupt public departments the stealings represented a far less percentage than would have been taken as profits if the same business were done for the public by capitalists.

"So much for the precious argument that, because some officials sometimes took profits of the people, it would be more economical to leave their business in the hands of those who would systematically do so! But, of course, although the public conduct of business, even if it were marked with a certain amount of corruption, would still be more economical for the community than leaving it under the profit system, yet no self-respecting community would wish to tolerate any public corruption at all, and need not, if only the people would exercise vigilance. Now, what will compel the people to exercise vigilance as to the public administration? The closeness with which we follow the course of an agent depends on the importance of the interests put in his hands. Corruption has always thrived in political departments in which the mass of the people have felt little direct concern. Place under public administration vital concerns of the community touching their welfare daily at many points, and there will be no further lack of vigilance. Had they been wiser, the people who objected to the governmental assumption of new economic functions on account of existing political corruption would have advocated precisely that policy as the specific cure for the evil.

"A reason why these objectors seem to have been especially short-sighted is the fact that by all odds the most serious form which political corruption took in America at that day was the bribery of legislators by private capitalists and corporations in order to obtain franchises and privileges. In comparison with this abuse, peculation or bribery of crude direct sorts were of little extent or importance. Now, the immediate and express effect of the governmental assumption of economic businesses would be, so far as it went, to dry up this source of corruption, for it was precisely this class of capitalist undertakings which the revolutionists proposed first to bring under public control.

"Of course, this objection was directed only against the new order while in process of introduction. With its complete establishment the very possibility of corruption, would disappear with the law of absolute uniformity governing all incomes.

"Worse and worse," I exclaimed. "What is the use of going further?"

"Patience," said the doctor. "Let us complete the subject while we are on it. There are only a couple more of the objections that have shape enough to admit of being stated."

OBJECTION THAT A NATIONALIZED INDUSTRIAL SYSTEM WOULD THREATEN LIBERTY.

"The first of them," pursued the doctor, "was the argument that such an extension of the functions of public administration as nationalized industries involved would lodge a power in the hands of the Government, even though it were the people's own government, that would be dangerous to their liberties.

"All the plausibility there was to this objection rested on the tacit assumption that the people in their industrial relations had under private capitalism been free and unconstrained and subject to no form of authority. But what assumption could have been more regardless of facts than this? Under private capitalism the entire scheme of industry and commerce, involving the employment and livelihood of everybody, was subject to the despotic and irresponsible government of private masters. The very demand for nationalizing industry has resulted wholly from the sufferings of the people under the yoke of the capitalists.

"In 1776 the Americans overthrew the British royal government in the colonies and established their own in its place. Suppose at that time the king had sent an embassy to warn the American people that by assuming these new functions of government which formerly had been performed for them by him they were endangering their liberty. Such an embassy would, of course, have been laughed at. If any reply had been thought needful, it would have been pointed out that the Americans were not establishing over themselves any new government, but were substituting a government of their own, acting in their own interests, for the government of others conducted in an indifferent or hostile interest. Now, that was precisely what nationalizing industry meant. The question was, Given the necessity of some sort of regulation and direction of the industrial system, whether it would tend more to liberty for the people to leave that power to irresponsible persons with hostile interests, or to exercise it themselves through responsible agents? Could there conceivably be but one answer to that question?

"And yet it seems that a noted philosopher of the period, in a tract which has come down to us, undertook to demonstrate that if the people perfected the democratic system by assuming control of industry in the public interest, they would presently fall into a state of slavery which would cause them to sigh for the days of Nero and Caligula. I wish we had that philosopher here, that we might ask him how, in accordance with any observed laws of human nature, slavery was going to come about as the result of a system aiming to establish and perpetuate a more perfect degree of equality, intellectual as well as material, than had ever been known. Did he fancy that the people would deliberately and maliciously impose a yoke upon themselves, or did he apprehend that some usurper would get hold of the social machinery and use it to reduce the people to servitude? But what usurper from the beginning ever essayed a task so hopeless as the subversion of a state in which there were no classes or interests to set against one another, a state in which there was no aristocracy and no populace, a state the stability of which represented the equal and entire stake in life of every human being in it? Truly it would seem that people who conceived the subversion of such a republic possible ought to have lost no time in chaining down the Pyramids, lest they, too, defying ordinary laws of Nature, should incontinently turn upon their tops.

"But let us leave the dead to bury their dead, and consider how the nationalization of industry actually did affect the bearing of government upon the people. If the amount of governmental machinery--that is, the amount of regulating, controlling, assigning, and directing under the public management of industry--had continued to be just the same it was under the private administration of the capitalists, the fact that it was now the people's government, managing everything in the people's interest under responsibility to the people, instead of an irresponsible tyranny seeking its own interest, would of course make an absolute difference in the whole character and effect of the system and make it vastly more tolerable. But not merely did the nationalization of industry give a wholly new character and purpose to the economic administration, but it also greatly diminished the net amount of governing necessary to carry it on. This resulted naturally from the unity of system with the consequent co-ordination and interworking of all the parts which took the place of the former thousand-headed management following as many different and conflicting lines of interest, each a law to itself. To the workers the difference was as if they had passed out from under the capricious personal domination of innumerable petty despots to a government of laws and principles so simple and systematic that the sense of being subject to personal authority was gone.

"But to fully realize how strongly this argument of too much government directed against the system of nationalized industry partook of the boomerang quality of the previous objections, we must look on to the later effects which the social justice of the new order would naturally have to render superfluous well-nigh the whole machinery of government as previously conducted. The main, often almost sole, business of governments in your day was the protection of property and person against criminals, a system involving a vast amount of interference with the innocent. This function of the state has now become almost obsolete. There are no more any disputes about property, any thefts of property, or any need of protecting property. Everybody has all he needs and as much as anybody else. In former ages a great number of crimes have resulted from the passions of love and jealousy. They were consequences of the idea derived from immemorial barbarism that men and women might acquire sexual proprietorship in one another, to be maintained and asserted against the will of the person. Such crimes ceased to be known after the first generation had grown up under the absolute sexual autonomy and independence which followed from economic equality. There being no lower classes now which upper classes feel it their duty to bring up in the way they should go, in spite of themselves, all sorts of attempts to regulate personal behavior in self-regarding matters by sumptuary legislation have long ago ceased. A government in the sense of a coordinating directory of our associated industries we shall always need, but that is practically all the government we have now. It used to be a dream of philosophers that the world would some time enjoy such a reign of reason and justice that men would be able to live together without laws. That condition, so far as concerns punitive and coercive regulations, we have practically attained. As to compulsory laws, we might be said to live almost in a state of anarchy.

"There is, as I explained to you in the Labor Exchange the other morning, no compulsion, in the end, even as to the performance of the universal duty of public service. We only insist that those who finally refuse to do their part toward maintaining the social welfare shall not be partakers of it, but shall resort by themselves and provide for themselves.

THE MALTHUSIAN OBJECTION.

"And now we come to the last objection on my list. It is entirely different in character from any of the others. It does not deny that economic equality would be practicable or desirable, or assert that the machinery would work badly. It admits that the system would prove a triumphant success in raising human welfare to an unprecedented point and making the world an incomparably more agreeable place to live in. It was indeed the conceded success of the plan which was made the basis of this objection to it."

"That must be a curious sort of objection," I said. "Let us hear about it."

"The objectors put it in this way: 'Let us suppose,' they said, 'that poverty and all the baneful influences upon life and health that follow in its train are abolished and all live out their natural span of life. Everybody being assured of maintenance for self and children, no motive of prudence would be operative to restrict the number of offspring. Other things being equal, these conditions would mean a much faster increase of population than ever before known, and ultimately an overcrowding of the earth and a pressure on the food supply, unless indeed we suppose new and indefinite food sources to be found?'"

"I do not see why it might not be reasonable to anticipate such a result," I observed, "other things being equal."

"Other things being equal," replied the doctor, "such a result might be anticipated. But other things would not be equal, but so different that their influence could be depended on to prevent any such result."

"What are the other things that would not be equal?"

"Well, the first would be the diffusion of education, culture, and general refinement. Tell me, were the families of the well-to-do and cultured class in the America of your day, as a whole, large?"

"Quite the contrary. They did not, as a rule, more than replace themselves."

"Still, they were not prevented by any motive of prudence from increasing their numbers. They occupied in this respect as independent a position as families do under the present order of economic equality and guaranteed maintenance. Did it never occur to you why the families of the well-to-do and cultured in your day were not larger?"

"Doubtless," I said, "it was on account of the fact that in proportion as culture and refinement opened intellectual and aesthetic fields of interest, the impulses of crude animalism played less important parts in life. Then, too, in proportion as families were refined the woman ceased to be the mere sexual slave of the husband, and her wishes as to such matters were considered."

"Quite so. The reflection you have suggested is enough to indicate the fallacy of the whole Malthusian theory of the increase of population on which this objection to better social conditions was founded. Malthus, as you know, held that population tended to increase faster than means of subsistence, and therefore that poverty and the tremendous wastes of life it stood for were absolutely necessary in order to prevent the world from starving to death by overcrowding. Of course, this doctrine was enormously popular with the rich and learned class, who were responsible for the world's misery. They naturally were delighted to be assured that their indifference to the woes of the poor, and even their positive agency in multiplying those woes, were providentially overruled for good, so as to be really rather praiseworthy than otherwise. The Malthus doctrine also was very convenient as a means of turning the tables on reformers who proposed to abolish poverty by proving that, instead of benefiting mankind, their reforms would only make matters worse in the end by overcrowding the earth and starving everybody. By means of the Malthus doctrine, the meanest man who ever ground the face of the poor had no difficulty in showing that he was really a slightly disguised benefactor of the race, while the philanthropist was an injurious fellow.

"This prodigious convenience of Malthusianism has an excuse for things as they were, furnishes the explanation for the otherwise incomprehensible vogue of so absurd a theory. That absurdity consists in the fact that, while laying such stress on the direct effects of poverty and all the ills it stands for to destroy life, it utterly failed to allow for the far greater influence which the brutalizing circumstances of poverty exerted to promote the reckless multiplication of the species. Poverty, with all its deadly consequences, slew its millions, but only after having, by means of its brutalizing conditions, promoted the reckless reproduction of tens of millions--that is to say, the Malthus doctrine recognized only the secondary effects of misery and degradation in reducing population, and wholly overlooked their far more important primary effect in multiplying it. That was its fatal fallacy.

"It was a fallacy the more inexcusable because Malthus and all his followers were surrounded by a society the conditions of which absolutely refuted their theory. They had only to open then eyes to see that wherever the poverty and squalor chiefly abounded, which they vaunted as such valuable checks to population, humankind multiplied like rabbits, while in proportion as the economic level of a class was raised its proliferousness declined. What corollary from this fact of universal observation could be more obvious than that the way to prevent reckless overpopulation was to raise, not to depress, the economic status of the mass, with all the general improvement in well-being which that implied? How long do you suppose such an absurdly fundamental fallacy as underlay the Malthus theory would have remained unexposed if Malthus had been a revolutionist instead of a champion and defender of capitalism?

"But let Malthus go. While the low birth-rate among the cultured classes--whose condition was the prototype of the general condition under economic equality--was refutation enough of the overpopulation objection, yet there is another and far more conclusive answer, the full force of which remains to be brought out. You said a few moments ago that one reason why the birth-rate was so moderate among the cultured classes was the fact that in that class the wishes of women were more considered than in the lower classes. The necessary effect of economic equality between the sexes would mean, however, that, instead of being more or less considered, the wishes of women in all matters touching the subject we are discussing would be final and absolute. Previous to the establishment of economic equality by the great Revolution the non-child-bearing sex was the sex which determined the question of child-bearing, and the natural consequence was the possibility of a Malthus and his doctrine. Nature has provided in the distress and inconvenience of the maternal function a sufficient check upon its abuse, just as she has in regard to all the other natural functions. But, in order that Nature's check should be properly operative, it is necessary that the women through whose wills it must operate, if at all, should be absolutely free agents in the disposition of themselves, and the necessary condition of that free agency is economic independence. That secured, while we may be sure that the maternal instinct will forever prevent the race from dying out, the world will be equally little in danger of being recklessly overcrowded."

THE END.

Made in the USA
San Bernardino, CA
06 May 2019